SINNERS & SAINTS

PART TWO

VERONICA EDEN

THE SINNERS AND SAINTS SERIES, PART 2

Copyright © 2021 Veronica Eden

RUTHLESS BISHOP

Copyright © 2020 Veronica Eden

SAVAGE WILDER

Copyright © 2021 Veronica Eden

All rights reserved.

No parts of this publication may be reproduced, stored in a retrieval system, or transmitted in any form or by any means, electronic, mechanical, photocopying, recording, or otherwise, without the prior written permission of the copyright owner, except in the case of brief quotations embodied in reviews and certain other noncommercial uses permitted by copyright law. For permission requests, write to the author at this website:

WWW.VERONICAEDENDAUTHOR.COM

This is a work of fiction. Names, characters, places, businesses, companies, organizations, locales, events and incidents either are the product of the author's imagination or used fictitiously. Any resemblances to actual persons, living or dead, is unintentional and co-incidental. The author does not have any control over and does not assume any responsibility for author or third-party websites or their content.

AUTHOR'S NOTE

Ruthless Bishop and Savage Wilder are dark new adult high school bully romances intended for mature readers. The Sinners and Saints series boys are all devilish bullies brought to their knees by a spitfire heroine, so if you love enemies-to-lovers type stories, you're in the right place. These mature new adult romances contain crude language, dubious situations, and intense graphic sexual/violent content that some readers might find triggering or offensive. Please proceed with caution.

If you like weak pushover heroines and nice guys this one ain't for you, but if you dig strong females and smug antiheroes, then you're in the right place! Hold onto your hearts, because these guys aren't above stealing.

Each book is part of a series but can be enjoyed as a standalone.

Sinners and Saints series:
#1 Wicked Saint
#2 Tempting Devil
#3 Ruthless Bishop
#4 Savage Wilder

Sign up for Veronica's newsletter to receive exclusive content and news about upcoming releases: bit.ly/veronicaedenmail
Follow Veronica on BookBub for new release alerts: bookbub.com/authors/veronica-eden

SINNERS & SAINTS

RUTHLESS BISHOP

BOOK THREE

ONE
Thea

Sexy selfie attempt number twenty and I still don't have a winner I totally love on my phone's camera roll.

"Just do it," I mutter, arguing with myself. "Spontaneity is a good thing. He'll like it. Be cool."

I've been going in circles for five minutes, getting nowhere as I pace my bedroom.

My school uniform hangs on the closet door from a funky sun-shaped brass hook, the plaid skirt in the school colors—evergreen and white—and the black blazer with the gold embroidered crest mocking me. At school I'm known by cruel names because I prefer wearing my uniform a couple of sizes too big to hide my body, unlike the girls who wear their skirts short enough their asses almost hang out and their blazers fitted to their petite waistlines. The other students are labelled cool because they break the uniform code with designer fashion, but I'm not because my rebellion isn't worthy in their eyes.

At least most of the time I'm invisible to them.

Narrowing my eyes at the uniform, I turn my back, where the riot of color on the other side of the room makes me smile. The wall is a pastel rainbow of baking-themed art with funny sayings like *bake the world happy* and *happiness is homemade*.

"Okay, focus. Send the photo," I coach.

My stomach protests with a wave of butterflies. All of my positive thinking flees.

I can't believe I'm losing an argument against myself. I blow out harshly, deflating my ballooned cheeks along with my nerve. A wayward auburn curl ends up in my eyes. With an impatient flick, I brush it aside.

It's taken me weeks to work up the courage for this step with Wyatt, the cute lifeguard at the summer retreat my parents sent me to. We had a sort of fling. Well, okay. Not really.

It was fling-like. *Fling adjacent.* We were on our way to flirting.

At least, that's what my friend Maisy assured me between yoga class and gourmet s'mores by the campfire.

The air hisses from my lungs in a soft, flat laugh that caves my chest.

You? Dream on. He was only being polite. As a staff member, he was probably contracted to be whatever the guests needed. Even appearing interested romantically.

I shake my head to dispel the depressing inner voice. Wyatt wasn't only being a nice guy, and I am a damn goddess he would love to be with.

Forget the short-girl-with-an-ass figure it's difficult to find jeans for, the stretch marks on my hips and boobs from puberty growth spurts, and the memories of shopping for bras when my friends were still playing with toys.

"A goddess," I repeat, letting the affirmation give me the mental hug I need to restore my confidence.

My tongue pokes out of the corner of my mouth as I hesitate to click on the message icon in his contact, where I saved his name with waves. As if I'd forget about how he looked in his red lifeguard trunks with a deep golden tan. Maybe I should go for a Facebook message or an Instagram DM first to double check I have his number saved correctly.

I shake my head. "Be bold."

This is my chance to keep our tiny spark alive before it snuffs out. I have to act fast. I arrived back in Ridgeview the week before school at Silver Lake High started, and Wyatt went home to Colorado Springs. The drive down is under two hours if this works out—but I'm getting ahead of myself.

First I have to buck the hell up and send the photo.

I've decided. Senior year is my year. I'm eighteen and it's time I stopped hiding myself from the world.

Mom can spout her crap until she's red in the face, but I'm not listening anymore.

A whine sounds at the locked door, followed by a muffled scratch.

"Not tonight, buddy. Go to your bed," I tell my rottweiler. He's an oversized lapdog that usually shadows me all over the house. He whines once more. "Bed, Constantine."

The dog makes a put out sound as his nails click down the hall.

My grip tightens on my cell phone. The picture I took is all right. Not my best, but like the hundreds of photos in a secret folder, it's the version of the girl I want to be.

Confident, sexy, and owning my curvy body.

Ah, the pipe dream.

I pluck at the sunflower yellow chunky knit cardigan I tugged on over the lace-edged romper that barely contains my breasts. It's designed to drape nicely on elegant bodies with long limbs and chests much flatter than mine. Instead, the romper fits to my big hips and rides up my thighs. Thank god for still photos where I can fake like I'm not trying to pick the material my ass is eating every two seconds.

Mom doesn't know I own the romper, or some of the other clothes hidden in the closet. I have to rotate my hiding spots because she is a notorious snooper.

Photo-me looks up from the phone screen with bedroom eyes, my lashes fluttered low over my blue-green eyes. My dark red curls are tossed over strategically to give my hair that bombshell volume, spilling down my neck and over one shoulder as I lean forward to show off my cleavage. My plump lips are puckered into duck lips. I can't help it, duck lips are my go to when I put myself on the spot in the hopes I'll capture something natural and effortless. It's me, and yet...not.

My gaze slides to the mirror and my shoulders droop as soon as I eye my reflection critically.

Mirrors and phone cameras must have a deal with the devil.

Somehow the reflection and the pictures never match up. Maybe the girl I am in my secret folder of photos exists only in digital format.

Squinting, I lean closer. Is that—? *Yup.* That's flour in my hair. I sink my fingers into my curls with an aggravated sigh and shake them out as I check the photo. Fan-flipping-tastic.

I thought I cleaned myself up after baking the rustic cranberry tarts I've been trying to perfect when I got home from school, but I must have missed some. What else is new? I'm almost always covered in some ingredient with my love of baking.

Okay, attempt number twenty-one.

This time I crop part of my face out of the frame and go for a coy smirk. Once I snap the photo, I drop out of the pose and perch on the arm of the floral print cushioned chair by the window, nudging one of my infinite recipe notebooks onto the seat.

"Not bad." I tilt my head and scrunch my lips to the side. The next dilemma occurs to me and my eyes widen. "Crap."

I'm already being bold with the photo, but should I say anything or just send the picture? What do people normally say when they send selfies revealing their thirst levels to their crush? Oh god, I'm going to screw this up. I'm so bad at this!

The glow of headlights shining through the window distracts me from my momentary panic as a dark silver SUV pulls into the house next door. The Bishop's place. I'm the lucky duck who not only has the school principal for a neighbor but also his vicious son, Connor Bishop. Most of the time he ignores my existence, but on days he doesn't, he's the champion of the crusade against me and my favorite sweaters.

"Oh freaking great," I mumble, ducking down in the chair so he doesn't look up to my window and think I'm creeping on him.

I'm not risking Connor seeing me in this romper, either. No free shows for that asshole.

The headlights cut off as he parks outside of the garage. Their house looks like it belongs in the Hollywood Hills with its sprawling paved terraces, huge arched windows, and terracotta tiled roof. It stands out against the other houses, like mine, that resemble mountain lodges and chalets with stone columns and dark accents. Almost everything in our town matches the same mountain vibe. Our neighborhood is comfortably upscale as far as Ridgeview goes, but Connor's is the biggest on the street.

Curling my fingers over the back of the chair, I peek past the sheer lavender curtains and watch him slam the door of the Lexus GX with a bag of soccer balls hooked over his shoulder. It makes his bicep flex, stretching his green varsity soccer shirt taut.

Why do mean boys always have to look like that? He's an angel-faced demon in disguise with his striking gray eyes, floppy light brown hair, and a dangerous, dazzling smile he uses to melt the panties off of his adoring fangirls. Not that I know what his charm-up-to-eleven smile looks like up close. I only get the cruel smirks directed my way when I have the misfortune of catching his attention.

Collapsing back into the chair, I bite my lip and push Connor Bishop from my mind. I'm a girl on a mission to flirt. He isn't messing this up for me.

As I tap my nails against my phone and tug my lips side to side in thought, different options scroll through my mind. *Hey cutie?* I shake my head. *No, that's too much. Hope you're having a good day?* I groan, scrubbing a hand over my face.

"Why are words so hard?"

The stuffed sea lion on the bed doesn't answer. I'm terrible at this stuff. A 4.0 GPA and all my baking skills, yet I can't flirt for shit. It's like I'm defective, missing a social skill or two because I listened to all the things Mom has always warned me about boys, and ran in the other direction when one spoke to me.

Except for one. But that didn't end well.

I cock my head to the side as a thought occurs to me while I'm wallowing in self pity. What would Connor say in this situation if he was going to sweet talk a girl he wanted?

My gaze flicks to the window where his bedroom light is on. I only know it's his room because he refuses to change with the curtains closed, the self-obsessed exhibitionist. I may have caught sight of his bare chest—*briefly*—a time or two over the years. He has abs, and that's just completely unfair.

Dropping my voice into a lower register and pretending to be all macho, I shoot my stuffed sea lion a sly look and say, "Baby, you light up the sky with your pretty smile."

A beat of silence passes before I make a sound like a dying animal in my humiliation. I sink further into the seat, wishing for the ground to open up and swallow me. Thank god no one actually witnessed that train wreck.

"I'm hopeless!"

With a sigh I scoot up and type out *missing your smile*. I chew on my lip. It's not bad. Maybe an emoji? But then again, emojis change meaning by the day.

"Ugh. No."

I jab the delete button, erasing the message letter by letter. Frustration mixes with a heavy bubble in my chest. It swells until it chokes me. Before I finish deleting the text, I let my phone slip from my grip to plop in my lap, rubbing at my stinging eyes. The mascara I applied is probably smearing, but I don't care. I can't get this right, so why does it matter anymore?

An innocuous computerized *whoop* sound makes me freeze. Oh no. Oh no, no, no. *Shit.*

Mortification crashes through me as I scramble to flip my phone. The evidence of my clumsy mistake glares back at me, punching through my stomach and making it plummet faster than concrete shoes dragging someone to the bottom of the ocean.

Thea: Missing you [Photo attachment]

The message sent. There's no way to unsend texts, because the technology gods like to laugh at us unfortunate souls who send embarrassing shit and regret it the minute it transmits. Maybe I'll get lucky and he won't see it.

How will I know, though? Wyatt never struck me as the type to leave his read receipts on. He could look at the text and I would never know.

"Fuck," I drag out in a harsh whisper.

What if Wyatt does open it and hates it? I already see three things wrong with my photo. I wish more than anything I could yank it back. Erase it from existence. Keep it tucked away in my secret folder.

I try to suck in a slow meditative breath through my nose like Maisy always instructs, but it catches in my throat while my pulse thunders in my ears.

A million thoughts scramble through my head. Pictures, too. *Thanks overactive imagination.* I see Wyatt with his longtime girlfriend when he reads my text. In my head, they laugh and I feel like the world's biggest idiot.

Squeezing my phone with sweaty palms, I search the internet, scanning articles and results with a jittery focus.

Does the throbbing-prickly sensation in my palms mean I'm experiencing an adrenaline surge?

How do I unsend a text message?

Can I delete a photo from someone else's phone before they see it?

In the middle of my fruitless searching, a notification banner pops up at the top of my screen for a few seconds before disappearing. Wave emojis bracket his name.

My heart stops.

He texted back.

TWO
Connor

My life is great from the outside. I'm the life of every party.

Until I'm forced to return home and face reality.

After dumping the bag of soccer balls from practice in the garage, I head for the kitchen. There's nothing good in the fridge when I raid it, but I snag a can of Coke. I need it after that practice and I'll likely be up late tonight.

"Connor," Dad acknowledges as he strolls past me, pausing to check his reflection in the microwave. "How was practice? The team shaping up to have a good year?"

I grunt in response, narrowing my eyes when I pick up a whiff of his cologne. It's not his usual, this one something heavier on the musky notes. My grip tightens on the can in my hand and I blow out a sharp breath, eyeing him up and down.

Dad's salt and pepper hair is slicked back and he has on a new tie, which he straightens in the murky reflection. I roll my eyes and turn my back on his stupid primping. If he's given up, he doesn't need to make it so fucking obvious.

A faint giggle drifts from the second floor hall, followed by a deep murmur.

My brows pinch together and I drag a hand through my hair, digging blunt nails into my scalp.

This family is such a fucked up nightmare.

Then again, who am I to judge my father when Mom does nothing to hide what she's doing either?

A year and a half of this shit and it still feels like the first time I walked in and found her on the kitchen counter with her campaign manager's pale ass pumping between her legs. My stomach rolls at the memory, the traumatic image permanently burned into my brain. At least back then she kept it a discreet secret. Now Damien eats dinner with us and spends almost every night in my mother's bed. Everyone on the block waves at our dear *family friend* when he comes around.

It makes me sick.

"Going to bed. Have a good night, Dad."

"Oh, Connor, don't forget." Dad gestures toward Mom's insane anal retentive calendar on the wall. Well, her personal assistant is the micro manager, I suppose, but Mom's no better

She trains her people well, and the rest of the world falls in line or faces the wrath of a socialite who fancies herself a self-made political woman. Dad peers over his shoulder. "Appointment tomorrow. Meet me in my office. I have a morning budget meeting with the school board, but I'll still be able to take you."

My lip curls. I cover it with a deep gulp of soda.

"Never forget." With a tight smile, I wave my phone, where the calendar reminder Mom's assistant programmed will go off soon. "Night."

I don't hang around for an answer before going up to my room and slamming the door behind me.

My athletic bag gets tossed in the corner as I cross over to my desk by the window, booting up my computer. I change into sweatpants and a t-shirt.

The quiet hum of my custom built tower and the glow of my double monitors sets my mind at ease. Soccer is fun to obsess over and keeps me in killer shape, but this right here is my real ticket to leaving my parents before they can leave me in the dust like they seem hell-bent on achieving this year once Mom's re-election campaign is over.

They're throwing everything about our family away, including me.

Fuck 'em. I don't need them if they don't want me. The trust fund granddad set up for me isn't accessible until I turn twenty-one, so I have an insurance plan in the meantime.

I won't rely on anyone. The only person I can trust to look out for number one is myself.

While the computer powers through the loading sequence at top speeds, I set my Coke down, open the desk drawer to retrieve my stash, then drop into the high-back orange and black gamer chair. The wooden box has a design on the lid of a trippy night sky burned into the grain that I thought was sick as hell when I was fifteen and a bit of a dweeb. Now I think it's kind of lame. Whatever, it keeps my bud dank.

Mom got all pissy when she found my old stash jar. We live an hour from Denver for fuck's sake, yet she still has a stick up her ass about smoking as if she wasn't sneaking into granddad's conservatory to get away from boring society parties doing the same thing when she was my age. I found her stale leftovers out there when I was exploring the estate during brunch years ago. I know what's up.

Smirking, I hold up a rolled joint. "Hello, beautiful."

The first puff after lighting up has me relaxing back in the chair, hooking an arm over the headrest as I hold the smoke in my lungs for a long beat before exhaling, sending it curling overhead. I take another hit and close my eyes, humming in relief. This is what I needed to unwind.

When my limbs tingle pleasantly and the edge of stress I carried throughout the day ebbs away, I get down to business. The joint dangles between my lips as my fingers fly across the keyboard. I run through my normal checks—bitcoin investments, skim a few Reddit threads, and a social media sweep for anything unsuspecting idiots dump online and later delete that I can save as receipts when I need to put them in their place.

An automated web crawler script I run when I'm not at the computer hasn't turned up much today, so I also do a manual scan to hunt down anything the script missed.

The corner of my mouth lifts when I come across one of the Coyote Girls on the cheerleading squad. Kamile, I recall, picturing last weekend when she drunkenly explained she was *kammy with a K* as she straddled my lap, trying to get with me at a boat party on Silver Lake. In the Facebook photo, she's posing with two teammates with a bright smile, but a telltale dusting of white powder by the corner of her nose means she'll be deleting this within the hour once someone points it out.

It's not powdered sugar.

Don't people know by now? The internet is forever.

Screenshot.

I pull up the program I coded myself to keep track of the dirty little secrets I collect. Maybe the encrypted dossiers are serial killer levels of detailed, but I'm not the king of blackmail because I half-ass it with word-of-mouth rumors. That's child's play. No, I keep extensive proof to back it all up. Every skeleton in the closet, every corrupt truth, I keep it all.

With a few keystrokes, I've made a new file for Kamile, populating it with notes on her extracurriculars, her GPA, and the screenshot with the direct URL address. She can buy me out of using it against her, but it will cost a steep amount. Doesn't mean I delete what I find. Knowledge is power and all that. Mine's backed up twice and protected by my secure protocols to ensure I'm the one holding all the cards.

"Tsk, tsk, Kammy. The hard stuff isn't worth it if it fucks with your future. Keep it herbal, girl. And this side of legal if you're going to post evidence of being a bit of a bad girl." As I'm doing a low-level search of the city for her name, a LinkedIn article pulls up for her mom, profiling the high-end rehab resort she heads in Ridgeview catering to celebrities and trust fund fuckups. A snort shakes my shoulders. "What will your mommy say?"

I knock back the last of my Coke and ash my joint in the empty can.

It's fear of what I know that keeps people on my good side. Not just the students at school, but the teachers, too. Hell, I even have a profile on Holden Landry's dad, Ridgeview's chief of police, and the first entry I ever put in my black book of information.

This all started when I was turning seventeen. I wanted to figure out how I wound up with a slap on the wrist after getting arrested on serious assault charges with witnesses. When I uncovered the truth, I needed to know more, until it shaped me into who I am now—obsessed with collecting everyone's secrets and lies. It's almost a compulsion at this point, something I can't turn off.

No one is real. No one is genuinely who they present themselves as. Everyone has something to hide.

The webs are spun all over this town, from my parents' affairs and what they did to keep me out of trouble to the deeper corruptions infecting the picturesque town nestled in the Rockies.

For every truth, there are two lies. And I'm the keeper of it all.

Aren't you proud of what you've turned me into, Mom and Dad?

I huff out a scratchy, deadpan laugh. A bitter aftertaste sits on my tongue at the thought. I take a deep puff on the joint to wash it away in a haze of tangy smoke.

What a twisted kingdom I've built for myself.

At my elbow, the phone screen lights up, the vibration buzzing against the desk. I let my attention flick to read the notification for a fraction of a second, more interested in finishing what I'm doing.

Reminder: *Anger Management Appointment; Doctor Levitt - Tomorrow, 11am.*

"Yeah, I fucking knew that," I grumble.

The corners of my mouth tug down as I grab my phone, intent on flipping it over. I don't need the reminder that I have court-mandated therapy—or why what happened was covered up, and I ended up with a shrink instead of in juvie for assault charges that magically disappeared. That magic being dirty hush money to grease the wheels and bribe the police chief. If I could get out of going, I would've figured out how to do that by now. Court-ordered makes it damn near impossible to escape. Faking it with Doctor Levitt gets me by.

Before I slam my phone face down on the desk, I get a new text. Assuming it's my boy Devlin bitching about sitting alone in his big ass house in the mountains in a roundabout way without saying how lonely he is, I swipe it open without looking. I've already got the perfect GIF to send that will cheer the mopey bastard up before I invite myself over.

It's not Devlin.

The tip of the joint burns down as I tap on the photo to see it full size.

My brows hike up in appreciation of the fine as fuck body this chick has. *Damn, baby.*

Her face is cropped, but I focus on the sexy little smile—*pink* glossy lips, fuck me—and take in the perfect tits practically spilling out of the little number she's got on. What is that, a one-piece nightie? Who knows, but it has lace and highlights every one of her curves.

My hands flex, the desire to grab those hips shooting through me. They look perfect for my hands to grip as I pound into her.

The number isn't one I recognize, but who cares? It doesn't matter if I deleted this chick's number. She's texting me about missing me and I sure as fuck am down to play with her to take my mind off the shit I'm dealing with.

I take one last hit of the joint before putting it out to finish later. Heat coils in my groin, my dick tenting my sweatpants while I admire the babe in the hot little selfie. Blowing out the smoke, I drop my knees open, grinding my semi against the heel of my palm and mumble,

"Shit, girl. Wish you were here with that dime body to take care of what you started in person."

There's a birthmark on her thigh, where the material rides up. I tilt my head, tracing my upper lip with my thumb in fascination. It's shaped like a sun.

Too many urges and scenarios run through my head at once, each better than the last. I could call her up and get her ass here now—I bet it will look amazing bouncing on my cock. But first I want to have some fun with the mystery texter.

As I get up and move to the bed, I dip my hand inside my sweats to pump my cock, dropping my head back and groaning with my eyes hooded. She's got me raring to go from one selfie, even with my buzz. Weed dick won't hold me back from enjoying myself with this chick.

I settle on the bed with my legs spread enough to pull the material of my pants tighter, outlining my erection. After clicking on the lamp on the nightstand, flipping up my shirt, and tugging the waistband low enough to show off that I'm trimmed, I rest my hand on my stomach and snap a photo to respond with.

A lopsided smile tugs at the corner of my mouth as I fire off my response.

Tonight just got a lot better.

THREE
Thea

The air feels as if it's been sucked from the room. Or maybe that's the effect of forgetting to breathe while staring at the super sexy photo Wyatt texted in response. My prior worries have flown out the window as I melt into the floral print armchair, eyes locked on the photo like I'm in danger of missing out on his delicious six-pack.

He texted back.

He. Texted. Back.

"Oh my flipping god." The words come out as a strained whisper.

A muffled squeal ekes out of me as I remember to drag in a huge gasp of air at last, before I pass out like a total basket case. Mark me down on the list of things that faint from overstimulation right below goats and the sweet dog in a viral video I watched from The Dodo who lives with a benign neurological condition.

My mind is the embodiment of the exclamation point on repeat. Several of them. A whole keysmashed parade of exclamation points.

Because Wyatt didn't just reply with an emoji or say he missed me, too.

Nope. Freaking *nope*! Containing the grin on the brink of breaking free is next to impossible. I should text Maisy and spill the good news. *Maise, your girl just successfully flirted and the world didn't die of embarrassment!*

I drop my phone in my lap and hide my face behind my hands, wriggling as I happy dance in place. The rollercoaster of emotions took me from the pits of anxiety and depression to clean off the track, launched into the sky by my elation that the boy I like responded. I can't resist scooping the phone back up and viewing the picture full-screen, biting my lip.

He's reclined on a bed with dark gray sheets, his green t-shirt rucked up to show off his abs and v muscle, his body lean and cut by athleticism. One hand is splayed low on his stomach, toying with his waistband, where I can see the outline of his erection—*and* his trimmed pubes catching the dim light. I swallow thickly. Wyatt's face is mostly cropped out by the angle, but I can still appreciate his jaw line and his playful smirk.

It sends an excited flutter through my belly as I picture his thumb stroking back and forth along the edge of his sweatpants before sliding under to squeeze himself.

Is he turned on because of the photo I sent? I can't know for sure without asking outright, but it's giving me a hell of a boost to think it's true.

The picture has me flustered, my cheeks engulfed in warmth while I wrestle against the urge to look away. Wyatt is a hot lifeguard who owned every one of my fantasies at the summer retreat, but this has my mouth watering on an all new level. The energetic *damn boy* sound clip from TikTok is going off in my head on repeat and it ain't wrong.

My gaze sweeps over his perfect body. He looks like he should grace the covers of magazines. It's not quite how I remember him by the lake, but maybe my memories are blinded by his beaming, boyish smile. He could have been hitting the gym a little harder since I last saw him.

Before I can spend more time dwelling on my memory versus the photo, a new text comes in, making me jump when the phone vibrates in my hand.

Wyatt: Still there, baby?

My eyes widen. *Baby?* A giddy thrill zips down my spine. If I had known it would be this easy to show him how I felt, I would have done this at the beginning of the summer.

"Curse you past Thea." I scold myself in a hush so Mom doesn't come snooping on my business. She thinks I'm studying before bed. "See what happens when you bravely squeeze the day!"

Well, seize the day. But I like my poster with bright citrus fruit and the pun version better. It's more colorful.

I'm still formulating the best way to respond when he sends another text.

Wyatt: Come on, sweetness. Don't show me yours and then get all shy on me when I return the favor.
Wyatt: You got me all warmed up. Are you going to leave me hanging like this? [Photo attachment]

Heat floods my cheeks again. He's grinning now, cocky and confident, and has a hand shoved down his pants. It's blatant and enticingly illicit, sending my heart rate into overdrive. Most of his face is still cropped out to give me a show.

What am I supposed to do now?

He asked a question. So should I respond or do I send another photo? He upped the ante by snapping a pic with his hand on his junk.

I scan myself, debating the most attractive way to match him. Rompers aren't exactly designed for easy access. I could go up the pant leg, I guess, or maybe dropping the straps off my shoulders, but then does it look like I'm too naked? I mean, yes, I would be tits out and everything, though I guess that's kind of the point. It's not like I have anything on under this.

The logistics twist my brain in circles for a few minutes.

I only planned as far as taking and sending the selfie. There was no strategy for what to do next if he answered.

My attention drifts back out the window where Connor Bishop's bedroom light is dimmer, but still on at the house next door. I bet he does this sort of thing all the time with the amount of girls always falling over themselves to flirt with him. An image of him pops into my head from the first day of school, where a pretty girl from the dance squad sat on his lap all through lunch, blushing every time he whispered in her ear. Yeah, with those full lips tilted in a smug curve? He's totally a pro at this stuff.

Maybe I should take a page from him to figure out how to be sexy while texting Wyatt.

A breathy laugh huffs from my lips while I drop my head back against the armchair. "Yeah right."

I can't match Connor for confidence, but W.W.S.F.G.D.? Because Secret Folder Girl—the version of myself I hide away on my phone's camera roll? She'd totally have this situation on lock.

Somewhere deep down, that girl is me.

"I can do this." Sucking in a breath, I nod.

This time it's live instead of when I last tried to flirt with pictures, where I could gather my confidence and walk away when it became too much to email back. But that was years ago now. It wasn't even—

Shaking my head, I push those dark memories aside. I can't let what happened then cloud my thoughts every time I think about other guys. My throat is tight when I swallow. Will it always be like this, the secret I carry following me and tainting every romantic experience?

"No," I say firmly, almost growling the denial.

Determined to get this right, I pop up from the chair and switch to the bed. I move my seal plushie out of the way, stuffing it behind the pillows so Wyatt won't see it and tease me. I'm playing around with different positions, slipping one of the romper straps so it drapes off my shoulder without fully popping a nipple out when my phone pings.

Wyatt: Are you being a bad girl, getting off thinking about me if I was there with you? I'm waiting to see what else you've got. Don't finish without me. Show me how you're touching yourself.

Thea: I wasn't!

Crap. I replied before I could think about whether or not it was protocol. Damn my lack of filter when I get going.

Wyatt: [smirk emoji] You weren't? Are you a good girl, then? Waiting for me to tell you how to make it feel good?

God. Heat pulses between my legs. My thumbs hover over the keyboard for a moment as I gather the courage to reply.

Thea: What would you do if you were here?

Wyatt sends another picture, this one a close up of his parted lips with his tongue licking across the bottom one.

Wyatt: First I'd want to lick that hot little birthmark on your thigh. Anyone ever told you it looks like a sun? I love the taste of sunshine.

I glance at my leg. Huh. I guess so.
It's not what I expected him to say and I tip my chin up, telling him as much.

Thea: Not a kiss on the lips?

The conversation goes quiet for a minute, then he sends a recorded voice clip. Just when I adjust to his pace, he changes it up on me. Holding my breath, I tap play.
"Oh, sunshine. You want me to kiss that sweet little mouth? Mm, I don't know if you could handle it." His deep, raspy chuckle makes my clit throb as his voice rolls over me. *"If that's what you want, I'd kiss you all over...starting with that fucking sexy birthmark."*
I've never heard him sound like this, so in charge and aware of exactly what effect his voice has on me. I'm more used to his kind smiles and enthusiastic laugh. There's a rustle and a faint groan. Is he—? I think he is.
He's totally stroking his dick while recording what he said.
It makes me warm all over, my skin electrified and sensitive to the ruffled material of my purple bedspread. My thighs squeeze together to get some relief from the sensual desire he stirs in me. I glance at the door to make sure it's still locked. Having Mom walk in without knocking right now would suck.

Thea: Then what would you do?
Wyatt: I'd have to touch those tits next. Stroke them nice and light until your nipples are aching from how tight they pucker.

I'm a little disappointed I don't get to hear these words in his voice, but what he says gets me hot anyway. Unconsciously, I've begun dragging my nails over the tops of my breasts, teasing the edge of the delicate lace lining the romper. My nipples demand attention, but I hold out, waiting to see what else he'd do.

Wyatt: Bet those nipples are pretty and pink. They hard for me, baby?
Thea: Yes. I need you to touch them.

Another photo comes through and I suck in a sharp breath. He pulled down his sweatpants just enough to reveal the base of his erection. His thumb and finger are curled around it. I lick my lips and shift around, debating grabbing a pillow to shove between my legs.

Thea: Would you kiss them next?
Wyatt: Yes. Pull down your top so I can suck on them. I'm going to bite them until you cry out.

Releasing a strained whimper, I peel off the thin straps and gasp when the air hits my bare skin. My nipples are pebbled, almost throbbing from how turned on I am. I palm my breast with one hand, pinching each nipple to simulate being bitten. My back arches and my clit aches with need. I almost drop the phone from my other hand.

Wyatt: Tell me how it feels.

A whine gets stuck in my throat while I fumble the phone, my typing getting sloppy as I keep rolling my tingling nipples beneath my palm to feel the tiny electric jolts it sends to my core. I wish he was here, laying next to me so I could smell him, feel his smile against my skin.

My stomach flips when he sends another recorded text.

"Fuck, baby. Can't even type straight, huh? You're so sexy." His voice is a hoarse growl over the faint slap of skin. He's jerking himself off harder. *"Show me."*

My heart thuds as I rub my thighs together to alleviate the tight coil of tension he's worked me into.

Thea: What?

His response is immediate.

Wyatt: Show me how I'm touching you, baby. I need to see you. Take a pic to prove you're being good and doing what I'm saying.

I sink my teeth into my lip. Can I do that?

This all feels so good, way better than I've ever made myself feel when I've touched myself beneath the sheets in the dark. I don't just mean physically, either. Talking to him was scary at first, but it's getting easier once it's clear he isn't waiting to laugh at me.

It's like he sees me, the real me from my secret folder.

My confidence rises and I take a picture of my tits squeezed between my arms, one hand pinching a nipple as my lips part on a gasp. The material of my romper bunches around my waist and the flush in my cheeks is visible.

After I send it, he replies with a recorded text that's a long groan. It takes another minute for him to respond.

Wyatt: Good girl. So good. Now, slide those fingers between those lips and suck them real good.
Thea: Like this? [Photo attachment]

My lips are wrapped around two fingers to the second knuckle, puckered and plump. The way I angled the photo, I left more of my bare tits in the frame than my face and the dirty result drives my confidence higher. I like how wanton I appear.

Wyatt: Holy fuck. Yes, like that. Fuck.
Thea: What next? Tell me how to make myself feel good for you.
Wyatt: Mm yeah, that's good, baby. You're killing me, you sexy as fuck little minx. Need those lips on my cock.

The mental image pulls another gasp from me. I push my fingers back into my mouth, imagining they're bigger and take another photo for him. This time when he replies, I get a dick pic, seeing proof of the effect I have on him. It's shiny, like he spit in his palm or keeps a bottle of lube handy. Pleasure coils deep in my chest because I did that to him, made him hard, made him masturbate to thoughts of being with me. I bite my lip around the shy smile curving my mouth.

Thea: So hot. You going to put it in me?

For a second, I squirm through a frisson of embarrassment. Is that good enough dirty talk? Should I have said cock or something?

The momentary worry disappears when his response comes through.

Wyatt: Fuck yes. So hard for you. Going to fuck your brains out, sweetness. Your fingers nice and wet? They're my tongue. Touch your clit, nice long strokes so you know exactly how I'm tasting you.

My chest caves with my sharp breath. I follow his directions, wriggling out of my romper and kicking the soft material from my ankles. I lay there for a moment, feeling the cool air of my bedroom on my nude body. The throbbing between my thighs is so heady that I don't think I'll last long once I start rubbing my clit. I'm ready to burst from the oversensitivity he's caused with our sexting.

Dragging my fingertips down my belly and stroking my mound, I let every sensation wash over me. My head tips back when I slide my fingers between my legs and do as Wyatt said, imagining his tongue licking my pussy. Shit, it feels amazing.

I spread my legs wider, getting into it. I've never done it like this, above my covers, the lights on, with total abandon. The world could explode around me, but my focus would only be on my body, on the pleasure I feel touching myself while pretending it's him.

Growing bolder, I bring my phone close and hold down the record audio button, capturing the breathy moans as I rub my clit.

"Wyatt," I whimper. "Feels so good. I'm close."

My thumb slips off the button and I pause long enough to send it before refocusing on what my body demands. The pleasure crests higher. My hips rock as I seek out my orgasm.

Wyatt hasn't said anything for a few minutes, but my brain is so clouded with the fog of touching myself that it takes me a while to notice. Maybe he was close and feels the same as I do, needing to reach oblivion.

The phone pings again, so I could be wrong. Who cares, as long as I keep feeling like this. I press harder, rubbing my fingers in a tight circle over my sensitive clit.

Wyatt: I want more of those sinful sounds you're making. Show me how good it feels, baby. Is your sweet pussy wet for me?

I don't know if it's because I'm so close to coming that I could be convinced of anything, or that I'm flying high on the way this has all unfolded, but I don't feel any shame or nerves anymore. Raising the phone with a wicked little grin, I get a good angle from above of my fingers dipped between my legs, knees drawn together. Just as I fire it off, the hot coil in my core intensifies.

"Ah!"

I drop my head back into the pillows while I stroke my fingers over my folds to gather some of the slickness coating my labia and thighs, gliding my fingers back over my clit. The waves crash over me, the intensity of the orgasm making me clench on the emptiness I wish were full of Wyatt's dick right now as I tremble. It feels incredible, definitely the best orgasm I've ever experienced.

Elation spirals through me, mingling with the aftershocks of pleasure skating over my skin, and I smile at the ceiling, stretching my arms overhead.

The abandoned phone buzzes on the bedspread with a new message. I roll onto my side and rub my thighs together lazily as I reach for it, enjoying the lasting effects of sensitivity and how wet I feel.

I nearly drop the phone with a surprised yelp. Wyatt upped the ante again with a Boomerang. The animated image plays when I open it and my mouth drops open as it repeats. Oh my god. I watch it four times, fascinated and turned on.

In the Boomerang clip he fists his cock with fast strokes and at the last couple of seconds before it starts over, come spills over his fingers.

Wyatt: Thanks babe [wink emoji]

I debate what to say next. Is there something universal that says thanks for the orgasm via text message? And can we set up a time to do it again?

Boldly, I lounge naked instead of getting up to get dressed as fast as possible. The confidence lingers. I roll onto my back and cross one leg over the other, hoping he'll say something first since he seems to be well-versed in this sort of thing.

My face lights up when he does reply shortly after the last of the afterglow fades.

Wyatt: Let me see how you look after you've come.

After everything we did tonight, this one feels easy now. I fluff my hair and recline against my pillows, tilting my face for a cute picture. There's a glow of life in my flushed cheeks and my sparkling eyes. It's one of the very rare times I like how I look in a photo on the first take.

Thea: Goodnight [heart emoji] [Photo attachment]

"Thea!"

A knock at my door makes my heart skip about eighty beats. My life force threatens to leave my body. I can feel the pull for it to float out of my mouth and drift through my ceiling. Poetic that I'd die young, sated, and totally freaking naked.

Mom jiggles the handle and knocks again. "Why is your door locked?"

"One sec, Mom! I'm changing for bed."

I shove my phone under my pillow and kick my romper under the bed. After hurrying into a pair of pink flannel sleep pants and a loose t-shirt sitting on my hamper, I check the mirror and hope she can't tell.

Unlocking the door, I peek through the crack. "Did you need anything?"

"Just wanted to make sure you remembered to study for your math test."

Mom crosses her arms, scrutinizing me in that silent motherly way that feels as if she's eating me alive. I shift on my feet, keeping my expression blank by sheer force of will. *Project calmness and she won't demand to come inspect the room.* Her gaze flicks over my shoulder, peering into what little I allow her to see of my room with me blocking the door.

"Of course I studied for it. I'm all done for the night," I assure her. Crap, is my voice still a little breathy? I clear my throat. "Anyway, goodnight."

I give her a kiss on the cheek and scurry back into my room, diving beneath the covers. A giggle bubbles up in my chest and I hide it in my stuffed sea lion when I fish him out.

Tonight was amazing.

FOUR
Connor

I'm either still lightheaded from smoking weed and jerking off, or going batshit fucking crazy because the photo my hot little mystery texter sent looks way too familiar. She's leaning back against a pile of purple pillows that are frilly, or some other girly shit, with auburn curls spilling around her beautiful face. The look she's giving me is…fuck, it makes me want to get off with her again.

Something about her prods at me as I languor in my post-orgasm haze with one arm tucked behind my head, feeling really damn good.

"Wait."

I sit the fuck up, dick still out and everything. Because I do know those blue-green doe eyes. Normally they're sweeping over me with sharp sparks of scorn when I tease her about the frumpy ass sweaters she wraps herself in. Not just scorn, but judgment, just like her nosy bitch of a mother.

"Well, shit." I drag the word out, followed by a short laugh of disbelief as I stare at the girl I've only ever known as my nerdy neighbor, Thea Kennedy.

A shy girl at school I love to torment just to watch her blush.

The same sexy as fuck little minx I just had an awesome sext jerk off session with.

I trace a finger over my lips and glance at my window. Her bedroom faces mine. I've caught her peeking once or twice while I changed, thinking those sheer curtains hide her. Might've even put on a bit of a show for her once I knew she liked to watch. Blinds are for pussies.

Who knew under those lumpy, shapeless sweaters in every color of the rainbow, she hides a body like that, with those luscious, seductive curves? It really is the quiet ones that are the biggest surprise.

I scroll back through our messages to admire the nudes and smirk. Her voice recording is still there, because she's a naïve thing that doesn't have them set to expire after listening. How cute. Between the photos and the recording, I could have an entire field day blackmailing her to do whatever I wanted.

The way she responded to me, obeyed me, makes it a strong temptation. My best friend Devlin would probably do it in a heartbeat, but he's a dark and twisted fucker. I maintain a rep that I could implode lives on a whim, when really I prefer to have a reason to destroy someone with the dirt I keep on people.

As I press the replay button, her breathless voice fills my room again.

"*Wyatt,*" Thea whimpers, innocent and sinful all at once. Her soft tone stirs my cock for another round. "*Feels so good. I'm close.*"

It had thrown me the first time I heard it, long enough to stop stroking my dick. She'd called out another man's name and a righteous bout of jealousy surged through me. I'd never been possessive over my hookups, but something about her in that moment made me want to hear *my* name falling from those plump pink glossy lips before she came.

Now things click into place with the blood flow returning to my brain. This is all a case of mistaken identity. She texted the wrong number. Whoever this Wyatt guy is, he's not me. And if I have anything to say about it, he won't ever get to hear Thea moaning his name like that.

The games I play with her at school are out of petty boredom. I need more of this side of Thea. Things just got a lot more interesting.

The next time she makes those sounds, it'll be because I drew them out of her.

My mouth curves in a mean smirk. I bet it will piss off her neighborhood busybody mother if she ever finds out her shy, mousy little daughter is naughty under those good grades and oversized granny sweaters. It's time for some revenge for what that woman did, sticking her nose where it didn't belong.

If I'm going to do this, I have to be strategic. I can't reveal myself yet. It will end this game too soon. Thea is the shy type who likes to get freaky in secret. She'll piss her pants and take off running if I come at this too hard.

No, I have to take it slow and steady. Figure out my play and the next three possible moves ahead to find the right moment to unveil that it's been me all along.

For now, I save her number to my phone and take care of the dirty tissues I dumped on the floor after cleaning myself up.

Thea doesn't know it yet, but with one racy selfie, she stepped into my world.

FIVE
Connor

By the next week, I've settled into a new routine. Wake up, text the little mouse that lives next door, take care of my morning wood with help from photos of Thea's sleepy eyes sparkling with mischief, shower for school, text her again—and so on throughout the day until I'm coming before bed to the image of Thea's perfect tits. The best part of the game is passing Thea in the halls or in classes we share, completely unaware I know how she sounds when she's about to come.

I've been keeping up the pretense that I'm this Wyatt guy she believes she's messaging.

On Tuesday, the soccer team has a practice scrimmage after school. Half of us play positions to cover one team, and the rest play against us. We're tied 1-1, but we're coming up on the end of the game.

There's nothing like the feeling of driving the ball toward the goal, the sweet grass-scented breeze in your hair, every nerve ending fizzling with energy. I love playing soccer. Always have, since my dad first put a ball in front of me.

My boy Devlin only has his head half in the game. I've pulled him up on it as captain once, but he keeps watching the girls track team. More specifically, the school's charity case sitting nearby like she's being subtle. Devlin got her kicked off the team because she pissed him off. Those two are bound to be fucking by the end of the year if they aren't yet.

"Dev!" I shout, dribbling the ball while avoiding two mid-fielders. "You better quit making moon eyes at Davis when I make this pass."

I check my periphery for him. One guy playing against us tries to break my footwork, but Devlin appears out of nowhere, like the lightning-quick devil I know, and picks up the pass I send him.

Satisfied laughter bubbles from my chest as Devlin's attack turns merciless, whipping past the other team's defenders and punting the ball with insane speed. It's how he got his nickname, the dark devil of Silver Lake. Together we're an unstoppable pair. The ball becomes a blur, cutting through the air and sailing past their goalie's outstretched hands as he dives for the save.

Devlin turns back to me, a sharp, wicked smirk in place. He jogs to my side at a lazy pace. I shake my head, grinning at my best friend. He's an asshole, but I love him. We get each other in a way the rest of the superficial idiots at this school don't.

"We could've cinched that goal faster if you hadn't been all goo-goo eyes for Davis. I told you last year, bro, you've got to just do her already, get your obsession out of your system." I hook an arm around Devlin's neck and rub my knuckles into his scalp. "Watching you two eye-fuck at lunch is not on my agenda for a second year in a row."

"Fuck off." Devlin shrugs my arm off. "I wouldn't touch Davis' cunt if it were the last one in the world."

I bark out another laugh. "Even you don't have that much self control. Pussy is pussy. You'd cave eventually."

Devlin rolls his eyes. "Whatever, prick. If you're so sure, you go fuck her."

"Nah. You called dibs last year." I hold up three fingers in a Boy Scout salute and solemnly intone, "Bro code is sacred."

I get smacked upside the head for being a good friend. Dick.

"All right, guys," I call. Sticking my fingers in my mouth, I whistle for the team to circle up on center field. They hustle over, wiping sweat from their brows with their practice jerseys. "Trent, you need to dig harder when the ball comes to our backs. Don't slack because it's practice, you lazy shit. Bad habits in practice make for bad habits in real games."

Trent snorts and flips me off while Sean, our other center-back, shoves him with a smirk.

"First official game of the season on Friday. No partying the night before. I don't want to hear any excuses—if I can manage, so can you." I point at a few of the guys who are hard-up to get through the week without getting wild. A few murmurs of assent filter through the team. "Aight. Go shower off the stink, you disgusting fuckers."

The team trickles toward the locker room entrance at the back of the school. Our coach waits for me to check in with him by the sidelines. He lets me run things since I made varsity captain last year, but offers insightful pointers I can't see when I'm playing the game.

Devlin hangs around, fiddling with his phone while I finish up going over the schedule with the coach. Something distracted him today. Whatever it is, it's been bugging him since yesterday. Maybe longer. He was weird over the weekend—weirder than usual. I'm used to most of his quirky shit after years of friendship, like his penchant for reading boring ass psychology books.

It was easier to weather Devlin's brooding moods when his older cousin was around. Lucas Saint was king of this school last year, a grade ahead of us and this town's golden boy with a golden arm. Too bad he pissed all that talent away to go to art school with his girlfriend.

With Lucas at college, Silver Lake High School belongs to Devlin and me. It's our senior year. He's our Devil Boy with his black hair, mischievous smile, and a wily streak the size of Texas. We're the perfect match of deviants.

"What time does it start tonight?" Devlin asks.

The corner of my mouth lifts. The Ridgeview police chief's son, Holden Landry, is organizing a fight ring. Because I have a copy of a positive drug test that would end Landry's football dreams along with footage of him getting blitzed at a boat party over the summer, Devlin and I are getting a thirty percent cut of tonight's winnings.

This is how things operate with us in charge.

"He's taking bets until seven. Pick me up at nine?" I grab the bag of soccer balls and sling it over my shoulder as we walk to the locker rooms. Devlin is distracted by his phone again, obsessively checking his messages. "I'll be at the usual spot down the block."

"You're like a junior high chick, the way you sneak out," Devlin says absently.

"You know what my mom is like. Most of the time I wish someone would see me sneak out and run a story in the gossip column." I gesture with my hands to highlight a headline. "I can see it now, Chairwoman Bishop's re-election campaign overshadowed by delinquent son." A wistful sigh blows past my lips and I elbow Devlin. "It would solve so many of my problems."

"At least she's around."

I bite back a reply. Devlin's parents duck out on him pretty often. I haven't seen them in three or four years.

Clapping my hand around his shoulder, I squeeze him closer in a half-hug. "Whatever. Tonight's going to be awesome."

The black shadow that passed over Devlin's features clears, replaced by a devious gleam in his dark gaze.

* * *

The scent of weed and beer tinges the night air. It's cooler than it was earlier now that the sun has gone down. September is still warm as hell during the day, but as soon as it's nightfall the mountain air turns frigid.

A joint dangles from my lips as Devlin and I move through the crowd, bumping fists with people here and there. A dirty bass line plays from a wireless speaker, the distorted sound flooding the woods at the edge of the abandoned quarry off Blackhawk Road. After it closed it was filled in. Now all that remains is a gravel lot at the base of the mountain. A few Coyote Girls, townies, and chicks from the two public schools dance on truck beds in skintight ripped jeans and cowgirl boots. Laughter spills through the night and a sense of wild debauchery threads through everyone's energy.

It's the perfect place for illicit partying in Ridgeview, the access road rarely used since the new highway was built. The only people that come through hit it up during the day for the old hiking trail that heads up into the Rockies.

I scan the crowd for Landry. Everyone is getting rowdy before the fights start. I've got something on almost every person here in my files, from my soccer teammates to the people who run in my crowd. Everyone is fair game. It's become an ingrained habit, one I don't plan on quitting anytime soon.

Landry is hanging by a classy white Jeep, thumbing through a wad of cash with a guy I don't know while he flirts with the hot girl sitting on the hood. Maybe he's a townie, but Landry hands him the cash, so he must run with him. He looks like an odd match to Landry, a punk with a leather jacket, messy dark hair, and a mean glint in his eyes when they land on me. I have no idea how Silver Lake's starting quarterback and this guy could have crossed paths.

I leave Devlin with the guys and head for the Jeep. The girl Landry's talking to lets her knees fall open and he steps between them with a wolfish grin. I recognize her as a poli-sci post-grad who joined my mom's campaign staff over the summer.

"Did you close out the call for bets?" I ask as I lean against the Jeep. The campaign staffer's eyes go wide when they land on me. I wink at her and tap my nose. "What mommy dearest doesn't know, right?"

"Uh, yeah," she answers with a strained cough.

To be extra welcoming since this is the first I've seen her at an SLHS party, I offer my joint. She hesitates, then accepts it, taking two hits and grabbing Landry to shotgun the smoke into his mouth.

"Nice," I say.

Landry flips me off without breaking the kiss with the campaign staffer. His friend rolls his eyes and stalks off with a grunt.

Being discreet, I record a short video clip of them kissing to add to my blackmail collection. Papa Landry would blow his lid at the scandals his son is wracking up. What would be more interesting is if Landry's younger sister shed her good girl veneer and proved to be even naughtier. With that tight little yoga bod she has, I wouldn't mind seeing what sort of trouble she could get up to.

Cute as little Maisy Landry is, my mind drifts to Thea and those dime curves she keeps hidden under oversized clothes. I thumb into our message thread. The last text she sent to "Wyatt" was a selfie with a cake she baked after school. I didn't give a shit about the cake, more interested in the fact her hair was tied up in perky pigtails. Fucking *pigtails*. I work my jaw as a bolt of heat shoots to my groin.

A surge of cheers drowns out the music, drawing me from my thoughts. People move in droves from where the cars are parked in the gravel lot into the tree line. The headlights spill into a clearing through the trees. I guess the first fight is starting.

Devlin finds me and we head over together. He hands me a beer and lights up a cigarette. We join the crowd circled around two guys duking it out, grunting when their punches land.

Fight Club rules apply, bare knuckles and no shirts. A few guys are positioned around the clearing to deal with any idiot filming for the likes on social media. Landry's leather jacket friend is one of them, pushing a hand through his hair as he narrows his cold gaze on a couple of chicks taking selfies near us.

One of the fighters in the ring is on the student council at school, with string bean arms, cheeks already pink with exertion and they've barely begun. Thanks to my weekly summons from my dad to the school office before therapy, I also know Mr. Student Council was accused of peddling Adderall last week. He swings with gritted teeth and manages to clock his opponent in the chin. The other guy stumbles back a step to regroup, then comes in with a quick one-two jab to Student Council's weakly guarded center.

The underground fighting is about letting out aggression. The betting is fun, but hardly any of us need the money. Ridgeview is a town that hit it rich in the gold rush era and the sun's been shining down on us since.

Devlin snorts, the sound dark and amused as Student Council successfully takes down his larger opponent, using speed against strength to maneuver the force of gravity on his side. The bigger guy goes down and Student Council wails on him, blood staining his teeth from a split lip, pure murderous rage blazing in his eyes.

It's violent, unhinged, and fucking glorious.

Landry steps into the ring and blows on a whistle clenched between his teeth. Grabbing Student Council's wrist and wrenching it into the air, he barks, "Winner. Next challenger in the ring in two minutes, or you forfeit your buy-in."

The crowd shuffles, waiting for the next person to step forward. Once they do, another match starts. Student Council goes down in two hits, knocked out and sprawled in the dirt.

As the following fighter enters the clearing, my phone goes off in my back pocket. Devlin exchanges a curious glance with me as I step away from the crowd. The name on the screen has me grinding my teeth. *Mom.*

I debate not taking it, feeling a muscle jump in my cheek from how hard my jaw locks. If I ignore it, she'll only hound me once I get home. Big fat FML either way. What a pain in the ass.

"I've gotta take this. I'll be back," I tell Devlin before I jog away from the party. Lifting the phone to my ear, I answer, "What?"

"Is that any way to answer your mother, Connor?"

"I could've not answered," I say dismissively as I pass the cars where some people are still hanging out and talking, and head for the old storage building.

"Where are you? It sounded loud when you answered." The judgement is clear in her tone.

Rolling my eyes and scrubbing a palm over my face, I lean against the rusty corrugated metal siding, kicking at the weeds popping out of the gravel at my feet. "People from school. We're hanging out at a friend's house."

She hums on the line, uppity even in her non-verbal communication. That socialite upbringing always shines best when she's disappointed by whatever way I'm embarrassing her now.

I don't have all night for this. "What do you want?"

"Have you checked the schedule? Angela should have updated the mobile calendar. The

children's hospital dinner benefit is coming up. This is your reminder that the entire family must be present. We have to show a united family front for the voters."

For the voters. I bring the phone away from my ear to scoff.

Everything she does is for her constituents. It's the only reason she wants me at this charity event and that dinner, all of these bullshit parties so she can trot out the happy family pony show. Meanwhile, that home-wrecker Damien sleeps in our house and makes Mom breakfast. He stupidly offered me coffee this morning and I threatened to dump the fresh pot over his head.

"Connor," Mom says on the line. I bring the phone back to my ear. *"We're almost there. We've worked this hard and all that's left is the finish line when elections come up. Understood?"*

"Roger." She can't see, but I give a sharp salute anyway.

Before she can add any other stipulations, I hang up and stomp back through the parked cars to the clearing in the woods. Adrenaline and anger rush through my veins. My breathing has picked up and my vision shrinks around the edges, focused on the ring.

Devlin steps in my path. His expression tightens around his eyes when he takes me in. "You good?"

"My mom," I say.

It's all the explanation I need with him. His dark brows hike up and he stands aside. He knows how I get after a call with her. I strip out of my henley and toss it to him.

"Give me your phone, too."

I hand it over and spot Landry's friend edging toward me. Pointing at him, I say, "Nah uh, dude. You might run with Landry, but he's not in charge here."

The leather jacket punk looks to Holden for confirmation. Landry nods and jerks his head to the ring. His friend picks at random and kicks one of the fighters back into the crowd. Before he's done, I'm stepping in, mouth pulled in a jagged, wild curve.

I square up with the guy who entered after Student Council was KO'd. He's bigger than me, bulkier, but he's tired. He swings and I dodge, smirk stretching wider. A flash of worry crosses my opponent's face. He backs off a couple of steps, trying to lure me in. I don't take the obvious bait, instead waiting for him to come at me again. When he does, I pop him in the chin.

A fist comes against my forearm as I block his blow, but I make a mistake in my stance, giving a clean opening for the guy to punch my face. Shit, I don't even care if I bruise. Maybe I'll get real lucky and it'll last long enough to make me look extra good next to Mom for her stupid fucking campaign benefit.

I spit into the dirt and swipe my hand beneath my nose to catch the trickle of blood. It comes away bright red, smeared across my knuckles. A minor blood vessel injury, nothing serious. When I chuckle, the guy backs off again, glancing at Landry.

No one wants to fight crazy. It's different than angry. Unpredictable. Dangerous.

Come the fuck at me, bro.

I lift a hand and wave him back for more. "Come on, I won't bite."

"No biting," Landry's surly friend barks.

A sharp laugh punches from my gut. I gesture to Landry's friend, appealing to my opponent. "See, no biting. It's in the rules. Let's fucking go, big guy. Time to dance."

The match starts back up and I go hard, unleashing everything I've got until I can see the fear creeping into my opponent's wide eyes. We go long enough that every one of his punches result from desperation as the crowd screams and cheers. Their shouts are drowned out by the pounding pulse in my ears.

Sweet oblivion comes when I use my fists to channel the anger out. I'm the kind of fucked up monster that takes enjoyment in making the guy I'm fighting think I might actually kill him with my bare hands. It's not his fault I'm like this, I don't even see his face when I throw a punch. Every time I do, I'm right back to that afternoon I caught Mom and Damien and lost it.

My next hit clocks the guy across his red, swollen cheek and he goes down in a slump. Everyone erupts in a deafening ruckus of screams, celebrating another win. Landry stands off to my left at the edge of the clearing, hands propped on his hips. He's probably pissed I didn't mention wanting in on tonight, only blackmailed him into a cut of the winnings. If he'd known, he would have made a bigger killing.

I stand over my opponent, panting. He's out cold. Damn, I wanted that to go longer. I glance up, scanning the crowd for the next challenger.

It takes almost the entire two minute allowance, but as the crowd grows restless, hungry for more brutality, someone else enters the clearing.

My mouth curves wickedly and I square up for the next round.

SIX
Thea

SWEAT beads along my temples and makes the baby hairs falling from my messy bun curl against my skin, sticking to the back of my neck as I walk Constantine through the neighborhood. *Something Beautiful* by Tori Kelly plays in my earbuds as we amble along in the uncomfortable afternoon heat, the soulful girl power song helping me forget any self-consciousness for my outfit. It's too hot out to cover up, so I'm in high waist yoga leggings and a billowy boatneck crop top over a sports bra.

Luckily, the neighborhood is pretty quiet this time of day. It's shortly after school let out, and too early for people to be home from work, so no one will see me like this. It's just me, my chunky rottweiler, and the sprawling manicured lawns bordered by natural landscaping rather than fence lines to avoid interrupting the effect of money at work. I swipe my arm over my forehead and emit a tiny groan. Maybe I'll whip up homemade ice cream when we get back. Pumpkin ice cream sounds so good right now.

Constantine doesn't mind the heat, happily keeping pace at my side with his tongue lolling out. I laugh when he stops to sniff a garden bed, coming nose to nose with a fat bumble bee that bonks against his snout and sends him into a playful tumble in the grass.

"Oh, Con, you silly boy. Come on. It's too hot to stay out for our usual walk." I give his lead a tug and continue down the sidewalk. "When we get home, we're making ice cream. How's that sound?"

Constantine gives me the cutest head tilt, his black ears perked.

A jogger rounds the corner on the next block and my steps falter. Shirtless, abs and pecs glistening in the sunlight, Connor Bishop looks like a god amongst men. His light brown hair bounces with his effortless running form, his long legs powerful as he cuts his path. Everything about his aura says *confident, knows what he wants, and nothing's stopping him from getting it.* It's an alluring sight to behold, addictive to be around in school—it's no wonder everyone flocks to him. He's really hot, but I could never want him.

No matter how attractive he looks, especially now, running toward me in nothing but basketball shorts, it doesn't forgive how he's treated me the few times he's paid me any attention since we were kids.

I force myself to keep walking toward my house. Self-consciousness creeps back in.

Why are these streets so long? Why are our houses both in the middle? Maybe he'll reach his before me and I won't have to worry about interacting with him. It's not like he's noticed me much this year.

We're almost home free, but Connor catches my eye after I close out of the playlist on my phone once I reach my driveway. I freeze, arrested by the full force of his attention. It's weirdly commanding, without him telling me to wait I'm obeying. He gives me a once over that floods my cheeks with warmth. *Oh my god.*

Does he think I look weird? A crop top is all wrong for me, I knew it.

No.

That's not true. My inner critic can shove it. I have a body and I can dress it any way I want.

I bet Wyatt wouldn't think my outfit is strange. He appreciates me. I'm already picturing taking a naughty selfie later where I lose the sports bra and flash my boobs, holding the hem of the crop top up with my teeth.

Knowing there's at least one person out there who finds me beautiful just as I am gives me the strength I need to face Connor.

Constantine plops onto his haunches by my side, dragging me from being under Connor's controlling spell. His cool gray eyes flick to the dog for a second before flying back to meet my gaze.

"Um," I mumble, twisting the leash in my hands.

Connor takes AirPods from his ear and studies me again, slower this time, dragging his gaze down my body. "Were you looking at me, neighbor? Here? Or maybe here?"

As he taunts me, he smooths a hand over his pec, then down his torso, hooking his thumb in the waistband of his shorts. His knuckles are red and there's a bruise on his jaw. It makes him look more dangerously handsome.

Air catches in my throat when I inhale too sharply. I fling my hands in front of myself defensively. "I—no, I—"

"Relax." Connor's voice is as smooth as the curve of his smirking full lips. He rubs his chin and rakes his teeth over his lower lip. "There's no crime in it." Each brush of his eyes is like a brand as they sweep over my legs and back up, lingering on my chest.

My breaths come faster. It's hard to ignore him when he's making sure I can't look away. Those gray eyes have some kind of magic that keeps me rooted in place. This might be the closest I've ever been to him.

A raspy chuckle drops from his lips. "Look at you, turning red, little mouse. Are you blushing from the heat or—" He steps closer, leaning in, lips nearly brushing my cheek "—because you like what you see?"

I jerk my head back as my heart thuds from his proximity and the rich, earthy scent of his sweaty skin. He really enjoys the sound of his own voice. For a second, his voice almost sounds like Wyatt's, but I brush that aside. It's simply that he's mocking me with his flirty oversexualization of everything.

"It's human nature to look. You know, with your dumpy clothes I never pictured you were hiding that underneath."

Connor gestures at my midsection, where my curves are on display. I suck in another sharp breath and narrow my eyes.

"Now, just what is that supposed to mean?"

He shrugs. "You should lose the bulky sweaters. They do nothing for you. About as much sex appeal as a bunch of grandmas playing bridge."

I open my mouth to tell him off for being such an ass, but our front door opens and Mom steps out, keeping to the shade behind the stacked stone columns. She lurks there, watching us. When I don't move, she crosses her arms.

"Thea," she snaps.

My mouth purses and I tighten my grip on Constantine's leash. He shifts at my feet, restless from the tension rolling off me. Is she kidding right now? Ignoring her, I swing a glare back on Connor.

"You're very rude."

He blinks, parting his lips like I've surprised him. Maybe he expected me to curse him out or slap him, like other girls at our school might. Loud, confident girls. But that's not me. I only raise my voice if there's no other choice. Bolstered by catching him off guard, I give him another piece of my mind.

"There's nothing wrong with the way I choose to dress, whether it's a potato sack, my favorite sweater, or this." I fist the hem of my shirt, revealing a tiny strip of skin. Connor impresses me slightly by holding out longer than I expected, but his gaze drops to my midsection after a few beats. "And besides all that, I dress for me, not you, or anyone else. You don't like my sweaters? Tough. So you can just leave me alone and go back to ignoring me."

I don't raise my voice, it even quavers a little at the end. Pride burns in my chest, pleased with myself for standing my ground and telling the jerk off.

This bravery has been growing since I first texted Wyatt, because I don't have to live in fear, hiding myself away. I would never have had the guts to stand up to Connor before. Saying how I feel is empowering, both new and unfamiliar.

It's short-lived when Mom appears at my side. My eyes widen as she waves me to follow impatiently.

"Thea, inside, *now*." Mom huffs when I don't immediately snap into motion. She's acting like Connor has a contagious disease with how embarrassing she's being. My life was already hard facing his teasing without her going all psycho mom on me. "I can't believe you went out like—" She cuts herself off with a frustrated sound. "Let's go."

I tug my arm from her grasp when she tries to take my wrist. "What's the matter? I'm coming, okay? Connor and I go to school together. We were just saying hello on my way back from walking."

Her livid expression says it all. God, what is her freaking deal? Doesn't she realize how insane she seems, dragging her grown daughter inside, away from a boy? Her lip curls and she shoots Connor a poisonous look.

"Stay away from this boy, Thea. I don't want you talking to him."

Connor watches the entire exchange with a bored expression, fingers tucked in the sides of his basketball shorts. He meets Mom's nasty gaze with an arrogant grin, like he knows exactly how much he pisses her off.

"See you later, neighbor," Connor says, eyes half-lidded and locked on me.

There's something about the way he says it that makes my skin break out in a ripple of hot and cold.

Mom releases a bitchy scoff and nudges me toward the house, Constantine following. As soon as we cross the threshold, she lays into me, saying what she refused to air in front of our neighbor.

"How could you go out dressed like that?" She flings her hand at me in jerky movements, indicating my top.

My temper rises. I kept my cool with Connor, but Mom sets me off. She never listens to me when I'm quiet. Arguing with her, I don't have any choice but to raise my voice, or she'd never hear me.

"There is nothing wrong with what I'm wearing, Mom!" I unclip Constantine and he trots off toward the kitchen, the sound of him lapping up water filtering through to the vaulted entryway where Mom and I face off with each other. "These are workout clothes and it was hot."

"Thea!" Her disappointed cry follows me as I go into the kitchen, picking out ingredients and pulling out the mixing bowls. Screw the ice cream, I need to shut my racing mind up. "I don't care how hot out it is, boys will see you dressing like that and think you're advertising you're welcome to their advances!"

If Dad didn't travel so much for work, maybe we wouldn't always be at each other's throats. But he's not here to create a buffer, currently away for another regional conference. I'm on my own against her.

"Do you hear yourself, Mom?" I whirl on her, slamming a whisk on the white countertop. Mom startles. I almost jump myself. Being so confrontational isn't my style. The burst of indignation burned hot and fast at what she said, and I just acted. "This isn't the flipping dark ages. No one is going to freak out because I'm walking around in leggings."

"They will if you're only *half dressed*! Your bra straps are—"

"Mom, so help me, if you are about to say something about my sports bra being visible, I will lose it." It's like I can't even breathe when I'm smothered by her. Constantine comes to sit by my feet, leaning against my leg. I turn back to my baking supplies, surveying what I grabbed on instinct as I continue ranting, getting on a real roll now that I've broken the dam. "Besides, boys need to learn to control themselves so I don't have to put myself out and be uncomfortable in the heat in order to keep their eyes off me. And why am I living in fear of a boy looking at me? Why is that so bad? It's human nature!"

Once it slips out, it occurs to me those are Connor's words.

Moving to the other side of the kitchen, Mom hisses at me, "They're out of control. None of them know how to behave."

"Seriously!" I toss my arms up in frustration. Talking to her is impossible when she gets on these topics. She's so backwards. "That is such a sexist idea that *I* have to change and be the one to protect myself, and that all boys are dick-for-brains animals driven by their impulses. It's a ridiculous argument, Mom, and it's complete crap."

Her eyes bulge and she opens and closes her mouth a few times, searching for some way to respond to my call out. I can't decide whether she's more pissed I said dick or that I disagreed with her. I stand my ground through it all, hands planted on the counter, armed with my baking supplies for fortitude. Having Constantine's solid weight against my leg helps, too.

When she turns a concerning shade of purple, she gives up on whatever she was going to say and rushes out of the room, leaving Constantine and me alone.

"Well," I say, glancing at the chubby rottweiler at my feet. "Let's bake."

Within minutes, I lose myself to the methodical process that quiets my mind and melts away my stress.

*　*　*

Baking cherry turnovers from scratch helped calm me down, but I'm still annoyed at Mom after finishing up my homework in my room later. The corners of my mouth lift as I twirl a pen between my fingers, sitting cross-legged on my bed. As irritated as I am, I'm so damn proud of myself for not only standing up to Mom, but also telling Connor off.

It felt good.

For those few minutes I embodied everything I aspire to be in my secret folder photos, and for once I wasn't sacrificing anything about myself to do it. Usually when I try to become Secret Folder Girl, I'm imitating other women who have made me stop and go wow, because they have that *it* factor.

It's been like that since my early teens, bombarded with images of the elusive idea of a perfect woman—as if anyone could live up to the fake ideals presented to us. Women are already wonderful the way they are. But I still struggle to accept that myself, even if I can dole out that advice to my friends.

Those old wounds are stubborn, scabbed over but never fully healing.

I shuffle my books to the nightstand and minimize the half-finished English paper for my favorite teacher on my laptop, opening a new browser window. The address I type in is ingrained, my fingers flying across the keyboard with muscle memory to type out my blog address.

The one I hid from Mom.

It loads, showing a feed of my latest posts—old photos of myself posed by the lake in a bikini that Maisy took for me, selfies in my bedroom trying on different outfits with short skirts or tying the tails of my blouse to reveal my stomach, and artsy crops where a hint of bra or panty line edge into the frame. Hundreds of posts blur past as I scroll the history of my blog, each with a photo.

I haven't posted to it in a long time, at least a year and a half. I didn't have to once I found someone to fill the void the blog plugged up in my aching heart.

Looking at these is kind of cringy now, seeing the phase I went through where I did my hair in half-braided pigtails in every photo, or the ones where I put on thick winged eyeliner. The cringe factor only lasts for a few minutes, then it's just like the muscle memory, the old photos from a few years ago reminding me how good they made me feel at the time.

The comments help that feeling.

I click on posts at random, seeing the numerous comments left by **Henry_Your_GoodKnight**.

Henry_Your_GoodKnight: *This is your best color. I'll picture you like this always.*

Henry_Your_GoodKnight: *Beauty beyond measure princess, but what really gets me is the way you smile. Your intelligent eyes say it all, love. You're longing for the world to show you all it has to offer.*

Henry_Your_GoodKnight: *Wish I could be there with you to experience your laugh. You'll always be my princess.*

His words were always like poetry. He seemed so intellectual and cool. The fact he followed me? Wanted to talk to me? It was a dream come true to have someone like him notice me.

I don't always end up deep down this memory lane. Usually I only look at the pictures, but once I read one of his comments, I find myself in an all-consuming black hole. One after the other, I relive being the sad little girl so desperate to love herself, to make sense of her changing body, to experience being wanted, that I latched onto the first person to give me that. A stranger on the internet who found my blog and gave me the attention I was so hungry for.

There's an echoing pulse of endorphins as I read through the emails we've exchanged, where I sent more...risqué photos when he asked for them. Nothing nude, but not entirely innocent, either. He was so good at talking to me, getting me to see things his way. But some part of me is uncomfortable with the idea the suggestive images are still out there somewhere. I couldn't bring myself to ever delete the emails, afraid I might forget the connection we had.

Maybe I'm stupid.

Maybe he doesn't think of me at all, even though he worms his way into my thoughts and brings my entire day to a halt.

Sometimes, when I'm feeling weak, I consider replying to an old email. Even if he doesn't respond, it would be an outlet. The temptation hovers at the back of my mind. I haven't taken things that far, though.

One of the earlier emails catches my eye.

To: Thea Marie <cupcakecutie22@gmail.com>
From: Henry Knight <henry.k.c@gmail.com>
Subject: a knight always comes for his princess

You're 15? Damn. Thought for sure you were older. By the way you talk and those pretty pictures, you seem closer to my age. I would expect to find you entering college with me this semester. That's not a big age difference, though. How do you like older guys? The idiots in your grade sound like their intellect is subpar to yours. They wouldn't understand you the way I do, princess. You must have one of those old souls, something too special to waste on boys your age. The connection I feel to you is unreal, it's hard to believe.

I used to feel just like you do. Tell me more about it. Tell me everything about you. I feel like I could reach through the screen and caress your cheek when you open up to me.

The world will show you what it has to offer you. It brought us together, didn't it? Now that I have you, I can't imagine you not being mine. Trust and it will keep offering you good things.

I guess I should sleep. It's 4am here. Thoughts of talking to you and imagining your laugh always keep me up. I want to touch your hair.
—Henry

Any time I talked to him, I felt his pain, too. He was like me. An old soul stuck in a body too mismatched to feel like we fit in with the world.

Henry was my first love. As much as our conversations skewed toward difficult, dark topics, or how many times he had to talk me into sending another photo, and another, and another...my sick heart was happy I had him.

I jolt when I hear Constantine barking downstairs. It's like a switch has flipped in my mind, the happy thoughts of love tainted by the logical side of me that judged myself the older I got. Releasing a rough sound of aggravation, I close out of everything, putting my face in my hands.

This is my crutch. My fall back. These memories are shrouded in shadows from a time I was tripping my way through growing up. If I had been able to express myself without fear of how much Mom would jump down my throat, maybe I wouldn't have turned to the internet for comfort.

I chew on the corner of my lip until it stings. "Ouch."

Pressing my fingers to my tender lip, I sigh. I used to think this was the most confident I could ever feel, but looking back at the old email thread, I feel in my bones how different it is from today, ever since Wyatt texted me back and took our fling to the next level.

I don't need to try to recapture the excitement I used to feel with my online boyfriend as I broke every one of Mom's rules, because now I have the real deal. It's only been a week, but Wyatt and I have messaged each other every day.

Popping off the bed, I put my laptop on the desk next to a stack of filled journals. I go on my tiptoes in the closet to reach behind an old box of binders filled to the brim with recipes I printed out from online to grab one of my secret stashes of contraband clothes. I lift the lid of the box covered in a sunflower pattern and unveil lingerie Maisy and I bought in secret when we went shopping for our summer retreat in the mountains. The material is soft and luxurious beneath my fingers as I touch the pretty bra and a sheer emerald green bodysuit.

I spend a solid half hour taking all new photos of myself, starting in my crop top, picking my mood up off the floor. When I've got several new pictures on my camera roll, I glance at the clock on my nightstand framed inside a porcelain rainbow. Perfect. It's about that time.

Picking the one I imagined earlier, where I've got a playful smile with the bottom of the crop top between my teeth, I send it to him.

My phone buzzes with a response right away. I bite my lip as pleasure fizzles beneath my skin. It's like he was waiting for me.

SEVEN
Connor

It's hours after the encounter with Thea at the end of my run, and I'm still obsessing over it. That was the closest I've ever gotten to her. Turns out, she smells like sugar.

And I wouldn't say no to a real taste.

After stripping out of my shorts, I almost texted her. She seemed to need the salvation of release with her bitchy mom breathing down her neck. The way she stood up to me, so quiet, yet so fucking fierce—I was rock hard and even her mom's arrival couldn't dilute the force of desire coursing in my veins. I've had people yell and scream in my face, threaten me, hit me, and all of it pales to the resolute way Thea held her own.

She doesn't fear me by reputation. We'll have to do something about that, won't we? She has no idea who she's getting tangled with.

Quiet, mousy Thea Kennedy interests me. I want to know what else there is behind the nerdy good girl.

I blame the thoughts of Thea when I enter the kitchen to grab something to eat for distracting me from realizing what was happening.

Mom and Damien look up as I pause in front of the fridge. He has a dish towel draped over his shoulder, a hint of a smile tugging at his lips, shirtsleeves rolled up as he dices vegetables at the island. Mom leans against the counter beside him, a glass of white wine raised to her lips. Her cheeks are tinged pink, the way they flush when she's been laughing.

It's domestic and turns my stomach as soon as I lay eyes on them.

"Hello, son," Damien greets.

My knuckles turn white as I fist my hands at my side. *Son.* No. Absolutely not. He has no right after what I caught them doing, after the beating I gave him for it.

I grunt in response, flashing him a glare. He always tries, and I never give him an inch. I'm in court-mandated anger management because he had to fuck my mom in our kitchen.

Mrs. Kennedy is to blame, too. That snooping busybody is the one who called the cops as a *concerned citizen* looking out for the neighborhood. The one thing Mom and I agree on is Mrs. Kennedy's position on both our shit lists. Without her, I wouldn't have been arrested and Mom wouldn't have bribed everyone involved to land me with therapy instead of juvie.

The faint scar at the corner of Damien's eye sends a sickening surge of pleasure into my stomach. I hit him so hard I fractured his brow bone. Mom's frantic screams still echo in my ears.

"How was school?" Mom asks, popping a cherry tomato in her mouth.

The laugh I bark out is jagged and loud.

"Let's not pretend you've ever been mom of the year. Cool? Cool." I wave a hand at the pair of them. "Go back to playing house with everyone who isn't part of this dysfunctional family."

Mom sighs.

Maybe I'd care if she ever acted like a decent parent.

This lovey-dovey scene can fuck all the way off. I have no intention of lingering around them, hell-bent on escaping to my room.

"Connor." Mom's clipped tone stops me in my tracks. Huffing, I half-turn back to her. She gestures to a manila folder sitting on the edge of the island, waiting in the spotlight cast by the pendant lights dangling above it. "Have a look through this. I've been wanting to talk with you about this matter for a while. It's important we go over it before the campaign benefit for the children's hospital."

My stomach churns with an uneasy ripple. She has her politician voice on, the false-sweetness belying the snake waiting in the grass to bite your ankle. Keeping an eye on Mom and Damien, I swipe the folder and flip it open, thinking I'm about to have some accusation thrown in my face. I've been expecting it with the bruise on my face and my knuckles still healing.

What's inside is so much worse than Mom being pissy over undeniable proof of me at an illegal fight ring.

The bafflement grows as I flip through pages of girls' photos followed by resumes, their entire lives profiled to the tits like they're security threats and it's necessary to know every minute detail about them. I suppose anything can be turned into a threat to a politician. My mom is the one I learned the lesson of *knowledge is power* from, after all.

"What is this?"

"Remember when I said we need to put on a united family front? Well, I also need you to have a girlfriend," Mom explains, distracted by Damien offering her a taste of the meal they're cooking. "A nice girl who will fit into the image we're cultivating. Polls are showing a positive rise in my numbers for voters wanting to see a legacy continuing on the horizon. Commitment is something they value and respect. I've taken the trouble of having these options prepared for you to choose from. They're already pre-approved and vetted."

The horizon. The problem with Mom is she doesn't just want to be re-elected to her office. She has a long-term plan. The endgame for her is the big one—the White House.

Controlling my expression to keep it blank is hard as disgust rolls through me, fighting back the urge to curl my lip. The entire folder is full of jersey chasing Coyote Girls. Not a single *nice girl* in the bunch at all, but all of them come from the crème de la crème families in Ridgeview. One elite name after another glares at me from the folder—daughters of old money like granddad's, real estate moguls, and Fortune 500 CEOs. Daughters of the people in

Ridgeview that hold positions of power and influence.

Half of them have hooked up with me. Hell, all of them want me to make them my queen. They recognize the power I hold at SLHS without adding in Mom's political clout.

But I don't date. Never have. Every one of the girls who come onto me are only interested in my name or my family's money.

"You can have your pick from any of the selections." Mom gives me a shark's smile. "Isn't that nice of me? It'll be the perfect boost for our family image."

How can she say that when she's standing in front of me with *him*, making a goddamn meal together from scratch?

I lose the internal battle not to show my cards, snarling as I slam the folder down. The contents spill out in a cascade, spreading over the island, some dipping into the prep station Damien has going.

"What family image?!" My voice rises as I jab a finger at Damien. "Your fucking boyfriend is right there, and you think I need someone? Maybe you should stop spreading your legs for that piece of shit and worry about having an actual family! Instead of fabricating whatever the approval polls dictate, wouldn't it be better to earn your votes the honest way?"

Mom crosses her arms and Damien casts a troubled look between us. *Go ahead and try it, fuckface. If you step in front of me, I'm knocking you out again.*

He takes a step closer and I raise my fists to a ready stance. "I won't hesitate."

Damien's eyes go wide. With a menacing smile that makes him shuffle back to put more distance between us, I stare Mom down for a beat before leaving the room.

"You will do this!" Mom calls after me, her voice changing from the saccharine tone to something more forceful, more true to her actual character.

It sends anger racing down my spine, but I stomp up the stairs to my room instead of fighting her. I might get what I want at school, but with her it takes work. She believes she has full control over me because of the money. Everything with her is an endless sequence of moves until I can back her into a corner, proving that the outcome I want is the right one. If I don't have smoke and mirrors, then my strategy blows up in my face.

My ragged breathing doesn't calm down until I've paced my room, going over possibilities I can present to get out of this stupid ultimatum.

Movement from Thea's curtains across from my window catches my eye and I creep over, keeping to the shadows of my bedroom so she doesn't see me watching. She's sitting sideways in an armchair angled toward the window, her bare legs crossed at the ankle and propped against the wall. Her head is bent, maybe reading something? Her foot bobs—she must be listening to music. There's something about the way she's sitting that amuses me. Is it even comfortable?

Watching her gives me an idea for getting around Mom's girlfriend project, because she won't sleep on this. I know how she gets. If I'm forced to do something, I'll do it on my terms.

I might as well have fun with it.

I have the leverage I need to make sure Thea has no other choice but to agree to become my fake girlfriend.

It'll get me closer to her sugar-scented hair. Close enough to really pin her under my thumb and discover what other secrets she has for me to steal.

Her nosy Mom will hate it. If she was freaking out about me standing close to her, talking to her, she'll blow a gasket at how I'm going to make sure Thea is corrupted and debauched in every way possible. I saw it in her eyes. She thinks I'm the worst kind of wild.

The perfect payback to Celine Kennedy has finally presented itself in the sweetest sweater-wrapped bow: her daughter.

Thea might be fun to play with, but everyone is a liar in some way or another. Apples don't fall far from trees.

EIGHT
Connor

THIRD period English is lit this morning.

Devlin is out for blood with his little charity case obsession. She crawled up to him like a lost dog, surprising me by handing over a paper and acknowledging his existence when she usually ignores all of us like the uppity ice queen she is. A hot ice queen.

But I honor dibs, so she's all Devlin's.

I had snatched up the paper she presented to him and made up a love note instead of the essay assignment with his name typed at the top. He got her to do his homework somehow, but he also wasn't taking it, declaring that he wasn't accepting proclamations of love and calling what she wrote sweet.

Now, I don't know what sort of kinky game he's playing with her, but whatever it is, it's brought a light to his eyes I haven't seen since his cousin Lucas left for college. Davis brought his wrath on herself by picking Trent's pockets right in front of us.

The laughter of our crew fills the room as other students filter in for class. Sean leans on Trent, howling with amused tears clinging to the corners of his eyes. Two of our friends from the dance team, Nina and Bailey, coo cruelly at Blair Davis while Devlin and I tag team her.

Fire flashes in her gaze. Yeah, she's a total fighter, even if she stays silent the majority of the time we're messing with her. "Listen—"

Devlin's voice is cutting as he interrupts, wagging a finger at her. "I don't like the way you look at my dick. It's not sexy to think you might bite it off because you mistook it for a hotdog."

"Oh damn!" I choke into my fist at the brutal burn. "Bro. That mental image. My eyes!"

Davis growls—actually growls like the trailer trash animal we call her—ready to fight Devlin. I'm kind of hoping she tackles him to the ground. He can take her, but it would be fun as hell to watch them wrestle. But our Devil Boy has her halting, balling her fists at her side.

"Whatever," she spits. "You're disgusting."

"Oh, come on, sticky fingers." Devlin props his chin in his hand, smirking because he knows he's won, kicking the trash in the mud once again. These two are out for blood this year. "I've heard you get up to way worse for anyone willing to pay. But not me. I don't pay for it, and I sure as fuck am not touching you with a ten-foot pole."

He goes on. The man loves a savage diatribe, but I miss the rest of it because Thea walks in. Today her auburn curls are braided, a few strands escaping. She hugs her books to her chest as she pauses in the doorway to say bye to Landry's sister. The school blazer is so big on her short frame, the cuffs of her sleeves become like sweater paws.

I want to unwrap her to get to the delectable body underneath. This lie of hers pisses me off, digging beneath the threshold of my patience.

Thea glances at me as she finds her seat at the desk in front of mine. Even more irritating than her fake frumpy armor is that the only recognition for me is indifference. Maybe a hint of judgement because she's caught some of how we're treating Davis.

She doesn't know I'm the one who gets her to come at least twice a day since she accidentally texted me.

Grunting under my breath, I turn my back on Thea to face Devlin at his seat behind me.

Davis sits stiffly in her chair in the next row over, sleek dark hair hiding most of her face as Devlin finishes eviscerating her by saying, "I don't want this. It's pathetic."

Everyone watches as he rips the essay to pieces and flings the torn shreds in the air. They float to the ground by Blair's feet. Our whole crew and the people that cling to us from the outer rings explode in laughter and coyote howls—the student body's way of honoring our school mascot when something goes down.

Devlin takes out his finished essay and sets it on his desk. Damn, he's an evil bastard. I snicker, sticking the tip of my tongue out of the side of my mouth.

Davis stares at the remains of the destroyed essay, her plump lips pinched at the corners as she fights not to react. The only reason we go at her as hard as we do is because she never does what we expect—doesn't cry at the nasty names, refuses to fight back unless it's Devlin, has never broken down, even after Devlin threw her lunch on the floor last year. She's ice through and through, but ice has to melt sometime.

With a restrained bite in her tone, Davis asks, "Are you still going to—"

"You shouldn't treat people like that." A familiar soft but determined voice speaks up.

My mouth curves into a dangerous smile as Devlin, Davis, and I turn our attention to Thea.

She's twisted around in her seat, cheeks tinged pink as she grips the back of her chair with white knuckles, practically touching my desk.

This is how I know she's hiding the same tendencies as her mom. I open my mouth to bite back at my little mouse for intervening where she doesn't belong.

"It's not right." Thea beats me by doubling down before I can snipe at her. She licks her lips, darting her gaze to me. I'm reminded of the encounter in front of our houses, when she told me off. It was cute then, but it's not now, here at school where she can publicly defy us. Her focus shifts back to Devlin and the rest of our crew hovering behind us. "So please stop."

Releasing a ruthless laugh, I lean close to her, clamping a hand over her wrist so she can't escape. Her sugary scent is intoxicating and I shift closer, whispering in her ear. "What's wrong, neighbor? Were you jealous we weren't paying you any attention? Your secret is how badly you want someone to pay attention to you, isn't it?"

She sucks in a breath, pinning me with her big doe eyes, stretched wide with embarrassed horror.

That's right, sweetness. I know everything. I've got your fucking number.

Literally. I smother a snort.

"You want attention?" I mutter. "I'll give you what you want."

Thea drags the cuffs of her blazer over her hands. Her face is flaming red. I lean back in my chair, smirking. Pulling out my phone, I kick my feet up on the bar on the back of her seat.

Our teacher bustles in, always with that grating go-getter vibe.

Coleman is in his late twenties, with clean-cut thick brown hair, a strong chin, and matching dimples when he turns a proud smile on the girls he calls on the most in class. He's playing at perfect all-American dreamboat, but I'm not buying his act. He's a try-hard phony if I've ever seen one. He turned up out of nowhere in the middle of the year in tenth grade and had the girls panting after him right away. It's always irritated me that Coleman doesn't take my rep seriously, but I haven't found anything on the guy to show him what I'm capable of, like the man is a ghost.

Or he's great at covering his tracks. Whatever the case is, I'll uncover it.

There has to be something serious for all the falsehoods he protects himself with.

"Let's get started," Coleman says.

Instead of paying attention to him, I pull up my messages.

Thea acts all perfect and innocent, when really she's as much of a corrupt deviant as any of us, and I've got the proof right on my phone from this morning when I got her worked up before school, and again before first period because I wanted to know how far I could push her.

If *Wyatt* can text Thea before first period and she sneaks off to a secluded spot to respond, what will she do if her secret sext buddy messages her in the middle of class? Time to find out. I click into our message thread, the corner of my mouth hitching up at the last message from her saying she was late for class and had to go.

Connor: Can't stop thinking about the sounds you made this morning. Your sweet little moans get me so hard, baby. I need to hear you all breathy and on the edge of falling apart again. Want to play a game?

A squeak sounds from Thea. She hunches her shoulders to hide her phone from the teacher as he explains the reading assignment. My cell vibrates.

Thea: Omg I'm in class right now!! [flustered emoji]
Connor: Be bad with me. I promise it'll be fun. Just lean back in your desk, spread those pretty legs and show me what color panties you're wearing.

Connor: Unless you're not wearing any, you naughty girl.

I shift in my seat, getting myself going from toying with her. My dick is half hard at the thought of her doing it. I flick my gaze between the text conversation and her back, inhaling when she sinks into her chair a few inches and slides both her hands beneath the desk.

Shit. I didn't think she'd actually do it. We're in the middle of class and I've got Thea Kennedy taking an upskirt photo. The sense of illicit mischief courses through me and I bite my lip to hide my pleased expression.

My pulse thumps in my ears as I watch every tiny shift of her body, until her legs widen slightly. Then my phone vibrates. Rolling my lips between my teeth, I check it discreetly. It's grainy and dimly lit, but I can make out dainty scalloped yellow lace.

She did that. She fucking did that. For me, during class, with Coleman strolling around the classroom.

A burst of lust mixed with pride rushes through me.

Connor: Good girl. Or should I say, bad girl? [smirk emoji]
Connor: Mm, baby girl, I want to come find you during the day at your school, pull your panties aside, fuck you good and hard until I cream in you, then smack that thick ass and leave you knowing I'll be in you all day.

Thea muffles another strangled yelp, crossing her legs tightly. It's too fun to mess around with her like this, to get her hot right under everyone's noses.

Our game is interrupted when Coleman pauses by Thea's desk as he strolls around the class and directs his question at her. "Can anyone give me their thoughts on the use of literary devices in the text?"

"I—uh, yes, I..." Thea trails off, flipping through her notebook, voice trembling. In her fumbling, she knocks the book we're reading off the desk.

Titters echo around the room. I cover the smug slant of my lips with my hand, propping my elbow on the desk.

"I have some thoughts," I offer. "You know, since she seems unprepared for class. The book uses irony and alludes to things going on in the world to drive the point that the political party twists the truth to exercise control, but I don't think the theme of propaganda is as universally applicable today. With social media always advancing and evolving, more voices are constantly in the mix from all over the world. People aren't complacent to mindlessly listen to manipulative party lines, or believe whatever the headlines read."

Coleman frowns at me, silent for a long beat. He sighs. "Yes. Good."

Thea drops her forehead to her desk and stays like that for a long stretch as the class goes on.

* * *

Before I make any moves, I need more information. I want to know my grip on Thea is ironclad. There's no way I'll let the little mouse escape the trap I'm setting for her.

I dump my athletic duffel in the corner of the bedroom and boot up my computer. As it purrs to life, I drop into the chair and scroll through notes I've compiled on my phone.

She's on my radar, no longer invisible. I'm paying attention to every move she makes, getting a lowdown on her from the classes we don't share, utilizing every access point I have to pick apart her life. From her friendship circle to her daily schedule, she won't make a move without me knowing about it. Holden Landry proved useful once more, giving me a play-by-play of Thea through the lens of her longtime friendship with his younger sister when I used the video of him at the boat party I've been keeping in my back pocket. Until he described a recent sleepover and how she filled out her skimpy sleep set nicely and I decked him.

I'm building a picture of how she presents herself—the studious, quiet good girl.

And I'm betting it's a lie. No one is that pure and innocent. As humans, we're all depraved beasts.

It's instinct. Our base nature. It lives in our bones.

Once my computer is ready, I waste no time getting to work. Hacking her network remotely is child's play. Their WiFi has basic, default firewalls that I break through with ease, allowing me access to connect my computer to any device in their house logged in on the network, dropping malware I've written to give me a backdoor in anytime I want.

There's no challenge, not like the things I faced when I was first developing these skills on my hunt to uncover the depth of Mom's misdeeds to cover up the assault incident. In the short time since that discovery, I've honed my talents in digging through people's lives.

"Gotcha," I mutter as I locate Thea's laptop, currently connected.

Her screen loads on my second monitor, a baking blog and Instagram open in two tabs on her browser. The calendar application is also open, and I grind my teeth when I see *Mr. Coleman's birthday, bake cookies* set as a reminder for tomorrow.

I never really noticed Thea before, but now that I have, it doesn't escape me that she's as infatuated with Mr. Coleman as every other girl in our class. Hell, the whole school. It still rankles when I think of today's English period. Watching her shoot her hand in the air, leaning forward to answer questions once she recovered from her mortification. Like she was eager to prove herself to our teacher. She might have hidden under her baggy uniform, but because I know what her perfect tits look like beneath the deceptive layers, it pissed me off to see her eagerness for any of Coleman's attention.

With a few swift keystrokes, I access the webcam, activating it. Her room appears on my screen.

Clicking my tongue and shaking my head, I lean back in my chair. "Don't you know any better? Come on, everyone knows to put tape or something over their camera these days. It's 101."

Her room is empty, the door ajar. A stuffed sea lion sits in the center of her ruffly purple pillows. It's every inch as feminine as I expected, splashes of color enveloping the whole thing.

The family's rottweiler sleeps on the floor next to her bed. He seems like a chill dog. I once fed him half of my burger when I was hiding out by our pool house, avoiding my parents when he wandered over. Thea shouted for him around the front of her house. He must have gotten out. She wasn't pleased to find her dog cuddled up to me—really, he was trying to push me out of the lounger, total chair hog—while I listened to her search for her dog for close to twenty minutes before she ventured into our backyard.

For the life of me, I can't remember the dog's name. Only her pet names for him. *Wookiee boy.* It made sense when he jumped down from the lounger, stretched his front half low to the ground, and released the weirdest warbling sound before trotting to her side.

I'm in the middle of scanning the colorful posters on the wall, reading their baking puns when Thea strolls in.

The corner of my mouth twitches up.

Flour is smeared across her cheek and dotting her apron. The sleeves of her sweater are rolled up and her hair is tied on top of her head by a big yellow scrunchie with a bow on it. The sun doesn't shine as bright as the excitement in her blue eyes as she leans over the desk to grab a notebook with pastel tabs sticking out to mark the pages. I drink her in, studying what she looks like when she doesn't know someone's watching. She pauses to pet the dog, giving him a belly scratch that has him stretching languidly before disappearing from the room.

Part of me hopes she'll come back. I have half a mind to start up a sexting session with her while I'm accessing her webcam for a double feature, picturing her wearing only the apron and nothing underneath.

But it's better for me if she isn't in the room. Even if she doesn't know how to prevent hackers like me from doing exactly what I'm doing, there's a chance she'd notice activity on her computer while I'm remotely accessing the files. I have to be quick, then I can play with her posing as Wyatt later.

Starting with the browser history, I download it to my files to comb through later. The page with Instagram open is her account—*@theactualsunbeam*. I scroll through the images, clicking at random. The whole thing is a mix of baking and floral aesthetic, mixed with an underlying obsession with positive optimism and self-love quotes. *Thick thighs save lives. Be kind always. Spread love (and cookies) around the world. Local goddess gang.*

She seems like a fucking woodland creature, too wholesome and good for this world.

Except I know the truth.

I unlock my phone, where the real Thea is. Picking a photo from this morning, I stare at what she shows me—the most stripped down, raw version of herself.

"Who are you?"

Shaking my head, I exit back to her Instagram profile and open Facebook. It loads to her account, login credentials saved.

A soft laugh puffs out of me. "It's like you want me to have easy access."

The Facebook feed isn't as personalized as her Instagram, mostly full of video shares of Tasty videos—damn, girl has a real sweet tooth—and tagged photos with Maisy Landry at a wellness retreat resort, some fancy cabin campground that screams glamping instead of real camping.

Skimming through her files, my annoyance rises. There's no protection against what I'm doing. Her security is so lax. This isn't even hard, any creep can learn to do it with shitty spyware.

"Fucking pain in the ass," I grumble, opening a new window to code in.

A short while later, Thea's computer has security protocols in place that rival the ones I installed for my own computer system. The only outside threat able to get into her stuff is me. No other little shit will spy on her with her webcam.

Only me.

NINE
Connor

At the end of the week, my good day goes to hell fast. I'm walking down the north building's hallway on my way to class when I stop in my tracks.

Thea stands with Mr. Coleman, chatting animatedly, her eyes all lit up as her hands move. Today's thick sweater is a peach color with bobbles. She almost drops the stack of books in her arms and laughs as Coleman steps closer to help her catch them. Too close. He leans into her space, his attention rapt as she continues talking.

The rush of annoyance rises so fast I almost go lightheaded.

Hell fucking nah, man.

My feet move before I've even formed a plan.

"Hey, baby, I was hoping I'd see you before lunch," I say, interrupting whatever Coleman was about to tell her. My arm slides around her waist and tugs her to my side, away from our English teacher. I nuzzle into her hair, shooting a flat look at Coleman. "Mm, you smell nice today."

"I, uh," Thea chokes out. I back off a little, but keep my arm around her. Her mouth keeps moving, but no words come out. She looks from me to Coleman, confusion etched into her features. "Connor?"

Pinching my collar and flicking, I say, "One and only."

"We can continue this discussion another time, perhaps. I'll leave you with your... boyfriend, Miss Kennedy," Coleman says, disappointment in her threading his voice. "Mr. Bishop, tighten your tie."

Fucking prick. I resist flipping off his back as he walks down the hallway. The milling students give us curious glances as they pass.

"You're still, uh. Holding me?" It comes out as a question. She licks her lips, glancing out of the corner of her eye at the attention we're drawing with this public display of possession.

"Good eye."

A beat passes, then she drags out her question. "Why?"

Yeah, might as well do this now. I've got enough info in place to make my move.

"Plenty of reasons. Your cute expression right now, for one. Felt like it when I saw you. And..." I fish out my phone and show it to her. On the screen is the last message she sent me from an hour ago—her school blouse unbuttoned in a bathroom stall to show me her mouth-watering rack in a lavender bra with ribbon bows. "I like the little game we've been playing, but we could be doing so much more."

Air hisses out of Thea and she sags. I shift my grip to hold her up so she doesn't collapse in the middle of the hall.

"What is that?" Horror fills her tone and the color drains from her face. "How do you have that?"

Releasing a dark chuckle, I put my phone away and cage her against the row of lockers. "What's wrong? You liked it so much before now."

She shakes her head in disbelief. "N-no."

"Yes."

"I don't believe you." Thea sucks on her bottom lip. "I've heard rumors."

I lift a brow.

She huffs. "You copied my phone somehow. Read through my private conversations."

"What makes you think you're interesting enough to be a target for something so elaborate? You're a nobody. Invisible. We don't notice you." I grasp her jaw, narrowing my eyes. "You're the one that started it when you sent me that pic of you in your nightie with your boobs almost spilling out. You wanted someone to pay attention and I did."

"I don't believe you. I think you're just making fun of me again."

A wild grin crosses my face. With a deft move, I pop a button on my shirt, then another. "Want me to strip to prove it? How much do you need to see? Abs?" I lick my lips slowly, making sure she's watching before I drop my hands to my belt. "More?"

In a flustered frenzy, she clamps her hands over mine, squeezing with more strength than I would've guessed. In my periphery, I feel the eyes of people openly staring at the scene we're making.

I laugh. "Feisty, huh? Can't keep your hands off me."

Thea lets go as if I've burned her. I prop my hands on either side of her head and crowd her against the lockers again.

"I'm not bluffing," I say. "I've seen more of you than I bet you've shown to anyone, sunshine."

"This can't be happening," Thea utters, more to herself than me.

"Damn, how horny are you, Bishop?" Sean taunts as he passes us in the hall. "You're hitting up the uptight nerds now?"

Keeping my eyes on Thea, I snort and play with one of the bobbles on her sweater. "I needed a snack and she was the closest chick around."

His sharp cackle makes Thea flinch, the sound grating as he swaggers down the hall. I grit my teeth and grab her, looking for somewhere private to talk. I can't hash this out with her and field interruptions demanding a different kind of show. She follows obediently.

"In here." I herd her into an empty classroom by my grip on her upper arm to get the prying, gossiping eyes off us.

It's one of the science labs, dimly lit by the half-drawn shades on the windows, the main lights off.

I never meant to do this in front of an audience. Humiliating her wasn't part of the plan, I only intended to make sure I had her in checkmate when I revealed myself. But when I saw her smile for Coleman, I just acted. Left my strategy in the dust.

"We're going to be late for next period," Thea says, her eyes flashing at me mutinously.

Christ, that look. You'd think I kicked her dog.

She tugs her arm from my grasp. "Please let me go."

"Who says I want to?"

"Me. I want you to, so you will." She skirts around me, stepping out of range to lean against a lab table in the deserted science room. Crossing her arms over her chest, she lifts her brows. "Why did you wait so long to reveal yourself? Why did you do it at all if I had the wrong number?"

Her soft voice rises, drawing a chuckle from me. I shrug, admiring another photo from our messages. It's one of her tamer ones from the last few weeks, but I love it. Her red hair looks fantastic in thick high pigtails while she sucks icing off her finger, grinning at the camera with a cheeky mischief she never shows at school.

"Because it was fun." I rake my eyes over her. "And hot. All I thought about every night was how you were just a short distance away, getting off with me."

"But I didn't know it was you! This is all wrong. I wanted—" A rough sound tears from her throat and she turns away, hiding her face. "You're disgusting."

"Disgustingly skilled at making you come, you mean." I slide my tongue along my lower lip as I taunt her. "You're so good for me, aren't you? I keep wondering if you'll do the same for anyone who pays attention to you."

I don't say it, but Coleman crosses my mind. The way he was leaning into her space before I interrupted makes me want to punch something. Preferably his smarmy face.

"Stop it." Thea pulls the cuffs of her sweater over her hands, twisting the material until it's stretched out and limp. She looks like I've shattered her world, the crestfallen expression killing her light. I frown, disliking seeing her face so shadowed. Her eyes lift to meet mine, glistening with wetness. "Why are you doing this?"

"Well, I was horny and high when you texted, so I think that's self explanatory, but—"

"Connor!" Thea sniffles, swiping a stray tear. The sight of her tears twists my insides. I don't want to make her cry. I don't know what's wrong with me, I don't normally care how my blackmail affects people. "What do you want with me? Hurry up and spit it out, so I can go."

"Go where?"

She shrugs. "First stop, ladies room so I can clean up."

I guess she means cry her eyes out that the real Wyatt isn't texting her. "And after that?"

"AP Chemistry."

My brows lift in surprise. "Not, like home or to cry to your gal pals under the bleachers?"

Thea wrinkles her nose. "No. The school day isn't over yet."

I cover my face with my hand and groan. "God, you're a nerd."

"Are you threatened by intelligent women?"

I scoff. "Hardly."

"If you have a problem with it, you'll have to suffer. I'm not changing what I do with my life for anyone."

"No. It's nothing." I shake my head. A lopsided smile tugs at my lips. "It's perfect, actually."

Mom won't be able to deny me. Thea is studious, wholesome, and appears innocent. I'm the only one who knows she isn't.

"Perfect for what?"

"For what I need from you. We're going to strike a deal. That's how this works when I have leverage on people around here." I stroll over and hook an arm around her shoulders. She's so short next to me that I could tuck her head against my chest. "You're going to do me a favor, and in exchange I won't tell anyone about this Thea Kennedy." I wave my phone. "Shame, really, she's way more entertaining than you."

Thea's mouth drops open and it's kind of cute, all indignant and affronted. I'm tempted to stick my fingers in her mouth to turn it sexy and bring one of my fantasies to life. They twitch against her shoulder, and I thread them into her hair instead.

"That's—like extortion, isn't it? That's horrible!"

My amused smile stretches. "Well, I'm not paying you. This is good, old fashioned blackmail, baby. So do as I say, or I'm going to play Russian roulette with my contact list and all the private pictures you've sent." I tsk, tilting my head. "You know, you should really be careful who you send nude photos to. Make sure you trust them and all that. Or that you've got the right number."

"But I...he put his number in my phone, I don't..."

"Damn, that's cold." I'm holding back from cracking up. "Either that was on purpose, or he's an idiot."

Her eyes flash with a burst of fierceness. "Wyatt isn't like that! He's kind and funny and dedicated to his job as a lifeguard." She gives me a once over. "Unlike you."

My eyes roll. "Sounds like a wet blanket. You need to accept that your lifeguard gave you a fake number because he didn't want you, or that he probably couldn't handle you." I poke my tongue from the corner of my mouth as my gaze travels over the curves I know hide beneath her frumpy uniform. "Not like I can."

"You haven't said what you need from me yet," Thea argues.

"It's easy, sweetness. I need you to pretend to be with me. Pose as my girlfriend."

She sputters, trying to get away from under my arm. I hold her tight. When she can't break free, she huffs. "Be your fake girlfriend? What the hell, Connor? I don't ever see you date."

"You're right, I don't. But this is important and it's all I need from you. It has to be you." I don't tell her I can't get out of it, so I'm forced to pick someone. "This is a good deal, so take it. I'm not asking you to memorize my favorite color, or even interact with my friends. You need me to not spread information about you around school, and I need you to do me this small solid until I'm done with you."

"Small! You're talking about a relationship. That's a huge deal to me!" Thea's mouth works as she formulates a response. After a minute, she flaps her hand. "You're not even asking! You're just demanding I let you control me by threatening me with blackmail so I can't refuse."

She bites her bottom lip and pinches her brows together. I set my phone on the lab table, curling my fingers into my palm to tame the urge to trace her pout.

"You really are as wicked as everyone says," Thea finishes in a hush.

I smirk. "Better fucking believe it, baby."

Horror morphs her pretty features as she leans as far away as I allow while she's tucked beneath my arm. She shakes her head. "Don't call me that. Don't call me that ever again."

"See, that's the thing, baby." I pause, dragging my teeth over my lip. "I'm going to call you that, because I do what I want. And I want you to be my fake girlfriend."

She tosses her hands in the air. "Why can't you ask some other girl! There are so many who would jump at the chance. They're—" Hesitation stops her, cutting off her words. Her blue-green gaze falls to the floor, lashes brushing her cheeks. "They're prettier, and actually want to be around you."

Thea doesn't think she's pretty? How can that be possible? What a load of shit.

This is taking so much work. Not only that, it's cramping my style and putting a wrecking ball through the ruthless cred I've built for myself in the last couple of years. I'm supposed to strike so much fear in the hearts of everyone in this town that I snap my fingers and they jump.

With a scoff, I put my hands on her shoulders to make her face me. "I can't use any other girls because they're all insipid and plastic. They'll read too much into playing domestic bliss for me. Fuck that." I step closer, toying with her hair, sinking my fingers into the strands framing her face. It's soft as hell, slipping over my skin. Her breath catches and she stares up at me. She smells so nice. "You, on the other hand, my sweet little mouse, are nothing more than a pawn and you know it."

It's heady to be so close after I've been imagining it. So many thoughts run through my head. Does she make the same sounds in person, or will it be different? Better? If I kiss her neck and put my lips on that sun-shaped birthmark on her thigh, will she tremble deliciously?

But instead of melting into my arms or wrapping her thick thighs around my waist, she struggles, turning her face away. Those pink, glossy lips set in a frown.

"Let me go," she demands quietly.

Stubborn little thing. I breathe out slowly.

I've never worked this hard for a hookup. Girls fall onto my dick. Shit, Thea fell into what we were doing easily. If someone wasn't into it, I'd always moved on to the next girl or three in line.

But I want Thea. I need to have a taste of her, and if I'm tying her to my side for the foreseeable future, I'll seduce her.

This close, her honeyed scent makes me want to swing her around, pin her against the desk, and kiss those rosy lips until they're swollen.

Trailing my hands from her shoulders down her back, I snake my arms around her waist, trapping her in my hold. She shoots a wide-eyed look up at me.

"What are you doing?" Her question comes out a little breathless.

This is affecting her, and I've barely done anything.

The corner of my mouth lifts as I lean close enough to press my lips to her ear, letting my hands roam when she stays still. I squeeze her hips and sneak my tongue out to lick the shell of her ear.

Thea sucks in a breath, shoulders shaking in a shiver. She bows her head, hiding behind her hair. "C-Connor."

The bell rings, but neither of us move.

"I'll still pretend to be Wyatt. You'll know it's me, but nothing has to change. I've really liked being your sexting buddy. We can keep what we have going. Why waste a good thing, right?" My lips brush her ear again. "And I make you feel so good."

The whimper that escapes her is music to my ears, drawing a grin from me. She allows herself to lean into me, touching my chest. My lids fall to half mast as she smooths one palm down my torso. I hum in encouragement. Screw next period.

"That's it, baby," I croon, squeezing her ass. "Give in. We'll have such a good time together. We can get started right now." I clap a hand on the high science desk behind me, chuckling when she jumps. She won't be acting like a scared mouse once I get my mouth on her. "Come sit up on this lab table and spread those legs. I want to eat you."

She sways into me, digging her nails into my shirt. Her voice is so soft I have to focus to hear it when she speaks. "You're crazy and entitled."

With that accusation, she launches herself at me, fingers scrabbling. At first I attempt to catch her, thinking she's trying to kiss me—*hell yes*, that's what I want.

But she's not trying to kiss me.

Thea snatches my phone and scampers back a couple of steps, breathing hard as she fumbles with the screen. I blink, trying to process what's happening.

"Damn it," she curses.

"Ah, ah." I wave a finger in disapproval. "You won't get it unlocked to delete your photos or your number."

"Yes I will." She flashes me a determined look, brows flattened.

The fire she keeps tucked away is like an ember at first glance, but it's blistering hot. I like it. Before she can do anything rash, like smash my phone—pointless, because I keep a cloud backup—I push off the desk and capture her in my hold. She makes a sound of protest as I toss my phone aside. It clatters on the lab table while I pin her arms.

Bringing my lips back to her ear, I bite out, "Don't test me. And don't be mad you liked it when you thought I was someone else." She shudders at my demanding tone. When I nip her ear, she fights to free herself, panting. A smoky chuckle rolls through me. "Fight all you want, little mouse. You're mine now."

"No!" Her attention darts to the door as her desperation climbs.

"Hoping if you go tattle to my dad I'll let you off the hook? Nice thought, but no." I rub my nose into her temple, fisting the back of her sweater. "Or…are you hoping if you figure out your real Wyatt's number, he'll respond like I did? Who else is going to give you what you need?"

She turns a glare on me, her mouth set in a mutinous line I'm dying to kiss. "No. You can't bully me into this because you have private photos of me. I'm never going to text you again." Her chin tips up and I grasp it between my thumb and finger, lifting it higher. Her small fists shift against my torso. "I'll—I'll block your number."

"That's so cute. Well, go ahead and try. But neighbor, I'm never far from you." A tiny sound catches in her throat. She shakes her head. I nod, pinning her with my unwavering stare. She needs to understand. "I control everyone's secrets, you know. That's why people are scared of me. You should be, too. Because I own you by knowing yours." I tilt my head and brush my thumb over her jaw. "You can play along like a good pawn and I'll keep taking care of that needy little vixen you keep under wraps—even from yourself, I think—or I can make your life fucking hell."

"Do you ever stop talking, or do you like the sound of your own voice that much?" Thea whispers, eyes bouncing back and forth, studying my face.

A burst of anger erupts in my chest. There's a sadness in her eyes that cuts me—pity. She should pity herself for the position she's landed herself in.

With a cruel laugh, I chuck her under the chin and hover my lips over hers, wrapping a curl around my finger. "You know, I've been really fucking nice about this. Nicer than I am with anyone, and you're shitting all over it with that attitude."

She grimaces, but her gaze doesn't leave mine. Silly little mouse, looking danger in the eye.

I release her, but she doesn't move, waiting to see what I'll do. Picking up my phone, I sigh in a mockery of being put out.

"Well, it's your choice. You've got real brass ones, Kennedy, choosing to face the entire school getting a good look at your tits. Guess I was right about you liking the attention." As I tell her this, I scroll through the address book on my phone. "I'll just keep sending your photos to my contact list until you submit."

"Connor, don't do this." Her throat works as she swallows. "Please."

I look up through my lashes, face bent toward my phone as I pick a number at random and start a new text message. Her gaze drops to my phone, then flies back up, silently pleading with me.

"That's not the magic word. You know what to do. So what'll it be?"

Thea releases a rough cry and rushes me again, catching me by surprise as her body collides with mine. My back bumps into the high tabletop and one arm bands around her automatically while she tries to get my phone a second time. I hold it out of reach above her head.

"Please! I don't want you to!"

My mouth curves into a smile that isn't nice at all and I cradle her face with my free hand, tilting it up. Her eyes are shiny with wetness. I can see how her strength is cracking, panic taking over. I smooth some of her wild curls back from her face.

"I wasn't kidding. You'll learn quick that when I say something, I'm dead fucking serious. Do you understand?"

After staring back at me for a beat, she plants her palms on my chest and shoves hard, wrenching away from me.

"Fine," Thea spits. Her chest rises and falls with each harsh breath she drags in, face flushed. She touches her hair with a trembling hand. "Fine. I'll do it. Just. Don't send my pictures to anyone."

I slide my phone in my pocket and close the distance she put between us. Tucking her hair behind her ear, I ask, "Was that so hard?"

Thea's eyes are consumed by an intriguing fire when she lifts them to face me, even when she's breaking. Quiet, frumpy, shy Thea Kennedy has fight in her. I'm going to have fun toying with it before I tame her.

"See you later, little mouse." I blow her a kiss before leaving her alone in the middle of the dark science lab, whistling with my hands in my pockets.

TEN
Thea

THE shock hasn't faded two periods later. Chemistry and French were both complete blurs. At lunch I'm still reeling from Connor's reveal, and his horrible threat if I don't meet his demand.

And I agreed.

I had to, or he was going to send my photos to people. There was no choice, no way to think my way out.

Fake girlfriend. Am I insane? We didn't even go over what that entails, or what the rules are, like when I'm supposed to start playing a role and if we have to act like a couple.

Back in that classroom, I put on every ounce of bravery, but in reality I'm so far from okay with all of this.

By some miracle, I haven't broken down yet. Once he left, I swiped my eyes and went to AP Chemistry, apologizing to the teacher for arriving so late.

Sighing, I pick at the carrots sitting between Maisy and I on the table in the cafeteria. My stomach gives a feeble protest. I'm not hungry for anything else. My insides are too twisted in anxious knots.

My best friend is so good at picking up on my moods. As soon as we met up at the stairwell by the library to walk to lunch, she launched into a story about falling down a YouTube hole of yoga videos last night.

Maisy Landry is a junior in the grade below me, but we've been close friends since the first day of camp when we were in middle school. It was a miracle to find out we lived in the same town. She looks like a stunning model with long tan lean legs, highlighted light brown hair, and warm hazel eyes. She's the kindest person I know. Her inner beauty makes her outer beauty shine even brighter. I've always loved her confident and laid back nature.

Right now I'm thankful she lets me retreat inside my head, unsure if I manage the occasional hum to show her I'm paying attention. I'm totally not listening, like a crappy friend.

"Are you okay today, girl?" Maisy asks, putting a hand on mine after her story ends. "We can move to the courtyard if you want. I can pull up a meditation flow playlist on my phone. It'll be great, we'll zen out before next period. Think we can get away with a nap, too?" She laughs, the sound light and airy, then crunches into a carrot. "My mom would freak if she found out I stopped being her perfect ideal of a goody-goody for, like, five minutes to cut class.

I'm missing out on a teenage rite of passage."

My reaction is delayed, but when her words register, I sit up straight. Rolling my lips between my teeth, I widen my eyes and nod at Maisy. "I'm okay. We're already here, we might as well stay. Tomorrow we should do that, though."

"Yes." Maisy drags the word out with a languid smile and wiggles her fingers at me. It gets me to smile. "All right, there's my girl. Want me to make us an appointment at the goat yoga studio this weekend? We haven't been in so long. We need to release our negative energy so we can soak in all the good vibes. And with that look on your face, we need to call in the big guns. Baby goats."

"Okay." I smile at her and take another carrot when she nudges the container toward me.

Maisy winks and a little of my worries ebb away for a minute. She's always had a calming effect, ever since she found me crying in the woods, lost on a hike, and guided me back to the campground.

A round of laughter sounds behind me. I hear Connor's voice, but I won't turn around. I won't.

The curiosity wins out and I peek over my shoulder.

Connor is at his usual table with the most popular students—Devlin Murphy, guys from the soccer team, pretty girls from the dance and cheer squads. He's holding court over his kingdom, talking with his hands, a big grin on his face. His eyes found me once, at the beginning of lunch when I walked in with Maisy. I haven't been able to look his way since, purposely putting my back to their table.

He didn't acknowledge me other than a quick look, so I guess I don't have to put on an act as his girlfriend today.

Blackmail, lies, and secrets. These are Connor's bargaining chips. It's how he and Devlin rule the school. They keep us all in line through strategy with no room for remorse.

Now I'm the latest victim.

My phone sits on the table in front of me, turned over so I can see the cupcake PopSocket on the back. I'm too afraid to scroll through my message history with Wyatt—who isn't even flipping Wyatt, as it turns out. If I look, it will only taint every thrilling memory of the last few weeks. I'll see the depth of how Connor manipulated me, the hot and sometimes sweet morning and evening messages twisted and poisoned by the truth.

How could I have gotten the number wrong?

It's a question I've been asking myself on repeat since the encounter with him.

Never in a million years would I ever want to be with Connor Bishop the way I *thought* I was progressing my relationship with Wyatt, upgrading from fling-adjacent to bonafide boyfriend and girlfriend status.

Goes to show me, assuming without ever talking about it. I'm so fucking naïve, playing right into Connor's cruel hands. My throat hurts, tight with emotion when I swallow.

I fight the urge to bury my face in my arms. It's pointless to hide from the truth—that my bully and my neighbor is the same guy I've been fantasizing about and having phone sex with. Well, text sex. But still. Lots of sexy stuff has gone down between us.

"Oh my god," I mumble in horror when it occurs to me I know what his dick looks like. I've seen him *come*.

This time I give in and cover my flaming hot face.

My hands burn with the urge to knead something to calm my breathing. I wonder if I can spend the rest of the lunch period in the culinary classroom to bake something before my next class starts. I'm in the mood for bread. Maybe Mrs. Horne will let me hide out there for a while.

It would be the first time I've ever skipped a class, but I think the circumstances justify a break before I crumble under the emotional pressure weighing on my shoulders, stabbing at my heart with fresh reminders.

"Oh great," Maisy says in a flat tone, grabbing my attention.

Usually she's hard to ruffle, so it takes a lot to draw a reaction like that from her. Her gaze is locked on the doors and I swing around to see what's got her twisted up.

A tall, imposing boy stalks through the cafeteria. Dark hair hangs over his forehead and he wears a leather jacket and heavy boots, completely disregarding the school uniform. His face is set in angry lines, mouth turned down as he glares at any student that dares look his way.

"Who is that?" I ask, not recognizing him.

"Wilder," Maisy says quietly. "Fox Wilder. He's in my grade, but he's supposed to be in yours. They held him back when he came back."

"Came back?"

"He used to live here." Her expression is distant and sad. "A long time ago, when Holden and I were kids. He was our friend."

Wilder sweeps his gaze over the room, landing on Maisy. It seems impossible, but his face grows angrier. Maisy lifts her hand, waving. Wilder jerks his head and moves to the corner where her older brother, Holden, sits with guys from the football team.

"I don't think he remembers you, Maise," I say carefully.

She remains quiet, sighing and crossing her arms. "Guess not. He's been cold every time I try to say hi, but he's been hanging around Holden since he moved back to Ridgeview. I don't know what I did. It was so long ago, we were only kids when…" She trails off and shakes her head. "Never mind. Oh crap. Drama alert."

Maisy nods with her chin and I glance toward Connor's table. My heart falls when I realize how quiet the center tables have gone, and *why*.

Blair Davis, the dark-haired scholarship student at Silver Lake High that seems like a punching bag for the rich, popular crowd, stands stock still in front of Devlin Murphy. He's sprawled in his seat before her like an evil king, expression hard and commanding. I watch as

Blair lifts the water thermos in her hand and dumps it over herself.

What the hell!

Heinous cackles erupt from Connor and Devlin's crowd of friends. Water drips from Blair's hair and her uniform shirt is soaked right through.

"Oh no," I mumble, already reaching for napkins from a holder on the table. "Not again. Why can't they leave her alone?"

"Assholes," Maisy hisses.

The whole cafeteria claps and taunts, cheering the drama on.

It fires me up that no one is willing to act. "I'm going to help."

"Wet dog alert!" Someone shouts from the other tables surrounding the central popular one. They call more vile things and make kissing sounds at Blair's back, like they're calling a dog.

Connor pops up from his perch on top of the table and slides in next to Devlin, muttering in his ear with a matching smirk as his friend.

He's just as vile and arrogant as Devlin Murphy, cruel and cold beneath the mask of the cocky jokester. All I see is someone who uses people and takes amusement in the torment he puts them through.

My chest burns with anger, both for Blair and at the boys at this school who think they can get away with murder. We aren't their toys. I navigate through the tables separating me from the middle of the cafeteria, clenching the napkins in my fist. I've never been one to resort to violence ever, but right now it's too much—his threats were bad enough, but seeing him laugh as his friend bullies Blair makes me snap. I could punch Connor and not regret it.

The bravado that drove me over to the scene wavers as I stand under the full brunt of Connor and Devlin together. They haven't even noticed me, both focused on Blair.

"Um." I offer the napkins to Blair. "I brought you these."

Connor goes stiff in his seat, inhaling sharply. I can feel the press of his eyes against the side of my face as I hold out the napkins.

"Thanks," Blair mutters, accepting my help.

I don't leave her side as she pats herself awkwardly. This is the second time I've stood up for her against them, and I don't doubt for a second that they'd double down in a more cruel way if I walked away. I shoot the pair of them a hard look, hoping they stop treating her so terribly.

As Connor explodes from his seat, I jump, clutching the napkins against my chest. In a blink, he's in my face, towering over me and invading my space.

"U-um, Connor."

"Were you invited over here?" Bishop demands.

I swallow. Is he saying I need to stay away when he doesn't need me to pretend to be his girl? This is so stupid! He should've told me the rules. My knuckles turn white as I grip the napkins tighter.

What if he sends my photos because of this?

The risk is worth it. No one deserves to be treated the way these people bully Blair.

"No. That doesn't matter, though." My chin tips up, spurred on by the fury simmering beneath my skin. It fights with the fear settling in my gut. Connor could destroy me within minutes. Game over. "Blair needed help."

"*Blair* needed help?" Connor mimics, circling behind me. My heart jolts when his hands clamp on my shoulders in a harsh and punishing grip. "You hear that, Dev?"

I want to whirl and scream at him, ask him what he wants from me if he's going to act like this when an hour and a half ago he said he needed me by his side.

"Sure did," Devlin says, voice like icy shadows.

With a deep grunt, he rises to his feet and I take a fearful step back, pressing into Connor's chest. Between the two of them, the poison I pick to kill me is Connor. He pays me no attention as he stalks into Blair's personal space, staring at her with his scary, dark eyes.

"Did you need help, Davis?"

Blair's jaw tightens, then she answers in a lifeless voice. "No."

Is this really happening? I gape at Blair, baffled that she would take Devlin's crap. I go to take a step closer to Blair's side, but Connor holds me in place, the warmth of his back burning through my sweater. My gaze bounces from Blair to Devlin and I part my lips, thinking I can appeal to him.

"Well—"

"You know," Connor drawls next to my ear, startling me. His fingers skate over my shoulders, down my arms, plucking at my sweater. "The only thing a girl next door is good for is warming my dick." He leans closer, covering my back with his chest, burying his face in my hair as he lowers his voice to a sinister hush. "You offering, neighbor? You can leave your granny sweater on."

Breathing is hard. His words crash over me, driving spikes into my heart. Why even threaten me if he's only going to be an utter bastard to me in front of his friends? I want to cry when I think of our messages, the way he swore I was the most beautiful girl he's ever seen. Making sure I can't forget that it's been him making me feel excited, wanted, *good*.

Tripping over my own feet, I stumble out of his grasp as soon as it loosens. "You... You—"

"Me," Connor declares, sweeping his arms to encompass it. There's no doubt he's thinking along the same lines as me. I can see it in his piercing gray eyes. "All me, baby."

He doesn't spell it out, but he's reminding me exactly who I've been intimate with. Who I've bared myself to. My heart aches, feeling like it's shriveling. Everything was a lie and it finally hits me, making me gasp with pain.

Shaking my head, my face crumbles in anguish. I can't look at him anymore. Turning on my heel, I rush for the double doors, wiping away tears as they stream down my face. Maisy calls for me, but I ignore her and burst into the hall.

* * *

I don't think of my world history class, heading straight for the culinary room, not stopping for anything until I sag against the door. Everything blurs at the edges, tunneling my vision. My chest feels tight and my skin is hot and itchy. I rub at my neck and shove my sleeves up.

Mrs. Horne is seated at her desk at the front of the room. She takes one look at my face, probably puffy and red by now. "Thea? Everything okay?"

It takes two tries to speak. "Yes. Please, can I spend some time in here?"

"Of course. I'll give you a pass when you're ready to go." She waves at the work stations. "Just clean up when you're done."

There's not another class in here until last period, the class I'm in.

"Thank you," I breathe, on the verge of tears again from her understanding.

I feel vulnerable, like a light wind could blow me over into emotional turmoil. The baking supplies call to me. I'm thankful this school has a thriving variety of courses available, because the cooking class is equipped with everything I need. It seems more like the set of a reality baking show than a high school class, but I don't care about it right now.

Losing my sweater and washing my hands at the sink in the back of the room, I grab one of the linen aprons hanging from a hook in the corner, looping the bib over my neck and knotting it around my waist. I put my hair up, borrowing one of the fresh hair ties Mrs. Horne keeps on her desk for anyone with long hair since I left the cafeteria with nothing. Maisy will take my bag with her.

My phone pings, but I'm not ready to look. Locking every stray thought behind a wall in my head, I get to work.

Once the ingredients are mixed, I turn out the dough by hand. As I work, my lungs stop burning and I can draw air in without feeling like I might pass out at any second. Kneading the dough becomes meditative as I follow a recipe I've memorized for a braided cinnamon sugar challah loaf, my favorite soft bread. I need a comforting bake, and the warm scent of cinnamon will make everything better.

I move on autopilot, and slowly my thoughts creep through the wall after I've calmed down from my panic. One by one, they slip free.

I should delete everything—the photos, our messages. And block his number while I'm at it. My breaths turn shallow and I focus on working the dough for a minute.

Sighing, I set it up in the proofing oven so it can rise. I debate mixing another so I can knead something else, brushing my hands off on my apron. My teeth drag over the corner of my lip. I peek at Mrs. Horne, but she's absorbed in grading at the front of the room.

I'm going to do it.

Pulling out my phone from my sweater, I carry it back to the workstation and put it down, bracing my flour-dusted hands on either side of it. Some dough is caked beneath my nails and around my cuticles. I tap my nails, chewing on my lip.

Come on, Thea.

But I can't. I can't bring myself to do it, not yet. My chest collapses as I release a heavy exhale, hanging my head.

"Stupid," I mutter.

My face prickles with heat as mortification slithers in and chokes me with long tendrils I can't escape. It's not just the nudes I can't face, but where I took them. In school, in *class* with that photo of my underwear. And, *god*, Connor was sitting right behind me when he asked for it. I swallow thickly. He's awful.

A bastard playing me for his pleasure, taking the torment to a new level.

"Thea?"

My head pops up. Mr. Coleman leans against the open doorway with a cardboard cup of coffee, mouth turned down in a frown.

"Is everything all right? I thought I saw you run from the cafeteria when I was getting coffee. I've been looking around for you." One of his handsome dimples appears as his mouth curves at my confused blink. He shrugs. "The student cafe serves better coffee than what they brew in the teacher's lounge."

"Oh. Um." I dust my dirty hands against the apron and flutter my fingers against my hair, hoping I don't look like a total mess. "I'm fine."

"Are you sure?" He steps into the room and weaves through the other worktables to get to me. His gaze shifts to Mrs. Horne for a moment, absorbed in her paperwork, before returning to me. With a soft smile, he puts his hand on my shoulder. "You can always come to me if you need to talk."

The heat filling my cheeks now is a different kind. Mr. Coleman is my favorite teacher, even above Mrs. Horne. He truly cares about connecting with us, and I admire him for it.

"Thank you." I'm smiling for the first time since that dimly lit science room. "You're so kind."

"You're at a difficult time in your life," he says, his voice soothing and warm. His eyes sparkle with his smile and his shoulders shake with a short laugh. "It wasn't that long ago for me. I want you to know I understand what you're going through."

I return his smile. I'm about to offer to bring him the second loaf of challah that my dough will yield when I catch sight of someone hovering in the door. My blood turns to ice and it becomes difficult to breathe all over again.

Connor looms in the doorway with a black, dangerous expression.

How long has he been there? Did he hunt me down, waiting for me to emerge?

He meets my eye and crooks his finger to call me over.

Can hearts turn into rabbits? That's what mine feels like, racing around.

He's the reason I ran to my sanctuary at school, and now he wants me to go to him just like that? That unfamiliar, violent urge returns. I draw a fortifying breath and rub my forehead, turning back to Mr. Coleman.

"Actually, I was, um." A nervous laugh escapes me. "Just cooling my head off, but I feel better now. I should get to class."

Mr. Coleman's expression shifts to something harder to read as he glances between us. "I'll write you a late slip. Come with me and we can chat about it on the way."

Connor steps into the room, silent as death. He picks up my sweater from the apron hook where I left it.

Frazzled, I swipe my phone from the worktable. "No, please. I'm okay. My boyfriend is waiting for me."

I pause, closing my eyes. It just rolled off my tongue. What is wrong with me?

Connor stills, too, watching me curiously. He tips his head to the side and lifts a brow. My stomach rolls unpleasantly.

Did I make a mistake? Isn't that what he wanted from me?

I open my mouth, but Mr. Coleman pats my shoulder. "Well, just remember what I said, okay? I'm always here for you, Thea."

With another awkward laugh, I nod and scurry across the room to Connor, where he seems to be kneading the material of my sweater, his hands flexing. He's locked in a stare with Mr. Coleman as I struggle out of the dirty apron, dumping it in the laundry basket.

"Good girl." He mutters so quietly I'm the only one who can hear it as he hands my sweater over.

"Marina, I have dough in the proofer," I say, sad to abandon my challah.

"I'll take care of it so it's ready to bake when you come back for class later," she says.

Connor puts his arm around my shoulders and guides me out of the culinary classroom.

We walk in silence through the hall for a minute before he stops. "We'll start tomorrow. You shouldn't have done what you did back there, the lunch room. You just butted in and…" He pushes out a harsh breath. "I got caught up, but I didn't mean to make you cry." His jaw clenches. "Clean slate?"

As if I could forget everything? Yeah, right.

Worst of all, if he really needed my help—before he broke my heart—I would have helped him out, no questions asked because that's the kind of person I am.

I huff, crossing my arms. "Are you kidding? You treated me like shit."

"I'm apologizing for it," he growls, turning cold gray eyes on me. "I don't have to. Would you rather I do business as usual and apply pressure until it hurts you even more? Don't forget, I'm the one with all the leverage."

A shiver runs down my spine. "It's a crappy apology. Are you going to spread my photos around?"

"No. As long as our deal stands."

I can't believe him. I've spent the last half hour sick out of my mind worrying my private photos would be all over school by the end of the day. But for whatever reason, he needs me.

Everything is on Connor's whim. This world is one where he does whatever—gets whatever he wants, and the rest of us simply exist to bend to his will.

"You're not forgiven for being an ass," I say, pushing his arm off my shoulder and walking away.

"Where do you think you're going?"

"Away from you." I turn my head just enough to see him from the corner of my eye. "Until tomorrow, when this dog and pony show starts."

He stares for a beat, then snorts and shakes his head. Turning around, he heads in the opposite direction.

"See you tomorrow, little mouse. Be ready."

ELEVEN
Thea

By *be ready*, Connor meant he'd be blocking my driveway in the morning, his dark silver Lexus GX idling as he waited for me, one hand resting over the top of the wheel as I stood there like an idiot.

He's throwing me in the deep end and we haven't even talked about the details. I wasn't inclined to message him anytime soon, so I thought he might find me before school to go over our...agreement. This is ridiculous and frustrating me to no end.

I stay rooted in my driveway, hoping Mom isn't peeking out the window for one of her random checks because I can't explain to her what I don't understand myself yet.

"Let's go!" Connor shouts through the open window, gesturing like *what* as he squints at me. "We're gonna be late if you don't get in the car."

"I didn't ask for a ride." I nod to my blue Mini Cooper. "I have my own car."

Connor snorts. "That is a doll car. Get in, now."

My lips purse. Damn him. He can't control me!

But he's right, we can't keep arguing or we'll be late. Groaning under my breath, I climb into the front seat, dumping my bag by my feet. The car smells like him—earthy and woodsy with hints of spice. It envelops me, making my stomach flip over in a weird way.

"Don't think this will be a regular thing. When are we going over the rules? I'm totally making this one of them."

"We will." He reaches out with his free hand after he pulls away from the curb, taking mine and threading our fingers together. I go still, surprised he wants to hold my hand when there's no one around to put on our act for. "And I am. Boyfriends drive their girlfriends to school. Can't look like a bad boyfriend leaving you stranded."

A sardonic laugh bursts from me. Connor tips his head to peer at me.

"Stranded? Please, I can drive myself. You humiliated me yesterday in front of your friends and made fun of my sweater, now you're holding my hand like you're sweet?" I yank my hand free and tuck it beneath my thigh so he can't get at it. I smooth my green plaid uniform skirt with my other hand, then prop my elbow against the door, resting my head in my palm. "You're still not forgiven. I'm only here because you're blackmailing me. I wouldn't come near you otherwise."

"You certainly were ready to come all over me before." The glare I direct at him drops the temperature in the car by a few degrees. He blows out a slow, strained breath and grips the wheel with both hands. "Okay. Whatever. Noted."

We ride in silence for a long stretch. The drive to school isn't long, and I realize I'm wasting a good opportunity for the details I'm desperate for.

"So what's our deal? Or rather, your deal that I have no choice but to accept because the alternative is...yeah, no thanks. Asshole." I shift a little to face him better as we drive through Ridgeview, turning onto the tree-lined road that leads up to the school. "When did we get together? How did it happen?"

Connor cuts a look at me from the corner of his eye. "We'll keep it simple so it's easy to remember. We've grown up as neighbors. Got together over summer or something. You're the girl next door, what's not to like about that?"

I frown as he hitches a shoulder. "That's unimaginative."

Amusement crosses his face. "We could always use the true version: you sent me a wrong number nude and I was like aight."

"You ass! We are *not* using that. And I wasn't naked."

"Yet. Shortly after?" Connor hums, shifting in the driver's seat. "So gloriously naked."

With a scandalized squeal, I swat his arm, overwhelmed by his proximity and what he's saying. He drives me to things I never do.

He laughs. The corner of his mouth tugs up in a crooked grin as he turns the wheel with the heel of his palm, entering the student parking lot.

"You want a whirlwind romance, or something? I'm just trying to make it easy. It's not like it's real."

The words slice me and I suck in a pained gasp.

It's not real.

Right.

For as big as his SUV is, I'm suffocated by being so near to him while my emotions spiral. Connor is my first actual boyfriend, but it's all fake. I stare at my lap.

"Is it cool if I drop you off here?"

I look up, blinking out of my depressing thoughts. He took the loop that cuts off from the student lot for pick ups and drop offs up the hill where the school stands flanked by tall pine trees. His friends gather in the parking lot at the base of the hill. Devlin Murphy's flashy red sports car stands out like a beacon, and a few people gather around it as he leans against the side.

We didn't get to cover much on the ride. Not knowing what to anticipate being Connor's puppet is grating on me.

"Don't want to be seen with your nerdy girlfriend? Too big of a dent to your shiny popular soccer captain image? I thought that was the whole point of this." The acidic bite in my voice surprises me.

"I, no," Connor says, furrowing his brow. He drags his fingers through his messy light brown hair. "I just thought—because of yesterday. I didn't think you'd want to show up with me yet."

The hot and cold nature of his cruelty and his unexpected consideration is giving me whiplash.

"Okay." I'm ready to escape the car anyway. I pop the door handle and grab my bag from the floor. "Thanks. Bye, I guess."

His voice halts me when I turn to join the flow of students making their way into school. "Wait for me after homeroom. We'll walk together to first period."

My brows wrinkle in confusion as I spin to face him. "We don't have first period together."

"The way to your first class has the most foot traffic. We'll get the rumor mill going early and by lunch they'll all have heard about it. You should sit at my table today."

"Uh, yeah, no. No thank you."

Did he forget the point he made about my discomfort with his friends? Or do guys just get over stuff that easily and he thinks I'll be dandy by lunch?

His expression darkens. "Yes."

"No." I fold my arms over the open window, lifting on my tiptoes to reach. "I already have standing lunch plans every day with my friends. And yours are very rude, so. That's that."

Connor releases an aggravated sound. "Just be in the hall after homeroom."

He pulls off before I can say anything.

I won't be waiting around for him. He needs to apologize to me for real to make up for yesterday before I play the perfect doting girlfriend. I only got in the SUV because I didn't want to be late.

* * *

After I part ways with Maisy at the end of lunch, a hand clamps on my arm from behind and a dark voice growls in my ear, making me yelp in the empty covered walkway between the north and south buildings.

"Somewhere you forgot to be?"

I toss an unimpressed look over my shoulder as my stomach clenches. "I told you I wasn't eating lunch with you."

He squeezes my arm. "I'm talking about this morning. We'll have to do it all over again tomorrow morning. Or—" My body collides with his chest as he spins me around to face him "—we take more drastic measures. Hold still."

Before I register what's happening, Connor tips my chin up, presses his forehead to mine, and holds his other arm up. He flicks his eyes to the side to check, then I hear the digital *click* sound of his camera. He keeps his piercing eyes locked on mine and kisses my cheek. I gasp, pushing against his chest. His arm is like an iron band around me as he licks my damn cheek like an animal, snapping away.

"What—are—you—doing?" With each word I struggle against him.

He chuckles against my temple, the deep and raspy sound unfairly making arousal pulse in my core, reminding me of the recorded voice texts where he'd say filthy things to me in the heat of the moment.

I push away from him, tucking my hair behind my ears to give myself a second to gather my wits.

"And," Connor drawls. "Posted. Hashtag bae. Better follow me back, or that'll look weird."

Annoyed, I whip out my phone and sure enough, I have a new follower notification on Instagram, a friend request on Facebook, and a photo tag with *@BigBadBishop*. Clicking on the post, I find three photos on a carousel. The first one where he kissed my cheek steals my breath for a moment because of how much we look like an actual couple. Then a sigh of relief hisses out of me. He didn't post the one where he licked my cheek.

"Why didn't we just do that in the first place?" I ask. "Seems a lot easier."

"Because my way was more organic. There are algorithms to fight against for visibility. Plus, photos can be doctored."

"If they can, I'll just say that it's not me in the ones you have." I cross my arms. "Easy peasy, we can go our separate ways."

Connor's smile isn't a genuine one, more like an evil shark's, marring his handsome face. That angelic face of his is a big fat lie. "Everyone knows I'm better than that. I'd never be so amateur that I'd spread something photoshopped. The secrets I collect are the real deal, baby."

The second bell rings, signaling that we're both late to class. He takes my wrist and tugs me into the north building, dragging me back to the same empty science lab.

"Do you ever go to class?" I ask, fighting back the memory of the last time we were in here together.

"You keep begging me to have this chat, so here we are." He pulls out a stool and perches on it, propping his heel on the bar. "This is your one and only reminder: you agreed, so you have to play along. No more ghosting on me if I tell you to be somewhere." He ruffles his hair, making it stick up a little, giving him a more boyish look. "What you have to do isn't even *hard*, just be seen with me and shit for credibility."

He makes me so mad. I'm normally level-headed. But around him? I grind my teeth and stalk up to him. Even seated on the stool, he's taller than me, but I don't let it stop me. I refuse to let him scare me as I poke my finger into his chest.

"Listen here, *Bishop*," I say firmly, using the name everyone calls him, "I might have agreed, but I want a real apology for yesterday before we go any further with this ruse. First you shatter my entire world with the truth, then you blackmail me, then the lunchroom! You hurt my feelings and I don't think I can stand to be around you whether you force me to or not until you make some kind of effort to treat me like I deserve to be treated."

In my head, my inner goddess is snapping and clapping at me for getting that out without my voice cracking.

Connor stares at me, his lips working, unsure how to respond. "You are..." He clears his throat, the wonder shrinking back into the shadows behind his mask. His voice hardens. "Something else, huh? I don't normally apologize to the people I blackmail *while* I'm doing it, if ever."

"I'm waiting."

"It won't change anything." His brows draw together. "You're still on the hook, or I'll start sending out your photos. I'm serious, Thea. I'm not a nice guy and I will hurt you if you cross me."

"You can continue as planned. After you give me a good apology. Then I'll help you." I hesitate, licking my lips, debating if it helps my case at all to tell him. "I would've, you know. Helped you. You didn't have to use any leverage, just asked and I would've."

It feels good to tell him that. Maybe if he understands who he's dealing with, he'll stop acting like a grumpy, controlling ass.

"Is that a trick?" He huffs out a scornful laugh and scratches the back of his head, muttering, "Better not be."

I lift my brows expectantly. He meets my gaze, unwavering. I'll wait all day if I have to.

"I'm sorry. Dick move on my part."

For the first time ever, in all the years I've watched Connor from outside of his luminescent bubble of popularity and fortune, he sounds genuine. Human. It's the small reassurance I need to do this.

"Okay," I say.

"Okay?"

"Yes. You may continue with your power trip."

Connor gapes at me, suspicion bleeding into the edges of his expression.

Checking the time on the clock above the door, I frown. If I miss any more of my classes, I'll be written up and sent to Principal Bishop's office. Setting my bag down, I pull out a notebook and a pen, prepared to take notes.

"What kind of girlfriend am I supposed to be?"

With a tiny shake of his head, he says, "Like a normal one. Just do whatever you usually do."

Easy for him to say.

I hold back a sigh. He's proven he's dangerous to spill my secrets to. I don't want to give him another one by admitting I've never had a boyfriend—a real, in person one, anyway. Swallowing, I consider my old online boyfriend, even though it was brief. There's always something that keeps me from counting him.

With my minimal experience, I don't know how to be in a relationship, pretend or otherwise.

Thoughts fly through my head, whispering to me how I'll fail at being a fake girlfriend as much as I would a real one. That Connor will find out how pathetic I am and probably destroy me worse for it. The ugly thoughts pick away at me, promising I'll never be the confident girl in my secret folder, driving away my inner goddess of self-love.

Fake, fake, fake.

Sad.

Unwanted.

My throat burns and I realize the rattling in my ears is my wheezing breaths.

"Are you okay? You look…"

He'll see it so easily.

Tossing aside my notebook, I close the distance between us in a panic. Connor's eyes widen as he cups my elbows.

"Just how long do you expect me to put on this song and dance with you? You never even told me when or how you want me to pretend. Just snap to it whenever you decide without an explanation."

Yes, I sound crazed. I don't care.

A bark of laughter drops from Connor's lips as he looks me up and down. He rises from the stool, herding me back a step.

"That's enough," he growls, grabbing my hips and pinning me against a lab table. "This goes until I say so. You're at *my* mercy here while I've got your dirty little secret in my power."

Ignoring his alpha male bullshit, I throw my next question at him without missing a beat to stave off the thump of my pulse. The words flood out of me with no way of stopping them when I'm worked up.

"How long is that exactly? I'm not just going to live some indefinite lie with no expiration date when it's your problem." While he's bewildered by my outburst, I wriggle away to pace. "A year? Three years? What about college? What—will it still be going on when we're in our twenties, and we'll be faking a marriage and two point five kids? And—"

Connor catches me around the waist, clapping a big hand over my mouth. His gray eyes are full of fascinated exasperation.

"Jesus. Are you some kind of wind up toy?" He removes his hand carefully, like he's worried I'll get started again. "What the fuck was all that?"

It's like I blink back to reality, once he interrupted the flow. My panic has faded in the shock of him grabbing me. I almost smile. Until I remember why we're here.

"I babble when I'm nervous." Folding my arms, I shrug. He steps back. "Seriously, Connor. I'm not blindly playing along without an end date. You can't keep using your leverage over me to keep me in line forever."

Connor rubs his chin, studying me. I can see the gears in his head turning. "Until graduation, then. We'll part on friendly terms as we prepare to go to college."

"That's it? Then you'll leave me alone and delete my photos?"

He smirks. "I don't get a parting gift for when I'm lonely at night?"

"Connor!"

An amused sound huffs out of him as he blocks my swatting hands, catching my wrists in his grasp. "All right, yeah. Fair. Although, little mouse, let me offer you some advice. Never trust anyone who has dirt on you. There's always an extra copy."

"Do you have extra copies?"

"Of course. Cloud backups." He taps my nose. "You can smash my phone and I'll still own you."

Biting my lip, I skate my gaze away. "So do I have to meet your parents? Are you going to meet mine?" I gulp the lump forming in my throat. "Look, I've—I've never had a real—"

I gasp. Crap. I wasn't planning on saying it, but then before I was aware, it was half out. Too late now. It's difficult to continue.

Closing my eyes, my words burst out of me all at once. "I've never had a relationship before, okay? I don't know what I'm doing here. If I'm going to do it with you, we need to outline every expectation, or I'll suck at this."

Silence follows my awkward admission. I crack my eyes open, wary of peeking.

Connor has his lips pulled to one side as he considers me. He reaches out, tangling his fingers with mine, playing with my hand. My breath turns shallow as he drags his finger over my knuckles. It feels nice.

"Not yet," he says, watching my reactions while he touches me. The soft caresses get my heart beating erratically. Whatever he sees makes him nod. "We'll take it slow. With the way you were texting me, I thought…never mind." His expression turns curious and calculating. "Have you ever been kissed?"

I shake my head, breath hitching.

He hums and cradles my face with both hands. "Do you want to be kissed?"

The timbre of his voice curls around me. I can't believe I ever brushed it off because I thought I was talking to Wyatt. The answer was right in front of me all along. Connor didn't modify his voice to hide it.

That deep voice does things I don't understand to my insides. It's the same tone he always used on the phone. The dark, sensual voice of my dreams.

Do I? My throat constricts. It will be my first. Connor will rob me of all my real firsts with this fake relationship.

My lashes flutter as his thumbs glide over my cheeks. He doesn't stop. The rich sandalwood and spicy scent wraps around me as he steps closer, angling his face toward mine.

This is crazy. I should still be angry with him for yesterday, even with the apology I can't get over how he made me feel overnight—being the person both behind my soaring heart and the one to send it crash landing into the ground.

But his touch is so soft and gentle. I picture how his lips might feel on mine and an ache tugs in my chest. I do want it.

"I—yes. But I don't want it to be fake."

Those gray eyes trap me for a long beat. I think he's going to kiss me anyway as his breath fans over my lips. My whole body feels alive, calling out for him.

Then he eases out of my space, back to business in a cool, collected tone. "No kissing. Okay. What about other PDA? It'll be hard to convince people we're suddenly together if I can't act like your boyfriend. Can I still text you?"

I'm dizzy from the almost-kiss not happening. "Like holding hands? That's fine. Um. I don't know about texting. I didn't know it was you. Obviously."

A rumble sounds in his chest.

"Wyatt," he bites out.

I'm no expert, but he sounds kind of jealous. My brows hike up. That can't be right.

"Fine. I'll leave it up to you. Ball's in your court." Connor grants me a cocky smirk. "Just like we started, with that hot little pic of your nightie you sent me."

Flustered, I sail right over the fact that text was never meant for his eyes. "What about when and where? Is this just for school?" I can't see why his reputation hinges on having a girl by his side—me, specifically. "Or outside of school, too?"

His expression closes off. "It's whenever I say it is. You'll do as I say and you're going to behave. Don't think you can get away with a long leash."

"So I'm just supposed to be at your beck and call when you need me to be your doll?" My eyes narrow. "That's not fair. I'm not some toy to pick up and toss aside when you feel like playing with me. I have a life."

In a blink he's in my face, growling as he corners me against the lab table once more. My throat throbs with my fluttering pulse, a spike of fear lashing me.

"And I own it now."

TWELVE
Connor

This is all some kind of trick to outwit me.

I'd bet anything on it.

What my little mouse doesn't get yet? I'm not letting her escape the trap I've locked her in. She stumbled into my depraved kingdom, and I'm throwing away the key to strand her here.

I crowd her against the tall worktable, muscles in my arms flexing. She puts on a frightened little expression that I don't buy. I haven't really scared her yet, not with the way she's fought back, a mouse facing off with a lion.

Thea is fascinating as hell going off on tangents in the face of danger, but I saw it yesterday when she stuck her nose where it didn't fucking belong. Apples and fucking trees, man. I can't forget it again. Can't let the cute little way her nose scrunches distract me from the truth. She keeps knocking me off balance, but if she thinks I'm letting her go or allowing her to call the shots, she's sorely mistaken.

She comes off genuine and earnest, but it's all a lie. Pretty wrapping to fool me into trusting her.

My little sunshine daisy has hidden thorns and roots to choke her king. Beautiful, but destructive.

Why do I keep letting her manipulate me when I'm supposed to be holding a guillotine over her head? This girl…

She's shredding my rep.

I have to stop rolling over when she pulls the pretty puppy eyes on me, or throws such sound logic when she should be cowering in terror that I find myself giving in rather than putting her in her place. Like the end date demand—there wasn't supposed to be one. Mom made a point about legacy and commitment, making it sound more long-term, but I had no way to tell her that without looking weak, not the formidable blackmail king she should fear. I can't keep her forever, and I let her steamroll me. I guess I'll figure something else out after graduation.

"Got it?"

Thea nods. "Got it."

"Great. Enough questions."

I shove down the annoying instinct that keeps catching me off guard, the one where I want to protect her. Like when I made her cry and immediately felt like shit for it. This is what lying bitches do, they get in your damn head and twist you up.

Other than Devlin, Thea is the first person to ever talk back to me and not fear me on sight from the image I've cultivated. In the face of domination and demand, she talks back with logic and a bravery I didn't know a shy chick like her could possess.

But after dumping everything in her lap yesterday, now I know how far I can push her before she breaks. It's information for later.

I put a hand on her waist. Damn, I really want to kiss her, need to claim that mouth. All this verbal sparring with her is getting me horny.

But she said no.

"We could be having so much fun with this, sunshine." I groan under my breath and bump my nose against hers. "You sure you don't want to keep playing our game? Advance to the next boss level? There are killer perks and achievements. I want to show you what it feels like to come on my tongue for real."

She makes a delicious sound, like she took me at face value for agreeing to let her make the first move, but can't handle the filthy words I'm whispering.

The inexperience was a shock after the things we've done when sexting, but it's intoxicating to know she's a blank canvas. I want to paint a masterpiece on it, show her what it's like to fuck the way we fantasized about. It's like I met two different girls, one confident and as devious as I am, and the one in front of me, trembling from a few words and my hand massaging her waist.

"I..." She shakes her head. "Connor. This is a bad idea."

My lips trail over her cheek in the lightest brush. "My favorite kind."

She laughs, breathy and soft. It makes my dick harder.

"They'll be your favorite, too. Let me show you how to live, sunshine."

Fuck yes, I think as she puts her hands on my shoulders, pulling me in.

The door bangs open, startling both of us. A shadow fills the door, back-lit by the bright hallway lights.

"Thea? Aren't you supposed to be in your world history class?"

Coleman.

He looms in the door, keeping to the shadows as Thea stiffens beside me.

"Mr. Coleman," she says.

Is that relief in her voice? I swing my glower to her, getting more pissed off by the second at the way she's focused on him.

What the fuck.

It takes a second for my brain to kick into gear, but once it does, Thea has danced out of my arms, drawn to Coleman. He falls back a step, the light in the hallway showing his smarmy face. The satisfied curve of his mouth ignites a rage in me.

What. The. Fuck.

Sure, he's a teacher, but this guy is always around Thea, especially when I'm alone with her. It's improbable he would just happen to be walking by her all the time. I followed him yesterday when he tracked Thea to the baking classroom. This is all wrong, blaring a dissonant clang in every bone in my body.

"Get to class, Mr. Bishop," he says in a clipped command.

I grin without a trace of pleasure. "Sure thing."

"Come on. I'll escort you to your class." He steers Thea down the hall with a hand resting lightly on her back. "You're really surprising me lately with this behavior. It's not what I expect from you."

Coleman walks off with Thea. She doesn't look back at me once. Nothing about this feels right.

Halfway down the hall, I catch her simpering. "I can explain, sir."

My stomach ices over. Goddamn it. I got swept up in her again.

Still suspicious and questioning why Coleman is always around Thea, I rub my jaw as I head for my car to smoke a joint. I have practice later, but fuck being here right now.

THIRTEEN
Connor

Practice is gruesome. Two guys have knelt in the grass at the sidelines to puke. A few more are sprawled and groaning across the field. Devlin's got a wicked gleam in his eye from the torture I'm taking out on the guys.

I stand on the center line with my hands on my hips, spitting on the ground. My throat is raw from shouting directions at them for the last forty-five minutes. "Shape the fuck up. This is not the team I know we are."

Which is true, because I'm taking all my annoyance out on them. For once, I don't want to be here, but I can't skip soccer.

All I want to do is get out of here so I can do more digging on Thea. I might be blackmailing her, but I still want to claim those pink lips. We were about to kiss, having a real taste of her was in my grasp. Then Coleman showed the fuck up and ruined it. She flipped a switch so fast, it's got alarm bells going off in my head.

I'll hunt down every secret she's ever hidden so I don't have any more surprises with her. Then I'll fucking devour her.

Devlin is in full Devil Boy mode with his own demons, enjoying the show. Damn sadist. He dribbles a soccer ball, flicking it from his toe to bounce off his knees.

"The hell did we even do?" Sean mutters to Trent as he helps him to the bench for their water bottles.

"Beats me," Trent answers, glaring at me as they pass.

I shake my head, not in the mood for my favorite pastime or my so-called friends. "Can't keep up? Quit popping your dad's oxy pills, then maybe you'll have some stamina. The pros go harder than this."

Trent lunges at me with a growl. Sean holds him back with a worried look, like he's afraid of what I'll spill about him. I grant them both a vicious grin. They back off, exchanging wary glances.

"Fucking psycho," Sean says in an undertone.

He better watch it, or I will spill his dirty deeds. Porn addiction, that one. Nasty shit, too.

"Another lap, captain?" Devlin asks as he cycles the ball from his toe, to knee, to chest, and over again with perfect control. Showoff. "If these guys can gossip on the field, they haven't had enough."

"Nah. Get the fuck out of my face, all of you." Flapping my hand in dismissal, I head for the showers. I don't care. "Game against Ridgeview East Valley coming up. Coach can deal with you."

Devlin follows, lacing his fingers and putting his hands behind his head. "You good?"

"Yeah. Just an intense day."

He pops my shoulder with the back of his hand. "You need anything?"

"I'm good. I just need to cool off. Unwind." I'm going to shower, go home, and pack a bowl. That'll do the trick to kill the edge close to choking me. "It's chill, bro."

"All right, cool. I'll catch you later." Peeling off from the path to the locker room, Devlin heads for the parking lot without showering.

I head into the locker room and rush through a shower. There's something else on my agenda when I get home.

* * *

Thea is what she seems at first glance. Sweet, kind, and all about a positive outlook. But that's bullshit.

Only forest creatures in cartoon movies are that pure-hearted.

She's a liar like everyone else, but despite the lies she gets my dick hard. I want her.

"I'll find you," I murmur as I poke through her search history thanks to the backdoor I left on her WiFi network. "Every secret. It's all mine, little mouse."

The clack of the keys are as soothing and relaxing as the bowl I smoked when I got home. I tore through two bags of Doritos and rode the high until the buzz wore off. Now I'm hunting for anything that will give me more insight into who I'm dealing with.

As I dig through her social media accounts, I find something new. One that wasn't in the recent browser history when I looked before. It's a blog site.

Once it loads, my stomach tightens.

"The fuck?" I mutter, bombarded by post after post of pictures.

She's younger, her face a little rounder. The newest post has a date stamp of almost two years ago. I'm guessing she's around fifteen or sixteen in these, but the blog archive goes back three years before that.

"For a girl who goes unnoticed, you sure did want to be seen."

By a rough count, there are hundreds of posts. Maybe thousands. When it was active, it looks like she was posting at least three times a week.

There's nothing too wild, but my brows jump up when I see a few that are questionable. Even though we're the same age, I feel skeevy looking at these. Sickos on the internet would have a field day with the gold mine she's offering up. It's not even password protected and private. Public fucking everything for all of her accounts.

My first thought is to lock this, but she could notice if she still accesses the site. It was in her search history, so she looked at it recently.

I was right. She was hiding more secrets. Everyone lies; haven't I learned that lesson enough times by now?

Somehow, victory doesn't taste great. A bitter tang fills my mouth as I click on a few of the posts, skimming the comments. It's a small relief that the blog seems inactive, but if she pulled it up recently, she might be thinking about using it again.

So help me, if she posts any of her pictures to this shit now, I will put her on lockdown and fry her devices so fast.

Ironic, since I'm using her nudes to blackmail her. A snort shakes my shoulders. Whatever, semantics.

My eyes narrow as I scroll through. Most of the comments make me scoff, but some of the creepier ones have my skin crawling. One username catches my eye.

Henry_Your_GoodKnight: *Beauty beyond measure princess, but what really gets me is the way you smile. Your intelligent eyes say it all, love. You're longing for the world to show you all it has to offer.*

"Yikes."

That one has internet predator written on it in neon blinking lights. I'm about to doxx this fucker for being all over her blog, on every post with multiple comments. The law can suck it. I'd be doing them a favor. Thea better not have given this guy the time of day.

Why the fuck would she subject herself to this for so long without blocking these basement-dwelling neckbeards?

I knew her security was lax as hell when I first hacked her computer, but doesn't she understand how easily this creep or any other on the internet could find her? She didn't even block her photos from download permissions or hide the metadata, putting her location on blast to any dickhead with half a brain.

Shaking my head, I close out of the window.

This girl is going to get me in a mess of trouble, throwing wrenches into my carefully laid plans. I'm supposed to be biding my time until I can break away from this place. All I needed was a fake girlfriend—one of my choosing—to show up when I needed her.

The plan was never someone seducing me with her curvy body, her addictive scent of fresh baked cookies that clings to her skin and hair, and that bright smile. How has a girl that exudes so much sunshine gone under my radar from so long?

Because it's all a lie. A girl like Thea is too good to be true.

I set an alert to notify me when she pulls this site up so I can keep an eye on her like a corrupt guardian angel.

Those protective instincts kick back in, rearing up with the urge to bust down her front door and stand between her and the world.

FOURTEEN
Thea

SITTING in the middle of my bed, armed with my stuffed sea lion, I'm throwing a pity party. I can't kick the down and dirty feeling. It's clung to me all day, ever since Mr. Coleman found Connor and I in a compromising position.

One where I was definitely about to kiss him.

How can I want to kiss my bully after all the crap he's put me through?

He's blackmailing you, girl!

My inner voice of reason sounds like Maisy today and I nod in miserable agreement. "I know."

But I did want that kiss. I would have thrown away my first on a fake, though, and that doesn't sit right with me. It's a good thing Mr. Coleman showed up when he did.

I flip my phone in my hands a few times, playing with the cupcake grip on the back. Messaging him has been on my mind, or at least reading back through it all. I think I'm ready to see it now.

"Right."

Taking a breath, I unlock my phone and scroll to the beginning.

After weeks of talking to him, the first photo I sent seems so tame. As I skim through the message history, my body warms up, my clit throbbing when I get to one of his dirtier messages.

Can't stop thinking about those sweet sounds you make. You make my cock so hard, I want to bury it in you so deep you'll never get me out, baby. Just you and me, fused together. How does forever sound to you?

"Oof," I mumble, cheeks on fire. "The boy knows how to use his words."

But I did, too. I thought it might make me cringe to read it back, knowing it was Connor on the other side of the screen, but some of it surprises me. Secret Folder Girl showed up, confident, aware of what she wanted. Talking to him like this—well, having phone sex—was easier.

I keep expecting my phone to ping. That's been the weirdest part in the madness of the last two days. I got used to anticipating his messages, got excited at the notification sound on my phone. But he's kept his word, leaving it to me to text him first.

It was hard enough to work up the courage to text *Wyatt*. I don't know what to say knowing I have to face him at school, that he's right next door.

What I need is familiar. Comforting. Safe.

I need to know I can walk away for a minute without someone like Connor breathing down my neck. Tossing my phone aside, I lean over to grab my laptop from the end of the bed and drag it over. Once it's loaded, I go to my old blog.

The beauty of posting these pictures was that I didn't know who was on the other side of the screen. It was an escape. The distance and sense of anonymity are what gave me the courage to be this version of myself, where I could experiment with the girl in my secret folder without judgement because no one knew me in person to realize how different I was in reality.

How much I fall short of the mark.

A comment on the second post catches my eye. It's from two days ago, but the last time I posted to this blog was years ago. "What?"

Missing these intelligent eyes and talking to you. Where have you gone, love? Do you miss me, too? I dream of finding you, coming to steal you away for the whirlwind romance the world has to offer you. It's me, I'm your world. If I held out my hand, would you take it? The thought consumes me.

Clicking on the other posts, I find a new one on each of them. It's the same username. **Henry_Your_GoodKnight**.

It's him. My old online boyfriend.

Mixed feelings swirl through me. It gives me a sense I'm wanted, desired, *seen*. But at the same time, there's something about the comments that makes my blood run cold and my heart beat faster.

Time has given me a different perspective on the nature of these comments. He was only a few years older, but still. The age I was in these photos and when I was enthralled with our late night emails? A cold sweat breaks out on the back of my neck and I work to swallow past my dry throat.

Opening a new tab, I find the folder in my inbox where I saved our emails, clicking on the last one I never answered.

To: Thea Marie <cupcakecutie22@gmail.com>
From: Henry Knight <henry.k.c@gmail.com>
Subject: ramblings to a princess in a tower

Love, you're all I think of. It's been so long, I fear I'll forget your perfect, porcelain face. Those innocent lips and your sea-blue eyes haunt my sleep. Why won't you answer me? I'll keep sending you messages. I won't stop. Ignoring me won't work.

Answer me, love. Talk to me.

I'll tell you what I really want. At night I sit up thinking about our conversations, the things you've told me. I want to hear your voice. Let me call you. We'll talk all night.

Once I hear your voice, I know you'll stay in my heart forever. If you do this for me, I'll reward you for being my princess again. We'll do what we talked about. I'll come find you, I promise. We'll live the life we planned out. I'll meet your every desire and give you what you ask for in those big sea-blue eyes.
—Henry

My breathing is ragged. I fan my fingers over my chest, rubbing.

I stopped because Mom was getting suspicious, and I was so scared of getting in trouble. There was no way I could let him call me in the middle of the night, with my parents asleep down the hall.

Closing the laptop, I climb to my feet. Pity party officially over. I will not sit around dredging up weird old memories to compare to the new ones.

The only comfort I need right now is comfort food.

* * *

A short while later, I'm elbows deep in baking to relieve the stress. The kitchen smells amazing. Two trays of finished double chocolate chip cookies sit to the side of our wide kitchen island, ready for baking once the first batch comes out, while Constantine sprawls at my feet, occasionally peeking up with a tiny whine to beg for scraps.

"I don't know," I tell Maisy on FaceTime, the kitchen iPad propped on the recipe stand.

She's in her airy bedroom, running through yoga poses with her hair in a sloppy bun. I finally broke down and explained I've been weird for weeks because of a mystery texter who wasn't Wyatt.

"I think I might've gotten myself into hot water. He's so zero to a hundred." I slice through butter, crumbling it with my flour and salt to make a batch of pastry dough. By the time I've baked through my feelings, I'll have enough for a full on bake sale. Maybe French club can host a fundraiser this week. "I mean, I'm crazy to agree to this whacky boyfriend and girlfriend thing with Connor, right?"

Maisy loses her balance and tumbles out of the handstand. "What!"

"Uh—"

Shit. I got wrapped up in talking while I was baking on autopilot. The plan was to tell her about the mistaken number debacle and keep Connor's name out of it.

Maisy freaks out, kicking her limbs in the air in a goofy dance. "Thea Kennedy has a boyfriend! What! And it's Connor *fucking* Bishop!"

She devolves into squealing while I shush her, frantically trying to muffle the volume on the iPad before Mom overhears from the other room where she's watching a docuseries on a big cat zookeeper.

"Shh, jesus!" I make a pained face as I flail my butter and flour covered hands around the iPad. "Oh my god, I'm going to end you! Please be quiet!"

"Okay." Maisy sits up, leaning toward her phone. "But for real?"

Blushing, I say, "Well, yes and no? It's not real. We're pretending. His idea."

"Tell me everything, girl!"

I laugh and wipe loose curls back from my forehead with my forearm, hesitating to figure out what to say.

Because that's the thing—I can't tell her everything. This is only the second time, ever, I've wanted to hide anything from her. She's my best friend and we've never held back from each other. We've pretty much been synced up on the same monthly cycle, both getting our first periods within days of each other the second summer at camp. Good times.

Despite our open friendship and deep connection, the only other time I've kept something from her was when I had my online boyfriend. I was vague on the details, calling Henry a pen pal instead.

Checking around the corner to make sure Mom is still absorbed in her show, I keep my voice low. "So, he asked—well, no. He's Connor," I start, laughing nervously. "He demanded I pose as his girlfriend because he doesn't date and doesn't want a real one, but he's got my pictures so what am I supposed to do? It's not like I knew I was texting those photos to him. Now he says I'm his until graduation."

"What? Why?"

"Right?" I shake my head. "It doesn't make any sense. I told him to pick someone else, but he, uh...was really convincing."

I suck on my lips, ignoring the tendril of heat when I think about how close I was to kissing him.

Maisy squints at me, her face filling more of the frame as she scoots across her floor. "You know his reputation, don't you?"

Sighing, I nod. "Yeah. Anyway, he wouldn't tell me when I asked for details. It kind of made me mad."

As I add cold water and mix the ingredients into a sticky dough, my anger grows. I frown when I look down and find I've taken it out on my dough. I pat it in penance.

"Sorry," I murmur.

"Are you talking to the food again?" Maisy snorts. "Goob."

"That's not what you say when I feed you my rustic tartlets."

Maisy moans and rolls onto her back, folding her hands over her stomach with a blissful expression. "They're so good. Screw school. We'll run away together, head for Venice Beach.

You'll open up a trendy bakery, and I'll teach yoga. We'll live in a really shitty one-room apartment, but it'll be close to the ocean, so who cares? It'll be *glorious*."

My breath puffs out on a laugh at her elaborate fantasies of leaving Ridgeview in the dust. "Yeah, I'll make you some soon."

"Goddess." Maisy blows a kiss at the screen. She pops up on her elbows. "Ugh. Mom's calling. I've got to go."

I grimace in sympathy. Both of our mothers are a lot to handle. "Good luck, girl."

After she ends the video call, my thoughts turn as I roll out and turn my pastry dough. A new sense of purpose fills me. I'm determined to get to the bottom of why Connor is so adamant he needs me by his side.

FIFTEEN
Connor

WHEN I meet Thea in the morning, blocking her driveway so she has no choice but to get in, I'm prepared for battle. It turns out I don't need to be. Other than rehashing the same argument about the merits of her doll car, she eventually gives in.

A few days pass where we settle into this new routine. I pick her up in the morning, she kicks up a cute little fuss about it, then when I remind her the clock is ticking she hops in. She still asks a deluge of questions, but is no longer resisting the deal. Her questions have my guard up. She's probably looking for any way out, but now she's approaching me with more logic and strategy.

Good luck, little mouse. You're going up against a master. You can't outsmart me.

She's acting like she genuinely cares and wants to help, but I can't believe that. I'm blackmailing her. Why would she help me?

Doctor Levitt would spout some crap about harboring trust beginning with small steps, like believing someone means what they say instead of looking for the lie, but people suck. We're all wired to save ourselves. Thea can't be as honest and straightforward as she seems.

As soon as we pull into the student lot in the morning, she scurries off before she's seen. Without meaning to, I've been arriving before the rest of my crew. Somehow, she gets me to consider her. She gets under my skin, bending me to her will. It must be that inexplicable instinct to protect her.

For now it's enough to add a few Instagram posts together to lay the groundwork. We can stay pretty DL until I need her on my arm for Mom's campaigning, but she stays in my head all day and my dreams at night.

Devlin's starting to notice. He busted my balls about it last night before our soccer match. He should focus on his own shit. I've seen glimpses of the kinky game he's playing with Blair Davis.

It's my fault anyway for pulling out my phone and looking at one of her photos in the locker room.

My days seem quiet and bland without her messages. I think I miss them, if that's possible. Me. Torn up over a chick. Unbelievable.

All I keep wondering is if she misses what we had, too. It wasn't always about getting off— she'd show me her baking, or slip in comments about her day. An amused sound punches out of me because she's really chatty for such a quiet girl once she breaks past her line.

The move is hers to make, but I hope it won't be long before she craves it too much to care that it's me. I wasn't kidding, I'm betting I'm the only one who can give her what she wants. Her stupid Wyatt couldn't handle her, not like I can.

I might not believe her word, but the physical chemistry between us? It's a firecracker.

Thinking about her texting me, *knowing* it's me this time... I trace my lip and cock my head. Anticipating the satisfying thrill is almost too much to handle.

I'm stalking the halls, looking for Devlin before first period when he didn't show in the parking lot, but something else makes me halt. Some underclassman crashes into my back and I swear I can see his soul leave his body when my scowl lands on him. The kid squeaks out some apology and disappears. I turn my attention back to what made me stop.

Thea. Standing awfully fucking close to Coleman.

Her secret blog I discovered flashes in my head. Is Thea better at this than I gave her credit for, putting on a good girl act to get attention? I knew it. No one's that naïve. And here I was, all protective over her when I saw those creepy comments. But she clearly has no qualms throwing herself at men.

Fake girlfriend or not, *teacher* or not, no chick of mine should be seen cozying up with another man. I need to do a deeper dig on Coleman to find something—anything on him that will keep him away from Thea. My suspicion from the other day hasn't faded.

She touches his arm for a brief second with a big smile, then gestures to the pastry-filled table beside them. Vague recognition crosses my mind. There was a new Instagram post Thea made this week of her kitchen exploding with baked goods with the caption *bake your feels away* followed by a yellow heart and a sun emoji.

To make matters worse, she's wearing the same sweater from the photo I was looking at last night. My hands ball into fists and my teeth clench. How many guys would she send a photo like that to, pulling the edge up to show off her stomach and a hint of her tits?

I've seen the fucking blog. That was a couple of years ago, but maybe she's had good practice since then and upgraded to the way she was with me.

Jealousy is an irrational emotion, but there's nothing I can do to stop it surging, calling on the vicious anger threatening to break free, threatening to break Coleman's face for looking at her. I don't fucking share.

I stalk the length of the hallway. If he didn't get the message the two times he's seen me all over her, I'll make it crystal fucking clear this time. She's mine and he needs to stay away.

"I think you'd be a perfect fit to head the winter formal planning committee," Coleman tells her, waving at the table. "You organized this so well. What do you say?"

"I don't know," Thea murmurs, blushing a pretty shade of red. "I'm not a great public speaker."

"This wouldn't be like that. I was the faculty advisor last year, and the students kept it informal, more like a club meeting. I think you'll do great."

"Really?"

Christ, she's so starved for attention, she needs him to praise her? I'm going to put my fist through a locker.

Thea spots me as I stop a few feet away and goes still. She picks up a wrapped pastry and takes a step toward me.

Acid feels like it's boiling beneath my skin, seconds from exploding. I have to get out of here. I might not listen much to that quack therapist every week, but the coping methods keep me in check.

Without acknowledging Thea or Coleman, I keep walking down the hall to cool off before I deal with them.

* * *

After I skip first and most of second period to go for a long run on the track, then grab a shower, I'm late to English class. Exercise helped, but I'm still on edge as I enter the room. The sight of Coleman is enough to have me teetering close to the uncontrollable anger again.

What's so great about him that the girls are always eating out of his palm? Until Thea, I didn't care about a young teacher getting his rocks off with the ego boost of high school girls fawning over him.

Coleman's eyes harden at my interruption. That all-American veneer cracks under pressure. Come on, everything about this guy screams creepy. How do the girls want anything to do with him? Their red flags should be flying around him.

"You're late, Mr. Bishop." Coleman pretends to be authoritative, but I'm not taking it seriously. "Care to explain yourself?"

My skin feels too tight. I almost lost complete control earlier. The thing about being a little unhinged is the breaking point is always a hairline trigger away.

"No," I snark, eyebrow raised.

"Excuse me?"

Coleman doesn't find my backtalk amusing. The urge to laugh bubbles up in my chest and I push it back down with serious effort. The humor helps cut through the red haze of rage.

A few muffled snorts sound to my left. Devlin and Blair have their hands covering their mouths, eyes sparkling. Everyone loves a little bit of anarchy to break up the monotonous bullshit of high school.

Their gazes meet in mutual interest and something passes between them. See? Fucking told him he had the hots for her.

Thea doesn't seem as impressed with my antics, a disapproving, worried frown marring her pretty features. I'm reminded once again why I shouldn't trust her. Why I can't want her like I do. Why does my dick not behave when I need it to? Maybe everything she does will stop messing with my head if I can hit it once and get her out of my system, like the mystery of what she tastes like when it's not my imagination is driving me insane.

Then I could get back on track.

Ignoring Mr. Coleman, I stroll by like I'm not late, enjoying the strangled sound of indignation he can't quite muffle. The closer I get to Thea, the more this morning grates on my nerves. Over and over it replays in my mind: her hand on his arm, her bright smile. I glare at her as the betrayal burns in my gut.

I should destroy her for that act of disloyal defiance. Blast her photos to the whole damn school. She's more trouble than she's worth to have my way against my mom and hers. I swear, I've never put so much effort in with a girl. No one ever fights me, questions me, defies me the way she does.

The brunt of my glare is a blow. Thea slouches down in her seat, shoulders hunched over.

As I drop in my chair, an aggravated sigh explodes out of me. Everything has gone to shit today.

It takes a minute to register the complete silence in the room. Glancing up at Coleman, I wave my hand.

"Well?" I snap my fingers, impersonating Coleman when he wants us to pay attention. The enraged look that flashes on his face has me biting back a smirk. "I'm here to get an education."

As titters move through the class, I feel Devlin nudge me from behind in support.

Mr. Coleman's jaw works. "Let's get back to the lesson. Can anyone tell me your thoughts on the protagonist's passage on page forty-three?"

Things are fine for the fraction of a second between the end of the question and Thea's hand shooting in the air, flailing her arm with an eager tremor to answer. Then the irrational anger rises like a tide in a hurricane, flooding through my system.

"Yes?" Coleman calls on Thea.

"I think the passage means that it's important to be true to yourself," she answers softly, her arm still hanging in the air.

I suck in a sharp breath. To rub salt in my open wounds, all I smell is sugar because she sits in front of me.

Be true to yourself? Something I know she isn't. The proof sits on my phone and that blog. Thea is full of secrets.

"Yes, Thea," Coleman praises, flashing his gleaming white teeth in an energetic smile. His praise earns a laugh from her, the sound pleased at his attention. "Excellent."

The pencil I choke in my grip breaks when I gouge it against the blank page in my notebook. I picture it's Coleman's face I'm stabbing. Bouncing my knee, I have to rein myself in before I grab Thea and drag her into my lap like I'm some deranged caveman. That's not my style, but she drives me to madness.

If I have to sit through an entire class like this, I'm going to end up with another assault charge to cover up. Thea will probably be the one to call the police this time, just like her Mom. Yeah, fuck this. I explode from my seat.

Coleman drops the pretense and stares at me with contempt, like I'm a bug under his boot he wants to crush. *Feeling's mutual, asshole.*

"Mr. Bishop," he snaps coldly. "You're disrupting—"

"Fuck off," I bite back. "I'm out of here."

"If you leave class, you'll earn detention."

Boo fucking hoo. I'll have Devlin erase it, or I'll do it myself with Dad's access credentials. Tossing up my hands, I make my way to the door, kicking Thea's bag out of the way. The door slams hard behind me, blanketing me in blissful silence.

It's broken by Thea's muffled squeak. I hear her through the door, like my stupid body is attuned to her. I stomp away from class, not interested in listening to her try to get class back on track.

She's messing with my head too much. This isn't good. If I can't keep a level head, my strategizing flies out the window.

Thea was hiding everything under her wholesome homespun wrapping. The desire for her is twisting me up and clouding my judgement. She's got an ass I want to take a fucking bite out of, luscious curves I could lose myself in, thighs I want to bury my head between and live there for eternity, and full tits I need in my hands or my mouth at all times. Like, damn. She is fine as fuck underneath those frumpy ass granny sweaters and her wallflower demeanor.

But behind it all, she's as much of a liar as anyone else. Because she's not really a wallflower, not with the way she challenges me. She's not shy and wholesome when I can see how she looks at Coleman.

My jaw aches from how hard I clench my teeth. The back of my neck is boiling hot.

The door opens and closes behind me. I don't turn around.

"Connor." Thea has to shuffle double time to catch up to my long strides. Her breath is short. "Connor, wait!"

I whirl on her, eating up her startled yelp. "What are you doing here, little mouse? Shouldn't you be in class like a good girl?"

The fear clears from her face, replaced by stubbornness. I hate that it excites me. That I'm anticipating her fight.

Want outweighs logic when it comes to her every time.

"I was worried. You didn't seem okay back there, and I haven't seen you since this morning when you walked past me without saying anything." She takes a step closer and puts her hand on my arm tentatively, like I'm a wild animal that might bite her. Smart. I am wild and I will bite her. "Are you all right? Do you need—"

I grab her shoulders and push her back until she bumps into the lockers, caged by my body. "What I need?" A dark laugh escapes me and I lean in. "I need you to stop with this innocent act. You're quite the vixen behind the nerdy exterior, huh?" I close the distance even more, leaving almost no room between us, growling, "I bet you think about being Coleman's teacher's pet, sitting on his desk with your legs spread for *him*. That make your pussy wet? You better not have fantasized about our teacher while you were my favorite little secret, and you damn well better not do it now. He can't have you, little mouse. You're all *mine*."

This is insane. I know I'm acting crazy and possessive, but this is what she does to me. It's impossible to control. I don't understand why she throws me off my game when no other girl has ever gotten me this hung up before.

Does she know the effect she has on me? Is this on purpose? I've been so tangled up, I kept forgetting to remember the strong possibility of her playing me while I was focused on the board, planning my next five moves.

"Mr. Coleman?! W-what, I'm not—I *wasn't* thinking—" She can babble all she wants. I don't miss the way her pupils dilate. She claws at my shirt in her blustering protest. "Why do you always say the most depraved things when you're jealous? Is your ego that fragile? I'm not even your real girlfriend, you territorial ass."

Liar, liar, pants on fucking fire, Thea Kennedy.

I chuckle, the sound rough and dangerous. That damn sugar-sweet scent is intoxicating.

Thea looks at my lips. A growl rips from my throat and I crash our mouths together, kissing her hard. She lets out a surprised sound, then melts into me as my tongue swipes over her mouth. God, her taste. It's better than I pictured. I release a tortured groan as she lets me in, kissing her deeper. My hands slide down her arms and I hold her waist, crushing her body to mine.

It's so much better than what I imagined.

The kiss is hot and demanding. She's a little clumsy at first, unfamiliar with the movements, but she kisses me back and that's all that matters. I cup her face, tilting her head and her arms wrap around my neck.

I'm beyond screwed because Thea Kennedy is an ocean I would gladly drown myself in.

The anger bleeds away, lost to the oblivion of glossy pink lips. It's never faded so fast before.

This calming effect she has on me pushes past every one of my defenses. It demands more of me than I've given anyone, even my closest friends.

A door slamming in the distance brings us back to reality. I don't know how long we made out for, but I want more. She tastes sweeter than the sugary way she smells.

Thea pulls back, blinking up at me in a daze. It's my new favorite look on her. My heart gives an odd squeeze.

Leaning against the lockers for support, she touches her lips, stunned. "That was my first kiss."

"Want a second?" I rasp. With a crooked grin, I move in again, touching her cheek.

Her small hand plants on my chest, stopping me. Her voice is quiet, but serious. "I can't do pretend with my emotions. I won't. Either I'm your pretend girlfriend and that's it, or…" She shakes her head. "We'll need to talk about the texting stuff, I guess. Maybe we can't ignore it and forget it happened. Right now, I can't trust you."

Trust.

Is this real? A strange sensation in my chest quivers and expands. Hope? Thea might be genuine in what she says. The thought bowls me over, painting my defensive actions today in a different light.

Swallowing, I move back, letting her go. Thea sidesteps me. Instead of returning to class, she walks down the hallway, lost in her head.

Maybe she's not trying to play me after all. Could she be as honest as she seems? The concept is foreign to me.

I watch her retreat, well aware of how fucked I am.

SIXTEEN
Connor

WEDNESDAY. My least favorite day of the week. Not because of cutesy hump day memes; those are hilarious.

No, on Wednesdays I'm treated to pure torture. My weekly appointments with Doctor Levitt. Worse, a standing lunch with my parents follows, something Dad insists on so we can spend time as a family. Total bullshit. An ice spike to the skull would be less excruciating.

Appearances.

All part of our happy family show.

The only reason Mom makes a point of joining us is because it gives her a boost in numbers when her campaign photographer follows us around and her social media manager posts to her official profiles with an update of how important family time is to Vivian Bishop. I swear it's her only motivation for anything she does. Damien waits in her back seat while we suffer through cardboard conversations.

Mom's been all over my case because the dinner at the children's hospital is this weekend. I still need to tell Thea.

But first, I need to smooth things over with her.

Yesterday surprised me. The kiss and Thea's words didn't leave my mind all night. At first I tried to go back to what I know, looking for the part where she pulled the curtain back. But it didn't feel right. I didn't want it to be.

I think this is what Doctor Levitt means about believing someone at their word. I only find that in her office, and even then it was a hard road to get to the point I wasn't bucking against everything out of my therapist's mouth. Therapy might be dull as shit, but some of it has stuck. It's nice to have someone speak their mind. I allow few people past my guard where I can take them at face value.

If Thea is showing me I can believe what she says, maybe I should try something new: apologizing.

Idling outside her house in the morning, I drum my fingers on the back of the passenger seat, waiting for her and dreading that it's a Wednesday.

What if she doesn't want a ride? Should I give her space?

It's not a concession I'd ever give anyone else. Things go my way, or they don't at all. But with Thea, it's different.

Once my anger faded, I was able to think clearer. I felt like a bastard because it wasn't her fault. And there was no way she faked that kiss. I was wrong. She's not playing me.

The kiss from yesterday repeats in my mind and I lick my lips. That wasn't an act for me, either.

I just wanted her, my secret vixen.

She's right about it. There's no forgetting what we've done. I never wanted it to stop, but she can't ignore what's between us either.

No, we need to discuss this before the benefit dinner.

Thea seems surprised when she emerges from the house, darting a glance behind her before hurrying to the SUV and climbing in. Her cheeks are pink.

"Hi," she says.

"Hey," I respond, putting the car in gear.

The air goes stale for a few minutes while I navigate onto the main road out of our neighborhood.

Planning to talk and actually doing it? Two very different moods. I'm wasting precious minutes trying to start a conversation, not used to thinking how what I say can affect the girl I want to talk to instead of just laying it out like the law.

"Listen, I—" Clearing my throat, I squeeze the steering wheel. *Come on, man, just spit it out.* "I'm sorry for being angry. That wasn't right or fair to you."

"Okay. Thank you."

She's distracted by braiding her wild auburn curls. Sighing, I continue reluctantly.

Doctor Levitt always says once I'm calm, I need to express my anger. Even if I don't want to be there, some things have stuck in my head.

"The thing is, I have trouble with my temper. You were right, I was jealous," I admit. My stomach tightens. I haven't told anyone other than Devlin about this. With a sidelong glance, I find Thea watching me. My throat bobs as I swallow. "I see a therapist. I have an appointment today. Every Wednesday."

I leave out that it's court-mandated therapy. It's strange to give up one of my cards after spending so long hunting the ones that belong to others. I hold so many of hers between her secret blog and the nudes, it's only fair to give her some of mine to prove I'm serious. I realize the tense set of my shoulders is because I'm bracing for Thea's judgement, but it never comes.

After a long pause where she peers at me curiously, her hand rests on mine on the center console. "I'm glad you have someone to talk to about how you're feeling."

"Yeah." I didn't expect this. She just rolls with it, taking me at face value. She trusts that I'm being honest without question, even after I've tricked her multiple times. "So. I'm sorry for what I said and how I acted. You deserve better, so I'll do my best."

She hums and squeezes my hand. "If you ever want to talk about anything, you can tell me. I'll listen if that's what you need. We might not be a real couple, but I'm here."

I don't love the reminder this is all fake, by my own doing no less, but I'm glad we're cool.

The acceptance feels so good, I'm out of it for the rest of the drive to school, my thoughts cleared and peaceful for the first time in I don't know how long. Thea's like a balm of warm light on my constantly shifting mind.

* * *

On my way to the office around mid-day, I curse, remembering an important thing I needed to tell Thea this morning. I got so caught up in sharing one of my own secrets with her, the benefit slipped my mind.

I thought we would have more time to ease into faking a relationship for the reporters and voters, but the event is this weekend. We've been wasting time with so much back and forth and fighting against the sexual connection distracting us.

I'm not supposed to text her, but I forgot to tell her this morning, too focused on apologizing. This is important and it can't wait.

Don't be too mad, sunshine.

Connor: Showtime this weekend. It's a formal event. Do you have that covered, or do you need money to buy something?

It takes a long time before three dots appear.

Thea: Don't think I don't notice how you're texting me. Your apology this morning doesn't change your promise.
Connor: Yeah, well. Not much choice when you pull a disappearing act all day and I need to get a hold of you. Do you need to borrow my credit card or not?
Thea: Shopping spree on your dime? That's big sugar daddy vibes. [laughing emoji]

My stomach dives off a cliff. Is she...flirting? She must not be that mad after all. Hope sparks to life in my chest.

Connor: You wanna be my sugar baby? Hell yes to those perks.
Thea: No! I don't know why I said that. It was a JOKE!

She sends me an army of emojis, filling the screen with the monkey covering its eyes. My mouth quirks up. It's cute when she embarrasses herself.

Connor: I'll give you more details on the drive home.
Thea: Ok [peace sign emoji]

A second later, she sends a selfie. She's in the library with Maisy Landry, a pair of earbuds shared between them. They make goofy faces for the camera. I'm warm all over, staring at Thea in wonder.

Since our kiss, things feel like they're clicking into place more easily.

The good mood Thea put me in evaporates as I walk into the administrative office. A scowl settles on my face while I wait outside Dad's office. My hands are shoved in the pockets of my black slacks, my school blazer tied around the strap of my messenger bag. The office secretary I flirted with to get Devlin out of a pinch when he was in the student records room eyes me in disapproval.

Suck it, Debbie.

I'd much rather drive myself over to the appointment, but Dad has always insisted. His door opens a minute later, and he emerges, buttoning his boring blue suit jacket. Seriously, whoever he's been seeing must have standards through the floor for Dad to jump right over their bar.

"Ready to go?" Dad asks.

I grunt, whirling to trudge from the hive of offices. Dad falls into step beside me. Outside, he clears his throat and I roll my eyes. Here it comes. The weekly lecture.

"Dad, save it. Come on."

We reach his Escalade and get in. He starts the ignition and sighs.

"I'm serious. This isn't like a few weeks ago when you stole the car for a prank." He pats the wheel in indication.

Devlin and I had the idea for mischief after school. Getting back at both our dads was glorious, stealing the Escalade from his parking space and going for a joyride to Denver to crash a college party. Dad was pissed. It fucking rocked.

I snort, slouching back in the leather seat. "What did I do wrong now?"

It's always me. True, I'm not an angel, but how are my actions always under a magnifying glass when I have two parents cheating on each other?

Maybe what I need to do is fake a private investigator profile and slip a tip to reporters on the local elections circuit. I've always thought about doing it, but not until Mom runs for something bigger, like Senate. I'll do it up with the works, a real pro job that'll fool anyone. The problem is, I don't want to be the one to take the seedy photos of my double home-wrecking parents. It's the same dilemma that trips me up every time I think out this plan.

Dad puts the car in gear and grimaces. "There're photos. Illegal fighting, Connor, really? You know how important appearances are to your mother. I don't have to remind you. A bad story like that could linger and be a roadblock in her political career."

Grinding my teeth, I draw in a slow breath. It was up to Landry and his boys to make sure no photos or video got out. Idiots.

"Yeah, Dad. It's only shoved down my throat every day." I jerk my head in annoyance. Great. I made progress with Thea, but today's session will probably suck worse than usual with my mood blackening like an oncoming storm. "Message received."

He sighs. "It's an important election year, son. You can't have any missteps."

How he can be so weak and pliant to Mom's scheming political shit is baffling. Maybe he got used to the silver spoon life and is too afraid to challenge her. After all, she's the reason he's the principal of an elite private school, and he enjoys the money we get from granddad on top of their cushy incomes.

The urge to punch the nearest thing strangles me. "So she gets to have everything she wants, and the rest of us better fall in line?" I smack the dash in frustration. "Why the hell are we putting up with this? It's stupid."

Dad grants me a sober look. "It's your mother. We have a good life because of her work. You'll go off to college next year thanks to your grandfather's money, so just do as she says until then."

"What the fuck ever."

How great is our life, really? It doesn't seem so peachy. Our family is fractured, all three of us just existing in the same house.

"She wanted me to ask if—" Dad cuts off and frowns. "Did you mother talk to you about finding a date for this weekend and, er..."

What he doesn't say is do I have a pretty puppet to play house with for the rest of the campaigning season.

"I have it covered." I should've never dragged Thea into my mess. Goddamn it. My jaw clenches so hard a muscle jumps in my cheek. "My girlfriend will be there."

I never told Mom I found someone and that I had no intention of picking from her folder. I guess part of me is trying to protect Thea from her, not prepared to subject her to the force of nature that spawned me. I'm a twisted fucker, but I learned from the best, I suppose. Apples and their goddamn trees.

When this started I was ready to throw Thea to the sharks, the same as I would anyone else. It didn't matter before, but now? I'm not so sure.

At first it was routine blackmail, playing with a pawn. Except I've had a real taste of my little mouse.

I'm going to earn her trust so that I can keep her after we get through this charade together. She can be an ally instead of a pawn.

* * *

Thea waits by the coyote statue in front of the school sign after the last bell.

Therapy wasn't as bad as I thought. Doctor Levitt was pleased when I explained how I worked through an episode and talked it out in the morning with Thea. She was on my mind all through the stilted lunch with my parents, helping me tune them out.

When Thea sees me, she smiles shyly, giving me a tiny wave. As I reach her, I put my arm around her shoulder.

"Is this okay?" I ask, steering her across the terrace.

Thea is hesitant, glancing around. People look, because I'm around and that's what they do. She doesn't seem used to being in the spotlight. "Yes. It's good to practice being comfortable with touching for our big debut. What sort of dress do I need to wear?"

Practice. Right. "Uh, I don't know. It's black-tie, so a fancy one."

"Fancy. Got it." She shoots me a shy smile. "Do you clean up nice in a tux?"

The corner of my mouth lifts. "You bet your ass I do. You ain't prepared, girl."

"Will there be dancing?"

"No, it's like." I gesture with the hand around her shoulder, then play with her hair. "A dinner thing. There's a cocktail hour and a banquet. The people going buy their plate and the funds are split between the campaign and the charity. It's boring as fuck. I snuck out for two hours last year."

Thea laughs. My smile grows. A few people watch us curiously as we cross the pavement on our way to the steps down to the student lot. As we pass, I give a few fist bumps to people that I recognize. Thea goes quiet and bows her head.

"What's wrong?"

"Nothing. It's just weird being so close to your popularity." She shoots me a wry look. "How do you get down a hallway to make it to class on time?"

She's joking with me. It makes me want to get in the car and just drive with her, go somewhere we can be alone.

Before we reach the steps, Coleman walks by. Thea stops.

"Have a wonderful evening, Thea."

"Thanks, Mr. C," she says, abandoning self-consciousness.

I grind my teeth, not liking the way he looks at her. "Come on, babe."

Thea turns her attention to me. Keeping half an eye on Coleman, I lean down and kiss the corner of her mouth, squeezing her close with my arm resting over her shoulders. She muffles a surprised sound, putting her hands on my stomach.

Possessive? Yes. Don't fucking care.

Coleman clears his throat. I pull back, smirking at the pretty shade of pink in Thea's cheeks.

"Gotta split, Mr. C." I mimic Thea's moniker for him in a sarcastic drawl. "My girl and I have a big date this weekend to plan out."

Coleman's look is unreadable, but I know I've won this round. He doesn't have a leg to stand on. I'll cut him off at the knees. Thea might be eighteen, but he's a teacher, so he needs to step about eighty steps back from her before I fucking snap.

"Thea," Coleman rumbles before leaving us be.

She narrows her eyes. Her defiant expressions are too adorable to resist. "Was that necessary?"

"Yes. Where were we?" I nudge her and we descend the steps to the lot full of top of the line rides. "How great I look in a bowtie, I think?"

Thea snorts. "So full of yourself."

"I'd rather be full on you, sunshine." I lick my lips and toss her a wink. She makes a delicious, scandalized little sound. "Say the word and I'm going to devour you."

"Connor." Her cheeks turn from pink to rosy. It's too easy to rile her up.

I unlock the car with the fob and open her door for her. She hops up and I climb in on the driver's side.

"What's the event for?" Thea asks, clicking her seatbelt.

"Children's hospital. A fundraiser benefit, sponsored by Mom's campaign. She gives a speech, blah blah blah." The engine rumbles to life and I pull out of the lot. "Really boring stuff. I hate that I have to go at all."

"So why do you have to?" She chews on her lip and tilts her head.

"Her platform and approval ratings center on her being a family woman. A leader, a mother, a wife." I scoff, knowing how much of it is manufactured to keep her numbers high over the guy running against her. "Pretty much everything comes down to politics. Trust me, I've tried to get out of these things. She's…difficult. Persistent."

Thea hums. "I know what that's like. Mine is always breathing down my neck."

My grip on the wheel tightens. I want to tell her I know all about how her mother is, but we've just got to a good place and I already gave up one piece of myself today.

"So if it's all about family stuff, why is it important for you to show up with a girlfriend?" She fiddles with the radio and stops on a song she must like, because she bobs her head to the upbeat music. "Is that why it's a fundraiser for the children's hospital?"

Thea is being nosy again, but it doesn't stir the same ire. In fact, I like her curiosity. She's asking good questions, strategic ones I would pose myself.

"Yeah. Real flimsy, if you ask me." I cock my head as I turn onto our street. "She doesn't have other children, so if I show up with you, it sends a subliminal message of her being a grandmother someday. Nurturing a legacy."

"Oh, so now we are having those two point five fake kids?" Thea taps my arm with a light swat. I park in my driveway. She certainly took that better than I expected. "You should've told me, dear. That will affect my outfit."

I sit back in my seat, angled toward her, totally aware of the crooked, dopey smile on my face. I don't do a damn thing to wipe it off. She keeps surprising me.

Thea winks—or, she tries to, it's sort of a pained blink with both eyes that does things to my heart that shouldn't be scientifically possible—and hops out of the car. "See you tomorrow."

"Bye, sunshine." I sit in the car, watching her all the way to her house.

The girl next door has me under her spell.

SEVENTEEN
Thea

Raised voices catch my attention late Friday afternoon as Constantine follows me out of the house. I stopped at the store to restock the baking ingredients that were getting low. Mom is out for the weekend on a spa retreat, and Dad is on a trip to Salt Lake City for a conference. It's just Constantine and I, which means the kitchen is all mine, so I've got all my bakes lined up until I need to play girlfriend for Connor tomorrow night. It worked out perfectly that my parents are out of town, so I don't have to explain the dress hanging up in my room or where I'm going.

"You need to keep him away from me." Connor sounds pissed as he stalks across his lawn to his Lexus GX. "I'm not playing. I don't want anything to do with him. Not eat his food, not talk about his day, not play happy family when we're dysfunctional as fuck! This is bullshit!"

Mrs. Bishop stands with her arms crossed, and the younger man I recognize as their family friend who comes to their house several times a week is beside her.

"Come back inside, where we can discuss this." Mrs. Bishop's tone is sharp enough to cut and her platinum, sleek bob sways. There's something about the set of her features that's disconcerting, like they're too perfect. "You're making a scene."

Constantine lets out a low *boof* and plants himself between me and our neighbors, standing sentry while I grab groceries from the trunk of my Mini Cooper. I shake my head with a wry smile. He's a seventy pound overprotective lap dog. He's not fooling anyone.

I grab the last bag from the car and catch Connor's eye. The turmoil in his gray gaze shocks me. He looks away, jaw working.

Is he embarrassed? I didn't think he cared what the world thought of him.

His mom gives me a shrewd once over, hyper aware of my presence. When she speaks again, she regulates her tone, sounding kinder. "Why don't you come inside, sweetheart? Dinner is almost ready."

I'm gripping the bag of flour and sugar, debating with myself. *Don't get involved.* But I can't ignore it, can I? It might not be my place to intervene, but damn it, the look on Connor's face like he's the only one in his corner hooks my insides and tugs hard. I won't stand by while he's hurting.

Not when I know how hard it can be to deal with parents.

Setting the bag of ingredients on the hood of my car, I cross the driveway to stand at his side. Constantine follows, laying down in the grass in front of my feet.

"Hi." I take Connor's hand and kiss his cheek, rising on tiptoe to reach. Turning to Mrs. Bishop, I wave. "I'm Thea. Connor's girlfriend. I live next door and go to school with Connor."

He's stunned silent, watching me from the corner of his eye. I'm standing so close, I feel it when his chest caves with the force of the relieved breath hissing out of him.

Okay, maybe that was rash. Oh my god, why did I kiss him in front of his mom before introducing myself? I clutch his hand tighter.

Mrs. Bishop's eyes narrow slightly, taking me in with a once over. I can't help but feel she's sizing me up and finding what she sees lacking.

Connor drops my hand, but before I can run to hide for being silly and intervening, his arm wraps around me, almost clinging to me. He's strong and warm, engulfing me in his rich earthy scent.

"Well," Mrs. Bishop says. Her eyes dart around the empty street. "We're having a family discussion before dinner."

"Mom," Connor snaps. He rubs my shoulder, hugging me close. His voice is hard, but his touch is gentle. "Thea is my girlfriend. She's my date for tomorrow night."

Mrs. Bishop's lips purse and she exchanges a look with their family friend. I've heard his name before—something with a D? She turns her attention to Connor, crossing the lawn to inspect me closely. She stops a short distance away, glancing at Constantine as he pops his head up. The vibe between her and Connor is charged.

Instead of cowering into his side, I put my arm around his waist so we're a united front, lifting my chin as she sniffs. That's a bitchy non-response if I've ever seen one, worse than my mom's false-sympathetic hums.

"You said I needed to bring my girlfriend," Connor says smugly. "Remember? Over that nice meal you were preparing with Damien."

The way he says Damien is almost a growl.

"I didn't realize the neighbor girl is who you were planning to bring." Mrs. Bishop folds her hands in front of her. "I thought you were seeing Nina Goldman. Or was it Anette Rossi?"

Popular girls far more perfect than me, ones that hang out with Connor's crowd and come from money, status, and power in Ridgeview. Not me, a nobody.

The effect of her dismissal is...wow. Is this what it's like to appear polite while silently screaming *fuck you*?

Message received.

Message shredded.

Putting on my sweetest smile, I lean into Connor's side. "We've only been dating since school started, but we have a really special connection."

Her eyes flash. I can see where Connor gets his haunting gray eyes. His are impossible to look away from. Hers are just disconcerting. It doesn't impress her, I guess, since I'm talking back.

I see you, Mrs. Bishop. I know what kind of woman you are.

Hopefully Connor doesn't mind I used the timeframe from when I first texted him. Mistakenly, but whatever. It's the truth.

"The heart wants what the heart wants. Doesn't it?" Connor snorts, caressing my arm. I don't shy away, melting into his touch. "I'm sure you and Damien agree."

If I thought she was intense and intimidating before, it's nothing compared to the deadly look that crosses her face now. Nothing changes about her plastered on smile, but the edges twist and shake, hinting at what lurks beneath.

Constantine remains on alert, watching Mrs. Bishop with an unwavering focus. I nudge him with my foot and he rumbles, laying his head on his feet. His ears are still perked, only pretending to be at rest. If I needed him, he'd protect me in a second.

"I'm looking forward to the benefit," I say. Connor kisses the top of my head. I thought the PDA might freak me out since we've been at odds until recently, but it feels right. "What a great cause your campaign is supporting."

"Is that right? I hope Connor informed you there's a dress code."

"He did. I have a gown." I smile wider. "It's all ready."

"Wonderful." She watches us for a beat, then turns to go back inside without saying anything.

Damien follows behind her. Once they're both gone, Connor winds both arms around me, burying his face in my hair. I slide my hands up his back, holding him. We stay like that for a minute, just hugging.

He peels back far enough to tip my chin up. "Thank you."

I'm about to lean up for a kiss when he squeezes my waist and lets me go.

Connor backs up a few steps, keeping me locked in his gaze, then he gets in his car and pulls out. I'm left alone in the middle of the lawn with Constantine.

"Come on, Con," I call, going to grab the grocery bag from the hood of my car.

He trots after me, panting happily as we go inside.

* * *

Later that night, I'm wrestling with myself, chewing my lips raw. A restlessness has settled and even baking for hours into the night didn't help me calm down.

The thing I need I don't want to do by myself.

"This is a bad idea," I mumble, staring down my phone as I pace my room. "Bad, bad idea."

My favorite kind, Connor's voice echoes in my head.

Blowing out a breath, I pick up my phone and do what I've been arguing with myself about all night—I text him. The contact no longer says Wyatt with wave emojis. Now it's updated with Connor's name bracketed by black heart and crown emojis.

The black-hearted king of secrets.
My secrets.

Thea: Hi. Are you up?

The response is immediate, sending my stomach into a wobbly flip of nerves. He doesn't bother with words, just sends a photo of himself, shirtless and sprawled in bed. I can see the edge of his lazy smirk. Just like the first time.

Licking my lips, I take a pic. My curls frame my face and I'm wearing a white bodysuit with illustrated peaches on it. On the backside it reads *peachy keen* across the butt. Maisy saw it when we were shopping and squealed, insisting I get it because it made my ass look amazing. Into the contraband box it went. Until now.

My heart skips a beat as soon as I send it.

Connor: Fucking hell, sunshine. I want you so much.

A nervous laugh escapes me. There's nothing like this, the way he makes me feel. A thrilling buzz travels across my skin as I settle on the armchair by the window, so I can peek at his across the way. Not only are the lights on, but I'm throwing caution to the wind. It's daring, being out of my bed.

I'm home alone and an aching need burns in my core.

Thea: What do you want me to do?
Connor: Touch yourself. Slide those fingers over your tits and down between your legs.

My breath punches out of me as I follow his command, stroking over my pussy. Sinking my teeth in my lip, I hook a leg over the floral-print arm and slip my fingers beneath the bodysuit. I'm soaking them already, feeling so turned on.

Connor: You wet for me?

Typing one-handed is always hard, but I manage.

Thea: Yes.
Connor: Mm. Slide one inside. I'm going to suck your finger clean and taste you.

I tip my head back, eyes fluttering shut as I work my index finger in slowly. My hips rock as I push deeper and pull it out, swirling wetness over my throbbing clit. Turning my head to the side,

I see a shadow filling Connor's window. My breath hitches and my whole body pulses.

Instead of a text message, my phone vibrates and Connor's name fills my screen with a FaceTime call. We never got that far before he revealed himself. The closest we came were the Boomerang clips and voice texts.

"Oh my god," I whisper, fumbling with my phone. "Shit."

I answer.

Connor's face appears on my screen as the video connects. When he sees me sprawled in my chair he pushes out a breath. "Fuck, baby. Look at you. Eyes all bright and hungry."

He puts a fist over his mouth, leaning against the window frame. He's naked and hard—I can see his erection bobbing from the way he angles the camera. Those gray eyes flick away from the screen, toward my window, before coming back to sweep over me. Desire flares in his gaze, sending my stomach into a pleasant dip.

"I, um." I'm trembling, certain my blush spreads from head to toe. "Hi."

"Hi, sunshine," he rumbles. "You texted me."

"I did," I breathe.

"What do you want?"

"I—I want to come," I choke out.

God, this is harder to do when it's live and I have no time to think about what to say. But Connor grins.

"Prop the phone on the windowsill and turn your chair." Swallowing, I get up to do it. "Good girl. Now, as cute as this peachy little number is, I want you to lose it. Bare yourself for me, baby."

I squeak, holding my breasts as I lean close to the phone. "Naked?"

"I've seen you before, remember?" He drags his teeth over his lip. "Strip."

Not moving right away, I put my hands on my hips. "I want to see you first. I..." The words clog my throat, but I push them out. "I want to watch you touch your cock."

The heat in his gaze grows hot enough I can almost feel it blistering my skin through the phone and across the distance between our windows.

Connor smirks at the camera as he shifts back to fill the frame with his incredible body. The muscles in his forearm flex as he takes his hardness in hand and strokes it, watching me.

"This what you wanted to see? Proof of what you do to me?" He twists his hand and he grunts. "With your sexy body and the way you always challenge me. Mm. Now strip."

Driven by the confidence and hot pleasure filling me at seeing how I turn him on, I peel out of the body suit, keeping my gaze locked on him through the video connection.

"That's it," Connor encourages with a deep rumble, working his hand faster. "Now you're going to sit back in your chair. Hook your legs over the arms and show me how wet that pussy is."

My heart stutters as I fall back in the chair. It takes me a second where I need to gather my wits. Connor moans as I absently play with my hard nipples.

"Want to break into your house and drive into you, shit."

I laugh, a little delirious before we've even done much. "This feels a lot different. I know you're watching me."

"Hell yes, baby. I'm not taking my eyes off you. It's just you and me. There's nothing to be embarrassed about," Connor croons. "Show me."

With a shaking breath, I spread my legs, resting them over the arms of my chair. Connor goes still, staring at me with such intensity, it's like I can feel him in the room with me. His eyes drink me in.

"Thea," he whispers hoarsely.

The reverence in his tone gives me courage to let go. I coast my fingers down my stomach, over my mound, and stroke my slick folds. I tip my head back with a soft sigh.

"That's it. God, I want to lick your pussy until you cry. But I won't stop, I'll keep going until I've made you come so much, you're wrung out."

My heart pounds and I shift my hips to roll against my fingers as I rub my clit. "Ah. Feels good."

"Yeah. Keep going."

I push a finger back inside and imagine it's Connor fucking me on his long fingers. My brows pinch. I need more. "Please."

"I'm right there with you, sunshine. You hear me? I'm kissing your neck and sucking on your nipples while I thrust my fingers in you."

Gasping, I pinch a nipple and buck against my hand.

"God," Connor bites out as his hand fists his cock. "See this?" Connor moves the phone so I can see how he's leaking pre-come over his knuckles. "This is you, baby. So hard for you."

A ripple of pleasure crests over my body and I cry out. Distantly, I'm aware of Connor cutting off a curse and groaning while I ride out my orgasm. As I come back down to earth, Connor chuckles. He's moved to his bed, covering his lap after tossing aside a used tissue. Blushing, I scramble for my discarded body suit and shift around to curl in the chair with more modesty.

"You feel better now?" Connor asks. His eyes are bright with amusement. "All ready for me to tuck you into bed?"

"I, um." It hits me hard. I just had phone sex with Connor. And I started it. So do I want him? Blinking, I push my hair out of my face. "Yes?"

His shoulders shake as another amused sound rasps out of him. "Sweet dreams, sunshine."

Whether he can tell I need the space after taking things so far with him, or he got what he wanted and he's eager to get rid of me, he winks and ends the video call. I melt into the chair and hide behind my hands. When I peek between my fingers, his shadow fills his window again, facing my bedroom. He doesn't hide behind curtains as he watches me because he doesn't have them. I close my sheer lavender curtains and dive into bed, not bothering with getting dressed.

"Well. That happened," I say to the empty room.

My heart races. I have to face Connor tomorrow and we just did that. Were my last two brain cells on vacation?

EIGHTEEN
Thea

As I pace by the front door, waiting for Connor to knock when it's time to go, my hands itch to sink into dough. I still don't know what happened the night before. I mean, I know the obvious. Phone sex. Really hot phone sex.

My cheeks heat and I fan my hands to cool myself off so I don't mess up my makeup. The elegant, beaded gold gown I'm wearing swishes as I pace. It's the prettiest thing I've ever worn.

I don't know what I want. I don't know why I started things with Connor last night.

A knock on the door makes me startle. "Oh god."

I open the door and gape. Connor stands there, one hand in his pocket and the other braced on the doorframe. His tuxedo is tailored to fit his body, and his floppy light brown hair has some product in it, styled to make him look even more dapper.

This isn't fair. My heart lurches.

He looks amazing. Irresistible. Then he smirks at me and I lose all breathing capabilities.

Sweeping his gaze over me, his full lips stretch into the charm-up-to-eleven smile I've never experienced the full force of. *Oof.*

"Looking good," he says, offering his hand. "Ready to be thrown to the lions?"

I have every intention of responding, but my tongue gets twisted. Connor takes my hand and tugs me against him.

"Don't worry, little mouse. I'll protect you."

Behind him, an expensive SUV is parked in the street. He waits for me to lock the door, then tucks my hand in his elbow, guiding me to the car.

"I'm nervous," I admit.

Connor pauses halfway down the walkway from my house. "Hey." He cups my face, smoothing a thumb over my cheek. "I'm the one who made you go. I won't abandon you. I'll be with you all night. Okay?"

I nod, feeling better.

My nerves spike again as we pull up to the hotel where the benefit is being hosted. Photographers and reporters line the plush carpet leading into the building.

Isn't Connor's mom running for city council? This is like a movie star or presidential welcome. It's a lot more attention than I expected for a local event, but this is Ridgeview

Everything is a big to do.

Connor squeezes my hand as he helps me out and tucks me against his side. Camera flashes and questions start up immediately as we turn to follow his parents.

"Just keep your head down or look up. Those flashes are blinding," Connor says.

"Councilwoman Bishop, this way! Are you hoping to beat out the funds raised from your election campaign last term tonight? Are you here with your family?" The reporter catches sight of me. "Miss, what's your name?"

Connor holds me close and strides past the press gauntlet without answering any questions while his mother lingers to smile. I peer over my shoulder before he pulls me through the carved lacquered double doors leading into an ornate, Victorian style parlor room.

"Cocktail hour is in here, then dinner through there." Connor indicates another set of doors inlaid with frosted window panes.

"This place is so fancy." I tip my head back to take in the deep colors and the intricate high ceiling, where crystal chandeliers dangle overhead. "Wow."

"I've always thought it was stuffy." Connor shrugs and swipes a piece of fruit from the spread of appetizers. "Remember our story if anyone asks."

"Okay." Interested in the table of puff pastries, I take Connor's hand and pull him over to inspect it. I pick one up and take a bite, moaning as buttery crust, creamy brie, and tart cranberry burst on my tongue. "Wow, this is so good. How did they get their pastry so flaky?"

Connor stares at me intently when I turn to offer him a bite. He parts his lips and I peek around us. He waits until I give in, feeding him. His lips brush against my fingers, sending a shiver racing down my spine. His gaze stays fixed on me as he chews.

"They're the top chefs in the country. Mom has them flown in for the event." His deep voice washes over me as he places his hand on the small of my back. He leans close enough to press his lips against my ear. "Moan like that again where anyone could hear you tonight, and I'll have to steal you away and stuff something in your mouth to keep you quiet."

A gasp tears from my throat as Connor strokes over my pulse with his other hand. Heat pools in my core at his words. "But, don't you have to be seen? They'll wonder where you went."

"Don't care. Not when you're making sounds like that while standing within reach," he rumbles, tracing the strap of my dress, slipping his finger beneath it. "No windows separating us."

How can that simple touch steal my breath and make my thighs squirm together? He watches me closely, granting me a wicked, devious grin. He knows exactly what he just did to me.

"You're so pretty when you blush."

"Connor, it's good to see you." A portly man with a whiskery white beard interrupts us. He holds his hand out for a shake and Connor takes it. I watch him slip on a mask, playing his part of supportive son. "What's next for your mother? D.C. I hope. There's a Senate seat that will open up once her next term on the council ends."

"She only wants to serve Ridgeview's residents and do her best for them right now," Connor says with a laugh I know is for show.

I hope that's the truth. To distract myself from over-analyzing last night, I spent a few hours researching the legislation his mom passed. What I found didn't impress me. Given the choice, she's not someone I'd vote for.

"And who's the lovely lady you're with?" The man takes an interest in me.

"My girlfriend, sir. I'm sorry, you'll have to excuse us. I see someone I was told to speak to." He inclines his head at the portly man. "You know how these things go. All hands on deck to woo the purse strings into bigger donations."

The man throws his head back on a laugh. "Too right."

Connor steers me away and we run right into Maisy's parents.

"Chief! Looking sharp," I say.

"Thea," Mrs. Landry says in surprise. "Darling, you look beautiful! I didn't know you'd be here."

"Oh, yeah. Maisy didn't say?" Chief Landry shakes his head, gazing past me to Connor, standing behind my shoulder with his hand planted firmly on my waist. "This is my boyfriend, Connor. His mom is Councilwoman Bishop."

"We're well acquainted," Chief Landry says, coughing when his wife elbows him.

He and Connor share a look.

"Well, have fun tonight, kids," Mrs. Landry says, ushering the police chief away.

It's deceptive at first glance, but Connor keeps himself between me and anyone we mingle with during the cocktail hour. I don't really get why, since I'm supposed to pose as his girlfriend. He won't let anyone talk to me for long, masterfully but abruptly extricating us from conversations when they get too prying.

When we sit down in the next room for dinner, he pulls my chair out for me. The room drips in splendor, with circular tables covered in white tablecloths and place settings more suited for a ball rather than a political charity fundraiser. This event pulls out all the stops.

Connor doesn't seem surprised as he takes his seat next to me. His parents are already at the table, Mrs. Bishop nodding as Damien leans over to speak in her ear with a tablet in his hand. He appears to be running the show as one of Mrs. Bishop's high up staff members.

"We'll do the speech between the soup and main course. Any later in the meal and I'll lose their attention and their wallets."

Her calculating demeanor changes as soon as the other guests who purchased plates at our table arrive.

"We went all out for you this year, Madam Councilwoman." It's the man with the white beard from earlier and he's taking his seat next to me.

Connor stiffens.

"Charles, it's an honor," Mrs. Bishop says. "Your support of the campaign is wonderful."

Connor leans close to me. "Friend of my granddad's."

As Charles sits down on my other side, Connor hooks his hand beneath my chair and gives it a subtle yank so my seat scoots toward him. Mrs. Bishop clears her throat across from us, spearing Connor with a pointed look.

Dinner goes on like that, peppered with awkward moments and tiny rebellions from Connor. His mother is doing a scary good job of keeping her cool. It's almost like Connor is pushing her to see how far he can go before she loses it.

I think it backfires, because all she's done is give me another taste of how she's polite but horrible while they have an audience.

"Charles, has Connor mentioned his plans for next year?" Mrs. Bishop asks as we finish the soup course. "Ivy bound. Maybe he'll be giving your company a run for its money in a few years."

As Charles chortles, he bumps against my chair. He keeps doing that and Connor doesn't like it. "Is he now? Of course he is. Spitting image of your father; I'm sure he's got a mind like his as well."

"What about you, dear?" It takes a second to realize Mrs. Bishop is addressing me. "Is it state school for you?"

"I haven't applied yet," I say.

"Mom. Don't you remember?" Connor laces his fingers with mine when I take his hand beneath the table. He brings our hands on the tabletop so they can all see us unified. "We're getting serious. I fell for the girl next door and finally got her to fall for me after nursing my longtime crush. I'm not about to let her go. Thea and I will get married after graduation and move to Paris for a year. She wants to study from the best pastry chefs. After that, we'll travel. Do humanitarian work."

For a second my heart takes a vacation until I remember tonight is fake. I swallow back anxious laughter.

"How romantic," one of the other table guests coos, about to swoon at Connor's steadfast declaration.

"Married." Mrs. Bishop might as well have said *drink sewer water* with that tone. "I'm thrilled to hear you're so committed to each other. And at such a young age."

God, she's just like my mom.

"I'm always thinking about the future, like you wanted," Connor says. He tilts his head and peers at me. "Always."

"Wonderful. You can apply to Oxford for a year abroad, then."

The tension at the table almost chokes me. Thankfully, Damien appears at Mrs. Bishop's elbow and she leaves to give her speech. Connor holds my hand through it all, stroking my knuckles.

My head is spinning by the time dinner ends. I slip off to the restroom to freshen up.

When I come out, a man with a press badge is in my face.

"Can I get a quote? You're here with Councilwoman Bishop's son tonight."

Connor materializes at my side, hand resting at the small of my back. "She is. What's your question?"

The reporter motions for a photographer hovering by a potted fern. "The policies your mother supported in the last year cut back on the education budget for Ridgeview. As students, how do you feel about that?"

"Oh, I was reading about this earlier. I think—"

"Those policies were put forth by the mayor," Connor says, polite but bland as he cuts me off. When I pinch his side, he deftly maneuvers me into posing for the camera with him. "Will that be all? Great. Bye."

As he guides me away, I dig my heels in and walk over by the coat check. The clerk is on break, so we're alone, shielded from the crowd by tall decorative plants.

"What is up with you tonight?" I demand. "You didn't tell me everything. Tell me the truth. Why am I even here? It doesn't seem like you need or want me at all."

"I'm sorry." Connor kisses me, cupping my face. "It's necessary. It's been harder than I thought it would be to play my part and keep you from getting sucked in by this tar pit. This isn't your world. I never should've gotten you involved in my shit." He rests his forehead against mine, closing his eyes. "I'm not really me tonight and you're not really you. Don't think of me like this."

There's a pleading edge to his voice. He seems unhappy and out of sorts. The pressure of tonight has put a strain on him that has him worn out from fielding questions and dealing with his mom. I've watched it weigh on him all night as tension wound through his posture.

He's reverted to being controlling tonight, closing off when things got hard instead of being the disarming guy who drives me to school in the morning, and apologized when he was wrong. Instead of the one who wished me sweet dreams last night.

It's Connor with his guard firmly up, refusing to let me back in. I thought we were making progress toward understanding each other better, that maybe he was changing his ways for the better.

This environment must be toxic for him, because it turns him into someone I barely recognize. He's that damn blackmail king once more.

I don't like this Connor, but I empathize with him.

I'm not really me tonight and you're not really you.

He wouldn't be here without the strict expectations of his mom. I want to do what I can to take away the look on his face, so I slide my hands up the lapels of his tuxedo and pull him in for another kiss.

Connor takes my mouth with a rough sound, holding me against him.

The kiss gets heated, and he tugs me into the coatroom, slamming the door behind us as we stumble through the muted light, bumping against coats. I clutch his shoulders and he grabs my ass, palming it through my gold dress while his tongue delves into my mouth.

Is this fake, too? Has everything tonight been for show?

The last time we kissed, it was intense. I feel the same trembling restraint shattering as Connor devours my mouth.

I need to know if this is real or not.

Because why am I lying to the people out there while we're hooking up in private? It makes no sense.

"You're the cure to this mad circus act I've been trapped in all night," he murmurs against my lips.

An ache pangs in my chest, but I snap my spine straight and plant my hands on his chest to keep him from diving in for another kiss.

"Wait. I'm not just going to play along and be your secret in private while pretending to be your fake girlfriend in public." As I lay it down, Connor stares at me, his expression hard to read. I prod him in the chest. "Why do I have to cater to you if you're just using me? Was last night anything or another game you'll hold against me?"

"Against you? What have I been doing all—" With a frustrated breath, he cuts off and swipes a hand over his mouth. His gray eyes harden. He's shutting me out, I can feel it. He takes out his phone and pulls up one of my tamer photos he's been dangling over my head. His knuckles turn white as he grips the phone. "You want to keep challenging me? Blackmail it is, then. I always keep my word. If you want out, you know what it means."

I fold my arms. I don't believe he would. "Do it. It's better than you pulling the leverage card when you don't like what I say. I'm a *person*, Connor. You can't control me like a chess piece."

He grumbles under his breath and puts his phone away. I called his bluff and it gives me a sliver of hope. I step close enough my chest brushes his body.

"This doesn't have to be a secret we hide. If you want me, you can ask me out for real and *maybe* I'll say yes."

Silence blankets the coatroom for a beat.

"Does that uptight mom of yours even let you date?" Connor narrows his eyes. "Does she know you're here?"

I lift my chin. "You didn't care before when you bullied me into this deal. I don't need her permission to do what I want."

Connor traces my lower lip. "There's just one problem with your cute little declaration."

"What?"

"I don't do girlfriends, remember? Never have. Wanting to fuck you doesn't change that. This is mutual back scratching to get my mom off my case."

"I don't believe you."

"You don't have to." He kisses me, lips moving slowly over mine. "But you do want this."

"Do I?" I sass as he herds me through the room until my back hits a wall.

"You're dying to know. I saw it in your eyes last night." Connor drags his lips down my neck and I gasp, tilting my head. "What do you say, my little mouse? Going to let me show you what it's like to become the irresistible vixen you are behind your phone?"

It's tempting. He's luring out the Thea in my secret folder. I want it, but I'm not done pushing my point. I won't give up. We can have this now, but I'm not letting this go.

Connor covers my mouth with his, nipping my lip. I dig my nails into his biceps. "Well?"

"Yes," I whisper.

The pleased sound he makes is downright sinful as he gives me one more searing kiss and sinks to his knees. He pins me in place with his gaze, gliding his hands under my dress, up my bare legs until he teases the edge of my panties.

It's intoxicating to have him on his knees at my feet.

"If you're such a good girl, you wouldn't have worn panties like that." He holds the hem of my dress at my hips, gaze feasting on what's beneath. "Those are the panties of a girl begging to get fucked."

I lean against the wall for support as he lifts my leg, kissing the birthmark on my thigh he thinks is shaped like the sun.

"Maybe I just like feeling pretty. For myself."

His chuckle vibrates against my skin, dragging a gasp from me. I lose my breath as he peels my panties down and stuffs them in his pocket.

"Now how do you feel? Wild?" He leans back to peek up at me. "Only you and I will know."

I bite my lip. "Free."

Connor grins. "Yes, baby. Hold your dress up."

He presses his face against my thigh as he strokes my folds with a teasing touch. I shift restlessly, needing more. His teeth sink into my skin and he licks my birthmark, pressing his thumb against my clit.

"Ah!" My head tips back.

"Love your sounds," he rasps. "So sexy."

As Connor teases me, he kisses my birthmark over and over, worshipping it with his tongue and teeth. Then his fingers slide into me and I have to let go of my dress to clap a hand over my mouth, muffling a moan.

"Feel good, sunshine?"

I nod, breathing hard when he pumps his fingers, filling me up. My insides twist into a tight coil of pleasure.

"Who's fucking you right now?" Connor growls. "Say my name."

"C-C—" Before I get his name out, he pulls out to spread my legs wider and descends on my pussy with his mouth. As he sucks on my clit, I whimper. "Connor."

"That's right, baby. Not Wyatt. Not anyone else," he says, making my body wrack from the sensation of his lips brushing my wet folds. "All me. Don't you forget who makes you feel like this." He swipes his tongue over my pussy. "Who gets you wet like this."

My knees shake as I'm overwhelmed by the sensations. It's so much and my toes curl. I can barely contain the sounds escaping me.

"Please," I gasp, angling my hips and reaching for his head, running on instinct and need.

Connor groans, eating me while his fingers dig into my thigh and ass. He pulls back to catch his breath and thrusts his fingers in me again, torturing my clit with his thumb.

"Oh my god," I whine.

"You'll always think of me, sunshine. Years from now, with your sweet college boyfriend who buys you flowers, with your wholesome husband who kisses you good morning—you'll think of me fucking you like this." He curls his fingers, hitting a spot deep inside that makes my body quake with pleasure. "Because you'll always be mine. No one else's," he growls. "I'll ruin you for anyone else, because I'm the only one who fucks you the way you like it, my dirty little mouse. There's no escaping me."

I fall apart on his fingers, tears pricking my eyes, almost losing my balance as I come. It's way more intense than I was prepared for.

Connor catches me in his arms, putting me on his lap as he slumps to the floor. I can feel his hard dick against my ass as we both pant. His hair is a mess. I'm sure I look just as debauched. He gathers me in his arms, in no hurry to take care of himself.

I'm about to speak when a commotion at the door has both of us jumping. Connor springs into action.

"Go. There," he points to the coats.

We shuffle into the shadows as an arguing couple comes into the coatroom. Connor holds me close, shielding me with his body.

"They're starting to notice," a woman hisses.

"You promised." That's a man's deeper voice, angry. "What do you expect me to do when I see you kissing him?"

"He's my husband. I'm still married to him."

Connor tenses, glancing over his shoulder. I can't see past him. He focuses on me once more with a mix of possessive protectiveness.

"I can't deal with this right now. It's already a risk to come in here. We'll talk about this at home. Do not mess this up for me, Damien."

My eyes widen as Connor steps closer, plastering his body against mine. "Shh."

The door slams. I don't dare breathe. Another piece of the Connor Bishop puzzle slots into place.

He cups my face, staring at me with resignation. "Let's get back out there."

"We're not going to talk about that bomb? Are you okay?" I wrap my fingers around his wrist. "Did you know?"

He's quiet for a minute. "I knew. Come on."

We emerge from the coatroom and I stop by the bathroom to check my makeup and cool off from the aftershocks of the earth-shattering orgasm he gave me. As I leave the bathroom, I freeze.

Connor watches me, leaning against the opposite wall. His hair is fixed, my lipstick wiped from his face. Without breaking eye contact, he pats his pocket, where he stuffed my panties.

"Get through the rest of the night and you'll get them back."

"Connor," I hiss. "Are you serious?"

He pops off the wall from his slouch and smirks as he closes the distance between us. He puts his lips by my ear and murmurs, "Be a good girl and I'll do that thing you like again."

Too flustered to respond, I spend the rest of the evening stewing on what we overheard in the coatroom with a million questions running through my head.

NINETEEN
Thea

At the end of the night, Connor walks me to my front door.

Principal Bishop has already gone into their house. Connor's mom and Damien rode in a different SUV, getting away with their secret without suspicion because he's her right-hand man. I can't believe what happened tonight, what we heard them arguing about.

After all my theorizing, I've finally worked out why he was forced to bring a fake girlfriend. I'm part of the elaborate distraction to further hide what Mrs. Bishop has been doing. Sadness pangs in my chest. The truth is worse than all the wacky reasons I thought up.

Connor brushes his knuckles over my cheek. Those intense gray eyes trap me in their hypnotic hold.

"Goodnight," Connor murmurs.

"Bye," I call as he walks away. A second later, I realize he still has my panties in his pocket. "Con—Damn it."

He's disappeared.

Unlocking the door, I slip inside. Constantine greets me, his whole hind end in motion as he tries to wag his tail nub. He dances around me in his excitement.

"Okay, okay. Come on, I'll let you out." I pat his head as I pass by him, kicking off my heels on the way to the back door and sighing in sweet relief as my sore bare feet hit the cool kitchen tile.

So many thoughts swirl through my mind.

On one hand, the girl I hide in my secret folder came out and it was overwhelming... and exhilarating.

I'm not ready to do it again unless Connor and I talk about our relationship, but I did like it. I do want more. Is it messed up that the boy who's been my bully for so long is the same one who gave me my first kiss and so many other firsts? Maybe, but I'm not going to psychoanalyze myself.

I wanted it, so that's all that matters.

Opening the door, I snort as Constantine tries to take off like a bullet, but skids on the back terrace and trips into a clumsy roll. He pops up a second later, perfectly fine and disappears past the pool of light into the backyard. I hear him rustling around as I lean against the open door to wait for him, hugging myself against the chill.

My mind goes to the fight between Mrs. Bishop and Damien we overheard in the coatroom. I know it's important. It feels like the key to understanding Connor and the way his mind works. He said he knew, but for how long? Did he recently discover the affair? My heart aches for him as I picture their family friend over for dinner and how that must have shattered Connor's trust.

He's hiding pain behind those cocky smiles and the way he jokes at school. Does anyone see that? I hope his best friend does, at least. I know how hard it is to hide a big secret eating you up and pretend everything is fine around friends. It's what I did with Maisy when I couldn't tell her about Henry.

Constantine returns in a seventy pound blur and sits at the back door, waiting for my command to allow him in.

"Okay. Come." The dog follows me inside and I offer him a treat from a jar on the counter—homemade peanut butter milk bones from a recipe I tweaked. "Take it."

Constantine crunches down and trails behind me as I climb the stairs to my bedroom. My thoughts turn as I change out of my gown and wipe the makeup off my face.

The light never turns on in Connor's bedroom. I watch from my chair for a while before I get into bed.

If Connor's mother is having an affair, why is she hiding it? She has the whole neighborhood fooled. Why is this a big secret?

I would hate to hide my love like that. But even worse, it breaks my heart that she's sneaking around in plain sight, hurting people. And Connor *knows*.

Maybe her affair has jaded him, giving him reason to avoid relationships.

"I'm going to figure this out," I mumble to Constantine as he snuggles with me in bed. I hug him close, stroking his soft fur. He stretches and flops half on top of me. "You big lump."

My arms circle around him. He's always my favorite to hug when I'm feeling down.

When I figure out what's going on, I'll confront Connor again to find out why he won't date me if he wants me. Isn't that what relationships are all about? I saw the look in his eyes tonight. It wasn't only lust.

And I refuse to be his pawn any longer.

TWENTY
Connor

It's impossible to get Thea out of my head. She's taken root, claiming every other thought as hers.

I was an idiot to think I could have one taste and get her out of my system. What happened in the coatroom was inevitable. It was only a matter of time before the powder keg between us finally went off.

That light in her eyes, the shyness burning away to reveal what she keeps locked up tight…

Thea isn't the kind of girl you hit it once and quit. She's the kind you grow addicted to, the kind that burrows beneath your skin and clutches your heart and your dick.

A weakness I shouldn't indulge in more than I already have.

There's nothing I want more than to keep her, both the secret fiery minx and the nerdy stress baker who babbles nonstop. I want to give her what she asked for—a relationship. A boyfriend. That's not me, though. And I'm sick to my stomach because there's always the chance my biggest worry will come true: that she's just like her mom.

I've been learning to let her in, to trust what she says. But what if I'm wrong?

After what she heard in the coatroom, she could tell someone.

Christ, how can I feel like this about the daughter of the woman who's caused me so many problems?

But I can't stop thinking about the other night, even while I'm supposed to be focused on the Monday night game.

My teammates run and shout around me on the field. The floodlights are blinding. Sweat drips down my temples, stinging my eyes. I'm so out of it that Devlin punches my shoulder lightly as the other team subs out players.

"Dude. What are you doing?" he asks, swiping black hair back from his face. "I've never seen you miss a shot so perfectly set up."

"Suffering." Between Thea and my mom, I'm going crazy. I drag a hand over my head and glance around. Several of our guys throw me dirty looks, as if I'm the only one who can carry the team because I'm the captain. I sigh. "Fuck, sorry."

Devlin squints at me. "Was that benefit shit this weekend?"

I grunt in response, nodding.

"Just get in the game. I've got your back." Devlin claps me on the shoulder. "It's almost over."

He's right. If I can stop dicking around, we'll finish this and stay in the running for the playoffs.

The ref blows his whistle and the game resumes. Family members and a group of Coyote Girls gathered on the sidelines cheer as we pick up the ball, zigzagging across the field to keep it in our possession.

Trent loses the soccer ball to the other team's striker, and I swoop back from my position at the center. Instinct and years of practice kick in as I mark the striker heading for our goal. The cheers and shouts on the sideline become white noise. The other team's player fakes me out with a spin, but I anticipate him and steal the ball before he can defend against me. A few of our guys whoop and holler for me, and the corners of my mouth tip up in satisfaction.

Devlin meets me at center field and together we move on offense, passing the ball back and forth as we cut down the grass toward the opposing team's net. Their goalie has his hands up, glancing between both of us.

This is what we're known for. An unstoppable pair with speed and skill.

As we're closing in on the goal, dodging defensive backs, Devlin sets me up so that the defensive players think he's taking the shot. They go to block him as I swoop in, stealing the ball and kicking it with precision. It arcs through the air into the back left of the net.

The sound of celebration erupts behind me as the timer runs down on the second half. I stand with my hands on my hips, dropping my head back and gasping to drag air into my burning lungs.

It feels good to finish this strong when my head is still so messed up. Thea's worked her unassuming roots into me, making me think she's harmless when she's got me entangled.

"Good finish, man." Devlin claps me on the shoulder, squeezing. "Don't let your parents' shit get to you. It's not worth it. Trust me." He grimaces, jaw clenching. "Just—" He gestures vaguely. I don't think I've ever seen him so at a loss for how to express himself. "Forget them. Find someone—*things* that make you happy."

"Uh huh," I say, squinting at him. "This wouldn't have anything to do with Davis, would it? You've been different ever since you had her in that cheerleader uniform at the last practice. You kissed her in front of everyone, bro. We all saw it."

Devlin shoves me without heat. "Pull your head out of your ass."

"Yeah. Sure." I laugh as we make our way to the huddle of our teammates to shake hands with the other players. "But I told—"

"Don't say it."

"So broody." I clutch my chest like he's caused me a fatal wound. "So cold."

Devlin shakes his head and plants a hand over my face to cut off my fake wailing.

* * *

After the match, I convinced Thea to meet me at my pool house to talk. She waits in the shadows cast by the edge of the building, peeking around the corner when she hears my footsteps drawing close.

"How was your game?" Thea asks, tucking a loose lock of hair behind her ear. She's wearing a thick tan sweater beneath a pale blue denim overall dress. Her white tennis shoes have hand-painted rainbows on the toes.

"We won." I unlock the door, running through what I need to talk to her about in my head, willing myself not to get distracted by her sweet scent.

"I've never seen one of your games. Are you good?"

I throw a cocksure grin over my shoulder. "I made varsity captain last year. I'm good. Our team is, too. Dev's a damn sight to behold, wicked bastard."

"Devlin Murphy?"

I hum in response as she follows me into the pool house. My room might be a sanctuary away from my parents, but I come out here when I need to think. A guest bed dominates the room and white cushioned ottomans are arranged in a small sitting area. In the other corner a large full-length mirror reflects most of the space, giving it the appearance it's even bigger.

Thea peers around while I sink onto the corner of the bed, leaning my elbows on my knees. She pauses by the mirror, blue-green gaze flicking to find me in the muted light through the reflection. A moment passes, crackling with this magic quality.

A tug in my chest feels like it has me tethered to her. The girl I was never supposed to have in the first place. The one I'd never noticed.

But that pull gets stronger until I'm gritting my teeth to stay where I am instead of going to her side.

This is what I mean by she's a weakness I shouldn't indulge in. This is a girl I would destroy, eating up her goodness, her warm light. A girl I shouldn't want, but I do. I've only had one taste, but I'd burn the world to the ground for her, damn the consequences.

That's a dangerous kind of devotion I've never experienced. Girls have always been a means to getting off and having fun. Never this intense storm of emotions I can hardly pick apart.

Learning to trust her is scary enough. But wanting her? I can't escape it.

Thea turns around and comes to stand between my knees. I swallow, cupping the back of her legs. Looking up at her, I skim my fingertips beneath the hem of her skirt. She shivers, placing her hands on my shoulders.

"You want to do more dirty things to me." She says it lightly.

"I do." I squeeze the back of her thighs, trailing my touch higher and closing my knees to trap her. "Very dirty things. They involve my tongue and your pussy until I have you crying my name."

She combs her fingers through my hair, dragging her nails gently over my scalp. Holy fuck, it feels good. My eyes fall shut and I release a soft groan, leaning into her body.

"We won't do anything else unless we're together. For real."

"Thea," I say firmly. "I told you, I don't do—"

"Girlfriends. I know." She stops touching me and pulls out of my arms. That mutinous fire is in her eyes again, challenging me. "You want me? Then date me. I'm not your hookup, and I'm not faking anything else for you, Connor Bishop."

God, I love it when she says my whole name all indignant and stubborn like that.

With a heavy sigh, I get up to stalk away, hoping to clear my head. It doesn't help; I can still smell sugar cookies and cinnamon. I peel out of my evergreen Silver Lake High soccer zip up and toss it aside.

"If it's because you're afraid, because of the thing with your mom…" She trails off with a conflicted look when I whirl around. "I just—we aren't our parents. Whatever their mistakes and shortcomings are, those aren't automatically ours, too." She blows out a breath. "I mean, I hope I never turn out like my mom."

She doesn't want to be like her mom. My heart thuds. It's the last fear holding me back with her.

I rub my forehead. Damn her solid logic and reasoning. I don't want to explain my family shit right now.

On top of that, I'm nothing but corruption. I would only taint her with it. Break her.

Staying away from her is too hard. I'm drawn back, taking her by the shoulders. The scent of whatever she's been baking today wraps around me. I lean in, needing to taste her lips.

"I told you." Thea pokes me in the chest to stop me, her voice quiet but not giving an inch. "I'm not the same as you. I can't turn it on and off. I like you. You *blackmailed* and bullied me, and I still like you, because under all that bravado for your reputation, you're hiding the guy you really are."

"I'm not. You're wrong. What you see is who I am. I lied to you. Tricked you because it amused me."

She tilts her head, studying me through her lashes. "You're not as cruel as you pretend to be. If you were, you wouldn't have cared what happened to me at the benefit. Even though you made me go. You put yourself between me and anyone else, keeping me safe in your own way." Sighing, she bows her head. "It's why I want this. Us. But if this is all fake for you, then I'm out of here."

Panic surges as Thea slips out of my grasp, turning toward the door.

"Wait." I grab her wrist. My voice is hoarse and my thoughts race with the burst of adrenaline coursing through my system. "Just—wait. It's not…I do want you." I push my other hand through my hair. "But I don't know how to have a girlfriend either, sunshine. I've only ever gone to girls for sex."

There's a long beat where she gives me her back, and I think she's going to wrench away to leave anyway. Relief pours through me as she turns to face me.

"We'll figure it out together. I'm sure we'll mess up, but I want to do it with you."

My throat grows tight. Why is this so hard?

Just take, like you always have.

I can't though.

"I'll corrupt you." Shaking my head, I step back, releasing her wrist so she can escape me. "I'm not good, Thea. I'm messed up."

I'm so fucked up in my shadows playing god that I spied on her. Toyed with her.

"Isn't that my choice to make? Besides, haven't you already shown me the dark side?"

Thea gives me a smirk that's all mischief. It looks fucking good on her, making my dick hard. That look should be illegal.

She takes my hand, bringing my knuckles up to press her lips against them, peeking up at me. "You said it yourself, I was hiding who I really am. I'm done hiding. Are you?"

A tortured groan tears from me. This girl...

Screw it. I'm done running from my problems and fears. Finished letting my fucked up family keep me from having someone that makes me happy. I tried to keep her away, but I'm not the noble hero. I take what I want, and if she wants me? I'm fucking giving her what she asked for.

Thea's right. This doesn't have to be fake. It never was. I'm a king of misdeeds. She'll be my queen.

The sunshine to my dark moonlight.

Together we make an eclipse.

I'll swallow her golden, warm light in my shadows, but she'll pierce through the blackest parts of my heart.

"Be careful what you wish for," I rumble, tugging her against me. "If we're doing this, I might never let you go."

"Do your worst. I can handle it."

"Yeah?" My cock throbs. I back up toward the bed and drop onto the corner of the mattress, facing the big full-length mirror. "We were interrupted before we could finish what we started the other night, before I devoured you. Come here."

She puts a knee on the bed and straddles my lap, her denim skirt riding up her thighs. I caress them, then unclip the straps of her overalls, peeling down the material so it pools around her waist. My hands bury under her thick sweater, pushing it up over her head.

Thea captures my mouth in a kiss and it's so sexy. Whenever she popped onto my radar before, I never would've pegged her for a first move girl. She proved me wrong with her mistaken number selfie, but I still thought of her as the kind of wallflower I'd have to coax to show me her petals in bloom.

She yanks on my shirt until it's over my head. Every second I part from her kiss is wrong, and I swallow her gasp when we come together again, both of us shirtless. It's so much better than the rushed coatroom quickie. Now I can take my time with her.

Growling into the kiss, I unclasp her bra, discarding it to the side. I've dreamed of her tits after all the naughty photos she's sent, and I'm finally going to get them in my mouth. Cupping and massaging them, I rip from the kiss to take a nipple between my lips. Thea's head drops back with a tiny cry. As I torture one nipple, then the other with my tongue and teeth, she starts circling her hips, the material of her skirt riding higher as she rubs her pussy on the hard ridge of my cock through my jeans. I suck harder on her nipple, dropping my hands to grab her plump ass, moving with her.

"Oh god!" Thea tenses, burying her face in my neck as her body shakes.

"You come all over my dick, baby?" I speak against her tits, snaking my tongue out to flick the tight buds of her nipples.

She whimpers, bucking against me. I slide a hand lower, between her legs from behind and stroke her soaked panties, watching our reflection in the mirror. We make a sight that has my cock rock hard.

"Mm, baby, you feel how wet you are for me? Turn around, you need to see this."

Thea climbs to her feet on unsteady legs with my help. I make her face the mirror as I strip her denim dress down her body along with her underwear. Her tits rise and fall as I guide her back between my spread knees, gaze locked with hers in the glass as I skim my fingertips over her flushed skin.

Her eyes drop and she turns her head away. A small sound escapes her.

"Hey, what's wrong?" I stroke her sides and can't resist squeezing her ass when it's at eye level. "I thought you were done hiding?"

"I...well, I don't normally have to..." Her stammering fades and she gestures at the mirror. "It's weird."

"It's not weird."

"It is. You've been with so many girls. All I see at school is your charming smile and the pretty girls that fall all over you." She tries to turn, but I hold her in place. "Can't we go back to what we were doing? I want to feel good."

Squinting up at her, I point at the mirror. "Look."

It takes a minute of her peering back at me pleadingly, but she faces her reflection.

"This is who you are, Thea. This is the girl I see. Look at her—*you*. You're beautiful. Forget everything else." I kiss her hip and trail a path to the sun-shaped birthmark I'm obsessed with, biting her skin lightly. With a tug, she lands in my lap. "Come back here."

Tension lingers in her body. I spend long minutes placing feather-light kisses over every inch of skin I can reach, holding her hair up as I focus on the back of her neck and shoulders. Eventually she melts against my chest.

An ember burns around my heart. I will make her see what I do—what I saw that first night we sexted.

While she's relaxed, I nudge her legs wider, so she's spread gorgeously for me. She's no longer paying attention to the mirror, but I am, watching the way her lashes flutter, the way she tips her head back when I caress her tits, and the way she arches when I tease my touch between her legs.

Time slows to a drowsy pace as I finger her, peeking at the mirror each time I grind my cock against her perfect ass. She makes soft sounds when I brush her clit and pump my fingers deeper. I know I'm driving her crazy, working her body with deliberate touches.

"Connor," Thea murmurs, sounding drunk and delirious as I keep her balanced on the edge and walk her back before she can come. "Please. *Please*. It's too much."

"Shh, not yet. It'll be so good, baby, I promise." I kiss her temple, licking the damp sweat beading her skin. "A little longer."

She whines, hips shifting with the slow pace I set, silently begging me to give her more. She's forgotten all about her hesitation with the mirror, all she can think about is the orgasm I'm keeping her a breath away from. With a devious grin, I fall back on an elbow, tugging my phone from my pocket with my free hand and pop back up, hugging her against me.

"Connor?"

"Right here. Now, baby girl," I rasp, smoky and hot against her ear, sending tremors through her body. "I know you want to come so bad, right?"

Thea nods, pushing her ass on my dick, distracting me for a moment. I grab my phone.

"I'll let you come. But we're going to try something. I'm going to play with your perfect tits, and you're going to ride my fingers until you come. Don't look away from the mirror. Cool?"

"I—okay," she says, blushing and biting her lip.

Humming, I kiss her cheek. "Good girl. There's one more thing you're going to do."

"What?" Her voice is husky with need.

I hold up my phone in front of her, setting it up on the camera app. Thea flicks her gaze over her shoulder, a cute wrinkle between her eyebrows.

"I want you to take pictures of yourself. Watch your face when you take your pleasure on my fingers. I want you to see everything I see when you come." Her eyes widen and I draw her into a kiss. "These ones are just for me and you. You can do whatever you want with them after—delete them, whatever."

The hesitation clears from her expression and she takes the phone. I drop another kiss on her shoulder as she shifts on my lap, holding the phone up.

"That's my girl. Don't stop watching."

I take my time working her back to the brink, teasing her sensitive pussy until she's back to whimpering, the click of the camera shutter punctuating her shallow breathing. It's so fucking hot. She's so wet, my fingers slip through her folds and slide into her easily, her pussy practically swallowing my fingers. This time I don't stop her from moving her hips, encouraging her to fuck herself on my fingers.

Heat pulses in my groin and it takes everything in me to let her have this instead of ripping my jeans off and fucking her hard until she screams. She needs this.

"You look so sexy," I say into her neck as I roll a nipple. "You see that?"

"Yes," she gasps, moving faster.

"God, yes, baby. That's it. Fuck my fingers until you come." As she bucks, I rub her clit with my thumb. My wrist cramps in protest, but I'm not stopping. Those high-pitched sounds escaping her tell me she's so close to falling apart. "You look so good."

The camera app clicks with shot after shot. At this point I think she's so far gone she's just snapping away with the burst option, but that's fine. She's focused on her reflection, eyes blazing with desire and pleasure, gasping as she soaks my hand.

With one more flick of my thumb on her swollen clit, she shrieks, falling back against me with a blissed out moan. I catch her with a grunt, falling back against the mattress as I gently stroke her pussy. She trembles and twitches in my arms, the phone slipping from her fingers and bouncing off the bed to the floor. The only sound in the room is our mingled breathing and her murmurs of *oh fuck, fuck, shit* as she rides the aftershocks of a damn good orgasm.

Once she seems coherent, angling her head to peek at me with pink cheeks and parted lips, I flip her over, grinding my cock against her. She cries out, too oversensitive for the rough material of my jeans, but I'm about to blow.

"Sit up," Thea murmurs.

"Baby," I plead, dropping my face into her neck. "Watching you lose it like that, I'm so close."

"You got to pick something and now I want to try something else." She kisses me. "You'll like it."

Grumbling, I roll us to our sides. She gets up, running her fingers through her thick auburn curls, looking sexy as hell. My own personal Aphrodite. I freeze when she kneels at the corner of the bed and motions me over, crooking her finger. As I sit up, I'm sidetracked by the sight of her back reflected in the mirror, her round ass stuck out.

Thea pats the bed. "Come sit here." Her tongue peeks out, swiping her lower lip. "I'm going to suck you."

"I—yes." I scramble to get my jeans and underwear off, sliding to the edge of the bed. Thea looks up at me from between my thighs, holding my dick and hovering her mouth over the tip and, *fuck*, it's my new favorite sight. "Are you sure you want to do it this way? I'll gladly jerk off on your tits if you're not ready for more."

"I want it this way."

Then she takes me in her mouth and I swear I ascend to a higher plane. Her perfect, pouty lips wrapped around my cock are a straight up electric stairway to heaven. She's tentative at first, licking around the tip. I thread my fingers through her hair, groaning as she sucks, taking me deeper. I watch her and the mirror. It's too much, I don't last long. Within minutes she has me coming with her name on my lips.

"Thea," I breathe.

She backs up with a yelp and I release a raspy chuckle, feeling too good to care if I get jizz on the floor. I grin at her, my golden sunshine. There's come on her tits and leaking from the corner of her mouth, a startled but pleased look in her eye.

"You're like a magic little sunbeam," I whisper, brushing a thumb over her cheek.

The shy smile she gives me fills me with warmth.

After we clean up in the bathroom, which leads to another make-out session because I can't resist her, we pull our clothes back on. It's late, after midnight.

On her way out, I give her the key to the pool house and watch as she picks her way across my yard, through hers until she reaches her back door. She glances back at me before slipping inside her house.

A smug curve tilts my mouth as I amble inside, thinking about the cliche of deflowering the neighbor girl.

Fucking worth it.

TWENTY-ONE
Thea

Connor saw exactly who I was in that mirror and made me face it so I knew, too.

He's given me secretive smiles at school this week and sent me good morning and goodnight texts every day. Last night we talked on FaceTime until I fell asleep, and this morning I saw he kept the call connected for another hour.

But I'm still alone at home on a Saturday at the end of the week.

I can't call Maisy to come over because she's out of town. I've already baked my way through lunch. I was ready for more until Mom yelled at me to stop taking up all the Tupperware and storage space in the fridge.

After trudging up the steps, I wind up bored after only a half hour of watching baking videos on YouTube. I roll on my back in the middle of my bed and look at the colorful posters on my wall.

"Maybe Maise posted a story of her yoga intensive." Flipping to my stomach, I grab my phone again.

What I find when I pull up Instagram sinks my stomach. My feed is full of photos. There's a huge party today up at Silver Lake Forest Estates. I don't know anyone that lives in the most elite gated community of Ridgeview, but Connor does. Devlin lives there. And Connor is tagged in a picture with him, armed with water guns.

At first my breath is stolen by how good he looks, shirtless and tan, abs for days and a swimsuit almost painted on his powerful soccer thighs. He's grinning, genuinely carefree. I recognize the smile because it's the same one he gave me in his pool house after he came with my name rolling off his lips.

But then reality sets in, along with my inner critic.

We agreed to be together in the pool house, but if I'm his girlfriend, why didn't I get invited to this party with him? I thought we made some progress. Things haven't changed if I'm sitting at home while he's out with his friends.

You're still his dirty little secret.

Not that I'd jump at the chance for a beach day, but it is unseasonably hot today and I've been baking since this morning. A swim in the cool lake would be nice, even if it means I'd stress over what to wear around the popular crowd.

With a sigh, I remind my inner critic that I don't hate every imperfection and inconvenience of my body. It's beach ready no matter what I wear.

Biting my lip, I spend twenty minutes going through account after account to find more photos, like a stalker. In each one I find, Connor is with one of the dance squad girls. Blair Davis is even there. I'm kind of surprised to see Devlin Murphy wrapped around her, and the reserved but happy expression on her face. She's cool with him after he made her dump water on herself in the cafeteria while everyone laughed? It wasn't that long ago, yet there they are, sharing an intimate moment someone captured for social media.

The more I scroll Instagram, watching a party I'm not at, the more invisible I feel.

Unseen.

Like always.

Will Connor only ever be mine when the moon is out?

I won't stand for this. I wanted to be together because I like him, not because I was happy to only be trotted out when he needed me.

Closing out of the app on my phone with a frustrated sound, I face plant into my ruffled purple bedspread, letting the darkness swallow me. Once I grant myself a few minutes to wallow, I get up and get my laptop from the desk. As I return to the bed, the positive posters on my wall remind me of my outlook. I turn my back on them and hunch my shoulders as I sink to the floor, opening the laptop.

"I'm not invisible."

Before I've finished typing the address to my blog, I stop. It doesn't feel right. The comments, or even the old emails from Henry aren't what I want right now. It's only a feeble bandage; it won't cure the wound.

I want Connor instead of my secret coping habit.

With a deflated exhale, I lean my head against the side of my mattress. What I want is in Connor's pool house, where we hid away from the world together under the moonlight. Where I felt free to be my true self, no more secret folders, no more splitting myself between who I should be and who I wish I was.

"Are you a clingy girl?" I ask myself, reasoning that I should leave this alone and do my own thing. I don't need him to entertain myself. With another sigh, I shake my head. "But you deserve the universe, so why settle when it doesn't make you feel good?"

Maybe this is one of those things Connor doesn't know to think about. He did make a point about only being with girls as hookup partners before. We're both tripping our way through being in a relationship, the first real one for both of us.

If I don't tell him, he won't know that this made me doubt everything.

After arguing with myself some more, I change out of the ratty old sweats I've been in all day into a stretchy jumpsuit with a pink flower print and sneak out of the house. I avoid Mom by the skin of my teeth as she's leaving through the garage door with sunglasses on. Once she's gone, I creep around the corner and slip out the back door with my phone and the key Connor gave me, cutting across our yard into his.

My heart races as I use the key to get in. Any second I'm ready for someone to ask what I'm doing in the Bishop's yard without an invitation.

Once inside, I leave my key by the door and go to the full-length mirror. It still smells like Connor in here. I lick my lips and sit down in front of the mirror with my legs to the side in a sensual pose, feeling the pinup vibe I have going on right now. I allow one of my straps to slip off my shoulder and angle my boobs forward.

After snapping a few pics, I pick one and send it to him. No caption. It doesn't need one. He'll know where I am.

It doesn't take Connor long to arrive. The door squeals when he opens it in a rush. I haven't moved from my spot by the mirror, and I watch him through the reflection, pressing my fingers to the glass.

"You came," I murmur.

"Did you think I wouldn't when you sent this?" He waves his phone and tosses it on the bed as he crosses the room to me. On the way he loses his black muscle shirt, leaving him in only his short swimsuit and a perfect view of the sculpted indents in his hips. "Shit, I've been thinking about you all day. About this."

He pulls me to my feet and swoops in for a kiss that leaves me breathless. His skin is warm from an afternoon in the sun.

Putting my hand on his chest, I lean back from his kiss. "You know, I opened Instagram to see if my friend Maisy had posted, but I saw the party at the lake instead."

"Yeah?" Connor is distracted, kissing his way down my neck. He hums against my heated skin and makes me shudder.

"Well, I was surprised to see there was a party. That you were there." My breath hitches when he finds a sensitive spot. "And...the girl you were with in the pictures I saw."

Connor stills. "What girl?"

"Bailey? She's on the dance squad." I suck my bottom lip into my mouth as he stares at me. "I'm not the girl you were with at the lake."

"No. You're not."

A sound rumbles in Connor's chest as he wraps me in his arms, picking me up. I squeal when he lifts me off the ground, surprised by his strength. He crosses the room and deposits me on the bed. Another growl leaves him while he fumbles with my jumpsuit.

"Always with the complicated outfits," he mutters, figuring out he needs to yank down the straps.

Once he has me down to my bra and underwear, he descends on the birthmark on my thigh, sucking on it until I'm pretty sure I'll have a hickey. I like that, the idea of him branding my skin with his marks. Proof that we had this moment.

Lifting his head, he pins me with his gray eyes. "If I wanted that chick, I wouldn't be here. Why would I want her when I only want a little beam of sunshine who drives me fucking crazy?" He keeps his gaze locked with mine as he licks my birthmark. "You're who I'm with. No other girl matters to me. Only you, baby."

My fingers claw at the bedding, a hazy fog of desire clouding my head. But this is important and I have to make sure he understands.

"How can I believe you really want me? You only kiss me in the dark." I sit up and face him in only my bra and panties. "The hall when no one was around. The coatroom. In here." My chest rises and falls. "You pretend I don't exist otherwise, like you always have." My voice cracks and my eyes sting. "I can't be invisible anymore, Connor."

"Sunshine," he rasps, cradling my face in his hands as his brow furrows. "I swear, I wasn't keeping you a secret. I'm sorry I made you doubt I want this. What will it take to prove it to you? I'll kiss you at school whenever I see you. You'll be dizzy from my kisses."

The fear clogging my throat vanishes. I give him a wet, breathy laugh. "You don't have to go that far. But a date to the dance would be nice."

"Dance?"

"Winter formal. It's not for a while still, but..."

Connor gives me a lopsided smile and climbs off the bed to sink to one knee. "Well, this is a little impromptu because my girl needs it, but I want you to imagine the flowers I would totally be presenting you with right now. Got it?"

I grin. "Got it. How many flowers?"

"The whole florist supply, obviously. Jesus, what do you take me for, baby? My girl gets the whole world."

For a first time boyfriend, he's definitely got the right idea. Has Connor Bishop been hiding a secret romantic waiting to be unleashed? The thought makes me smile wider.

"Do I now?"

"Mhm. Now hush so I can ask you a very important question. Thea Kennedy, my bright sunbeam," he starts and I cover my face with my hands. "Hey, look at me. You're gonna miss it." He pries my hands away and holds my hips. "Can I take you to the dance?"

I lean in to kiss him. He lets me for a minute, humming as he sucks on my lip. Then he pulls back and lifts his brows.

"Well?"

"Oh, you wanted an answer? I thought it was a given."

"*Tch*. Girl, please." He pulls a face and clutches his chest dramatically. "You've got my angsty teen heart on the line here. Put me out of my misery."

Laughing, I slide my arms around his neck and kiss his nose. "Yes, Connor Bishop. You can take me to the dance."

"That's my girl. Now where were we?"

Connor takes my mouth and guides my legs around his waist, lifting me from the bed in a smooth move. He carries me back to the mirror and presses my bare back against it without breaking the kiss. I'm dizzy with want, my body thrumming. My hips roll against his muscled torso. He undoes the clasp on my bra with a deft flick of his fingers and buries a hand down the back of my underwear to squeeze my ass.

"Mm, these are nice. Silky. Loose 'em." He lowers me to my feet and smacks my ass. Spinning me to face the mirror, he helps me out of them as I brace a hand against the mirror. I moan as my bra drops along with my panties. "Look at yourself. That's fucking hot."

My skin prickles with excitement.

In the reflection, Connor stands behind me, still wearing his trunks, which are tented as he grinds his hard cock against my bare ass with a groan. He pulls my thick curls off my neck and sinks his teeth into my pulse point, sending a hot burst of pleasure straight to my core. With his other hand, he rolls one of my nipples between his fingers before dragging his fingers down my body to dip between my legs, sliding through the wetness already coating my thighs.

"Oh shit," I gasp, bucking into his touch and back against his hardness. "That feels—ah! So good."

Connor's rough chuckle does things to my insides, twisting them in knots of lust. He makes me wild in a way nothing else ever has. With him, I forget to hate what's in the mirror, only face it with bravery as he pushes the proof of his attraction against my backside. He loses his swimsuit and pulls me against his chest, feeling all of him.

It's unlike anything I've ever imagined, and I'm lost to the heat of his body, his firm muscles, his cock brushing my own flushed skin.

"Watch yourself while I make you come," Connor commands.

My eyes almost flutter shut, too overwhelmed by everything, but he chides me with his lips against my ear, murmuring his encouragement.

"Look, sunshine. See how your pretty blue eyes get all dark when I touch you here?" His fingers circle my clit and it's all I can do to stay standing. "That feel good?"

"Yes! God, yes." I lean my head back against his shoulder, obeying his demand to watch as he kicks my legs a little further apart and cups my pussy. I bite my lip, tempted to rock against the pressure of his palm until I come, my hips shifting restlessly as he teases between my folds. "Connor. Please."

His amused huff fans over my neck in a hot breath. "Listen to you beg for me. So needy."

When he slides a finger in me, I lose my breath, scrabbling at his arms. He adds another, filling me. I give into the temptation, meeting each thrust of his fingers until my toes curl against the carpet and I'm relying on him to hold me up.

It's too much to take, and as Connor sucks on my neck, I fall apart with a moan. He keeps working me, teasing my clit, my swollen folds, and dipping his clever fingers inside until a second orgasm shocks me. This time I do almost collapse, but he supports me with ease. His heavy-lidded gaze meets mine in the mirror and the slow curve of his mouth into a smirk has me matching his expression.

Pressing up on my toes, I kiss him, smiling into it. The kiss is sweet for a moment while he gives me a second to catch my breath, then it turns heated as I start to tug at his hair. He squeezes my breasts in both hands, trailing his lips down my neck to my shoulder.

In our frenzied kisses and touches, we end up on our knees in front of the mirror. My back is slick with sweat, overheated and sensitive to every touch.

His hand covers my jaw and throat, pulling my head back for a filthy kiss. Our eyes meet and he presses his cock between my thighs, brushing against my throbbing pussy.

"You want it?" Connor thrusts slow and dirty, making me gasp at the sensation of him gliding against my folds between my legs.

"Yes." I moan, leaning against him, my skin burning up. "Please, I want you."

"Easy, baby. Put your hands here." He arranges me how he wants me, hands planted on either side of the mirror on the wall. "Don't look away."

Connor disappears for a moment, rummaging through drawers. I hear a foil packet tear and watch in the reflection as he rolls a condom on. He positions himself behind me, takes my hips, and finds my gaze in the mirror.

"Okay?"

This is nothing like things were with Henry. Connor always checks if I'm into it and doesn't pressure me. If I didn't want this, I know he'd stop and slow us down.

"Yeah." I'm ready, so turned on.

"Good." He grins and bends to kiss the center of my back. "I'm going to wreck you, sunshine."

The first press of his cock at my entrance makes me choke on a gasp, my fingers scrabbling at the wall. He hushes me, dipping a hand between my legs to rub my clit. He takes his time, focusing on working me close to the edge as he eases in. I'm so full. It's tight, his cock thicker than his fingers, but when he moves his hips and presses his fingers harder against my clit, I drop off a cliff into pleasure. My breath fogs the mirror as I press my forehead against the glass.

"Goddamn, baby. Squeezing my cock so good already. Fuck." He starts a slow, torturous pace that draws my orgasm out and grips my hair. "Look at me."

My gaze snaps to his.

Connor looks like a king of debauchery and devious pleasure. His lips are parted, gazing at me intently, gray eyes full of unwavering want. He tightens his hold in my hair—not enough to hurt, just to control the angle of my head. I like it, being at his mercy. His thrusts pick up and my mouth falls open on a silent cry of pleasure.

He falls forward with a rough, possessive sound and my body arches against his, sinking back into his lap as he lowers to the ground to pump into me faster. His scent is all around me, musk mixed with a hint of spice, making me dizzy.

"Fuck, Connor," I breathe, reaching back to hold on to his hair as I roll my hips to meet his thrusts.

"You like that?" Connor rasps in my ear, squeezing my breasts. He bites the shell of my ear and drops a hand to my clit. "Right there?"

My entire body shakes as my core convulses with pleasure, cresting over my body in waves of ecstasy. I'm delirious and flying high with his arms locked around me. It feels perfect.

Connor groans in my ear and I feel him twitch deep inside my body. He hugs me close, not letting me go for a second as we come back to earth.

"Fucking amazing," he murmurs in my hair, caressing my skin with the tips of his fingers. Gathering me in his arms, he takes me to the bed and kisses my forehead before ducking into the bathroom. A minute later, he comes out and climbs in with me. "Come here. You okay? I wasn't too rough, was I?" He smooths my hair back, taking stock of a spot on my neck he probably left a hickey on. "Are you sore? We can get in the shower or the hot tub if you are."

Shaking my head, I snuggle into his embrace. "No. Just want to lay like this."

"You've got it." He kisses the top of my head and holds me tight.

I fall asleep with his fingers combing through my hair, my head resting on his chest, feeling blissed out.

TWENTY-TWO
Connor

A few days later, I can't take the shit in my house anymore. Damien keeps arguing with Mom about the benefit "incident". He means that Mom put on her happy wife mask. Get over it, bro.

Dad's been scarce, most likely off with the librarian from school he's been spending time with, making the house feel like the inevitable train wreck we've all been barreling toward: Damien and Mom getting married. That's what she keeps promising him, anyway.

Damien as my stepdad? No fucking thank you.

It's after one in the morning and they're at each other's throats. I have half a mind to stomp to the master bedroom and tell them I have school in the morning.

Their shouts filter past my bedroom door and drown out the music I'm blasting. Jesus. I shake my head, entering a new file in my encrypted program full of people's secrets, adding an old incident report of Landry's friend with the leather jacket, Fox Wilder.

"The fuck kind of name is Fox?" I mutter, swigging from my near-empty can of Coke as I input the data.

Holden's dad coughed it up when I pressured him to run a search or I'd start letting his skeletons out of the closet. It didn't turn up much. My access and leverage only extend to the Ridgeview Police Department he heads. There's a report on a car accident that killed his parents and landed little Fox Wilder in the foster care system, whisking him away from Ridgeview at a young age. The rest of the files are sealed or missing, which is weird. I only put a medium amount of effort in before I give up.

Whatever, I have enough to shake him down if he ever steps out of line with me. With that leather jacket and the giant chip on his shoulder, it's only a matter of time before he stirs trouble in this town.

"You're making me crazy, Vivian!" Damien screams. "I've put my entire career at risk because I love you, and you're acting like that's nothing."

Mom's response is muffled by the heavy beat drop on the song playing on my speakers, thank god.

"Why are we still waiting for this? Why am I always the one sneaking around like your mistress? I thought you were in love with me!" Damien wails. Actually full on bleats, the sound of his betrayed misery like some dying animal. Maybe this will be their breaking point.

"Divorce isn't going to ruin your political career!"

All right, screw this. I'm not staying in here. I'll head out back to smoke until they've worked out their shit. I know from sickening experience that the bigger their blowouts, the more frenzied their makeup sex is.

No one should have to listen to their mom like that, let alone walk in on it like I did when I first discovered them. It's fucking gross.

I can't wait to save up enough to move out. My trust fund inheritance from granddad won't pay out for a while, but I've got my thumb in a bunch of pies. I won't wait around. I'll do anything I can to get the hell away from my mother's chain leash. The bitcoin investments are growing, and I've been dabbling in learning how to make an app. After I saw Thea's vulnerable security on her computer network, I've been thinking about creating something for desktop and mobile that will protect the same secrets I mine for.

"We're not having this discussion again," Mom snaps as I head downstairs on my way to the back door.

Damien's shouts follow me when I slip out back with a joint, my head pounding. I should leave the back door open so their argument can wake up the whole neighborhood.

Sprawling on a lounge chair, I sigh in relief as I light up, taking a deep drag on the joint. I fold an arm behind my head and play around with making the smoke curl into shapes. As the high sets in, I relax.

I pull my phone out, the joint dangling from my lips as I text Devlin, sending him a GIF of a sad frog in black and white with the lyrics from Simon & Garfunkel's *The Sound of Silence* to convey my despair.

Connor: Darkness is my only friend. [skull emoji]

Devlin doesn't answer, but I'm not surprised. He got Blair Davis to move in with him. I have no idea how he went from dangling dollar bills on fishing wire in front of her at the beginning of school to *living* with her, but that's where they're at. Grumpy bastard is probably balls deep in her, so I tuck my phone away and finish the joint.

My gaze trails to Thea's house and I sit up, surprised to see a light on. I didn't think she'd be up this late.

With a lopsided smile, I stalk across her yard, keeping to the shadows as I creep around. The back door is unlocked when I test it. Sneaking in drives away my melancholy, the mischief putting my mood in high spirits. The smell of warm sugar hits me and I almost groan.

Around the corner, Thea is a delicious mess, covered in flour and dough as she presses a cookie cutter to a slab of cookie dough. Her hair is piled on top of her head in a bun, she has tight spandex shorts on that make her ass look divine, and a loose pink cropped t-shirt. I pause to watch her, my captured sun bathed in moonlight. The light I chased and caught for a few stolen moments.

"Boo," I say, laughing when she jumps with a strangled shriek.

"Connor, what the hell," Thea hisses, flashing a look at the ceiling where her mom probably is. She flutters her messy hands over her shirt, letting out an embarrassed laugh. "You scared the crap out of me."

A deep *boof* sounds and I lift my hands as her rottweiler charges into the room, heading straight for me.

Shit. Maybe sneaking in wasn't my best idea when she's got an attack dog protecting her.

TWENTY-THREE
Thea

My heart is still racing from the jump scare of Connor sneaking into my house in the middle of the night, like some dark prince of depravity.

"Con, wait," I say.

Constantine halts, huffing at Connor.

"Thank you. Bed." The dog lets out a lazy rumble, sniffing Connor's hand as he lowers it to his side, before trotting back to his bed in the corner. "Good boy."

"You mean me, sunshine?" Connor gives me a grin that's all bad boy on his handsome face and traps me against the high counter of the island, arms planted on either side. A thrill shoots through my stomach. He buries his face in my neck, inhaling deeply. "Mm, you smell like fresh baked cookies."

"Well, that's what I'm making. And no, you're not a good boy." I smack his hand as he tries to steal a cookie from the cooling rack. "Those are for the French club."

"But I've got the munchies, and your baking is the best." Pointing to the dog, he wrinkles his brow. "You named your dog after me? Something you want to tell me? Like a crush you've been nursing on your sexy neighbor for years?"

"Wipe that smug look off your face. His name is Constantine, not Connor." I go back to cutting my dough with my set of Paris-themed cookie cutters while Connor goes over to the dog, petting him. When I look back up a few minutes later, he has Constantine on his back, tongue lolling out of his mouth as he gives him a belly rub. "Traitor."

Connor chuckles and returns to my side, sneaking pieces of cookie dough scraps as I get the next batch in the oven.

"What are you doing in here, anyway? It's late."

Connor shrugs. "Saw your light on. Missed my girl."

He shoots me a charming smile, but a tightness lingers around his eyes. I offer him a cookie from the sad pile, and his expression turns more genuine as he takes a bite.

"Oh, god, yes." Connor moans, wrapping me in his arms as he chews. "So good. You should totally make special brownies. We'll get baked and it'll be delicious."

I snort, wriggling out of his arms to get started mixing another batch of dough to pop in the refrigerator before I take out the dough currently chilling.

"What are you doing up so late? You said goodnight two hours ago."

I shrug as I measure out the ingredients into a big mixing bowl. "Couldn't sleep. Baking helps clear my head."

"I know something else that'll help you sleep," Connor says, planting himself behind me, teasing my arms with tickling touches. He runs his nose up and down the back of my neck, distracting me. His tongue swipes across my skin and he presses his hips against mine so I can feel him, drawing a gasp from me. "Works like a charm."

"I have to finish these."

"Can I help?" Connor picks up the rolling pin, wielding it like a sword instead of a baking tool.

"Here, you can mix this." I set him up with one of the bowls and start another so I can chill more dough at once.

We work in comfortable quiet for a while. Having Connor here is nice, like I'm letting him into my haven, but he's more of a hindrance than actual help. He keeps stealing kisses and eating the dough, and he's much messier than I am. But his muscles come in handy for mixing, since the one thing I don't have is a standing mixer. I'm having a good time with him anyway as we murmur over batches of rolled out dough.

I like this. I like who Connor is here, in the moonlight. He's more real with me alone in the dark, but at school he's still the vicious king of secrets the students and teachers fear. Knowing what I do about his family situation, I think I understand why he's so hell-bent on being the keeper of people's deepest secrets. But I hope he'll drop that wall someday, to share this Connor with the world.

The one who paints Nutella on my cheek so he can hold my face while he licks it off, making my heart flutter with joy.

While we're working, he keeps making vulgar things with the excess dough scraps—boobs, a dick, the poop emoji. He makes me laugh so hard I have to crouch down and muffle my amusement so Mom doesn't hear and come to investigate. Constantine watches our antics from his bed, his deep brown eyes dancing back and forth between us.

As I'm rolling out the next dough, this one a chocolate shortbread I plan to dip in white chocolate, Connor smacks my ass with flour-covered hands.

"Hey!" Holding my arms up, I twist to find a big flour handprint on my black workout shorts. "I'm so getting you back for that."

"Can't be helped. You've got these hot little booty shorts on."

"You have no self restraint. Just a one-track mind."

With a chuckle, Connor jumps out of reach when I swipe at him with the flour from the bowl by my rolling station. I hunt him around the island and he flashes me a sneaky look as I make my move, trapping me in his arms before I can dump flour down his shirt.

"Got you," he murmurs before kissing me.

I shift around in his arms to kiss him properly, our tongues sliding together. He kisses the curve of my smile, unsuspecting until I smash flour in his hair.

"What the—" Connor's eyes are wide in shock as I choke on my victorious laughter. "Okay, Kennedy. I see how it is."

"Wait—babe, don't!" I retreat before he can retaliate against me with the jar of Nutella, my hands raised in surrender.

He narrows his eyes, but concedes. "Okay, truce. But I get another kiss."

After Connor claims his bounty with another kiss that leaves me breathless, he lets me return to baking.

"You really like this stuff," he says, leaning against the sink as I put another tray of cookies in the oven. "You're good at it, too."

I toss a quick smile over my shoulder, flushed from his praise. "Thanks. I've always loved it. Before I could even reach the counter. When I was little, my grandma used to pull up a chair so I could watch and help while she taught me her recipes." I nod to the notebook I have on the other side of the island. "That one has a lot of her old ones in it. I've tweaked some over the years. I'm always tinkering with them."

His mouth quirks up at the corner as I tell my story. "Is that what you're always carrying around? I swear I see you with a different notebook every day."

"Yeah. I've probably filled hundreds of them by now. Mom used to get so annoyed when we'd be out grocery shopping or whatever and I'd beg for a new notebook I saw." I shake my head. "But I have enough to open my own bakery someday. It's my dream. Feed the world with happiness. And sugar."

"Yeah? That's cool. You'll do amazing at it. Does your grandma approve of your improvements to her recipes?"

A pang pierces my heart. "She did, but she's passed. Right before freshman year."

"Oh. I'm sorry, baby." Connor pops out of his relaxed position and wraps me in a warm hug. "Come here."

"I'm okay. I still miss her, though. We've always shared a love of baking and it just hits me some days that even if I make her signature creamy puff pastry recipe, it still won't be her love going into it, you know?"

He hums and strokes my back in comforting circles.

"What about you?" I tip my head back to meet his gaze. "What do you think you want to do with your life?"

His head cocks to the side. "Something with computers. I like working with them and I'm pretty good. I guess it quiets my head the same way baking does for you."

"Computers?" My nose crinkles with my teasing grin. "You know, I think that qualifies you as a nerd. I seem to remember you calling me that once or twice."

Connor taps my nose. "Takes one to know one."

"Sure," I drawl. "There's no way mister popular soccer captain isn't harboring self-loathing going around calling his sweet neighbor a nerd. Not at all."

"Savage little thing, aren't you?" He nips at my neck in revenge, torturing the sensitive pulse point until I'm putty in his arms.

The timer on my phone goes off and I leave his embrace to take out the final batch of cookies. A tendril of warm pride blossoms in my chest as I survey the room. Every surface in the kitchen is covered in cookies and the traces of our midnight baking. It felt amazing to have him here, even if he snuck in. I can't remember what nasty thought drove me out of bed, my mood soaring high after spending time with my boyfriend doing my favorite thing in the world.

Connor studies me as he leans his hip against the counter. His playful demeanor has shifted to something more serious. "Why don't you ever let anyone see you, Thea?"

The question takes me by surprise and slices into my heart, digging at one of my oldest wounds. *Invisible.* "What do you mean?"

"You're always so quiet, but you have all these opinions about everything." He rubs his jaw and shrugs. "And you've shown me more of yourself, even before you knew it was me."

Heat floods my face. I was so desperate to keep my sputtering flame with Wyatt alive, I really did dive in head first to it when I got a response.

As I'm struggling to respond, Connor adds in a soft voice, "You're brave, so why do you hide it?"

My stomach bottoms out. I take a second to gather my thoughts, wiping my hands clean on a dish towel.

"Well, I'm brave in my own ways. To me, bravery is about showing myself I can do something I'm afraid of. Like standing up for someone when no one else will." My mind flashes to Blair Davis. "It's not about showing off or making myself look good. I don't have to be in front of a crowd to consider myself brave. I don't really care what anyone else thinks, I just answer to myself."

Connor stares at me for a beat, then he huffs out a laugh. "Don't ever let anyone tell you you're not amazing, because you are."

"I don't. I've told you about a hundred times I didn't care what you thought, didn't I?"

My pleased grin stretches when he snorts and mutters to the dog. "You believe this? Boyfriend status and I still get attitude."

Constantine doesn't answer, only continues to snore, deep in sleep after dozing off an hour ago. I bustle around the kitchen, packing the cooled cookies into containers to sort through them for French club. Once I'm done, I gape at the time.

"Wow, it's late. Almost three."

Connor hums, sliding his arms around my waist. "The perfect time for mischief."

"Or sleep." I tip my head back and pucker my lips. He gives me a quick peck, then comes back for more, deepening the kiss. I mumble against his lips, "Need. Sleep."

"Need. You," Connor shoots back, palming my ass. "Come with me. We'll sleep out in the pool house. I don't want to go to bed without you."

It's tempting. I'd love to sleep with his warm arms locked around me and his lips nestled against my skin. Mom would kill me, though. She knocks every morning if I'm not up first, and then she barges in my room anyway.

"I want to, but we can't."

"Come on, baby. I want to fall asleep with you and wake up the same way." He keeps kissing me until I'm dizzy. "Then we'll skip school tomorrow. We'll sleep in, get coffee and donuts, and have an adventure. Run away with me. Sound good?"

I hum, brushing our lips together, entranced by the fantasy of a dreamy date day.

Then the second set of lights flick on and a sharp gasp cuts through my happiness. "What. Is. Going. On. In. Here?"

I fly away from Connor, almost tripping when he's slow to let me go. Mom stands in the arched entrance to the kitchen in a robe, murder in her eyes.

"Do you have any idea what time it is?"

She takes me in and I'm painfully aware of how this looks—making out in the kitchen in the middle of the night, a baking bomb left in our wake, and his flour handprints on my ass. This is my worst nightmare. She's already on my case all the time about what I wear, demanding I dress modestly. Now she discovers me in comfortable but way more revealing clothes than she'd ever approve of me wearing and seconds from climbing my boyfriend like a tree.

Hopefully she can't tell we've had sex, or she'll blow her lid. I've tuned out enough of her lectures about my *sacred gift*—gag. She never listens when I insist virginity is a bullshit social construct designed by the patriarchy.

I have no regrets about sleeping with Connor. None. It was amazing and he treated me like a queen.

"Thea," Mom hisses. I know it's bad when she's so angry she can't even raise her voice. "Get to bed, now. And you." She swings on Connor, pointing at him while she holds her robe closed. "Get out of my house before I call the cops."

"Second time's the charm, right?" Connor gives Mom a cocky smirk.

I stare at him with my eyes wide in terror. *Do you have a death wish?* I ask with my expression. He winks at me. Winks! Across the room, Mom's nostrils flare. I brace for the incoming rage. Talking back to her never goes well.

"You think I won't? You're trespassing. Get. Out." Mom grabs the landline—the one she refuses to get rid of because 'it works perfectly fine'—brandishing it at Connor. "They should've locked you up before. You're not just a vicious miscreant, you're a troubled boy."

"You flatter me." Connor is still leaning against the counter, not worried that Mom starts dialing. "Tell Chief Landry hi for me. You know, I talked to him earlier? We're good friends now."

A vein in Mom's throat bulges as her throat contracts with her swallow, her face turning a scary shade of red.

"Yeah, yeah." Connor pops off the counter, hands up. "I know you have a real penchant for calling the cops." He lowers his voice to a mutter as he makes a show of gathering his things—things he doesn't have. "Regular ol' Karen you are, Mrs. K."

On his way out the back door, Connor blows me a kiss, sealing my fate as grounded forever.

"I'm sorry," I spit out before Mom can speak. "I won't bring him here again."

I turn to go to bed, but Mom plants herself in front of me. "I told you to stay away from him."

Frustration at being treated like a perpetual child spears through me. Huffing, I square off with Mom.

"You don't get to dictate everything in my life. Connor is my boyfriend." She opens her mouth, but I hold up a finger. "And no, I won't stop seeing him. My life is mine, Mom."

"You stupid girl," she seethes. "Fine. Wait until he breaks you, throws you away. Then you'll see how rotten boys are."

Surprisingly, she doesn't try to ground me.

"Jesus, Mom. Do you even listen to yourself?" Rubbing my forehead, I cast a glance around the kitchen. "I'll clean up tomorrow. I'm going to bed."

Her poisonous gaze tracks me as I leave the kitchen. While climbing the stairs I can hear her fuming to herself.

It makes me sad. I don't remember my childhood being awful, other than her obsession with my body and her little nitpicking comments about my outfit choices, so why is she like this now? She was never overly affectionate with me, but she treated me more human when I was a little girl than she does now.

It seems like she's getting worse and she hates that she can't control me because I no longer cower in fear of whatever she wants to say about my body to keep me in my place.

TWENTY-FOUR
Connor

STICKING it to Thea's mom as I strolled out of her house in the middle of the night is one of my top five hashtag swag moments for myself in the last year. I was feeling really damn good about myself, knowing that not only was I pissing her off by my mere presence, but that I also had Thea on my side.

And I know that woman has been fuming about how I'm corrupting her daughter ever since. The next morning she was drinking coffee under their portico, glaring at me as Thea climbed into my ride.

I leaned over and kissed Thea long and hard until she pinched my side. Her mom's face was fucking priceless before I pulled away from the curb.

What can I say? I don't do well with overbearing parents telling me what to do. Celine Kennedy can shove her judgement up her ass alongside the broomstick.

Over the next two weeks, Thea and I spend our time together at night in the pool house as our relationship slowly grows. Her work ethic is bleeding into mine because she won't let me distract her until both of our homework assignments are finished. But once they are? She's all mine.

My friends accept her when we show up to the parking lot in the morning. I miss Devlin being around, but I don't mind that he's been skipping out on us. He's happy and he needs it. I can't fault that. We'll pick up when he comes up for air from his own bubble with Blair Davis.

It feels good to walk into a school I rule with the world's prettiest sunbeam under my arm, talking my ear off about the upcoming dance.

I've already got a plan in the works. She's been putting her all into heading the committee to organize the dance, so I'm going to make sure her night is nothing but magical.

* * *

Half-absorbed in my phone as I follow the flow of foot traffic between classes near the end of the day, it takes me a minute to realize the crowd forming ahead is because some drama is going down. The students blocking my way titter meanly at the scene. I don't have time for this.

"What, don't have anything to say? You a mute?"

Some meathead football player pushes someone shorter than him. I can't see clearly through the crowd. A cheerleader I recognize from that boat party before school stands next to him, smirking triumphantly—*Kammy with a K*, my mind supplies.

"Gonna go cry about it?" Kammy teases in a nasty tone. "Should've thought about that before you butted in."

They must be picking on someone. A dealer that shorted them on product, or one of the nerds who make bank selling homework.

I switch directions, planning to take the stairs to the second floor to get to my computer science class, but a familiar voice has me halting in my tracks and flying into protective mode.

"Please leave me alone. I didn't do anything to you."

Thea.

"Move," I demand in a deadly voice.

The underclassman in my way might have shit himself when he saw me towering over him before he scurried out of my path. Others spot me and part, lowering their gazes, too afraid to look a crazed beast in the eyes. By the time I bust through the crowd of onlookers, the football player and Kammy are tugging on Thea's sweater. Fierce rage overtakes me.

Thea stands her ground while they bully her and it eggs them on. They're probably pissed off she's not reacting how they thought. I can see it in their eyes: they want her tears. Her humiliation.

I won't stand for this. No one treats my girl like that.

"The fuck you think you're doing?" I cut in, putting myself between them and Thea. Her hands touch the back of my school blazer. "Messing with my girlfriend?"

"Bishop," the football guy says in confusion. His puny, juiced up brain can't fathom why I'm here. That's what steroids will do. "What's up man?"

"Connor," Thea murmurs behind me. "It's okay."

"No, baby, it's not. I saw what they were doing to you." Swinging back to the other two, I snarl. "Touch her again and I'll destroy your whole life. Then I'll break your arms." Thea tries to sidestep me, but I block her. These two don't even deserve to look at her. My gaze flicks to Kammy. "That goes for both of you."

Kammy and her footballer shuffle back a step at my feral look. I don't have to spell it out for them. Everyone knows when they cross me, whether they realize it or not, I've got dirt that will bury them before their life even gets off the ground.

"All of you, actually." I raise my voice, moving my attention over the crowd watching us raptly. "Thea is off fucking limits. If you mess with my girlfriend, I'm coming for you."

Once I'm satisfied that I've struck enough fear in everyone, I let Thea out from behind me, tucking her under my arm. "Tell me what happened."

She frowns at me. "It's not worth it."

"It is. Tell me."

Her gaze travels over the crowd. She takes my hand and I allow her to lead me away. "Let's just go. The bell's about to ring and we'll all be late."

I toss a glare over my shoulder at Thea's bullies, one that says *I'm watching you*. Kammy's face pales and she yanks on the footballer's arm to get out of there.

Once we're away from the crowd, I dig my feet in.

"What are you—? Hey!" Thea yelps as I tug her into the empty stairwell at the end of the hall. The door clangs shut, enveloping us in its echo that fades into silence.

I cradle her face, examining her.

"I'm fine."

"Tell me what happened."

She huffs. "It's stupid."

"It's not. I'm sorry I wasn't there. I promise I won't let anything like that happen to you again."

Thea lifts her brows. "Yeah? You know, not that long ago that was you, too. It's only been a little over a month since you humiliated me enough to send me running from the cafeteria crying."

Her words stab into my gut in a fatal blow. Fuck, I was such an ass to her. Hanging my head, I give her another piece of myself.

"I'm sorry. I've always been a dick to you because of your mom. I..." Now that I'm saying it out loud, now that I *know* her, it sounds so idiotic. How could I have thought this was okay? With a sigh, I push out the rest of my words. "I thought you were like her. Anytime I noticed you, it was because you were intervening and I took it badly."

Her beautiful features twist in conflict. "What do you mean, because of my mom?"

I rub the back of my head. "About two years ago is when I first discovered my mom and Damien's affair. I walked in on him fucking her in the kitchen."

Her nose wrinkles and she wraps her arms around my waist. "Connor... That must have been awful."

"Yeah, it wasn't peachy." I gather her closer, bolstered by her soothing touch. If she's in my arms, she can't hate me, right? "I lost it. Totally went berserk. I beat the shit out of him while my mom was screaming. It was a whole ass scene."

A sad laugh punches out of her. "What happened next?"

"Well, I was so focused with raging on him that I didn't realize I'd chased him all the way out of the house. I was on my front lawn, punching him until his face was a bruised and bloody mess. Then I guess your mom came out and saw it happening. She called the cops, shrieking like a banshee. You've seen how my mom is with appearances. Not even her own side piece gets in the way of her goal, so you can imagine how she felt that I not only caused this huge scene in front of the neighbors, but that I was pulled off Damien, cuffed, and carted away in the back of a squad car."

It actually feels great to get off my chest. Only my parents, Devlin, and my therapist know the full story. I thought Thea would hate me when I told her the truth about the source of why

I bullied her, but it feels right to confess it to her. I'll do whatever I have to in order to make it up to her for being a bastard.

"God," Thea says. "I'm sorry you had to find out like that."

"I'm sorry," I repeat once more. "I took it out on you and that wasn't right."

"I forgive you. We're moving past it now."

A relieved breath hisses out of me as I hug her. After tipping her chin up to kiss her, I feel like I can give her another shard of myself.

"I should've gone to juvie, but my mom bribed Chief Landry and a judge. They made the assault charge disappear, paid a fine for disturbing the peace, and I got slapped with court-mandated anger management."

Thea stretches to brush my hair, trailing her fingers down the side of my face. "I'm glad you didn't have to go away."

The corners of my mouth tip up. There goes my sunshine, lighting up my day with her silver linings and positive outlook.

"Now, are you going to tell me what happened, or do I have to go find out from someone else?"

She snorts, pushing her palm over my face. "No. Don't go bothering anyone, either. It was nothing, I swear. I didn't laugh when he was making fun of an underclassman and told him to stop. He turned on me instead."

I take a step toward the door, intent on hunting down the footballer and putting his head through a locker, but Thea stops me.

"I'd rather kiss you again before I'm late for French class than have you go attack someone to avenge me."

Well, when those are my options, how can I resist giving my girl what she wants?

"Come here then." I herd her against the wall, swallowing her giggle as I seal my mouth over hers.

We're both late to class.

* * *

Later the same week, I'm sneaking around Thea's backyard again.

We started in the pool house, but when she said she had to leave, I wouldn't let her go. So I'm following her, staying low in case her mom is around.

"This is such a bad idea," Thea murmurs for the third time since we slipped out of our haven in the pool house. "I swear, Connor, if you get caught, you're on your own."

"Ouch, baby," I whisper back. "You know what I say about bad ideas."

"Yeah, yeah. Your favorite kind. I know." She peeks around inside the dark house before carefully opening the door. "Just—don't make a sound until we get to my room, or she'll suspect something."

I smother a devious laugh and follow her lead.

Once we sneak upstairs and make it to her room, Thea collapses against the door with a strained sigh.

"Oh my god. I can't believe we pulled that off. She's usually all over me when I come in late."

I plant my hands on either side of her and lean in for a kiss. She goes pliant, releasing a tiny moan. Leaving her against the door, I slowly draw away, smirking at the blissed out look on her face.

"So this is your bedroom. Looks different when I can see the entire thing, not just your flower chair or your girly bedspread," I tease, taking it all in.

It's the first time I've seen it in person rather than through a phone or computer screen. The room is full of feminine touches, from her positive food pun themed posters to her little rainbow clock on her nightstand. It's got this soft, warm vibe to it that feels like Thea. Bright and welcoming.

"It's not girly." Thea swats at me as she passes by on the way to the closet. She rummages for a moment, then pulls out a hoodie she stole from me last week, holding it to her nose as she sniffs it. "It's just a bed."

I pluck the hoodie from her and she pushes out her plump bottom lip. Goddamn, she's so cute.

"I was looking for this." It's from a concert I went to with Devlin and his cousin Lucas over the summer. I shoot her a sly look. "If I remember right, I sent you home from the pool house wearing this the other night."

"You did." She tilts her head all coy. "I've been wearing it to sleep in. It smells like you."

"Yeah?" I hand it back, eager to see her wearing my clothes. "Make you feel like you're in my arms?"

She nods as she peels out of her outfit to change. I rake my teeth over my lip, dropping on her bed to watch.

As she lifts her hair out of the neck, she catches my eye and squints at me. "No. Don't even think about it. We can't have sex in here."

"Not even a little?" I spread my legs and adjust my dick. She's so hot, wearing only my hoodie and panties. It's big on her, almost hitting her knees. "Leave the hoodie on while I eat your pussy."

She turns red and I chuckle, grabbing the hem to tug her closer.

"You're so vulgar," she says, exasperated. Her hands rest on my shoulders as I tease my fingers beneath the hoodie. "We have to go to bed."

"Baby, that's what I'm angling for." I cup her ass and tug so she lands on my lap, straddling me. "You're so irresistible. I'll never have enough of you, even if I fuck you five times a day."

"We had sex twice in the pool house today." The end of her sentence dips into a moan as

I massage her ass and lick the shell of her ear. "Seriously, we can't. She'll hear. There's no way I can be quiet."

I love that I drive her so wild she can't control herself. We fucked in the pool house shower earlier so she could moan as loud as she wanted while I drove my cock into her.

With one last graze of my teeth over her throat, I let her escape across the bed. She takes a minute to compose herself while I kick off my shoes, then shuck my jeans and t-shirt so I'm only in briefs. As I lay back against the pillows, her stuffed sea lion captures my attention.

"Who's this little guy?" I pick it up. It's softer than I expected and I hum, dragging it over her bare leg. "Why a sea lion? I pictured a girl like you would have something magical, like a unicorn or something cute to go with the rest of your bedroom decor."

It's a question I've wanted to ask since I saw it on her webcam, but couldn't without raising suspicion about why I knew she had it.

"It is cute! Give me that." Thea snatches the stuffed toy, her smile fond as she smooshes its lumpy body. "I don't know. I was like, seven, when I got him on a trip to the aquarium. I liked how funny their bodies were. He was round and I liked it."

My gaze goes soft as my heart swells. I might be new at relationships because I wasn't interested in chicks after my family's money or the status of dating me, but she isn't like that at all. She's just herself, this incredible light.

Thea is the only girl I've never hated the idea of letting in, sharing my life with, *keeping*. When I think about the future now, it's one that includes her.

"Ready to fight me for the covers?"

Her question draws me out of my dazed thoughts. She has her fists up in a mock boxing stance. I cover her hands with mine, correcting her so she won't end up with broken thumbs if she ever throws a punch.

"Like this. Remind me to teach you to fight."

"What if I don't want to fight? Make cake, not war."

Thea nods sagely, crawling into my open arms as we settle into a comfortable position. I spoon against her back, nuzzling into her neck.

"For self defense, then." My voice turns drowsy and I stifle a yawn. "Important stuff, baby. Everyone needs to know how to protect themselves."

"Okay," she murmurs, reaching over to turn out the light.

As the room plunges in darkness, I roll my hips against hers, enjoying the feel of her ass tucked against my dick. "Mm, goodnight sunshine."

"Night." She finds one of my hands and tangles our fingers together, holding our joined hands over her heart.

It's the most comfortable I've felt in a long time.

* * *

At dawn, I wake up before Thea, spending a minute enjoying watching her in the pale morning light. Her face is smashed against my chest, and she wasn't kidding about the fight for the covers—she has all of them cocooned around her while I'm left with a measly corner.

I carefully brush her hair back and kiss her forehead before climbing out of bed. Rustling through my pockets of my pants, I take out the small, polished moonstone I've been carrying around, intending to give it to her. I got it when I was a kid, when Dad took me to a nature museum. It was one of our last outings before he began to drift.

The shimmering light blue stone reminds me of Thea. She's my sunbeam, but I love the way she shines at night, like this stone.

After tugging on my jeans, I flip open one of her recipe notebooks on the desk and take a fresh page. I borrow one of Thea's pens to draw a heart on the page, put it on her nightstand, and place the moonstone in the middle.

Resisting the temptation to crawl back into bed and wake her up with my tongue, I slip out of the room and manage to sneak out unnoticed. Once I make it out, I send her a good morning text.

TWENTY-FIVE
Connor

AFTER soccer practice finishes, I shower as fast as I can to pick Thea up from the dance planning committee. It's one of the last practices we'll have this season before the playoffs start now that it's November.

"Is your ass on fire?" Devlin jokes as I fly through the locker room.

"Shove it, I'm late to see my girl!" I toss my stuff in my duffel bag as I drag on a clean Silver Lake High Coyotes t-shirt.

"You saw her an hour and a half ago," Devlin points out as he sprawls across the opposite bench. "Made out with her until we had to drag you off her so she could go."

I level him with a flat look. "And where was Blair while this was going down?"

Devlin drops his gaze, grinning stupidly. Yeah, I've got him. I saw the way he was all wrapped up in her in the parking lot when he went to get his gear.

"Aight, I'm out," I call to the other guys in the locker room. "Let's keep it tight and finish the season strong."

A few whoops and hollers follow me as I duck out of the room and head for the one the dance committee is using for prep duties. I can't wipe the dopey grin off my face as I yank the door open, planning to sweep Thea off her feet and kiss her.

I freeze in the doorway, jealousy rocketing through me fast enough to make me sick to my stomach.

Coleman stands too close to Thea, leaning into her space as he points out whatever is on the papers she's presenting to him. Creep.

Dealing with this was hell when we were faking, but now that she's my girlfriend? I'm even more possessive of her. He gives me a bad vibe and I don't want him near her.

Stalking into the room, I make sure I'm as loud as possible, dumping my athletic duffel on the floor. The other students on the committee throw me dirty looks. One of them is Maisy Landry, squinting at me over the clipboard she's marking.

"Hey, babe. Practice finished early. Perks of being captain." I slide in, draping an arm over her shoulder, subtly pulling her away from our teacher. "Ready to go?"

"Hi. In a minute, we're just figuring out the logistics of the refreshment tables and the DJ." She flips through her papers, mumbling to herself.

I touch her hair, pulling it out of her face while she's working. I know I'm being territorial, but I can't help it when it comes to her. Coleman's hand twitches every time I touch her.

"Mr. Bishop, this meeting is for planning committee members and faculty advisors only, I'm afraid," Coleman says in mock-sympathy. Yeah fucking right. He's trying to kick me out so he can perv on my girlfriend. "If you'd like to wait outside for—"

"Actually, come here," Thea says, tugging on my shirt. "I need your help and everyone else is busy with their own tasks."

I smirk at Coleman as she leads me across the room. His lip curls and he looks like he wants to strangle me. Not very becoming for an educator.

"Hold this up for me? Yeah, like that," Thea directs, stepping back and pinching her chin as she studies the balloon archway decoration I'm holding up. "Okay, good. We'll weave the clear ones through to spell out SLHS and fill those with silver glitter. It'll be perfect for the photo op as people arrive."

I peer overhead. "You did all this?"

Thea nods.

"It's awesome."

"Thanks. This is just the test version, but I saw a really cool photo online."

"People are gonna love it. Look, come here." I motion her over with my head as I hold up the archway. "Take a selfie so you can see."

As she holds up her phone, I kiss her cheek. She's grinning in the photo, her face scrunched adorably from my attack kiss.

"There. See?"

"Yeah." Her voice is warm as she studies the photo. "It looks so good. Okay, perfect."

"Send me that one. I'm totally posting it."

Thea shoots me a beaming smile as she shuffles her papers. I set the decoration down and lean over her shoulder to see the logistics.

"Put the tables with food over here and the DJ here," I say, pointing out spots on the page. "Mom made me go to this rally once and that's how they did it. Something about the natural flow."

"Oh! That's perfect." Thea makes a mark on the page, drawing little symbols of her own making. "Awesome, now we can go."

Coleman has been watching us the entire time. While his attention is on us, I take her face and tip it up for a kiss, sliding my gaze to him. A muscle in his jaw jumps.

I wind my fingers with hers. "So are we good to go?"

"Yes." She pulls away to cross the room.

I shoulder my bag and take Thea's as she talks to Maisy. They both come over. Her friend sizes me up.

"Maisy is coming over so we can go shopping."

"Cool." I hold a fist out for her to bump.

She holds out, then taps her fist against mine.

Coleman hovers while Thea delegates last minute questions from the other planning committee members. As she returns to my side, he stands in our path.

"Is there anything else we can knock out today?"

"No, but I'll call the DJ to confirm tonight." Thea doesn't pick up on his intensity. She's too kind to suspect anything is wrong. "We'll move onto the other tasks at the meeting next week."

"Well. I have to say, Thea, I knew you were the right choice for this. You're perfect." His gaze is unwavering as he stares her down, like he's waiting for her recognition. "I have to commend you for a job well done so far."

I exchange a look with Maisy. She's put off by Coleman, too, so I know I'm not imagining this weird feeling.

"Thank you," Thea says.

"I just know that because of your hard work, you'll always have all the world has to offer you," Coleman says in this haunting voice that makes every hair on my body stand on end. "You won't have to wait for it anymore."

What the fuck?

An uncomfortable sense of déjà vu washes over me. I recognize those words. They were one of the creepy stalker comments on Thea's blog.

I'm taking a step before I know it, edging between them to protect Thea. Coleman can't quite smother the frustrated sound that catches in his throat.

"Come on, or we'll totally miss all of our shopping time," Maisy says, hooking her arm with Thea's and ushering her ahead.

I cut a glance to the side, making sure Thea is leaving.

"What? No we won't," she says. "Relax, the dresses aren't going anywhere."

"Let's just get out of here." Maisy twists around. "Boyfriend? Your chauffeur service is required. My brother already left."

I hang back for another beat, meeting Coleman's gaze with a challenge. He seems to snap out of the psycho trance he was in a second ago talking to Thea and sneers at me.

"Get out of here before I give you detention, Mr. Bishop."

I give him an arrogant snort. "For what? Standing?"

Without waiting for his answer, I head out. The slithering feeling knotting my stomach doesn't leave as I catch up with the girls.

"So that was weird, right?" Maisy asks once we reach the parking lot.

"Hmm?" Thea takes her bag from my shoulder, rummaging for her phone. "What was weird?"

Maisy's gaze darts to me and we both look at Thea.

"Do you have conversations like that with any of your other teachers?" Maisy questions.

"Seriously, I think what he said to you was over the line."

"I guess not. Mr. Coleman's really cool though," Thea says. "I've always felt like I can talk to him."

"That guy?" I shake my head.

"Thank you!" Maisy looks at me in a new light, no longer judging me for being her friend's boyfriend she doesn't know.

"He's my favorite teacher," Thea says firmly.

"I'm questioning your taste."

Thea pokes my arm. "My taste includes you, too."

"Smile and eyes," Maisy cuts in, studying me. "Twelve out of ten, but butt? Eh, six out of ten."

"What's wrong with my ass? Have you ever seen a soccer player's ass up close, little Landry?"

"Absolutely nothing wrong back here," Thea assures me, biting her lip around a smile and tucking her hand in the back pocket of my jeans, boldly giving my ass a squeeze.

I give her a smile, but it doesn't reach my eyes. I can't shake the dark web of thoughts clinging to me.

We climb into my Lexus GX and I waste no time pulling out of the lot. As soon as I drop them off, I'm setting out on the hunt to dig up the comment triggering my memory to check it against Coleman's words.

* * *

Hiding my suspicion from Thea and Maisy on the ride home was hard. I didn't want Thea to think I was in a bad mood, but I was itching to get on my computer and dig through her blog. A sick feeling has lodged in my gut and I have to double check if I'm right.

My knee bounces as I wake my system from sleep mode, and my fingers pound the keys harder than necessary as I type in my login.

I go straight for her blog, Coleman's words playing in my head like the eerie tune of a rundown carousel ride.

The same thing repeats in the comments.

Henry_Your_GoodKnight: *Your intelligent eyes say it all, love. You're longing for the world to show you all it has to offer.*

Henry_Your_GoodKnight: *Do you trust me, princess? Your knight waits for you. My precious doll. Say you'll take my hand and I'll show you all the world has to offer.*

Henry_Your_GoodKnight: *Missing these intelligent eyes and talking to you. Where have you gone, love? Do you miss me, too? I dream of finding you, coming to steal you away for the whirlwind romance the world has to offer you. It's me, I'm your world. If I held out my hand, would you take it? The thought consumes me.*

The timestamps are recent. My overprotectiveness for Thea goes into overdrive, but I have to know what I'm dealing with first.

Gritting my teeth, I take the IP address and trace it. The search runs for a second, bouncing around before telling me it routes to the Ukraine. That isn't right. I know it.

There's no way in hell Coleman says the same exact thing to Thea that this Henry Knight guy says all over her blog.

"Fucker," I grit out. "Know how to mask yourself with a VPN, huh? I'll find you."

I switch to searching for Coleman instead. One way or another I'll tie him to the Henry Knight username and gather everything I need to prove to Thea she needs to stay away from him. Basic search engines only turn up his LinkedIn and results that don't match him. I slam my fist on the desk, frustrated beyond measure.

How can he have wiped himself from the web? It's damn near impossible these days to fly so under the radar. Leaning forward with a deep inhale, I pull up the Ridgeview School District database and use Dad's password to login to the admin network. Coleman's employee file has to have something. I click through only to find his previous employment history won't open.

Closed records.

"That's not shady at all," I mutter, trying to find a workaround to access it.

All I get is his ID photo and his start date. The name on his file makes me suck in a breath. *Shit.*

H. K. Coleman.

"Too close to be a coincidence. What does H stand for?"

The deeper I search, the more roadblocks I come up against. My hair must be standing on end from practically ripping it out of my head because I'm not getting anywhere.

It's like Coleman showed up without any trace of where the hell he came from. I've never been able to find anything useful on him. No one is that much of a ghost.

When I'm about to give up, a search result on my third try with new keywords catches my eye. Next to the link is a thumbnail of Coleman smiling with a group of students. *Mostly girls,* I note with clenched teeth.

The link says North East Regional Award for Excellence. Beneath that, the description goes on to preview the article.

Local students from Thorne Point Junior Academy commended for their fundraiser work, along with their advisor, Harold K. Coleman.

An icy sensation drags down my back like vicious nails. Harold. If my name was Harold,

I'd go by Henry, too. I swear to god, if Coleman's middle name is Knight...

My violent thoughts race too fast to sort out. I click on the link while my heart thuds.

An auto-download triggers.

"Shit!" I fumble with the keyboard and mouse, but I'm too slow to stop it. Within seconds, the file downloads and runs an install package. "Mother fuck—no!"

Goddamn it, I'm better than this. I know not to click on unfamiliar links or download fishy files, no matter how funny an angry desktop goose sounds. Learned that the hard way thanks to a trending TikTok video. Wasn't worth it, twelve out of ten wouldn't recommend.

Whoever this is, they're good. They confused a major search engine to show their download within the results, luring anyone looking hard to find Coleman once they put together enough of the puzzle. That is top level shit. I have no idea how they pulled it off.

An 8-bit crow animation flies across my screen, the little black bird mocking me. The screen goes dark and flashes with a skull. Once the crow lands on top of the skull, the whole monitor display glitches into pixelated distortion before returning to normal.

I'm looking around for the crow, ready to drag its ass to the trash can icon, when a chat window pops up. There's no way anyone should have access to my system. Whatever was in that download package, it infiltrated my firewalls.

Dolos: Looking for info on Harold Coleman?

I hesitate to answer, rubbing my jaw. This whole thing feels hinky.

Dolos: Time's ticking. Answer now.

When I don't respond, they message again.

Dolos: Connor Alexander Bishop. Ridgeview, Colorado. Senior at Silver Lake High School. Varsity soccer captain. Son of city council chairwoman Vivian Bishop. Active social media presence. Girlfriend, Thea Kennedy. Oh, she lives next door. Cute. Should we keep going?

"Jesus." I push back from the desk and scrub my face.

Within seconds they were able to doxx me and get a whole picture of my life. Not just mine. Thea's, through her connection to me. This is a professional who knows what they're doing.

If they're on my system, they could get into my blackmail files or find the backdoor to Thea. Not happening. I drag myself back and release a ragged breath.

Connor: Enough, I get it. I'm here. Nice work on the search result embedding. You got me.
Dolos: Glad you're paying attention.

Connor: You have details on Coleman?
Dolos: We do.
Connor: And??? Give it to me. I need it.
Dolos: That's not how this works. First you need to do us a favor. If you're successful, we'll give you everything you're searching for.
Connor: And if I refuse?

They can give it to me now or not at all. I don't have time to play games. I'll get it on my own.

Dolos: You can try. You'll never find what you're looking for. Coleman has friends in high places with deep pockets that helped him disappear the last time we had him pinned down. We're the only ones with the info. It's no longer public record.

Sighing, I pinch the bridge of my nose.

Connor: Who are you?
Dolos: Unimportant right now. Are you ready to make a deal?
Connor: Yes. Whatever gets me dirt on Coleman.
Dolos: Your task is retrieval. Locate Coleman's house, get it back with proof, then we'll be ready to do business.

An image attachment comes through the chat. It's a necklace. A heart locket with the initials CT engraved on the front. After seeing those comments and the way Coleman's creep factor turned up to eleven today, the sight of the locket makes an uneasiness settle in my gut.
Who the hell are these guys and how are they connected to Coleman?

Connor: Get the necklace and you'll give me what I need?
Dolos: That's the deal. Take too long and it expires.
Connor: Wait! I'll need time. Coleman is evasive and good at covering his tracks.
Dolos: Fine. By the new year, or we'll have to introduce ourselves to that pretty redhead.

I stand so fast to slam the desk, the whole thing almost overturns. A growl tears from me as I grab for the monitor to stabilize it. The desk left a dent in the wall. I type with all the force of the anger coursing through me.

Connor: Touch her and I'll kill you.
Dolos: Better get to work then.

My screen goes black and non-responsive. When I do a hard reset to reboot the computer, the chat window is gone.

"Damn it!" My throat burns as I drag in air, breathing hard to regulate the fury.

Once I have myself under control, I collapse on the bed. The first thing I do is run a search for *Dolos*. My snort jerks my head when the results populate. It turns out Dolos is from greek mythology, a god of cunning trickery and deception. Fitting.

"Edgelords," I mutter.

Next I text Devlin. I'm going to need help to pull this off. I doubt I can get Chief Landry to convince a judge to issue a warrant for Coleman with circumstantial evidence, even if I emptied my investment accounts for the bribe.

Connor: Feel up for some recon?
Devlin: Playing Batman again?
Connor: This is bigger than that. I'll explain. I'm on my way over.
Devlin: Can you give me like an hour?
Connor: This is serious, man! You can get your dick sucked later.
Devlin: My parents just left town again sometime today, dude. You're killing me [skull emoji]
Connor: You can last a few more hours. Bring her with us if you want, Blair might have more insight into what I need to plan.
Devlin: Which is?
Connor: Surveillance. Probably some B&E.
Devlin: [smirking devil emoji] That does sound like something she'll know about.

Some of the tightness loosens in my chest. I knew my best friend would have my back. Grabbing my keys and wallet, I head out the door. On my way, I text Thea to check in on her.

Connor: How's shopping? Find the one?
Thea: Pretty sure I can't show you the dress before the big day.

I snort, leaning against the driver's side of my car.

Connor: Babe, that's a wedding dress. You angling for wifey status?
Thea: [flustered emoji] Stop teasing me!

My heart does a little flip. She always gets me smiling.

Connor: Have fun. I'm going to hang with Devlin. Call you later?
Thea: Ok [heart emoji]

Climbing into the car, I pull out and head for Devlin's place to figure out a plan.

TWENTY-SIX
Thea

The last month has been such a whirlwind. Before I know it, it's the week of the dance. Between my planning committee duties, studying, baking about a million pies for the Thanksgiving dinner at the local shelter, and trying to have a life, time has slipped by me.

Everything is in chaos at school with the semester ending, midterms looming next week, and the excitement for the winter formal at the end of the week to give the students a break before our winter vacation.

Connor and I have barely had time to sneak away to our secret haven in the pool house over the last few weeks. He was wrapped up in his own thing with the end of the soccer season, and being there for Devlin when his relationship with Blair ended abruptly after Thanksgiving.

They're back together now, or at least that's the impression I got when I walked in on them making out in the English classroom before anyone else arrived. Those two burn hot and fast, like exploding stars. I quickly stammered an apology, but I'd already seen Devlin's hand fisted in Blair's hair, holding her head back, and the huge hickey on her neck. They didn't even stop, just gave me matching smirks as I backed out of the room and bumped right into Connor's chest.

The gymnasium is in a state of havoc as the committee members direct our helpers with the decorations. Connor promised he'd bring the soccer team to lend a hand, and I'm waiting on them to drape the silver and white fabric Maisy and I picked out to transform the room into a winter wonderland.

We're both working on lifting a table onto the stage for the DJ, but we're struggling with just the two of us.

"It's too heavy," I say.

"Oh!" Maisy pops up from her squat and heads for the door. "Hang on, I see my brother in the hall. Holden!"

Maisy's brother stops and leans against the doorframe. Behind him, Fox Wilder looms like a deadly shadow, scowling at Maisy.

"'Sup?" Holden asks.

Maisy tugs on his arm, a force of nature of her own making when she wants something. "Come here a sec. We're trying to lift this, but it's too heavy. I need to borrow your football muscles." She peers over Holden's shoulder and latches on to Fox's wrist. "You too, Fox."

She wrangles both of them, but Fox doesn't seem happy about it. His sharp, eerie gaze tracks her as she leads them over.

"How long is this going to take?" Holden asks, dragging his feet. "I'm hungry. We were going to get food."

"Just a minute. You're wasting your own time by complaining about it."

Holden groans, dropping his head back. "You're such a pain in the ass."

"Deal with it, my god." Maisy flips her hair over her shoulder and sticks her tongue out at her brother. "Two minutes, or I'll tell Mom where you've been going on weekends."

"Fine," Holden grumbles.

"Okay, help us get this over there," she directs, kneeling to grab the end she tried to lift with just the two of us.

I get into position as Holden comes to help me support my side. Fox doesn't move. Maisy looks up over her shoulder. Her brows hike up. He towers over her, intimidating as hell with that cold expression, his dead eyes shooting daggers at my sweet best friend.

Maisy is the kind of girl everyone likes, so how can he look at her with so much hatred?

Fox is scary. Bad boy is written all over him, from the motorcycle he rides around town on to his complete disregard for any rules. He looks dangerous in his leather jacket and messy dark brown hair. It's hard to believe this guy is someone Maisy could've been friends with; he's her total opposite.

"Aren't you going to help us?" Maisy sighs. "It won't take long. Then you can go back to pretending I don't exist."

"Maybe we can get it with the three of us," I say, trying to break up the suffocating tension between them. "Right, Holden?"

He grunts, gaze flicking between his surly friend and his sister.

"Fox, come on. Please?" Maisy won't give in, frowning at him when he narrows his eyes. She lowers her voice. "You always used to—"

His furious growl cuts her off. "No."

My heart leaps into my throat. I shift to jump to my feet, but Holden puts his hand on my arm to keep me in place, watching the exchange between Fox and Maisy.

"No?" Maisy sighs, never one to get angry or spiteful. "Okay, it's just...if you helped, we'd get it done faster. Then I'll leave you alone."

Fox moves at last, getting in her face. "Always such a goody-goody."

Maisy's shoulders tense and she hugs herself, glancing away. Fox laughs, the sound an awful, cutting bark.

"Yeah. That's what I thought." He takes a lock of her hair, letting it slide through his fingers. "Didn't your daddy teach you to run from monsters? Get it through your fucking head."

Turning away, he kicks over a bucket of metallic silver paint we need to make the signs. It skims across the gym floor, creeping close to Maisy's flats. Meeting her gaze, he smirks cruelly at the look on her face.

"What are you going to do about it? Cry?" Fox speaks in a deep, biting voice as he mocks her. "That's all you are. All you'll ever be. Maisy Daisy the Crybaby."

Maisy stands her ground, even though I can tell she's upset. She lifts her head.

"What happened to you?" Her whisper is watery. "You were my friend, too."

"Playtime is over," Fox growls. "Fuck off, daisy. Stay out of my way."

He storms off, tearing down a mylar fringe curtain Maisy hung.

"Are you fine being friends with that jerk when he treats your sister that way?" I ask Holden.

"I don't control him. Couldn't if I tried. He's not even my friend, he just showed up again and started hanging around me."

I shake Holden's hand off my arm and go to her side.

"Holden, get the paint," I say while I wrap Maisy in a tight hug. "Are you okay?"

"Yeah," Maisy says softly, tucking her face in my shoulder. "I don't understand why he hates me so much now."

"Maybe it's best if you stay away from him. He seems..."

"I know." Maisy groans. "I'll go pick up another can of paint."

"Are you sure?"

"Yeah. Holden? Give me a ride to the hardware store."

Holden stops mopping up the silver paint. On their way out, he puts his hand on Maisy's head and ruffles her hair, leaning close to murmur to her. She nods as they pass through the door.

With a sigh, I motion over two students from the planning committee. "Can you two work on this? We'll get more paint for the signs. I'm going to find someone to help lift this."

As I'm pulled in different directions, Connor appears in the double doorway with Devlin and the rest of the soccer team at his back, all dressed down in their SLHS athletic gear. I push out a relieved breath and wave him over.

"Your very hot labor team has arrived," Connor drawls. He captures me in his arms and drops a quick peck on my lips. "Give us your orders."

Smiling softly, I dip my fingers beneath his t-shirt, smoothing them over his skin. "Thanks for helping."

"Of course, sunshine." Connor winks. "What my girl needs, she gets. Ain't that right, Dev?"

Devlin huffs out a laugh, shaking his head. "Yeah. Real attentive lover type, you are."

Connor clicks his tongue and shoots me a finger gun.

"Okay, if a few of you could head to that corner to set up the photo booth station," I say, addressing the soccer team. "We need help to hang the decorations from the rafters, so speak to the custodial staff. Then the rest of you will help with the draping."

"You heard her, guys. Chop, chop," Connor says.

He doesn't move right away, keeping me in his embrace. His gaze darts around, sweeping the room like he's looking for a threat.

"Has Coleman been around?"

"He went to pick up the lighting rental. Why?"

"Just checking." He's being evasive and keeps looking around, as if he expects something to take him by surprise.

Connor is odd like that for the rest of the afternoon, on edge and wary of everything. He barely leaves my side, hovering over me as soon as he finishes the tasks I give him. Despite my shadow, we're able to get most of the decorating done, and I walk out of the gymnasium at the end of the night feeling a sense of accomplishment.

With the logistics taken care of, I can finally allow the excitement for the big dance to creep in.

TWENTY-SEVEN
Thea

Seeing the room all set up and walking in the night of the dance are two different things. It steals my breath as Connor and I pass through the shimmering curtains draped in the entrance.

For once, I feel completely confident. Like the goddess I'm always telling myself to be, dressed in a flowing pink dress that makes me feel amazing, my hair down in soft curls, and my handsome boyfriend escorting me. The flower crown he presented me with when he picked me up helps with the goddess vibes, a beautiful mix of yellow anemones and pink roses sitting on my head. He'd said he wanted to give me the sun, but this was the closest he could get to suit a queen. My heart hasn't stopped glowing with warmth since.

Connor's hair is combed and styled the same as it was the night of the benefit for the children's hospital, and he looks so good in a gray suit that complements his eyes.

"Wow, it really came out nice," I murmur in awe.

"Of course it did. You were the brains behind it all." Connor kisses my cheek. "Nerds, right? The best."

"Oh, now they're the best?" I tease. "Your tune's changed since I found out about you being a computer nerd."

"Like I said. The best."

He chuckles, drawing me toward the balloon installation—a pearlescent white and silver arched confection—to set us up for a selfie. He wraps me in his arms from behind, playing with the material of my dress, and I lift my hand to touch his face as he leans over my shoulder.

Once he takes a couple of us smiling, I turn his face to mine for a kiss. We take a few more photos, then dive into the fray of the dance. It's perfect and amazing.

"Thea! Oh my god, you look so pretty!" Nina, one of Connor's friends from the popular crowd, gives me a big hug. Her friend Bailey holds up her phone and takes a photo of the two of us. "Bishop, take one of the three of us."

These girls were never outright mean to me, but they never made an effort before I began dating Connor, either. I was invisible to them. We've reached a point where we briefly talk in the mornings when we all pull into the student lot.

Bailey hands off her phone and comes to pose on my other side.

"You both look amazing, too," I say.

"Thanks," Bailey says as she squeezes me between her and Nina.

They work it for the camera as Connor obediently captures us. I hesitate for a second, then laugh as we get into it.

"Just what the world likes, hot chicks rubbing up on each other," Connor says.

"Connor!" My cheeks heat.

He laughs under his breath, handing the phone back to Bailey. "Just calling it like I see it."

The girls giggle and go through the pictures he took. More of his friends join us.

When I see some of mine, I peel away from his side to talk to them. I'm in the middle of talking to a girl from my culinary class when Connor materializes next to me, looking annoyed.

"What's wrong?" I follow his gaze to Mr. Coleman, deep in conversation with a girl from our class.

Connor's hand fits to my waist, guiding me further away. "Let's go grab a table over here."

His friends join us. For a while we watch the photo booth nearby, laughing at the funny ideas people come up with.

I'm having a great time, but Connor's good mood chips away as the night goes on.

Not long after, all of his friends have left us alone at the table while they spread out, grabbing refreshments and dancing.

I hold Connor's hand and play with his fingers while he zones out. "Want to make plans for winter break? We haven't had all that much time together lately."

It takes him a minute to register my question. He's distracted, glaring across the room at Mr. Coleman while he hovers at the edge of the dance floor, smiling at the students having a good time.

"What?"

"I was just saying, maybe we could go to one of the holiday markets or something? Like a mini date adventure."

"Uh, yeah. We'll figure something out." He gives me a smile that doesn't reach his eyes before he settles back in his chair, watching Mr. Coleman while he chaperones.

I drop his hand and rise from my seat to get a drink.

"Where are you going?" Connor's voice stops me before I make it two steps.

"The refreshments table. Do you want anything?"

He gets up and hovers at my back, more like a bodyguard than my date. "I'll go with you."

Getting tired of this putting a damper on our night, I spin to face him, tilting my head. He looks fine, but something is bothering him.

"Are you okay? Things started out great, but you've been weird since we got here."

Connor blinks. He cups my face, his brows pinched. "I'm sorry, baby. I'm fine."

"Are you sure? You can tell me if you're not having a good time. I don't want you to suffer for my sake."

"Yeah, of course. I'm here with you, aren't I?" He bends his head down, kissing me tenderly. "I'm sorry. Let's go dance."

Connor laces his fingers with mine and draws me onto the dance floor as a slow song starts up. The worry plaguing me eases when he smiles at me, a real one this time. Nearby, Blair and Devlin dance together. She looks amazing tonight in her sleek dark gray dress that sparkles when the light hits it, and Devlin looks very dapper beside her in his suit. The two of them are absorbed in each other with twin smiles full of fondness.

"You look beautiful tonight," Connor murmurs, pulling my attention back to him. "Have I told you that yet?"

A slow smile pulls at my mouth. He slides his arms around my waist and rests his forehead against mine. We stay like that through two slow songs, swaying in a tight circle, floating in our own world.

"I'm happy," I whisper, placing my cheek on his chest.

"Yeah? Me too, baby." Connor kisses the top of my head and squeezes me in a tight hug. "All I want to do is make you happy."

"I'm glad Wyatt gave me the wrong number. You're who I'm supposed to be with."

Connor gives me an intent look that pierces through me. The room goes still and my heartbeat speeds up at the way he stares at me.

"Thea, I—" He stops, then takes a breath. "Sunshine, you're my world. I lo—"

Someone bumps into us as the music changes into a faster song, knocking my balance off kilter. Connor catches me.

"Hey! Watch it!" He turns to me. "You okay?"

"Yeah."

The moment we were having is broken. Whatever he was about to say, he lets it go.

Smirking, he says. "You ready?"

"For what?"

"This."

He gets me breathless and laughing as he twirls me around. After a few songs, we're gasping, leaning on each other as we grin bright enough to light the entire room.

"Thirsty?" Connor asks. When I nod, he says, "Be right back."

While he's getting us drinks, I spot Mr. Coleman nearby and head for him.

"Thea. You look lovely tonight." Mr. Coleman's hand lifts for a second, then drops. He curls his fingers into his palm. "Very beautiful."

Blushing, I laugh off his compliment. "I just came over to thank you for pushing me to do the planning committee for the dance. It was fun to work on." I gesture around at all the committee accomplished. "I think the dance turned out really nice."

Mr. Coleman gives me a warm smile. "You're perfect." Clearing his throat, he nods to the dance floor. "Really, I'm so impressed. I knew you'd be perf—"

"Here's your drink, babe." Connor interrupts Mr. Coleman's praise, inserting himself between us and giving Mr. Coleman his back. His face is twisted with tension. "Let's go over there."

Mr. Coleman's expression hardens. Connor ushers me away with a hand at my back, pushing a little harder when I don't move fast enough for him.

"Connor, it's rude to interrupt. And stop pushing me." I step out of reach. "I was having a conversation and you just—"

"Thea, listen," he snaps, then closes his eyes, smothering a frustrated sound. "Sorry. Listen, he's bad news. You have to stay away from him. I turn my back on you for two seconds and you walk right into danger."

"Danger?" I scoff, growing annoyed with his feud with our teacher. "Are you serious? Is this you being jealous again?"

"Don't fight me on this." Connor backs me against the wall, on the outskirts of the dance. His jaw is set in determination. His tone brooks no argument as he lays out his demands. "Stay the fuck away from him."

"How do you expect me to stay away from a teacher I have to see every day for class?" I fold my arms. "He's my favorite teacher. I'm sorry if you feel threatened by that, but I was only—"

"Threatened." The sound that drops from Connor's lips is caustic, far from amusement. "I'm not worried about you crushing on him. I'm worried about what that sick fuck could do to you. It's him I don't trust, not you. I'm trying to *protect* you." He holds my shoulders in a tight grip, pinning me against the wall. "This is serious. I promise, I'll tell you why soon."

I'm not having this. "You don't have to make up wild excuses. If you're determined to ruin our night and not have a good time with me, you can leave."

Connor's jaw works. He's stunned silent. Breathing hard, he balls his fists. "Fine. *Fine*."

"Hey!" Blair Davis pulls Connor off me.

"Stay out of this!" Connor growls before he registers who he's talking to.

Blair narrows her gaze on him and gets in his face, prodding him in the chest. She's fierce and brave, no longer the girl who let anyone get away with the horrible things they did to her. "Quit being such an asshole! You need to stop acting like a god around here. Got it?"

"You don't know what you're talking about," Connor says through clenched teeth. "You're supposed to be on my side here."

"I know exactly what it looked like: you holding your date against the wall against her will. I don't care what you say," Blair snaps. "Try that shit again, and I'll make you regret it. And I don't give a damn if you're Devlin's friend. I'm not scared of you. Hurt her again, and I'm coming for you, Bishop."

Connor looks so pissed off at the accusation he hurt me. His eyes cut to me for a beat and a muscle in his jaw jumps. He storms off, leaving me feeling empty. Tears prick my eyes as he slams his shoulder into Mr. Coleman's on his way out.

I didn't expect him to actually leave. I only wanted him to stop being so controlling.

I thought...

Sunshine, you're my world.

The tears fall, splashing down my cheeks. If he meant what he said, then why did he give up so easily?

Worst of all, I'm worried about what he might do. After he told me about his anger management, I looked up the symptoms and what could happen if he lost control. I don't want him to hurt himself.

"It's about time I returned the favor for all the times you stood up for me," Blair says. "I thought you guys were together. Did he say something to you?"

I look up from wringing my hands to find her peering at me sadly. My lips part, but no words come out, clogging in my throat. I shake my head, on the verge of shattering.

She sighs. "Are you okay?"

I shrug, a wet breath hiccuping out of me.

"Shit," Blair mutters. She rummages through her clutch and pulls out her phone. "Here, look. This always cheers me up."

On her phone, there's a pug dog account on Instagram.

"Watch the video in the third post."

Despite everything, watching the pug dog fly into a pile of leaves, tongue lolling out, does make me smile. A soft, breathy laugh escapes me.

"Thank you."

"Come on," Blair says. "Let's get something to drink."

She leads me toward the refreshment table, rubbing my back. Without Connor here, the dance doesn't seem as magical. The decorations seem childish.

Mr. Coleman catches my eye, but keeps his distance while Blair is with me. Once I wipe my tears, I'll ask him for a ride home so I can go out looking for Connor.

* * *

Blair helped me calm down, showing me more dog videos and keeping me distracted. When Devlin came to stand at her side, looking at her like she hung the stars in his sky, they insisted on giving me a ride home with them, complete with a pit stop for pizza.

I'm glad I went with them. Getting pizza while all dressed up lifted my mood. They kept my mind off everything as Blair and I argued about the merits of pineapple on pizza against Devlin's firm belief that fruit didn't go on pizza.

The wariness I used to have toward Devlin has slipped away. Beneath his brooding outer shell, he's intelligent and has a wicked sense of humor. Spending time with him, I think I understand him better. Devlin isn't the cold, brutal devil he presents himself as, he's selective about who he lets in past his walls. He and Blair are a sight to behold when they get going, everything about them pointing to *power couple*.

It's nice to see how different they are now. In the back of the limo, they murmur to each other. Devlin holds Blair in his arms.

I peek shyly in my peripheral vision, pretending to mess around on my phone.

They seem happy. The way Devlin looks at Blair makes an ache settle in my chest, both with happiness that someone can love that deeply and with a pang of want. I thought Connor looked at me like that tonight, but the way he left has me questioning whether we're okay or not.

The limo is close to my house. My grip tightens on my phone.

Devlin cuts into my thoughts. "Bishop probably didn't mean what he said. That's why he wanted us to make sure you got home safely. He's…" A sigh escapes him. "I know how his head works. If he loses control, he acts without thinking."

There seems to be something else he's not saying because he shifts around. Blair puts her hand on his thigh and squeezes. They share a look and Blair gives a tiny shake of her head. Devlin shrugs. I blink at the odd exchange.

"Well, thanks," I say as the car pulls up to my house. The lights are all dark. I guess Mom was too tired to stay up late judging me after her snide comment about what boys expect at the end of a dance. She hasn't figured out yet that Connor and I are way past that point. The only thing on my mind is changing out of this dress so I can head out in my Mini Cooper to look for Connor. "I'm sorry I had to cut your night short. I hope you liked the dance."

"It was great," Blair says. "Typical teen scene isn't really my thing, but it was nice to try it on for a while."

Devlin snorts at some private joke between them. He turns his attention to me. "He means well."

I grant him a tight smile and climb from the limo, knowing I won't get any sleep tonight until I know Connor is safe and not doing something self-destructive. Something was bothering him all night and I need to find out what it was.

TWENTY-EIGHT
Connor

When the limo pulls away, I step out of the shadows as Thea walks up to her door.

"I'm sorry."

She jumps, hissing out a strangled, "Jesus, Connor." Looking me up and down, she frowns. "I'm glad you're not out doing something stupid. I was really worried about you."

My breath punches from me. I go off like that and she's worried about me?

I'm such an asshole. My girlfriend is right in front of me, stunning in the moonlight in her pink dress and white wool coat. Tonight was the one thing she asked me for and instead of making her night magical, I was on the defensive. I was too focused on the plan to break into Coleman's house in a few days that I pushed her away. It was only for her protection, but now that I see the sadness in her eyes I know I fucked up.

With a sigh, I scrub a hand through my hair. "Sorry. I messed it all up. I didn't mean to ruin the night. I had to get out of there, or I was going to put my fist through the wall, or..." I shake my head.

She doesn't want to hear about me punching Coleman.

I hold out my hand, heart hammering in my chest. "It doesn't matter. I was wrong and I shouldn't have left you alone. I want to show you something to make it up to you. Will you come with me for a drive?"

Thea studies me for a long beat where I think she's going to refuse. She should, after the way I treated her.

"Where are we going?"

I swallow in relief.

"I want to take you to a special place. It's where I go when I need to cool my head."

The wariness in Thea's gaze softens. "Promise me one thing."

"Anything."

"You don't dictate my life. You can't tell me what I can and can't do. You know why I hate that."

My gaze cuts away. I do know. She's told me about her issues with her mom being controlling and conservative. I can't help that in my effort to protect her from the threat Coleman poses, and from the mysterious hacking group using her as incentive to do what they told me to, I became forceful with her.

Controlling is the only way I know how to be. Without it, I turn wild. Learning to give that up when I know I'm keeping her safe is a daily challenge.

She takes my hand in both of hers, her eyes bouncing between mine when they fly back to her. The sight of her causes a pang in my chest with her flower crown, those big doe eyes, and the tilt of her pouty lips.

I open my mouth to swear to her.

But I can't.

The only choice I have is to lie, and that frustrates the hell out of me. I don't want to lie to her, but I can't freak her out with this, either. Bile rises in my throat, keeping me from betraying her.

This is all for her own good. I can't stop the plan now. Once I get into Coleman's house with Devlin and Blair's help, then this will all be over. I'll give Thea anything she wants afterwards, even if she demands I walk away from her.

It'll kill me to leave her when I'm in love with her, but this will be the last promise to her I ever break.

Thea isn't the meek girl I used to think she was, but I won't hurt her by scaring her with the monsters waiting to take a bite out of her.

It's a huge risk, putting everything between us in jeopardy.

Instead of the promise she wants, I aim for a little honesty, because it's what she'll listen to.

"I can't promise you that yet." At Thea's crumbling expression, I rush the rest of my explanation out. "I want to, baby. So badly. But this is really big. Bigger than dirty politics and cover ups. I swear to you, I would never control you like she tries to. I know you're strong and capable of making your own choices. Please. Trust me?"

"We've had good communication to solve our issues before," Thea murmurs. "I trust you with my secrets, and you trust me with yours. So why are you keeping something from me?"

Damn her logic. She has me there. Forcing out a breath, I scrub the back of my neck.

"Everything I do is to keep you safe. Can you trust that?"

Thea studies me. "I know you'd never hurt me."

"I wouldn't. Just—give me a few days, okay? I swear, I'll tell you everything."

"Okay. As long as you tell me." She gives me that fierce look full of fire that I love. "Don't think I'll forget it."

A weak laugh leaves me as I gather her in my arms, inhaling her sugary scent mixing with the flowers. "You? Never. You're too sharp for that."

I stay like that for a minute, breathing her in while my stomach unknots. I can't mess this up. She's my everything. The only good thing to ever happen to me.

She presses up on her toes, kissing me with so much tenderness that my breath comes out shaky. I lean my forehead against hers and tell her what I wanted to earlier.

"I'm in love with you." Her gasp is soft and she goes still. Before she says anything, I go on in a reverent tone. "I didn't notice you. All these years, and I never looked twice at you. But you were right there the whole time, living next door." I lean back to meet her eyes, tucking her hair as I pour my heart out. "I see you now, Thea. You're so bright, I don't know how I ever missed it. Your light glows, in the day or at night."

"Connor," she whispers, eyes wide and shiny.

The corner of my mouth lifts and fondness fills me. "You make me feel like the moon, desperate to chase the sun. You're all I want to look at, sunshine. All I want to catch."

The smile that breaks out on Thea's face is stunning. A laugh escapes her and she winds her arms around my neck in a hug.

"I love you, too." Her voice is muffled against my chest.

Taking her hand, I back up a step. "Let's sneak out for that drive. I want to show you my favorite place."

We hop in the Lexus and when Thea turns to me, I shoot out a hand to cover her eyes. "Don't look around. Keep your eyes shut."

She laughs, brushing her fingertips over my knuckles. "Why?"

"Don't want to ruin the surprise I put together for you."

Biting her lip around a smile, she covers her eyes with her own hands.

"Are they closed?" I squint at her.

"Yes!"

"Good. No peeking."

Shifting the car in gear, we drive off, leaving the neighborhood. The streets of Ridgeview are quiet this late. It's past eleven as we drive the winding roads leading up into the mountains that overlook the town. When we reach our destination, I back the car in.

"Keep them closed still," I say as I open my door.

"Okay," Thea drawls, tipping her head back against the seat. With her eyes scrunched tight, she lifts the flower crown from her head and rests it in her lap.

It's cold up at Peak Point. We're the only ones here and I made sure it would stay that way. It's the most popular place to hook up, but I come here for a different reason. I blow into my hands as I round to the back, opening the trunk so we'll have the perfect view. Inside the SUV, I built a nest of blankets, pillows, and a strand of battery powered Christmas lights to make it festive. When I click them on, they blink in multicolor.

Once I'm satisfied with the set up, I go to Thea's door and open it. "Take my hands. I'll guide you. That's it—watch your step."

I want to kiss the crinkle in her nose as I walk backwards toward the rear of the SUV. When I have her in position, I lick my lips.

"Okay. Open."

Thea's lashes flutter and she takes in the sight of Ridgeview lit up at night, tiny lights filling the valley below us from the high vantage point.

"Wow," she breathes.

"Yeah." I'm looking at her instead of the town below. "I know it's just Peak Point, but it's my favorite place. I sit up here for hours when I need to cool my head."

"It's so pretty at night."

"Seeing it all lit up and small reminds me that whatever I've turned into a big problem doesn't have to be in the scope of things."

She turns to me with a smile. "I love it."

"You'll love it more when you turn around. It's too cold." Nudging her by the shoulders, I show her the fort I built in the back of the SUV for us. Her delighted laughter echoes off the tree tops as I help her climb in. "Let's warm up."

"Thank you. This surprise is amazing," Thea says once we're comfortably entwined and burrowed in the blankets to keep out the biting chill. She traces my jaw. "I love you."

"You make me fall in love with you over and over." Cradling her face in my hands, I hover my lips over hers. "The world doesn't matter. Only us. Right here. Only this."

"Only us," Thea repeats, her eyes hooded.

I slant my mouth over hers. She plays with the hair at the nape of my neck as we fall into the pile of blankets, kissing like the world could end and we still wouldn't stop, wouldn't part from each other.

My hands slide into her coat to get at the curves of her body. She arches against me and a faint moan fills the back of the SUV. I take her mouth again, a rough sound catching in my throat.

This is my favorite place now. Right here, with her in my arms.

Layer by layer, our clothes come off as our bodies tangle together. We close the door to engulf ourselves in a cocoon of our own making. The chill from outside is forgotten as we heat up the back of the car.

"I want you," Thea begs as I kiss a trail from her breasts down her stomach, settling between her legs.

"Soon, baby." I stroke her hips and place feather-light kisses over her thighs, then her folds, teasing her until she shakes. I give her a long lick with my tongue where she needs me, enjoying the broken sound that flies past her lips. "First, let me worship you."

Gripping her thighs, I bury my face between her legs, licking and sucking until Thea is crying out, rolling her hips to ride my face. The sounds she makes while she comes have me grinning against her pussy, my face a mess as I flick my tongue against her clit.

"Love making you fall apart like that," I rasp, shooting a cocksure look up the length of her body.

"Please, please, I need you now." Thea tugs on my shoulders, half sitting up to capture my lips in a kiss, moaning into my mouth when she tastes herself on my lips.

Without breaking the kiss, I roll us over, grinding my cock against her. Fuck, her body feels incredible and I can't wait to drive into her. I fumble around for my pants to get the condom, finally forced to stop kissing her to tear the packet and roll it on. She makes me so wild every time, I'm close to the edge before I'm inside her.

Thea sits up on her knees with a spark of determination in her eye that's so sexy. The look in her blue-green gaze has my groin tightening with a coil of heat. Before I can go to her, she straddles my lap, bracing her hands on my shoulders and sinks down on my cock.

We both release a groan, leaning into each other for a moment. Nothing can touch us. It's me and her, the way I want it to always be. My hands find her hips, squeezing as she starts riding me at a slow pace.

"God, you're incredible." I kiss anywhere I can reach—her neck, her chest, between her breasts as they brush against my jaw. "My beautiful sunshine."

Thea winds her arms around my neck and drops her forehead against mine, meeting my gaze as we move together, making love in the back of my car beneath the moon.

My breath grows shallow and I sink a hand into her hair when the pleasure becomes too much to withstand, gritting my teeth to hold on for her a little longer.

"Thea," I whisper, tensing.

"Yes. Let go with me." She tips her head back with a moan and I feel her squeezing my cock, driving me over the edge.

We're both left panting by our orgasms. I stroke her hair and pull the blankets around us, keeping her in my lap.

If I could freeze time, I'd pick this moment to stay in forever. Right where I belong.

TWENTY-NINE
Connor

Weeks of planning brought me here, sitting shotgun in one of Devlin's dad's cars—one of the lower end luxury models to blend in—parked near Harold Coleman's house.

Tonight, I'm breaking into my English teacher's house for a group of mysterious hackers obsessed with crows and skulls.

He lives on a quiet street on the outskirts of the town center, with only a handful of other houses on the block. Most are decorated for the holidays, lit up and festive. His is the only one that's not decked out, except for a sad little lawn sign that says happy holidays with a snowflake on it.

Winter break starts tomorrow. We picked tonight because Coleman would be stuck late at school with meetings to close out the first semester. Blair's tailing him as our lookout, Devlin's the getaway driver, and my job is breaking in to get the locket the Anonymous wannabes demanded before they give me the dirt on Coleman.

"You're sure about this? The time to back out is now." Devlin rests his hand over the wheel. He's a ride or die friend, no matter what I say he's down to back me.

I think about how pretty Thea was the other night at the dance in her gauzy pink dress, then later, even more beautiful beneath blinking Christmas lights in the back of my SUV. My heart squeezes.

"No doubts, bro." Devlin and Lucas both found their queens in Blair and Gemma. I'm doing this to make sure mine has her place of honor by my side. I'll do whatever it takes to protect her. "I'm going in there."

Devlin gives me one of his sadistic grins. He's living for this epic mischief making. This is bigger than any of our pranks.

"What do you think you'll find?" Devlin muses.

I suppress a shudder. I haven't wanted to think about it, braced for the most depraved shit my twisted imagination could think of.

"The truth. Probably a sad as fuck, lonely life."

Devlin hums in agreement.

I haven't told Devlin and Blair everything. I glossed over the details about Thea, but to a creepy online persona. Devlin is the one who guessed Coleman has an interest in Thea going off my short fuse and his own observations.

Blair's been ready to cut off Coleman's balls ever since, sitting in third period English like she's prepared for battle.

We're waiting for her confirmation in the group chat on our phones before I go. Her criminal tendencies and pick-pocketing talents have come in handy planning out the logistics of tonight.

"What's the psychology behind a predator?" I ask.

Devlin cocks his head in thought. He has a strong interest in psychology, always carrying a book with him.

"It always comes down to power. But in this case, it's like the victims aren't people. They serve their purpose fulfilling a sexual desire. A predator is a hunter. They know to set themselves up for success by working on a victim who is vulnerable and already susceptible to being manipulated into doing whatever the predator wants," he says after a minute. "It's abusive."

The answer has my blood boiling. Thinking of Thea in that frame of mind, her window right across from mine.

Damn it.

Our phones ping at the same time. When I check, I shake my head.

Blair: All this sneaking around brings back memories [smirk emoji]

Devlin's answer pops up in the conversation.

Devlin: [smirking devil emoji] you just wait until we get home, little thief.

"Can you two not flirt in the group chat? You're nauseating with your lovey-dovey sap shit."

Devlin just smirks while Blair sends a selfie of her leather-glove covered middle finger in front of her face to our group text. A minute later, she hits us up again.

Blair: Ok, meeting started. Timer begins now.

With the go ahead, I tug a beanie on and put up the hood on my black hoodie.

"Gloves," Devlin says, handing them over.

"Thanks, man. For everything."

"You're family. We go to war for family."

"You big fuckin' sap. Love you, bro."

"Shut up. Go be a badass."

Saluting him with a crooked grin, I get out of the car and act like I belong here.

The house is quaint, with blue shingles and a porch. It pisses me off how easily Coleman gets to blend in when he's a fucking creep preying on young girls. Who knows how many? The thought turns my stomach. I'm here for a locket, so I can only guess Thea isn't the only honey pot he's tried dipping his claws in.

Gritting my teeth, I check if anyone's around before I slip toward the back door to pick the lock.

Blair let me borrow her kit of picks and drilled me until I could pick Coleman's brand of lock with my eyes closed. It comes in handy that Dev's girl has a history of criminal tendencies. I kneel at the back door and get started, carefully working it until the knob gives way.

"Gotcha." Tucking away the tools, I step inside, leaving the lights off and illuminating the way with my phone.

The inside of Coleman's house tells a much different story than the charming young teacher persona he puts on at school. My lip curls as I move through the dated kitchen to a living room with grime-stained walls. This place looks fine from the outside, but it's a shithole. He must've got it real cheap because it looks like it was a crack den. Empty take out containers and instant dinner dishes sit around, making the place smell rank. They're at least two days old.

"Fucking gross," I grumble, scanning the room.

There are no signs of a partner or roommates. The place is sparsely furnished. Every inch of the house screams shut in bachelor.

Coleman clearly spends a lot of time on his computer. It's a setup like mine and the only corner of the room that seems frequently used. A serious system with big monitors, like a skeevy command base. I picture him sitting there typing that shit to Thea and ball my fists to control the wave of fury crashing over me. Blowing out a breath, I cross to the computer and tap a key.

The display wakes up and I smirk. "Thanks for the easy access."

I plug in an encrypted drive and type in a keyboard shortcut to bring up a command prompt window, giving me admin control. With a few more keystrokes, his hard drive is downloading for me. While that's running, I head into the other rooms to search for the necklace and hunt down anything else I can find.

The house is a single floor bungalow, so there are only so many places for Coleman to hide his sinister corruption. I start with the bedroom, which makes me gag.

Black silk sheets? Is he fucking kidding?

As the creep factor climbs, so does my anger. I take pictures of everything to paint the image of Harold K. Coleman, perverted douchebag degenerate. The darkest monster I've ever met. Considering the secrets I know of the people in this town, that's saying something.

"Going to have to shower eighty goddamn times to get the vibe of this place off me."

The closet has nothing interesting, so I try the bureau, pulling drawers out and rifling through ratty pairs of sweatpants and stained graphic t-shirts. What a man-child.

When I don't find anything, I'm about to look under the bed, but the third drawer down on the left makes me pause. The grain on the bottom of the drawer is a shade off from the others. I shine the flashlight from my phone closer, furrowing my brow. I pull out the drawer on the right side to compare, putting my hands in both.

"Shit."

The one on the left is slightly higher. It's a fake bottom. I take out the stacks of clothes, taking care not to mess up the order so Coleman doesn't suspect anything. There's a tiny tab at the back. When I pull on it, I'm able to remove the false cover.

My heart stops.

A row of necklaces sits in the drawer on black velvet. All matching.

At first I suck in a breath, thinking I've found the locket. But no, these aren't silver. They're gold plated. Cheap. Each heart pendant sits on a slip of paper with Coleman's handwriting.

Girl's names.

These are disgusting collars of ownership for every girl Coleman is manipulating. He probably sends them as gifts to make the girls feel special, when he's got six other duplicates. If they feel doted on, he must have an easier time controlling them to do whatever he wants.

Acidic bile rushes up my throat.

"Jesus fucking christ." My teeth clench hard enough to crack.

It takes a long minute to control the powerful instinct to punch through the wall as hard as I can as an outlet for the rage.

I snap several photos on my phone, documenting closeups of the name tags, each necklace, and the hidden compartment in the drawer. My phone vibrates with an incoming call, sending my heart into an awful adrenaline spike. It's Thea.

My chest goes tight and my attention drops to her necklace, second in the row. What a cruel twist of fate that she ended up vulnerable and pliant to fall into this monster's trap. "I'm sorry, baby."

I grip my phone tight, rubbing my forehead with the back of my hand, and let her call go to voicemail. I can't afford to get distracted when I need to be ready for Devlin and Blair's signal while I search. If I answered, I don't know if I'd be strong enough to keep this secret from her. As soon as I give the crow guys what they want, I'm telling Thea everything.

And I'll never let her near Coleman again. She'll be safe.

Once I know she's protected, I'm coming for Coleman. The proof of his evil is here. If Landry won't listen to me, I'll go over his head. Whatever it takes to put Coleman away for his crimes.

He won't hurt anyone ever again.

Putting everything back the way I found it in the drawer is one of the hardest things I've ever done. Every part of my being screams at me to grab the necklaces, that it's wrong to let Coleman keep these like he hasn't been caught. With a rough sound, I turn my back on the bureau.

A single nightstand sits beside the bed. I head there next.

For a minute, I stare down at the dark wood, rubbing my fingers to gear up to continue the search. I force out a ragged breath and brace for the worst as I open the first drawer. My nose wrinkles at the tube of lotion mixed in with an inhaler and other odds and ends. There's nothing else, so I go for the second drawer.

At first glance, anyone could mistake it for a junk drawer.

But amongst charm bracelets, a headband, two leather cuffs, and a picture keychain I find a silver locket. *Trophies.* Before I do anything, I pull up my phone camera and grab several shots of the drawer's contents.

My hand shakes as I take the locket, checking it.

The initials *CT* are engraved on the silver heart.

This is the one.

My gaze flicks from the bed back to the drawer. He keeps them right next to where he sleeps. An uncomfortable shudder wracks my body.

"I will end you, if it's the last thing I ever do," I growl, stuffing the locket in my pocket.

I have what I came here for, but I want to keep going. As soon as I finish the bedroom, my phone buzzes, signaling my time is up. Opening the group chat confirms it.

Blair: On the move. 15min ETA.

A second later, Devlin revs the engine outside.

"Damn it." I cast a glance around the room I was checking.

Connor: 2 mins [sweat smile emoji]
Devlin: Now. Christ, only you would use emojis at a time like this.

Gritting my teeth, I rush into the living room to check the download status. A relieved breath leaves me. It finished. I've got it all. Ejecting the thumb drive and closing out of everything, I put his computer to sleep the way I found it.

Once I'm outside, I cut through the shadows and bushes, emerging on the street as if I was there all along. Moving quickly, I slide into the passenger seat of Devlin's car. He doesn't wait until my door is fully closed before pulling away, peeling down a side street and shifting gear.

It's not until we're five minutes away that he speaks. "Did you find it?"

"Yeah." I stare out the window, fist covering my mouth. "I'll show you when we meet up with Blair."

Devlin scoffs, shaking his head. "Knew he wasn't right."

While he drives, I reach in the back and take out my tablet from the backpack on the floor, plugging in the encrypted drive. I push off my hood and drag off the beanie as the thumb drive connects. My throat goes dry and scratchy once I get into Coleman's files.

It doesn't take me long to find. She's right there in a photo on his local drive, along with other girls. Each photo is labeled with a name. Thea, Charlotte, Jen, Alicia...

My nostrils flare before I finish checking all the names. Some are tame, like Thea's, but others are far less so. I almost throw the tablet out the window, but I control myself. Instead, I put the photos in a folder to separate them from the ones I can stomach, where the girls aren't baring themselves to this disgusting asshole.

With images like these, he could do anything with them. Start a porn site. Sell them. A sharp pain stabs in my gut as nausea rolls through me.

Steeling myself, I sift through what's left in the folder.

In Charlotte's photo, she's wearing the same locket burning a hole in my pocket. She's a pretty blond, around the age Thea was in her blog photos, maybe a little younger.

In Thea's photo, the metadata tells me it's three years old, from when she was fifteen. She's in her room, the colorful baking pun posters visible behind her. She's not nude, but her outfit is revealing and the way she poses is suggestive. I shift uncomfortably in my seat, plagued with the skeeze feeling again.

The thought of Coleman having this photo, and others like it, makes me want to scream and go fucking wild. If I was unleashed on him right now, I'd kill him. No mercy.

It's no wonder Thea started dressing in less form-fitting clothes after going through however long of dressing like this for an older man she didn't know on the internet.

In the same folder, there are saved transcripts from conversations. I can't look at any at the moment, too wired by my anger to face more of Coleman's depravity poisoning these young girls. Regulating my breath is difficult. Thankfully we're almost to the abandoned quarry.

Shame there isn't a fight tonight. Then again, I'm so ready to go off, I might be a danger to myself and others, like Doctor Levitt warned me.

Devlin pulls in, parking behind the rusted old storage building next to the car Blair is leaning against. He cuts the engine and we climb out.

"Did you get it?" Blair asks.

Without a word, I unlock my phone and hand it to her, jaw clenched.

"Shit," Blair hisses, scrolling through the photos. Devlin leans over her shoulder, scowling. "What a sick dickhead."

"I'll kill him." I stalk away, grabbing one of the broken old pieces of steel littering the ground around the building.

"Bishop," Devlin calls.

"Just—give me a minute, man. It's too much. If I don't get it out, it'll eat me up."

He and Blair exchange a glance. They leave me alone as they go through what I found on my phone. Seeing the way Devlin rubs Blair's arms when a chilly breeze moves through the clearing makes me ache to speed across town to tuck Thea in my arms.

Releasing a harsh yell, I swing the metal with all my might against the ground, leaving a deep dent in the gravel. I lose myself in it for several minutes, pouring the torrent of emotions into destruction. By the time I come back to myself, I'm panting.

"Feel better?" Blair asks lightly as I walk back to them.

"Much." With a sigh, I toss the busted up piece of steel aside into a patch of scrubby weeds and drag a hand through my hair. "So. Yeah. Coleman."

"Coleman," Devlin repeats in a dark tone.

"Dead man fucking walking," I utter harshly.

"Exactly," Devlin agrees.

All three of us are pissed off by the pictures I took. I'm glad I have the two of them with me so I don't have to deal with this alone. Now that the adrenaline and fury are under control, I'm itching to get out of here so I can send proof, get the unsealed files from those hackers, and finally tell Thea what I've been keeping from her.

"Did you take the locket?" Blair holds up my phone, showing me the photo of the trophy drawer.

My lip curls. I pull out the necklace by the chain, the pendant dangling in the air.

She leans in to examine it. "What do you think those guys who hacked your computer will do?"

"They seem pretty dangerous." I shrug. "And they wanted it fast. If they don't do something by next week, I will."

"I knew he was a creep, but thinking of sitting through class with him is—ugh." Blair shakes off her shudder, burrowing into Devlin's side. He wraps his arms around her. To anyone else it might look like a normal embrace, but Devlin's knuckles turn white from how tight he clings to her, like he's preventing her from disappearing on him after he almost lost her. "I'm so grossed out right now."

Devlin props his chin on Blair's head and cuts his gaze to me. "Ready to head home?"

"Yes. I have the proof one way or another. Time to do what I do best."

"You're a real piece of work when you go into blackmail mode." Devlin smirks, tossing me a set of keys. "Here, take that one. I'll pick it up tomorrow."

"Thanks," I call to them as Devlin opens the passenger door for Blair. "No one I'd rather commit a crime with than you two."

Blair snorts, glancing up at Devlin.

"Go be the Batman to your girlfriend." He nods to me before he gets in the driver's seat and revs the engine.

I watch as the wheels throw gravel and dust while Devlin pulls out of the quarry.

Getting into the car Blair had been driving, I grip the wheel tight. I'm a man on a mission as I turn the ignition and drive home.

THIRTY
Thea

When my call goes to Connor's voicemail, I hang my shoulders in defeat. I thought things would be better after our amazing night in the mountains, but I haven't been able to get a hold of him for days. Every time I look across the space between our windows, his light has been off.

"You've reached Bishop. You know I don't check this shit, so I don't know why you're bothering. Text me."

There goes my plan to invite him with Maisy and I to the holiday bazaar downtown. Winter break is off to a great start with my boyfriend back to avoiding me.

With a sigh, I set my phone next to the rainbow clock on my nightstand and flop on the bed, hugging my stuffed sea lion.

An unpleasant flutter fills my chest.

Could Connor be bored with me? If he is, why would he tell me...

I close my eyes and just breathe for a second to stop the racing thoughts and nasty inner voice that makes me doubt everything. No matter how hard I try, I can't keep it at bay.

You're not good enough to keep someone like him. He'll forget you soon enough.

I swallow past the lump in my throat. The thoughts chew me up, leaving me raw and vulnerable. Curling on my side, I hug the sea lion tighter, burying my face in the plush fuzziness.

I can't go back to being invisible. Not to him.

After a few minutes of breathing through the thorns twining around my heart, pricking at every insecurity, I get up and pat my puffy cheeks.

"This calls for double chocolate fudge cupcakes."

With a sniffle, I text Maisy before the evening yoga sessions start at the wellness and recreation center she volunteers for.

Thea: Great British Bake Off marathon after your class?
Maisy: You got it, dude. Which season?
Thea: [hiding monkey emoji] All of them...?
Maisy: Oh lordt. Should I cancel class? The yoga moms can survive one day without their warrior 2 and downward dog.

Thea: No, no. I'm going to bake us cupcakes until you get here. See you after class!

Maisy sends me two peace sign emojis and promises not to eat all the cupcakes this time. I pull on the hoodie I stole from Connor, press the neckline to my nose, and close my eyes. It feels like he's hugging me when I wear it.

Downstairs, Constantine follows me into the kitchen while I tie my hair back in a pony tail. A few minutes later I have the oven preheating, my supplies are out, and the cupcakes are underway.

I'm still feeling sensitive about Connor as I'm mixing the batter when Mom walks in, eyeing me critically. I'm too tired to fend her off if she says anything about wearing my boyfriend's hoodie.

"Mom," I say in greeting while she pours herself a glass of wine. It's not her first of the day.

"What are you making today?" she asks after a minute of stale silence.

An exhale leaves me, unwinding the tension in my shoulders. It's okay. She's going to be normal and not attack me.

"Double chocolate fudge cupcakes. Extra gooey." I direct my hesitant smile at the mixing bowl. "Would you rather have peanut butter or cream cheese frosting?"

Mom says nothing. I look up to find her gaze narrowed on me in disappointment.

"Yeah..." I trail off. "You're right. Peanut butter would probably be too rich with the chocolate. Still, I'm kind of craving it, so I guess I'll make a batch of both."

I'm desperate for a scrap of normalcy with her. It's always made me crazy that I can't have the same bond with her I had with grandma. Part of me wonders if she's resented me all these years because I liked baking and she never did, so grandma and I had something Mom couldn't get from her.

"Are those for that horrible boy next door?" The acid in her voice stings.

A weak protest catches in my throat. I was wrong. She's primed for attack after all, and I'm too drained to clash with her.

Mom continues before I can push any response out, planting her hands on the island between us. "Look at you, like his little housewife baking away. You have to understand, Thea. Men aren't trustworthy." Her voice drops to a horrible, grating whisper as she tears into me. "His doting is all a lie. He doesn't want you. All of them are the same—only after one thing."

"Mom, can we not?" With a frown, I shut her out, keeping my spine straight as I work on the batter. "I'm so tired of having this argument."

Circling the island, she pinches the sleeve of Connor's hoodie and yanks. "We clearly need to have it. You must've given him what he wanted, so now he'll drop you. If that's all he does, you'll be lucky."

The words cut deep, blow after fatal blow.

She hasn't bothered me with this in over a month, so she must have been bottling it up to dump on me all at once. I clutch the whisk hard enough the handle leaves an indent in my palm.

"Mom, please," I whisper in a tight voice, holding back the tears pooling in my eyes.

I've held out against her for so long, never giving in. But everything she's saying pulls on the same fears that haunted me in my bedroom when Connor didn't take my call.

"You're going to end up just like my sister."

I blink. "Wait—what?"

Mom closes her eyes. "You had an aunt. My younger sister. Momma's favorite."

This is news to me. I knew Mom and grandma had bad blood between them all the way up to when she passed away, but this is something Mom has never talked about.

"She met a boy when she was in high school, about your age. I'd gone off to college and couldn't keep an eye on her." Mom's lip curls, gulping her wine. Now she's so close, I can smell it on her breath. Her eyes are too bright. "She was always dressing for attention and it caught his eye. He was older, but it doesn't matter. They all want one thing. He got it from her, all right. Left her dead in a ditch for it once he had her body."

"Mom," I breathe. "Jesus."

Everything about her strictness with me, why she's always nagged me to dress conservatively, becomes crystal clear. But it doesn't mean Connor is like the man who hurt her sister.

She's silent for a beat, eyes glassy. "Too infatuated. Thought he hung the moon. Just like you."

"I—Connor isn't like that. He's always been sweet and gentle with me, even when we—" I cut off. Crap. "He's a good guy, Mom."

She folds her arms and nods like she has all the confirmation she needs. "You should've listened to me in the first place."

With the satisfaction of the final word and making me feel small on top of telling me about her sister's death, she takes her wine—the glass and the bottle—and leaves me alone, crying over my cupcake batter.

THIRTY-ONE
Connor

THERE was nothing I wanted more than to go straight to Thea after I left Coleman's place. But first I have to know what the mysterious hackers have on him. Once I get all the concrete evidence, I'll take every damning piece of it to her.

Damien didn't even register as I blew through the kitchen and took the stairs two at a time to my room. Slamming down in the chair at my desk, I hook up the encrypted drive and my phone to input what I found at Coleman's house. I pull out the locket and set it next to the computer as I work.

It occurs to me when I'm halfway through adding the new information on Coleman to the file in my app, I have no idea how to contact Dolos. No sooner does the thought cross my mind, a chat window pops up in the middle of the screen.

"Backdoor? Those douchebags." I try to navigate away or close the window, but the only access I have is the chat window.

An irritated sound rumbles in my throat. This is pissing me off. My system isn't easy to hack. I pride myself on the security measures I have in place to prevent compromises, but they're able to slip past them with ease.

Dolos: Well? We know you infiltrated Coleman's residence tonight.
Connor: The fuck? Were you watching me the whole time?
Dolos: Someone had to check you were doing as we said.
Connor: I thought you didn't know where he lived?
Dolos: We didn't. You found it, we traced your phone.
Connor: Whatever. Give me what you promised.
Dolos: Proof first. Take a picture.

Blowing out a breath, I lift the locket as my webcam connects. I peel off the electrical tape I cover the camera with and hold the locket close.

Dolos: Good.

A second later, a compressed file labeled HKC comes through, along with control of my computer again. I hold my breath as I double click to open it. Once it's ready, air hisses from my lungs.

"Holy shit."

It's all there. Reports, police records, employment history. Between the stuff at his house and the files documenting his previous two employer records—both with complaints of sexual harassment and inappropriate conduct with minors in his charge—I have more than enough to make a move.

I'm so focused on combing through the information in the unsealed files, I almost miss the new message blinking in the chat window.

Dolos: Now we start the next phase. Stay put.

"What? No." My brows pinch as I type.

Connor: Fuck that. Wherever you are, you can suck it. He's here and he's a threat.
Dolos: You will do nothing.

I don't answer to these assholes. I'm getting fed up with them telling me what to do. Screw waiting, it's time to act.

Dolos: Don't be an idiot when you still have that cute little neighbor to think of. We hate making threats against the innocent ones.

Fuck.

Connor: Fine. What's the next phase?

They don't answer. The window disappears and the screen goes black, flashing with a laughing skull being circled by another 8-bit crow.

"Assholes." I reboot my computer once again, really hating their idea of goodbye.

Every part of me revolts at the thought of sitting on my hands. I've done enough of that. If I don't do something, Coleman has more chances to hurt Thea.

Why should I sit around and wait for whoever the hell these guys are when they're somewhere else and I'm here in town with a monster hyper-focused on my girl?

I'll die before I let the crows or Coleman touch her.

All I want to do is protect Thea. She won't slip through my grasp.

THIRTY-TWO
Thea

In the morning, I feel like a husk. Maisy stayed up with me half the night after we gorged our way through the cupcakes, then ate frosting directly out of the mixing bowl during three full seasons of feel-good bake off competition. She helped me through the shock of finding out I should have an aunt.

Grandma never said anything. Maybe Mom forced her to hide it from me, but my heart aches for her, losing a daughter at such a young age in a horrible way.

Groggy, I roll over in bed. Maisy is starfished, arms and legs spread to take up most of the mattress while I'm curled against the edge. It's funny that such a kind-hearted, giving person can be such a bed hog. I somehow end up fighting her skinny butt for space every time we've shared a bed over the years.

With a groan, I nudge her. "Up. Or move. Whatever you want, just do something because I'm about to fall off."

Maisy cracks one hazel eye open, squinting at me. "Demon."

"Maise." I laugh as she burrows further under the covers.

"The sugar coma I'm coming off of might be the end of me. We had a good run, bestie." She shuffles over, reaching out blindly to drag me closer. "How are you feeling?"

"I'll be okay, I think. Thank you." I massage my forehead. "It was a lot on top of an already emotional state of mind."

Maisy hums, hugging me. "Do you still want to go to the holiday market? Instead we could do a face mask spa day. Meditate it out? Or do I need to pull out the big guns with goat yoga?"

A sleep-tinged, husky chuckle rolls out of me. "Actually, I think I'm going to shower and head next door. I want to see if Connor is home before we go to the holiday market."

"Mind, body, and spirit self-care bonding with a friend passed over for the power of a good dicking," Maisy teases, pinching my sides where I'm ticklish.

I flail in my attempt to escape. "Maise, no!" I wail, clawing my way to freedom while she tortures me with precise attacks. "God, you're the worst! You know it's not like that!"

Laughing, she sits back against my headboard. "I know. The vagina needs its own worship to achieve the zen of self-care, too."

"Oh my god, you're such a weirdo." I flop on my back, head dangling off the bed. "Love you."

"Love you back," she sings. "We'll meet up later by the entrance to the bazaar?"
"Of course."
"Sweet. Dibs on the shower first."
"Go ahead. I'll take one later.

As Maisy heads for the bathroom, I try messaging Connor again.

Thea: Are you around?

No response comes by the time she's done.

* * *

An hour later, I'm standing outside Connor's house after lunch time. I don't know what I expected when I knocked on the door, but it wasn't Mrs. Bishop answering instead of him. She's dressed down, rather than the power suits I typically see her in. Maybe she has off from city council duties today.

"Oh. Sorry, I don't mean to interrupt your day, Mrs. Bishop."

Mrs. Bishop leans against the door frame, rather than welcoming me inside. "Vivian, please. What is it?"

"Is Connor home?"

She sweeps her gaze over me, pursing her lips. It's the most expressive reaction I've witnessed since that night in the coat closet at the benefit dinner.

"Come inside." Without waiting, Vivian turns and walks deeper in the house.

I follow, unable to shake the uneasiness clinging to me. "Is he here, or...?"

"No. Left early and wouldn't say where he was going." She stops and turns on her heel when we reach the kitchen. "You can wait here for him. Would you like some tea?"

"Okay." I take a tentative seat at the island. "Thank you."

She smiles without moving the upper half of her face. It's disconcerting. "Be right back."

I'm not waiting long before she returns with a manila folder. She must be working from home. She paces on the other side of the island.

"Sorry again for interrupting." I gesture at the folder she's flipping through. "I haven't heard from Connor in a few days, so I was worried and wanted to stop by to see if he wanted to go to the holiday market downtown."

Vivian lifts a brow with her attention on the contents in the folder, but doesn't answer.

"I'm going to make you an offer," she announces after a stretch of awkward silence.

"I'm sorry?" I lick my lips nervously.

Snapping the folder shut, she plays with it as she studies me with a tight expression. "You've worn out your usefulness for the campaign's family-centered message. Leave my son.

Stop seeing him. Don't call or text him."

"What?" The air sucks from the room as I grip the edge of the counter. "Why would I do that? Connor and I—" I close my mouth. It sounds stupid and cliche saying we love each other to his mom while she's trying to drive me away. "I won't do it."

She sighs like I'm a big inconvenience. "How much do you want?"

"You can't pay me to stop dating Connor." I gape at her. "That's horrible."

Vivian coos at me, the sound derisive. "That's how the world works, darling."

I straighten my spine. "No thanks. No matter how much you try to bribe me with, I wouldn't do that to him. I don't like lying."

"Well, aren't you good at playing wholesome?"

"*Playing*?"

I'm about to jump up from the stool when she smirks. "Connor doesn't want or need you. Why do you think he hasn't contacted you?"

Denial clogs in my throat. No. He wouldn't ghost me. He's too proud for it. If he wanted to end things between us, he'd tell me to my face. I shake my head.

Vivian clucks her tongue. "With your…promiscuous proclivities, you don't foster the right kind of image. It's best for everyone if you disappeared from his life."

"Disappeared? Promiscuous proclivities?" My head is spinning. "What are you talking about?"

She tosses the folder across the counter. It lands between us, pages spilling across the gleaming granite. They're…*me*. Photos of myself. Dread seeps into every inch of my skin as I stare at printed pages from my blog.

No. No, no, no. This can't be happening.

"I'll take your stunned silence as agreement." Her words tear me from my stupor. She clicks a pen, poised over a checkbook she pulled out while I was in a daze. "How much will it be?"

What a horrible woman. I'm never voting for her.

Sucking in a fortifying breath, I face her. "If Connor doesn't want me, why would you have to pay me to stop seeing him?"

I'm proud that my voice only shakes a little.

Vivian taps the tip of her silver pen against the blank check. "Insurance."

My lips part. Forget this, standing up to her is pointless. I swipe the pages from my blog and hop down from the stool.

"I have to go," I say.

"Those aren't the only copies, dear. Be smart. Tell me your price, or I'll show my son."

A wild laugh escapes me as I back away from her. "You think you can blackmail me?" It's kind of hilarious, actually. I wish Connor was here to see this. He would get a kick out of it. "Bye, Mrs. Bishop."

Heart in my throat, I get the hell out of there. On the way, my phone rings. I wait until I'm in the Bishop's driveway before I pull it out. When I see who it is, a sound catches in my throat.

"Connor!" I answer, pressing the phone to my ear in a white-knuckled grip.

"Thea? Are you—? I'm almost home. Can you meet me in the pool house?"

I turn back to face his house, my stomach roiling. The last twenty-four hours weigh on my shoulders after facing off with his mother and my own.

"Yeah." I sniffle, wiping my nose. "Of course. Are you okay?"

"We need to talk."

My stomach drops.

The call cuts off.

"Connor? Connor! Damn it."

I almost drop the phone as the printed pages slip from my grasp, cascading all over the driveway. Doubt engulfs me as I crouch to gather the pages blaring my secret.

Between the ideas both our mothers planted in my head, I dread what Connor needs to talk about.

THIRTY-THREE
Thea

There might as well be a singed path in front of the pool house from the serious, stressed-out pacing I did in the last ten minutes waiting for Connor. The entire time I had myself half-convinced we're breaking up, like both our mothers want.

My inner critical voice wreaks havoc, running rampant with the worst things I think of myself, clawing at my mind with one berating thought after another.

Not enough, silly girl, my mind chants.

The anxiety has ratcheted so high, I'm sure any second I'll puke up all the sugary confections Maisy and I gorged ourselves on last night. Double chocolate fudge cake is coming back for a gruesome revenge.

I threw out the printouts I took from Vivian, but what if she already told Connor?

The tense, resolute expression on Connor's face when he finally rounds the house to the backyard with a laptop and thick file in hand doesn't help alleviate any of those poisonous thoughts. I smother a sound that should belong to a dying animal, not a girl seeing her boyfriend for the first time in days.

The last time we were together, we talked about loving each other. Now I'm certain those were our last happy moments. Something in my bones braces me for the impact of this conversation shattering my heart.

One smile from him could save it.

"Hi," I say hoarsely when he's close.

Connor doesn't smile. The first crack in my fragile heart splinters, catching me off guard.

"Come inside." He glances around, watchful of our surroundings. "We need to talk."

"Yeah, about that," I croak, wringing my hands. "You're kind of freaking me out. Maybe you can put a girl out of her misery over here? I've had a rough couple of days."

"You and me both, baby," Connor rumbles, reaching for my hand and squeezing it.

It's a brief ray of light breaking through the clouds of despair hanging over my head, but it helps me breathe a little easier and soothes some of the anxiety, bringing me back from the brink of an emotional breakdown. Once we're inside, he sits me down on the bed, kneels in front of me, and opens his slim laptop with a grim expression.

The tension is killing me. I haven't fully calmed down from what his mom tried to pull, let alone the bomb dropped on me last night.

"Your mom wants to bribe me to stop seeing you." I put one thing out there, shoving the weight off my shoulders so I have help bearing it before it crushes me.

Connor stills, dragging his attention from the screen to stare at me. He pinches the bridge of his nose.

"Fucking bitch. Don't listen to her. Whatever poison she tried to feed you, it's bullshit."

My body sags in relief. "I thought—when I couldn't get a hold of you. I thought you didn't want me."

"Thea." He puts the laptop on the floor and slides his palms up the sides of my thighs. "I want you. I love you. Everything I've been doing is for you. All of it. I'm ready to tell you why I've been distant the last few days."

I lean in, resting my forehead against his. The earthy scent unique to him twines around me as he strokes his thumbs against my legs.

After a minute, he taps my thigh and picks up the laptop again. "We have to prioritize this. Time is running out and I'm not waiting around anymore."

"What is it?"

Connor sighs. "You know I'm good at weeding out people's secrets?"

I nod.

"Back when you and I...well, before I revealed myself to you, I did some digging. It wasn't hard to access for someone like me. I told you I'm good with computers."

"What are you saying?"

"It's better if I show you what I stumbled on."

Connor turns the laptop, the screen full of several windows showing photos of necklaces, email transcripts, and Mr. Coleman's photo.

"What is this?"

"Something sinister. Chief Landry won't listen. That's where I was this morning, begging him for an arrest or an investigation after I did all the damn legwork. 'Evidence obtained illegally is useless'." Connor pulls a face, imitating Maisy's dad's gruff voice. "Bullshit, right? Whatever, like hell I'm waiting around. We'll get him ourselves if we have to."

"You're throwing a lot at me," I say, head jumbled by the battering my emotions took and wary of where this is going. Connor has always had trouble with my favorite teacher.

"Coleman," he clarifies, watching me as he taps his laptop screen. He gestures to each of the windows as he talks. "If I didn't have the comments to compare the conversations to, I might not have figured it out, and then he said that freaky shit to you. It threw up red flags."

My lips part to interrupt, but he goes on before I voice my questions.

"I couldn't tie him to the creepy knight username concretely with an ip address match at first—bastard's damn good at covering his tracks—but there are these insane hackers also onto him, and they sent me on a wild goose chase to get one of Coleman's trophies back. They gave me the unsealed files once I did, but I'd already seen enough after I broke into his place."

"Broke in?" I yelp, pushing my fingers in my hair. He broke into our teacher's house? "Oh my god, Connor. What are you talking about?"

"I had to." He squeezes my knee. "I'd do anything to keep you safe."

There's so much to unpack. Between his confusing explanation and the information overload, I'm speechless. One window in particular pulls my focus and my body freezes.

The relief I felt moments ago vanishes. He already knows my secret. An instinctive refusal rears up, leaving me feeling exposed, but I swallow it back, trying to keep a level head.

He sees you. All of you.

"How did you find that?" With a shaking finger, I point at the browser window with my blog loaded.

"I hacked into your computer and it was in your recent browser history." Connor shoots me a look that says *not the important thing here,* and jabs his finger on the screen over Mr. Coleman's face. "I don't care about the blog. Although, really, if it's private you should've password protected it, but what matters is it was key in figuring out—"

"You hacked into my computer." The disbelief spiraling through me is profound. My voice is quiet, but he goes still at the monotone in it. "You spied on me! What gives you the right?"

Connor exhales in exasperation, brows pinched together. "Is that really what you're focused on when I'm showing you all this evidence that Coleman is an online predator? He gets off grooming his victims, knows exactly how to talk to them. He's a psycho."

"A *what?*"

My mind screams in denial at the word *victim.* It's not true. As much as I try to keep calm, a raw anguish overtakes me.

Ignoring the predator accusation for a minute, I hold my head in my hands. It feels like my secret has been wrenched from me, but it was mine to tell, not his to hunt down. "This is too much. If you knew about my blog, why didn't you talk to me about it sooner? Not that I have to explain anything to you, but it's a sensitive and personal escape for me."

Flashes of my conversations with my online boyfriend pop into my head, cut in a harsher light.

I was the one to give us that label. Henry never did. *No. It can't be.*

It hurts too much to think about. The only thing my brain can focus on is the lesser, but still stinging pain of Connor hacking my computer. Desperation to shut those old questions about Henry behind an iron wall has me pushing all of my anger on Connor.

"Damn it, Thea. It was before we were really together. I'm sorry I did it. I wasn't spying. Shit, I know it was wrong, baby. But it helped me find him. What Coleman was doing to you for years. Others, too."

Others. Doing to you. I shake my head, air catching in my throat. I'm not a victim. I stopped answering the emails. I never sent nude photos.

But Henry still controlled you.

The blog was my safe place to escape the nitpicking from Mom about my body. Henry poisoned it, his infection spreading deep until he had me in his web.

A pained noise escapes me.

Connor sets the laptop aside and picks up the thick file, flipping through to show me. "He's taught at two schools before he showed up in Ridgeview. He was fired from both after sexual harassment reports and complaints for inappropriate conduct."

Focusing on the pages as he talks is hard. I barely take in any of the information. My mind keeps chanting *no* over and over.

"He doesn't even hide how he favors his female students. And he was all over your blog comments even though you're inactive, then he's so focused on you at school. Think about when he showed up here. He's going to make you his next prize."

An unpleasant hot and cold sensation flies over my skin. This is insane. How could Henry and Mr. Coleman be the same? It's so much to think about. I can't accept it.

There's only one thing I can control right now: how I feel about the man I love invading my privacy.

Isn't that what Henry did?

Gritting my teeth, I shove the thought back into a mental abyss. *Stop it.*

Connor is acting like he was justified, as long as he got to find out his version of the truth. Forget who it hurts along the way in his search.

I'd rather deal with Vivian Bishop and my mother at the same time than face the truth—Connor spying on me.

This is the blackmail king of Silver Lake at his best.

Is this all I am to you?

"This is serious."

"I know!" Connor shouts. "That's what I'm trying to tell you."

"You had no right to worm your way into my secrets without my permission. Your jealousy of Mr. Coleman is out of control. You've been obsessed with him for months." I give a forceful shake of my head as I grasp at straws, unable to believe. "You could've fabricated photos to get him fired because you don't like him."

"Are you hearing yourself, Thea? You know me. Would I really put that much effort in when I could get rid of him in other, easier ways? I'm telling you the truth. It's far scarier than anything I could've made up about him."

"But you hacked my computer," I repeat, unable to let it go. It's the only thing I can process in this mess.

Twice in the last day I've defended him as a good guy. But he's been lying to me. I swallow, struggling to choose logic over the shaky emotions threatening to drown me. We always talk out our problems, but how can we work out a betrayal like this?

I thought we tore down our walls to be together. If he's still hiding behind his, I can't be with him. I want Connor, not the ruthless blackmail king.

Maybe it's time his whole damn castle burned down.

As soon as the thought hits me, I push it aside. That's not us. My emotions are wreaking havoc on my mental state. These aren't rational thoughts. If there's one thing I've learned with Connor, we both need clear heads.

He cups my face with one hand and I push out of his grasp. He forces out an aggravated sound. "It was—I'm trying to protect you!"

"I didn't ask you to!" My yell echoes in the pool house.

I'm trying to stay calm, but it's impossible. The evidence he's forcing me to face is slicing me apart at the seams. My mind races in different directions, a base instinct seeking some way to control this so it stops hurting so much, to hide and go back to ten minutes ago before there was a possibility I could be a victim. That's not me. I don't want it to be.

Tears of overwhelm prick my eyes, turning my voice watery. "I've forgiven you for a lot, but I can't look past you invading my privacy and lying about it. I don't believe you. You're just playing god because you're obsessed with everyone's business, just like my mom and yours. You're too afraid to make your own life better, so you just ruin everyone else's!"

Connor jerks his head back as if I slapped him. "Why are you so focused on the hacking? So you kept a blog for your pictures—so what? Doesn't every girl do that these days?"

When he says it like that, it makes the insecurities I've struggled with about my body and feeling invisible seem so small and insignificant. Posting to the blog and finding Henry are the only things that helped me through that time in my life. How can he say it was fine to have my blog but tell me I was groomed by an online predator because of it?

And my abuser is Mr. Coleman? Rejection surges in my head. Maybe what I had with Henry wasn't normal and made me feel weird, but Henry *isn't* Mr. Coleman. He can't be. That would mean—

Before I can face the thought of sitting in class with Henry as the teacher instead of Mr. Coleman, I shut down, going completely numb. I wring my hands, taking unsteady breaths in through my nose to calm myself, like Maisy instructs me when I feel like I'll fly out of my skin.

"Are you okay?" Connor asks, backing off when he sees the state I'm in.

I shake my head, unable to formulate a verbal response.

"Here." Jaw tense, Connor pulls out a photo of a teenage girl that's so similar to the kind of photos Henry would ask for. "He has these on his computer—it's a big set up like mine, dual monitors. I have an encrypted copy of his hard drive, where I found this. I don't know whether he keeps them to himself or sells them or what, but he has more than one. We have to stop him."

Looking at it causes a riot in my body. I shy away.

Every photo I've ever sent Henry flashes in my head, along with the discomfort and uncertainty I felt every time I pushed back, only to be convinced to do what he asked. My stomach hurts. I block every thought about Henry from my mind, too vulnerable to think of those memories.

"Please," I whisper, throat burning. "I don't want to, Connor. I just want it to stop. It's too much."

A rough sound escapes him as he gathers me in his arms. "I'm sorry, baby. I don't want to hurt you with this. Just—fuck, okay, I know I messed up, but I'm trying to fix it. I don't want him touching you." Leaning back, he tries to hand me the evidence again. "Just look at the pictures in the file. He's got these creepy as shit trophies and necklaces with names. *Your* name!"

Another memory floats to the surface, murky and heart-stopping. There was a gift Henry said he had for me. Something special to show he cared. My stomach plummets.

"I have to go. I-I can't be here right now."

Connor growls, fisting his hands in his hair. "Thea!"

Pushing him back, I spring up from the bed. He stands from his kneel, following me as I pace across the room, whirling back, only to spin away again as thoughts run through my head.

"You asked me to tell you," he says. "I swore I would, and now you don't want to hear it."

"This isn't what I thought you'd say! How did you expect me to react to all this? I'm not—I'm not a—"

I can't force the word out. It sits on the tip of my tongue, driving daggers into me.

"Jesus," Connor snaps, throwing his fist into the wall when he can't control his temper.

I jump at the force of it, heart in my throat. I can't stand by and watch him injure himself with self-destructive behavior. It breaks me out of my spiral.

"What are you doing?" I rush to his side, taking his wrist to examine his red knuckles and the damage left behind in the wall. "Why?"

Connor clenches his jaw and a muscle twitches. "Seemed like a good idea."

"It wasn't." Sighing, I drop his hand. "I really can't do this right now."

"Look, we'll start over at the beginning." He holds up the file. "You have to listen."

It's too much to handle with Connor pressuring me to face a truth I can't cope with. I run my fingers through my hair and swallow past the searing heat in my throat. "Please. I can't."

"Thea, *listen* to me." He drops the file on the bed. "Let me explain."

"No! You should've told me right away instead of this. I thought we told each other everything." I'm near a breaking point, lashing out to protect myself from what I can't look at directly. It crushes me to see the disappointment on his face. My chest heaves and my voice grows small. "I thought we were past the lies and games."

"It's not like you told me about this, either!" As soon as he says it, he jerks his head, holding a hand out to me. "Fuck, I didn't mean that. I'm sorry. All of it was to protect you from Coleman. This isn't what I wanted, baby."

Connor takes my hand as I rush toward the door. I tug free from his grip.

"Don't leave."

"I need to go. I just want to go lay down. I'm supposed to meet Maisy at the holiday market later. I came here to invite you, but...I think it's best if we both cool off. I need time and space to process this."

"Thea, please." He captures me in his arms and spins me around. "I'm sorry I ambushed you like this."

I lean back against the door. Everything feels too confusing. "You hurt me with your lie."

He releases a ragged breath, gray eyes filled with the same anguish plaguing me. "I never want to hurt you. Ever."

Despite the disappointment and anger, for a second I stay in his arms. A lump forms in my throat. I can't turn off the love I feel for him. I allow the safety of his strong embrace to be the balm I need.

"Let me go. We'll talk later. I just need to go be alone for a while. I'll think about what you said."

Connor's arms tighten around me before he steps back. We stare at each other for a beat, then I turn the knob.

"Wait," he says. "Here, take this with you." He pushes the thick file into my hands. "Look at it and call me when you're ready to talk." Taking my chin in his thumb and finger, he stares into my eyes. "I'm sorry I kept this from you. I'm sorry for hacking your computer, for everything. We'll do this together, like we should've from the start."

"Fine. But I need time." I pause on the threshold, glancing back. "Please don't do anything reckless."

The sight of Connor watching me walk away from him, face etched with the suppressed rage he battles against sears into my brain.

It's only once I make it inside my house and step under the blistering spray of hot water in the shower that I let the tears free.

THIRTY-FOUR
Thea

A week that started off with an amazing night in the mountains has turned into the hardest of my life. I had an aunt that lost her life too young. My boyfriend's mom cares more about her political career and image than her son's happiness. My *boyfriend* admitted he spied on me.

And the accusation of something even worse. Someone stalking and grooming me for years. *Victim.*

The word causes my chest to cave. Crying in the shower hasn't made my fear of the word fade. Or what I'm blocking behind brick walls in my mind. They're cracking fast, crumbling to dust no matter how much I want to keep hiding from it.

The only thing the shower helped me see clearly was that I shouldn't have lashed out at Connor. I was putting all the blame on him because I was so scared to face questions I've asked myself about Henry.

It hurts that Connor spied on me, but as I pick through the denial with a clearer head, I see the real problem is Henry. What he really was. What he did.

I don't think I can stress bake my way out of this one.

Once the initial anger faded, burning off fast, I understood I was scared in the pool house. Afraid to face the truth beneath the surface all these years.

Some part of me knew it wasn't right, but I always pushed it aside. Now the burn of pain and humiliation is blistering. It's something that could happen to anyone, but I never thought it would be me.

I sat under the spray until it ran lukewarm, leaving my body pink and tender. It didn't wash away the feelings slithering beneath my skin.

Online boyfriend. It was the easiest way to explain away that I was talking about private things with someone I'd met on the internet. Easier to say we were together, because sending photos and having the intimate conversations we did...pretending to act out fantasies. I swallow thickly, shying from the thought. The things I did with Henry were the things couples do. I did them because if I didn't, he'd break up with me. But that doesn't make it okay.

What he did to me was wrong.

He used me. Abused me. Manipulated me when I was vulnerable, making sure I felt like shit if I refused to give him what he demanded. Punishing me for it with his silence until I was running back into his arms like a good little pet.

Henry was not an online boyfriend.

He is a predator.

Not only did he feed on my insecurities about my body—he made them worse. He actively whispered in my ear to knock me back in the dirt whenever I felt strong enough to overcome the negative thoughts, dragging me down with his claws into a pit of despair where he was the one in control of my happiness if he felt like giving it. *If* I did what he wanted.

Fear, that was how he controlled me.

A wheeze cracks my throat as I sit down hard on my bed, digging my fingers into the damp towel wrapped around me.

After a long minute, I lick my lips and take a deep breath.

"I am a victim," I say hoarsely, wincing at the word once more.

Saying it out loud makes it real. I can't run from it when it lives in my bones, lurking in my memories. I tremble on the bed, my knuckles white.

Did I bring this on myself? I responded to his attention in the first place.

As soon as the thought enters my mind, I vehemently refute it with a sharp jerk of my head. "No. I will not blame myself."

Nothing I do will change what happened to me. I was at a vulnerable age that caused a perfect storm. Mom might have driven my negative feelings about myself, but we both aren't to blame for this. Henry preyed on me. He is the only one to blame.

Acknowledgement of it all hurts. It's embarrassing to think a smart girl like myself could be duped. The truth I never dared face rakes me raw.

This is still a lot to think about all at once. I don't know if I can do it by myself without breaking down. Before I'm swallowed by my emotions, I finish getting dressed.

After a quick search online, I find therapists in the area who can help me process this. I save a list of potentials to the note app on my phone. Whether I decide to seek out therapy or not, I want to be prepared when I'm ready to cross that bridge.

For now, I need to get ready or I'll be late. Maisy is expecting me at the market. It's one of our favorite holiday activities to do together. I'm not missing out on it when it's exactly what I need—another afternoon with my best friend, hot chocolate with cinnamon and marshmallows, and something normal to take my mind off of all this for a while.

* * *

In the car on the way to meet Maisy, more memories and thoughts worm their way through the decimated remains of the mental walls, painting everything in a new light. It makes my heart beat hard and my palms sweat.

I want to stop thinking about it, but it's like being dumped in ice water. Every time my mind jumps off it, the wet clothes remind me how tightly they cling to my skin. I don't know how I lasted in denial about this for so long.

Would I ever have figured this out without Connor? Or would I have buried it deep down, pretending it was harmless, when in reality it was a poison flaring up when I least expected it?

Maybe I was an idiot.

With a sigh, I park the car. I'm not an idiot, but my mind is still jumbled. I'm beating myself up for something I couldn't control.

I knew I was uncomfortable in some way talking to Henry, but I always brushed it off in order to please him, too worried to let go of the connection to him. What if I didn't find someone else? I didn't want to go back to being invisible again.

"It will be okay," I murmur.

I grab my bag as I climb out of my car and follow the trickle of people walking to the holiday market. I didn't have time to hide the file I took from Connor before I left, and I couldn't chance Mom snooping, so I left it in my big purse and brought it with me. I might have come to terms with the truth about Henry abusing me, but I still need more time before going through whatever proof Connor handed over. Too much at once is devastating.

Besides, I'm here to take my mind off of this and enjoy the market with Maisy.

As I'm walking with the crowd, a couple catches my eye. I roll my lips between my teeth and push down the pang in my chest. I just need some time with Maisy, then I'll talk to Connor.

"Hey!" Maisy waves at me from the arched entrance wrapped in boughs of fir and festive ribbon. She's wearing maroon yoga pants, knee-high boots, and a vintage boho-style fringe poncho with a dark green fair isle pattern. Once I'm close, she does a double take. "Whoa, dude. Are you okay?"

I put on a little makeup to cover up before coming, but I guess it doesn't do much to help my swollen eyes. If I get into it now, I'll definitely break down again.

"Yeah. Still raw from everything." I offer a smile as I adjust the chunky scarf poking out of the neckline of my white wool coat. "I just want to have a good time."

"One good time, coming up."

Maisy hooks her arm with mine and leads us down the stall-lined main street. The folder sits heavily in my bag. My plan is to ignore it while Maisy and I stroll around the lively market.

The heavenly scents of spiced meat, cider, cinnamon, cranberries, and pine trees fill the air. It's everything *winter* and it smells amazing, lifting my spirits.

Maisy leans into my side, fluttering her lashes as she rolls her eyes back dramatically. "Oh my god, it smells so good."

"It does." This time my smile comes more easily. "First stop, hot drinks and pie pops?"

She snaps her fingers and points at me. "You read my mind."

We veer left toward our favorite stall to kick off our yearly tradition. Maisy gets a hot cider and I ask for extra marshmallows in my hot chocolate. We toast each other, tapping our cherry pie pops before laughing into the huge bites we stuff in our mouths. It feels really good to laugh. The tart burst of fruit on my tongue makes everything feel a little better.

"Ready to roll?" Maisy blows on her cider. "I think for this year's prank gift, I'm getting my mom one of those carvings with moose crap."

I snort as we amble with the flow of traffic, pausing at a few stalls to check out the wares on display. Maisy has a tradition where she tries to annoy her mom by getting her the weirdest gift she can find every year, acting like she really thought her mom would love it. Neither of them will give in or back down, so Maisy forges on with her mission.

"Trying to outdo that hideous cross stitch from last year?"

"She didn't even blink at that! I thought she would, I mean it was so detailed. How do you stitch shading for a bull's balls? A true artist at work."

"That thing still gives me nightmares."

Maisy muffles a proud laugh as she sips her cider.

A couple bumps into me at the next stall, not apologizing for being so wrapped up in each other they don't notice me. My heart gives another feeble pang. The man's cologne smells similar to the earthy one Connor wears. With a polite smile, I sidestep the pair to check out the crystals and gemstones on the shelves. Maisy makes a sound like she found one she likes, and gets lost in a conversation with the vendor about crystals for empowering and boosting yoga practice.

I tune it out as I poke at the pretty stones on one of the tables. The basket at the end of the row stops me. It's full of moonstones, reminding me of Connor once more.

Gulping the dregs of my drink, I slip outside to toss the cup, putting him from my mind. I bump into someone.

"Sorry!" I put my hands up to brace myself and catch my balance.

"Thea." Mr. Coleman gives me a handsome smile. "It's so good to see you outside of class."

"Mr. C." The high-octave surprise in my tone has him tipping his head. My bag suddenly weighs a thousand pounds with Connor's file inside sitting like a brick. All the accusations float up to the forefront of my thoughts. They test the impression of the cool, kind teacher I thought of him as, small fissures running along the facade. An uncomfortable pitter-patter moves through my chest. I edge back a step, putting more distance between us. "Uh, hi. You're here, too."

"I am. The holiday bazaar in Ridgeview is one of my favorites in the area. I'm a real sucker for the mulled wine." He chuckles and reaches out to pat my shoulder. "I hope your break is going well."

He pauses when I flinch and step back again. Henry flashes in my mind and my skin crawls.

Maisy saves me from answering, slinging her arm over my shoulder. "They had such a good deal on rose quartz!"

"That's great," I say in a strained voice. "Well, bye Mr. C. Enjoy the market."

I feel his eyes on my back as Maisy and I keep walking. Can't I get one afternoon away from my problems?

Apparently not, because every couple-oriented ornament, holiday song, and activity at the market bombard me the further we go. Damn Connor for owning my thoughts. One of his hugs would feel so good right now.

"Oh damn, look how long the line is." Maisy motions to the bathrooms, where she pulled us after the last stall. "Don't wait up."

"Are you sure? I don't mind."

"It's fine. Go ahead." She points at me with a sly smirk. "Keep your eye out for a good prank gift for me."

"We can meet up by the tree display in the middle when you're done," I offer.

"Perfect."

Leaving Maisy, I tuck my hands in my coat pockets and continue browsing. I'm looking at a vendor with wooden holiday ornaments when I spot Mr. Coleman again at the next booth, enraptured by the jewelry. The necklaces in particular have his attention.

Uneasiness whispers in my mind. Connor swore he was dangerous.

I abandon the laser-cut ornament with baking tools dangling beneath a pie to sneak closer, observing Mr. Coleman's actions. He touches the jewelry with a meticulous focus, stroking each pendant. It brings up the memory of the necklace Henry planned to send me. After selecting one, he stands in line to pay.

A woman runs the stall, but she hands off Mr. Coleman's necklace to her teenage daughter while another customer asks her for help. I bite my lip as Mr. Coleman's eyes light up. He leans closer to the daughter, talking to her. She's flustered but peeks at him shyly as she packages his purchase. His hand brushes hers as he takes the bag.

The corners of my mouth turn down. Glancing around, I follow him, keeping several feet behind so I can duck out of sight.

Mr. Coleman meets up with a girl from Silver Lake High, a sophomore, I think. She doesn't seem wary as they chat, but I can't stop watching. He gives her a serene smile, all his attention focused on her. Whatever he says makes her giggle.

She kind of looks like me. Similar shade of red hair, same white coat I have on today. I swallow as Connor's voice fills my mind.

He's so focused on you at school.

Maybe it's because I'm used to him in one setting and now he's out of that box that has everything feeling so off. It's not that he's doing anything crazy, but now that I'm watching him with Connor's words in my head, it feels questionable.

He could be Henry. Imagining it sends my stomach into an uncomfortable flip.

I shake my head, sucking in air.

This is ridiculous. I'm hiding behind a large quilt in the middle of the holiday market, stalking my teacher.

I ball my fists, but I don't walk away, tethered to my hiding spot. Because what if it's not as harmless as it appears? Henry is in my past, but if he's not? Then the danger is even more real.

Mr. Coleman gives the bag to the girl. She's delighted as she pulls out the necklace he bought. She tries to give it back, but he must insist because he curls his fingers over hers, closing the jewelry in her hand.

Without hearing their conversation, I'm jumping to conclusions about what's happening. Is it the first time he's given her a gift? Is he grooming her?

I'm lost in my head, but when I zone back in, the quilt hiding me is pulled aside as another shopper debates between two choices. His attention is on me. He caught me. Crap.

Mr. Coleman nods to the sophomore girl and walks over to the quilt vendor before I can brush off following him or give him the slip into another stall.

"Hello again."

"My mom loves these quilts." As soon as the words are out of my mouth, I want to dive under the blankets hanging around the hut. Curse my nervous babbling.

Mr. Coleman's brows lift. "Is that so?" He pinches one of the smaller throw sized blankets hanging behind me, reaching over my shoulder to do it. My spine goes rigid. "Ah, yes. It's made nicely."

He doesn't leave, so I'm forced to make small talk as he fondles the blanket over my shoulder. "Are you enjoying the market?"

Mr. Coleman hums. His gaze slides back to me. "You could've asked to walk with me if that's what you wanted instead of following me. There's no harm in it outside of class, right?"

What? No, that's not what I wanted. It's a really odd response. Back at the pool house I wasn't thinking straight, but face-to-face with Mr. Coleman, I'm on high alert.

The way he's honed in on me that makes my heartbeat spike in a horrible way. I want to walk away.

"I was kinda wandering aimlessly. My friend is in the bathroom line, but we're meeting up. I was just killing time."

He watches me for a long beat. *It's not a fixation*, I tell myself, clinging to desperation. He doesn't have to be Henry. That monster can stay in the past where he can't hurt me anymore.

"Well, enjoy yourself." Mr. Coleman steps back, dropping his arm from feeling up the blanket. "If I don't see you again, have a wonderful holiday."

"Bye." Not waiting, I hurry away, hoping Maisy is already waiting at the tree display when I get there.

I came out today to get my mind off all of this, but it followed me here anyway. Maybe I should tell her we can come back again another day.

When I make it to the tree display, I circle it twice. She isn't there yet. I check my phone and curse under my breath. The battery is on 1%.

"Seriously? Unbelievable."

Pawing through my bag, I don't find the charger, remembering I left it in the car. I chew my lip. If I hurry, I can grab it and make it back here. The coffee shop has outlets I can use. I shoot Maisy a text before my phone dies to let her know to meet me at the coffee shop instead, then leave the cheery holiday festival behind to return to the parking area.

The late afternoon sun cuts across the street as it falls closer to the ridge line in the distance. I have to charge my phone before it gets dark, or Maisy and I might miss each other.

My plan goes up in smoke when I reach my car. Mr. Coleman is parked a few spots away, and the sophomore girl from before is with him. They climb into his car.

"Oh no."

If Mr. Coleman is Henry, I don't want him to hurt anyone else.

I squeeze my bag against my side, feeling the heavy file stuffed in it. Making a decision, I unlock my car and slide in. Something in me can't leave the girl alone. I'd never forgive myself for abandoning someone potentially in danger if I could do something to help.

As Mr. Coleman pulls out, I follow in my car, hoping he doesn't spot me tailing him in the rearview. The whole way, my fingers tap on the wheel and I scrape my teeth over my lip until it's tender and raw.

"It'll be fine," I repeat over and over.

THIRTY-FIVE
Thea

THE drive isn't long. Mr. Coleman pulls off onto a residential road not far from downtown. There are a handful of houses on the short dead end street, a patch of woods beyond that. Most are decorated for the holidays with lights and lawn ornaments, but Mr. Coleman's car pulls into the driveway of the one house on the block without festive trimmings.

Feeling too conspicuous, I park my car a few houses away, scooting low in my seat so I go unnoticed. I hold my breath as they get out of the car, prepared to dart across the street to save my lookalike. Mr. Coleman gestures with one hand as he talks, the other tucked in his coat pocket. My heart shoots into my throat as the girl beams and follows him inside.

"No! Don't go inside! Shit." My knee bounces as my worry rises.

I can't just walk up to his door. He already caught me following him once today. What can I do?

Rubbing my forehead, I finally reach for the folder in my bag. My hands shake as I open it, fully ready to believe Connor.

The name on the records has me releasing a choked sound—*Harold Knight Coleman*. Henry's email was *henry.k.c*. The initials are the same. I frantically flip through the photos and copies of reports in the file as my breathing turns shallow. With shaking hands I lift a photo of myself, one I remember emailing to Henry when I was fifteen.

"Oh my god. No."

I didn't want it to be true, because thinking about it already hurts. The overwhelm crashes back into me and I squeeze the edges of the folder until the pages crinkle. God, I sat in his classroom when he had my photos, *knew* who I was.

A strangled sob escapes me.

The next photo in the file is a row of gold heart-shaped necklaces against dark velvet, each with a name card. One of them has my name on it, just like Connor said. Shit.

I can't run from the agonizing truth any longer.

Mr. Coleman was the monster all along. The one who kept me from growing out of my insecurities, making them fester with his manipulation and abuse. He is Henry, my abuser.

And now he has another young teenage girl in his house.

My chest feels tight.

Connor was right. I wish I hadn't hidden behind denial and listened to him.

I want to tell him, but when I grab my phone, it's dead. I never plugged it into the car charger on the drive over, too worried I'd lose track of Mr. Coleman's car. Now I'm kicking myself. When I try the power button, the battery icon blinks on the screen, mocking me in its uselessness. I can't even call Maisy's dad about Mr. Coleman to make a report about what happened to me.

Glancing from my phone to his porch, I blow out a breath. I can't wait for the phone to charge. The sophomore girl is still inside. He could be trapping her right now. If I leave to get help, will it be too late for her? Maybe I can knock on the doors of other people on the block. But how long will it take?

There's one thing I know for certain: I won't stand by and let Mr. Coleman harm any other girls like he hurt me. I've seen the folder. Hell, I *lived* the folder.

I have to do something.

Stuffing the file back in my purse, I take the bag and grab the all-in-one tool from the glove box Maisy insisted I have. It's for car accidents, but it could do damage as a weapon in an emergency. Climbing out of the car, I shove it in my coat pocket as I hurry to the closest house across from Mr. Coleman's. I knock on the door, but there's no answer. I knock again, shifting restlessly on my feet.

"Come on. Damn it. Why doesn't anyone answer their doors anymore?"

I run to the next house over, trying there. No one answers. This is wasting time.

Shaking out my hands, I head for Mr. Coleman's house. I keep low as I sneak around, peeking in windows carefully. Inside, it's rundown with cracks in the plastered walls. My breath catches at the sight of the dual monitor computer surrounded by an array of old takeout containers. I still don't see anyone, so I continue around the side of the house. Voices from inside drift out through the old, grimy windows.

"...sure you have to go right away? I insist, stay for a quick cup of cocoa," Mr. Coleman says. "It'll warm you up from the chill."

Only part of their conversation is audible as I strain my ears, crouched beneath a window.

"...supposed to get back, but..."

"Don't be silly," he says, closer to the window. I hold my breath. "There's no rush, right?" There's a slight pause, then, "That's the holiday spirit. Never too much cocoa. I'll put on some music, too."

She must have agreed. I shift around, but in the fading light I misjudge the distance between my hip and the recycling cans near the window, accidentally knocking into one.

"Crap, crap, crap," I hiss, steadying them before they make too much noise. Hopefully Mr. Coleman didn't hear that. Or if he did, writes it off as a wild animal.

Holiday music starts playing. I try to peek in another window to see if I can gesture to the girl to warn her off, but it's too dark inside to see anything. Why aren't any of the lights on?

I skirt around to the back door to see if I can hear better. Before I reach the handle, a hand covers my mouth as I'm grabbed.

"*Mmph!*"

Lips press against my ear, making my skin crawl when I hear Mr. Coleman's husky voice. "You came, princess. I thought that was your little blue car in my mirror. Following me, sneaking around out here playing naughty games? Well, if you insist. I'll have to punish you later."

White-hot panic rushes up my spine. I kick and thrash, but he's strong. I try to scream, but his hand muffles it.

When did he come outside? Oh god, this can't be happening!

"Ah, ah. You came to me. I'm your knight, princess. Stop fighting it." His demeanor has changed from earlier, bordering on manic. "I've been waiting for you. I've wanted to tell you for so long—every day in class. Having you chase me at the market was so thrilling. I knew you must have realized it and couldn't stay away any longer." He presses his nose into my hair as I struggle. "But you're making this hard for me by misbehaving."

I'm your knight, princess.

No.

No fucking way.

He's spouting words he's typed to me a hundred times over. A sickening sensation travels through my body.

This is worse than every nightmare I've ever had come to life.

Mr. Coleman keeps my arms pinned tight. I'm too short to crack my skull back into his. I try to bite him, to yell, but he squeezes my face hard enough to hurt.

Everything in my body screams in protest at his harsh grip. I feel violated all over again, worse this time with his hands all over me. His breath is hot on the back of my neck as he grunts against my frantic flailing.

No!

Escaping his hold is impossible, but I manage to worm my fingers into my coat pocket. They slip on the smooth handle of the all-in-one tool. My chest caves with a desperate, smothered cry.

Please, please.

When I have it, I release a wild sound, swinging as hard as I can with limited motion. Mr. Coleman grunts as I catch him in the leg with the hard tip meant for breaking glass. But it doesn't work for him to release me like I wanted. I didn't strike hard enough.

He wrenches the tool from my grasp and throws it aside in the dead grass. That was my only weapon against him!

"Mmph! Mmmph!" My protests come out as muffled grunts.

His voice is a low growl in my ear as he lifts me from the ground. "You'll behave, pet. I don't want to punish you too harshly, but I will."

Terror spears through my body as he crushes me against the back door, covering my back to pin me there. My nostrils flare with each panicked, labored breath.

He has me inside before I can fight him off. I try to scream again, to warn the sophomore girl, but with his hand over my mouth and holiday music playing, I go unheard.

My pulse races as he shoves me through another door, then down a short flight of steps into a basement off the kitchen. I squirm to reach for something I can use against him. Anything to stun him long enough to escape.

My feet jar as he drops me back to the ground, sending me stumbling from the jolt. A second later, he shoves me against a workbench with shelves of cubby holes. My bag drops to the ground as I try to break his hold. In the struggle, my head knocks into a shelf, spreading a jarring pain in my skull and making my vision swim. Everything goes black around the edges, a strange pulse in my head leaving me woozy.

He watches me with calculating, narrowed eyes, then steps back. Without his disgusting hands holding me up, the dizziness gets worse and I slump against the table, then collapse to the floor. I try to form words with my heavy tongue, but everything goes black.

Open your eyes! Get up!

Cracking my eyes open takes effort. I think I try it multiple times as I sit on the dusty floor because distorted flashes of Mr. Coleman slip through the throbbing in my head. Watching me. Getting a tool and extension cords. His back to me as he climbs the stairs.

Now! Escape now!

When I come to, I'm alone. I don't know how much time it's been. Seconds? Minutes? Hours? I scrub a hand over my face and climb to my feet. My head still hurts, but the dizziness that made me black out has passed.

It can't be long if my head is still tender. I wince, carefully prodding at my skull.

The room grows dimmer as the last of the daylight outside fades into dusk. No lights are on, swallowing me in shadows and darkness.

My chest heaves as my breathing speeds back up. I race up the steps, but the door is locked. The music is turned down lower. I smack my palm against the door.

"Help! Hey! Help me! Let me out!" As I scream, I jiggle the doorknob. No matter how hard I yank on the handle, it doesn't budge. My palm stings from banging so hard.

Mr. Coleman's muted voice travels through the door, sounding far away. I pause to press my ear to the door. "...no problem. Tell your parents they can borrow from me anytime. Goodnight."

The extension cords. That was why she came in? I thought—

Shit! I wanted to help the other girl, but now Mr. Coleman has *me*. How the hell am I getting out of this?!

My nerve endings feel flayed from the dread choking me.

Was it a mistake to want to help? I didn't have any other choice. A swollen lump lodges in my throat as I press my forehead to the door, breathing through the rush of emotions.

Princess.

Repulsion rushes over my body. How could I have thought that pet name made me feel special at fifteen? Now it only sends wave after wave of nausea through me. I'm trapped by my abuser. What will he do to me?

At least the other girl got away. That's the only silver lining I can cling to right now. Mr. Coleman took me instead.

I'm sorry, Connor. I'm sorry I messed up so badly.

If I hadn't shut down in denial, I wouldn't be here right now.

I wish Connor were here. He has stepped in so many times, not trusting Mr. Coleman around me. But wishing for him won't save me.

I have to save myself.

I'll get out of this. I have to.

Be brave.

THIRTY-SIX
Connor

AFTER cooling off by beating shit up with my bat at the abandoned quarry for a couple hours to give Thea space and get my thoughts off my major failure, I'm worn out but feeling less like I'm about to split apart.

The late afternoon sun dips low, creeping behind the ridgeline as dusk falls, casting long shadows across the weed-choked gravel lot. Thea asked me not to do anything stupid, so I came out here to work out my frustration rather than put more holes in the pool house wall.

With my head refocused, I'm ready to try talking to her again. I told her I'd let her come to me, but we don't have the time. Two hours to calm down is long enough.

It was a mistake to ambush her with all the information at once, especially after she told me what Mom did to her. I should've come at it from a different angle, starting with Coleman. Keeping everything from her was killing me, so it poured out all at once.

Worse, I hated the panicked look on her face and the tears in her eyes as she left. I hate making her cry.

I sit in my Lexus GX with the door open and call her to find out what part of the holiday market she's at. It goes to voicemail.

"Hi! You've reached Thea. I'm unavailable at the moment, probably because I'm up to my elbows in cake batter. Leave a message and I'll call you back soon!"

I lift the phone away from my ear, scowling at it. I almost never get her voicemail when I call.

A bad feeling slices through me.

When my phone pings with a message, I relax. She's fine, it must be loud at the market. Missed the call. That's all.

But it's not Thea when I open it. The text is from a contact in my phone I don't remember putting in—the name blank except for a skull and crown emoji.

"Those crow bastards," I grumble, opening the video clip.

As the CCTV footage plays, my heart stutters to a stop. *Fuck.*

It shows Thea following Coleman at the holiday market, then talking to him. He's standing way too close to her for comfort. The last angle isn't clear, but there's a girl getting in Coleman's car with him, driving off. She's wearing the same wool jacket as Thea's. My mind jumps to the worst.

Nothing else matters but getting her back.

"Goddamn it!" I pound my fist against the wheel, flying into motion. "This can not be happening right now."

How can Thea be in the exact danger I was trying to protect her from? How could she get in a car and go anywhere with Coleman after what I tried to show her?

I should've followed her instead of cooling my head. My heart beats in double time as I fight off the sick sensation of failing her.

I can't lose the girl I love.

We have so much ahead of us still, our entire future together.

I pull out of the quarry in a spray of dust and gravel. The tires skip over the road in a high-pitched squeal, and the lingering scent of burnt rubber tickles my nostrils. I push the gas harder, speeding toward my house. I need a weapon before I go save her from him.

And I *will* save her. She's the most important person to me.

If I'm the storm tearing through everything, Thea is the sunlight that breaks through in my wake. A sun captured by the moon, eclipsed by love. She pierces through my darkness with her light.

Thea is it for me. She's the girl I plan to marry. The only queen I want by my side. I'll spend the rest of my life groveling for every mistake I've made if it means we make it out of this.

I'm close to breaking my teeth from grinding them so hard as I take corners too fast. The car screeches as I brake hard in the middle of the street, throwing it in park while I burst from the car to run across the lawn to my house.

Nothing registers but my goal: Dad's gun safe.

It's in his study on the first floor. The door hits the wall when I fling it open, but I don't care. I go to the desk, open the bottom drawer, and punch in the access code. I looked over Dad's shoulder when he was showing it to me before he took me to the gun range to learn how to shoot.

The 9mm Glock sits in the foam casing. Wasting no time, I take it and get bullets from where he keeps them.

Once I'm back outside with the gun tucked away so I don't give the neighbors a heart attack, I get back in the SUV and floor it toward Coleman's to rescue my girl. On the way, I call Devlin.

"*Yo. What's up?*"

"Get the cops to Coleman's," I demand, speeding through a red light at an empty intersection. I need to make it there before I get pulled over for reckless driving. "Do whatever you have to. Call in a suspected shooting. Start a fire. I don't care, just do it."

"*Whoa, slow down,*" Devlin says. "*The fuck are you on about?*"

I smack the wheel. "He has Thea!"

"Shit. Okay, got it."

I push the car faster, hoping I'm not too late.

THIRTY-SEVEN
Thea

WHILE I scramble in the darkness, searching the workbench for another weapon to defend myself, the basement door opens. My stomach lurches. A dim, flickering bulb blinks to life, casting the basement in sickly yellow light.

Oh god. He's back.

"Kicking up all that fuss and not behaving. Tsk, tsk," Mr. Coleman says in an eerie tone as he descends the rickety wooden steps. "I don't know if you deserve this gift or not. But you've always been my special princess, haven't you?"

Shoulders rigid with terror, I spin to face him with a strangled cry, my head throbbing with dull pain from the sudden movement.

Mr. Coleman stands between me and the exit. I feel blindly behind me and wrap my fingers around a small tool handle—tiny screwdriver, maybe? I don't know. It feels like the kind used on computers. I can't look, not willing to risk drawing his attention to it.

It won't do a lot of damage, but it's all I feel behind me without continuing my search.

He reaches the bottom step, presenting me with the same necklace from the file half-spilled out of my purse on the dingy floor. It's a gold heart dangling from a dainty chain.

"Mr. Coleman," I try, my tongue sluggish. Maybe I can talk my way out in order to escape from this monster. "Why are you doing this?"

Ignoring my question, he glides across the floor. "I didn't want to say anything earlier, but your eyes are all swollen and bloodshot. I know the result of crying when I see it. I'll make it all better." He speaks in a soft, reverent tone. "Princess, are you ready to take my hand?"

Fuck, what can I do? He has me cornered. He's too far away to stab without losing the element of surprise, and too strong if I run without diverting him first. I need to get to those stairs.

"The other girl," I whisper.

"Hmm, yes. I thought about keeping her, but then you came right to me. I'd much rather have my prize instead. I knew you couldn't stay away forever. You don't have to be jealous of the others."

He's not just manic—he's delusional. He thinks I want him. A fierce wave of nausea upsets my stomach.

I need something to distract him. There's a paint can on a bench next to the worktable, just out of reach while his attention is on me. An old rolling chair sits at the edge of the pool of yellow light. Maybe I can knock him off balance?

While I'm searching for something else to use against him, Mr. Coleman steps closer. I jump aside in revolt, but he traps me with a terrifying chuckle, his chest touching me as I lean back against the worktable until it digs into my back.

"Where do you think you're going, pet?"

Another panicked noise catches in my throat as I try to edge away. My nails dig into my palm around the screwdriver's handle.

Wrong, wrong, wrong, my mind clangs.

"You...you said your name was Henry," I babble, mind racing to figure a way out of this without ending up like my mom's sister. I'm so scared of what he'll do to me, the fear making it hard to move. Whenever he was mad because I didn't do what he wanted, he would flay me with words once I crawled back. Now, he could do so much worse. "And that you were only three years older than me. We stopped, I-I stopped answering."

Mr. Coleman touches my hair and I flinch with a frightened sound. "Shh, my darling. I know it's upsetting to find out I lied, but they were little lies. Necessary ones. You were so young, so I didn't want to scare you off. Not when our souls were speaking so clearly to one another."

Bile rushes up my throat.

His eyes dance back and forth between mine. He cocks his head. "I know you felt it, too. Every class, I longed to reach out." His mouth curves into an ugly, lopsided grin. "You're always so eager for me."

I shake my head, unable to speak. The tears welling in my eyes wobble, blurring my vision. When I blink, they burn hot paths down my cheeks.

"Don't cry, pet," he says in a light, haunting tone. "I got you this gift, see? I want to show you how special you are to me. You'll wear this and know you're mine."

So special he has several other matching ones for however many girls he's done this to.

As he leans back to fumble with the chain, he spots my purse on the floor with the file sticking from it. One of my photos peeks out far enough to see what it is. He lowers the necklace, staring at the picture.

Ice shoots through my veins.

"What's this?" Mr. Coleman sounds annoyed, sending my heart tripping over a beat in fear I've made him mad. He snatches the bag, digging the folder of evidence out.

"No, don't!"

His face turns to stone as he flips through the file while I'm plastered against the worktable in horror.

"Why do you have this, Thea?" I didn't think it was possible, but his creepy factor ratchets up another degree when he turns his gaze back on me, eyes dead and soulless. He sighs in disappointment. "I can't let you leave here now, princess."

"W-Why? That would be bad. Wrong. Please." My voice trembles. Every part of my body quakes in fear. "It's fine. I won't tell. You can let me go. We'll pretend nothing happened."

He barks out a sharp sound, shaking his head as he comes close again. "Nothing, is it? You're ruining our nice evening together."

"Please," I whisper hoarsely. "You don't have to do this."

"Princess," he says as he strokes my cheek, leaning close enough to nearly brush his lips over mine. With a sharp intake of air, I jerk my head to the side, but he grips my chin in a punishing grip and yanks me back. His touch feels like barbed wire tearing through my gut. "What makes you think I can resist when I have you here? You ran right into my arms."

I shake my head in denial, struggling to free myself from his hold. Maybe if I play along again, he'll let me go. It might give me enough time to grab the paint can if he doesn't think I'm going to run. He was always more receptive when I made clumsy attempts to take initiative in his games. It makes me sick to my stomach, but I can do this. I fight back the nausea rolling through me and force my body to relax.

"It's just..." My voice is scratchy and small. *Come on, Thea. Do this and maybe you get to escape your nightmare and live.* "It's just, my mom. She's strict."

Mr. Coleman coos to pacify my false worries. "We'll sort it all out, princess. We'll leave town if we have to. If no one understands us, we'll just go."

"Or, we could just wait until graduation. My friends are here." I'm grasping for anything to make him disregard me as a flight risk or a threat enough to back off. As soon as I have space, I'll distract him and run. The door isn't locked anymore. It's left open at the top of the steps. "We'll make it like a game. Secret meetings."

Using something so close to my love story with Connor rakes hot coals over my heart, but I'm so stressed out and scared. I'll say anything to appease the man caging me against the worktable.

Mr. Coleman hums in consideration, studying me. I think he likes the idea. "A game."

I nod eagerly. "Yes! No one will know we're t-together. It'll be fun. Our little secret, just like our emails."

"Yes, you're onto something there." He taps my nose and finally takes a step back. "Right under everyone's noses. No one will know I've fucked you on my desk, had you on your knees beneath it with those incredible lips sucking my cock. Mm, princess. This is a wonderful idea. I always knew you were my favorite of my girls for a reason."

His grin stretches into something hideous as I swallow my gag. At last he turns his back on me as he ruminates on his disgusting fantasies of having me. While he's distracted, I snatch the nearby paint can, heart thumping violently. It's not as heavy as I hoped, maybe half-full, but I throw it as hard as possible. It smashes into his head, disorienting him.

The papers in the file spill to the floor as he stumbles, catching himself on the rolling chair. It crashes as his body weight collides with it.

I don't wait, dashing for the stairs to get to the kitchen, still armed with the screwdriver.

A grunt and heavy footsteps are right on my heels. I push my legs to move as fast as possible so I can outrun the monster chasing me.

"No you don't!" The sound of his feet pounding on the creaking wooden stairs will haunt me forever if I make it out of this alive.

I scream as his weight collides into my back once I've made it through the basement door, tackling me. We land against the kitchen table, shattering a glass in the fall. It cuts one of my palms as I try to push him off. From this angle, the best I can manage is stabbing the small screwdriver clutched in my grip into Mr. Coleman's leg, squeezing so hard the handle hurts the bones in my hand. He lets out a furious shout as we thrash against the table.

"You're all mine, princess." He hisses into the back of my neck, breath humid. "Your knight will take good care of you."

A heavy bang sounds nearby. Mr. Coleman growls.

Pinned in place with my stalker panting against my neck, I fear for my life. Tears stream down my face while I struggle, my breaths coming short and fast, burning my lungs.

My heart breaks in a splintering mess.

I wasn't good enough. Not strong enough or fast enough. Not brave enough. I didn't escape.

Am I about to end up like my mother's dead sister after all?

THIRTY-EIGHT
Connor

Thea's Mini Cooper is the first thing I spot when I whip onto Coleman's street. I park crookedly behind it and check the handgun once I load the full magazine. There's no time to waste. It's past dusk now, making it easier for me to sneak around Coleman's house in the dark.

The cops haven't arrived yet.

"Where are they?"

Five to six minute response time, my ass. I made it in under fifteen minutes breaking every speeding law. With a muffled, aggravated exhale, I circle toward the backyard.

No lights are on in any of the windows. I strain my ears, listening for any sign of life in the house. It's hard to focus when my pulse won't stop pounding over everything. If they aren't here, he could've taken her to a second location.

Thea has to be here.

Keeping low, I creep up to the back door, gun squeezed in my grip.

All bets are off once I hear a shout. The back door is locked when I grab the knob. There isn't a window to smash to reach in and unlock it. Coleman's house is older, maybe I can—

Thea's scream followed by a crash makes my heart stutter.

"Fuck!"

Stepping back to center myself, I kick next to the knob as hard as I can. The old wood cracks, but it's not good enough. Nothing will keep me from getting in this fucking house. With a grunt, I kick again, then another. The frame breaks as I bust through the door.

It's mostly dark, the only light coming from an open basement door, but I make out Coleman pinning Thea to the table in the middle of the kitchen. He wrenches his head up, glaring in my direction. I slap my hand against the wall and flick on the light. Coleman squints as the brightness blinds him momentarily.

"Connor!" Thea screams, desperate and pleading as she struggles beneath her attacker, craning her neck to see me.

"I'm here!"

Coleman snarls, bracing his forearm against the back of Thea's shoulders to keep her in place. There are splotches of blood on her white coat—*hers or his?* She chokes on a sob, nails scrabbling for purchase on the table amidst broken glass.

The sight of Coleman on top of her, the tears staining her blotchy cheeks, her terrified cry, it all makes me wild with the need to protect her.

"Get the fuck off of her!" I lift the gun to make the threat clear, my savage yell echoing in the room. I hope the neighbors hear the commotion of the break in or the goddamn police get here soon.

"What are you doing here? Leave, or I'll call the cops," Coleman sneers. "You're not wanted."

"Nah, man. Not a chance in hell." I bark out a laugh. "The cops? Already on their way. Besides, you think they'll care about busting in your back door when they find out what the fuck you like to get up to? They already know. You're finished." I level the gun, aiming at Coleman. My tone turns deadly. "Now get the fuck off."

Coleman ignores the gun pointed at him and plasters himself over Thea's back, messing up my clean shot. He angles his head and shoots me an evil smirk. "You won't do it. You're nothing but a spoiled, cocky pissant playing hero."

Beneath him, Thea growls, my fierce fighter not giving up. She bucks, but he still holds her easily, keeping her at a disadvantage.

"You think I won't?" I advance two steps, hissing through clenched teeth. I'm done playing around. "I've been itching to kill you for weeks, since I first broke in. This," I gesture with the gun, encompassing the room and the situation, luring him into believing I'm crazy and untrained in handling a firearm, "fucking escalates that mood. I won't even flinch when I put a bullet in you."

My gaze slides to Thea for a fraction of a second, meeting her glistening eyes. She shakes her head slightly, not drawing any more attention to herself. I try to communicate that it will be okay. I'll get her out of this.

Swinging my focus back to Coleman, I take careful aim. "Sunshine, tell this degenerate sack of shit I'm a little unhinged. And the thing is, *Harold*, you're all over my girl. She doesn't seem happy about it. I'm not happy about it, either. You have three seconds. Three...two..."

Before I get to one, I squeeze the trigger. I fire while aiming close enough to Coleman in the hope it will spook him so Thea can get away. The gunshot is sharp and piercing.

Coleman does startle, staggering back against the wall, howling and holding his ear. Thea yelps, rolling away as soon as he moves. She drops to the floor out of sight behind the table. Coleman's hand comes away shining with blood from where the bullet grazed him.

"You little piece of shit." He charges across the room.

I fire again, but miss. Coleman barrels into me. My hip hits the edge of the cheap tile counter, sending a shock of pain through my body as we struggle for control of the weapon. In our wrestling, I get a solid punch in, but Coleman drags me to the ground. The gun slides across the floor when he slams my hand down, weakening my grip.

We both dive, but he gets there first.

Shit, shit.

"Thea, run!" I shout. "Get out of here!"

Her shoes squeak against the floor as she moves.

Coleman jabs the gun under my chin, bruising my skin with the force of it. His expression is crazed, perfectly coiffed hair hanging in his face.

"You're done. All I have to do is get rid of you, then she's mine."

Even if I die here tonight, at least she'll be safe.

I struggle, pushing against his wrists, managing to move his aim. The gun fires and intense blistering agony bites into my upper arm.

"Fuck!" I slam my head forward, glancing off Coleman's chin, then slump over when I put too much pressure on my injured arm.

Holy shit that hurts.

"Connor! No!" Thea wails from somewhere in the room. "Stop it!"

Damn it, why is she still here? I told her to escape!

Coleman gets up on his knees and points the gun at my face. Fuck, this is it.

Then a loud *whack* has Coleman's eyes rolling back in his head as he collapses to the side, revealing Thea standing over him with a bright blue kettle, panting.

"Oh my god," she breathes as she drops it and crashes to her knees beside me. Her hands flutter over my hoodie where it's warm and sticky. "He shot you. Oh my god. We have to stop the bleeding."

"It's fine, come here." Grunting, I clutch her close with my uninjured arm, stroking her hair. She flinches when I brush over a lump. I'm woozy and aching, but the only thing that matters to me is her. "I'm sorry, Thea. I'm so sorry. I shouldn't have let you leave."

"No, shh, I'm sorry," Thea whispers, hugging me until I wince. "Shit. God, I'm sorry I didn't listen. I should've listened. I came here alone, it was so stupid, but I had to help her. I couldn't let him hurt her like he hurt me, I—"

"You're safe now. It'll be okay, baby."

She fusses over the wound, finding a dish towel to help stem the bleeding, and helps me sit up. I can't tell if it was my shoulder or lower, my whole arm throbs. I can move it, so I don't think he hit bone. If I'm lucky, it was a graze or a clean through and through. We shuffle further away from Coleman's knocked out body.

"Can you stand? We have to get you to the hospital."

"Yeah." I lean on her for support. The red staining her pristine coat catches my eye. "The blood on your coat, are you—?"

"I'm fine. Just a little banged up." She shows me her palm, where a shallow cut has mostly clotted over. "Broken glass. But I stabbed him with a screwdriver I found in the basement."

The corner of my mouth lifts. "That's my girl. Resourceful even in a crisis."

Her lower lip wobbles as she pauses, really taking me in. "I love you so much."

A band constricts around my heart. I almost lost her.

"I love you, too." With a rough sound, I gather her in my arms, kissing the top of her head. "Won't ever stop. My heart beats for you, sunshine."

"How touching."

We spring apart as Coleman climbs to his feet, the gun in hand. I step in front of Thea, shielding her as he takes aim.

"Come here, princess," he commands.

A small sound catches in her throat. She buries her fingers in the back of my hoodie.

"You willing to die for her?" Coleman's voice is creepy as fuck, completely psychotic. "I've shot you once, now I'll finish you."

"I'm not letting you near her."

Narrowing his eyes, he stalks toward us. I back up, keeping her behind me as we move into the next room.

The front door flies open and flashing lights illuminate the shadows in the living room. Shouts come from the front and back of the house.

"Freeze! Hands up!"

About fucking time.

Coleman's eyes go wide as he whirls to face the cop and the gun trained on him from behind. More responders pour in from the front.

"Put the gun down on the floor slowly!"

"Officers, this is a misunderstanding." Coleman shifts his demeanor, putting on his good teacher act. "This punk broke in."

Thea and I shuffle out of the way. I stay in front of her, hands up to show I'm unarmed.

"Drop the weapon!"

I meet his gaze and smirk. "Game over, bastard."

Watching Coleman's expression crack as the authorities disarm and cuff him is satisfying. Thea takes my hand while we are ushered outside. I'm never letting go again.

* * *

It's a madhouse on the quiet residential street outside of Coleman's place a short while later. The road is crammed with squad cars, an ambulance, a news van, and the neighbors watching the scene unfold.

Coleman is in the back of one of the police cars as the cops secure the scene and take our statements.

Thea and I are seated on the back of the ambulance as the EMT patches my injured arm. They cut my hoodie off and Thea wrapped the blanket they gave her around me to keep the frigid night air at bay.

Mom's going to have a goddamn field day when she gets wind of this. Deranged teacher, wounded protecting my girlfriend. Sympathy vote, here she comes.

"GSW, male, eighteen." A paramedic standing to the side checks off on a tablet. "We need to get you to the hospital for a CT scan so they can confirm the bullet isn't lodged in your arm."

The paramedic rolls her eyes as I lift the oxygen mask off and toss it aside.

"Fuck that, I'm not going anywhere. I feel fine." I hold Thea closer, tucked beneath my good arm. I'm not ever leaving her side. "Not without her."

"Connor, they're just trying to help." Thea rests her bandaged hand against my stomach. It shakes slightly, the shock and adrenaline wearing off. Troubled shadows cloud her beautiful eyes and I want to drive them away. "Don't give them trouble."

"I want to see Chief Landry's face when he gets here so I can look him in the eye when I tell him I fucking told him so."

"It doesn't matter now. As long as they stop him from attacking and abusing others." Thea puts her head on my good shoulder and I cradle her close.

I can't stop touching her. It's vital I feel her in my arms, to know she's okay.

"Who are they?" Thea murmurs.

A black SUV rolled up a minute ago, stopping near the ambulance. The windows are tinted. It doesn't seem like regulation, and the car model is way too expensive for a government budget.

"Feds?" I squint as the doors open and one by one the agents get out. "Maybe some kind of elite prodigy squad, they don't seem old enough."

They're not like the FBI agents shown in the movies at all, despite dressing the part with long dark coats and sunglasses at night. All four of them are tall, imposing figures. Tattoos creep up the side of some of their necks and onto the backs of hands as they adjust their sleeves and cast assessing glances around. One with thick, slicked back blond hair gives orders to one of the other guys with inky hair and a contemptuous frown.

"Ten minutes. In and out," the blond agent says curtly. He addresses the most hostile looking guy in the group. "Keep it clean."

A dangerous vibe rolls off them and people give them a wide berth as soon as they move like shadows through the bustling scene, spreading out. Agent Grumpy heads in the house, while the rest follow the domineering blond dude who must be in charge.

The agent stops an officer by planting a hand on his chest. The officer is annoyed until the fed removes his sunglasses and speaks too low for us to hear. Whatever he says, it has the officer heeling to his chain of command, jerking a thumb behind him at the squad car where Coleman is in custody.

He motions to another officer and Coleman is yanked from the car, then marched over to the group of feds. As he gets closer, Thea tenses. I clutch her in a hug. He can't get her now.

Coleman goes willingly enough, until he sees who he's trudging toward. He freezes.

"No." He loses his cool, paling. Struggling against the officers, he tries to get back to the car. "No, no!"

"Is that any way to greet me?" The lead agent asks with a sadistic gleam in his eyes. He holds out his hands. "I told you we'd find you. No point in running."

Coleman hollers in protest as the two other intense agents grab his arms. They have no problem containing him. Their boss gets in Coleman's face, grabbing his jaw and forcing his head back. The curve of his smirk is lethal.

With a sharp nod to his guys, they drag Coleman to the SUV and shove him in the back seat. One pulls out a knife as he slides in with him.

My brows jump up. Are switchblades FBI regulation? Thea finds my hand around her waist and grips it tight. I stroke my thumb over her knuckles to soothe her while we watch.

The lead agent flicks his gaze at us. He motions in our direction, then stalks off toward the house.

After watching his boss' back for a moment, the remaining agent comes over. I blink in surprise when he stands in the pool of light from the open ambulance. This guy can't be much older than Thea and I, maybe two or three years at most. He has tousled dark brown hair and a sick neck tattoo of a crow in flight. His coat is open, revealing ripped black jeans.

There's no way these guys are real FBI.

"Need a statement. Shoo," he says to the EMT working on me. The EMT gives the guy an unimpressed look. He chuckles and nods his head toward the house. "You have a problem with it, you can take it up with him. Trust me, he is in a pissy as fuck mood right now. Rough target for him to finally get his hands on."

"Fine." The EMT points at me. "Don't think about leaving the scene. Coherent or not, you need to see a surgeon as soon as possible."

"He's not going anywhere," Thea assures him, squeezing my hand. "I'll make sure of it."

The fed imposter grins at her, winking. "You're cute as a button."

A growl rumbles in my chest. He lifts his hands in surrender.

"Just sayin', man." Once the EMT moves away, he gives me a once over. "Should've waited. Our way was a lot cleaner than all this fuss. Here."

He hands me a thumb drive and doesn't wait for an answer before walking back to meet up with the other guys.

"Do you know them?" Thea asks.

"I think so."

When I look up, the imposter agents are piling into the SUV with a drawer from Coleman's bureau and the computer tower. All the evidence of Coleman's crimes. The doors slam, then the SUV peels out and speeds away.

Something tells me Coleman won't make it to jail.

Whatever. The only thing that matters is Thea's safety. I lean my head on hers, breathing easier when a hint of her sweet scent hits my nose.

THIRTY-NINE
Connor

As the anesthesia from surgery wears off, I wake up groggy in a hospital room. Thea is by the bed, holding my hand as she dozes, her head resting on her folded arm. Her hand is re-bandaged.

"Hey, man," Devlin says from a chair by the window, Blair asleep in his lap with her head on his shoulder and his coat draped over her.

"Time is it?" My tongue moves sluggishly and a gross metallic taste makes me grimace.

"Late. You got out of surgery at eleven and it took a couple of hours for the drugs to wear off."

Out in the hall, I hear Mom's grating voice, followed by Dad telling her to keep it down. She's arguing about using this to turn around the approval ratings after they took a hit. The gunshot wasn't a fatal injury, but Mom is here to put on her show anyway.

Rolling my eyes at her ridiculous bid for a boost in her numbers, I angle my head to get a look at the bandage covering my upper arm. It's stupid that I'm even in the hospital. I told the paramedic I didn't want to come, but Thea insisted to be on the safe side. I couldn't refuse the pleading look she gave me.

"What's the damage?"

"Stress fracture and stitches, but you're lucky. It went in and out and missed anything vital. Minor fragments and the residue left behind, but the nurse said most of it was the force of impact to the tissue from close range."

"Still hurts like a bitch." I flop my head back to the pillow, easing my frustration by brushing Thea's hand with my thumb. "Did you bring my computer?"

"Yeah, hang on." Devlin nudges Blair, his smile tender as she makes a quiet sound. "He's up. Want to sleep still?"

"No, I'm awake." She moves off his lap, wrapping the peacoat around her shoulders. Her gaze shifts to me. "Glad you didn't die."

I snort, then regret it when it makes my arm throb. "Hi to you, too. Dev, can you also get the flash drive from the pocket of my jeans?"

Devlin gets my laptop out from a bag by his chair, then rummages through the plastic bag containing what's left of my clothes in the corner. At all the movement, Thea startles awake, gripping my hand tighter. Her wide eyes relax once she realizes where she is.

"Hey," I say softly. "Okay, baby?"

"Yeah, I was having a bad dream." She presses her forehead to the back of my hand. "It wasn't real."

"It wasn't." I pat the bed. "Come here."

"No, I don't want to hurt you." She gets up, gesturing with her hands. "You just got out of surgery!"

Gripping her wrist, I tug until she falls into an awkward position, bracing her arms on either side of me.

"Do I seem like I'm a severely injured invalid?" I run my good hand up her side. She no longer has the blood-stained coat on, down to a fuzzy yellow sweater and tan pants. "Come here, baby. I need you close."

"Fine, but if the doctor comes in, I'm not taking the blame for any trouble we get in."

"I'd break every rule just to have you close."

She settles on her side next to me in bed, kissing my cheek. "I'm so glad you're okay."

"I'm more glad that you're okay." I cup her face and pull her closer, capturing her lips in a kiss. Her body trembles as I hug her against my uninjured side, feeling the remnants of tension bleeding away. "It'll all be okay now. He can't hurt you anymore."

She makes a soft sound of agreement, pressing her face into my neck. A hot wetness against my skin makes me squeeze her as tight as I can, trying to pull her pain onto my shoulders to help her bear the weight of what she faced tonight. When things have calmed down, I'll be whatever she needs to support her through dealing with the emotional fallout of knowing she was a victim of grooming.

"Here." Devlin brings the laptop and flash drive over, setting it up on the tray table.

I pull the tray closer with Thea's help.

"What do you think is on it?" she asks.

My brow creases as I open the folder on the drive. From the scraps I know of the guys impersonating federal agents, it could be anything. "Let's find out."

"Financial reports." Devlin leans over my shoulder from the other side of the bed.

Not just financial reports. I jerk forward, trying to sit up, only to grit my teeth at the discomfort it causes. Some of the machines connected to me throw off warning beeps before settling down as I lay prone.

"What's wrong?" Thea bounces her gaze from the screen to me. "Don't move so much, you're going to hurt yourself."

"They're statements of my accounts." I nod to each file. "Trust fund and the private accounts."

The ones I use to grow my bitcoin investments.

"So they're watching you?" Devlin clarifies.

"No. Well, yes, probably. The balances are all tripled from when I looked at them last. That was only a few days ago."

Whoever the hackers are, they're powerful.

Devlin and Thea give me matching expressions, brows rising high. Blair whistles from the visitor's chair across the room. I was close to my goal before, but this is beyond. With this much money, I no longer have to wait to escape Mom's bullshit. A disbelieving laugh huffs out of me.

"Holy shit," Thea murmurs. "That's a lot of money."

I already know what I'll do with some of it. My gaze slides to her. Her dream is to open a bakery. I'll make that happen sooner than she planned.

A commotion at the door draws our attention. Thea's mom bustles in, arguing with the nurse on her tail. Thea tenses at my side.

"No, I will not stay out!" Mrs. Kennedy snaps. She takes one look at the two of us in the hospital bed and her lip curls. "Thea! Let's go. You're coming home right now."

"I'm staying here." Thea sits up, but remains by my side. "I'm where I belong."

"You are not. Get away from that boy right now." Mrs. Kennedy shakes her head violently. "When I heard from Maisy's father what happened tonight with your teacher, hours later, I—"

"Mom." Thea sighs and squeezes my wrist. Sliding from the bed, she goes to her mom, taking her by the shoulders. "You can't keep smothering me. What you told me yesterday? The way you did it? You should've told me a long time ago instead of the way you handled it." She lowers her voice, but remains firm and strong. "If you had, maybe I wouldn't have questioned everything that was normal about myself. I didn't understand why you were so strict with the way I dressed because you weren't open or honest about your sister."

"Thea," Mrs. Kennedy whispers, throat working. "I only wanted to keep you safe, but you still ended up in danger."

Swiping away tears, Thea goes on. Her voice quivers with emotion. "I'm not blaming you. Or myself. It's no one's fault but Mr. Coleman's for manipulating and preying on me in a vulnerable state. He's the actual monster to blame for hurting me. It was a perfect storm, but I can't go back and change it now."

Pride blooms in my chest watching my girl stand up for herself and not allowing what she went through to bring her down. She's so strong, even when the world is crushing her. I didn't think I could love her anymore than I already do, but the warm glow fills me up from the inside.

Her mom is rendered speechless, expression crumbling. "I didn't hear from you and I was so scared."

"I know. I'm sorry, it was a crazy night and I forgot to call you once it was all over. Learning about the truth and getting attacked by him on the same day was a lot to handle." Thea rubs her mom's arms as she collapses against her, crying into her neck. Thea meets my eyes over her hysterical mother's shoulder. "I'm okay, I promise."

"I'm sorry," Mrs. Kennedy cries. "I'll do better."

"Okay. Shh, it's okay," Thea soothes. "Why don't you head home? You've seen I'm safe. I'm not sure if I'll come back tonight or stay here."

"Will you call me?"

"Yes. We have a lot to talk about."

Sniffling into the tissue Thea hands her, Mrs. Kennedy nods, calming down. The door opens again and my mother steps in, phone pressed to her ear. Dad's right on her tail, going to sit in the visitor chairs with a weary sigh.

She gives Thea and her mom a dirty look. "Damien, I'll call you back. Handle it." Hanging up, she addresses the room. "Here's the story when the reporter arrives in the morning—"

"Mom." My severe tone cuts her off. "Take your image worries and your campaign and shove it up your ass."

"Connor," she hisses, attention swinging between everyone in the room. "Are you cranky from surgery?"

"Vivian, give him a break," Dad complains.

Nice sentiment, but too little too late, Dad.

"The come down's a bitch, but no. I'm done playing your political games. I'm not your dancing circus bear anymore, effective immediately."

"We can talk about this later." She sniffs importantly. "When you're feeling better."

"Now's good for me. The thing is, Mom, you have no way to control me anymore. You want the car back? Take it. I'll buy a new one when I move out."

She narrows her eyes. "With what money?"

It's clear from her expression. She thinks she's got me.

I turn the laptop. "The trust fund from granddad is very generous." He never told her how much he set aside for me. "And from personal investments. I don't need you. You can't keep me under your thumb. If you try controlling me, I'll release the detailed documented account of your affair with your campaign manager."

Color drains from her face and her smug look falls before she plasters another blank mask in place to cover for the slip. It's not as detailed as I make the threat to sound, but my reputation precedes me. She believes my bluff. Still, I go for a final blow.

"Everything. I'll leak it to your political rivals and the press."

"Fine," she snaps.

Thea returns to my side, taking my hand. Together we stand as a united front against my overbearing mother. Nothing has ever felt better.

FORTY
Thea

THE finishing touches on the sour cream donuts are perfect. They smell amazing and I can't wait to see Connor's face when I show him my awesome skills icing these gunshot wound confections, especially with my hand still a little sore from the cut on my palm. It's almost healed now, along with my other bumps and bruises from that night.

The donuts are more gruesome than my usual style, but it's worth it to make Connor smile. I set my piping bag aside and lick excess red glaze from my fingers. With the decorating done, I take off the apron protecting my sheer blouse and the high waist fitted goldenrod corduroy skirt with buttons down the front.

Another one of my resolutions: I'm no longer dressing to hide my body. Once I found out the reason Mom was always on my case, it chased away any remaining self-consciousness, allowing me to dress in whatever feels good. I'm moving forward, not letting anything that happened stop me from enjoying my life.

Every day Connor tells me how beautiful I am, echoing my inner goddess of confidence.

I don't have to choose between Secret Folder Girl and myself, I can just be who I am because I'm enough.

Things are finally settling down. It almost felt weird to start the second semester after such a whirlwind over winter break.

When Connor was discharged from the hospital, we combed the internet, news stations, and talked to Maisy's dad for any information on the people who took Mr. Coleman into custody. Almost a month later and we still haven't heard anything.

Connor told me about the necklace he broke into the house to retrieve and how intense the hackers were about it. He is certain those guys killed Mr. Coleman for revenge. They did seem dangerous. But that man is a monster. He won't be free to attack any other girls.

As for myself, I have an appointment with a therapist specializing in cases like mine to begin working through the trauma I went through. The first thing I did the morning after the hospital was call Maisy over and tell her everything I'd kept from her. She hugged the life out of me, promising to be there for me. It felt good to be open with her and get it off my chest. Pushing the truth out was hard, though. It came in starts and stops, interrupted when I couldn't speak from my throat tightening with emotion.

I'm a little nervous to continue unpacking the things I haven't looked at directly about how Mr. Coleman abused me. The pain is so fresh it sometimes blindsides me out of nowhere. Victim. It's still a weird word in my mouth, as if it doesn't feel like it should belong to me. But does anyone feel like they've achieved the arbitrary required level of trauma before it feels like the right word? Maybe no one ever feels like it's theirs.

I'm learning to accept the shape of it, because I can't erase it or pack it away in my brain behind walls.

Not thinking about it won't make it go away. It's something I have to face in order to move forward. It doesn't have to change who I am or define me.

This is another facet of myself I will learn to treat gently.

I'll find my new normal with the support of my loved ones at my back.

Constantine nudges my leg with his snout, huffing at me when I lift my brows. His big brown eyes dart to the counter and back to me.

"One more piece, you little pig." I feed him a morsel from the broken bits of cake that didn't make the final cut. I scratch under his chin as he chomps happily. "Good boy. Let's take these outside for everyone."

Lifting the tray of bullet wound donuts, I head out back, where Connor and our friends lounge on the terrace around the blazing fire pit. My heart swells at the sight of them all. It reminds me I'm not invisible or alone.

Everyone has a quilt wrapped around them, Devlin and Blair curled together in a cushioned loveseat, Maisy sitting cross legged barefoot on a lounge chair, and Connor holding one side of his blanket open for me to nestle beside him.

Constantine comes when Blair calls him, flopping at her side while she grins, snapping pictures with her phone. His tongue lolls out, drawing a laugh from me at his blissed out expression. We've been bonding over our love of dogs. Now when she sends her friend Gemma dog posts on Instagram, she includes me in the group chat and begs me for pictures of Constantine all the time.

"I come armed with baked goods," I announce.

"Yes!" Maisy unfolds her legs and snatches a donut from the tray. She takes one look and cracks up. After taking a big bite of her bloody donut, she hums in bliss. "My sugar queen."

"I think you mean mine," Connor says in an amused tone. "What's so funny, little Landry?"

Maisy points her half-eaten donut at him. "Dude, you have got to drop that. I might be younger than my brother, but I can still kick ass."

"Play nice," I shoot over my shoulder, offering the tray to Blair and Devlin.

He examines the choices with a smirk. "Oh, I like these. Nice eye for detail."

Blair takes two donuts, biting into the first while admiring the second, nodding in agreement with her boyfriend. "Gruesome. These are rad as hell." She closes her eyes and hangs her head back. "Tastes so good."

The corner of Devlin's mouth lifts and he leans into Blair's space to give her a languid kiss. Seeing her enjoying herself always makes his chiselled features soften in fondness.

I set the tray on the ottoman between Connor and Maisy, taking a donut for myself and Connor.

"Come over here." He lures me to his side with a charming, crooked smile that pulls heat into my core. He knows exactly what kind of effect it has on me as he tugs me down onto the wide cushion, enveloping me with the blanket. "That's better."

"What's that?" I ask, nodding to the real estate page he has loaded on his phone. "Looking for an apartment already? I thought you were joking when you told your mom you'd move out."

He tucks his phone away before I get a good look at the property he was checking out. "It's nothing. I'm just looking right now, but once I find the perfect place, I'll show you."

Narrowing my eyes, I do an impression of one of his favorite memes. "Keep your secrets, then. Donut?"

He takes it while I bite into mine, staring at what I made for a long beat. "Your baking is taking a turn for the gory, huh?"

I try to contain my grin, but I lose the battle. "Do you like it? How does the blood taste?"

"You tell me."

He swipes his finger through the decorative frosting and holds it up to my lips. Cheeks hot, I part my them and dart my tongue against his fingertip. His gaze is locked on my mouth, dragging his teeth over his bottom lip.

"I'm about to haul you off to the pool house."

I tap his chest with a light smack, lowering my voice. "Don't tease me, then!" Wrapping the blanket tighter around us, I drop my hand to his lap, running it over his semi-hard dick. "You brought this on yourself. We're hanging out with our friends."

With a groan, he drops his head back. I break a piece off my donut and feed it to him. He chews for a minute.

"It's delicious, baby. It always is with you."

Maisy, Blair, and Devlin sound off in agreement, reaching for seconds.

There's nothing like feeding the people you care about with something you baked with love. "I'm glad you all like them."

Surrounded by our friends and wrapped in Connor's arms, my heart is full of the brightest joy. It breaks through any shadows, lighting me up with an ember of warmth that makes me feel stronger.

"Face mask self-care day tomorrow. You in?" Maisy points between Blair and me.

"Wouldn't miss it," I say. "Do you like face masks, Blair?"

She blinks, glancing at Devlin. He rubs her arm, dropping a kiss on her shoulder.

"Uh, sure. I've never done one."

"Oh my god! *Girl*. I'm about to change your life. This is it, this is our bonding moment.

Come with me." Maisy gets up, taking Blair's hands. "This can't wait. We're doing this right now. Come on, Devlin. You're doing one, too. We'll film it and put it on our stories. Baby's first face mask!"

Leaning against Connor, I laugh at Blair's perplexed expression. "Go on, she doesn't have an off switch when she decides to do something. It doesn't take long and it feels good."

"Take lots of pictures," Connor says. "I want proof of our Devil Boy in his true form."

Devlin flips him off.

Maisy snaps and points at Connor. "You're right. Is your hair long enough for pigtails? They'll look like horns. It'll be bomb."

"Aren't you, like, quiet at school? What the hell?" Devlin asks, bewildered.

"Not around people that know me," she says.

"Never underestimate the quiet ones, bro."

I shake my head. "You did. Look where it got you."

"Yeah?" Connor pulls me on his lap, trapping me in his strong arms as he puts his lips by my ear. "It got me a lapful of this."

I laugh and yelp as he attacks my neck with kisses. No matter what happened before, I'm safe and loved now. The shining truth of it glows in my chest.

"Okay, enjoy the make-out time," Maisy says as she herds Devlin and Blair through the back door. "Don't get too frisky. Or do. You know, self-care. Peace, bitches."

"You heard her," Connor murmurs, angling my head back for a languid kiss. "Mm, you always smell sweeter when you bake. I love it."

I shift around on his lap so I can face him, looping my hands around his neck. "How does your arm feel? I know you think you're superhuman, but the sling only came off a couple weeks ago."

"It's good." He takes my hand that was cut and brings it to his lips, kissing each of my knuckles. His gray eyes meet mine, full of warmth. He's quiet for a moment, taking me in. "You hold my heart in your hands. Promise you'll take care of it, okay?"

I give him an impish smirk, cupping his jaw. He drops another kiss to my healing palm. "Like take it for walks and keep it fed? Easy, it's just like caring for Constantine."

Connor wraps his arms around my waist with a playful growl, dragging his mouth over my skin. "You know how I like to be fed, baby."

"My heart is yours, too," I say after he stops teasing me. "It always will be."

When he kisses me again, we lose all track of time, warmed by the fire and our love.

EPILOGUE
Thea

December, 11 Months Later

Squinting from the cryptic note Connor gave me to the numbers above the row of shops on the main street in downtown Ridgeview, I huff. After a quick kiss good morning, my boyfriend disappeared from our apartment, leaving behind a handwritten note that sent me on a wild scavenger hunt all over town. He loves these games, and I usually end up delighted by his surprises, but I would have enjoyed it more if we spent the morning cuddling in bed instead of roaming all over Ridgeview.

"This can't be right."

I glance up and down the street, standing in front of an empty storefront with big windows covered in paper. The shop sits between a florist and an art gallery, both decorated for the holidays. It was recently for sale. I secretly passed by it every day on my way to work making pastries at the coffee shop, imagining how nice a mural would look on the wall inside. It would be a big sun and moon celestial painting surrounding the name of my future bakery—Eclipsed Tarts Baking Co.

The sign in the window reads *Sold*.

So much for my big dream. It was too expensive, anyway. Commercial leases in Ridgeview have pretty much put my plans on hold until I sell a kidney to get my startup.

Connor has been offering to get me going. I keep turning him down because he does so much for me. He already pays for our apartment. In a year he's grown his finances even more, officially a self-made man from releasing an app he built that took off for its uses in preventing security breaches and identifying threats, especially predators. He doesn't want what happened to me to happen to anyone else if he can help stop it. He has been amazing in helping me cope with the fallout of my trauma, and I'm proud he put his skills to use for something good to help others.

But his scavenger hunt note led me here, promising my path to the future if I open the door.

"Okay. Here goes nothing." I pull a face, bracing as I twist the knob. "Please don't let me get arrested for breaking and entering."

"You're too cute for that," Connor says, grinning from across the room. He's leaning against a polished wood counter with the sleeves of his henley pushed up, painting a very attractive picture. "You're about twenty minutes later than I expected."

I hold up the paper as I enter the building, glancing around. It's lit in warm muted light by the thin kraft paper covering the bay windows. "Leave better clues, then."

"What? Which one was hard?" Popping out of his slouch, he plucks the note from me as his arm finds its way around my waist. "Number seven? No way, I made that one obvious."

"Number three!" Gripping his biceps, I press on my tiptoes to kiss him. He tilts his head, a smirk playing in the corners of his mouth. "Hi. Going to tell me what mischief you're up to today?"

"Thinking about it." His hands slip inside my coat, fitting to my waist over my long black skirt with big sunflowers printed on it. He dips into the high slit with one hand as his other teases beneath my cropped sweater, tracing exposed skin. "Thinking about something else, too. Especially when you wear this."

"When aren't you thinking about that." With a sardonic smile, I shrug out of my white wool coat—a replacement from the one I had last year—and drape it over the counter. It looks newly built. I don't remember the photos on the real estate website having anything inside, but now it seems like whoever owns the place has been getting it ready. "Are we allowed to be in here? I saw the sign out front. I know you love bad ideas, but—"

"We're allowed. This is actually one of my better ones."

He follows me as I explore the main room. I imagine how I'd paint the wall, make the one behind the counter a chalk wall with an artistic display of the daily menu, and fill the back one with a similar poster mural of inspiration and positivity just like my old bedroom. I have one in our apartment that grows every time I find something new to add. It would look perfect in my bakery to create an uplifting environment that will make people smile.

"Do you know who bought this place?"

Connor tucks his hands in his pockets. "I do."

"What are they going to put here? It looks like a shop."

He hums as if he's pondering, wrapping his arms around me from behind. "A bakery, I think."

"Really?" My face falls. A second later, I shake my head and turn in his arms. "That's so great. Maybe I can get a job here instead of the coffee shop!"

Connor's smile turns fond. "Baby. The building is for you. I bought it."

It takes a moment for his words to register as I'm lost in the process of how to quit my job. I blink, digging my fingers into his shirt. "Wait what?"

He chuckles, kissing my cheek. "I'm saying it's yours, all of it."

"You…" I gape, gaze flying around the room. "And you built…"

"Yes. You kept showing me your Pinterest vision board, and I had Maisy help me design the style you saved most."

I'm speechless, mouth working helplessly. Tears of joy prick my eyes. "Oh my god."

"I want to give you the world. Help you achieve all of your dreams." He brushes a knuckle under my eye to catch a stray tear. "Do you like it?"

"Like it? I fucking love it, you crazy, wonderful man!" Laughter bursts free as I crash into him, hugging him tight.

"Oh, f-bomb. I know I got it right when you start letting those slip." He kisses the top of my head. "Love you, sunshine."

"I love you, too. This is the best surprise. Oh my god." I can't stop saying it. "I'm opening a bakery."

"You are." Connor grins into the kiss he gives me. "I have one more surprise."

"Okay, but you probably should've led with that one. I don't think you can top this."

His gray eyes gleam. "We'll see. Close your eyes."

Tugging the sleeves of my sweater over my hands, I cover my eyes. A few moments later, Connor is back, cupping my elbow. He takes a shaking breath, drawing my attention. He's usually confident no matter what he does.

"Okay, you can look."

When I lower my hands, Connor kneels on one bent knee in front of me, thumbs stroking the sides of my legs. My eyes go wide.

"Are you—"

"Not if you interrupt with your classic nervous babbling."

I mime zipping my lips and tossing away the key. It makes him huff out a laugh, a tenderness lighting up his handsome features.

"I've known you're the girl I'd marry since you first challenged me every step of the way with your not so quiet stubbornness and logic. You're my perfect match"

As a watery puff of amusement escapes me, he pulls out a velvet box, popping the lid back to reveal a ring that steals my breath. It's two rings fitted together, a sun captured by a moon. An eclipse, like he describes our love. In the center is a pearlescent moonstone. A lump clogs my throat.

"Connor," I whisper.

He lifts his gaze to meet mine, taking one of my hands. "Thea, I'd wait until the end of time for you. But I need you to know you're it for me. There's no one but you."

I release a garbled, incoherent sound and fall into his arms. He catches me as we collapse to the floor, lips locked together. When we part, he rubs his nose along my cheek, hands cupping my ass.

"What do you say?"

"Yes, obviously."

He snorts, taking my hand once again. With his eyes burning into my soul, he kisses my ring finger and slides the engagement ring into place.

"I love you so much," I say. "I didn't know it was possible to be so happy."

"Let me keep surprising you. I'm not going to stop now." He makes me squeal as he holds me tight, climbing to his feet. My arms wind around his neck. "We have a lifetime of surprises ahead of us. Together."

Together.

When I'm happy, he lifts my spirits higher, and when I'm aching, he holds me while I cry, offering his strength until I restore my own. He takes care of me and I take care of him.

"As long as I'm with you, I feel like I can do anything."

"You always could." He sets me down on top of the counter and braces his hands on either side of my hips. "You prove that every day."

I bite my lip around a wicked smirk I've picked up from dating him in the last year. "I'm about to prove something else. With my tongue."

"God, yes." Connor steals a quick kiss. "Hold that thought, though. They're all waiting to come in."

"Who?"

"Our friends. They all helped get the bakery together, so keeping the proposal a secret from them was impossible. Gemma wanted to camp out behind the counter all sniper style to capture your reaction."

As he explains, he types out a text on his phone. A minute later, the door opens and everyone in our life spills in. I hop down to meet them, hugging Maisy first before she makes it across the threshold.

"Dude. You're getting married."

"Holy crap," I mumble into her neck.

When we part, the loud rev of a motorcycle cuts into our celebratory moment. We both look up as Fox Wilder glares at Maisy from across the street, sitting on his bike. She stiffens, breaking their tense staring match first.

While she examines her feet, Fox's sneer fades. He meets my eyes for a beat before driving off. Once the roar of his bike dwindles, Maisy sighs.

"Is he still bothering you?" I ask.

"No. Yes? I don't know. It's senior year, but he hasn't grown up from his stupid feud. At least Holden graduated with you guys, so now Fox doesn't seem to be around every corner as much, throwing what we don't have in my face." She shrugs, tucking her highlighted brown hair behind an ear. "I just wish things could be like before, when we were kids...when we were friends. This is so stupid."

"Don't let him get to you. And if he's still bullying you, Connor and Devlin will kick his punk little ass."

Maisy snorts at the fierce expression on my face. "Okay, come on, killer. It's your day. My petty life dramas can wait."

Hooking her arm over my shoulders, she steers me inside where the rest of our friends are elbowing Connor in congratulations. His gray eyes fall on me and his smile grows. He pulls me to his side as Lucas Saint's girlfriend snaps photos with her camera.

Over the summer while they were on break from college, she helped me grow more comfortable with my body by modeling for her any chance she needed me. She has a real eye. When I see myself in her photos, it feels as if I've bared my soul to the lens, never worrying if there's a difference between the mirror and the photo because I love myself, even on the days it's hard and those dark thoughts creep up on me. When they do, I take myself through the affirmations my therapist had me write out to process those painful thoughts.

Blair slides up next to me and Maisy squeezes in on the other side.

Gemma hands her camera off to Lucas. "Group shot, babe. Girls first, then the guys."

"You've got it." He holds up the camera. "Work it, ladies."

Connor elbows Devlin, grinning. "Damn. We are lucky bastards."

"Fucking truth," Devlin murmurs, with eyes only for Blair.

The door opens again and my parents come in. Mom gives me a tentative smile. I motion her over and show her the ring. As soon as Connor and I graduated, we moved out of our houses to live in the apartment he bought for us. Things have been somewhat bumpy and slow learning to be honest with each other, but they're improving. We're getting to a point we can be a mom and a daughter again. Dad is taking less regional jobs and they've started seeing the same therapist as Connor to work through her suppressed grief for her sister.

Someone plays music from a phone and we bring in take out and snacks from one of the nearby shops on the strip. Tucked against Connor's side, I soak in the love our friends and family share with us.

"You and me," I murmur to him, stealing his chip, then a kiss. "Always and forever."

"Ends of the earth, to the moon, wherever doesn't matter. I'll love you."

He takes my hand and pulls me from my seat on the counter he built, leading me to the middle of the room. Our friends cheer and hold up phones to record us as Connor sweeps me into a dance, twirling me in the middle of my future bakery.

EPILOGUE
Thea

Paris, Six Months Later

"Where do you think you're going? Get back here, I'm not done with you yet." Grabbing Thea by the ankle, I drag her across the bed and latch my mouth over her nipple while tracing her sun-shaped birthmark. She squeals, writhing in the sheets as I tease her. "I need to fuck my wife silly before we go anywhere."

"Silly achieved," she breathes, wrapping her legs around my waist and rolling her hips against me. "We reached it three rounds ago, you insatiable monster."

"I can't help it when it comes to you. Marrying you doesn't change that."

I reach across the bed to take another chocolate covered strawberry from the plate by the open window, the Eiffel Tower in view. Warm, breezy June air billows through the curtains, kissing over our sweaty skin. We've been in bed all morning, indulging in alone time. Chilled champagne sits in a bucket beside the strawberries. Eloping in Europe was a damn good idea.

Our friends are out exploring the city today, or shut away in their own hotel room in Blair and Devlin's case, leaving us to enjoy our honeymoon. Devlin married us as our officiant and Gemma photographed the intimate ceremony. Thea has never looked more radiant than she did reading her handwritten vows from a yellow notebook with a rainbow print on it, her promises penned between the pages of her favorite recipes.

The official wedding isn't until September back home in Colorado, but Thea was going crazy planning a wedding and opening a bakery at the same time. It was time I made good on a promise I made over a year ago, when we first began. Even if the idea to whisk her to Paris was something I pulled out of the air, she's been dying to visit real patisseries.

It was worth it for the look on her face. I love surprising her. I'll never stop doing it.

We might be young, but we both know what we want. What's the point in waiting around?

Feeding the strawberry to Thea, I say, "Well, then I'll just have to do my daily worship with my tongue at the altar between your thighs."

She moans as the chocolate cracks, sucking on the juicy strawberry. Her eyes widen and she sits up, flailing her hands.

"Pause! I've just had the best idea for a fun Valentine's day private order adult line.

Where's my notebook?"

I sprawl across the bed, propping my head on my hand, enjoying the sight of her naked ass as she moves to get one of her recipe journals. Her auburn hair spills over her shoulder while she scribbles the idea down.

"Babe, the bakery doesn't open for another two weeks and you've already got a whole menu."

"I know, I know. But this is too good." She spreads her hands dramatically. "Chocolate molds of your partner!"

"You're going to make this into a chocolate replica?" I stroke my cock, shooting her a sly grin. "How much testing will be involved?"

After setting her notebook aside, she shuffles back to me on her knees, straddling my hips. "Oh, plenty."

"I like this idea." I skim my palms up her thighs to cup her tits. "Now you're definitely not escaping. I need you again."

Thea's head falls back when my cock sinks into her body. She moans softly, riding my dick at a torturously slow pace.

She's so fucking beautiful it carves an ache into my chest.

I squeeze her waist, bucking up with a sharp thrust that has her mouth dropping open on a gasp. "Like that?"

"Always," she murmurs, bracing her hands on my chest as she leans in for a sensual kiss.

Always. Our whole future together. I can't wait for all of it.

With the girl of my dreams—my *wife*—in my arms, the world is perfect.

SINNERS & SAINTS

SAVAGE WILDER

BOOK FOUR

PROLOGUE
Maisy

10 Years Ago

"That's not fair!" I cry, chasing after my brother and our best friend. "You can't win just because you're nine, you jerk heads!"

Their laughter echoes as the three of us run down the quiet street where we all live. They're both a year older and bigger than me, meaning the boys can outrun me easily. It makes me so mad! Girls can be just as awesome at things as boys. I'll show them.

"Holden!" I yell at my brother's back as frustration bubbles up in my chest.

"Suck it up, Maisy. You lost!" Holden shoots a mean grin over his shoulder. "Maisy Daisy is a crybaby loser!"

"I am not!" I shout loud enough that a few birds startle and fly away from the towering pine trees behind the houses on the block.

Fox slows down, trailing Holden far enough that I can catch up. Once I'm beside him, he bumps his shoulder into mine and shoots me a secretive smirk. Some of the frustration leaves me.

"I'm not a crybaby," I mumble sourly.

A huff of laughter escapes him and he gives me a sly look from the corner of his eyes. They're like the ocean, dark blue and mysterious. I really want to see the ocean again someday. Both our families went last summer and it was my favorite trip, hunting for seashells and cool rocks with Fox and Holden as the waves crashed against the beach in California. I loved it so much, I made a bracelet of the stones Fox gave me. I never take it off.

"You're not," Fox agrees. After a pause, his mouth curves into the trickster smile he gets when he wants to make trouble. It's a smile that always draws me in for his sneaky plans. "Let's get him back."

I grin. "Deal."

After high-fiving, he wraps an arm around my shoulder to tug me closer, whispering in my ear. He's warm and smells like the sweet summer grass and a little like the motor oil from his dad's garage. They must have been working on his dad's motorcycle before he came out to play. My nose scrunches at the mix, but I don't pull away.

"You distract him, and I'll find a beetle," he instructs.

I have to cover my mouth to keep my excitement from sneaking out and giving us away. It's a perfect plan. Holden stayed up late one time and saw a scary movie about an army of mutant insects that freaked him out forever. Now he's terrified of beetles because of one of the scenes.

Nodding, I try to wink at Fox, but I end up blinking twice. Lame. He grins, shaking his head and messing with his dark brown hair as he slips away to hunt through the neighbor's bushes.

My brother has stopped running, waiting for Fox and I near the end of the street.

"Holden," I sing-song, skipping to quickly close the distance between us. "If you don't stop being so mean to me, Fox says he won't trade the Flareon he caught in Pokémon last week with you." I stick my tongue out to sell my taunting distraction. "And I won't show you how to build a cool treehouse on Animal Crossing."

"What?" Holden hisses. He brushes the long ends of his floppy light brown hair from his forehead agitatedly. It's the same shade as mine. People used to think we were twins even though he's older. "You both promised. I need those for my challenges!"

Fox walks up, not giving anything away except for his hands tucked behind him. "What are we playing next? You beat us both to the finish line, so you pick."

Holden shakes his head. "Not yet." He whirls on Fox. "You swear you're going to trade your Flareon with me?"

Fox tilts his head. "Yeah, dude."

Holden relaxes and mulls over what he wants to play next.

"Hide and seek?" I suggest, unable to hold back a tiny smirk as I practically squirm with anticipation of what's to come.

"No, you lost. You don't get to pick." Holden sighs. "But hide and seek does sound good."

"Yeah?" Fox grins. "I was thinking the same thing. Can you hold this for me while we hide from your sister?"

Before Holden can finish nodding, Fox grabs his hand and shakes out a round striped beetle into Holden's palm. It's a harmless potato bug, I think. My brother looks down and his brown eyes go wide. A scream tears from his throat as he flails his hand around to get the bug off. The tiny little thing drops to the ground, wriggling in confusion for a moment before scurrying away while Holden freaks out, waving his hand around like it was poisoned.

"Got you!" I cheer, giving Fox a triumphant high five. "That's what you get for cheating."

Holden's face twists in embarrassed irritation. He swipes his hand on his jeans, over his freak out now that the bug is gone. "You guys suck!"

My delighted laughter breaks free, making me double over and hug my belly when a cramp twinges. Fox leans against me for support as we fall into hysterics at our revenge prank.

"Whatever," Holden grumbles, waving a hand to act like he's all cool. We totally got him. "I'm going home to play Xbox. This is boring."

Satisfaction fills me to the brim as I watch my brother jog across the street to our house.

Holden can be such a whiny butthead sometimes, but Fox likes him anyway. I do too, because he's my brother, and he's not *always* a jerk. The three of us have grown up on this street since before I can remember. Our mom and his parents work together and they're close friends.

"Maise, come look."

Fox has wandered over to the grassy field at the end of the block. The tree the three of us challenge each other to climb every week sits in the middle. Beyond the tall grass and wildflowers, the woods stretch up into the hills at the base of the Rocky Mountains. I walk over, automatically reaching up to catch one of the lower branches of the tree and swing back and forth like a gymnast.

"What's up?" I try to get higher, but the bark bites into my hands.

He pops up from the tall grass and reaches for me, tickling my stomach, making me shriek and wriggle until I'm forced to let go of the branch or keep suffering his attack.

Once I'm on the ground, I curl into a protective crouch so he can't mess with me. "What the heck?"

Fox snorts. "You make it too easy."

"There are rules, Fox," I point out, standing up. We have them written down and everything in a notebook with Pokémon stickers on the front. I huff importantly and recite the sacred rule: "No tickling when a climber is in the tree."

The corners of his mouth lift and his eyes are bright. "Yeah, you're right." He taps my nose. "Sorry."

"What did you want me to see?"

"I found this."

Fox holds up a wildflower he picked, his crooked smile turning proud. It's dainty with thin light purple petals, not like the white daisies we usually see. A small gasp escapes me as I take it.

"It's so pretty." I touch a soft petal carefully. "What's it for?"

"You're *my* daisy."

Fox waits until I tear my attention from the flower to look at him in surprise. He's serious, his eyebrows wrinkled as he stares at me. Reaching out, he circles his fingers around my wrist. I watch, wide-eyed as he leans down and places a kiss on the wildflower clutched in my hands.

"I'm going to marry you someday," he promises.

A feeling like butterflies fills my chest as I stare back at him.

"Okay," I whisper.

He grins and tugs on my wrist. "Come on. There's something else I want to show you. It's in my dad's garage. I wasn't supposed to find it, but I did when Dad went to answer a call and left me alone." We walk a few steps, then he stops us. "You have to promise not to tell anyone. Even Holden. Got it?"

I nod. "Promise."

Flying on the giddiness making me dizzy, I follow Fox, like I always do.

* * *

A week later my world feels crushed.

I sit outside my house with my knees tucked against my chest and my arms wrapped around my skinny legs. Holden is at the end of the block throwing a football at our favorite climbing tree over and over. Across the street, the crooked for sale sign stuck in the Wilder's front lawn mocks me.

The *someday* he promised me won't come.

Fox Wilder is gone.

ONE
Maisy

THERE are less than two months until graduation and Fox picks now to start messing with me again.

Well, no. He actually chose a couple weeks ago, but I slam down hard on that memory before it can assault me.

I squeeze Sam's hand tight as we descend the steps from Silver Lake High School to the student parking lot at the base of the hill where our classmates hoot and call to each other while revving the engines of their expensive cars. The warm breeze moving through the pine trees carries the seniors' rowdiness high above the school's sprawling mountainside campus.

Fox Wilder's eyes don't leave me for a second as he leans against his motorcycle with his arms crossed. Whenever his attention is on me, I know something horrible is coming. I can't decide if it was better to be ignored by my oldest friend, or to be his plaything with a target on my back.

Once he got it through my head last year that he despises me for some reason, he mostly left me alone. But that's over now. Almost every day for the last two weeks he has some new twisted way to fuck with my head.

This time I don't have my older brother or my friends to watch out for me, so I'm on my own to stand up to his bullying crap.

The leather jacket he wears stretches tight over the muscled arms I know hide beneath. He shifts his rigid posture, poised on his hunt for my pain and humiliation. Despite the warm spring weather, he's in all black from his jacket to his jeans to his boots.

Everyone else abides the preppy SLHS uniform—black blazers embroidered with the school's gold crest, slacks for the guys, and evergreen plaid skirts for the girls. There are some who bend the rules for a shorter hem, a loose tie, or more fashionable shoes, and then there's Fox, who never pays attention to the dress code, always the outlaw king of his own world.

No one can tell him what to do, not even the school faculty. They're as afraid of him as everyone else in town.

His stormy dark blue gaze is hard and angry as usual, thick brows set in a permanent scowl. It's the only way I've known my old friend since he returned to Ridgeview last year like a ghost coming back to haunt me with the heartache I've carried since he left Colorado.

At first it killed me to be reunited only to feel the impenetrable wall Fox kept around him, allowing only a select few in. Holden was one of them. But not me.

I don't know why, but it's clear he can't stand me now. I know I'm not as impulsive thanks to Mom's obsession with public image, but I'm not so different from the girl he used to know.

I brush my fingers over the bracelet I've worn forever, the braided leather soft from age. It has three stones Fox found for me on a beach in California the year before our lives changed.

Fox was my friend, too.

The bitterness that rises in the back of my throat tastes awful and I roll my stiff shoulders. Looks like I'm in for another extended yoga routine tonight to ease the ache in my body from being wound so tightly. My heart hasn't gotten the memo, giving a hopeful flutter every time Fox is around. As if he'll suddenly get over whatever reason he's holding a grudge against me.

Lost cause, girl. Let that energy go because it ain't manifesting no matter how hard we will it.

The truth stings, but I've learned to survive with this knife hanging over my head.

Fox was ripped from my life for ten years, then blew back into this town like a violent storm, fast and without warning. I've been holding my breath for over a year waiting for the damaging force to strike once he turned those scornful eyes on me. I used to know everything he wasn't saying behind them, when he was my closest friend. But now? I don't remember what I did to make him hate me so much and he won't give me the chance to fix it.

"Are you okay?" Sam asks with a sweet, curious look, startling me out of my thoughts. He brushes his thumb over my knuckles, all shy and polite. The corner of his mouth hooks into a boyish smile that should make my heart pound, but I've got nothing. "You went all quiet on me, beautiful. Tell me more about the sights you want to see on your road trip after graduation."

This thing with Sam Blake is...new. Really new. I don't know if I'm ready to call him my official boyfriend yet, but he's been asking me to hang out since the year started and I needed a distraction from the heavy weight of Fox's stare constantly following me everywhere at school.

Rumors about me have spread like wildfire through this drama-thirsty school. Attaching myself to Sam quelled them. For now, at least.

We weren't together when Fox and I—*no*. Nope. Not thinking about that.

Sam took me out to see a movie last weekend and did the whole pick me up at my house and shake Dad's hand thing, like I'm some maiden in waiting. He's been driving me to and from school and whenever he sees me in the hall he takes my hand and carries my books without asking. Sam is...nice. The kind of guy my parents love because he's perfect on paper in every way. Good grades, good manners, good family

I think I'm panic-dating him. Fox catches my eye again as we reach the parking lot and my body goes hot and cold all over at memories I need to forget. I really needed that distraction.

"Um, yeah, I'm great," I spit out, turning a bubbly smile on Sam.

He returns it with a wider one, the corners of his brown eyes crinkling. The color isn't as intense as Fox's dark blue gaze, which is fathomless enough to drown in when his focus is locked on me.

Crap, what did he ask? Don't read the freak out in my eyes.

"Zion," I blurt once the question registers. "Sunrise yoga in every national park I can hit."

There's more to the cross-country road trip I've been dreaming of for years, but each time I talk about it in detail Sam's eyes glaze over. My best friend Thea is the only person who cares as much as I do about my goal, and knows why I want to take the solo trip to spread my wings before I'm forced into a college my parents chose, just another part of the full life story they laid out for me as soon as I was born. The older I get, the more they try to control what I do with their expectations.

I wish I could close my eyes and go back to when I was a wild little girl who could climb trees and run free.

"Cool." Sam pulls his key fob from his pocket and unlocks the souped up blue BMW X5 parked near where Fox is watching our approach. Sam glances at me and pushes his fingers through his sandy blond hair. "Are you sure you want to take the trip by yourself? It doesn't sound safe. Maybe I can come with you. We can make it like an adventure. Just the two of us."

We're close enough now that Fox can hear our conversation. His vicious snort makes my stomach churn and my shoulders rigid.

"I'm sure. I can handle myself." I offer Sam a tight smile. "Thanks though, that's really sweet."

"Bet."

Sam is unaffected, or totally oblivious to how much inviting himself on my road trip annoyed me. Another cutting bark of amusement sounds from Fox.

Ignoring him, I get in the SUV while Sam puts both our bags in the back seat. I check my phone for messages, finding two new texts from Thea asking if I want to come by the bakery she's opening in June. Her fiancé, Connor Bishop, bought the building for her as a surprise to help her achieve her dream. They're both a year older than me, like Fox and my brother, but Fox was held back when he enrolled at Silver Lake High.

I tap out a quick reply to let her know I have volunteering and a yoga class to teach after that. Her response comes a minute later, all flowery emojis and cutesy hearts because my best friend is literal walking sunshine. My mouth curves in a fond grin at her positive energy. I smooth my fingers over the other bracelet I always wear, a brass bangle with a smooth round inlay of rose quartz. Its nurturing properties remind me of her.

Sam slides into the driver's seat and reaches across to prop his hand on my headrest, absently playing with a lock of my light brown hair from my high ponytail. "Want to come to my place?" His voice dips lower into a flirty tone. "We can do our homework, then chill in my hot tub."

The quick leer he flashes me almost has my eyebrows flying up. Wow, even the nice ones are obvious.

"Can't." I twitch my head so my hair slips through his grasp, playing it off like I'm still checking my phone. His hand drops to my leg instead, brushing my skirt up slightly and stirring another flash of irritation. "I have to be home by two so I can make it to the library on time for my volunteer shift. I don't like to let the kids down, you know? They love story time."

"Fine."

I purse my lips and dart my gaze out the window, only to meet Fox's piercing scowl a few feet away. My stomach gives another lurch of dread. He's paying too much attention to my every move, but nothing has happened yet. That can only mean—

The engine makes an awful sputtering sound as Sam presses the ignition button.

"What the—" Sam's brows pinch in confusion and he tries again.

The same thing happens and my teeth clench together. I can feel the intent press of Fox's entire presence in my periphery, but I won't give him the satisfaction of knowing he's wrecking my day. *Again.*

When Sam tries the push start button a third time with no change, I force out a sigh. "I don't think it's going to start."

"Yeah, I guess not."

Sam seems at a loss for a moment, ruffling his hair. He gets out of the SUV and eyes the front grille like it might bite him. The parking lot is emptying out fast, leaving only us and the cars of students who have after school activities.

When I hop out to see if I can help, Fox is right there, a huge wall of leather, muscle, and heat blocking my path. I stand my ground, refusing to let him intimidate me. He gives me a cool stare through the thick messy dark brown fringe hanging over his forehead. His mouth curves into a vicious smirk when he catches me staring too long at his lips.

My cheeks heat. Stupid memories. I jerk my head toward the front of the BMW so I don't have to face him or my momentary lapse into insanity. Or nostalgia? I haven't decided yet, I just know what happened at that party has brought me nothing but torment no matter how good it felt to be wild and impulsive.

"Car trouble?" Fox taunts with an edge of satisfaction in his deep voice. He doesn't spare Sam an ounce of his attention. "What a shame. Those upmarket models really aren't made to last."

Sam's head pops up from beneath the hood and he hesitates, taking in how close Fox is standing to me, almost keeping me prisoner against the side of the car. Like most of our classmates, he doesn't mess with Fox. For every new rumor about me, there have been two for him. People love to talk, everything from speculating he has a different girl every night to mob ties that bankroll him. I heard someone yesterday morning whispering that he killed a man when I was walking to my freshly vandalized locker—*thanks, Fox.*

"Yeah. It won't start."

"I can take a look," Fox offers with a merciless grin that highlights the hard-edged asshole he's become. "I know my way around cars."

My eyes narrow in suspicion. This was totally all him and he's enjoying the spectacle. Goddamn it. Why is Fox so hellbent on torturing me?

"Thanks, man. Have at it." Sam waves his hands with a relieved breath. "I don't really know a lot about cars. My dad's dealership handles all the maintenance."

I shake my head. "It's fine. We can figure it out. Or call a tow service."

"But babe, you said you had to be home in time for your volunteering thing," Sam points out.

Is Sam crazy? Fox is the reason the car won't start, and he's just going to let him back under the hood as easy as that?

The hate-filled look Fox gives me tells me he knows he's won yet again.

He steps around to peer under the hood beside Sam, shouldering him out of the way and looking comfortable with the engine parts, like he belongs with his calloused fingers working out the mechanics. Now he has witnesses as he gets his fingerprints all over the engine, touching every single part and leaving us with no way to file a police report against him to prove he did it.

I edge closer, watching his long fingers carefully to make sure he doesn't pull any tricks. There's a scar on his knuckles, maybe from the work he does on his bike and cars, or maybe from fighting. Knowing I'm watching him, he shoots me a look through his lashes as he checks the connection of the clamps on the battery.

I huff. What if he decides to do something worse than drain the battery or steal spark plugs or whatever the fuck he pulled?

Fox's parents died in a fatal car accident when I was eight and I don't like the heartless gleam in his eyes as he works.

For the first time ever he scares me.

Does he hate me enough to really hurt me?

My heart gives a weary, aching thump. Tears sting my eyes and I touch the stones in my bracelet. I already know the answer to that.

Fox is all rough with sharp edges and an air of danger now. There's no trace of the mischievous smiling boy I used to know, the one I loved getting into trouble with.

Ever since he came back, I thought he was still in there. He has to be, or so I've believed for a year.

Maybe everyone in this town is right. Fox Wilder is a black shadow. Mysterious, terrifying, and bad news to anyone who crosses him.

And somehow, I'm the person he hates the most.

TWO
Fox

THE sight of the missing spark plugs from the engine tips the corners of my mouth up in gratification.

Poor, perfect little Maisy Landry isn't going anywhere without the parts sitting in the pocket of my leather jacket. The guy she's started hanging out with doesn't have a clue what I've done.

This is nothing. I could do so much worse to her than fuck with her idiot boyfriend's car and fan the flames on the rumors about her by spray painting *EASY* on her locker. I *should* do worse.

It's what she deserves. Liars always get what's coming to them. And Maisy? The biggest liar of them all, prancing around the school like a goody-goody, fooling everyone with her act to hide what she's really capable of.

I trusted this girl once. Once upon a time she was my best friend—I thought I could tell her anything and believed a promise mattered to her. I carry the guilt of the biggest mistake of my life every day, the poisonous weight infecting my veins.

"I think we can take it from here," Maisy says tightly. "I'll just call my dad to help us out." She pushes out a breath and adds on as an afterthought, "Thanks."

The fucking fakeness slides beneath my skin like needles. Her dad is the goddamn chief of police in Ridgeview, a position he didn't earn on merit. Their lives have been so privileged after mine was torn apart. I almost release a bark of laughter at the thought of her dad helping with the car after what he's done.

Richard and Jacqueline Landry are the reason I broke every piece of myself, stamping out any ounce of goodness to become the cold, vengeful monster I am now.

"Always running to your daddy, little daisy," I sneer low enough that only she can hear me while her boyfriend is distracted with texting. "Think he can protect you from me? Try again."

Maisy stiffens. Good, I hit her where it stings. I'll always be able to get to her. There's no escape from my wrath.

She should be glad I didn't tamper with the brakes, like the fate my parents met ten years ago. As usual, thinking of them sends a sharp stab of emotion lancing through me, my throat burning with the old ache. My hands flex on the frame of the SUV and I drag in a breath through my nose. I hate Maisy and her whole family, but that would be too easy of an out for any of them.

If they're gone, they can't live with the misery like I have.

The thirst for revenge has driven my actions for the last decade as I bounced around from foster home to foster home before I found a new family of brothers just as broken as I am. Without their help, I wouldn't be here. They took in an angry, grieving punk and shaped me into the darkness I shroud myself in so I fit in with them. When the world fucks with me, now I'm adept at hitting back harder with no mercy.

Every day I think of my promise to my parents' ghosts. I want the Landrys to know what they've done to me when I rip apart their lives and make them face the truth of their actions.

Maisy hovers at the side of the BMW, attention locked on me. Those hazel eyes haunt my thoughts more than I care to admit. She doesn't trust me anymore either, not after the things I've done to her. Well, she did beg for my fucking attention every minute since I got back to town, and now she has it.

Careful what you wish for.

"What's wrong, crybaby?" I use the old nickname her brother and I taunted her with every chance I get. I love the way it makes her lip curl, but she refuses to let anyone at this school see the real Maisy she hides beneath the shiny good girl veneer. "Is this cutting into your time to ride your boyfriend's dick before you fix your hair all prim and proper and go read to kids at the library? That's the rumor going around about you."

The one I had a hand in starting.

"How do you know I volunteer at the—" Maisy snaps her mouth shut, shock flickering on her face before she closes off her expression.

It doesn't matter, I can still read every line of her body. She barely pays attention to the cookie-cutter dude who's supposed to be her boyfriend as she squares off with me. For a second, I can't help the way my heart thuds. The fire in her expression is a small glimpse of the girl who was my entire world.

"You know what, Fox? Never mind, I don't care. You can get fucked, asshole." There's a steel in her tone that makes my pulse pick up. Was I waiting for her to fight me back? A rush of the forbidden desire I shouldn't feel shoots through me as she continues. "No matter what you do to me, I'm not going to be afraid of you."

My teeth clench. *Keep telling yourself that.*

"Whoa, beautiful." Her boyfriend isn't glued to his phone anymore. His name is something with a B, but I don't give a shit. It's unimportant to me. The wholesome vibe is condescending as fuck while he looks at Maisy in surprise for the bite in her tone. "That's not like you."

Maisy's mouth tightens and a harsh sigh rushes out when she reins herself back behind her mask. Everyone around here looks at her and expects a sweet, well-behaved girl. They have no idea who she really is, but soon they will.

"If you were paying attention instead of checking your Instagram for likes, you'd know he deserves it," she mutters with a frown.

An echo of the memory of her nails digging into my skin as she panted for more tingles my nerve endings. I left my marks all over her not that long ago. The marks can fade, but she can't erase me.

There's no way this guy knows how to touch her to drive her wild, but that's her problem. I won't touch her again. It was just another way to show her what she'll never have while covering my tracks at the party so no one caught the real reason I was there.

As I stare at her, battling the thoughts of the way she smelled pressed against me, I see another hint of the girl I thought I knew. The only one I've ever wanted, but I can't fucking have anymore because she betrayed me by breaking her promise. That girl is gone and all that's left standing in front of me is a liar. Anger thunders through me as I cut off the memory of the sounds she made.

Maisy Landry isn't my friend anymore. I'm the demon she should run from. She means nothing to me other than the weak link in her family that I'm going to break. I can't forget that.

Pushing back from the engine, I drop the pretense of helping. "Guess you're screwed. Sucks to be you."

"Wait, you seriously can't help?" Boyfriend-with-a-B-name calls as I turn my back to head for my bike. The few people left in the lot give me a wide berth, too scared to get in my way. "Babe, did you have to piss him off? He could've fixed it."

The side of my mouth kicks up and a snort escapes me. I don't hang around for her answer, swinging a leg over the motorcycle parked nearby and slipping the helmet on. The growl of the engine drowns out all the sounds around me, clearing my head.

Without looking back at the one person I never thought would hurt me, I pull out from the parking lot, the constant searing pain of my decayed broken heart keeping me going.

THREE
Fox

Driving along the road that winds through the rolling hills, I clench my jaw hard enough to feel the pressure pulse through my skull. I'm surrounded by tall pine trees, rocks jutting from the ground, and fresh mountain air whipping against me as my bike rounds the bend with a roar. None of it is familiar like it should be. All it does is make me miss the smell of the ocean and the misty cove on the coast of Maine that was my sanctuary from my nightmares.

Colorado doesn't feel like home anymore. The truth hit hard when I came back last year, but I don't want to go back to Thorne Point yet. I can't, not until I've accomplished what I'm staying in Ridgeview to do.

It's the only reason I came back—to destroy every member of the Landry family for ripping mine away from me.

The trees thin out as I near the shipping district. Dusty gravel crunches beneath the tires of the bike when I pull in to the entrance to a row of warehouses. The one on the end is mine. The whole thing.

Colt helped me out, even though I didn't ask him to. When I got to town without a plan for where to stay, an address pinged on my phone and I followed it here to find an envelope taped to the front door of the warehouse with *To Foxy, Love Dolos* written on it. A key was inside.

The thought of my foster brother has my head shaking in wry amusement. He's always got his nose in everyone's business, from spying on their devices to charming everyone to lower their defenses before they're aware of it. It's one of the reasons Wren Thorne gained so much power in Thorne Point, with his loyal band of psychos at his side. The Crows rule every secret in the city, stretching beyond that to control the east coast.

A phantom tingle spreads across my chest where a crow wearing a crown, perched on a skull is inked into my skin, hidden in an intricate ocean design that stretches halfway down my arm.

When the DuPonts welcomed me into their home as their scuffed up project to improve their image to their other socialite friends, I had no idea it would lead me to the Crows. Colton DuPont didn't have to accept me, let alone bring me into the fold with his closest friends, but he did it with an easy grin and a protectiveness that always makes me feel guilty for being grateful for.

It's the kind of protectiveness I should've been able to provide the little sister I was supposed to have, but I never got that chance because the life I should've had was stolen from me.

I park my Harley in the garage on the first floor of the converted warehouse, next to my matte black Charger. The lower level serves as my work space when I need to clear my head by sinking into grease and metal, or whatever odds and ends I can get my hands on. Once I cut the engine, I sit for a second, resting my hand on the one scratch I couldn't bring myself to buff out of the chrome.

Tracking down my dad's bike was hell after our assets were split up and sold off, but I managed to hunt it down right before I turned eighteen last year. The DuPonts set me up with a trust fund to make up for everything lost to me with my family's death. It was a drop in the bucket to them. The money is helpful, but it's the bike that matters most.

I remember the day I accidentally dinged the gleaming metal, shortly after Dad started allowing me into the garage to teach me how the mechanics worked. He wasn't mad. I swipe my thumb over the old imperfection as his face fills my mind, the features blurred from time. At least I can still hear his booming laughter.

Riding the motorcycle, I still feel close to him, keeping the memories of us working on it together alive. It's the only piece of him I have left.

Releasing a harsh exhale, I dump the spark plugs I stole on the workbench in the corner and head upstairs to the studio apartment. I peel out of my leather jacket and toss the keys to the bike on the counter of the industrial kitchenette. I lose my t-shirt next using it to swipe at the sweat beading my tattooed chest. It's always sweltering near the summer without air conditioning.

There isn't much inside, just enough to keep me comfortable along with the odds and ends I've built myself—the reclaimed wood and steel I used to craft a coffee table and the palette platform the bed in the corner sits on. I've always been good with my hands and the tinkering empties my mind when I can't sleep.

It's an old habit I couldn't kick after so many years of growing accustomed to not having a lot in the foster system. The DuPonts indulged me, allowing me to build things from the materials I found. They'd called it art, but half the time I picked up scraps of steel at the junkyard.

I pass the leather couch in the middle of the room and brace an arm against the large window panes. The shipping district is practically a wasteland compared to the bustling heart of Ridgeview. It's far from the residential areas of town.

This place is perfect, appearing shady as hell from the outside. It allows me to come and go without worrying about neighbors to watch me. Plus, it's a welcome reprieve from the whispers that follow me everywhere in town. A muscle in my jaw jumps as I lock it.

The Wilder name has become a curse. I'm the resident black shadow this town fears. Whispers about. Everyone remembers that a Wilder means bad news.

When someone sees me—the spitting image of my parents—the same lies as the ones told about my dad in the days following the accident spill free. People called Dad a troubled, reckless, suicidal drunk who was a danger to himself and others. But it's not true. None of it.

My parents were murdered and powerful people in this town covered it up.

Secrets, lies, betrayal, revenge...this town is stained in blood.

But who I am now is not the same broken, naïve kid that left this town. I have teeth now and I bite hard enough to make my enemies bleed.

The Landrys as good as pulled the trigger and I'm going to prove it. Then I'll make them pay.

Too tense to focus on anything, I change out of my jeans and head for the workout area I've pieced together at the other end of the apartment. Pushing my body until it's ready to break from punching the bag is the only other way I can shut my brain off before the constantly simmering rage boils over.

I lose track of time, only aware of the aching protest in my muscles, the sweat dripping from my body, and the rhythm of my breath as my fists strike the punching bag.

It's only when an incoming call cuts off the playlist of angry music for the third time that I finally stop, inked chest heaving when I catch the bag on the backswing to steady it. Swiping damp hair out of my face, I pick my phone up and shake my head, accepting the call.

"Colt. I'm busy."

"That's not how I taught you to talk to your big brother." Amusement laces his tone. Always the jokester. *"You've turned into such a little shit since you left Thorne Point."*

"I've always been this way." I mop the sweat from my face with a towel, slinging it around my neck as I cross to the kitchen to grab a water. "But you already knew that."

He hums in agreement. *"Not for lack of trying on my part to get you to lighten up. I swear, you and Levi are related somehow. You're both cut from the same cloth of angst-ridden edgelord."*

I scoff. Colt's friend is one of the few people who scares the shit out of me. He has no morals, no limits, and a serious obsession with knives.

"I've got a new lead for you," Colt says, turning serious.

Ice spreads across my nerve endings. I'm already moving to the laptop and files spread out on the coffee table, holding the phone between my face and shoulder. My voice is rough when I answer. "Yeah?"

"Are you by your computer? You'll get a push notification with an encrypted download package."

"On it." I drop the phone to the table, switching it to speaker phone. The file he mentioned pops up on the screen. Once it opens, I suck in a breath, reading quickly. "You're sure?"

"Yeah. When you sent the copied hard drive I was able to dig this up. It was actually hard for me to seduce it into telling me its secrets, and that's saying something. Whoever encrypted this didn't ever want this to see the light of day. I'll send over whatever else I find."

I scan the information again. There was already someone lined up for the police chief position, preparing to transition only a week before Richard Landry was named the new chief. I suspected it—how else could I explain how Richard and Jacqueline ended up in positions of power, living in one of the most upscale neighborhoods in town without a fishy reward for their involvement—and yet seeing it in black and white makes my skin crawl. This is the biggest break I've had in my efforts to bring my parents justice.

It made it easier for them to cover up what was done to my family.

My heart pounds. Going to that party was worth it then, and not only because I found out what makes Maisy moan. She was just my cover so no one caught me sneaking around the home office.

"Thanks, Colt. I owe you."

"*Pay me back later. Preferably with a sexy new waifu to beat it to.*" He laughs at the disgusted sound I make. I don't know how he gets off on hentai because the fake cartoon boobs do nothing for me. "*Kidding, I get the good shit on my own.*"

"Whatever," I mutter.

"*Later, Foxy.*"

He hangs up before I can tell him off for calling me by his nickname for me. "Asshole."

It doesn't carry much heat. Without him, I'd still be floundering in my hatred with no direction. It's only thanks to Colt and his friends that I now have another piece to the puzzle.

Rubbing at my jaw, I pull up the photo album on my phone. It also means I need to move forward with the next plan, the one that's formed in the last couple of weeks. I went after Holden's future first, but Maisy is the real chink in her parents' armor.

Photos of her fill my phone from when I followed her to learn her habits after the party, once I decided it was her turn to pay her pound of flesh. At first I ignored her because it was too painful to look at her, but now she's got the attention she begged me for.

It surprised me how much she stacked her extracurriculars. Volunteering at the library to read children's books, AP classes, teaching yoga, for fuck's sake. I would've guessed with how her parents were paid off, she could have her top pick of any elite college. Holden did, before I eliminated it, and as far as I could tell his only qualification to beef up his college application was playing football.

Memories from last year swirl to the surface as I look at a photo of Maisy leading a yoga class.

I'd been walking with Holden, flooded with how much I resented being around him. Just like Maisy, he turned into someone unrecognizable. It was almost hard to believe we were friends once, but nine year olds are different from douchebags at eighteen. Maisy appeared in the gymnasium doorway to stop him, wearing a crooked smile that still made my heart turn over without my permission. She ignored my scowl to ask for help setting up the stupid winter dance.

Maybe it was a moment of weakness, or maybe it was because all I could think when I saw them together was that my mom was pregnant with a little sister I'd never know the night she died, but Maisy managed to latch onto my wrist as she dragged us both behind her, reminding me of the force of nature she used to be.

Holden groaned, dropping his head back. "You're such a pain in the ass."

"Deal with it, my god," Maisy sassed back, sticking her tongue out at her brother. "Two minutes, or I'll tell Mom where you've been going on weekends."

"Fine," Holden grumbled.

It was better to help her and be done with it than lose my bargaining chip—the secret fight rings Holden organized, raking in cash from the other hopped up, over privileged kids in Ridgeview. I'd stood frozen for a moment, glaring at the doll she was now instead of the wild little troublemaker I was familiar with, but she'd sighed and asked if I was going to help.

"It won't take long," she said, lowering her gaze. "Then you can go back to pretending I don't exist."

I had almost laughed. The one thing that was impossible was pretending she didn't exist. I tried, shit didn't work. She stayed in my goddamn head, refusing to be forgotten completely. I was about to turn around, but she wouldn't give in or get the fucking hint.

"Fox, come on." Damn her voice. All it did was make me remember what we had a long time ago. "You always used to—"

"No." The furious growl cut her off.

"No?" Maisy sighed. "Okay, it's just...if you helped, we'd get it done faster. Then I'll leave you alone."

It was too much. The docile politeness wasn't her. I hated it as much as I loathed her parents. I still didn't understand why she acted like that until I started catching the glimpses through her mask.

Where was my wildflower?

Moving at last from the rigid statue I'd become, I got in her face. "Always such a goody-goody."

When she tensed and hugged herself, I let out a cutting bark. "Yeah. That's what I thought." I took a lock of her silky light brown hair, allowing it to slide through my fingers. The faint floral hint of her favorite shampoo had me grinding my teeth. "Didn't your daddy teach you to run from monsters? Get it through your fucking head."

Kicking over a bucket of paint the student committee was using to decorate with felt good, channeling the pent up fury threatening to burst free. It had skimmed across the floor in a shimmering metallic smear. The shock of pain that cracked her sweet mask drew a cruel smirk from me.

"What are you going to do about it? Cry?" My deep, biting tone mocked her. She stood her ground, but she wasn't unaffected. Tears gathered in her hazel eyes. "That's all you are. All you'll ever be. Maisy Daisy the Crybaby."

"What happened to you?" Her whisper was watery. "You were my friend, too."

"Playtime is over," I growled. "Fuck off, daisy. Stay out of my way."

I had stormed off, tearing down another decoration on my way out of the gym.

Maybe if she'd listened to me that day, I would have left her out of my plans. Now they center around her. I swipe to another photo of her smiling brightly with the redhead she's friends with.

Maisy Landry won't know what hit her. I'll attack her reputation, her spirit, and when she thinks she can't break anymore, I'll destroy her future. Liars don't get to enjoy their futures.

Another photo of her fills my screen. My mouth curves with deadly precision.

Get ready, little daisy. We're only getting started.

FOUR
Maisy

People sidestep me in the hall at school a few days later. I'm like a rock in the middle of a river, forcing everyone to go around me because I'm frozen, glaring at my locker. The words spray painted on it are a slap in the face.

LIAR.

The big bold black letters stand out against the green metal door. The worst part is it hits home in a way I don't expect. It's not the first time my locker has been vandalized in the last couple of weeks since Fox started paying attention, but this shines a light on an ugly truth: I am a liar. That's how I feel, anyway. Always obeying my parents' expectations instead of making my own choices. He sees it somehow. Knew exactly how to get under my skin.

Someone snickers, bumping into me on purpose and I shuffle on my feet to keep my balance. Their whispers have become the norm lately. All it took was one party for people to stop seeing me as the nice girl with good grades. They don't care if it's true or not when the gossip is juicy and entertaining.

Everyone lives for a good downfall story.

It doesn't matter. I repeat it in my head enough times for it to feel true. None of this matters. Just smile through it. Play along. Ignore the whispers.

Someone laughs louder and says my name as if I'm not standing right in the middle of it all, listening to the lies grow bigger. *She's secretly a nympho and the prude thing was an act. She's sleeping with one of her teachers. She's Wilder's personal sex doll and in exchange for doing his homework he lets her suck his dick.* I'm done with this.

Turning on my heel, I head for the custodian office with my head held high. Whether I look down or not, my classmates' stares bore into me, so I might as well keep my chin up. It's just a locker.

I'm polite when I ask if a janitor could come to my locker. One of them follows me back. A crowd has formed around it, snapping selfies and laughing.

"Move aside," the janitor says.

People I've never seen or talked to before swagger away, smirking at me like I'm on display in a zoo.

"Again?" The janitor asks in a tone that makes me ball my hands into fists.

It's this side of judgmental. Just my luck I got the same janitor who spent two days last week scrubbing *EASY* off my locker the first time it was vandalized. The thing about high school is that it's not just the students who love to gossip. The staff are just as bad if not worse.

The urge to get upset and fight against these rumors is there, sitting in my chest, waiting to be unleashed. I breathe through it, feeling the bars of my cage bumping against my back. If I make a bigger scene, Mom will only bring her wrath down on me for putting a dent in our family's image. Totally more important than standing up for myself, right?

With her promotion to CEO and Dad's to police chief came more eyes on us, which meant tempering my impulses. The words on my locker ring alarmingly true. Most days I barely feel like I know myself because of the image I've been trained to portray.

Instead of opening my mouth, I shrug and plaster on a sweet smile. That's the best I can manage right now. His gaze lingers on me for a beat too long before he turns back to examine the locker and mutter into his radio about the cleanup.

What they think they know doesn't mean anything, these people will never see the truth. It's only high school, it's not forever. I'm almost done here. Of course, rumors have a way of sticking in Ridgeview. It's a big town, but not that big. People love to talk.

* * *

On my way to meet up with Thea after school, an impulse grips me. It doesn't happen a lot, but when I'm in this part of town, I can't fight the pull to drive down the old street where we used to live. Maybe it's stronger now because of my run in with Fox in the parking lot.

If Mom or Dad knew I came here they'd kill me. When Holden and I got our licenses, they forbid us from coming back here, as if our childhood home was tainted. I never understood why, it's a nice area where we had block parties with our neighbors.

"Just to see. It's been a while," I murmur to myself, turning down the road instead of going straight.

Like always, as soon as the familiar houses pass by I'm overcome with a wave of longing. After Fox left Ridgeview, we moved to a new house because Mom got a big promotion at her pharmaceutical company. I still don't get how someone from the research department becomes CEO, but no matter how many times I've tried to wrap my head around it I can't make sense of why it happened. It was supposed to change our lives for the better—that's what Mom and Dad told us. But it didn't. The last good times we had as a family were left behind on this street.

My life has been good, but a piece of me was torn out when Fox went away. Everything changed, and the piece hasn't slotted back into place since he's returned, like the damn thing has warped, no longer fitting where it belongs.

After I pass both of our old houses, I slow the car to a stop at the end of the block by the field. It's overgrown with fresh wildflowers, dotted by a few bees and butterflies floating on the breeze above the blooms. If I close my eyes and concentrate, I can hear an echo of laughter. My throat is thick when I swallow. So many memories...

I get out of the white Audi Q7. It's really Holden's car, but he lets me use it whenever I need it, which has come in handy since he never left for college like he was supposed to. It's not fair that my brother got a car and I didn't, but there are way bigger problems in the world than not being gifted a car. Dad refuses to let me have my own and it's putting a serious damper on my road trip plans. He's not going to stop me from going on that trip, though. I've played by their rules and given them what they wanted. The road trip is my one chance to spread my wings before I go back to being a picture-perfect Landry for the college they picked out for me.

It's warm out, the late afternoon sun peeking through billowing clouds to kiss the tall grass. I brush my hands over it as I pick my way through the field to get to the tree. It doesn't look as big as it did when we were kids. I used to be so proud I could climb it. The bright green leaves rustle on the swaying branches as I press a palm to the bark.

The time Fox dared me I couldn't climb our tree flashes in my mind. Quirking my mouth up, I picture how determined I was. I climbed higher than I ever had, almost to the top. Proving him wrong felt good, until he had to come up after me to get me down. We went branch by branch with his guidance. He kept checking if I was okay, squeezing my hand as he helped me reach the ground.

My phone vibrates in the pocket of my school blazer. I pull it out and sigh. It's a text from Mom checking in on where I am now that school is out for the day. They know my volunteer and yoga class schedule. Outside of that, I have to let them know what I'm doing, even at eighteen.

Maisy: I'm on my way to Thea's. I'll come straight home after that.

I hold my breath as three dots appear, hoping she won't decide to check my location by creeping on my phone. She doesn't do that often, but I haven't given her any reason to doubt me lately, keeping my free-spirited urges reeled in. When Dad does it, he's being overprotective like usual, but with Mom... It always feels like a collar pulled tight around my neck.

The instinctive urge I sometimes have to just *go* rushes through me. I could just get in the car and drive. The road would decide where to take me and I'd follow the wind until my heart felt free of the heaviness.

Mom and Dad would be furious, but I'd be happy.

Mom: Be home in time for dinner.

Air gusts out of my lungs in relief. While I'm typing my reply, the heavy rumble of an engine catches my attention. I put my phone away as I turn and my heart drops into my stomach when I see a matte black Charger speeding down the street, screeching to a halt right behind the Audi. It stops inches from smashing into the back bumper.

Oh shit.

It's Fox.

I've been wondering where he's been. He hasn't been around school since he messed with Sam's car. Things like his attendance record and grades don't seem to matter to him while he comes and goes as he pleases.

Fox gets out of the Charger and stalks toward me with his handsome features set in a deadly scowl. The hair on my body stands on end as he quickly eats up the distance with long, powerful strides. Before I can breathe, he's in front of me, forcing me back against the tree. The bark digs into my shoulder blades.

"What the fuck do you think you're doing here?" he growls, making my pulse thunder.

The scent of rich leather, earthy wood, and the faint hint of motor oil surrounds me.

My gaze flies around the empty field, then returns to meet his cold glare. I open my mouth, only to gasp when his fingers lock around my throat. A tremor runs down my spine while heat spikes low in my stomach, making me squirm to rub my thighs together. He doesn't miss it, a rough sound rumbling in his throat as he presses closer so the hard lines of his chest connect with mine. I struggle, testing the limits of his grip, but he's too strong for me to break away.

That's what I should want to do—get away. But…curiosity keeps me in place. This is the first time his hands have been on me since that night at Jenna's party two weeks ago and my body remembers. Vividly.

The marks he left on my skin have faded. My stomach dips when I think of him doing it all again.

Fear and desire fight for control. It's so wrong that Fox can touch me like this and stir excitement, but some part of me craves it even as he torments me.

There's no one here to stop him. Even if there was, I don't think it would change anything. No one holds authority over him. If he wanted, he could easily slide my school skirt up and do whatever he wanted. My clit shouldn't throb at that thought, but it does, *god*, it does. It's so messed up.

He doesn't choke me, but his hold is firm, pinning me to the tree in case I was planning to run.

I might be scared of what he could do to me, but I'll never run from him. The brooding jerk can have my fear, but he doesn't get my surrender.

Somewhere deep inside, there's a small part of him I recognize. I saw it last year, when I caught sight of him smiling at the holiday market in town. It was the same as the boyish smile that used to charm me to do anything when we were kids. I cling to that hope whenever I hear the rumors and whispers flying around about him.

"Fox, what are you trying to—"

"Why are you *here*?" he grits out furiously through clenched teeth.

Narrowing my eyes, I shove the fear aside. "I'm not allowed to exist now? Last I checked, you don't own the street or this field. I'm not trespassing. If I want to visit our tree?" I lean into his hand and my heartbeat flutters when his grip flexes. He's serious, but so am I. "I will."

Fox's dark blue gaze flashes at my defiance. He glances down the line of my body, lingering at the sight of his fingers wrapped around my throat. His mouth tugs into a smirk. "You never could resist trouble. You always loved the thrill."

He digs his thumb into my pulse point, making it crystal clear he could snap my neck with little effort. I struggle to swallow, fighting to drag in a full breath while he controls my air. He can probably feel my racing pulse. Then his thumb eases off to trace up to my jaw. The gesture is at odds with the contempt in his gaze, but it makes my hands grab at his leather jacket, curling into the supple material. For a moment he seems to freeze, like he's curious what I'll do.

Fox leans in until our lips almost touch, then waits another beat, watching me through his hooded gaze.

Is he going to kiss me this time?

This is the closest he's come to me since the party. I just want things to be right between us. If he's ready to move past his grudge, then I'll forgive and forget his cruelty so we can go back to how things should be between us.

Licking my lips, I strain toward him with want.

He releases a gruff, arrogant sound of amusement. "Do you seriously think I'm going to kiss you?"

The cutting tone makes me flinch.

"I..."

"How pathetic."

Oh god, I'm an idiot. The alarm returns, winning out over the fog of desire. I can't believe myself right now for losing sight of common sense. This is that damn party all over again, the intoxicating invisible tether cinching tight between us, but all it brings is heartache. How could I forget?

Fox scoffs. "You look so fucking desperate right now, little daisy. It's a terrible look on you."

Hurt stings the newly opened wounds and I shrink back against the tree. How could I think he was ready to move past why he hates me? He didn't that night he finally acknowledged me. I swallow the hot embarrassment and glare at him.

"Fuck you," I mutter.

His grin is scary. "You make me want to end you. Right here, right now. There's no point in dancing around it."

My eyes widen. The reality slams into me once more. Fox can and will hurt me without a second thought.

"Why do you hate me so much?" I whisper, despising the painful fire in my throat. "*Why?*"

Fox's lip curls and he brings his mouth to my cheek. "Stop acting like you don't know. It's making me sick. Everything about you makes me so goddamn sick."

My chest collapses with a hoarse breath. The acidic hostility in his tone is unmistakable.

A phone rings and he curses, tearing away from me. I lean against the tree, unsure of what he'll do if I move. Whoever is calling makes his sharp jaw tic when he clenches it. His glare finds me once more.

"Get out of my sight before I change my mind," he commands. "Don't let me catch you here again. You won't like what I do to you."

The thought of staying away from the tree drives a white-hot lance into my chest. I want to argue instead of letting him win, but I'm still reeling from allowing myself to think for a second that he wanted me. God, he's right. I am desperate, but all I want is to make things right between us.

When I haven't answered, he takes a threatening step toward me, his glare intensifying. "Got it?"

I hate this.

Heart lodged in my throat, I manage a stiff nod before I walk to my car on trembling legs. I won't run. I refuse to let him believe he can control me like that, snapping his fingers and barking commands to make me hop fucking to it because he said so. I deal with it enough from Mom and Dad, but no one gets that power over me.

Behind me, I hear the deep murmur of his voice as he answers the phone. "You got something new for me?"

Glancing over my shoulder, I watch him pace by the tree, pushing a hand into his messy dark hair in agitation. The hint of a tattoo is visible at the neckline of his t-shirt. Curiosity tugs at me. I didn't get to see it at the party, but I caught a tiny glimpse of black feathers.

I don't stick around long enough to listen. Once I reach the SUV, I get in and drive away in a shaken daze. I don't even roll the windows down to let my fingers ride the waves of the wind whipping by the car. Dad would be really annoyed if he knew all his lectures about safe driving were flying out the window in the face of self preservation.

It doesn't make sense how Fox Wilder can simultaneously draw me in with magnetic force while also throwing off dangerous vibes that make me want to get away.

Nothing makes any damn sense to me anymore. It has to be the fact that there's so much history between us. Throw in his grudge against me and...whatever it was that went down at the party, the line between us is mottled and blurred by the ferocity of our feelings. One minute he ignores me, the next he's pushing me against the nearest flat surface to ignite a fire in me with his body, only to turn around and lash out at me in punishment. I never know what to expect from him.

Gripping the wheel hard enough for my knuckles to turn white, I head for Thea's bakery. My racing heart doesn't slow.

Fox is the only person who gets under my skin and riles up my easy carefree spirit. He makes me want to fight him. I'm more of a peace and love type of person, but when it comes to Fox, a fierceness I didn't know I possessed breaks free.

I should stay away from him—it's what he wanted. But I can't. Not until I know why he hates me enough to forbid me from coming to our tree.

FIVE
Fox

2 Weeks Ago

The party sucks. It's nothing like Wren Thorne's extravagant and hedonistic parties, but I wasn't expecting much from the spoiled brats of Ridgeview.

Whatever, that's not why I'm here tonight amongst the kids of the most influential and powerful people in town. Just need to blend in until the time is right, then I'm getting the hell out of here. Except right now I stand out too much to do what I need to.

People side eye me and mutter when I walk through the kitchen to another room where the pounding beat of music fills the huge house. No one will kick me out, though. They're all too chickenshit to cross me. If my fierce scowl isn't enough, the rumors about me are, so they let me crash.

"Bet he's got a dumping ground spot out at the old quarry," someone whispers loudly. "Buries all the bodies of people he's offed for the mob out there."

"No way," a girl responds, giving me a once over from the corner of her eye. "He's so hot. He can't be a hitman."

"He totally is! It's how he made all his money."

Rolling my eyes, I slip past them. The rumors in this town are getting stupider by the minute.

I grab a beer bottle to look less like an angry shadow and prowl around the party, keeping an eye out the entire time. People don't stand in my way because they recognize that I'm a predator who could tear them apart. When I spot the girl throwing the party—the daughter of the mayor, who has a habit of bringing his work home—I begin to make my way toward her. Her gaze trails me up and down, the heat flaring in her eyes easy to read. The corner of my mouth twitches in triumph.

Like a bad boy, do you?

"I don't remember inviting you," she says in a fake tone meant to entice me.

My shoulder hitches and I take a swig from the beer bottle. "I don't like playing by the rules."

She releases a breathy sound and inches closer, pressing her tits against my arm. If this all turns out to be a waste of my time, I'll be pissed I had to put up with her. Swallowing back the snarky comment climbing my throat at how she was making out with some dude from the football team thirty minutes ago, I give her a lazy smile that makes her flutter her lashes flirtatiously.

"You've got a sweet place. Is your dad someone important?"

Buying my act, she flaps a hand, leaning into me harder as she fires off questions rapidly. "I guess, but who cares? Did you bring your motorcycle? Can you give me a ride?"

I trace a thumb over my lip. "I did."

Didn't mean I was going to let her touch it. I barely let the guys back east touch my bike.

Girls like her have never interested me. That goes for most of them, actually. Even amongst Wren's mismatched band of Crows, the girls that hung around never held my attention. There was only ever one girl who had my heart. Just one, but she crushed it to dust in her little fist.

The mayor's daughter keeps doing most of the talking and flirting while I stand there leaning against the wall, tuning out half of what she says to scan the room. Now that I'm blending in, the attention is off me. Good, that'll make it easier to get into the home office.

The plan is going fine until all the air in the room sucks out when I catch sight of who just entered through the front door out of the corner of my eye. Maisy fucking Landry, hair down from the ponytail she favors and dressed in a loose crop top that exposes her flat tanned stomach and tight blue yoga pants that hug her ass and her long toned legs. *Goddamn, daisy.* My focus splits, snagged by the need to watch Maisy's every move and stick to what I'm here to do—use this chick to gain access to her dad's computer.

For now I ignore her. It's been the best way to deal with the raging pain that sears my chest from the inside out every time I look at the liar. If I don't, I teeter on the brink of losing control and burning this whole fucking town to the ground.

Ridgeview, the town that turned on me and my family ten years ago. This was our home until it got my parents killed. I've waited this long and the time has finally come. I'm out for blood and I'm going to get it if it's the last thing I do.

Maisy scans the room and stops on me and the girl dragging her manicured nails over my chest. We lock eyes and I let my mouth quirk into a savage curve as I wrap an arm around the girl's waist, hauling her against my body. She squeals and releases the fakest moan.

"You want that ride now, baby?" I ask.

The chick doesn't notice that I'm not looking at her. She nods. "Let's go upstairs."

"Lead the way."

Maisy's nostrils flare and she rips her attention away, stalking through the party with an angry grace that makes my blood thrum more than the chick melting against my side. I force out a breath, trying to get my head screwed on right. I'm not here for games.

Once my decoy takes me into her room, I let her kiss my neck and I put on a show of throwing her on the bed roughly. She giggles when she bounces. I cover her body with mine and hold her hair while she writhes beneath me. She doesn't see it coming when I use Levi's trick with a pressure point to knock her out cold. I shift her onto her side in case she had too much to drink and put a pillow beneath her head. Sitting back on the edge of the bed, I smirk, glad I made the craziest of the Crows teach me how to pull that off.

I set a timer for twenty minutes on my phone and make my way into the home office at the end of the hall. The vibrating thump of music drifts up as I head straight for the expensive computer in the center of the luxuriously furnished room—just as swanky as the rest of the house. It shouldn't shock me after the years I've spent amongst the people the DuPonts associate with, but Ridgeview has this way of slapping their wealth in people's faces.

Reaching into my back pocket, I pull out thin gloves and get to work copying the hard drive. The computer has no password set, so I don't have to utilize the skills Colton taught me to get around it. I huff out an empty laugh. People are too fucking trusting that nothing can touch them when they're at the top.

I finish downloading the entire drive to a USB as a backup and pocket it before my alarm goes off. Making sure I haven't left a trace of what I've done, I slip out of the room and head for the staircase.

Maisy is waiting for me at the top of the steps, glaring down the hall. Damn it. She can't blow my cover. I return her glare as I stalk toward and she lays into me as soon as I reach her.

"So you'll talk to other girls, just not me. Right. Got it."

Sticking to ignoring her, I pretend she's not there as I shoulder her out of the way and head downstairs, tucking the copied hard drive deeper into my pocket. I got what I came here for, now I can get out of here.

"You can't even look at me anymore," Maisy accuses when we reach the first floor, gripping my elbow with an unexpected amount of strength.

I glance down at her hand. She always was strong. She used to hate it when Holden and I treated her like she couldn't do the same things we did because she was a girl.

This close, those blue leggings are even harder to resist. The urge to take a bite out of her ass is strong. Fuck, why are they so tight?

"I'm over this," she says, getting in my face while I hesitate. Her familiar determination and steel spine make me ache to crush her to me in a hug and push her away harder. "What have I done? Why are you so ready to throw our friendship away?"

It feels like as soon as I look down her body, everything I've ignored calls to me. I've rejected and avoided how beautiful she is—god, even more than when she had my heart ten years ago. I've disregarded how much my mouth has watered at her tight body for a year.

When I don't answer, her brows pinch and she keeps pushing. "Goddamn it, Fox. If you don't talk to me, then I don't know what I'm apologizing for. We can't keep going on like this. It's killing me."

The catch in her voice makes me ball my fists.

A thousand and one memories of when we were kids blindside me. Her hazel eyes pierce through the intricate ocean artwork inked into my bicep and chest, straight into my heart. Then every inch of me turns to ash when I remember the most important thing—she broke her promise.

If she wants my attention so bad, she's going to fucking get it.

I slam her back against the wall. A few people look our way. The party has all but faded away, my focus narrowing down to my old friend.

"You can say you're sorry while you choke on my cock," I growl, face inches from hers as I cage her in.

Surprise crosses her face for a beat before it bleeds away, replaced by a look that has my dick hard in seconds. She slides her arms around my neck, watching me with as much arousal as I feel rushing through me, tempting me with her sweet scent of flowers and coconut. I bite back a groan and grasp her waist. My thumbs skate over smooth skin beneath the hem of her short crop top, exploring her bare belly. I brush the underside of her tits, unable to hold back a grin that she's not wearing a bra.

"That gets you hot, doesn't it?"

"Yeah, it does," she says without any shyness. She gives me a crooked smile when I stare at her. Leaning closer, she murmurs, "There's a lot that gets me wet. Going to keep going to find out?"

Holy shit. Heat pools low in my gut at the confidence she has. I thought she was going to cower and freak out at the rough treatment and dirty words meant to make her blush.

I picture her on her knees with those pretty lips wrapped around my dick, tears streaming down her face while I fuck her lying mouth until she's wondering whether or not I'll pause long enough to let her breathe before I come down her throat. Want crashes over me.

Ignoring her was stupid. Hate fucking her is so much better.

My hands drag down her sides to palm her ass. These yoga pants are sinful as fuck, skintight and leaving nothing to the imagination. I trace my tongue over my lower lip and picture peeling them off her with my teeth.

"Fuck, little daisy," I rasp in a smoky tone as my hands roam her body, claiming every inch with my touch. "You've grown up."

Maisy presses up on her toes, tilting her head. She wants to kiss me. Through the haze of lust, I shut down the way my heart thumps at an old dream coming true.

I stop her before her lips touch mine, holding her neck and jaw. Disappointment flashes in her golden eyes, but this isn't a romantic reunion of long lost friends. This is all physical, that's fucking it. Smirking, I direct her head to the side and close my mouth around her pulse point. I torture her neck until she's melting against the wall, releasing these soft sounds that drive me insane.

A few people have already seen us tangled together, but we're too wrapped up in an overwhelming flood of need to stop. The broken dam that held us back from this drowns us. Anger colliding with lust is a heady mix. The only thing I'm vaguely aware of is that we can't do this in the hallway at some house party, but I can't tear myself away long enough to take her somewhere private. Releasing a growl, I pick her up. She yelps, clutching at my shoulders as I grab her ass in a possessive grip.

Someone howls like a coyote, whatever the fuck that's supposed to mean.

I walk into the first room I find—a bathroom. Compared to the rest of the house, it's not that big, but I don't care. The enticing little monster in my arms digs her nails into my skin and it pulls all my focus back to her.

We knock over a decorative basket of hand towels as we get lost in the storm of each other. It's violent and passionate and fucking addictive. I drop her, pinning her hips against the counter as I return to biting and sucking at her neck. She arches against me, proving what those hours of yoga are good for. The thought of how my marks will be all over her neck make me grind my erection into her stomach.

Maisy pulls on my hair and wraps a leg around mine as she buries a cry into my chest. "I need you to—"

Before she can finish, I push a hand down the front of her leggings, finding her folds slick as my fingers glide across her pussy. I don't waste any time on teasing her, sinking a finger inside and leaning back to watch my fingers flex through the thin fabric of her pants and the way it makes her mouth opens on a breathy moan.

"Oh god!" Maisy moves against my hand and slides hers under my shirt to brush against my abs. She moves down to my black jeans, over my hard cock. When she rubs it, my eyes hood as I press into her. "We could've been doing this all year, you stubborn jerk. If you'd just talked to me. We've wasted so much time."

"Shut up," I command harshly, thrusting my fingers in with enough force to make her suck in a breath. "No talking."

"You're talking," she taunts with a gleam in her eyes.

I slow down for a second, gaze flicking up and down her body before I meet her eyes. "You want me to make you be quiet, or are you just hoping I'll punish that mouth by making you choke on my cock?"

"Promises, promises," Maisy snarks.

Sassy little brat.

I wish we had more time to explore. Breaking her until she submits would be something I'd want to do over and over.

The side of my mouth tips up. It's the only warning she gets before I push another finger in her pussy and fuck her hard with my fingers. She fists my shirt and grabs the edge of the counter, only able to hold on, head hanging back and small cries escaping her when I hook my fingers up. I'm relentless, not stopping until her eyes fly to mine, pupils blown wide from arousal.

"Fuck, right there, I'm—" She breaks off with a strangled sound and her pussy clenches down on my fingers.

I used to think I knew all of my favorite sounds and faces she made. Watching her come easily slots into the top favorite spot and it pisses me off even more that we can never have this again. We were made for each other, but she ruined that.

"Turn around."

Maisy's eyes flash. With a smug smile, I grab her chin with the same fingers I had buried in her pussy a minute ago. I touch her lips with my thumb and she licks it. The fact she likes it rough, likes my demanding nature makes me groan.

"Turn the fuck around."

I jerk her body around without waiting for her to do it. One of my hands runs up the back of her leg while my arm wraps around her shoulders to crush her back against my chest. I grab a handful of her ass in a harsh grip and dig my cock into her back. The want I feel for her is overwhelming to battle. My touch roams her body, squeezing her neck, then dropping to her waist as I pant against her temple and grind against her.

I hate Maisy, but god, I want to fuck her so badly. There's nothing I want more in this minute than to sink my cock into her pussy and make her scream my name.

Moving to tighten my arm around her, I drop my head to her shoulder. "I could fuck you right now and you'd let me, wouldn't you," I rumble into her neck, enjoying the way her body shudders against mine. "That's what I thought. Let this be a lesson, because that will never fucking happen." She stiffens in my arms as my tone turns cruel. "This changes nothing. I still hate you."

I don't know if I shocked her into silence at last, or if she's reeling from the contempt in my voice, but she stays still as I unzip my pants and take my dick out. A groan vibrates in my chest as I pump myself, pressing the tip right against her ass. It doesn't take long for the heat in my gut to coil tight as my orgasm hits. With a hoarse sound, I come, painting her ass with it as I hold her hip hard enough to bruise.

She remains quiet as I stumble back, leaning against the wall to catch my breath. In the mirror above the counter I can see the pinkness in her cheeks, her lashes lowered to sweep against them. My gaze drifts down to her yoga pants stained with my come.

It's a fucking beautiful sight that will remain burned in my brain long after I break her. Pushing off the wall, I leave her to figure out how to clean up, banging out of the bathroom into the party. As I move through a crowded room, I get elbows and smirks from other guys who were wary of my presence here at first.

"Get this man a beer, he just deflowered the yoga prude," one of them says.

A round of cheers follows.

"Damn, bro, first Jenna, then Maisy Landry in the same night?" Another guy claps my shoulder, leaning in. "Jenna hasn't come back down to the party, either. What did you do to get that kind of stamina?"

"Screw that, I want to hear about Maisy." The first guy shoves a beer in my face that I don't take. "That yoga shit is hot. Was she flexible?"

As he asks, Maisy comes into the room. Her cheeks flush as all eyes turn on her. She folded down her yoga pants to try to hide the stain I left. A satisfying smirk settles on my face.

"Very pliant."

The guys in the room laugh while hurt fills her eyes. She hugs herself as they throw around more lewd comments, looking at her like she's their next meal.

It pisses me off, but I stare her down, drinking in her pain and humiliation.

I lied to her when I said it wouldn't change anything.

This changes everything. I'm done ignoring her.

SIX
Maisy

It took the entire ride over, plus one of Thea's magical soul-restoring hugs and her beaming smile before I was able to shake off the dark cloud of what happened at the tree. At least enough to resemble a well-adjusted, functioning person who isn't wrapped up in berating myself for falling for another one of Fox's tricks.

The look on his face...

Do you seriously think I'm going to kiss you?

Ugh, he needs to stop living rent free in my mind. Shoving him from my thoughts and locking the last hour away behind a mental wall of concrete, I shift my focus to painting this mural with my best friend.

Stevie Nicks' soothing voice serenades us from my phone as we work. I hum along to the melody of *Dreams* and laugh when Thea pauses her section of the mural to dance with her arms overhead, swinging her auburn curls around as she's feeling herself, no longer afraid to show off her curves. Minute by minute, I'm beginning to feel more normal, chilled out by hanging with Thea. I realize as I guide my paintbrush along the celestial mural design outline that I've been carrying so much negative energy in my heart ever since this situation with Fox escalated. It has me missing last spring, when Thea and I went to the yoga studio every weekend with baby goats.

Fox's dark shadow has infected the bright light in my life, shrouding me with his damn grudge.

"Yoga this weekend?" I suggest, rubbing the smooth piece of quartz in my brass bangle. I need something positive in my life to reset myself. A fresh nightly meditation plan is already forming in my head. I will get back to a zen headspace where Fox can't infect my bubble of happiness. "I've been slacking and your girl needs some serious best friend time."

Thea lights up. "Yes! I've missed going with all the stuff on my plate to get the bakery ready to open."

Her energy is so great right now. It's clear to see how happy she is, and that makes me glad for her. She deserves to glow like a goddess.

Smirking, I tip my head to the side. "Sure it's not because you get railed on the reg by that good D?"

Thea whips toward me, her cheeks pink as she fiddles with the engagement ring Connor gave her six months ago. The guy bought her a building because he wanted to support her goals, like what an incredible proposal. "*Maise*. Jesus."

I fall back out of my position on the floor, cracking up. I'm the most myself around her. It always surprises people who expect me to be quiet and prudish, but I'm not like that at all. Not the real me, anyway.

"You know I fully support your wild sex life. It's self-care. I just like living vicariously through you since it's just me and Righty." I wave my hand and waggle my brows when she releases a tiny shriek. "Well, and Sir Good Vibes."

"I still can't believe you named your vibrator that." She shakes her head in amusement. "You're so weird. I love it."

"Love you back, goob." I blow her a kiss. "Where's your man?"

"He's building me a desk in the office. There's still the city inspection, and the oven delivery got moved back, and, oh my gosh, the applications. I need to get those up, but I keep forgetting." She gets that overwhelmed look once her ramble ends, the one that happens when she takes on too much. She blows out a breath, lifting a stray curl from her face. "How am I ever going to open this bakery on time?"

All she's ever dreamed of is opening this place.

"Say the word, girl. My offer still stands—we can run away together and live our best life in Venice Beach. A shitty one bedroom apartment and the ocean, that's all we need."

I'm only half-teasing. The other half is kind of serious.

"That was always your wish." Thea purses her lips to the side. "You'll get to go on your road trip." She comes over and hugs me from behind. "They can't take it away from you, or any of your other dreams. You're going to do everything you want to with your life, and the choice is *yours*, not theirs. Don't forget that."

My breath catches and I latch onto her arms as she gives me a squeeze. Once again the truth of the words spray painted on my locker hit me.

Damn, she's too good at reading me. We've always had a strong connection, ever since I first found her bawling her eyes out on a hiking trail in the woods at the summer camp we met at. She was lost and I helped her find her way back to the campground. We've been inseparable friends ever since, from middle school onward. I can't imagine my life without her friendship.

"Thanks, dude," I mumble.

"Anytime." She holds up her pinkie and I lock mine with it. "No matter how much I'd love to go to California with you, Ridgeview is my home. But I'm always down for a visit if that's where you go."

A heavy sigh leaves me. I play with the braided leather bracelet, touching the stones. "Yeah. You're right."

It's not just that I have this untamed need deep inside to leave at the drop of a hat, or even that I actually want to run from my problems. It's that the choice isn't mine, and that's what I crave when I fantasize about pulling onto the interstate and following it as far as it'll take me.

"That reminds me! I found a neat thing for you on Pinterest last night. I meant to text it." Thea grabs her phone and shows me a pin she saved on must-see cross-country road trip spots and tips for routes to take to make the most of the trip. "See? With this you can hit more places."

"Thanks, girl. This is good."

I haven't gotten that far, but Thea is more of a planner. All I know is I want to go. It's this hungry need that tugs at the inside of my chest whenever the wind moves my hair and I see a bird taking flight.

"Have you brought it up again to your parents?"

Shaking my head, I stare into my paint tray. "Not yet. Not since last time."

If I can't convince them to give me permission, I'm going after graduation. They can't stop me. No one can.

"It'll work out." She claps her hands. "Think good thoughts!"

My mouth quirks into a soft smile. "You're the best."

We get lost in painting again, singing along to the rest of the Fleetwood Mac playlist.

"Are you okay?" Thea asks after a comfortable silence.

"I—yeah," I push out, hoping she can't hear the strain in my voice. We both know each other too well to easily hide our emotions. Last year it was her hiding from me, but now the tables have turned. I think I'm starting to get why she kept quiet about her drama for so long. "Why wouldn't I be?"

She turns her big blue eyes on me and my heart leaps into my throat. Crap. She totally sees through me.

Reaching out, Thea takes my hand. "Are you sure? I don't want to push you, but it seems like there's a lot weighing you down. I've never seen you like this. I know your parents can be a lot to deal with, but you've been so quiet lately. Like your light's gone out."

My throat tightens. "It's nothing."

I force out a laugh and wince at how brittle it sounds, grating on my ears. It seems stupid to moan about rumors and someone spray painting my locker, so I haven't brought it up. Then there's all the stuff with Fox. When did my life get so complicated?

"You don't have to worry about me. There's a lot on your plate."

She frowns, squeezing my hand. "Full plate or not, you're my best friend. You can talk to me about anything. My therapist encourages me to picture pouring water out of a jug when I'm having trouble talking about my problems. We start with little things, and then it gets easier. I always feel a lot better after I've let it out instead of holding it all in like I used to, when…"

Thea trails off, but she doesn't have to finish. I know how hard last year was for her. It's behind us now and no one can hurt her anymore. She's shining brighter without the darkness that crept into her life.

Releasing a sigh, I shake my head. "It's not a big deal. Not yet, anyway." Just way too complicated to untangle. "I promise, or I'd already be spilling my guts about it. I'm just looking forward to graduating so I can get on with my life, you know?"

She nods. "Okay. Does this call for cupcakes?"

"My favorite kind?" I add hopefully. "And face masks when we're done with painting."

"Of course. I'll bake it all better after we finish this."

As Thea picks up her paintbrush again, I make a silent vow to tell her once I figure this out for myself. I fill in the sun and moon that make up the logo while she works on the Eclipsed Tarts lettering.

The song changes to *The Chain* and Connor dances his way into the room on the chorus, shoulders dropping to the drum beats as he lip syncs the lyrics into a hammer. His antics make us laugh.

"Your new office is officially sexy," he announces with a charming lopsided grin, winking at Thea. He shoots me a nod. "'Sup, little Landry."

I flip him off. "What did I say about calling me that? Dude, I will kick your ass, no hesitation."

Connor is as cocky as ever, the star ex-soccer captain of Silver Lake High with floppy hair and intelligent gray eyes. At first I thought he was an asshole with a bad reputation, too full of his own swagger who was going to break my girl's heart, but he turned out to be the perfect guy for my best friend.

His grin stretches and he gestures to my crystal bracelet as he sets down the hammer on the counter. "What happened to all that peace and love zen hippie shit?"

A smile threatens to break free, but I keep my expression serious to sell our usual song and dance. "I'll make an exception for you."

"Won't you two ever learn to play nice?" Thea asks fondly. "You're my two favorite people in the world."

"We just like to tease, sunshine." Connor draws her close for a kiss that makes her melt in his arms. He pulls back and smirks at the expression on her face. "She's family. A little ball busting is healthy."

He means it, too. Their group of friends that has absorbed me as a package deal with Thea consider themselves a family, one they chose. The guys can be somewhat intimidating with how intense they all are, but deep down they're good. They each love their partners and they're fiercely protective—that's good enough in my book to vibe with them.

"Oh, Dev got back to me in the group chat." He shows Thea his phone. "His summer break from college starts next Friday, but Oakridge College doesn't break until a few days after. He's going to wait until Blair, Gemma, and Lucas are done, then they'll all drive back to town together."

Out of all their friends, Thea and Connor both opted out of college. They don't need it when Thea's been baking her whole life and Connor is a loaded savvy computer nerd. The dude made bank because of a security app he created.

"Sounds good. Fam picnic in our favorite spot once they're all back?" Thea suggests.

"You know it, baby."

Connor steals another kiss while I grab my phone to change out the playlist. A text notification pops up at the top of the screen, sinking my stomach. Mom. My allotted amount of freedom is up for the day.

Mom: You have 15 minutes to get home before I have your father trace your location and pick you up.

"Shit," I say under my breath. It grates on my nerves the way she summons me. I can feel the damn bars of my cage slamming down. "I've gotta go. Sorry, girl. I'll see if I can come back tomorrow so we can finish painting, okay?"

Thea gives me an understanding look and I shrug. She knows my parents are overbearing. One of the reasons we bonded so easily as friends was because we both could commiserate over nosy mothers. She's managed to make peace with her mom, but I don't see that in my future. Not with how mine treats me like a doll—something to look at, a pretty prop to keep her reputation shining, but back on the shelf I go when I don't meet her expectations.

I hug Thea goodbye and fist bump Connor before heading out.

Lately it seems like it's more often than not she exerts control over me. At least last year I was allowed a longer leash.

Then again, that was before my parents knew Fox was back in town. Now I can't breathe without them needing to know about it.

* * *

The door slams behind me and I tense as it reverberates off the cream marble floors and the high ceiling of the foyer. Crap, I didn't mean to do that. I'm wound too tightly, annoyed at being called home before I was ready like I'm a damn child.

"Is that you?" Mom's voice drifts from the kitchen, where the savory scent of cooking fills the first floor.

"Yeah." Swallowing back what I really want to say, I add, "Sorry I cut it close. We were still painting."

Reluctantly, I go into the kitchen and take a seat at the large island in the middle with the same marble as the foyer. Mom was obsessed with making our new house look like it could be a palace from Greek mythology compared to our old one. It was nicer in my opinion since it actually fit us, unlike this oversized, too fancy monstrosity with a ridiculously over the top security system. It always feels cold and empty, no matter how many fruit bowls and flowers she puts out.

Mom has a folder with the Nexus Lab company logo on it, standing at the end of the island. She flicks her eyes up at me briefly. "As long as you're not late. You need time to study."

My gaze cuts to our cook, who is preparing dinner. Lana doesn't pause in sautéing vegetables, familiar with these lectures she gets a front row seat to. Mom pays her three times the going rate for an in-home chef and made her sign an ironclad NDA to keep her mouth shut about whatever she overhears in the house.

It's yet another thing that changed when my parents got promotions. We used to cook meals together. Holden and I had a running contest to see who could catch the most food in our mouth when Dad would flick us a piece. We became obsessed with the game after a night out at a Hibachi restaurant. We haven't done that in years.

"I already have my acceptance letter to Northwestern," I say on autopilot, like I have ever since the thick envelope arrived a few months ago.

The words taste like ash on my tongue.

If I actually cared about going there, I imagine it would be really exciting to have an early acceptance. Impressing a college I don't give a damn about leaves me feeling empty. I can almost smell the salty ocean air and feel the warm sand—my imaginary happy place filling me with the kind of joy I should feel about college.

Mom turns a page of the report in front of her, releasing a quiet, unimpressed sound of acknowledgement.

I curl my fingers into my palms, concentrating on my breathing. "Isn't that what matters?"

"Of course. But so does finishing what you start. Are your latest grades in my inbox?"

The line of tension in my shoulders winds tighter. I stare at Lana's prim white chef uniform and focus on the snaps and sizzles of the vegetables in her pan. "Yup. I forwarded it when the student portal updated this morning."

"And you're still on track for Valedictorian?"

"Yes."

Not that I care. Finishing my senior year at the top of the class doesn't really matter to me. What I really want is freedom to explore this world, to go on an adventure where I don't know what awaits me next.

Mom turns another page. She looks the same as always. Her sleek light brown hair that Holden and I get ours from is cut in a fashionable bob, her lips painted red, and her pantsuit pressed to perfection. Even though she never changed her style, something about that summer ten years ago took away my loving parent and replaced her with this woman who hits me with one expectation after another.

I used to be free to run around untethered and untamed, discovering the world around me without a worry of the rules. Now my whims are silenced and if I don't think first before acting, I get an earful while I'm stuck in this gilded cage of a house.

LIAR. The inescapable words from my locker are burned into my brain.

Reputation. Respect. That's all that matters to her now, and Dad's gone along with it ever since he became chief of police.

If they get wind of the rumors and everything else happening at school, Mom will blame me. I don't want to know what else she can take away from me then, so I'm doing everything to make sure she doesn't find out.

"How long until dinner?" I ask.

"Twenty minutes," Lana answers.

"Great. I'm going to change out of my uniform."

"Tell your brother to come down for dinner," Mom says.

I can't escape the room fast enough, hugging myself as I jog upstairs to the landing above the foyer that leads to the bedrooms. At the third door, I knock loud enough to be heard over the thudding base beat vibrating Holden's door.

"What?" he shouts over the music.

"Dinner in twenty. You're cordially invited."

More like our presence is required or else.

"Whatever."

Holden's been in a pissy mood ever since his football scholarship was rescinded over the summer. He was all ready to fly the nest as fast as he could—something I don't blame him for—but his dream was crushed.

Part of me is relieved he's still here so I don't have to face Mom and Dad alone, but then guilt swarms in my stomach. Playing football at Ohio State was a big deal to him. I'm no stranger to desires being so close, and yet just out of reach when they're yanked away.

Now he's at Ridgeview Community College, the only school he could enroll at on such short notice. It's not a bad school, but for most graduates of Silver Lake High School it's a different world than a prep school that educates future politicians and lawyers. Power, that's what comes out of Silver Lake High.

I open my mouth to ask if he wants to do something this week after school, but his music turns up, drowning out the world. Leaving my brother alone to brood, I continue down the hall to my bedroom.

Once I'm inside, I lean against the door. This is the only spot in the whole house that feels like me. It's bright and airy, with a macrame wall hanging on a piece of driftwood over my bed. Above it on the ceiling, there's an old roadmap I tacked up there. I light the incense on my desk and breathe in the floral-infused scent. On a shelf above it, my crystal collection is lined up. A jar sits at the end of the shelf full of rocks, agates, and small geodes. They're all ones I found with Holden and Fox years ago. I've kept them all, including the ones I made into a bracelet.

I touch the old braided leather on my wrist, running my fingertips over the stones in the jewelry.

Heaving a big sigh, I peel out of my school uniform, dropping the blazer in a heap on the floor, followed by my skirt and blouse. I run my fingers through my hair, gathering it up into a messy bun.

Swapping out the lacy bralette and panty set I wore to school for a simple green strappy sports bra, I skip underwear and slip on a pair of gray flowy yoga pants with a slit in the legs that cinches with a cuff at the ankles. This is how I'm most comfortable and it's already working to relax me. I put on a meditation playlist, roll out my mat, and lose myself to a quick flow of stretches that ease the tension in my body from this afternoon.

As I breathe deeply and arch into a low lunge, my mind drifts where I don't want it to when I look at the old bracelet on my wrist.

Fox.

What is it about him that I can't ignore?

Ex-friends really do make the best—or the worst—enemies.

They know how you think. They know all your secrets. They know what will hurt you the most.

Fox hasn't known me for ten years, but he still understands how to cut me deepest. Except this time he's the one pushing me down in the dirt, not the one kissing my scraped knees.

I exhale and switch positions. Even if he was fine ignoring me for so long, I don't think I could ever do the same to him.

At first all he did was ice me out throughout junior year to push me away. I thought we would make it all the way to graduation like that, but then the party happened. After that, he's been everywhere, around every corner, always watching me.

A switch flipped and I finally have his attention—just not in the way I expected.

Fuck, little daisy. You've grown up.

The memory of his deep growl against my flushed skin makes me gasp and lose my balance from tree pose. I plant my feet on the floor and cover my face against the wave of heat traveling down my spine, thighs clenching.

Belatedly, Sam pops into my head. That should speak for itself that it took me this long to think of him. Pursing my lips, I tilt my head to the side. It's not like we're officially together, but it doesn't make me feel great that I was ready to kiss someone else before the guy who wants to be my boyfriend has kissed me, even if Sam doesn't get my heart racing like Fox does.

With his hypnotizing stormy gaze, his sharp jaw, mysterious tattoos, and those muscles he steals my breath. I can't deny that I'm attracted to him. My stomach twists in excitement, a coil of desire thrumming in my blood. His hands felt so rough on my neck and I liked it. He doesn't ask for what I want, he just takes unapologetically.

Heaving a sigh, I nod. It's time to be honest with Sam. It was never going to work out with us. He was a distraction that didn't even work. I shouldn't have used him.

I grab my phone, then hesitate. "Can't text him. That's too shitty. Ugh, phone call it is. This is going to suck."

My eyes close as the phone rings. He picks up.

"Hey, beautiful. This is a surprise. Did you miss me?" The flirtatious tone makes me frown.

"Uh, hey. Listen... Man, this is awkward, but I don't want to hold out on you."

"What is it?"

"I don't think it's going to work out between us." I chew on my lip, willing him to get it. "Like dating. I just wanted to be honest with you that I wasn't feeling it."

Sam lets out a sharp laugh. *"Wow, you really know how to let a guy down easy."*

I hate the swirl of guilt.

"This is probably a bad time to tell you I had a sweet date night planned for us this weekend. I already cleared it with your dad."

I blink. That was news to me.

Ugh.

Who the hell does that?

My parents eat it up. They're obsessed with Sam. This is exactly why he doesn't fit who I am. I know I'm making the right choice by stopping this before it goes too far. We haven't even kissed, though not for lack of trying to get into my pants on his part.

Who I date can't be a decision I make based on what makes my parents happy. My heart needs to be happy.

"Yeah, sorry dude. That's totally not happening."

"You'd really sleep on all this?"

The phone vibrates and I pull it back to find a photo of his shirt pulled off and his basketball shorts sitting low. I lift a brow. Yeah, nothing. Not a flutter, not a tickle, not a swoop. He does absolutely nothing for me.

"Um, yeah I guess I am. It frees you up to find someone who will appreciate, uh...all that."

Sam laughs again. *"Damn, girl. I'm trying to keep you and you're already setting me up with someone else."*

"Look, it's not really you, it's—"

"Don't." I startle at the force in his voice and the change in his easygoing demeanor. *"Don't do that. It's cool. Can we still be friends?"*

"Yeah, of course." I smile in relief that he understands. "I'm sorry we didn't work out as something more."

"Don't be sorry. You're too pretty for that."

I have no idea what to say to that. Awkwardly, I end the call after saying goodbye and drop back onto my yoga mat. One of the many weights on my chest evaporate, letting me breathe a little easier.

Thrown off from my meditation zone, I end up drifting over to the window to open it to let in fresh air. I reach for the latch and freeze.

A painfully familiar matte black Charger is lurking at the end of the street. Unease sits in

my chest as I wonder if he's watching my house now.
　　Isn't there anywhere I'm safe from him?

SEVEN
Fox

WATCHING Maisy search through her bag three times the following week for the assignment due makes me want to laugh. It's a big one, a research paper worth a percentage of the grade. She's putting on a good show of appearing calm, but I can see the gears turning in her head going from confused to frantic.

Look all you want, it's not there.

I shredded that shit, then stashed it in the shiny white Audi Q7 she drove to school today. She's in for a nasty surprise when she discovers the gift I left her. It was child's play to swipe the research paper from under her nose this morning when she was pretending to pay attention to her preppy boyfriend's recap of what he plans to pick for his fantasy football league.

The teacher, a pinch-faced older woman who always looks like she just caught a whiff of dog shit, stalks back and forth along the front row of desks. Maisy tucks her head lower as she goes through her bag for a fourth time while I stretch out in my seat beside hers, swiping a hand over my mouth to hide my amusement.

"I know I put it in here," she mumbles.

A vicious streak of satisfaction shoots through me. I'm still angry she showed up at the tree last week. Finding Holden's car parked there as I turned down the road made me furious, but when I saw her long honey-brown hair blowing in the wind I saw red. She deserves this and more.

Our teacher stops in front of Maisy's desk and raises her brows. "Are you prepared for class, Miss Landry?"

"Yes."

"Then hand in your research paper. Everyone else is prepared. You're holding us up and I don't have all day to wait for whatever excuse you're going to give me next."

A round of titters sounds through the room. Maisy's shoulders hunch at the weight of their eyes on her. She's not familiar with being under a negative spotlight from the teacher and it shows in the discomfort radiating from her.

She drags her teeth over her lip. "Right. I just...seem to have misplaced it. Maybe it's in my locker."

The teacher rolls her eyes. "Like I haven't heard that one a thousand times in forty years," she mutters, crossing her arms and leveling Maisy with an unimpressed look. "This certainly isn't behavior I expect from you. Just because you've already been accepted to colleges doesn't mean you should slack off. Your final class rank and GPA will reflect in your transcripts."

Whispers break out among the other students in the class and Maisy shifts in her chair, clearly uncomfortable. All this humiliating attention is getting to her, showing who she is behind the curtain—not the girl at the top of the class who seems perfect in every way. The corners of my mouth tip into a callous sneer.

"I know." She rifles through her things again, brow furrowed. "It was really here, I swear."

As Maisy grows flustered over her mysteriously missing research paper, she catches my smirk while I play with a pen. Realization dawns on her face and the curve of my mouth sharpens.

"I'll print off a new copy and turn it in tomorrow," she says in quiet defeat.

You can try.

I fiddle with my phone when it vibrates with a text I've been waiting for.

Colt: Hard drive is toast, nice and crispy [GIF of a marshmallow roasting over a fire]

A quiet huff of triumphant humor leaves me. It catches Maisy's attention and she flashes me another accusatory look, her hazel eyes burning. There's nothing she can do but take what I dish out to her. Even if she tried to get back at me for this, the faculty wouldn't touch me. She has no way to fight what's coming to her.

It almost makes me feel bad. Almost, but not quite. Because all I see when I look at her is my childhood best friend at eight, with her eyes bright and cheeks flushed as she fucking *promised*—

My fist clenches beneath the desk. No. There's no feeling sorry for the crybaby. She made her choice and now she'll pay for it.

"It'll be marked late," the teacher says before moving on, stopping in front of me. She lifts a skeptical brow. "I suppose you think you're above the final weeks of school as well, Mr. Wilder?"

"Not at all, miss."

She blinks in surprise at my response. The teachers here have grown to expect me being a silent dick all the time, but I'm not here for them. I'm only here for her.

Eyes locked with Maisy's, I hand over my assignment—which is really her paper, reworked a little. If she does manage to remember some of what she wrote and turn her project in, she'll be flagged for plagiarism and fail. It will be another hard hit to her class ranking and a black mark on her academic record that her college will frown on.

"Well." The teacher scans the first page and nods. "At least you finally put some effort into your school work. Better late than never."

That's right, miss. Maisy Landry does good work.

Not that I give a damn about the grade—it's just taking it from her that brings me the sick satisfaction I care about. Just like I'll take everything else away.

As our teacher carries the stack of papers back to her desk, Maisy stares at me. I rake my gaze over her. She huffs and turns in her desk to face the front, probably wondering what the hell happened to her assignment.

This is all petty shit in the grand scheme of things. Compared to what I've done when I lived in Thorne Point with Colton and Wren's crew, it's nothing. But it's all according to my new plan. Maisy is a rusted chain, ready to snap. I took care of Holden first, but she's more satisfying to break, slowly chipping away piece by piece until the fake good girl crumbles before me.

And she'll know without a doubt it was me crushing her to dust.

VERONICA EDEN

EIGHT
Maisy

This place is descending into madness, I swear. Eyes have burned into me in all my morning classes, eager for the show when I search my bag for assignments due only to find they aren't there. I've never been unprepared for class or turned my work in late once in my life, not even in kindergarten. Missing one paper is one thing, but every piece of homework due today isn't where it should be in my bag and I'm getting really sick of the muffled laughter behind my back.

At lunch I slip out to the parking lot, avoiding the snarky whispers that follow in my wake. I hope my research paper is there. It could've slipped out of my bag in Holden's Audi and I didn't notice. *Please let that be the case.*

Turning it in late is already going to be a hit to my grade point average. I'll still be in the top five percent, but Mom only cares about me maintaining number one. It makes her look good if I'm Valedictorian when I graduate, and if I lose that spot? Goodbye road trip I've been working so hard to convince her and Dad to let me take.

When I reach the car, I open the door and immediately rear back from the smell that hits me. "Ugh! What the hell?"

It's awful, the entire interior reeks of rotting fruit and sickly sweet soda, baked for hours in the car under the hot summer sun. This has to have been like this for a while, after I got to school. Sam met me at the car this morning and talked my ear off before we turned to walk inside together. It probably happened right after.

The driver's seat is covered in trash and rotten debris. Banana peels so ripe they're black are dumped into the cup holders of the center console and apple cores spill off the seat to the floor.

Holding my nose from the awful trash-plus-heat sauna stench, I pick up one of the banana peels and drop it to the ground with a revolted jolt. It's *sticky*. I wipe my hand on my plaid uniform skirt and scrunch up my face in dismay.

On closer inspection when I prod the black interior seats, they're soaked with the soda that was dumped over this whole mess. From the seats to the wheel to the dash, everything is covered in so much soda that whoever played this prank on me must have been prepared with several bottles. And mixed in with it all is a pile of shredded paper. One corner pokes out and through the smeared print, I can make out the title of my research paper.

Now I know where it went.

Groaning under my breath, I dig around in the back seat for a bag, then hunt down extra napkins from the glove compartment, glad Holden and I grabbed burgers at our favorite place yesterday. My nose wrinkles as I swipe the trash into the bag and clean up the soda as best as I can. It will need to go through a full detail service to really take care of it. Holden's going to kill me. I'll be lucky if he ever lets me use his car again. It will leave me completely stranded and at the mercy of others who can offer me rides.

Tears well in my eyes as I dump the trash in the can at the edge of the parking lot, right next to the vending machines where the culprit most likely bought the soda. What did I do to deserve this? Nothing warrants this.

There's only one person here who hates me enough to come at me like this. After swiping angrily at my eyes, my fingers clutch the braided leather bracelet, nails scraping over the stones woven into it. Stones I love because they're special to me.

Damn Fox Wilder. He's not going to beat me. He wants me to break and cry for him, but I'm not running just because he's put a target on my back.

Trudging back up the steps, past the school sign flanked by the SLHS coyote mascot statues, I head for lunch. As soon as I walk through the door, I stall. Every eye on the room is on me and conversations lull to a stop. It's weird and disconcerting knowing an entire room full of people were probably talking about you behind your back until you happen to walk in.

At the back corner of the room, Fox sits by himself, scowling at his phone.

My smile is wobbly, but I pull it into place like armor as I walk deeper into the room. The conversations slowly begin to pick up again.

Sam isn't in my lunch period, so I usually float around from table to table. I've always been kind and polite, but never made many friends in my own grade. The people I talk to are more like acquaintances. Today that divide feels more isolating than ever.

It doesn't hit me until now, with the rumors getting worse, how much I've kept myself separated from my classmates. I have no close allies I can trust because all of my true friends graduated last year. I miss lunches in the courtyard with Thea, Connor, Blair, and Devlin.

"Hey, Maisy, right? Come here for a minute."

I pause by the table of rowdy guys. Some of them are on the soccer and football teams, some are just jock by association. The one who stopped me is a guy I recognize from Jenna's party.

"Yeah, that's me," I say, tucking my wariness behind a mask of sweetness.

His friends elbow him and they shush each other, chuckling to themselves. I want to take a step back, but I hold my ground.

"So," the guy from the party drawls. I'm pretty sure he hangs out with Sam. "You free Friday night? I heard you and Sam Blake broke up."

"I have to volunteer at the library on Friday, then I teach yoga classes until pretty late." I shrug and tilt my head. "So I'm not free, sorry."

"That's cool, later is better for me." He gives me a flirtatious once over. "I'll pick you up and we can go up to Peak Point."

My shoulders stiffen as his buddies make lewd noises. Peak Point is Ridgeview's notorious makeout spot, a lookout point in the mountains where everyone parks in the shadows to hump in their cars.

"What?" My tone is frosty, but they don't notice, too busy congratulating each other while their friend propositions me.

"Don't be shy, baby." He stares openly at my breasts. What a pig. "I want the wildcat you were at Jenna's party. The easy one, not the prude."

There's nothing I can do to stop the way my body jerks in response. These rumors are out of control.

"You've got the wrong girl," I say, crossing my arms, no longer willing to play nice. "My answer is still no."

"Don't be a cock tease, those lips are begging to suck my dick."

Fuck this.

If I wasn't doing everything to make sure my parents let me go on the road trip, I'd deck this guy. Screw peace and love, he totally deserves a fist in his face to wipe off that smug look he thinks is so sexy. With a tight smile, I turn away.

"Hey! I wasn't done talking to you!" he calls after me. "Don't ignore me, bitch!"

Glancing around the room, I'm struck by the amount of attention on me from the surrounding tables. Beyond that, Fox watches all of this go down from the corner of the room, no longer occupied on his phone. His expression turns hard once my gaze sweeps over him.

How much did he hear?

The guy's friends at his rowdy table join in, slinging names at me. *Slut. Easy. Prude. Bitch.* The chants catch on until the whole room is shouting.

Which is it, guys?

Eyes stinging, I stare back at Fox.

Take a good look. You turned me into the crybaby. Are you happy now?

Again, I clutch my wrist, covering the leather braided bracelet carrying the stones he gave me. Neither of my bracelets make me feel strong right now. The one with the stones Fox found on the beach during our vacation used to make me believe in anything. After he was gone, wearing it felt like it was my last connection to him. I'd whisper my dreams to it at night as if I was talking to him. It made me feel close to him.

A tear slips down my cheek, then another. Mean laughter echoes around me, but I keep staring at Fox. He leans back against the wall in his corner, kicking one booted foot on the bench seat. His smirk is savage.

For the first time ever, I consider ripping off the bracelet I've worn since I was a little girl and throwing it down at his feet.

NINE
Fox

By the end of the day, it hasn't gotten old. We only share a handful of classes together, when I bother to show up. But this idea is way more gratifying than I first thought.

I'm surprised she's still standing after the lunch room turned on her. It just means she can take more and it sends a sick sense of satisfaction through me.

As Maisy sits in World History, staring helplessly into her bag like it'll give her answers, I stifle a silent laugh that shakes my shoulders. Petty playground bullshit or not, this is fun. More fun than I've had in years. The more she gets worked up, the more I enjoy the show.

"Did the dog eat your homework?" I taunt, making sure she's watching as I put another paper with my name and her effort in the basket on the teacher's desk.

Maisy stiffens, darting her gaze away. After all the other students hand in their assignments while she remains seated, red as a tomato, I saunter back to my seat, this time right behind her. I'm in such a good mood, I can't resist giving the ends of her hair a tug and she whips around to glare at me.

"What is your problem?" she snaps.

The corner of my mouth lifts. It's another crack in her calm, kind facade if she's showing some spirit to bite back. She waits, but I don't have anything else to say to her. Crossing my arms over my chest until my leather jacket creaks, I lean back and give her a cool stare.

Squinting, she leans toward me over my desk, hissing under her breath through clenched teeth. "You're behind this. It's got you written all over it. I'm getting sick of these pranks."

"Behind what?"

Her mouth tightens and her knuckles turn white as she grips the back of her chair. "You stole my homework. All of it. I thought you wanted nothing to do with me?"

A girl in the next row does a double take when she realizes there's drama stirring and who it's between. We're drawing more eyes on us as the teacher writes out the schedule for the upcoming final exams on the chalkboard.

"Or maybe…" Moving too fast for her to register before I'm in her face, I grab the side of her neck and clamp down hard so she can't move. The sharp inhale she sucks in is music to my ears. "You're just making excuses because you're tired of being such a fucking goody-goody all the time."

Hushed voices sound all around us while Maisy's breathing turns harsh and strained. I tilt my head, studying her. Her eyes have gone wide and she seems on the verge of breaking. Just one more push...

"Come on, you can't keep fooling us," I croon. "It's what everyone's thinking. They all know you're a liar. It's what your locker says this week, right?"

"No!"

Maisy shoves away hard, breaking my hold on her. Her desk topples to the side with the force. The room shrinks away, my world narrowing down to the girl who broke my heart and ripped my life apart.

I shoot to my feet and grab her shoulders, digging my fingers into her blazer. "What's wrong? Does the truth hurt?"

At all the commotion, the teacher whirls around with a shout. "What the hell is going on here? We're in class!"

Shock ripples over Maisy's features. She glances around, realizing how many phones are trained on us, probably recording. Paling, she turns to the red-faced teacher. He stalks down the aisle of desks to reach us.

"Get your hands off her, Wilder. What's gotten into you, Miss Landry?"

The teacher spares me a disgruntled look, then unloads all his disappointment on the little liar in my grip. I hold on for another beat, just to prove I'm in control. He doesn't ask me again. I let her go and she shrinks back a step while I stand my ground.

"I'm sorry, Mr. Brewer." Maisy's back to her fucking simpering mask, casting her gaze at the floor demurely. It pisses me off more than usual. "I didn't mean to make a scene."

"This kind of behavior is unacceptable. Disrupting class, fighting." He shakes his head, peering between us. "School policy deems fighting on school grounds a suspendable offense. But..." His glare softens when it leaves me and lands on Maisy. "Seeing as it's the first time you've been involved in this kind of trouble, I'll let you off with detention. That goes for both of you, everyday for the next week."

Barely resisting an eye roll, I stalk from the room. The teacher calls after me, but I'm done. I make it halfway down the hall before the sound of footsteps reaches my ears. I angle my head back and find Maisy following me. My brows lift.

Cutting class? That's a first.

"You're not even going to say anything, asshole?"

She grabs my arm once she's close enough and pulls hard to yank me around. It only works because I wasn't expecting it. As soon as I plant my feet, I become an immovable wall.

Cheeks pink, she takes a step into my space. "How'd you do it?" When I don't offer up an answer, air hisses between her teeth. "My research project that took me two months to do isn't on my cloud drive anymore. At lunch I found it—" She breaks off with a disgusted sound and glares at me. "How the hell did you do it, Fox? *Why* did you do it?"

I ignore her, staring over her head. Growing more frustrated by the minute, she pushes at my chest and releases an agitated little grunt when I don't move.

"Which is it?" Maisy demands. "I just want to know so I can stop getting whiplash. Cold shoulder and ignoring me again, or all your damn focus on me to toy with me in these demented mind games?"

That catches my attention. Smirking, I crowd her against the lockers, enjoying the startled but challenging look on her face.

"You want my attention again, daisy?" It comes out as a deep, threatening rasp. "Is that what you really want?"

Her mouth sets in a firm line. "Don't call me daisy."

I grab her waist tight, shoving a knee between hers to keep her pinned in place. Her legs clench together around my thigh and she buries her teeth in her lip, holding herself as far away from me as she can. A dark chuckle rolls through me. I trace my bottom lip with my tongue as I study her face for every reaction.

"Are you sure? Because the way you're squirming on my leg suggests otherwise. You like it when I pay attention to you, even if I make it hurt." Her face flushes and I edge closer, pinning her whole body with mine. A faint sound escapes her, but she lifts her chin stubbornly. The feel of her soft chest is familiar and draws a growl from me. "People say I'm a bad boy. Shouldn't that make you want to run instead of rub your pussy on me hoping I'll get you all dirty again?"

This close, her intoxicating floral and coconut scent tempts me to repeat what happened at the party a few weeks ago. Make fresh marks on her to remind her of me long after. Fuck, as soon as I allow the memories in, I'm drowning in her all over again.

"Fox," she whispers hoarsely.

Watching her face closely, my grasp flexes on her waist and I move my leg so it connects with the apex of her thighs. Her breath catches and she shudders. She digs her fingers into my shirt and manages to shove away from me by bucking her hips and twisting out of the hold I had on her. The only reason she gets away is because I'm momentarily impressed she handled herself so well when I had her cornered against the lockers.

The door to the bathroom a few feet away slams shut once she flies through it and a bark of laughter bursts from me at how easy she is to predict. But she doesn't get to run from me. I'm not done with her yet.

Not after she looked at me with all that forbidden want in her hazel eyes.

Stalking down the hall like a nightmare come to life, I follow her into the bathroom. It's straight out of a swanky hotel instead of a high school, with wood paneled stalls and granite countertops. Nothing like the grimy public schools I was bounced through in the system before the DuPonts came along.

"You finally figured out you should run when I'm around. Too bad I wasn't finished," I say as the door shuts ominously behind me.

Maisy jumps in surprise by the row of sinks. "Dude, this is the girls' room. You can't—"

"Well isn't this a familiar scene for us."

While she's caught up, I move, herding her. It cuts off her protest. She backs up twice for every one of my long strides. The edge of my mouth curls up when I have her where I want her, trapped in the far stall.

"I go wherever the hell I want."

Maisy's throat works on a swallow. She keeps a wary eye on me as I advance on her until her back hits the wall, my chest brushing hers. I can feel the rise and fall with each of her breaths. She's not backing down still. Interesting.

"You should get out of here. It's almost the end of the period. Someone will see you."

"Yeah?" I grab her throat, enjoying the flash in her eyes. There's something dark and depraved deep inside her that likes it when I'm controlling, dominant, and demanding. "You should be trying harder to get away from me right now." Leaning in, I brush my lips against the corner of her mouth. "I dare you to scream."

She jerks against me, whipping her head to the side. She speaks to the wall. "You're so messed up."

"Only because you made me this way," I mutter as I bury my nose against her temple, inhaling her sweet floral scent.

I shouldn't want you at all…but part of me still does.

My heart thumps and I cover the ragged breath that knocks out of me by pressing into her, taking her wrists and wrestling them over her head. I hold them in one hand and put my lips to the shell of her ear as she struggles and wriggles.

"Is that fight real or fake, baby?" I nip at her lobe and plant a hand next to her hip, tracing the edge of her plaid skirt. "Funny how you aren't screaming for me to stop. So either you want me to take whatever I want from you, or…"

I trail off and her expression says it all when I peer down at her. Defiant, but underneath it there's a hunger burning in her pretty eyes. One that calls to the same insatiable lust brimming inside me, making my dick hard.

It shouldn't. This girl destroyed me once.

I let her in that night at the party and used her body because it was a good cover. A moment of weakness I allowed because hating her in person rather than from afar was its own form of agony.

Yet my cock stiffens and I'm filled with the desire to taste her mouth, to swallow those breathy sounds she makes when she's close to coming. It's the one line I haven't crossed.

"If you were really going to hurt me, you would've done it by now." She's only half confident, but she stares me down. "I'm not afraid, so do your worst."

She's right.

This time I can't blame needing extra cover. I just want to take from her.

As I stare at those full lips, drawn inch by inch to close the small gap between us, the door clangs open. I still, remembering where we are. Maisy goes rigid, eyes wide as someone turns on water at the sinks. I release her wrists and grab the back of her thighs, lifting her. She manages to muffle a squeak, dangling until she realizes what I want her to do.

A smirk tilts my mouth when she's forced to wrap her legs around my waist rather than hanging there off balance. Adjusting so I can support her more easily, I mime a finger to my lips to tell her she better be quiet. She grants me the tiniest nod and the wicked sensation spiraling through me shouldn't excite me as much as it does.

Dirty, dirty girl.

No one at this school gets to see this version—the wild child. As I skim a hand down her side and bring my mouth back to her neck, I almost laugh, giving us away. She hides the vindictive little promise breaker well. Just like she hid the hickey I gave her. I'll just have to mark her all over again. I look forward to catching hints of my secret claim on her.

I bite her neck and hold her tight to absorb the force of her response, her back arching and her thighs squeezing tighter around my waist. Shit, she likes it rough. My cock throbs in my jeans and I send up a silent prayer of thanks for uniform skirts alongside the skintight yoga pants she favors outside of school.

Licking a trail up her neck, I stop at her ear, speaking in a smoky whisper. "If they catch you right now, they'll know you're not the good girl you pretend to be. I'll ruin that pretty reputation and show them who you really are."

She rests her forehead on my shoulder, whimpering as she places her hands on my chest. Sweeping her hair aside for better access, I nibble on her pulse point. Her nails dig into me hard and I grunt, reaching down to squeeze her ass through the skirt in retaliation. I find a new spot of her throat to torture, one that makes her writhe and mash her face into the muscled juncture between my shoulder and neck. Her lips brush over my skin inside the collar of my leather jacket and I falter from sucking on her skin at how good it feels.

Damn, I'm getting caught up in this, like last time. The line is blurring further and I need to bring everything back under my control.

Distantly, I'm aware of the running water stopping and footsteps leaving the bathroom. Thank fuck.

Once the person is gone, a wicked grin settles on my face. "You managed to stay quiet enough." I pin her back to the wall and slide my fingers up her leg, beneath her skirt while grinding my erection against her ass. "You must really hate yourself as much as I do to let me do whatever I fucking want to you. Does the thought of getting caught like this make you wet?"

"If you hate me that much, then why are you hard?" Maisy accuses, spitting like an angry viper. "That makes you a liar, too. You said this wouldn't happen again."

My grin turns lethal and I crush my chest to hers to feel her shake. "You think I can't still hate you while I fuck you? Watch me."

As she trembles, chewing on her lip, my touch travels all the way up her smooth thigh to her hip. I blink, drawing a circle with my fingertips over her skin. Her *bare* skin. She's not wearing any underwear.

A brittle laugh forces out of me and I *tsk*, moving my hand between her legs to stroke her. She's wet as hell. I bet if I looked, she'd be glistening. My mouth waters without my permission and I clench my teeth.

"What a pretty mess you are for me, daisy," I murmur.

Mortification creeps into her expression. She can't deny that no matter what I put her through, she still would beg for more if it meant I would touch her. Desperate little thing. It just makes me want to double my efforts against her.

I pinch her clit between my fingers, keeping her on a razor thin line between pleasure and pain. She gasps.

"Fox, please—"

I interrupt her strangled cry with a hard tone. "Was this for him?"

She blinks. "Who?"

"Your boyfriend. That preppy idiot you're always with."

"Sam? No." She swallows and plays with the collar of my jacket, some of the fog of arousal fading. After a moment, she shakes her head. "I just...I prefer to be like this." Her challenging gaze darts up to meet mine. "It's not for anyone but myself. I like the freedom."

My chest grows tight and I force out a breath. I wasn't expecting that, or the honesty in her soft voice. This isn't supposed to be some sweet moment between a romantic couple. We're anything but that. We're the opposite, brutal heartache and wild destruction. Ruinous and destined for tragedy.

We'll never get back what we once had. I can't trust her and she should fucking run from me, because I won't stop trying to end all her perfect happiness, even now, with my cock hard between her toned thighs and her bare pussy dripping all over my goddamn hand.

I shake my head and rub her clit, intent on making her cry out for me. "What will he say about you allowing another man's hands on you like this?"

Maisy's eyes flash. "He's not my boyfriend. He never was." My fingers move in a circle, dipping lower. She struggles to get her words out. "We were just—hanging out. I broke up with him after...after the day at our tree."

Another laugh punches out of me as I fight off the wave of possessiveness that rises. She stifles a moan while I tease her slick folds and I lean in, licking a stripe up the column of her throat.

"Whatever you say." It doesn't matter. I don't care. She's not mine anymore—maybe she never was to begin with. As I attack her skin with my teeth, my tone turns meaner. "I'm still not going to kiss you, no matter how bad you beg me. I'm going to break you apart, and then leave you here."

"Fine. If you think that's what will hurt me, you're wrong." Fire burns in her gaze and she tips her chin up. "Bend me all you want, I'm flexible. But I won't break for you."

Her nails dig into my body again, right into the ocean and crowned crow inked over my heart. She's not going to be intimidated by me. I like it, her fight reminds me to see past her mask. As long as she understands this means nothing, then she can give me as much fire as she wants.

I shift her in my arms again, setting her ass on a bar on the wall for extra support. My hand goes to her throat, holding her while I slide my fingers through her wet folds. She releases a shaky breath, spreading her legs wider.

The determined, reckless look on her face sends me right back to ten years ago. That's my Maisy sitting before me. The one who isn't bound by anyone's rules but her own.

This girl…

I rake my teeth over my lower lip and sink a finger inside her without warning. She chokes when I squeeze her throat to stop her cry.

"Look at you. Feel that? You're soaking my hand. Getting off on the danger."

I thrust my finger deeper, adding a second. Every sensation feels new and heady, making me want to chase her down this rabbit hole to the very end.

Maisy wraps one hand around the arm at her throat and the other grips my leather jacket as she arches, riding my fingers. Fuck, it's a good look on her—cheeks flushed and lids heavy, she looks hedonistic. Free. Something I can't have anymore, a girl I vowed to never want. She broke her promise, and I'm breaking mine.

The grin I give her is sharp and ruthless. "What does it say about you that you'll let someone who despises you so much I can barely breathe around you do this to you?" I twist my fingers, hooking them into a spot that makes her lips part on a silent moan, her lashes fluttering. Her pussy clenches on my fingers as I drive them deeper. "How far would you actually let me go? Are you hoping I'll rip this skirt off and fuck you with my cock next?"

"God, just—shut up and make me come, Fox," she bites out. "Fuck! Don't stop, I'm really close."

An unhinged rumble vibrates in my chest as I grind my erection against her thigh so she can feel it. She claws at me, burying her face in my neck. A sharp pain makes me jolt, sending a spark of pleasure down my spine. She bit me back. When she tenses and comes with a muffled sound of ecstasy, I stare, just as struck by it as I was that night a few weeks ago.

The satisfaction of breaking her in a new way is tinged in bitterness because this can't keep happening—I want what I taunted her with too badly. Once is a mistake, twice is a bad habit. Fucking her is the one thing I refuse to give her, even if a thousand fantasy scenarios of making her scream by driving my dick into her tight heat rush through my head.

The bell rings as I step back, taking in how shattered she is. Her pretty features are twisted in orgasmic bliss at my hands. It drives a spike of ice into my heart. I slid too far down the slope, losing the upper hand by getting too wrapped up in this game.

Panting heavily and ignoring the throb in my hard cock, I take another step back. Her eyes finally open and she peers at me through her lashes. Another burst of possessiveness rears its ugly head and I grit my teeth, stuffing it back down to smother it before it can fully form.

I swipe the back of my hand over my mouth. My voice sounds hollow when I find my words. "Everyone here calls me a black shadow. They're not wrong, Maisy. When you call a boy a monster enough times, it starts to stick. What I touch turns to ash. Now that includes you."

I hold her gaze for a beat, then back out of the stall, leaving her exactly as I warned I would.

TEN
Maisy

The past several hours have left my thoughts a chaotic mess and my heart heavy.

After the bathroom door banged shut behind Fox, what happened hit me hard. I said I didn't care, but my bravado faded as soon as he was gone. I was disappointed in myself that I could sink so low right after he bullied me. Was it really worth it? Shame slid through me as I scrambled out of the stall, splashing cold water on my cheeks. It was no use, what we'd done was written all over my open face. I couldn't hide it, or how much I enjoyed it.

This was the same as the night at the party, down to the way he left. At least this time I didn't have to walk out to a gauntlet of people who knew just by looking at me.

I've never been someone who shies away from my desires, but it's the fact I keep fucking around with him when he's tormenting me that eats at me.

Today was such a shit show.

From the stinging humiliation of not being prepared for class with no explanation for how my finished assignments were gone from my bag, to the whispers and side eye looks that dug into my back as I passed. Discovering the mess in the car followed by the cruel taunting in the lunchroom. Topped off by the bathroom when I tried to face Fox head on because I wasn't going to just let him get away with it. I was done taking his crap laying down. His tampering with my school assignments irritates me way more than what happened after, but all of it is one big pile of suck sitting on my shoulders.

It was a miracle I made it through the last class period of the day on autopilot by keeping my head down until I could escape. I went through the motions of the yoga sessions I led at the studio in the health and wellness center, glad it was a day I was allowed to use Holden's car instead of relying on someone to give me a ride. Although if I didn't drive today, his car wouldn't have been the scene of one of Fox's disgusting pranks. I stopped to have it cleaned before my first class. He'll never know.

I'm staying behind as long as I can to work out my frustrations of the day, avoiding going home where I'm sure my parents have already heard about my detention. If they find out what else I was up to on school grounds, they'll blow their lids.

The last of my seven to eight late class trickles out, leaving me alone with a wall of mirrors and an emptiness eating away at my insides. I feel so adrift, and while that normally wouldn't bother me because I thrive better on the unknown, this feels different, like a heavy weight pulling me down, keeping me in the dark murkiness where it feels like I'll never get out.

It's getting worse the closer I get to graduation. Between Fox and my parents my problems threaten to drag me so far down I'll drown.

There's no way for Fox and I to be together. Maybe I was holding my breath in the hope we could still be friends—or *more*. His old promise of *someday* is something I still think about. I never forgot it, even if he has. Knowing his touch, I've been hoping to have that promise come true even more.

"No." I scrub my hands over my face. "Not in the cards."

My old feelings for him and the fact I find him hot can't cloud my judgement of how he's treated me. It's not okay.

That can't happen again.

After today at school and last week at the tree it's even clearer.

The harsh way Fox called me desperate echoes in my head. Is that why I let it happen? Why I didn't tell him to stop and allowed him to go as far as fingering me where anyone could have found us?

But you know what? No. It was a choice I made and I have to live with the fallout. In the moment, I wanted it and I refuse to let the guilt over it all fester. I'm not going to beat myself up feeling bad about anything. That's not my style.

Annoyed that this has taken over my mind for hours, I move into a flow, continuing even when the playlist switches off. I don't need the music to lose myself in twisting my body. I keep moving as my breathing syncs with my heartbeat, pushing away the fact Fox somehow destroyed my classwork so thoroughly, then violated Holden's car with it followed by the sinfully good exhilaration of his touch paired with his cruel words making me come so hard I couldn't move.

It feels good to keep pushing my limbs, stretching and arching through the flow.

My mind doesn't empty. Did I want to be caught, or did I just want to stay in his strong arms and let him torture me with his addictive pleasure?

The heat that floods my cheeks is searing and I cover them with my palms, closing my eyes while I concentrate on breathing. When I open my eyes, the fierceness I keep tucked away in my heart is there in my reflection.

I need a way to fight back against him so he sees I'm not the liar he's accused me of being. I won't be scared of him anymore because it's getting me nowhere. I thought he was capable of hurting me, but he's had the opportunity and hasn't taken it. That has to give me the only hope I can cling to. There must be a way I can find out how to get through to him so he'll stop hating me. I twist the leather bracelet around so I can see the stones.

If I can just get close enough to figure out if there's any scrap left of the boy I knew, I'd be able to break through his wall and fix this. Fix *us*.

Centering myself, I move into a handstand split against the mirror, using it for balance as I practice perfecting my inversions. My shoulders burn as I curve my spine and spread my legs.

The lights cut out.

My heart skips a beat as I suck in a breath, trying to adjust to the darkness. I keep working. It's not the first time the custodial staff turned the lights off on me. Besides, I have a key. Yoga in the dark is nice.

I work to get my breathing back in sync, feeling the exertion in my shoulders from supporting my weight. After I focus for a minute, I notice that something feels off. The hair on the back of my neck stands on end and a shiver travels against my exposed stomach not covered by my tight crop top.

The air thickens and my pulse speeds up, along with my breathing.

A touch comes from out of the darkness, nearly startling me out of my skin. It's a barely there, familiar brush of fingers right over my center that echoes the memories from earlier. My heart stutters in my chest. I tremble, but remain frozen in position. Is my imagination going wild? There's no way he's really here right now, no way he touched me.

I swear I hear a deep chuckle in the pitch black shadows. Then the lights flicker back on. Breathing hard, I carefully force my limbs to move out of the handstand split. My shaking knees make me crumple to the floor and I lean my forehead against the mirror, my breath fogging the glass. My heart is racing when I rest a hand over it.

Did I imagine it or not? It doesn't matter.

The message is loud and clear—*I can get to you anytime I want*.

It should terrify me. So why is there a needy ache between my legs?

* * *

Braced for hell when I get home a short while later, I'm met instead with a weird phenomenon. Mom and Dad aren't mad, they're disappointed.

"So, I'm not grounded?" I stand on the steps with my yoga mat under one arm and my gym tote, ready to escape to my room. When they met me at the door, Dad spared me a quick *don't make it a habit after you've worked hard* and left me alone with Mom. "The last time I got a detention you grounded me for a month."

The last and *only* time I'd ever gotten detention. It was freshman year, earned because I wanted to nap outside beneath the sun during the lunch period, which made me late for class. It was DEFCON 5 when Mom got wind of it, so I was expecting much worse this time.

She still hasn't yelled, or done the scary calm undressing that is even more terrible. She frowns at me.

"I'm not thrilled, don't misunderstand," she explains. "You caused a scene, and that is deeply disappointing."

Tiny invisible knives prick at my skin. "Sorry. I'll go upstairs and do my homework over. It won't happen again."

"I wasn't finished, Maisy Grace." She puts a hand on the banister, lines forming around her mouth. "I can't have you involved with that boy. I know he's to blame for this, just like his rotten drunk of a father."

My throat tightens and a hot lash of anger rushes through me. How can she talk about someone she was friends with like that? Mom and Dad believe every rumor about him.

"Fox? That's what you're pissed about? Not that I was fighting or that my GPA will drop because of my missed assignments and allow someone else to take the top spot you need me to have?"

Her mouth pinches. "Those things are important, but nothing is more serious than my warning to stay away from him. I thought I made that clear. Everything we've worked for to provide paths to success for you and your brother are wasted if you let that boy infect your life."

"*That boy*, Mom? Do you even hear yourself? He was my best friend. Holden's too. *Your* friends' son." I grip the strap of my tote bag. "Holden was allowed to hang out with him without you and Dad intervening, so why do I have to avoid him? It's impossible when we have classes together, and he—"

I cut off. I can't tell her about what's been going on because I don't want more rules from her.

My parents don't like Fox. If they find out there's more going on than me slacking on homework, they'll do something to get the school to expel him. I want to be able to handle this on my terms.

"Yes, and look where that got your brother," she says shrewdly. "Drafted to play for one of the top schools in the country, but he flushed it down the toilet by associating with trash."

A disbelieving scoff rips from my throat. "Jesus, Mom. Tell me how you really feel. You can't seriously believe that a college like Ohio State really looks that deeply into their incoming students, especially the athletes they accept."

One manicured brow lifts skeptically. "You're naïve if you think otherwise. This is what I've tried to teach you. The world is always watching. What you do matters—every move you make. Do not make the same mistake as your brother."

God, Holden and I really have become pawns to her if that's all she cares about. I open my mouth to protest, but she's not finished.

"You need to do damage control to get your life back on track. You're so close to graduating, Maisy. I won't let you throw it away because of your impulsive tendencies." Her nails tap on the banister as the gears of her mind turn. "What we should do is call that sweet boy, Samuel Blake. Invite him over for dinner. Why hasn't he been around lately to take you out? Your father and I like him."

"You've got to be kidding me," I mutter low enough she doesn't hear. "I don't think that's a good idea."

"Why not? He's perfect for you. He's a handsome and intelligent young man from a wonderful and well respected family."

"Mom, I broke up with him. It wasn't going to work. He's not someone I see myself with."

I'd tell her he doesn't make my heart flutter, but I don't think she'd give a damn about things like feelings.

"You did what? When was this?"

"Last week."

She gives me a look full of displeasure that calls on my urge to leave. Not just to run upstairs, but to get out of town.

"Maisy."

How she can make my name sound so cutting, I'll never know. I smother the urge to snark back and say *Mom*.

"You are such a disappointment. Go to your room."

Forcing out a breath, I turn to face her fully. "So which is it, Mom? Am I grounded or not?"

"Go," she snaps. "We'll finish discussing this later."

My feet slam on the steps, echoing in the foyer. The weight on my chest gets heavier and heavier.

"Maise," Holden calls from his open door.

I stop. He's sitting on the floor, leaning against his bed. Five o'clock shadow covers his jaw and his brown hair is a mess, but he doesn't look as down as he's been since my senior year started and his future halted in its tracks. Must be one of his rare good days.

He motions with his head for me to come in and I do, shoulders sagging as I dump off my stuff from the yoga studio inside the door. I collapse on the floor beside him, dragging my knees up.

"Did you hear?" I almost don't want to know.

"A little. Not all of it." He motions to his headphones sitting on the floor. "Just the last part."

I hope that means he didn't hear what Mom said about him. Acid sloshes in my stomach. Holden puts a comforting arm around my shoulder and I tip my head back against his bed.

"Do you wish things were different?" I ask. "That you'd gotten to go to Ohio State, like you wanted?"

He grunts. "Yes and no. Ridgeview Community College isn't so bad."

"Even though you've been sulking about it for two semesters straight?"

He chuckles and pinches my shoulder. I punch his leg in return and he smirks at me.

"I started talking to some of the people from my classes instead of avoiding them and I realized the other day that it's pretty freeing actually. Not having to deal with the pressure they've put on us."

God, I want that. It's like this year Mom has taken what she divided between us and put twice as much on me as her last horse in the race.

"I don't think it'll work out like that for me. They won't even let me go on my road trip."

"So take it later. Who says you have to chase everything in your life now? You've got time."

I stare at the sports paraphernalia all over his room, wondering if he believed the same. "It's not even about the trip. I just hate being smothered and never getting to do what I want. Why does my life have to be so planned out?"

Holden ruffles my hair. "Just chill."

"Easy for you to say." I rub my lips together. "Can I ask you something?"

It feels nice to have my brother back after he's shut me out most of the year, but I don't want to piss him off.

"Shoot."

"Don't be mad."

He rolls his eyes. "Spit it out."

"When Fox came back last year, why did you hang out with him?"

"Uh…" Holden blows out a breath. "I don't know. We didn't really go back to being friends, he just sort of became my shadow. The guy grew up to be a real dick."

I suck on my teeth. "So what, he made you look good for the kids you shook down for money with your bets out at the quarry?" Holden's brows fly up. "Oh, don't give me that look. I knew exactly what was going on out there. It's not a great kept secret when it hits the Silver Lake High rumor mill."

He rubs at the back of his neck. "I guess. It didn't hurt and he helped enforce the rules." His mouth tips into a lopsided grin. "Especially when your friend Thea's guy showed up. Dude could really lay them out."

I didn't care about Connor's fighting skills, I was hungry for more about Fox. This is the first time I've gotten Holden to open up about him since his return. "What was he like?"

He shrugs. "Like I said, he was a dick. Didn't talk about much—only cared about the fights, his Charger and his motorcycle."

I'm quiet for a moment. "It's the same one his dad had. Remember?"

"Yeah," he says somberly, momentarily lost to the memories of our childhood. "Listen, I know you're not going to like this, but he's different. We were kids then. He's not that same kid we knew at all. Got it? You should avoid him. I don't want him messing with you."

I almost snort, but I keep it in. Holden has missed so much while he's been brooding over his own problems. I climb to my feet and grab my stuff, pausing at the door.

"Thanks for making me feel better."

Holden gives me a jerk of his chin on my way out.

I go to my room. Plopping on my bed, I stare at the roadmap I pinned to the ceiling, mulling over strategies for how I'll get closer to Fox without him realizing what I'm doing.

First I need to figure out why he only shows up to school half the time, or where he goes when he cuts out early. As far as I know, it's random. Determination settles in my bones.

Before he knows it, I'll be inside his walls and we'll hash out the negativity between us.

ELEVEN
Maisy

Sneaking out on Friday night is the best idea ever. Another day of detention after school left me restless, and annoyed that I had to serve it alone—Fox didn't show. It was straight home after that. Mom's judgmental stare was too much at dinner and I was going stir crazy in my room while the sun was still shining outside, begging me to have some fun.

Luckily, Thea is best friend goals and loves me. When I messaged her, she and Blair helped me sneak out past our security system undetected.

As we peel away from my house, I reach forward to hug Blair from the back of Thea's Mini Cooper, arms wrapping around her seat to reach her. "You guys are the best."

Blair used to stiffen at my hugs—or anyone's affectionate touch who wasn't her boyfriend's—but now she gives me a husky laugh and reaches up to squeeze my wrist. "Who doesn't love a little jailbreak. Keeps life interesting."

I laugh. From the story Devlin tells of how they ended up together, she can get down and dirty, going as far as attempting to steal his car and earning a reputation for being a smooth pickpocket.

"I'm so glad you're back from school."

"Me too," she says.

We head for downtown Ridgeview, where the guys are meeting us to see a movie. My phone is off, so there's no worry of Dad tracking me down at Mom's command. Freedom feels damn good.

"Where's Gemma?"

"Her and Lucas and his parents drove out to Denver for the weekend to see her brother," Thea says.

I remember him. Our brothers both played football together for Silver Lake High. Gemma's really cool, someone who has an energy that matches mine and killer confidence I admire. It's no wonder her boyfriend Lucas, Silver Lake's ex-football quarterback, is off the deep end in love with her.

Once we reach downtown and park, the guys meet us in front of the theater. Connor and Devlin both have eyes only for their girls as the three of us head for them arm in arm with me in the middle. The guys look like the angel and devil that might sit on your shoulder, with Connor's lighter features and charming smile and Devlin's dark everything—hair, eyes, presence. When they're together, you know trouble is going down.

As soon as we're close enough, Devlin steps forward to cup Blair's face for a deep kiss that makes me and Connor whistle at them to tease. They both flip us off without looking or breaking their kiss. Chuckling, Connor slides his hand around Thea's waist and drops a trail of fluttering kisses across her cheek to her lips, lingering with a pleased hum.

Without meaning to, the memory of Fox's lips brushing against the corner of my mouth, but never connecting springs into my head. My cheeks heat and I clear my throat.

"All right, save the making out for the movie you're only going to half watch."

"Jealous? C'mere, I'll kiss you, too," Connor teases.

Rolling my eyes, I walk ahead of my friends. "I'd rather kiss Thea. She's way cuter than you."

Connor makes a sound like he's dying, then stops partway through to make an intrigued sound.

A round of laughter sounds behind me as we go into the theater. It's not that crowded inside, most of the seats in the dim room left open. Devlin immediately pulls Blair down one of the rows with only a few seats that will end up shadowy as soon as the lights go down. She smirks as he tugs her down into his lap. Two rows ahead of that, Connor leads Thea to a seat, whispering to her to make her giggle. I go one more row in front of them to give them some space to cuddle.

The movie starts and I get sucked in. It's about halfway when someone slides into the seat beside me.

It's Sam.

"Thought that was you I saw," he says, dropping an arm across the back of my seat.

"Uh, hey," I whisper.

I try to pay attention to the movie, but wariness sets in as he inches closer. At first he grazes his fingertips over my shoulder, toying with the thin straps of my summer dress. I don't want to cause a scene, but I'm not cool with this. We broke up.

"Sam," I murmur, shifting his arm off. "What are you doing?"

His hand lands on my leg and he shoots me a crooked smirk. "Don't be like that."

"Like what, dude?" I keep quiet, but an irritation edges into my tone. His fingers tease the bottom of my dress and I smack his knuckles. "Knock it off."

"I've been thinking. We should try again." He tips his chin down—what is that, puppy eyes? "I don't think you gave me a solid chance. We only got to go on one date before you broke it off. I can't get you out of my head."

"That sounds like a you problem. Sorry, but I'm not interested in anything more than friendship with you."

"What's wrong, baby?" Sam's voice gets harder and he leans in to mutter in my ear so no one but me can hear. "You need a party atmosphere and an audience? Aren't there enough people in here to put you in the mood?"

Stiffening, I realize he means Jenna's party. I can't believe I thought this guy was nice.

Annoyance slides right into rising anger. "You weren't there. You have no idea what you're talking about."

He scoffs, twirling a piece of my hair. "All I need are the rumors. You pretend to be all innocent, but we both know you're not. Otherwise you wouldn't have had 'easy' spray painted on your locker. Quit playing hard to get because it's not cute anymore."

Now I'm really pissed off. "Sorry, Sam. That's not how I let my *friends* talk to me. We're done."

Slamming my hands down on the armrests, I get up and stalk out of the theater. He follows and it makes me grit my teeth. I'm vaguely aware of the rest of my friends—my real ones—trailing after us. They've got my back.

"Maisy, wait—" Sam puts his hand on my arm, but he's interrupted when someone grabs him.

"I don't think so. That's enough," Devlin bites out in a dangerous undertone, reminding me why he and Connor had full control of our school when they were seniors last year.

Connor closes in on Sam's other side. He has a terrifying gleam in his gray eyes that matches Devlin's. Blair and Thea come to my side, Thea taking my hand and squeezing while Blair levels Sam with a cool stare.

"Uh, hey," Sam says, losing some of his confidence. "I don't think we've met, I'm Sam. Maisy's boyfriend. If I'd known we were doing a group thing tonight, I'd have been here earlier."

Connor snorts, but there's nothing amused about it. "Yeah, no. I was watching the whole time. You ain't shit, touching her when she said not to. That isn't gonna fly, is it Dev?"

"Fuck no."

Despite what led to this, I'm fighting back a grateful smile. These guys treat me like I'm family. Like I'm someone they want to protect. This is what family does for each other, what my real one used to feel like before everything changed.

"Thanks for the backup, guys," I say, stepping forward to stand in front of Sam. "Listen, dude. You and I aren't happening. I don't know how much clearer I can be."

He clenches his teeth, nostrils flaring. "You're taking this slut's side? She's just a cock tease."

"Yo," Blair snaps.

"Slut shaming, wow," I deadpan, blinking slowly. "Cool. So hurtful."

His words don't sting at all, but now I'm glad I broke up with him. I knew I didn't like his vibe.

"Only a coward tries to tear a woman down with derogatory terms," Thea says.

"Just calling it how it is. She can fuck around at a party, but acts too good for it from her boyfriend."

Connor whistles low. "Look at that attitude. Don't you know who we are?" Sam jerks against Devlin's tight grip and Connor grins. "Girls? Meet us down at the bakery."

Thea takes my hand again and pulls me away.

I rake my fingers through my hair. "I don't need you to fight battles for me. He's not worth wasting your time on. I can do it myself."

Devlin glances at me. "We won't break him, but there's no avoiding this lesson. Want the first punch?"

Sighing, I shake my head. There's no saving Sam from his fate after he was such a dick. My gaze meets his.

"We're done, got it? There's nothing between us. No feelings, no friendship." I put my hands on my hips. "And definitely no fucking. I don't sleep with anyone who tries to use a woman's sexuality against her."

A deep laugh leaves Devlin as he and Connor drag a struggling Sam around the corner into an alley. The girls come to my side again.

"Are you okay?" Thea asks.

"Yeah. He's just an asshole. I thought he was nice, but… Guess not."

"The nice ones are always surprise douchebags because they hide it to get their reward," Blair says. "At least when they're a bastard up front, you know what you're getting."

"Right. And he had my parents so into him."

"They should've dated him then," Thea says.

We start to walk toward her bakery a few blocks away and I tip my head back to peer at the night sky. The early summer air is warm.

"So," Thea says, pulling out the sound. "Everything's fine at school?"

With a wry smile, I squeeze her hand. "Yes, Mom. The rumor mill is always looking for something juicy to tear someone else down, but it doesn't mean anything. You know that. People like Sam can be shocked I hooked up at a party, but that was my choice."

"Who with?" Thea leans close. "You didn't tell me this."

The growl of a motorcycle coasts down the street and I almost laugh. Impeccable timing. Fox drives by and it's like my whole body feels it when he turns his head our way. The helmet is blacked out, but I feel the sweep of his gaze.

"I hooked up with Fox." My heart is in my throat. *More than once*, but I don't add that. "Fox Wilder."

"What?" Thea gasps. "Oh my god. For real?"

"Yes." The memories flicker through my mind. The rich scent of leather, woods, and the tang of oil. The peek of his tattoos. His hands on me, rough and demanding, familiar and new. "It just sort of happened."

"Called it," Blair murmurs. "That dude is always looking at you like you belong to him and him alone."

"Hah, right. He still has a grudge against me."

Blair smirks secretively. "Hate sex is a wonderful thing."

I swallow. She's not wrong.

"It won't happen again," I say, staring down the street as his bike turns the corner.

Not until I fight my way through his misplaced anger.

* * *

It figures the first detention Fox shows up for is the final one of our sentencing for fighting in class. The teacher said nothing when he followed me into the room after the final bell, hooking my curiosity. The faculty never challenge him. They let him get away with everything.

The thoughts are short lived when Fox takes the chair next to me, surrounding me with his distracting masculine scent.

All week I've sat alone for detention, but now I can't escape his gaze as it locks on me. He watches me, tracking every move of my hand as I write out an essay explaining the school policy. He doesn't do the essay and the teacher isn't paying attention to us.

We don't speak, but it feels like he's saying a lot with the way he's focused on me. If he thinks it scares me, he's wrong. I'm done letting him intimidate me. Raising my head from my essay, I lift a brow. The corner of his mouth kicks up into an arrogant smirk.

"Such a good girl," he rasps, leaning into my space. "Perfect little daisy."

He can call me whatever he wants. I refuse to let his jabs hurt anymore. At first they were a shock, but they've lost their power over me once I decided I was stronger than he thought. I'm not a crybaby—never was. Unaffected, I turn back to my task and pretend he's not even there.

But he doesn't like me ignoring him. Bullies always get frustrated when their efforts are wasted. It's how to best them. I can feel his restlessness as he shifts in the seat next to mine, brooding gaze boring holes in the side of my head.

Which is it, I want to ask. *Cold shoulder or not*. He can't have it both ways.

Without warning, he snatches my wrist, making my pen drag across the essay. I turn a scowl on him, then freeze. His attention is zeroed in on my bracelet, tracing the braided aged leather and poking the stones woven into it. The stones he found for me on the beach.

My breath stutters out of me. "What are you doing?"

This time it's his turn to ignore me. His thumb slides beneath the bracelet, tugging the material taut. My heart clenches and fear tears through me, worried he wants to take it from me or break it.

"Don't!"

Slowly, those volatile dark blue eyes lift to me and his mouth tilts into a heartless smile. "Chill. You can keep your stupid rocks."

"You don't scare me anymore," I whisper, cradling my bracelet safely out of his reach. "No matter what rumors you spread, or what nasty pranks you pull, or the degrading names you spray paint on my locker."

Fox huffs sardonically. "That's what you think."

Going back to the essay, I don't take my attention off the notebook in front of me. "Shaking in my boots."

"You will be when I'm through with you."

I turn to him and smile sweetly. "Does it involve cornering me in a bathroom again?" I bite my lip. "I don't know, that turned out pretty good for me."

His jaw clenches, accentuating how sharply chiseled his features are while his gaze drags down my body, lingering on my lips when it travels back up. "*Tch.* What is it about looking danger in the face that gets you so hot?"

"Must be those handsome eyes of yours," I sass.

He swipes his fingers over his mouth and I hide a smirk. Some of the teasing nature leaves him as he leans closer, the harsh threat clear in his tone when he murmurs, "Watch it, or the next time you're alone in the dark in your yoga studio, I won't stop at a single touch."

My lips part. Abandoning the essay, I put down my pen and turn in the chair to face him. "So that was you. I could report you for that."

"You don't have shit on me that would stick. And even if you did, I'd make it go away. You might have powerful parents, Maisy, but I'm no good boy. I like to live in the shadows." He grasps my chin and angles my face up. "I'll do anything to get what I want."

I swallow, steeling myself to keep from shying away from the ice in his dark blue eyes. Hearing him say my name in that cold, detached way drives a spike into my heart, leaving me bleeding out all over him and the table. I thought we were making some progress, but the banter from a minute ago has disappeared.

Leaning closer, Fox's voice drops lower with a chilling promise. "Or maybe you should be more careful of the roads you take." His mouth curves without a trace of humor. "You wouldn't want to get in an accident. You could get hurt...or worse."

"Are you threatening me to scare me?" I hiss, my eyes widening.

He squeezes my chin harder, bringing his face inches from mine. A tiny inkling of fear skates down my spine, followed by a spark of excitement. My body has its wires crossed.

"If you got in an accident, you could lose everything. The good grades, your perfect life, your future. How would that feel, to have that ripped away?"

My heart beats wildly as he pulls away. For several minutes I sit there trying to get my breathing under control. The danger in his gaze is burned into my brain. I feel his stare as I gather my composure.

I still don't know why he hates me so much. I have to find out before he crosses a line he can't come back from. So far his bullying and lashing out at me have been tough, but a storm I've weathered.

My mind shies away from the thought of him actually hurting me. That's not the Fox I know. No matter what people say about him, I don't believe he'd do it.

"All right. You're free to go," the teacher finally announces.

After I gather my things, he pauses in the door before he lets us leave. "I'll expect the behavior of model Silver Lake students from now on. Especially from you, Miss Landry."

I ball my fists against the unfair bias. "Yes, sir."

"I mean it. This is not the kind of thing we expect from you, like we do—" He glances at Fox warily. "Anyway, don't allow your personal differences to bleed into your time here on campus."

Fox huffs behind me, the strong lines of his chest practically pressed against my back. If he takes another step forward, we'll be touching.

Once the teacher moves out of the way, I hurry past. Fox passes me with a grunt, striding ahead with his phone pressed to his ear. Suspicious of who he's always talking to, I try to stay close to listen, but I can't keep up and he easily loses me.

On my way out, I remember that I don't have a ride home. I take out my phone and text Thea.

Maisy: Can you give me a ride? Detention just ended, but Holden has the car today.
Thea: Sorry, babe! We're both busy.

When I try the others, they're also unavailable.

"Crap," I mumble, glancing up from my phone when I reach the parking lot.

Fox straddles his bike, helmet in his hands. He cuts his gaze to me, then looks away. He's going to strand me here, too.

As I turn to head back up the steps to the school, his voice stops me.

"Get on," he growls.

"What?"

He can't be serious. The whiplash is killing me. One minute he's threatening me, the next he's barking commands at me.

"Too scared, crybaby?"

The corners of my mouth turn down. "Like hell I am."

Not when he tries his best to intimidate me, not in the yoga studio, and not now.

Fox narrows his stormy blue gaze and holds out the helmet. "Get on the bike."

His voice brooks no argument, demanding I do as he says. To get on his motorcycle with the one person in this world who claims he hates me. I breathe out slowly and rub my lips together in consideration.

I will not be afraid of Fox Wilder.

Mind made up, I close the distance between us and accept the helmet. He stares at me for a moment once I have it on, eyes drifting down to my skirt. A throb of heat pulses between my legs. Is he remembering my secret little rebellion?

He tears his attention away while I swing a leg over the rumbling bike behind him. It's more powerful than I imagined, vibrating through my legs and making a gasp rush out of me. I think he laughs, but I'm too busy thinking about where I have to put my hands.

Fox angles his head, giving me another challenging look over his shoulders. So today is one of the days he's fine with touching? Fine. I'm not backing down. He should really get that by now. Setting my jaw, I wrap my arms tight around his waist, our bodies melded together from hip to shoulder.

It feels…right. Like that warped piece I've been missing finally found a new way to fit us together.

"When you get wet from this, try not to get it all over the leather," he drawls in a sultry tone.

"I'm wearing underwear today, you ass."

A little scream leaves me as he revs the engine and takes off like a shot. I hold on tighter, riding the buzzing thrill that zings through me. The longer we drive, the more I drop my guard, enjoying the ride.

It's exhilarating, calling to my adventurous heart. I want to reach out and coast my hand along the sharp waves the wind creates as the bike moves fast around the bends in the road, but that would mean taking my hands off Fox.

Instead of taking the road that would lead to my house faster, he takes the side of a fork that heads higher into the mountains. I release an excited yell into the sky and feel his shoulders shake with amusement.

I'm struck by the urge to tell him about the road trip I want to take, even though he was a dick in detention. He's the one who gave me the idea in the first place, back when our families took a vacation to California together. He and I found a roadmap and plotted out the way from Colorado to the coast, coming up with all these plans for how we were going to go on adventures when we were older. We were going to do it together.

Other than Thea, he's the only one who might understand why it's important to me.

The memories of our friendship always outweigh his actions of the present, reminding me of what we once had. Of who he can be when he's not hating me.

Riding on the back of his motorcycle, I press a smile into his leather jacket and wish it could be like this always.

This is how we're supposed to be. Just like this. Free and untethered, an open road ahead of us.

***

The exhilaration of being on the motorcycle clinging to Fox ends abruptly once he pulls up to my house. A line of tension stiffens his back as I step off and I freeze when I find Dad and Holden watching from the front step beneath the arched stone portico.

Dad's expression shifts from surprise to something I don't understand when he looks from me to Fox.

"Thanks for not leaving me stranded," I say, handing the helmet back.

Fox doesn't answer, just studies me for a beat before revving the motorcycle and speeding off.

I don't make it in the front door before my brother and father are in front of me.

"What were you doing with him?" Dad demands.

He's always been overprotective, it's why he often goes along with Mom's strict parental decisions, but he doesn't raise his voice like that to me. Between the two of them, Dad's remained more himself than Mom, but the weird edge in his voice has my steps faltering.

"We had detention. Remember?" I make to move past them, but they both plant themselves in front of me. "He just gave me a ride home. I didn't think you were here." Lifting my brows, I glance between them. "Um, can I go inside now? Seriously, you're giving me double vision with this whole 'grr men of the house' vibe."

"Don't give me the attitude, young lady," Dad grumbles.

"My maiden virtue is perfectly intact." I make a show of bowing. Holden coughs to cover a snort while Dad's graying brows flatten. "Chill, guys. It was just a ride."

They finally move when I nudge my way past them.

"I don't want you anywhere near him," Dad says, expression stern.

He used to smile so much. I miss it. Most days I just want back the man who would laugh with us.

"I agree," Holden says. "I told you, I don't want him to hurt you."

Everyone around here is a broken record. It's like they all forgot about Fox and just believe what the town says—that he's bad news and a twisted monster, troubled like his dad. It's all bullshit.

I whip around, tired of it all. "Why, Dad? Tell me."

The cagey expression doesn't bode well, turning my stomach into a knot. Whenever I've pressed about Fox and his family in the last year, even to bring up good memories, my parents get like this. At first I thought they were just upset—they lost their friends as much as Holden and I did—but now I'm wondering if it's something more.

Could they be hiding something?

Maybe Fox isn't the only one who won't be honest with me.

"Why," I repeat more firmly. "I'm not a kid, so stop treating me like one."

He opens his mouth, then scrubs a hand over it, shaking his head sharply. Turning his back on me, he sets our Fort Knox-worthy security system. "Just stay the hell away from him, Maisy. Pretend Fox Wilder never existed in the first place and all our lives will be better for it."

My stomach swoops as I think of everything my family doesn't know about between Fox and I.

Too late.

TWELVE
Fox

Regret filters in and out as I pull into the garage at the warehouse. Once I park the bike, my thumb finds the old ding in the chrome and I rub it.

I don't know what made me fold and give Maisy a ride. Instead of stranding her, I hesitated. Something about that stubborn expression cracking at the thought of being stranded, alone. I couldn't take it, so I gave her the ride.

Her broken promise stole my dad away and I enjoyed driving her around for an hour. The feel of her arms locked around me and the echo of her body plastered against my back lingers. The sound of her joyful yell as my bike cut through the mountain roads plays on repeat. Every minute is burned into my brain. For a short while, it was like everything was how it should be.

Feelings I've suppressed and rejected for so long unfurled in my chest, refusing to be smothered completely.

A heavy breath leaves me.

The girl I used to climb trees with loved being on my bike. And I fucking liked it.

She still wears that same damn bracelet from when we were kids. I recognized it as soon as I snagged her wrist for a better look. My skin prickles with awareness. She wears the stones as a reminder of the ocean, and I tattooed it on my skin. I remember the day I found those stones for her.

The rocks and shells we picked have piled up in our bucket. My concentration was focused on the damp sand in search of more. Holden trailed behind me, climbing a rock jutting from the sand while Maisy poked her nose close to a tide pool at the base.

"There are tiny fish," she said. "Come look, Fox."

Before I went to her, a small cluster of stones caught my eye. One was white with black lines running through it, another waas blue, almost like seaglass, and another was orange with speckles. As soon as I spotted them, Maisy filled my head. I scooped them up, dusting off the sand. They were cooler than the finds we collected in our bucket, and I knew I had to give them to her.

"Here," I said when I reached her side by the tide pool. "Found these for you."

She took them with a murmur of thanks and her eyes lit up. "These are so cool."

There was a weird warmth in my chest and I rubbed at it. When her gaze lifted to meet mine, it was like the butterflies she loved to chase in the field at the end of our block lived inside my ribs.

"I love them. Thanks, dude."

"Yeah. They made me think of you."

She held up the blue one. "This one looks like your eyes."

Holden's laugh sounded behind me. "You gave the crybaby pretty stones?" He nudged my shoulder. "Lame."

"Shut up, Holden," Maisy said.

"You're jealous," I added.

"Am not." He shoved me harder. "Whatever."

Maisy and I snickered as Holden trudged down the beach, back to the area our parents were set up. Her attention returned to the stones I gave her and her mouth stretched into a wide grin.

Again, I try to suppress the same warmth trying to unfold and take flight. The past is better left buried. She needs to let it go...and so do I.

My mouth fills with a bitter taste as conflict plagues me. I keep allowing my judgement to be clouded, holding back when I should be enacting my revenge.

It's getting harder to keep my focus around her. Maybe I never should have touched her. If I didn't know what the coconut and floral scent tasted like on her skin, didn't know how to bury my fingers in her pussy and curl to make her breath hitch I wouldn't be in these situations where my goddamn dick takes over and makes me forget to hate her.

Every time I think I know what she'll do, she turns around and does the opposite. When I corner her, she lets me have her body. I threaten her and she...*flirts* with me. It's got my head all kinds of fucked up.

What is wrong with me? Why is there a part of me considering giving it all up if I could have another minute of those moments together on the bike?

Blowing out an exhausted breath, I get off the motorcycle and plug my phone into the speaker set up on the workbench. The song blares through the sound system, filling the garage with the heavy beat of drums and guitar riffs. Colton didn't have anything new that would help me out when I checked in with him after detention. Until he gets back to me, I'm at a dead end. The urge to work with my hands to clear my head wraps around me like a vice.

First I lose myself in tuning up the Charger, my thoughts swirling endlessly. As my fingers become coated in grease from changing the oil, I try to push Maisy's tempting body out of my mind. Those addictive hazel eyes aren't going to ruin anything, not when my goal is to crush her.

The only reason I came back to Ridgeview was because I'm out for blood. Nothing will stop my rampage against this town that turned on me. Time is running out for my plans. There are only a few weeks left until graduation.

It hits me then, after I finished with the car, while I'm making a piece of scrap metal bend to my will to become whatever my hands demand it create, that I've been more affected by allowing myself to touch Maisy than I was aware. I cut those thoughts off with a grunt.

I hate Maisy and everything she represents. She chose her parents over me. She lied to me and broke the promise she swore to keep the secret I showed her. There's no way I can trust her, forgive her, or fucking have her ever again.

I told her I could hate her and fuck her, but it was so much easier to hold onto that feeling when she wasn't in front of me all the time. Before those sounds began haunting my dreams, making me want old desires I burned out of myself years ago. Before I was faced with the same stubborn determination and wild spirit that I loved in her when we were kids.

Goddamn it. I didn't try hard enough to cut my feelings for her out of my heart. I can't want her. I won't betray my family's memory.

Longing for the misty ocean air at the cove in Thorne Point winds around me. I wish I could go there now. Instead, I rub at my chest where it's tattooed as a permanent reminder. The sound of the waves crashing against the rocks on foggy mornings always helped when I couldn't run far enough from the demons in my nightmares. Wanting Maisy Landry more than I hate her and her family is the worst nightmare I've ever faced.

When working in the garage isn't doing what it usually does to clear my head, I head upstairs and spend the next hour pushing my body until I'm drenched in sweat and panting raggedly. The smack of my fists against the punching bag becomes the only sound I'm aware of as I picture Richard and Jacqueline Landry's faces, throwing hit after hit. With a fierce growl I throw another jab.

I put my body through hell, punishing it for my mistakes. My chest burns with each breath I drag in, but I keep going, sweat droplets rolling down my flushed bare chest. Damp tendrils of dark hair hang over my forehead as I take another swing at the bag. Each brutal punch is penance, an apology to my parents' ghosts.

Levi's gruff voice becomes my conscience when my form becomes too sloppy, reminding me of the time I spent in the boxing ring with him back east. Colton's friend would be pissed if he caught me right now. The guy is like a machine, with deathly focus on honing the weapon he's crafted his body into. Not all of us hit the bag to be the terrifying demon whispered about throughout Thorne Point—the rest of us just need to shut our brains up for a while.

Dropping my head back and propping my hands on my hips, I take heaving breaths and close my eyes. I scrub a hand through my hair and flick my gaze to the coffee table, where my laptop and the efforts of my hunt for the truth lay. I can't wait for Colt.

I grab a quick shower, leaning my palms against the wall while the hot water beats over my head. My dick gets hard because I let my mind wander again and Maisy's sexy smile and those fucking yoga pants taunted me even when she's out of reach. I don't touch myself, rejecting the attraction to her.

Once I'm out, I throw on a loose pair of joggers and sit on the couch, opening the laptop. It loads to the last thing I was working on—a PDF backlog of medical journals my parents have been mentioned in or interviewed for. They praise my parents and Jacqueline Landry for the advancements their research team achieved. My brow furrows in concentration as I continue to skim through them.

The other side of the screen has my efforts to track down an incident report. It's been a dead end so far, and what Colton was able to mine from Ridgeview Police Department's server isn't promising. If I can't pin Chief Landry with the incident report, it could be another dead end. I could look into CCTV to place the Landrys there, but there's no guarantee recordings from a decade ago were kept this long. Colton's working on hacking his way past firewalls to turn up old bank statements to find out when and how much they were paid off to keep quiet. For all I know they hired a hitman to do the dirty work for them while those greedy bastards reaped all the benefits of eliminating my parents.

I've been trying to remember what my parents were working on, but those memories are blocked by grief and betrayal. All I remember is wanting to show Maisy what I found in the garage, but no matter how hard I focus I'm unable to picture what was in the hidden stash and files I showed her that day I picked a daisy for her.

Something in my gut keeps pushing me to follow this thread. The key to what got them killed has to be in these journals and in their research.

THIRTEEN
Maisy

With a few weeks left until graduation, I'm no closer to figuring Fox out. After his threats during detention before last weekend, he's backed off. It's like being back to his cold shoulder again, his walls higher than ever whenever we're in the same vicinity.

It's crazy, but I actually miss his attention, even when he's promising my downfall. I also miss riding on the back of his motorcycle. Once was enough to make me fall in love with the thrill. I want to do it again to feel that rush of freedom. It didn't hurt that it was Fox I was holding onto, or that he didn't take me home immediately.

He still knows me so well and it makes my heart pang.

Instead of hunting me, he seems to be focused on the other thing that occupies most of his time. He acts increasingly shady—which is saying something given the way people in this town call him a black shadow—taking calls in the middle of class and disappearing. The teachers do nothing to stop him. They couldn't control him if they tried.

No one controls Fox.

School lets us go early on Friday for the holiday weekend. We have off on Monday and one thought keeps snagging in my head—a three day weekend is plenty of time for Fox to stir trouble. My curiosity buzzes with the need to know what he's been doing and where he goes. If I can find out, it might help me get past his walls to finally make him listen to me so we can work through this thing between us—his grudge and the way our bodies are drawn together by a magnetic lure full of heat.

At the end of the day, I'm absorbed in texting Connor as I head for the parking lot. He's planning another crazy surprise for my best friend.

Connor: Don't worry about the tickets. I'm taking care of everything. What matters most is that our closest crew is there. [GIF of money raining down]

A grin crosses my face as I type my response.

Maisy: Dude, she's going to love it.

He is done with waiting to marry Thea. He's taking her to Paris to elope and bringing our whole group of friends as a surprise.

The way it calls up the need for adventure in my heart has me excited to pack a bag. I'm glad Dad is wrapped up in the parade logistics for Memorial Day in a few days, so I can duck him easily. Mom will be the tricky one to evade. If I can get far enough away, she won't be able to get me before I jet out of the country. Holden better help, because I'm not missing out on this chance to experience the world. I bite my lip as a giddy squeal works up my throat.

This gives me the same heady feeling as thinking about my road trip plans. The crush of excitement is a full body experience, tingling in my fingertips to my toes as I bounce with the happiness I can't contain.

Paris. Thea's always loved it and wanted to go. I'm excited just to leave the city limits of Ridgeview. I haven't been out of town since our family vacation in California.

The sight of Fox's matte black Charger parked not far from my car makes me pause in my mini mental celebration.

Glancing back, I find him on his way down the steps to the parking lot at the base of the hill. Keys in hand, the locks on his car disengage. He doesn't see me because he's scowling at his phone intently.

It's not like him to unlock his car from so far away without doing a sweep of his surroundings. Sometimes he acts like Dad does, on high alert for any threat, always checking the exits. I thought it was a cop habit, but when he does it, he doesn't look like a cop.

Opportunity calls to me. I rub my lips together, thumbing the corners of my phone case, a photo of the California coastline printed on the back. It's always reminded me of the day Fox gave me the stones on my bracelet. Instinct flutters across my awareness, whispering for me to take a chance. Mom hates my impulsiveness, actively working to rein it in, but I shove the thought of her aside as I close the short distance to his car and open the back door before the idea fully forms.

I'm going to find out where Fox goes all the time. Instead of following him, I'll stow away.

After throwing a quick look over my shoulder to check that he hasn't noticed me, I slide into his back seat. The rich scent of leather, wood, and that faint hint of motor oil that I secretly like best surrounds me, but I don't have time to appreciate it.

There's a big canvas duffel bag, a tool box, and what I think is a small drone. It's a really weird mix of supplies to keep in a car and none of it makes sense to me, making me burn with the need to know what he's been up to. It's a little cramped and I'm thankful for my obsession with yoga to help me twist my body into a comfortable enough position on the floor behind the passenger seat. Shrugging out of my uniform blazer, I use it and the bag to cover myself in case he checks back here.

Hopefully he doesn't look, because in my impulsive rush, I didn't think about a good reason why I'd be camouflaging myself against the dark interior of his muscle car.

There's no more time to think about it when the driver's side door opens and he gets in. I hold my breath, drawn to the powerful presence he exudes.

Fox isn't someone that doubts himself. He acts and expects the world around him to fall in line to accommodate him.

As the car begins to move, I wish I'd arranged myself so I could see him. It's disorienting to be shrouded in shadows beneath my blazer and the supplies he keeps in the back seat. I have no idea where we're going. He doesn't speak or turn on the radio, like he can't bother with any distractions. I imagine his expression—his sharp, handsome features locked in permanent grim determination, square jaw set, stormy blue gaze unwavering.

Wherever we're going, I sense that Fox will get what he wants. It's a palpable feeling that fills the car and almost chokes me in my hiding spot.

I try to track where we're headed by the number of turns, but he takes so many it's hard to remember the order. I'd never be able to replicate it. Dad wouldn't be happy after all the times he's drilled me with the necessary things to do if I was ever kidnapped, but I always write off his insistence that it could happen on his overbearing parental paranoia. It seems all the times he made me practice with him when I was younger, not long after the Wilder's deaths, haven't paid off because we could be anywhere in Ridgeview and there's no way I could pinpoint our location.

Despite the complicated route he takes, we don't drive for longer than twenty minutes. The car finally comes to a stop and I hear Fox release a weary sigh. I really want to peel back my blazer and peek at him, but I smother the urge. I doubt he'd be thrilled to find me sneaking around and spying on him from his back seat.

Belatedly it occurs to me that I left Holden's Audi at school and I have no idea where Fox lives. My eyes go wide, but I'll tackle the problem of getting home without anyone—Fox or my parents—figuring out about my little adventure later.

I almost jump when a door opens. The car shifts as someone slides into the passenger seat, the back of it pressing into me slightly. Whoever it is seems small, not heavy enough to make the seat crush me between the foot well and the bench seat. I regulate my breaths, glad again for all the meditation I do to know how to find my calm place as I strain my ears to listen.

"You're late," Fox grumbles.

"Sorry." It's a woman, her soft voice trembling at the edges. She keeps shifting in the seat and I guess she's not entirely comfortable around him. "It's not easy to leave in the middle of my shift without someone noticing. I did what you said so no one followed me."

"That's not my problem."

"You don't understand. They're—my employers aren't what they seem. If they find out about this, I won't just be fired."

Familiarity tugs at me as I concentrate on their voices. Something about her voice—I recognize it.

"I know all about what they're capable of." Venomous loathing drips from Fox's voice.

He's silent for a beat, then his sharp baritone is closer and I picture him crowding into her space the same way he does to me when he wants to be intimidating. "And I don't give a fuck. Not my problem."

The woman squeaks and I think she presses back against the window to get away from him. "I don't want Mrs. Landry to find out."

It's an effort not to suck in a shocked breath. Lana. The person in his car is Lana, our family's in-home chef.

What the hell? What is she doing here? Why is she talking to him?

I want to burst out of my hiding spot and demand answers, but I corral the irrational urge in favor of self preservation and listening for more information.

Nothing makes sense. I swallow, being careful to inch around to hear better while Lana sounds like she's trying to get tears under control. My fingers clench around my school skirt as I try to understand what's happening.

"Are you going to give me what I want or are you going to keep crying about it?"

Fox's patience is running out. There's movement above me—he's digging through the canvas bag. It makes a little bit of light pierce the shadows I'm hidden in. Whatever he takes out makes Lana release a low, panicked sound. My mind races to figure out what he took out of the bag. A tightness in my stomach has me picturing a gun.

"I'm not playing around," he says in a deep, detached tone. "You're going to give me what I want, or I'm going to make your life harder than what they might do to you if they found out you helped me."

"Yes—yes, okay," Lana says hoarsely.

I've never heard her like this. She's afraid. Not just of Fox, but also of my parents. What she said before echoes in my head. *If they find out about this, I won't just be fired.* What more can they do to Lana other than fire her for meeting with Fox? The NDA they've made the household staff sign is ironclad, but I always thought it was because Mom cares so much about our public image with her prominent position.

Unease twists my insides into knots. Whatever is going on, it's serious. Once again I'm hit with the suspicion that he isn't the only one hiding things from me.

"Good. But I'm taking a thousand off the price we agreed on because you just pissed me off."

Lana makes a distressed sound. "No, please! I—I need it all for my daughter's treatment. We don't have the insurance coverage, *please—*"

Fox growls something too low for me to make out, but it makes Lana settle down. My heart lodges in my throat. Lana has a daughter? She's never told me about her. Not that we're close, but there are some days when Mom's lecturing me that she feels like the only one who knows my secret hell. Do I even know her at all?

I miss some of their conversation while I'm lost in my swirling thoughts, but when I refocus my blood turns to ice in my veins. Lana is giving him the details to our security system.

She's telling him how to get past the one thing I thought protected me from him.

"It has to be this weekend," Fox says. "I can't get around the Landry's security system, it's why I'm paying you. They'll be at the mayor's Memorial Day party, like you said. I'll do it while they're there."

Shock filters through my system. He wants to break into our house in a way that we won't be able to detect while we're at Mayor Taylor's party? We've been going to the mayor's house for his holiday weekend celebration for years, ever since Mom and Dad got their promotions. It's stuffy to be around all the rich assholes in town gathered in one place compared to when it was only my classmates for his daughter Jenna's party, but I've always gone. How am I going to go while knowing he is trying to get into the house?

Fox would really go that far to get to me? Does he have any limits?

My throat thickens and it becomes hard to breathe for a moment, my vision going fuzzy at the edges from the force of the dizziness crashing into me. I close my eyes tight and try to breathe through the bout of panic without alerting them to me hiding in the back seat. An ache sears my chest.

When I get myself under control, the car is quiet again. Lana must be gone.

With the kind of access she sold him, he could get at me anytime he wanted. My stomach knots as I brush my fingers over my leather bracelet, touching the stones. I don't have anything in my room he could possibly be shocked to uncover. Nothing he could use against me to start more rumors about me at school. None of this is connecting the dots to make a clear picture.

We're moving again. Fox takes fewer turns as he drives. I stare through the sliver of light bleeding into my hiding spot without seeing. My throat stings with the questions swarming it, needing an outlet. I want to kick his seat and scream at him, demand to know what the fuck he's planning. To let me in.

This feels bigger than his efforts to bully me. It would be crazy for him to pay our cook so he can bypass our state of the art security system. He's able to get at me more easily than that, something he's proved time and again in the last few weeks.

He said something about my parents that sits like lead in my stomach. He knows what they're capable of. The way he said it makes chills break out across my skin. Hate like I've never heard before, deep and vicious and deadly.

"Shit," Fox spits before taking a sharp turn that snaps my attention back to him.

I'm jolted by the force of it, scrambling to brace myself so I don't go flying across the floor in the back. He curses again and the tires of the Charger screech as he speeds up suddenly. We whip around another bend. I can't hide anymore. I have to know what's going on.

While he's distracted by driving, I carefully move the bag and drop my blazer, remaining crouched low out of his periphery. Trees fly by the windows in a blur and the car speeds down an incline. So we were up in the mountains, I guess. Behind us, I hear the rumble of an engine. We're being followed.

Fox seems irritated, but not about to lose his head. He doesn't have his leather jacket on, the black t-shirt stretched around his powerful biceps. For the first time, I get a sense of his tattoos. The intricate design of a wave covers most of his left upper arm and disappears beneath his sleeve. It makes my throat burn and my wrist tingle against my stone bracelet to know he has an ocean tattoo. I want to see the rest of it, to discover what those feathers I glimpsed near his neck are.

He pushes a hand through his dark hair, tousling it. I can just make out his profile, jaw clenched. A muscle tics in his cheek as he flexes his white-knuckled grip on the wheel, the veins in his forearms protruding. He darts pissed off looks at the rear view mirror and clicks his tongue.

"Pain in the ass," he grumbles.

My pulse thunders as he drives away from the tail following his car. He's skilled but we're moving terrifyingly fast, whipping around corners. It makes my nails dig into the dark interior, but I'm only partly worried. The other part of me is flooded with the thrill. Adrenaline courses through me and I have to keep reminding myself to stay low and not jump up to whoop.

I doubt he would appreciate my enthusiasm for his driving while he's being followed, and that's not even touching the fact I'm hiding in his car.

As he's taking another turn, his body twists to check over his shoulder.

The exhilarated smile falls and my heart drops into my stomach as his eyes lock with mine.

Fuck.

Fox sees me.

The growl that sounds from him might as well be the roar of an infuriated bear. His expression twists into a violent scowl as he faces front. He says nothing and my heart pounds.

"Fox," I whisper.

He ignores me, but I catch the way his whole body tenses. The wheel creaks beneath his grip. I fall silent, limbs stiff from being in my hiding spot for too long. Watching his profile, I ease off the floor onto the back seat. He makes another displeased sound that makes my heart thud, catching my gaze in his rear view mirror. It lasts seconds before he cuts away to look at the road, but it could've been an eternity.

Now that I'm not hiding beneath it, I see what's inside the duffel bag: dark clothes, some kind of techy tracking device, and binoculars. There's a gun and my heart clenches. The mental image I conjured was right and emotions collide in a confusing swirl. The only thing missing is fear. Fox has a gun and it should scare me, but it doesn't.

Glancing behind us, I see the tail. A big black SUV speeds up, gaining on us. It doesn't have any markings or a license plate from this angle. They're getting closer and my eyes widen.

"They're going to ram the back!" I shout.

Right before it happens, Fox makes a hairpin turn down an alleyway as we reach the outskirts of the residential center of town. The SUV can't follow with the same precision Fox has in the Charger. He takes advantage, making a series of quick turns as soon as we reach the end of the alley.

We're able to lose the tail, but my heartbeat doesn't stop racing because Fox doesn't relax. I'm not out of danger yet.

FOURTEEN
Fox

Fury rockets through me, an unruly fire in my veins that draws on every violent tendency I have. I need to punch something, but first I had to deal with the fucking tail. People are starting to take notice of my digging. I expected it at some point, but I thought it would be later, when I had more proof gathered.

It doesn't bode well that they found me so quickly, whoever they are. Security for the Landrys, maybe. Or if I'm really unlucky, they could've been cops in the chief's pocket, as dirty as he is with a goddamn license to act under the guise of the law. It's possible the cook didn't follow the route I mapped for her exactly, or she's being watched. The specifics aren't important right now. I have a bigger problem in my lap.

I throw another furious look at Maisy in my back seat through the reflection in the mirror.

"I think you finally lost them," she murmurs, craning her neck to peer out the rear window like this is an afternoon joyride.

The urge to lock my fingers around her throat and squeeze for her goddamn actions has me damn near ripping my steering wheel off in a death grip. How dare she hide out in my car. Another surge of rage thunders through me, swallowing the long-dormant feelings that have been nagging me since our detention.

My lying daisy couldn't resist sticking her nose where it doesn't belong and now I'm screwed. The plan to get in their house to go through their personal computer for their secrets is a bust. I paid off the cook for nothing, because now Maisy will warn her parents of what I was going to do. It's what she did before when she broke her promise.

I drive for several minutes in silence, leaving the center of town and heading toward the shipping district where my warehouse is. I won't take her there, but I can't do this downtown where there are witnesses.

Once I find an empty parking lot near a hiking trail, I pull in. Maisy doesn't move while I cut the engine. The energy buzzing beneath my skin becomes too much. I explode from the car, yank open the back door, and grab her, ignoring the little yelp she makes as I drag her out.

"Hey—"

"No," I bark, slamming her back against the frame of the car. "*No.*"

Maisy has gotten too comfortable. Ever since I let her on my bike and gave her a ride home, she's becoming an insolent challenge, forgetting what I've promised to do to her. I shouldn't be that surprised, since promises mean nothing to her. My lip curls. I'll make sure she doesn't forget who I really am, just like I won't forget who she is—a liar.

"I'm sorry," she says in a rush, eyes wide and hands up in a defensive gesture. I want to rip that goddamn bracelet from her slim wrist. It's as much of a liar as she is, making me want things I can't have. "I just…"

My teeth grind and I pin her with my whole body. "You just *what*? Thought it would be cute to sneak around with me? Think again. I told you, little daisy." My fingers flex on her upper arms, digging in. "Playtime is fucking over."

She tips her chin up, her favorite defiant move. "Why do you have a gun?"

I drag in a sharp breath. She never acts like I expect her to. Every fucking time.

"I told you. The rumors about me aren't wrong. I'm dangerous."

Run. I want to scream it in her face. But if she did, I'd chase her, hold onto her with every ounce of strength. I can't let her go.

How can I hate her so much but need her within reach at the same time? Is it the echo of the deep connection we once shared, or something more that twines us together?

"What made you think you had a right to get in my car?"

Maisy frowns and squirms against my immovable body. "I'm glad I did. You've gone too far," she accuses. "You can't get to me by going through Lana. Leave her out of this and just come at me."

A hollow bark of laughter punches out of me and I shake my head. It annoys me when Maisy acts like she doesn't know anything.

"I don't need your damn cook to get to you."

"Then why did you pay her for information on the security system on my house?" Her eyes narrow. "And you shouldn't have stiffed her, either. It sounds like she really needs the money for her daughter."

Now she pretends to care about others and wants to lecture me on bribing ethics. My brain can't even process the ludicrousness of it. The version of her that's kind and caring is another lie.

"I'm not telling you that," I force out gruffly.

There's a mutinous little pinch to her mouth that snags my attention to the shape of her lips. A harsh breath leaves me as a new need pushes at my senses. It takes more effort than I want to admit to tear my gaze up, fighting back the ridiculous desire to crash my mouth over hers.

What the fuck is wrong with me? I will not kiss her. I should be shaking her lithe body and demanding she never pull a stunt like this again.

"And more importantly," she continues like I didn't sidestep her question, "why were you being followed like that? If you didn't take the alley when you did, they were going to hit you."

I don't have the answers she wants. I barely have the answers I want for myself. If I did,

I wouldn't give them to her. But as my head clears enough for more thoughts to slip past the anger, one blaring truth becomes inescapable. I've been reckless with my life. It's never mattered to me if this hunt ends with my death. That's how far I'm willing to go to uncover the truth for my family.

But that disregard for life doesn't extend to Maisy. For all that I hate her and her family, the thought of her death is unacceptable.

The wrongness of it clangs in a jarring blare, still echoing in my head when I met her eyes in the car.

Whoever followed us is connected to the same sick people in power that have this town in their claws. They're dangerous, capable of making murder look like an accident. They don't care who they have to get rid of. If their greed is threatened, they'll go to any length to make sure they stay on top.

No matter what I feel for her, I don't want her dead. Hate is intense, but it's a passionate emotion that is as all-consuming as love. In some ways hate is love, equal in intensity from how deep it runs.

I loved Maisy before I hated her. Maybe it never fully went away, just shifted around to become this bigger, more complicated emotion that controls my heart when I look at her.

"I don't know," I finally say. It's like I'm hearing my voice from outside my own body, reeling a bit from the possibility I'm still in love with my ex-best friend. "They definitely weren't looking for a friendly chat if they caught us."

Her throat works as she swallows. Fear mixes with the bright exhilaration lighting up her hazel eyes. Something unlocks in my chest, a crack in my fortress that allows me to see her right now, separate from her parents.

For one too long, heartbreaking moment, my head fills with flashes of worst case scenarios. The SUV driving my car off the road, taking us somewhere to detain us, or skipping all of that to put twin bullets in our heads—all of it ends with Maisy dead in my mind.

No, my mind revolts against it. A tremor runs through my hands. She can probably feel it. The thought of her broken and gone from this world is wrong. My throat closes over and I blink against the staggering wave of refusal crashing down on my head.

This never started as an *us* situation, but now that I've had the thought, it won't leave. It's messed up as hell, considering the dirt I've been looking for on her crooked parents. But it was always me and her, back then and now.

Fuck it.

Something inside me snaps and I lose control of myself. I can't hold back anymore, taken over by a single driving need to kiss her, to hold her close and erase the images in my head of what it would be like if she was gone.

My hand fists in her hair and my mouth slams over hers. She stiffens for a moment, then makes a small sound as her lips part for me. A rough, broken noise scrapes my throat as I plunge my tongue into her mouth, claiming her in a way I've always wanted to but haven't let myself.

It was a line I wasn't going to cross, but that's out the window now that I'm kissing her. I never want to fucking stop.

Maisy wrestles her hands up from the crush of my chest against her and puts one palm over my cheek as I devour her in a soul-wrecking kiss. The other buries in my hair. My heart beats hard as I try to tuck her back into it, where she used to belong. She kisses me back, writhing against me like she's trying to climb into my body—or maybe draw my darkness into herself.

We kiss until we're breathless. It's pleasure and pain, teeth and tongue, and the wild sounds we both make. It's beyond perfect.

The only thing I'm aware of is how my world rearranges. I've existed like everything is upside-down for so long, but Maisy sets it right side up again.

And it kills me, because I can't have this.

* * *

In the end, I didn't use the information I got from the Landry's cook. I couldn't risk it, unable to trust Maisy not to warn her parents or stay home from the mayor's party to catch me. After kissing her, I ripped myself away and demanded she get in the car. Stunned, she listened for once, touching her lips. I drove her back to school in silence and left her by her brother's car before peeling out of there like my tires were on fire.

The kiss has plagued me all week.

I've avoided the Silver Lake High campus, thrown myself into my search efforts, alternated between working in the garage and beating the hell out of my punching bag, and punishing my body with more reps than usual on the bench press until I collapsed into bed.

The days bleed together, but she still won't get out of my head. The only saving grace of laying low is that whoever followed me hasn't found the warehouse yet.

Sleep brings no relief, my dreams full of the kiss on repeat and more, so much fucking more that I can't have. Old dreams that used to be all I wanted—a field of wildflowers, a white veil, and her glowing smile. Last night my subconscious trapped me in the bathroom from that party last month, only this time she wore her school uniform without underwear beneath her skirt and I fell to my knees to bury my face between her legs.

This world is too cruel, ripping my parents away and showing me exactly what I've always missed in Maisy.

The same damn girl who was my best friend and the catalyst to the destruction of my world.

She didn't have to be perfect for me, but the way she fits against my body and responds to every touch calls me down to my fucking soul. I've never looked at another girl the same way I'm drawn to her. It's something I can't deny anymore—I want her. Period.

It's only because of her social media I figure out she's not even in Ridgeview. She's in Paris for the weekend according to the photo of her and her redheaded friend in front of the Eiffel Tower. Her friend is in a flowing white dress and is flashing her ring finger. The caption reads *the bestie tied the knot in the most romantic place in the world*. I've been so wrapped up in my head, unable to stop thinking about her, that I didn't even notice when she managed to skip town thanks to her friends sneaking her out. Bet her parents love that surprise, judging by the cryptic comment Holden left on her photo to enjoy the fun while it lasts.

After another brutal workout that leaves me numb, I strip out of my basketball shorts and grab a shower. The steam shrouds me and the water pounds over my head as I brace against the wall.

This shift in awareness has left me floundering in all my plans. There's nothing else I've wanted for ten years than to see the Landrys stripped down to the bone, but now I'm hesitating. I can't. I'm not giving this up. But realizing how much I want Maisy makes this harder.

I'm still pissed at her. She still broke a promise she made. Turned her back on our friendship. For so long that broken promise cut me deep.

Then the heavy-lidded look on her face after I tore away from the searing kiss floats to the surface.

Releasing a heavy sigh of resignation, I press my forehead to the tile and thump a fist against the wall to distract myself. Damn it. I'm so fucked.

I imagine her sweet floral and coconut scent, the way her skin tastes, and I'm a goddamn pathetic goner. Reaching down, I groan as I circle my fist around my erection. My cock swells as I remember how her tongue slid against mine with no hesitation, so fucking eager. If I'd kept kissing her, I would've slipped a hand beneath her skirt—no underwear again, I hope with a thrum of excitement racing down my spine—and found her pussy wet and glistening for me. Another rough sound passes my parted lips and my breathing grows heavy as I stroke my dick.

She's not afraid of me and still runs headfirst into danger once she sets her mind to it. God, why does it make me so hard that she's still defiant and wild?

Licking my lips, my eyelids fall to half mast as I stroke myself while the heat builds low in my gut. I picture everything at once, her on her knees until they're red and raw while I fuck her face, her lithe body arched in pleasure as she rides me in the back seat of my Charger, twisting her around on her hands and knees as I take her from behind with that damn school skirt flipped up to reveal her ass begging for my palm to slap it mercilessly until she's crying out, her flushed skin tender. I want Maisy every way my fantasies paint her.

"Fuck," I bite out as I come, the orgasm rushing through me.

I stand there for a moment, watching my release swirl down the drain. My throat is thick when I swallow. The guilt is only a mild throb, unlike how it used to be in the times I've given into my weakness for her and allowed fantasies to take over. I shut off the water and get out, scrubbing my body with the towel until my skin feels raw, as if I could wipe away jerking off to thoughts of her. No matter how hard I drag the towel over myself, it doesn't work.

Maisy Landry is branded on my fucking skin and she won't be erased without a fight.

My phone rings once I'm dressed. It's late on the east coast, but Colton and the rest of the Crows keep odd hours to carry out their misdeeds. I answer as I collapse on the couch, the apartment lit only by the dim glow of my laptop screen.

"Yeah?"

"*Would it kill you to say hello?*" Colt snarks.

"Probably." His husky laughter sounds at my blunt tone. "What's up?"

"*No dice, they didn't have plates to run.*"

"Shit. Figures."

"*They're professional for sure. They know the tricks to avoid CCTV and mask themselves when they can't. I lost their route when I tried to track it.*"

My fingers ball into a fist and my lip curls. Damn it. I need to figure out who was following me so I know what I'm dealing with now that someone is aware of my presence in Ridgeview.

"*You'll have to lure them out on purpose to find out who they are.*"

"Or I'll just keep following the money. They'll keep coming out of the shadows to protect the empires they've built for themselves on the blood of others."

Colt hums in agreement. I put the phone on speaker and set it on the coffee table next to the laptop. The browser window I left open makes me hesitate. It's Maisy's Instagram page. I scrub a hand over my mouth as anxiety digs its claws into me. It unsettles me that she made it out of town without me knowing about it.

"Did your alerts go off when Maisy flew to Paris?" I ask hoarsely, fighting back the weird feeling in my gut.

There's a long pause. "*No. She's not in Ridgeview?*"

"No. She went to Paris with her friends while they elope or some shit."

Colt barks out a laugh and mutters, "*Bishop. That suave little shit gives me a run for my money sometimes.*"

Who the fuck is that? A vague memory of the cocky asshole who knew how to fight better than anyone in Holden's amateur fight ring last year tugs at the back of my mind. I wait for Colton to elaborate, but he moves on, keyboard keys clacking faintly.

"*Don't worry about it. I'll know when they're back.*"

The unease crowding my chest doesn't go away. If people know I'm digging around to unravel the secrets of the elite and powerful in Ridgeview, they could know she was with me the other day. Even her last name won't stop the greedy bastards from making sure their pecking order remains intact. It doesn't make sense, but I have to make sure she's safe. I can't drop everything here and fly out to France, but I have the connections to make it happen.

"Listen." I rake my fingers through my damp hair. "I need another favor."

"*A favor.*"

He drags it out, tone shifting from playful to something more serious. He's going into crow mode, treating me like one of their clients instead of his foster brother. My chest tingles with awareness where the black bird is inked into my skin, perched on a skull and hidden in the design of the waves. The detached, calculating nature creeps into his chuckle when I sigh.

"Yes. I want you to use the resources at your disposal. You guys have the reach. I just want you to do what you can to make sure Maisy is watched and gets home unharmed."

"Helping you while you're in Ridgeview for your revenge is one thing, but outside of that, what you're asking..." Colt trails off for a moment and clicks his tongue disapprovingly. *"You know the rules, Foxy. Can't break them, even for family."*

Annoyance flares. "Don't call me Foxy, asswipe." I tug on my hair. "Come on, Colt. I'll owe you one again."

"You sure you want to owe me more than once?" I can hear his smirk in his tone. *"You know the price of favors owed in Thorne Point."*

A gruff sigh leaves me. "Yes."

There's another long pause, then Colt laughs. *"Done. Your little flower is safe with me, brother."* A low, sinister voice filters over the line in the background. Wren Thorne, the ringleader of their group. *"I've gotta go. You know how the big guy gets when he's in a mood."*

We share a laugh and I picture Wren's fierce scowl. He's not someone to be messed with.

The anxiety fades away at last. I end the call and stare for long minutes at her social media pictures on the computer screen. There's work to do, but I don't move.

This is insane. I don't understand why I have this urge when I still don't fucking trust her. She's a goddamn liar, just like her parents. Yet here I am, selling myself out to a group of psychos with skewed morals and a code of loyal brotherhood I know the consequences of in order to keep her safe.

Forcing out a breath, I drag both hands through my hair and stare at the industrial rafters overhead. When I turn over the idea of giving it all up, everything in me revolts. Not happening. I've spent too damn long wanting to know the truth about my parents' deaths and I'm not done yet. Her parents are behind it and they have to be brought down.

Tracing my tongue over my lower lip, I nod slowly, mind made up.

I won't stop, but...I'll do what I can to protect Maisy from afar. I'll stop focusing my efforts on taking her life apart. Separate her from my vendetta against her parents. I'll quit bullying her at school. It's all I'll allow myself.

A hollow laugh escapes me at the weight lifting from my shoulders now that I'm acknowledging this. I can't outrun it anymore, or bury myself in messing around with scrap metal and engine grease, or pretend what happens when I'm around her is something else than what it really is. What it's always been.

For every minute I've spent hating her, I hate myself a little more because I've never been able to let her go.

The truth is, I never stopped loving her.

It's existed beneath the surface all these years. I can't cut her out of the hold she's kept on my heart since we were kids. It's why her betrayal sliced me open, hurt so much worse because I love her.

This damn thing I feel for her is still real, overwhelming and impossible to smother. Even my hatred is love for her, as fucked up as that is.

After the harrowing images my brain supplied of what could've happened if I didn't lose that tail and how things would end if we were caught, I know that even if I've been willing to ruin her life, I won't let anyone else do the same. I won't be the reason she gets hurt because she's impulsive and never learned to stay out of trouble.

The instinct to protect her is bone deep, woven into my being. She's mine and no one else can have or hurt her. Only me.

It scares me that I feel so deeply for her—the good emotions and the bad.

I have to stay away from her, or the things I've bottled up beneath the hate and my grudge all these years will explode out of me. I won't be able to control myself. The attention she's been begging me for will consume her like an untamed fire.

I'm in love with Maisy, but I can't ever trust her again. If I give her my trust, it opens my heart up to feel the agonizing pain of her betrayal once again.

FIFTEEN
Maisy

Once my whirlwind adventure in Paris to watch my best friend marry the man of her dreams ends, I face my front door with a sense of dread. Three days away from home was amazing. It was the trip of a lifetime, leaving my free-spirited, travel-hungry heart full. I made memories I'll cherish forever. Yet even amidst the splendor of a foreign city, Fox and what I learned last weekend never left my mind for a second.

The frantic kiss, the car chase, his rough hands on me, and his bribe with Lana—all of it demanded my attention. Even while Thea and Connor were exchanging their vows and rings while Devlin officiated, the thoughts were there, luring my attention away from being present in the moment. I kind of hated myself for being a crappy friend during one of the most important milestones in my best friend's life. We need to sort things out between us soon, or I'll go crazy from feeling like I'm living a double life.

My lips tingle at the memory of Fox claiming my mouth. All this time I've been braced for his storm to impact me. My heart wasn't prepared for what it would feel like when we finally collided.

He refused to kiss me for weeks, despite how he relentlessly took and took from me. Something broke and shifted at last. His walls are eroding and I have to slip inside before he builds them back up stronger than ever.

Staring down the door to the house, I clutch my bag tighter and breathe through the strong urge to turn around and go anywhere else in the world, as long as it gets me far away from this cage. But I can't leave things unfinished with Fox.

Not after everything I've found out.

Not after that kiss gave me hope that he's not out of my reach.

I've barely gotten past the security system and through the front door before the wall of judgement and anger hits me. My parents stand in the cold foyer staring me down. Holden sits on the staircase to watch over the mother of all lectures I can feel brewing. His light brown hair stands on end like he's been running his fingers through it repeatedly. I meet Mom and Dad's gazes and my heart gives a little stutter.

They're furious.

Deep lines bracket Dad's disappointed frown and Mom is so angry she's become a statue.

It's a scary habit of hers to go as still as possible while her fury rises to the surface, pouring out of her in an unavoidable tirade when it crests.

"Hey guys," I say, clutching the strap of my travel bag like a lifeline.

Silence. Absolute and impenetrable.

Oh shit.

The last time she was so mad she couldn't speak was when I went camping and showed up late to a press conference for her company's new research project without telling her. Not only did I show up late, I was still sweaty and wearing the red dust of the trail instead of the smart business casual outfit she ordered me to wear. There's nothing Mom hates more than being embarrassed by my actions.

"Maisy Grace Landry," Mom finally says when I begin to shift my weight.

It's all she offers, making my name sound like a vicious curse. Dad pinches the bridge of his nose and takes over.

"What were you thinking?"

I blink. "I was thinking my friend invited me to his surprise elopement and I wasn't missing out."

"You couldn't have waited until their actual wedding in September?" Dad grumbles.

"Of course not." I narrow my eyes. It annoys me that they've never had close, genuine friendships in the last decade. They don't understand what you do for your real friends anymore. "I can't believe you'd ask me to skip my best friend's wedding."

Dad slashes his arm down, his voice rising. "And I can't believe you'd think it's okay to go gallivanting around the world without telling anyone."

The hurt racing across my senses is blistering. I duck my head and ignore the stinging in my eyes.

"I'm eighteen," I say in a low voice. "I don't see the big deal."

"You still can't do things like this without asking permission, Maisy. I thought someone kidnapped you." His expression turns haunted and I pull a face at his paranoia. "It's unacceptable. I can't prote—"

"Your road trip is officially off the table," Mom cuts in, folding her arms. I look from Dad to her, trying to keep up with why he'd need to protect me, but the road trip steals my focus. "Your childish actions have proven you're not a responsible adult."

My chest rises and falls with each strained breath. "How?"

"Running away from home. Do you know how that makes me look?"

The force of my scoff shakes my upper body. "Are you fucking kidding me? I went out of town for the weekend. Let's not alert the damn media over a vacation."

Mom's laugh drives ice into my veins. "You left the goddamn *country*, Maisy. Don't be cute."

"Guys." Holden's expression is troubled. "You can't baby her forever. What's the problem? She's home safe. Isn't that what matters?"

My throat grows thick with emotion for my brother standing up for me. We have our squabbles, but when it comes down to it, he's got my back.

"Stay out of it, Holden," Dad snaps. "This isn't up for debate. She needs to learn."

"What—that I'm expected to never experience life, just watch it from inside this glass bubble?" My voice is scratchy and the tears are falling freely now. Swiping angrily at my cheeks, I stare at them. I gesture to the security keypad on the wall above a video screen showing a grid of the house's entry points. "What are you going to do when I have to go to college, move off campus to watch me to make sure I behave?"

"Paris was your one wild trip," Mom says with finality. "So you definitely don't need to take the road trip you wanted. You will behave as I expect you to while you live under our roof. If you don't agree, you will be escorted by a bodyguard to and from the house, and all the security codes will be changed so you can't sneak out."

Holden's brows shoot up as air wheezes from my lungs. A bodyguard? That's crazy. This is the most excessive, overprotective, controlling decree my parents have ever set.

Pissed off beyond belief and at my limit, I spit out an agreement and push past them, running upstairs to my room. If they're so eager to treat me like I'm their prisoner, that's what I'll be. For now, while I make a plan for getting exactly what I want—my freedom from their insane expectations.

* * *

In the last week before graduation, Colorado is blooming with life. Bees and butterflies float on the fresh mountain air, kissing the wildflowers in the field around me. I stretch out on the blanket and turn a smile to the sun.

Since I've been home, I've been a good little prisoner. I stick to my schedule, not a toe out of line. I wear the good girl shell that appeases my parents, acing my final exams and filling my time with studying, feeling like I've given myself a lobotomy to shut off the adventurous side of me longing to go, go, *go*. It's boring as hell, sucking my soul out to smother everything that makes me who I really am. The time I spend at the yoga studio is my only outlet for all the frustration building up.

I don't look for Fox, even though every part of me is dying to get to him before he can shut me out again. It's been too long. I'm worried I'm losing my chance with him all over again and it pricks at my emotions. I won't lose him again, not when I'm so close to getting him back. He belongs in my life, and I belong in his.

Today is usually my volunteer shift at the library, but I got someone to cover for me. Once Dad dropped me off in front of the building, I hugged and kissed him goodbye, then ducked out the back doors where my friends were waiting in an SUV to pick me up. When I confided in Thea about what happened after I got home from Paris, she made it her mission to jailbreak me, offering to let me couch surf at her apartment with Connor. I'm not about to be a third wheel to the newlyweds, though. As much as I love and appreciate her support, I want to win this battle on my own.

My parents would be livid if they found out we're having a picnic near Peak Point in the mountains in a field that overlooks town. I'm probably chancing that permanent babysitter they threatened me with, but I needed to get out in nature to recharge myself.

Thea and Blair are stretched out on either side of me on the blanket, watching Connor and Devlin kick a soccer ball nearby while Gemma and Lucas share another one, snuggled together and murmuring to each other in a snarky tone. Those two love fighting each other, and I recognize it.

I think it's how my connection to Fox has evolved. Something in my blood sings when he comes at me and I don't shy away. Instead, I take him on and ride the thrill of surprising him.

We watch the guys pass the ball to each other. When they were at Silver Lake High, they were known as a wicked duo on and off the field, and those sharp skills are still evident as Devlin pulls a move with his foot that sweeps the ball from the ground to bounce on his knee while he smirks at Connor before returning it with a midair kick.

"You showy asshole," Connor taunts with a wide grin as he goes for the ball.

"Losing your touch? That one was easy to get," Devlin snipes back with a deep laugh.

"Never."

Blair shifts around and I laugh under my breath at the look on her face. It's one that matches Thea's as Connor dribbles the ball with some fancy footwork. These two are totally into their soccer player partners while I'm just admiring the athleticism and fluidity in their movements.

My blood only races when I think about calloused hands, scarred knuckles, and the faint scent of motor oil mixed with leather.

Tracing my lip with my tongue while my cheeks heat, I roll over onto my back and flip my crop top higher to feel the warmth of the sun on my stomach, careful not to let the bottom of my tits out. If I was alone, hell yeah I'd take advantage and go for full nip freedom, but for now I'm content like this.

A playful growl sounds to my left and when I peek from the corner of my eye, Gemma is straddling Lucas, wrestling with him. The corners of his mouth kick up before he switches their position and pins her arms overhead.

"Caught you, sweetheart," he croons, kissing a path up her neck. He nips her skin. "I'll always catch you."

"Love you, caveman." She laughs, bright and happy. It's easy to see how much they love each other.

The guys come over to the blanket. Devlin reaches us first, tucking Blair's hair back before he kisses her. Connor flops next to Thea and tugs her half on top of him, cupping her face and drawing her down to press their lips together. Watching both couples, longing hits me and I pluck at the leather bracelet I always wear. I wish I could have what they've all found, but my heart is destined to weather the storm that is Fox Wilder.

I don't care what's happened between us in the last year. We can move past it all after I fight for him.

Maybe if I can find out who would follow him and nearly run an orphaned nineteen year old off the road, I'll be able to help him. I purse my lips to the side in consideration, glancing at Connor and Thea. There used to be a rumor about his reputation as a king of blackmail around school. It's how he got Thea involved with him in the first place, because he was blackmailing her when she accidentally sent nude photos to him thinking he was a lifeguard she flirted with at the summer wellness retreat we went to.

"Hey." I sit up. "Can I ask you something?"

Connor leans up on his elbows, relaxed in his sprawl beside Thea. "'Sup?"

"Do you know anything about Fox?"

His brow lifts and he ruffles his floppy hair. "Maybe." His gaze slides to Thea, and whatever silent thing she tells him, he nods, scratching at his nose with his thumbnail. "I've got a file on him. I keep tabs on everyone in town. If they've got skeletons, I find them."

"Cool. Well, can I, like...have it?" My friends all stare at me. They've seen how he used to glare at me while they were in school with me, but I haven't told them much about what's been going on since then. "You know we used to be friends, when he lived here as a kid. The Wilders were our neighbors and close friends. I've been trying to find out what happened to him after he left Ridgeview." I swallow. "After his parents died in an accident."

"That's so sad," Gemma murmurs.

Lucas gathers her close, rubbing her arms comfortingly.

"I know," I agree.

"I'm sorry," Gemma says.

I offer her a lopsided smile, appreciative of the sympathy for the hell Fox has been through.

"Yeah." Connor hitches his shoulder. He pulls his phone from his pocket and starts typing. "I'll get it for you. What I have is thin. I was never able to dig up too much on him, and since I was—" His gaze zeroes in on Thea again, burning in its intensity "—occupied last year, it was enough for me. It's mostly old stuff from an incident report, and half of it was redacted by your dad and his work buddies when I got it from him."

My brow furrows. "What do you mean? Why would my dad give you a police report?"

"Well," he hedges. "I mean, I'm no saint, you know?"

"Connor Bishop," Thea says with a chastising bite, elbowing him.

He coughs, murmuring to her under his breath, "All right, jesus, baby. You don't have to break out the elbows. I'll tell her." Turning back to me, he presses his tongue into his cheek. "So, it's not a very well kept secret. I'm surprised you haven't heard anything."

"About what?" I push.

"The chief is known for taking bribes and looking the other way. I held that knowledge over his head to get what I needed on your punk ass biker to make sure I could keep him in line if I needed to."

My brows fly up in shock. "Um, what?"

"It's true." Devlin shrugs and turns his attention to Blair and runs the back of his knuckles over her cheek in a loving gesture. She blushes, nuzzling into his touch. "I've had to utilize it before. It's probably one of the worst kept secrets in town."

"Yeah, even my dad tells me about it," Lucas says. His father is a lawyer. "He jokes with him about it when they get together for poker nights at my parents' place on the lake."

Dad has always been a good guy to me. He's protective, but deep down he's the man who used to smile and laugh with me. How could he take bribes? My world wobbles and I twist my fingers in the blanket. I gulp as I remember once again what Fox said to Lana—that he knows what my parents are capable of.

They're definitely hiding things from me. Now I'm sure of it. That's the only thing that makes sense to explain why they've always been so strict.

"You said his name is Wilder?" Devlin asks.

"Yeah."

"I recognize it. Is he related to anyone that worked for Nexus Lab?"

"Yes. His parents and my mom worked in the same research department."

"They used to be mentioned a lot in the science journals at my parents' house. I remember reading about the articles on their drug research," he says, somberness creeping into his voice.

For the most part, Devlin is relaxed and happy, but I remember before he and Blair were together. When I'd see him in the halls at school, he seemed to carry the weight of the world on his shoulders. His name is well known in this town for his parents' famous medical clinic. I've met them once or twice when Mom has corralled Holden and I to attend events for her company. They're a cold and unfeeling couple who barely seem like they're married, let alone parents.

Blair puts a hand on his arm and whispers something to him that clears the shadows from his expression. He leans into her for support, closing his eyes.

"Can I borrow the journals?"

Devlin snorts. "Sure. They're barely ever there, so I can get them for you if you want. I doubt they'd miss them."

"Thank you."

I'll take anything I can get to find out who Fox has become and discover what he's involved in.

SIXTEEN
Maisy

By the time I'm home, the file Connor sent is waiting in my inbox. I download it from the link he sent with the password he provided and settle in to learn everything I can about Fox.

He wasn't kidding, there really isn't much to go through. But what is there makes my breath catch. I rub the stones in my bracelet.

The first thing I read is the incident report from the accident, which is littered with bold black lines hiding vital information. It's hard to believe that mere days before this horrible thing happened Fox and I were playing with Holden and making one of my happiest memories in the field by our tree.

My brow furrows. Dad's signature is on the report, but I don't remember him being on duty that night. The harder I rack my brain, the clearer it becomes. We were out for dinner, which wasn't out of the ordinary for us. It was at the hibachi restaurant Holden and I loved so much. I think...we were celebrating Mom's promotion, but it wasn't officially announced until a couple of weeks after everything happened. How could Dad be at dinner with us, but sign off as the officer in charge of the case?

"Why don't the page numbers line up?" I murmur to myself in confusion as I realize I'm reading page 8 after page 3. "Where's the rest of it?"

It doesn't seem right for pages to be missing. For a fatal car accident, there should be a coroner report and an analysis of what remained of the car after the fire was put out. A scanned handwritten note attached to the last page declaring the crash an accident states the rest of the file is sealed and the case is closed—signed *Chief Richard Landry*. I press my lips together.

I wonder if half of what's in the report are lies given what Fox said to Lana and what my friends told me about Dad taking bribes. I want to know why most of the report is missing, some parts redacted by thick black lines. What are they hiding if it was an accident?

There's another related document from the Ridgeview Police Department in the same file releasing Fox into the state's foster care system. This is signed by Dad, too. My stomach flips unpleasantly. Dad is the one who sent him away. How could he do that to his friends' son? We could've taken him in if he didn't have any other local family.

After the first placement, it looks like there was a trail of foster homes. The dates hurt my heart. Six months. A month and a half. Three weeks. Two days. One after the other, an endless revolving door kicked him out, mixed with two short stints in a detention center, painting a bleak picture of what an unstable upbringing he experienced after he lost his parents.

A letter catches my eye from one of the shortest times spent in a home. As I read, everything blurs from the tears filling my eyes. A few lines stand out.

Fox is a danger to himself and others...can't get along with the other children...extreme grief and anger. He is a troubled child beyond help...getting into fights...the violence is too much to have in my home, so I unfortunately can no longer act as his state-appointed guardian.

After that it cuts off, leaving a weird gap between when he was fifteen and now. It's like someone wiped him clean out of the system.

This wasn't the life Fox was supposed to have.

All of this is heartbreaking to look at. I rub my forehead as I click through, wishing there was more and glad that there isn't because this is already a lot to handle. My heart sits in my throat, aching as I think of what he went through.

He was all alone. He had no siblings or other family to take him in.

A tear streaks down my cheek. It always used to be me, him, and Holden against the world. Holden was the brother he never had. I was...

You're my daisy.

My chest constricts at his voice in my head, but instead of the way it sounded when we were younger, his deep, raspy voice whispers to me.

That was torn away when he lost his parents. Everything he had was taken from him.

Guilt twinges in my stomach for reading this about him without him telling me directly, but I know from where we stand right now he'd never let me in to tell me this on his own. He's guarded now in a way he never was before tragedy tore through his world. I had to know this. It's one more thing I can add to my list of apologies he's holding over my head.

With some of the answers in front of me, I finally understand enough to fit the jagged pieces of the new Fox into the shape of the one I used to know so well. Of course he's angry. I get it now. Who wouldn't be when faced with so much grief and countless people who are meant to protect him gave up on him, labeling him troubled and dangerous?

What he told me about calling a boy a monster enough times making it stick carries a heavier, depressing weight to it now that I know.

Taking a shuddering breath, I scrub my hands over my puffy cheeks. I wish he would've opened up to me instead of shutting me out when he came back. He didn't have to be alone anymore, but I understand. He's been alone for so long that he's learned to only rely on himself. What's the point in trusting the world around you when he has so much experience of it shitting on him to prove he's the only one who can look out for himself.

I jump when my door flies open, scrambling to open the window with a yoga YouTube video I had waiting to hide what I was looking at. Mom barges in without asking and I ignore her, throwing all my focus into the instructor stretching her body at sunrise on a beach in California.

"*Deep breath in, feel that energy filling your heart chakra, and let it out,*" the instructor narrates while she moves to the next pose in the flow.

"Maisy."

Releasing a small aggravated breath at the interruption, I flick my gaze to her. "Mom."

Jailer. I keep that to myself, not wanting to give her incentive to slap me with a freaking bodyguard to babysit me.

She narrows her eyes. "Why do you look like you were crying?"

"It's nothing," I lie, reaching for another to get her off my back. "I'm on my period."

Her nostrils flare, but she accepts the cover story. I pull my hair into a ponytail, but the next words out of her mouth have me freezing partway through.

"Get ready."

"For what?"

"We're going out to dinner."

"I'm not really hungry." I don't say it's because Thea made an entire feast for the picnic earlier since I snuck out to be there.

Mom gives me a triumphant look that makes me tense. "If you cooperate, I'll reconsider the road trip."

I wait for her to elaborate more, but she turns on her heel and leaves without closing my door. A bout of irritation skitters across my patience. Nothing agitates me more than her opening my door to bug me with her commands, then leaving it open on her way out. How hard is it to just close the door like when she found it?

Whatever, more importantly I'm going to do as she says because I want to go on my road trip. I've been making plans, but everything will be so much easier if I don't have to do it behind her back.

* * *

Understanding hits me as soon as we arrive at the ritzy steak house downtown. Tonight is all about image and reputation. Probably another lesson so I don't "run away" again. This is the worst way to teach me, stirring my resentment of my parents.

Because Sam Blake is here, waiting for us in front of the restaurant in slacks and a dress shirt.

"Samuel," Dad says warmly. "Good to see you, son. We've missed you."

"Chief. Mrs. Landry, you look beautiful tonight," Sam greets, saving me for last. His voice drops lower. "Maisy."

I watch in horror as he shakes Dad's hand. Boyish dimples appear beside his broad smile as he puts his hand at the small of my back without my permission.

I throw an accusing glare at Mom, but her expression says it all—do not make a scene.

Road trip. Road trip. Road trip.

It's worth it.

Gritting my teeth, I shove down the urge to throw Sam's hands off of me. I wish Holden didn't have a paper due for a summer class so I wasn't here alone. Actually, I wish I could've done Holden's paper for him so he could be here, because at this rate I'd much rather stay home doing homework than sit through this torture. Mom and Dad finally got what they've always wanted from me. Who knew all they had to do was trap me at a public place with a douchebag almost-boyfriend?

"Shall we?" Dad suggests, guiding Mom inside.

Sam follows suit, nudging my back. I shoot him an unimpressed look, chanting about my road trip in my head. My feet feel like lead blocks as I trudge into the restaurant.

Of course Mom picked the most upscale establishment in town to set the stage for this puppet show. The mayor and his wife are dining at their table in the prime corner booth. Lucas' parents, the Saints, are nearby. So is Connor's mom that he doesn't talk to, the city council chair. I hear she's been angling for the mayor's office if her run for senate doesn't work out.

Every prominent face of the elite and powerful in town fill the steakhouse and they don't miss Mom and Dad's arrival. Several of them wave, or stop us to say hello while we're escorted to our table by a host. This is how the upper echelon of Ridgeview works. They all rub elbows with each other and pour on the smarmy charm, trading favors and securing deals outside of their offices. It makes my stomach turn, but when I take a step back from the mayor's table, I only put myself more soundly in Sam's embrace.

As we finally take a seat, I'm directly across from Dad and everything I've read up on Fox comes rushing back. Anger sparks to life in my chest and I use the menu folio as a cover to peer at my father over the top edge without him noticing.

He's aged, but maintains the handsomeness of his younger years, making him look distinguished, like someone who belongs in his position in the police department. Like someone who should be trustworthy that upholds the integrity of the law. Instead of the warmth of when I was a little girl, his clear blue eyes have become sharp, and his mouth sets into a more natural frown these days. Now all I see is the imposing man meant to protect this town.

But how much protecting is he really doing if police reports are suspiciously missing information?

The time he and Fox's mom took the three of us to an amusement park for the day flits across my memories. He was always ready to get us to smile, whatever it took. I still don't get how the guy who used to fling tiny bites of food in our old kitchen for Holden and I to practice catching in our mouths is the same man who could put Fox in foster care. That's not the man who raised me and I don't know how to process it.

Distrust tugs at my senses as I watch Dad's tight smile while Mom asks Sam about his college plans.

"University of Illinois in Chicago? How wonderful," she praises. "Maisy has an early acceptance to Northwestern University."

"You must be proud." Sam shoots me a smirk that's supposed to be nice. I want to punch it. He drapes his arm across the back of my chair, playing with my hair. "Northwestern isn't far from where I'll be. Same city."

"It's not," Mom agrees with a calculating gleam in her eyes. "You'll be able to visit each other without having to carry on your relationship long distance."

"Relationship?" I blurt.

That wasn't on the table. I will not sit here while my parents basically set me up in an arranged situation with Sam for the sake of my road trip. Literally, fuck that. I'll go on my road trip without their permission and give them two big middle fingers as I drive west without ever looking back. Screw college, screw their life plans and expectations, screw everything.

"I'm just glad I won't have to be far from you, beautiful," Sam murmurs, taking my hand and bringing my knuckles to his mouth.

It takes a monumental effort not to curl my lip at him. I succeed—*barely*—but I can't control the way my spine snaps straight. Sam notices, his eyes narrowing slightly. Seriously, how can he sit here putting on this nice guy act for my parents after the crap he said to me?

I'm sick of it by the time our salad course is cleared. There are only so many thinly veiled comments about our future together that I can stand before I'm on the verge of screaming in the middle of the restaurant. Bet Mom would love that.

Pushing back from the table with a graceful motion instead of the hard shove I want to give, I turn to Sam. "Can I talk to you for a minute? Outside?"

The arrogance in his gaze mocks me. Asshole. He checks with my parents before answering, making me fume even more.

He waits for Dad's nod before he finally answers. "Sure thing, beautiful."

"Excuse us."

I don't wait for my parents to respond before I leave the table. My simple, but elegant dress swishes with each purposeful stride to freedom. It's a pretty shade of blue with thin straps that braid together in the back, but I wouldn't have picked it up for myself, preferring to shop vintage when I can. My style drives Mom crazy because I'm always in what's comfortable, like my workout clothes, or my favorite second-hand finds instead of the designer labels she wants me to wear.

The summer sun is just dipping behind the Rockies when I burst out onto the terrace in front of the steak house. It's chillier than earlier, the cooler evening air prickling across my skin. I rub my arms as Sam strolls out behind me, relaxed with a crooked grin and his hands in his pockets.

"You can wipe that smug look off now," I tell him. "There's no one around to watch the show."

He purses his lips like he's considering it. "I don't think so. I'm getting what I wanted." He closes the distance between us, snagging my waist before I can step out of his reach. He traps me against his body and murmurs in my ear in a low seductive tone that makes my skin crawl. "And if you play nice, I'll give you what you want, little slut. I've as good as got your daddy's permission to fuck you, so you're not getting away this time. No friends to step in for you, so just bend over and take it, yeah?"

"Get the hell off me," I snap, stepping on his toe hard to get him to release me.

"Ow! You bitch!"

Fury burns through me, hot and blinding. He clearly didn't learn the lesson Devlin and Connor inflicted on him. Screw peace and love in his case. He hasn't changed at all.

I stab my finger into his chest. "Tonight means nothing, got it? I'm only here so I can go on my road trip before my parents trap me in the life plan they've laid out for me." I look him up and down with disgust. "And if you ever think I'd let you touch me after calling me a cocktease and slut shaming me, you're dead fucking wrong. I will never let you touch me."

"You're the one who's wrong about that. They said you were easy and like it rough." He raises his hand to hit me, spewing vile bullshit as he swings. "I'll *make* you mine and have you screaming my name so loud—"

The blow doesn't come. I didn't realize I closed my eyes when I braced for the impact because I couldn't dodge out of the way, but as I open them Fox stands between me and Sam, digging his fingers into Sam's arm hard enough it looks like he's seconds from breaking the wrist if he squeezes harder. Sam's mouth hangs open in shock because Fox seemed to materialize out of the shadows with barely any sound.

Relief and annoyance spiral through me. On one hand, this is my fight and I will handle it myself. It wasn't cool when Devlin and Connor stepped in to defend my honor at the movies, and the same applies when it's Fox. On the other, a baser part of me is dancing around at his rescue.

"If you ever raise a hand to her again, I'll fucking kill you," Fox growls in a deadly undertone. His whole body is tensed for a fight, like a predatory animal ready to spring free of its cage. "There won't be any piece of you left for anyone to find." His grip tightens and Sam releases a pained groan as Fox leans in, speaking through clenched teeth. "I will make you disappear."

God, why does hearing him threaten Sam like that make my heart race and heat throb between my legs?

SEVENTEEN
Fox

I had to cut in. It's lucky I was parked in a discreet spot on my Harley, waiting to pick up a Nexus Lab employee ID badge at the back of the restaurant from a waiter I bribed to steal it for me. Maisy didn't notice me at all. The minute I saw her come out, followed by the guy she swore wasn't her boyfriend while I had my fingers buried deep inside her, possessiveness and protectiveness rushed through me. It's exactly why I've been avoiding her once Colton confirmed she made it back to Ridgeview.

Seeing the douchebag all over her drove fire into my blood, but the second he raised his hand to her, I was off my bike and catching his arm before he could slap her faster than I've ever moved in my life.

Maisy hovers behind me, releasing a tense breath. I grind my teeth. It doesn't bother me for her to see the true monster I'm capable of being, but a weak part inside of me that refuses to be stamped out flares with worry that she'll finally run away.

"Are you okay?" I ask.

"Fuck no, you're about to break my arm, you psycho," Blake bleats, contorting his body to get away.

With a grumble, I put more pressure on the tendon beneath my thumb. The corner of my mouth kicks up at the pained sound he makes, twisting to find relief that isn't coming. Levi taught me every trick he knows to make someone fucking hurt.

"I wasn't talking to you, shithead." My gaze moves back to Maisy, waiting for her answer.

"I'm fine." She steps forward. "But I had this, you didn't have to—"

"I did."

There's no room for argument in my bitten off response. The days spent avoiding her haven't changed a damn thing, the need filling my chest still very much alive. When it comes down to it, I won't let her get hurt. I'll protect her. It's instinctive, soul-deep, and undeniable.

The flood gates that kept these feelings at bay during the years I spent hating her with every breath have cracked and crumbled. They're open and there's no going back.

Maisy is mine, even when I can't have her. She's always been mine.

And I'll be damned If I ever stand by and allow another man to lay a hand on her like this fucker tried to. I wasn't kidding when I threatened him with death for touching her.

That's how far I'll go for the people I want to keep safe.

The moments of Blake lifting his hand to smack her fly through my head again, and with a savage growl I maneuver his wrist to a painful angle.

"Dude!" he shrieks, free hand scrabbling uselessly at my leather jacket.

"Okay, scary tough guy, enough," Maisy grits out. "I appreciate your help, but I can take care of my own problems."

"No, daisy," I mutter, dragging Blake by my hold on his wrist so I can step closer to her. Flowers and coconuts touch my sense of smell and my mouth quirks up at the sides. I bend my head down so she can hear my low promise. "He wanted to touch you. That makes this my problem, too. You're my problem."

Her breath catches as her eyes fly up to meet mine. The seriousness evident in my gaze makes her lips part. My attention falls to her mouth and an intense yearning to kiss her right now pours through me.

God, I want to steal her away, put her on the bike behind me, take her back to our tree to pin her against it like before while I peel this dress up, and—

"How touching," Blake snarls, breaking the moment. He struggles to escape, but I have a good grip on him. "Is it the leather that does it for you? His motorcycle? You hide it well, pretending you're this perfect ideal. What will your daddy say when I tell him?"

"Tell him what?" Maisy cuts him off with a glare. She holds out her arms. "This is the real me. You have no idea what I'm really like because you didn't want to get to know me. I don't care what you or anyone else thinks of me. I thought you wanted to be my friend, but you're such an asshole, Sam."

He releases a caustic laugh. "Friend? Bullshit, I just wanted to fuck you after all those rumors that you finally stopped being such an uptight good girl. That's the only reason I was nice to you, I fuckin' earned the right to—"

Before he can spew more shit, she cocks her arm back and punches him. Blake can't move far thanks to my iron grip on him, so he takes the full force of her fist to his cheek with a groan. Laughter puffs out of me at the fierce expression on her face.

"Like hell you earned anything with me, you entitled dick," Maisy says furiously. "What I do with my body and who I decide to do it with is my business, not yours. So stop trying to comment on it like you have any right to my body because of some fucked up notion you got in your head that if you were nice to me I'd reward you."

"You should use your whole body. Turn your hips and torso with your momentum," I suggest, raking my gaze over her.

"What?"

She turns to me, still spitting mad. It's a damn good look on her, sending another bolt of heat shooting to my groin.

"Your form is good, but you're smaller than him with less muscle tone to power your hits."

Her eyes narrow dangerously, and another chuckle leaves me. "I said less tone, not that you aren't strong." A beat passes as I take her in. Every stunning inch. I can't hide the reverence in my voice. "I know you're strong. If you do it that way, you'll pack a harder punch without sacrificing speed."

Her eyes soften and a pretty pink color tinges her cheeks at the compliment. I swallow back the happy rumble that starts climbing my throat, cutting it off before it can escape. She keeps making me forget, drawing me in with magnetic force to something I can't have.

"I can't believe you'd rather spread your legs for this bad boy act, slu—"

We both release irritated sounds. Blake doesn't get to finish, breaking off into a scream when I twist his arm in my punishing hold, yanking hard to stretch it, and then angling up until there's a sickening *pop*. A vicious grin crosses my face as he stumbles away from us in agony.

"Holy shit," Maisy whispers, staring wide-eyed at the sight of Sam Blake's dislocated arm.

This time she doesn't look ready to run. There's no fear in her hazel eyes, only a bright intensity that echoes the violence brimming in me.

"What the fuck?!" Blake yells, trying to cradle his injured limb. "You—Your dad is inside. When I get him and report you for assault, it's over for you, Wilder."

I stare at him with an unwavering threat that makes him freeze. "Fuck off, Blake, before I do something more serious to your car than making sure it doesn't start the next time you get in it." When I take another step toward him, he scurries backward like the coward he is. "A dislocated arm will be the least of your worries. Be glad I didn't break it."

"Get out of here," Maisy says. "And don't ever come near me again, or I'll file a restraining order for harassment."

Blake looks between both of us standing side by side and mumbles, "Screw this."

Then he leaves us alone in front of the restaurant in the fading twilight. I turn back to her, unsure of what I should do or say. It's unlike me. I swallow as my head fully empties for the first time in a long time. She looks beautiful tonight, her soft light brown hair framing her face and skimming the bare skin of her shoulders. My fingers twitch with the urge to reach out and thread through her hair.

"Next time, you need to leave it to me."

I blink out of my stupor. "Not happening."

Her lips purse and she crosses her arms. "Yes it is. I don't want you to fight my battles for me. I appreciate the help, and the…" She trails off as a flush creeps into her cheeks. Coughing, she darts her gaze away, brushing her fingers over her leather bracelet. "The thing you did. Not that I think violence is the answer, even though I decked him. I mean, he deserved it by that point," she hastily tacks on, throat working as her lashes lower. "But I don't need a man to save me, you feel me? I can stand up for myself."

Fuck me. A rush of heat races through my body. Maisy is turned on by what I did to him. I drag my teeth over my lower lip and file that away to fantasize about later—the only way I'll let myself have her. In my fantasies, I don't run the risk of her betraying my trust.

"Let's get one thing straight here." I step close enough that the soft material of her dress brushes against my chest. Grasping her chin between my thumb and finger, I tilt her face up. "I have no problem with a woman fighting her own battles, but don't expect me to stand idly by if I'm around. Either I show you how to protect yourself, or I do it for you. Like I said, you're my problem. So if someone threatens you, I will step in to take care of it."

Her hazel eyes are luminescent, almost gold in the amber glow the restaurant casts off. Her breathing turns shallow and her pupils dilate at my dominant tone. For a beat, she looks at my mouth with so much longing, all I want to do is crash my lips against hers.

"Even if the threat is you?" Her voice is soft and alluring, but her eyes harden when I begin to close the small distance between us to claim her mouth. "Or do you not count in taking responsibility for your actions because of double standards? That would undermine every sexy word that came out of your mouth."

Well, shit. She's got me there.

"You're right," I rasp, caressing her bottom lip with my thumb.

Now that she's safe, I can walk away. I need to, before I slide further down the treacherous slope and do something stupid again, like kissing her within an inch of her life.

"Maisy."

We both turn at the sound of Jacqueline Landry's bitchy tone. Her parents stand outside the restaurant's doors. It's the first time I've come face to face with them directly since I moved back to Ridgeview.

I don't release Maisy right away, fighting against another wave of possessiveness. It's stronger this time, latching onto me and making me want to never let her go. Richard Landry looks about ready to pop a blood vessel at the sight of his precious daughter standing so close to me, and his wife actually looks annoyed she didn't plot to make sure I was in the car with my parents that night so she could've avoided this moment. Maisy tenses, grasping my shirt in her fist as a tremor runs down her spine. What was once a simple revenge plan has gotten complicated by what I feel for her.

She presses gently against my chest and steps away from me. My hand falls to my side, chest burning with an acute tightness.

"Where is Sam?" Jaqueline demands in an icy voice, because asking anything is beneath her.

"He had to leave," Maisy says. Lowering her voice so only I can hear, she adds, "Crying shame."

I snort.

"You've been out here too long and you left before the entrees were served," Jacqueline says. "People inside started to take notice."

Maisy shrugs. "Sorry. I'm not that hungry now."

Jaqueline's detached gaze flicks to me for a moment. It's hard to believe those eyes are the same color as Maisy's, which are full of life. "Then I guess you don't feel like going on your trip."

Maisy bristles beside me. I take a step, but she shoots a hand out to stop me.

"Don't," she murmurs. "I have to take on this fight for myself, too."

I look back to Jacqueline and Richard. The coldness in her eyes is awful. I remember when she would buy us ice cream, and the time she drove us to the aquarium for a class trip when my parents were out of town. She used to look at me with the same fondness as she had for her own children, like I was another son to her. The malicious way she looks at me now harbors no warmth, like if I say something she doesn't like she won't hesitate to end me if it threatened her greed.

Meeting her gaze, I know beyond a shadow of a doubt this is who took my family from me.

EIGHTEEN
Maisy

"Fox, wait!"

After staring at Mom for several tense heartbeats, he turned and walked away toward the shadows past the pool of light outside the restaurant. I'm not finished with him yet, not by a long shot. I need to talk to him before he shuts me out again. I want to know what he meant about me being his problem and why he stepped in between me and Sam when he was actively tormenting me not that long ago.

"Maisy, get back here!" Dad calls as I go after Fox. I move faster to outrun him, expecting him to restrain me if he has to, but it doesn't come. "Please! Jackie—"

"We won't make a scene here, Richard," Mom says cryptically.

I'm not turning back, not even for the desperation in Dad's voice. They can't keep me from him. I'm fighting for him and they won't stop me. For once, Mom's insane need to control every aspect of her image is working out for me to escape so I can chase Fox.

I'll deal with the fallout when I get home later. I'm sure I'm in for hell from her for ruining her meticulously orchestrated night by running off. Let people start another rumor, see if I care. There are more important things happening right now than maintaining the image she's obsessed with.

When I reach the shadows, I don't see him. Crap. Did I miss him? How does he move so quickly and quietly so it's hard to follow his path?

A pair of strong arms circle me from behind and I'm whirled around. I release a tiny gasp before my back hits the brick wall of the restaurant.

"What are you doing, Maisy Daisy?" Fox rasps in a smoky tone, lips brushing my temple while his hand closes around my neck.

Unlike before, this time his hold is almost...gentle. His thumb swipes the underside of my jaw, guiding my face up.

For a moment, I can't speak. My throat closes over with the emotions choking me up. He's called me daisy, and by my name a few times, but never the full nickname from our childhood. My hands automatically rest on his chest, clinging to the material of his signature black muscle shirt beneath the leather jacket to anchor myself so I don't float away in the sea of memories attacking me. I didn't expect how it would make me feel when I used to hate it so much, but hearing it now infused with so many things—wry amusement, sultry teasing, *affection*—I have to swallow a few times and force out a ragged breath.

"You're more interesting to be around than my parents." I want to pull him closer. A snort shakes his shoulders and a hot puff of air travels over my neck. "I need to talk to you."

"No."

The arrogant way he decides it makes me bristle.

"Yes," I insist, twisting my fingers and tugging on his shirt.

"I didn't plan on you."

I don't know what he means by that, but it sounds like the admission cost him.

He sighs in resignation, tracing his nose down the side of my face, as if he can't keep away from me anymore than I can stay away from him. It's impossible. The world knows we're meant to be like this, so it gave us an invisible cord that ties our hearts together.

My whole body protests when he pulls back, allowing the cool night air to get between us. It feels like he's putting the cavernous divide back in place. His eyes are hard to read in the dark, but they still pierce through me.

"I have to go." His mouth twists. "There's something I'm late for."

"So take me with you. We really need to talk. You said I was your problem and I want to know what you meant."

He pushes out a breath, cutting his gaze to the side as he drags his long, calloused fingers through his tousled dark hair. His jaw works while he shakes his head.

"No."

That damn refusal again. I tighten my grip on his shirt, ready to jump across the deep invisible crevice he separates us with.

"Don't."

"What changed?" My words come faster and my voice cracks. "Why did you hate me so much and do everything you could to make my life hell, but now you decide you'll protect me?"

The more I push, the more I feel him closing off. My one chance to get past his walls is slipping away. He steps back, prying my hands from his shirt. He won't even look at me.

"Why?" I yell. "Just tell me!"

Fox moves aggressively, pinning me to the wall. "Why?"

A harsh sound passes his lips as he grips me by my upper arms and cages me against the bricks with every inch of his hard muscles. His controlled composure breaks and everything he keeps locked away pours out of him.

"*Why?* Because you broke your goddamn promise, Maisy!"

There's so much anger bleeding out of him, I expect the red stain to be all over my dress and shoes when I return to the light.

His voice grows hoarse and gravelly. "You know that! Stop acting like you don't!"

"What?" I sputter, caught off guard as confusion swarms me. "What are you talking about?"

"You promised me. You swore not to tell Holden or your parents when I showed you what was in the garage."

Fox breathes heavily, digging his fingers into my upper arms. The brick bites into my back through the thin designer dress. I ignore all of it, because what he said triggered my memories. It's all coming back in a visceral rush that threatens to swallow me whole.

"The day you gave me the daisy," I whisper, my eyes widening.

There's something else I want to show you. It's in my dad's garage. The image of Fox at nine floats to the surface of my mind as we stood in the field by our tree. *I wasn't supposed to find it. You have to promise not to tell anyone.*

I remember that day now. I haven't thought about it in so long because it was too close to when I lost Fox.

He took me into the garage and I thought he was going to show me something to do with the mechanics he was learning from his dad. But I was wrong.

His excitement was infectious, and I loved following him into trouble. It gave me a thrill like no other. He never told me I couldn't do something because I was small or a girl. He liked it when I came along on our adventures.

Everything looked normal at first. Fox jogged over to his dad's motorcycle and ran a proud hand over it. "I'm going to take you for a ride on this once I'm allowed to drive it."

I nodded eagerly. I wanted to feel the wind in my hair while I got to hug him really tight.

Then he took my hand and led me to the other side of the garage where his dad usually kept a stash of his favorite beer in a mini fridge. We opened the door and instead of beer bottles, there were trays of small tubes with labels on them. As far as I knew, our parents weren't allowed to bring their work home from their lab.

"A science experiment?" I asked.

He shook his head and carefully prodded one of the tubes. "I think it's this." He let the door to the refrigerator shut and moved a box of tools out of the way on the workbench, pulling out the folder hidden there. "It says it's a patent."

"Synthetic opioid formula trial," I read aloud on one of the section headings. The page had a scientific diagram on it. I couldn't pronounce some of the longer technical words, even though I read a lot for my age. "How come they have it here? Why is it hidden?"

"Dunno. Cool, right? We never get to see their work. They always say I'm not allowed to visit when I beg them to bring me to their lab for take your kid to work day."

We only spent a few minutes marveling at Fox's discovery of his parents contraband drug trial stash. I remember one of the pages in the packet having a long list of numbers that I wrote off at the time, but now that I'm thinking about it, I remember dollar signs and lots of commas. Whatever they had been hiding in the garage was worth a huge amount of money to the company.

"I-I did promise." And I did break it. "I'm so sorry."

The echo of guilt flares as fresh as it was when the words slipped out of my mouth in my excitement to tell my parents about my new favorite day at bedtime. Once they tumbled out, I couldn't steal them back.

The memory of the weird, tense look they exchanged makes my breath catch. They told me not to tell anyone else what I saw. To forget it even happened. It was the first time Mom ever became controlling with me, but we're so far down the path now that I'd pushed the memory far behind all the other bad blood between me and Mom. The expression on her face scared me that night.

Grabbing onto his biceps, I will him to hear out my explanation. "Wait—I did tell my parents when I said I wouldn't, but they already knew." I felt really bad about it, but our parents were close friends and it made sense that they knew, because Mom worked with them. "They didn't seem surprised by what we saw in the garage."

He's angry all over again. It rolls off of him, nearly suffocating me. I sense he's ready to shove me back out behind the iron walls he built around his heart once more. How could I have forgotten about that day?

"You picked them over the promise you made me."

"I was too excited to tell them about my day. It wasn't on purpose, it just slipped out."

"The secret of what they were hiding got them killed," Fox grits out through clenched teeth. I can feel the vibration of his deep voice through his chest against mine. "Their car crash wasn't an accident. They were murdered along with my baby sister."

Another wave of shock crashes over me. I'm on the verge of shattering, stuck between the old memories and the truth coming out.

"Sister?" It comes out strangled.

"Mom didn't want to tell anyone yet, but they just found out she was having a girl." His voice is shaking. "I was supposed to have a baby sister."

Did I unknowingly contribute to his family's death? Even if my parents knew, did I put everything in motion to get them in trouble by spilling a secret that wasn't mine in the first place?

Ice freezes my veins and I slam my eyes shut to block out his expression. It hurts my heart too much. This is why he's hated me. This is how our friendship was destroyed.

Fox hasn't only been living with the grief of losing his parents to tragedy all these years. It's so much worse than I ever could have imagined.

"Murdered." The word tastes like ash on my tongue, but I force it out.

My eyes open slowly and I stare at his unyielding jawline as my thoughts turn. The police report. The investigation was ruled an accident, the coroner report missing. I knew it was suspicious that there was information missing from it and that Dad's signature was all over it. Fox's weird behavior and the way he's been lurking around town bribing people makes sense now. I've finally figured out what he's been up to.

"You're trying to prove it."

It takes him a long time to answer. He studies me, not letting up on his punishing grip. "Yes."

"How? You're nineteen."

"That doesn't concern you. I have to do this. I won't let the people that did this to my family get away with it. They don't get to enjoy the power they got by killing my family." His conflicted tone breaks my heart as he breaks off, swallowing audibly. The sorrow threatens to drag me under. "You helped them by breaking that promise. No one would've found out what they were hiding."

"That's not true. I told you my parents already knew!" I have to believe it's not true, rejecting the idea that I inadvertently helped hurt them.

Fox grunts as he bears down on me, finally releasing my arms in favor of locking his fingers around my throat as he gets in my face.

"Why do you think your Mom was promoted to CEO out of nowhere? Check the damn dates. That's the level the people behind this are working at." His hand flexes and I struggle to draw my next breath. "That's what your broken promise did."

My heart crushes under the weight of guilt. "I was eight! We were just kids!"

"Tell that to my dead parents!"

Fox smacks a palm against the brick over my head and backs away with a frustrated noise. I reach up to rub my neck. My throat burns like I've swallowed thousands of knives, but not from his rough handling.

"So you hate me because you think I helped the people that did this?"

The question hurts because part of me actually wonders if I'm remembering the events of that day wrong and I did inadvertently have a hand in it all, but I force it out. Fox gives me a low rumble in response.

"You seriously believe I would hurt you so deeply when I've always lo—" I clamp my mouth shut as he crushes me against the wall with his body once more. Both of us are breathing hard. I lick my lips and tilt my chin up. His searching gaze tracks the movement. "I would never hurt you like that."

"Then why did you break your promise?"

Fox sounds gutted and it stabs a knife into my stomach. I shudder at the way everything about him seems torn to shreds. He's carried the weight of this pain on his shoulders for ten years and it's killing him.

It makes me want to take all of his anger and grief and hurt. I'll bear the weight of it for him. I just want to take it away so he doesn't sound so utterly damaged by the world.

Reaching up, I cup his face. His cheek turns hard, a muscle jumping beneath my palm. But he doesn't pull away. I dig into the flare of hope that gives me.

"I'm so sorry. I didn't mean to." Determination fills me, giving me strength. I wait until he meets my gaze in the dim shadows. "My heart knows yours, Fox Michael Wilder. It always has.

I never ever forgot." I lower my voice. "Did yours forget me?"

"No. Never." It comes out on a broken growl.

"Then you have to know I wouldn't betray your trust to hurt you on purpose. I'm not your enemy. I'm sorry, Fox."

As soon as the words leave me, I wind my arms around his neck and hug him. He remains stiff for a long stretch of seconds. I close my eyes tight, hugging him harder.

Slowly, his muscular arms come around me until he's crushing me into his embrace. He buries his hands in my dress and holds me.

It's like he's not used to the touch anymore, as if he hasn't had a real hug for ten years when I last threw my arms around him for having my back or making me laugh. My heart squeezes when a barely there tremble shakes his broad frame.

A soft, rough noise leaves him, then he breaks away, putting distance between us. He scrubs a hand over his jaw while I lean back against the brick wall so my knees don't give out. I can feel the shift, the energy cleansed from the decaying thing that used to hang in the air like venom between us.

But when he speaks, low and gruff, my heart finally splinters.

"I won't mess with you anymore. That's done now, so you can go on to live your life." He pauses, tugging harshly on his messy dark hair. "But we can't get back what we had before."

NINETEEN
Fox

The undeniable sincerity in Maisy's apology caught me off guard and I still feel the echo of her hug hours later in the middle of the night. It's created a deep-seated yearning in me. A wish that I didn't pull away so soon, that I kept holding her and got to kiss her one more time.

All these years I thought she knew she lied and broke her promise, but she swears she didn't remember until the truth came out.

I trace my thumbnail over my lower lip as I stare at the laptop on my coffee table.

Can I really believe her? My heart riots against my rib cage, telling me I can't trust her so easily. She could turn around and stab me in the back again. It's not something I could survive a second time.

I tamp down those thoughts and squeeze the back of my neck. She couldn't fake that sincerity.

If I accept her apology...she could truly be my daisy again.

As soon as it crosses my mind, my chest caves and I lean back against the couch. Focusing on what I got from the waiter at the restaurant is impossible. I'm supposed to be using the duplicated ID badge to gain access to Nexus Lab from the inside to dig up dirt on Jacqueline. Every time I try, I circle back to Maisy, as inevitable as the shifting tides of the ocean I miss so much.

And her.

Because I still miss her.

"Pathetic bastard," I murmur to the industrial walls surrounding me.

Something did hit me hard earlier tonight while standing outside the restaurant. For the last ten years I've formed my vendetta around the entire Landry family. I punished Holden and Maisy as ruthlessly as I want to go after their parents. But as I had her chin grasped in my fingers and stared them down, everything sharpened with clarity.

The real problem has always been Richard and Jaqueline. Not my old friends.

I've been so stubborn and sure of my grudge against the entire family that I might have sabotaged my own efforts to bring them down. Instead of wasting my time with the schoolyard shit I came at Maisy with and the strings Colt helped me pull with Holden's college football draft, I should've been focusing all my attention on the two people who actually had a hand in this.

Hating Maisy for breaking her promise was the old pain of a kid broken by loss and torn away from the only friends I had.

I swallow past the lump in my throat and rub at the burning sensation in my chest.

Without being clouded by anger and anguish, I'm able to think back on the day I found the wild daisy for her and took her to the garage. I remember how much I wanted to learn to ride dad's Harley as fast as I could and imagined all the places I would drive Maisy. We had so many adventures planned, including the most important thing I promised her.

I'm going to marry you someday.

I swipe my fingers over my mouth and let the old love I felt for her crash with the love it's grown into in the background, behind every intensely passionate thought I've ever had toward her.

Hate. Love. Betrayal. Longing.

The secrets of this town tore into the path we were set on, but somehow it couldn't fully destroy how deeply connected I am to her. If I told her that, she'd probably have a name for it, like fate or destiny. My mouth curves into a lopsided smile as I picture scoffing and telling her fate was for fantasy stories.

Knowing now that she never meant to hurt me makes a sludge-like sense of guilt settle deep in my gut. I've been such an asshole to her. I hunted her for sport, like the psychotic bastard I've honed myself into, put my hands on her, and sabotaged her grades and social standing. I wanted her to hurt and I made it happen, driving her fear and tears when she's been resilient against my efforts to take her life apart. All because she's fucking brave and wanted nothing more than to earn my friendship back.

My throat works on an uncomfortable gulp. I don't like the feeling creeping through my veins as I consider all the horrible things I've done and said to her. It makes what I told her tonight ring more true—we can't get back what we had because I'm afraid to trust her, but also because I can't look at myself in the mirror for what I've done to her for the sake of revenge.

I rub my face and release a sigh, sagging deeper into the aged leather of my second-hand couch. I do want to accept her apology. It's lifted a solid weight off my shoulders and I finally feel like I can breathe easier without every breath being tinged with so much darkness.

But some part of me still hesitates. Once trust is broken, it's hard to heal it. Even if I want to erase it with her apology, the withered parts of my heart are wary, more comfortable behind thick walls of impenetrable stone to remain hardened. It's the only way to protect it from reliving the pain.

Instead, I need to do what I said I would—stay the fuck away from Maisy. She can go on with her life, and I'll keep living this half-formed existence, destined to spend my days missing the girl who makes my heart feel like it could beat without hurting. I'm no good for her.

Decision made, I turn my attention to the information on my laptop leading me to a shipping warehouse. I have work to do and it's time to stop hesitating. Jacqueline and Richard will pay for what they've done.

TWENTY
Maisy

HEALING a broken heart is impossible, but self-care keeps me going. I throw myself into my routine. That means plenty of yoga, face masks with the girls, and hanging out with the rest of our friends at Thea's apartment when I'm allowed out. Plus I spend time centering myself in nature when I can convince Holden to go on a hike. A nightly session with Sir Good Vibes helps to blow off steam and I totally don't picture calloused hands running over my skin. Absolutely not.

It all recharges me, but I'm still trying to find a way to breathe without Fox again.

He doesn't think we can even be friends. It's worse than the first time I lost him, because now I know why he couldn't even look at me when he first came back. This time he wasn't ripped away from me, he made the tear himself.

I haven't seen him in days. He never showed for finals and hasn't come to any of the graduation ceremony practices.

After what he said to me, I didn't bother looking through the medical journals Devlin dropped off a few days ago. They've been sitting by my rolled up yoga mat in the corner of my bedroom, mocking me. Instead of reading them myself, I want to give them to him, but first I'd have to pin the stubborn elusive jerk down to offer them to him.

As predicted, I caught a load of shit for running off from the restaurant and causing an unwanted scene for my parents the other night. Since Fox left me there alone, I called Holden to come pick me up. I've never seen Dad look so mad. He was livid, more angry than Mom, who regarded me with a cool and dispassionate look the minute I walked through the door. She didn't even bother berating me, like I expected, simply announced that the road trip was off the table again. I stood there grinding my teeth, quelling the desire to stand up to her as she informed me that if I didn't get my impulsive, childish urges under control then she'd send me to a private disciplinary school that specializes in rehabilitating troubled brats of the influential and wealthy instead of the college they made me apply to. The admissions paperwork was already completed. I wanted to call bullshit, but the threat in her empty gaze was very real. After she was satisfied with my stunned silence, she spun on her heel and went into her office.

Then Dad tore into me for putting myself in danger for a solid twenty minutes. He wouldn't hear any of my arguments in Fox's favor or that the most danger I was in was stubbing a toe in the dark. He's the one who decided I wouldn't be leaving the house except for school and my yoga classes, and that I couldn't go anywhere on my own. I'm not even allowed to do my volunteer shift at the library. Dad made me pick—yoga or reading to the kids, and as much as I love their little faces, I need yoga or I go crazy from bottling up my energy every day.

The reminder of their ability to control my life stung.

It could've been worse. They could've actually shipped me off to the mysterious disciplinary school. I'm at least glad that Holden is my new warden, escorting me everywhere now that his summer class is over for the summer. He told me he feels bad, so he's been far more lenient than my parents expect. If they had hired a bodyguard, like they threatened before, I definitely couldn't have pulled sibling sympathy for an easier time. My brother doesn't say anything when I spend half our time together with my nose glued to the map app on my phone, dropping points for where I want to go on my road trip.

I'm biding my time until the moment is right to make my move.

On the day of graduation, I'm one step closer to freedom. I just have to get through the ceremony, then I'm hitting the road. Mom can threaten me all she wants, but there's no way I'm letting her send me to a disciplinary school. The cage they've kept me in for so many years is becoming too much, suffocating the wings I need to spread. An itch crawls across my skin, growing worse by the day.

"Stop fidgeting and stand up straight," Mom hisses so no one else will hear her perfectionist nagging.

We're standing off to the side of the school on the path that splits to lead to the football field, surrounded by a sea of green and white graduation gowns that match the one I'm sweating in and the families of the graduating class.

It's my high school graduation and I feel...nothing.

Shouldn't I care more? I can't find any reason to. Thinking back on my last four years, I'm troubled by how little of my own interests I've explored. My senior year was a complete bust. The only bright spots are the times I spent with my friends when they were still here with me before they graduated, and the only memories worth reliving that give me a thrill are the times Fox was focused on me.

"The ceremony hasn't even started yet," Holden says. I shoot him a grateful smile and he winks. "Give her a break for five minutes, Ma."

"Like the break I've given you, Holden?" Mom says sharply. "It's been such an awfully long break."

He clenches his jaw at the reminder he's missed the mark on how high she expected him to jump by ending up at a public community college. A few people glance our way curiously and Mom's spine goes ramrod straight while she plasters on her CEO smile.

"We're so proud of you," Dad says.

Really, I want to ask skeptically, *even though I didn't make Valedictorian?* As if she can hear my thoughts, Mom's mouth pinches.

"Thanks, Dad."

"Well, at least you're graduating. We would have liked to see you earn the top spot in your class." She speaks out of the side of her mouth as she nudges me toward the group of students lining up by one of the teachers. "It's disappointing that you've deviated so much from what your goals were."

I couldn't hide my grades when she has a rule about keeping her updated with them, but I'm not even that annoyed anymore at Fox for messing with my class rank. It's just a grade, so what's the big deal? My life isn't over or ruined because I got an A minus instead of an A plus. It took a deep meditation session to come to that realization and once I did the weight lifted from my shoulders, leaving me lighter. I should thank him for making me face it.

"Valedictorian wasn't ever something I'd pick for myself anyway," I mutter.

Mom flashes a severe look that warns me to back up. *They're all your goals*, I want to snap, but I drag in a measured breath and let it the fuck go. *Just make it through the ceremony*, I remind myself. Then I can finally get a break from their dog and pony show.

"We'll meet you after, sweetheart," Dad says. "We'll be cheering for you."

They leave with Holden to find seats with the rest of the families heading for the football stands.

Fox still isn't here. My brows draw together and my heart gives a pained little pinch. I don't know if his number of absences this year disqualified him from being able to walk in the graduation ceremony, but I was hoping to see him.

I'm still hurt that he could give up so easily on friendship, or the fiery thing building between us. When I'm around him, he makes me feel safe, despite being a stubborn asshole. He's always seen my wild side without telling me to tone it down. He's the only person who makes me feel alive and I want him in my life, no matter what that looks like. After the initial despair from my shattered heart dulled, a new grief formed a pit in my stomach.

My fingertips find the old braided leather and smooth stones of my bracelet.

Fox shouldn't have to do what he's doing alone. I want to help. If I can do that, maybe it will be enough to make amends for breaking my promise. Even if I was just a kid, it's been eating at me that I had any part in hurting his family or him.

My thoughts continue to drift as I follow the rest of my classmates into the school to line up like we did yesterday in practice. Glancing at the rows of lockers and classrooms as we're led through the hallways, sadness trickles through me. My parents might be proud, but can I say the same thing?

High school should be a time where I started to learn who I could be. I should've been making memories and discovering my own voice. It's the chance to start to explore independence and shape my values and goals in life. But I didn't get to do any of that.

A boy bumps into me that I don't even know and it only makes me regret that we never got the chance to be friends. I frown and mumble an apology that he waves off, picking up his animated conversation with his buddies.

If I could do it all over again, without all the rules and pressure to perform in the precise way my parents wanted, what would I have picked for myself?

As soon as I think about it, I'm hit with a realization that almost brings me to my knees. Air rushes past my lips and I clutch the polyester gown hanging off my shoulders. Someone gives me a funny look, but I barely register it.

Mom and Dad haven't just controlled me for years to make sure I follow a life plan they set out for me—I let them. I helped them by not fighting back hard enough. I gave in and went along, strangling my impulsive urges and curtailing every whim I've ever had.

Whims are for children and you're a grown woman now.

Mom's favorite criticism fills my head. Funny how I could be a grown woman but also still be treated like a kid by my parents. Whatever manipulation they had to pull to keep me in line, doing what they thought was best for me—what made them look good—was fair game to them.

How many times have I cut away pieces of myself in order to do what I've been told so I'd be seen as this perfect goody-goody?

Big parts and small, ones that didn't seem noticeable and ones that hurt to shave away from who I really am. Everything from not dying my hair a fun color to only picking classes they wanted me to take, instead of choir and women's history and a rock climbing elective introduced last year—because anything I wanted wasn't as important as maintaining the path they wanted me on. I did it to keep the peace, in the hope I'd one day be granted the reward to take control of my own life. I did it because deep down, I didn't want to disappoint them if my good behavior was the only reason they paid attention to me.

Because I was afraid.

I put myself in my cage as much as my parents did. That needs to end.

My throat closes as I glance through the open doors to the stands where families are seated, trying to search for my parents and my brother.

The ceremony is about to start. My fellow graduating classmates stand with me in line, waiting to be led out onto the football field on a bright, sunny summer day.

I'm supposed to be here. Expected to. But this is not where I want to be right now.

Time to stop pretending to be the good girl. That was never me.

"Where are you going? We're about to start," Jenna Taylor says when I step out of line.

I glance over my shoulder at her. This is the first time she's ever spoken to me directly. She's the mayor's daughter, the one that threw the party Fox was at two months ago. It feels like a million years ago now. I was so jealous when he took her upstairs. The emotion swept through me like an angry tide, overtaking me to the point I just couldn't stand by and take his crap anymore because that wasn't who I was. I guess I should thank this girl for pushing me to find my backbone.

"I have to go to the bathroom," I lie. "Be right back."

She pulls a face. "Don't you care if you miss the beginning? This is like, your thing."

"What is?"

"School. Smart nice girl shit? I don't know, you've always seemed like a huge priss since you never partied all four years here and only focused on school."

I lift a brow. "Assume much?" Hitching a shoulder, I gaze past her at the other students in line. Most of them don't know the real me and never bothered to look beyond my reputation or the rumors. "If you'd ever taken the time to talk to me, you'd know that isn't me at all." Her brows jump up and an embarrassed blush creeps across her cheeks. I wave a hand. "I'm pretty glad this is all over. I don't actually care about any of this, or missing the beginning."

Or missing the entire pointless thing, I think as I leave to sneak off campus.

As much as I want to smash out of my imaginary cage and take what I want—hitchhiking if I have to—there's something more important I have to do first. *Someone* more important.

Once I make it around the corner to the side hall that leads to a terrace, I fish out my phone and text my brother. He drove separately from me and our parents, so he's my only hope of getting out of here in a hurry.

Maisy: Meet me at the courtyard by the north building.
Holden: Uh, that's not the football field. Why, what are you doing? Are you okay?
Maisy: I'll tell you when you get here. Hurry!
Holden: Fine, on my way.

I blow out a relieved breath and lean against an Aspen tree. It doesn't take Holden long to arrive. I ignore his confused expression and rush over to him.

"Holy shit, are you okay?" he blurts as I grab his arms. He cups my elbows to balance me. "Isn't the ceremony about to start?"

"Yes, fine," I say in a hurry. "Forget about the ceremony and give me your keys."

His grip on my elbows tightens. "Why?"

I hang my head back and swallow my annoyance. I don't have time to explain this, but he's never going to help me if I don't give him something.

"There's no requirement that says I have to walk in the ceremony. I'd rather go hang out at Thea's bakery instead of go through all the stuffy traditions."

Holden gives me a flat expression. "Right," he drawls. "Except, I totally recognize the look on your face. Cough up what you're not telling me, or I'm not giving you shit."

I sigh. "Holden."

"Nah-uh. Give me the real reason you want to ditch."

Damn it. Fine. "I'm going to see Fox."

His gaze hardens. "Seriously? I don't think that's a good idea. After he's been treating you like crap, you just forgive him? You should listen to Dad and just stay away from him."

"Well, I can't." Staying away from Fox was never in the cards for me. The desperation flooding my voice makes him pause. "Just—Can't you trust me that I know what I'm doing? He needs my help and I'm going to give it to him."

Holden lets go of my elbows and steps back, scratching his chin. "I still don't want to let you go." He holds up his hands when I open my mouth. "God, you're annoying when you get your head stuck on something. Are you sure? Mom and Dad will be pissed and you're already skating on ice so thin it's cracking. I think they're serious about that disciplinary school."

"I know. But I'm sure." I offer him a half-smile and hold out my hand for the keys. "It's time I stop letting what's expected of me dictate my life. It's making me miserable and I'm done with feeling like crap to make everyone else happy."

Conflicted emotions flit across Holden's face, but after a few moments he nods. "Okay. I don't want to, but I hate seeing how unhappy you've been this year. Just be careful around that guy."

"He's not a threat to me. He never really was." My throat burns as I think about those case files again for the accident and what I've learned from Fox. "I'm going to fix what broke between us."

And help him prove his parents were murdered.

Holden drops the keys to his Audi in my hand and the taste of freedom bursts on my tongue. For a second, I wish I could just *go* and never stop, but I fight back the familiar urge. First, I have to find Fox and help him. My road trip escape will have to wait indefinitely until then.

"Maise," he calls out as I turn to go, already tugging off the polyester graduation gown over my dress. When I look back, his brows dip and he scrubs a hand through his light brown hair. "I'm sorry I've been a shitty brother."

"You haven't been. You've just been dealing with your own stuff."

"Still." His shoulders sag with his sigh. "I could've pulled my head out of my ass for five minutes to see how hard this year has been for you, too. Or how all your smiles are fake. I've been a selfish bastard, but that stops now."

I swallow past the lump in my throat. So someone did notice, he was just too torn up about his own problems and crushed dreams to let me in for some solidarity. "It's fine. We'll talk later. I've got to go."

"I'll cover for you with Mom and Dad."

"Thanks, Holden."

TWENTY-ONE
Maisy

SKIPPING out on my high school graduation ceremony to search for Fox—and most definitely pissing my parents off in the process if Holden can't make up a good excuse for why I'm not there to receive my diploma—is all good in theory.

In practice?

I have no idea how I'll find him. It's hard enough to trail him whether he knows he's being followed or not—he's good at covering his tracks. If I hadn't stowed away in his Charger, I never would have gotten the slip on him. My fingers tap out a random beat on the steering wheel of Holden's car as I drive aimlessly for a few minutes through the rolling hills on the winding road at the base of the mountains.

You can figure this out. Think. Where would he go to look for the pieces of the puzzle he needs to prove his parents were murdered?

Nexus Lab. It's the best I can start with for now, considering what Fox showed me in his garage when we were kids.

On my way to the pharmaceutical company where Mom now holds the highest position of power, my phone dings with a text notification. The bluetooth connection shows it's from an unknown number on the console screen in the dashboard. My brow furrows. Maybe it's the fact I know Fox is trying to prove his family was murdered, or maybe it's the adrenaline rush still buzzing from making a decision for myself to leave my graduation ceremony, but a random text from an unknown number has my stomach rippling with suspicion.

Once I reach a red light, I snag my phone from the cup holder and check it.

Unknown: 1207 Rolling Rock Drive, Ridgeview, Colorado 80304

"Huh."

The address isn't for Nexus Lab. It's the opposite direction, on the other side of town near the shipping district full of warehouses and not much else. Is this Fox's number? It has to be. I suck in a breath, the horrible thought crossing my mind that he could be in trouble and this is his way of asking for my help.

As I input the address to the GPS feature on Holden's car, a fierce determination settles in my shoulders. *I'm coming, Fox.*

The first thing I notice when I arrive is that I don't see his Charger or his motorcycle. But an SUV that looks just like the one that tailed us the day Fox met with Lana is here, along with a whole matching fleet.

I hope Fox is the one who found them instead of the other way around since they didn't seem all that open to a friendly chat when they tried to run us off the road. But I have no clue how he managed to locate these guys when I didn't see any identifiable plates in the chase. I pull the car into an open spot and look down at the outfit I'm wearing—another one of Mom's designer picks, paired with my lowkey rebellious disregard for wearing underwear or a bra.

"Just gonna roll with it and hope for the best," I mutter as I leave the car.

The warehouse is isolated on a no outlet lane with no others nearby. I don't come to this part of town often, but I follow the row of SUVs around the corner. An eighteen wheeler is backed up to an open bay door and I catch sight of Fox. My steps falter as I head for him and the man with a clipboard he's talking to.

Always aware of everything, he spots me before I even reach them and his eyes tighten at the corners. Hot and cold tingles run across my skin and I suppress a shudder from the intensity in his gaze.

He's not wearing his usual leather jacket, ripped black jeans, or the heavy combat boots. Instead, he's dressed in a sharp suit and it's actually pretty distracting because he looks hot. Warmth pools low in my stomach, and I can't decide if I prefer him rugged and rough, or clean cut with the sinful edge lurking beneath his hard blue eyes.

I glance between him and the warehouse employee, plastering on my brightest smile. The older guy seems wary of me despite my nice dress, studying me with a small frown as I stick my hand out. This isn't my world at all, but I'm not letting that stop me from getting sucked in if it's part of helping prove the Wilders were murdered.

"Hey! I'm M—"

Fox sucks in a breath and takes a small step forward. It's a subtle move, but I catch it and correct myself.

"Millie. Intern," I add when I spy the Nexus Lab ID badge clipped to his jacket. The guy with the clipboard raises a brow. I gesture toward Fox with my thumb. "Sorry I'm late. They keep sending me for coffee runs when I'm supposed to be assigned to his side to learn about the department."

Fox relaxes slightly, but is still wound tight. "Right. I forgot to mention her when I called to arrange our meeting." He pauses and shoots me an assessing glance that seems to go straight to my soul. "She's new to all this."

I almost laugh, but stop myself, keeping my friendly smile in place as I sink into the role of eager intern. The clipboard guy shakes my hand, then strokes the trimmed stubble growing around his mouth.

"You were saying," he prompts.

"The higher ups are looking to double check and tighten communication between departments," Fox says. "I'm here to audit that and confirm the shipments through each distribution network."

While they talk, I let half of my attention drift around the warehouse. There's not much to see. Only a few employees mill around packing boxes and transporting them on forklifts into the truck waiting at the bay door. The logo for Nexus Lab is all over the place and I realize this is a shipping warehouse for the company's manufactured product. This is the first time I've ever been to one of the other sites of the company. Usually I only go right to Mom's corner office at the sleek building nestled at the base of the mountains, but something nags at me as I take everything in.

The quantities are off from what I would expect. Most of the boxes carry the same label for a synthetic opioid rather than a variety. The company is supposed to be one of the top pharmaceutical manufacturers in the country, so why would they be making such large amounts of the same thing? And if this is the shipping department, shouldn't there be more here than the sparse equipment and a handful of employees? It's all weird.

"This hasn't been an issue before," the older guy says. "As far as I know, the company likes it this way."

I glance between the skeleton shipping crew and the number of boxes full of synthetic drugs being piled into the truck. There's no way there's such a high demand for only one drug when they're meant to be making all kinds of things.

Fox holds up his hands with a crooked smile that makes my knees go weak. "Don't shoot the messenger. I'm just doing my job, same as you, man."

"Right. Okay, come this way."

He takes us through the procedure they follow at the warehouse and shows Fox his clipboard so we can match it to what Fox has in a list on his phone. A large portion of the shipment is heading for the same two places—an address on the west coast and one in the northeast. That doesn't seem right. I wish I knew more about Mom's company to know if there are medical companies in those locations that would order such a large amount of the same drug.

"So, as you can see," the manager says, slapping his clipboard. "All in order."

"Right," Fox agrees. "Thanks for your cooperation."

He nudges the small of my back and we head for the bay door. The manager stops us before we make it out.

"What department did you say this was for again? I'll need to write it in the log. Protocol and all, you know how they are."

Fox barely reacts, but I go rigid, thinking we're caught. He calmly offers his ID badge for the guy to copy the information to his clipboard. Whatever is on it, the manager is appeased and sends us on our way.

"Thanks for your cooperation," Fox says.

My thoughts race as I try to work out the puzzle in front of me. What is Nexus Lab really up to? Isn't it illegal to flood the market with this much of one drug? There are regulations for what they're allowed to produce, I'm sure of it.

If this massive supply is making it to the legitimate market at all, that is. I don't like the thought as soon as it crosses my mind.

Fox grabs my elbow and leads me outside, his grip hard and unyielding. He doesn't slow his long strides and half-drags, half-carries me out the door and around the corner behind a pile of shipping palettes.

"What the hell are you doing here?" he demands through clenched teeth, dropping the cool and collected act.

"I came to help. The address sent to my phone... I was already skipping the grad ceremony to find you, but I thought it meant you needed me."

"Needed you?" Fox drags his fingers through his hair and jabs his finger back toward the building. "You almost blew my cover."

I cross my arms and frown, eyeing him up and down. "Which looks flimsy at best." I flick his badge. "This doesn't look fake or anything, even if it passed for a legit one. How did you get this anyway?"

He grumbles something under his breath and pinches the bridge of his nose, ignoring my question. "How the fuck did you even get here?"

"The address sent to my phone, I told you." I show him the text. "You haven't given me your number, but when you sent it I knew it was you."

"You thought—" He breaks off with a curse, pulling a face as he glares over my shoulder. "I'm going to kill Colt for bringing you here. I told him to stop surveillance tracking," he mutters. I have no idea what or who he's talking about. Turning his attention back to me, he shakes his head. "I didn't send for you, Maisy. You can't help."

"Like hell I can't. I want to."

Standing my ground, I silently dare him to tell me what I can and can't do. I've had enough of playing by the rules and doing what's expected of me.

Fox blows out a breath, treating me to the same once over I gave him. Except his eyes drag much slower over my body, lingering at my chest for a beat before lifting to meet my gaze again. His head jerks with the force of his snort.

"Always so fucking stubborn."

Somehow he makes it sound like it's a trait that gets under his skin and makes him fond of me at the same time.

"You shouldn't be here." He rubs his mouth. "I can't let you get involved in this."

"You can't do all this on your own," I reason. "I know you said we can't be friends, but I want to help. Two heads will be better than one."

It sounds like he mutters that he already has an additional head, but he continues pinning me with his stare, working his jaw as he considers my offer. I have to sweeten it so he sees how much I need this as much as he does.

"With me, you get more access. I have the incident report from the night your parents..." I trail off, not wanting to say it. An ache of sorrow moves through me for the little sister he never got to meet. Licking my lips, I go on. "Look, helping you is the only way I can think to make up for my broken promise. Will you let me?"

The shadows in his eyes kill me. As soon as the impulse grips me, I take a step, bringing our bodies close together. I touch his chiseled jaw lightly and press up on my toes to kiss him.

Fox allows it, releasing a low rumble as my lips slide against his. He doesn't let me in, so I start to pull away, but then he grips my waist and unleashes his storm on me. My heart sings when my back hits the wall of the warehouse as he claims my mouth with a deep kiss that sweeps me up in its possessive force.

This time when I pull back, lips swollen and tender, the shadows have cleared.

We gaze at each other and his thumb moves back and forth at my waist. With a sigh, he rests his forehead against mine. "There's so much you don't know still."

"So tell me. Don't push me away again. Let me in."

Fox's throat works with a swallow. "You want to help so bad? Fine," he murmurs in resignation. "Just remember—you asked for this."

TWENTY-TWO
Fox

Continuing my search for the truth with Maisy at my side wasn't the plan, but she does everything her way. I almost laugh because I should've known better than to try to control her free-spirited nature. Maisy is only controlled by her wild heart.

After leaving the warehouse, I led her to a place to stash her brother's car. As soon as she slid into the passenger seat of the Charger, my grip tightened on the wheel as my mind jumped back to the last time she was in my car. We drive to the diner near the interstate where I want to stake out a meeting Colt intercepted the details of.

The whole ride over, she had the window down with her arm hanging out to ride the waves of the warm air with her hand. More than once my attention snagged on the old leather bracelet she wears, the one with stones I gave her. She still never takes it off.

"I've never been on a stakeout before," Maisy says after we've been parked for twenty minutes. She digs through the glove compartment. "We should've stopped for some snacks."

I run my tongue over my teeth. "Stakeouts usually require quiet and concentration." I gesture with the hand resting on the wheel to the target. "So keep those pretty lips shut before I find a way to make you be quiet."

Maisy shoots me a look full of heat at my threat and I bite back a groan. God, this is torture after so many days away from her. The faint scent of sweet coconut on her skin is killing me.

"All right, grumpy." With an impatient huff, she falls back against the seat and props one leg up against the door to get more comfortable. "You don't have to be so bossy."

"You don't have to help," I remind her, trying to find something to distract myself from admiring the length of her toned legs as the hem of her dress lifts higher from her position. "You're only here because I'm allowing it."

Letting her in is probably my worst idea ever.

After what she said at the warehouse, I considered that I'd been going about this wrong by pushing her away. She should learn the truth about her parents. Besides, by keeping her close I can keep an eye on her. She'll either be an asset I can use against her parents, or if she picks them over me I'll be aware of it before she betrays me again.

My gaze drifts to her for the third time in five minutes instead of where my focus needs to be and I bite down on the inside of my cheek. If she slouches anymore, I'll be able to see right up her dress. A bolt of heat shoots to my dick. Damn little temptress...

Maisy draws me in with this crazy force made of the fabric of the universe. I drag my teeth over my lower lip and give her a subtle once over, wondering if her habit of forgoing underwear leaves her pussy bare beneath that dress. The last time I had her in my car, I couldn't stop the fantasies from coming and they're back in force now as the arousal builds, clouding my head with a hunger for her to ride my cock until she screams for me.

This time the want is even more intense, now that she's forced her way back into my life, demanding to help after I kept her at a distance. She won't let me go and it does things to my heart that make it twist around on itself and thump hard.

Blowing out a breath, I rest my hand on the gearshift between us and barely brush my fingers against her smooth thigh while fighting off the desire to drag her across the center console into my lap where I could kiss her.

After a couple of minutes, she adjusts in her seat, bringing her closer to me as she scans the area we're staking out. "So what are we on the lookout for?"

"I had a tip off for a meeting going down here today. I don't know who with, so I'm prepared for anything. Whoever it is, I'll document it."

"Cool. Got it."

I consider how dangerous it is to poke the sleeping bear while I hunt for the truth, but she would only prove to me once again that I have zero chances of keeping her out of this anymore.

"When the meeting goes down, I want you to make sure you duck out of sight. You understand?"

She peers up at me. "Why?"

"You know why," I mutter, clenching my fists. She lifts her brows questioningly and I sigh. "To keep your face hidden. That will protect you if we're spotted. I'm less recognizable in this suit, but I'm not taking a chance that anyone will recognize you and connect your face to your parents."

"Okay." She stares at me and reaches over to put her hand on my leg. "We're doing this together. You and me, the way it always should be."

I look at her from the corner of my eye, resting my elbow against the window while tracing my lip with my thumb. "Yeah."

A bone-deep truth settles in me. I never should've blamed Maisy. We were just kids back then. The breath I release feels like it yanks away the last dredges of my years-long grudge, leaving me lighter and less shrouded in so much pain.

The car goes quiet again as we settle in to wait. I pass the minutes by running through everything I've learned so far in my head. The accident was covered up and Richard Landry helped with his new position as police chief. Jacqueline Landry becomes CEO mere weeks later. Both of them became richer and Nexus Lab grew from a small regional lab to one of the nation's top suppliers in the last decade.

Maisy's breathing slows as her head droops, hitting my shoulder after a few minutes. She's asleep. I still for a moment, then adjust my position to support her head better. She'll complain if she gets a stiff neck from falling asleep that way. Her floral and coconut scent wraps around me the same as her hug did the other night, making my lips twitch with the urge to smile.

This time instead of being a distraction, I find myself centered like she's a guiding light. I watch her sleep for a minute, then shift my attention to wait out the meeting.

For a while there's no activity, then two cars pull up. I shift around carefully without dislodging Maisy from my shoulder. Surprise lances through me. The first man, I don't recognize. He's a big, mean looking guy with a barrel chest and buzzed hair in a cheap suit. The other is Richard Landry.

Shouldn't he be with Maisy's family? I check the time and guess the graduation ceremony ended.

Richard is agitated, hands jerking sharply as he talks to the man he's meeting with. There's a quick exchange of something when they step closer together. Money, probably. And I caught him in the act of accepting a bribe.

Using my phone, I discreetly record everything. Colt will get the footage and analyze it on his system for me. Instead of leaving as soon as the coast is clear, I wait, allowing myself to watch her again. Her lips part and I want to trace them. Unable to help myself, I caress her cheek, careful not to wake her.

"Mm, sorry," Maisy says in a husky whisper as she stirs not long after. "I didn't mean to fall asleep."

"It's fine. I got what I needed while you were out."

"Did you?" She sits up, taking her warmth and comfortable weight with her. I have to restrain myself from drawing her head back to my shoulder. Her expression twists into an adorable pout. "Man, I didn't want to miss it. This totally ruins the badass cred I'm working on. I've got undercover work down, but choked on the stakeout."

I snort. "Yeah, you're definitely ready to take on corruption with those skills."

Colton would get a kick out of her. For the first time ever, I picture what it would be like to introduce my foster brother to my daisy. It puts a smile on my face as I start the engine and pull onto the road. Maisy's hand goes out the window again, coasting on the air as I pick up speed and race around the winding road.

More than once, my attention darts to her. She seems content with her hand in the wind and her hair. It's times like this I see the girl who held my heart in her small hands when we were kids.

"Do you remember California? When we went on vacation?" she asks after a short stretch of peaceful quiet. I hum in response, flashing her a curious look. Her attention is on her hand, expression distant and tinged in sadness. "That was such a good trip. I still have the shells and rocks we collected. Remember when I turned the stones you picked out for me into this?" She holds up her wrist with the leather bracelet. "I miss the ocean."

A pang hits my tattooed chest with the same ache I've felt. "I do, too."

"You do?" There's a catch in her voice that lights a fire inside me.

Licking my lips when I feel her gaze on me, I rest my hand over the top of the wheel and willingly open up to someone for the first time in years.

"When I lived in Thorne Point on the east coast, there was a cove I would go to when I couldn't sleep. I stole my foster brother's car to get to it, and he caught me." I laugh at the memory of Colt squinting at me and calling me a punk-ass little twerp. "He let me borrow it anytime I wanted after he saw the haunted look in my eyes."

"Nightmares?"

"Yeah. They come and go, usually around the anniversary, but going to that cove helped. I miss the salt air on my skin. So much so, I tattooed it there."

Maisy leans toward me. "Exactly! I've been planning this road trip. I want to hit up as many national parks as I can between here and the west coast. I'm going to do sunrise yoga in each one and really connect myself to nature."

As she explains, I'm struck by nostalgia, remembering how many hours we'd spend pouring over roadmaps and making plans for the adventures we would go on. It was me and her, ready to take on the world. All of our dreams used to intertwine until we didn't know where hers stopped and mine began. We were so close.

I find myself smiling. "You're finally taking it. I remember how important it was to you."

"Yeah." She bites her lip around a smile, hazel eyes bright. "Not yet, though. First I'm helping you, then I'm hitting the road."

When the impulse strikes to punch the gas, I follow it, shifting gears and opening up the engine. Maisy yelps as her back hits the seat, then throws her hands up. It's clear to see what the thrill does to her as it rolls through her whole body, as alive as she is. She smacks the roof overhead and lets out a whoop while I take a bend.

We drive like that until we hit the shorter roads that twist around the boulders dotting the hills.

"Will you give me a ride on your dad's bike again? I loved it."

Air catches in my throat. "You knew it was his? Not just the same model Harley, but *his*?"

"Yeah. I'd recognize it anywhere. You used to idolize it." Her eager smile softens. "I'm glad you have it."

"It was hard to track down."

There's a beat of quiet where we're both in our heads.

"I'm sorry you were alone for so long. I wish you never had to leave here." She pulls her hair out of her face and glances at her lap. "I missed you every day."

"I wasn't always alone," I admit, throat constricted from the pain in her tone. "For a long time, it felt like all I had was me." My life has gone so wrong, but not every second of it was bad. "The foster system wasn't good to me, it was like my past followed me like a bad smell." My grip flexes on the wheel. "Most of the families were afraid of me."

"Why?"

"I was so angry all the time. I fought anyone I could." I clench my teeth, then relax when she reaches out to take my hand. "It wasn't until I was fifteen that the DuPonts took me in after I'd been bounced around so much. Then things finally started turning around."

"They were good to you?"

"Yeah. Kind of socialite snobs, but they had an older son. Eventually I found he was in my corner, and with him, there were others."

"I'm in your corner," Maisy says mildly, squeezing my hand.

I grip her small hand in mine. "I know that now. Colton, my foster brother, had friends. They brought me into their circle and treated me like family. Honestly, after so many years of what I went through, I was against it at first. In the system you learn fast that nothing belongs to you and no one really wants you."

Her fingers tighten around mine. "Fox..."

My shoulder lifts in a shrug. "That's the system. These guys, though, they cracked through my *fuck you* shell before I realized that they'd accepted me as one of them."

"Are they who you were with at the holiday market last year?"

I blink. "What?"

Last year Wren, Colton, Levi, and Jude had rolled into town out of the blue around the holidays. I thought the Crows had come for me, but Wren said it was strictly business and I understood the lethal hardness to his eyes. His sister. He'd been on the crusade since she died, searching for her fucked up teacher that preyed on her not long after I started living with the DuPonts. We met up briefly at the local holiday market downtown, but I only saw them for a few minutes before they left in a rush when they finally found the bastard.

"Yeah. How did you know?"

"I was there with my friend Thea." A complicated expression contorts her beautiful features. "That day was pretty crazy, but before that I was looking for her and saw you with those guys. It was the first time I'd seen you smile genuinely since the last time I saw you, before..."

She doesn't have to finish, I catch her meaning. I haven't smiled much since returning to Ridgeview. It seems I only do when it has to do with her.

Curiosity brims in her gaze as she studies me. I can sense her hunger to learn more about what my life has been like in the time we've been apart. When the connection between people is as deep as ours was, there's this sense of possessiveness that's hard to kick. I know I've felt it around her, too.

It's not until we're almost at my warehouse that I realize I wasn't on guard with her, driving on autopilot. That more than anything else tells me I'm ready to trust her again, when I rarely let anyone in. The patched up wall around my heart finally crumbles.

"I want to show you something."

"Okay."

I take the turn off for my place. She's the first person in town I've brought here. Once I pull in and park the Charger in the garage, she gets out.

Vulnerability burns in me as I follow her around my workspace while she takes in my abstract pieces.

"This is where you live."

"Yes."

She brushes her fingers over the bike and glances at me. "I'm serious about that ride."

Some of the vulnerability bleeds away and I smirk, dragging my gaze over her body. "As long as you promise not to get the leather dirty, little daisy."

A flush colors her cheeks and she finds the steps leading to the studio apartment. I follow her up, sinking my teeth into my lip as her ass sways.

"Love what you've done with the place. Big Batcave vibes," Maisy says with a crooked grin. "Down to the workout corner."

I chuckle, glancing around to try to see what she sees with her fresh eyes. "It serves its purpose."

She hums and explores, examining the coffee table and skating her hand over the back of the couch. While she looks around, I take off the suit jacket and toss it on the arm of the couch and pull the tie loose. Her gaze tracks my movements, lingering on the flex of my arms. The corner of my mouth lifts and I slow down.

It's so clear now, with her fitting right into my space as if she's always belonged here. I never should've blamed her. Anger blinded me and festered in my heart until it was an unruly beast. It's still there, but she tempers it with the way she balances me. The hope that I haven't fucked myself over by hurting her arrows through me.

I want to make this right. I have to.

Reaching for her hand, I sit her down on the couch and park my ass on the sturdy coffee table I made with my own two hands. My knees bracket hers. "There's something I need to say."

The apology doesn't come easily. I prefer actions over pretty words, but for her I try to get it out.

"I'm...sorry. For being an asshole to you, for hurting you, and all the times I tried to scare you." Her brow creases, but she doesn't pull away, giving me the strength to go on. "I see how wrong I was now. I never should've put the blame on you." I meet her gaze and swallow at how much could be showing in my eyes, not hiding from her anymore. "If you can forgive me, I want to do better. I want to trust you. All the rage and grief and pain blinded me for so long—years. I couldn't believe you were as good as you seemed when I came back when I formed this picture in my head, but you are. You've shown me time and again that you're still as good-hearted and kind and real as when we were kids."

"Fox," she whispers, stroking my knuckles with her thumb. "It's okay. It's behind us now, right?" I nod and she smirks. "Good. Because I'll kick your ass if you try to push me away or treat me like crap again." She holds up her fists at the ready. "Use the momentum from my core, right?"

Lips twitching, I scrub my face. "I'm sorry I wanted to destroy you. It's all I've been planning for years—you and your parents and Holden. All I could see was that my parents were dead and your family had this great life. I wanted it to hurt as badly as I did, but I…I couldn't do it." I clear my throat. "When it comes down to it, I can't truly hurt you. I would rather protect you or die, because I…"

My words dry up. Good thing, too, because I was likely to let it slip that I'm still in love with her. Always have been. As much as I want to rush and take everything I want with her, I know I can't scare her off. This is my one chance to keep her and I'm not giving it up.

When Ridgeview is in ashes, it'll be Maisy at my side.

"We're a mess, huh?" She gives me a soft smile. "I'd rather have you in my life than go back to living another day without you, no matter what it means to keep you."

A rough sound escapes me because I feel the same way. My heart never stopped belonging to her.

Maisy leans forward, winding her arms around my neck as her lips find mine. She tastes sweet when my tongue pushes into her mouth. My fingers bury in her hair and I yank her forward so she has to straddle me. Fuck, how did I ever think I could live without this perfect girl?

I groan when I slide a hand up her dress to push it up so it's out of the way and find out I was right about her naughty secret. No panties stop me as I palm her ass. She moans into the kiss, grinding down on my cock as she tugs on my hair. I haul her closer and nip at her lip, growling when she gets me back by digging her nails into the nape of my neck. My girl is wild and untamed and my dick is so fucking hard for her.

Leaning back, she licks her lips. "There's something I want."

"Yeah?" I trace her lips with my thumb and curse under my breath when she takes the tip into her mouth.

She nods and speaks against the pad of my thumb. "I want you to fuck my mouth. Like you promised before. I want you to take control of me."

"Shit." It tears out of me and my grip on her ass flexes. I didn't promise, I threatened. "You want me to stuff your mouth with my cock, baby?"

Instead of answering, she takes my hand and swallows two of my fingers, keeping her eyes locked with mine. Heat rockets through me and in one motion I stand, bringing her with me. Glancing around the room, I spot a towel on the floor by the bench press. It'll have to do. I want her on her knees, but I don't want the concrete to hurt her while she takes me down her throat.

Carrying her to the corner of the room, I let go so she slides down my body in the most sinful, sensual glide. There's a damp spot from how wet her pussy is on the front of my suit pants and I drop a hand to rub my erection, grinning with a feral edge. Maisy steals another kiss and grabs the towel, folding it a couple of times and dropping it on the ground. She follows, gazing up at me from the floor.

Holy. Fuck. That is a beautiful sight.

"Fuck my face, Fox."

I hiss, pausing in unbuckling my belt to grip myself. If she's not careful, she could send me over the edge before we get anywhere. I never let other girls in, because they weren't her, and now that I get to touch her again it's got me worked up as hell. She reaches up to help.

Gripping her hair, I tilt her head back as I glide my cock across her lips. She grins up at me with this wicked look that makes my hand flex in her hair. Without warning, I force my way into her mouth and she accommodates me, opening wide to take me. My head tips back, but I keep my gaze on her, testing her limits with a few shallows thrusts. It feels so goddamn good, the perfect amount of heat and suction.

She curls her tongue around me and bobs her head in time with my thrusts. I let her lead for a minute, fascinated and turned on by the sight of her perfect lips wrapped around my cock. My fantasies have nothing on the real deal.

A sharp pinch at my hip makes me blink. She lifts her brows as if to say *are you going to do it?*

Grinning, I tighten my hold on her hair. "Open wide, daisy."

Warmth floods her gaze as I take my first sharp thrust. She likes this. The rough treatment, the way I take control—it gets her hot.

"Bet that pussy is fucking drenched for me, isn't it?" She nods as best she can while I control the pace. A savage need overtakes me. "Show me, baby. Stroke that pretty pussy and show me how wet you are for me."

Maisy's pupils dilate and her hand flies between her legs, diving beneath her rumpled dress. Her lashes flutter at the first touch and she spends a little too long fingering herself. I yank on her hair to get her attention and punish her by going deeper, hitting the back of her throat. She chokes and sucks in a breath when she can, adjusting to the new depth.

"Show me," I growl.

Tears cling to her lashes as she lifts her fingers to show me. They're glistening, her hand covered. With a rumble vibrating in my chest, I capture her wrist in my free hand and bend down to suck her taste into my mouth. Next time we do this, she's going to suck my cock while I make her sit on my face and I won't stop eating her until she's a sobbing mess for me.

I release her wrist and speed up my thrusts to the point she has to concentrate on when to suck in air before she passes out. Her hand goes back to rubbing her clit and her thighs shake. Pleasure races down my spine and my balls draw tight. I'm close.

Maisy moans, tears leaking from the corners of her eyes, one hand gripping my leg for balance and the other buried between her thighs as she takes her own pleasure. My thrusts pick up and I gasp for air as I drive my cock into her mouth. It's too much. Fuck, it's *too much*, and I release a loud groan as my orgasm hits.

Her nails dig into my thigh and she swallows my come, throat working as she meets my gaze with hazy pleasure burning in her gorgeous hazel eyes. The flush in her cheeks darkens and she bucks her hips, crying out around my cock as she comes.

It takes us a minute to come back to ourselves. When we do, I scoop her up from the floor and kiss her, holding her against my body.

I never want to let her go. Even if it meant never getting the justice I've been seeking, I'd live in this moment for eternity if I could.

She pulls back with a dazed smile while I tuck my dick away and pull the suit pants up. As she's wiping the corners of her mouth and catching her breath, her phone goes off on the table. She grabs it and her eyes go wide. "Shit. Can you give me a ride back to Holden's car? He just warned me that his distraction didn't work out so well."

I want to say no. I need to taste her. Strip her down and lay claim to every other inch of her—spend hours rediscovering my daisy. But I nod.

Smirking, I strip out of the suit pants she stained and grab a pair of jeans from by the bed across the room. "Let's take the bike."

Maisy's hazel eyes light up and it calls to a deep part of my heart to bring that side out of her.

TWENTY-THREE
Maisy

There was no sense of dread when I returned home, like I've already burst from my metaphoric cage and allowed my wings to fly free. Maybe it's the lingering thrill of riding on the back of Fox's motorcycle, or maybe it's how unchained and right I felt taking him in my mouth. Either way, I won't let them put me back in the miserable place they've kept me for years. And when it comes down to them and helping Fox? I pick him.

Once Holden texted me, I knew I had to get away from Fox's studio apartment fast so Dad couldn't track my phone and know how to find him. It was just as exhilarating as the first time to ride on the bike, my arms locked around him as we zoomed down the roads.

Before I got off the bike, he took my phone and put his number in, kissing my cheek before he drove off.

My parents and Holden aren't home yet when I get past the security system. I don't waste a minute, seizing the opportunity to get what I can to help Fox before they get back. My best bet for snooping on what my parents could be hiding is in the home office.

Mom uses it more often than Dad, but I know he's brought home his work before. He's the one with more power and I can't get the sight of his signatures on the Wilder case files out of my head. His secrets might have lurked in our house for years. It makes my suspicion spike as I sit down in the expensive leather office chair, turning on the computer. I wonder what else I can find on Nexus Lab that Mom might keep on this computer as the busy CEO.

I tuck my phone against my shoulder and ear as I wait for the computer to boot up, calling the one person I know who can walk me through this fast. I've never been more thankful for my best friend to have married a computer genius than I am right now.

"*'Sup, little Landry?*" Connor answers, like the cocky ass he is.

"I don't even have time for you right now," I say with a smirk. "Walk me through copying a hard drive. The fastest way you've got, preferably."

That piques his interest. "*What are you up to?*"

"Clock is ticking here."

"*Are you doing something illegal?*" There's a grin in his tone. "*I'm in.*"

"You'd better be." I throw a glance at the door with no idea how much time I have before they get home. "Come on."

"*Aight, relax. I've got you. It's easy.*" It sounds like he's stretching. "*Do you have a flash drive or an external?*"

I search the drawers of the large desk and come up with one. "Yes."

"*Good, so here's what you need to do.*"

He walks me through the steps and it goes faster than I expected. A question occurs to me as the progress bar hits the halfway mark of copying the drive to the flash drive.

"Will I be able to access everything?"

I know Dad's password because he let me buy concert tickets for a show Thea and I went to. I didn't want Mom to know. Hers are a mystery to me, though, and I'll need them if I want to get into the pharmaceutical company's files on the drive.

"*All the settings will copy, so anything not encrypted or password protected is fair game.*"

I bite my lip. "So I'll need the passwords."

He laughs. "*Maybe. Depends on the level of security on them. What are you getting up to, hippie chick?*"

"None of your business, Bishop. Keep this to yourself."

"*Cool, cool. Your little snooping secret is safe with me.*"

For now is left unspoken, because Connor loves collecting information and has a penchant for blackmail. Not that he'd actually use it against me. He collects information to protect the people he cares about, too.

The computer dings when the hard drive is copied. "It finished. Thanks."

Swiping the flash drive, I go to my room and stash it in a vintage blue suede purse with fringe. I catch sight of myself in the mirror and pause. My lips are still pink and slightly swollen from earlier and my dress looks like a mess. I shift, rubbing my thighs together and still feel the tingly echo of how much I liked what Fox and I did.

The front door opens and closes, low murmurs from Dad and Holden drifting through the foyer.

"Maisy Grace Landry," Mom calls ominously. Her voice only raises enough to carry without outright yelling. "Downstairs. Now."

Sighing, I head for my execution.

When I reach the top, Holden shoots me an apologetic expression. I give him a subtle nod. It's fine, I knew it was going to be tough to avoid this, even with him running interference. Leaving my high school graduation ceremony probably meant when my name was called, there was a wave of confusion when I didn't get up and walk to the stage to accept my diploma. Bet Mom really loved that embarrassment. I picture the other parents in the stands whispering.

"Get down here," Dad snaps.

Oh good, they're both upset. Mom I expected, but Dad's always acted out of an overbearing sense of protectiveness. I don't make it down the steps before they tear into me.

"Where were you?"

"What were you *thinking*?"

They both speak at once and my gaze bounces between them. Mom narrows her eyes and shoots Dad a look that has him stepping back. Lines form around his mouth with his severe frown as he folds his arms.

"What ridiculous notion did you have that made you think you could get away with walking out on your graduation ceremony?" Mom hisses. "They called your name for five minutes before they finally moved on. Why would you do this?"

Jutting my chin, I cross my arms. "There's no rule that says I had to attend. They'll mail my diploma. Why is that so wrong?"

"You are so childish," Mom says coldly. "Go to your room."

"Go to my room?" A sound of disbelief escapes me. "I'm not twelve. You have to stop treating me like a baby."

"When you stop acting like one, you'll be treated accordingly," Mom shoots back. "Your actions today reflect on all of us."

"So what!" I explode, descending another step. "Who cares so much that you got a side eye for five whole minutes? There are more important things than reputation!"

"Reputation is *everything*," she argues, gesturing between me and Holden. "One child can't maintain his college acceptance and ends up in a public community college, and the other is a goddamn wild child I can't control no matter how many rules I have to lay down for you to become a proper example."

"I actually like my classes," Holden mutters, expression clouding. "I'm…glad I lost the football draft to Ohio State."

I could hug my brother right now. This is the first time he's stood up to their tyrant rule over us, too. I think we're both done with the bullshit. The anger is expanding in my chest, climbing my throat. I won't swallow it back or let this go. I'm eighteen and I've done every single thing they've ever wanted—studied hard, gotten the grades they demanded, and put myself in the boxes they wanted.

"Oh, shut up, Holden," Mom says haughtily.

My laugh is caustic and bitter. "God, Mom, do you even hear yourself? Who fucking cares!"

"Maisy," Dad barks.

"No, Dad! Seriously, the world isn't ending because I skipped out today. You guys are the ones acting crazy for thinking that."

"We didn't know where the hell you were or if someone had taken you," he says angrily. "I looked all over."

"You didn't try to track my phone, like usual, warden?" I shout. "Shocker, it's usually your go to."

His expression darkens. "That was to protect you."

"From what?" I rush the final steps and throw my hands out. If I get him worked up enough, maybe I can make him admit the things he's done. "Where is the threat? If you can be honest with me about why we have such tight security and why you think it's okay to track my whereabouts by my phone, I'd be willing to listen. But I can't do this blindly anymore. You're suffocating me." The breath I take is sharp and painful. "I can't be a doll anymore. I have my own feelings and thoughts."

He opens his mouth, conflict flooding his gaze. He's going to tell me something important.

"Every choice and sacrifice we've made for you has been to set you on the best path to have a good future," Mom cuts in, exchanging an unreadable look with Dad.

Damn it.

I face her and am struck by how much I have bent myself into whatever shape she demanded. "If you really loved me, you'd let me pick what I wanted for myself. Everything you've forced on me I've hated. And none of it has ever been good enough to satisfy you, just makes you demand more and more of me. The grades, the clothes, then you forced Sam on me as another way to keep me under your thumb. Why are you so obsessed with him?"

"He's a perfectly good match for you. He's from a well-respected family on our level. We're in talks with his parents and we all agree, you'll date and after you both graduate from college we'll talk about marriage plans."

"You expect me to marry him? Hell no! I'm not having some arranged marriage. Dad, are you seriously going to let that happen?"

Dad can't look me in the eye.

"Mom, come on. That's too much," Holden says warily. "You can't make her to do that."

"Maisy will do what I think is best," Mom says.

"I can't anymore. You can't control every aspect of my life."

Her mouth pinches. "You're just a child. You can't possibly know what's good for you."

"That's the point I'm making here! I need to make these decisions for myself." I stand up straighter. "Starting with this one—I'm not going to Northwestern. I never wanted to go there. I want nothing to do with Sam Blake, so you can toss that out, too. I'm going to make my own life plan instead of following the one you forced on me."

It feels good to finally get that off my chest.

Dad shoots a worried look at Mom and she steps into my space, putting her hand on my shoulder. Her nails dig in slightly.

"Jackie—"

Dad doesn't get to finish.

"Well. Then pack your things." Her voice is so cold. It's hard to believe she's my mother with how little emotion is in her voice when she stares at me. "If you don't have any plans to go along with these choices, then the disciplinary institution it is."

I grit my teeth and jerk away from her. "No."

"Yes."

"You can't make me. Holden gets to go to community college, but I have to get shipped off to some shady finishing school because I had an original thought instead of one you fed to me? No fucking thanks."

"Yeah, that's not fair," Holden says. "Why can't she just pick?"

"Because I said so," Mom says.

"Let's not be hasty, Jackie. I don't want to force that on her."

Dad tries to reason with her, but I've never seen her like this. Ruthless, that's what she looks like. She was playing nice before, but now the gloves are off.

"Shut up, Richard. This is necessary."

I back up, inching toward the stairs. "You're insane if you think I'll let you send me anywhere I don't want to go."

"You will do as I say," Mom says.

"I won't! I'll get a lawyer. I'm eighteen, you can't do that to me!"

A vein pops out in her temple and a flush creeps up her neck. "If you won't obey my rules, then you'll be cut off." She's livid now, her threatening voice shaking. "I give you enough liberties as it is. If that's what it takes to make you behave, then that's what will happen."

"Go ahead," I challenge, putting a foot on the first step. "I'm leaving. You won't listen, so I'm gone. I'll cut myself off." Swinging to Dad, I add, "If you track my phone, I'll throw it away and get a new one because parents don't invade their kids' privacy and lives like that."

"Maisy Grace!" Mom yells after me.

I'm so fucking done.

With my chest heaving and adrenaline from the fight rushing through my veins, I run up to my room and slam the door. I need to make this quick, or Mom will pull something crazier, like putting a security lock on my door or overruling Dad to send me to the disciplinary school against my will.

I grab the first bag I find in the closet and throw clothes inside with my laptop, then snag my purse with the flash drive. The medical journals from Devlin go in next, followed by my jar of rocks and my favorite crystals tucked carefully between my clothes. Glancing around the room, my throat goes dry. I can't fit everything in my bag.

In one motion I strip the rumpled designer dress overhead and fling it onto the floor, standing nude in the middle of my room with the evidence of what I did with Fox two hours ago dried on my upper thighs. It feels good to stand there like that, like I'm shedding a skin that was too tight and I've finally burst free through the constricting seams.

For a minute, I consider going to stay with Thea, but I don't want to intrude on her and Connor. They're still enjoying their time together as newlyweds. As much as I love my best friend, there's somewhere else that's calling me.

As I pull out my favorite yoga pants with slits in the sides that cuff around my ankles, I call Fox, searching for a shirt with my breasts out and proud. Nothing will keep me down anymore.

He answers on the first ring. *"Hey. You good?"*

I don't have a penny to my name. No savings, no car, no phone if my parents cut me off for this stunt.

And I've never felt more alive.

"Yup. So, is it too soon for me to move in?" I joke, grabbing a fitted crop top. "Come get me?"

There's only a brief silence before his deep voice filters through the phone. *"I'm coming."*

Nothing has ever made me smile wider or made my heart soar as high.

TWENTY-FOUR
Fox

Two coffee mugs clink on the table when Maisy sets them down next to my laptop in the morning. "Walk me through what you know so far."

For the second time yesterday, her arms were wrapped around me on my bike after I picked her up at the end of her block when she left her home. She told me Holden helped her out after a blowout fight with her parents.

The sensation of her embrace created a steadfast ember of warmth in my heart. I've fought on my own for a long time, even struggling to let Colton in completely. But with Maisy, it feels like the world has opened up from the blinders I've had on.

Once we got back to the warehouse, I kissed her, then went down to work in the garage. She watched, perched on the steps until it got late. We ordered pizza that I went to pick up and stayed awake until the early hours of the morning talking. I told her more about what it was like growing up in foster care, about my favorite cove in Thorne Point, and the story of how I managed to track down my dad's Harley and bought it back. My heart ached when she described what it was like after I had to leave town, then told me the story of when she met her redheaded friend, and how much her road trip plans meant to her.

At some point we finally passed out in the middle of the conversation, trying too hard to soak in each other and make up for all the lost years.

This morning I woke up with her tucked against my side, her face smashed into my shoulder and I spent several minutes gazing at her, lightly brushing her tangled hair aside. After getting up, I heard her rustling in the sheets and she joined me in the workout corner, running through yoga poses and stretching her lithe body while I went through my own routine. I thought I'd hate having someone else in my space, but with her it just fits as if we've always been like this. When we were done, she showered and I ended up on the couch with my laptop.

Instead of taking the coffee, I pull her down into my lap on the couch and get distracted for a moment, kissing the side of her neck as my palm skates over the strip of her stomach exposed by her tight crop top. I can't decide if I like this version or one of her loose flowing ones better, but I'll never get tired of having easy access to her tits. She arches when I push beneath her shirt to tease a nipple.

"Mm, focus, or we won't get anything done today," she says in a husky tone.

"Can't help it," I rasp against her neck. "I resisted everything for so long, but it's like putting a starving man in front of a buffet."

Her lips meet mine in a lazy kiss that has my arms banding around her waist. "Come on." She speaks against my mouth. "Lay it all out."

"I want to lay you out."

Her shoulders shake with her laugh. "Later."

"Fine."

Releasing a calming breath to encourage my erection to go down, I adjust her so she's not teasing me with every tiny move, settling a hand on her hip. She grabs the coffees and offers me one while I gesture to the laptop.

"I always knew that the accident was faked," I start. "I was with my dad when he checked the car, it was only a day or two before. They weren't supposed to go out that night, but they'd been arguing about something. I tried to listen, but they dropped it when they saw me trying to sneak down the steps. It wasn't until I started to dig into everything to connect the pieces that things didn't line up and I started to get suspicious of the circumstances surrounding their deaths."

"Why do you think they had those samples hidden at your house? Is that what they were arguing about?"

"I don't know. The best guess I have is they were trying to protect their patent. My working theory is Jacqueline must have gotten there first and the company rewarded her for it by appointing her CEO. It's quite the promotion."

She nods with a troubled look. "We went out to dinner to celebrate her promotion that same night. It wasn't announced publicly, but she already knew."

That's news to me. I nod slowly, swallowing. She puts down her coffee cup and laces her fingers with mine.

"When I started looking into Nexus Lab to find answers connecting back to my parents, I found something weird that gave me the first clue something wasn't right. The previous CEO just disappeared off the face of the earth. Officially he took early retirement about twenty years too early—he was in line for Forbes 40 under 40. It's like someone got rid of him in order for Jacqueline to take the position, jumping straight from R&D to the top. It was the same when I looked into your dad with a miraculous promotion. I've been trying to follow the money to trace it back to what happened and how my parents ended up dead because of it."

Maisy listens attentively, asking questions for clarity as I take her through what I've gathered. I let her in on what I was doing at the restaurant the other night before school ended, bribing a waiter to give me a stolen employee ID badge, which led to finding the remote shipping facility Nexus Lab uses when I accessed the employee's schedule. I show her photos Colton enhanced for me that I took discreetly at the warehouse. I'm only slightly surprised when she doesn't shy away from the facts I've found that paint her parents in the worst light.

"Someone else was supposed to become the chief," I explain. "He was in the process of taking the position when suddenly your dad was sworn in. Your dad's been known to take bribes and has maintained a corrupt office as chief. He was who showed up at that meeting we staked out. I think it's because he already knew how to play dirty that someone put him in that position of power."

She sits up. "I know. I brought stuff that might help fill in the blanks. I copied the computer at the house before I skipped out. And the police report from the accident, although some of it is redacted."

My brows jump up. Colt assured me he'd wiped most of the important things from the system so that I could dig before someone covered their tracks more than they had. "How did you get that?"

"My friend Connor. He knew about some of Dad's corrupt ways and used that knowledge to squeeze it out of him to get information on you, or he was going to expose Dad as a bribable cop."

I'm starting to get why Colt has taken such a liking to Connor Bishop. The two of them are practically cut from the same cloth.

"So Richard really gave it up?"

"I guess. I don't think Dad thought anyone would look too closely at a closed case accident report, or maybe he thought it would be more suspect to withhold it like he was trying to hide something. My dad's signature is all over it, though, even on the night of the accident when he had an alibi because we were out to dinner."

"That's the problem I have. I can't prove their involvement without proof of payment or something more concrete. The alibis put them in the clear."

"As smart as the alibis are, there are still holes. It didn't make sense why pages were missing. Why hide things when it's supposed to be an accident? It's what first made me suspect his involvement in covering it up because it was closed so fast." Her brow creases and she looks at the laptop. "But this explains why Mom was always so uptight and a total bitch to me. She didn't want to risk anything casting doubt on her if it threatened her power. They've both changed, but she's so different from when I was little."

Frowning, I pull her closer, tucking her hair behind her ear and brushing my fingers down her cheek. I used to resent her for growing up with her parents and her brother, but I can't imagine how much Jacqueline and Richard's greed has poisoned their relationship with Holden and Maisy. I don't see the woman who was sweet to me when I was a kid anywhere in the soulless woman she is now.

"Do you think my parents actually killed them, or were they the ones who covered it up?"

I've asked myself that same question over and over. "I don't know. I just know they were involved somehow."

"I'm sorry," she whispers. "I hate that they could hurt you."

"It's not your fault." I know that now and I don't want it to weigh on her.

Opening up to tell her this feels like I'm in a twilight zone. It's not just that I've let very few people know the full story—only Colton knows the full extent. But sharing it with her makes it feel like I have someone I can lean on. I bump my nose beneath her ear and squeeze her tight in an embrace.

"The truth is coming out," I murmur. "One way or another."

She makes a soft sound in agreement, turning to kiss me.

"I also brought these," Maisy says, getting up to rustle through her bag at the foot of the bed. She comes back with a stack of magazines and perches in my lap.

It's the science journal I've been looking up online. I lift a brow.

"A friend of mine, his parents run that medical research clinic in town. He got them for me."

"You have helpful friends. I should've gone after them instead of you."

She smacks my chest and puts the stack of magazines on the table. "Maybe I can scope out the company if I play it like I'm stopping by to see my mom? She had an important meeting on the calendar that she's spent a month preparing for. Maybe I'll convince the guard to let me wait in her office since I'm her daughter. I can snoop around and see if I can get us more."

"Let's find out." I adjust her in my lap, reaching around to switch windows on the laptop. My brows furrow at the map. "That's weird. I have tracking on her phone, but she's not there."

Maisy's brows dip. "She's really strict about her work hours, she should be there."

"Hang on."

I type a few keys to trigger the tracing Colton hooked me up with. It takes a minute for the scanner to pinpoint her signal, but once it does we both lean in. The address she's at isn't anywhere near where she should be, on the opposite side of town in the middle of nowhere. It's not far from the shipping warehouse I snooped around at, but further off from the rest of the shipping district.

"Switch to street view on Google maps," she suggests. "I want to see where she is."

I plug in the address and Maisy tilts her head as we take a virtual tour. It's another warehouse, this one much shadier looking than the shipping facility. The tin siding is covered in rust and the roof looks in disrepair.

"Wait. Go back, I recognize that logo."

"This?"

I navigate back to the front of the building. On a rolling bay door in faded, peeling letters is SynCom.

"SynCom," Maisy says in a dull tone. "Fox, that logo is on her paychecks."

"What? Why wouldn't Nexus Lab be the ones paying her?"

"They are. It's done through this, I think. I was with her once at the bank and she had me hold a stack with this stamped on it."

"There must be some kind of investor or something that owns Nexus Lab privately. I'll find out if this SynCom is a holdings company and see what this means."

"We make a good team." She beams at me.

I rub my mouth. "I should've been working with you instead of against you this whole time. I would've gotten more answers sooner."

"I told you at that party, jerk," she teases, elbowing me. "We could've been doing so much this year—kissing and kicking ass—instead of wasting all this time."

I hum at the memory of my wild daisy at that house party. That first taste was everything. "Did you keep those pants?"

"Maybe." She blushes. "I was going to throw them out because they're stained, but…"

A slow grin stretches across my face. The tight leggings she has on now are similar, hugging her legs in a deep green color. Only a thin barrier separates her ass from my lap.

Cupping her face, I draw her in for a kiss that quickly turns dirty as our tongues glide together. She twists her flexible body to reach me, ending up straddling my lap and grinding on me. I groan against her lips.

"There's something we didn't get to do yesterday and I can't hold out any longer."

Her lids are heavy. "Do your worst."

The echo of the last time she said that to me when I cornered her in the girls' bathroom sounds in my head. I hoist her into my arms and carry her to the bed, dropping her down hard enough to bounce. She stretches, lifting her arms over her head. With a wicked grin, I crawl over her and kiss my way down her neck, over her hard nipples, biting them through her cropped shirt to earn a cry. I continue lower, licking into her exposed belly button on my way to her waistband.

Peering up, I take in the incredible sight of her propped up on her elbows, watching me. "I'm going to taste your pussy."

"Yes," she whispers, her knees falling open to allow me room to settle between her legs.

A hunger that's nearly feral overtakes me as soon as I hook my fingers in the waistband of her snug yoga pants. I yank them down with rough tugs and fling them behind me while she giggles. Smacking the outside of her thigh to quiet her, I use my grip to pull her leg open for me. Once again she's not wearing any underwear. My mouth waters as I sink to my elbows between her thighs.

The first swipe of my tongue over Maisy's wet folds makes me groan and dive in for a second taste. It's better than I imagined when I pictured doing this for the first time. She arches off the bed with a high-pitched cry as my tongue drives her wild. I grab her hips and find every way to make her pant and moan. When I slide two fingers into her, she clenches around me, gripping me with her tight heat, making me want to drive my cock into her right now.

"Oh, fuck!" Maisy hooks a leg over my shoulder, hips bucking as she rides my fingers and my face. "I'm so close!"

I growl against her slick and swollen folds, sucking and licking until she clenches her thighs around my head with a hoarse cry. I don't stop. I keep feasting on her like I have to savor every single taste, curling my fingers inside her and pumping them. At first she tries to get away, only to let her legs drop open while pushing her pussy against me, coming undone again. I force orgasm after orgasm out of her until she's trembling.

"I need you," she begs. "Please, I need you right now. Don't keep me waiting anymore. We've wasted too much time on waiting."

I still don't stop, not until I'm good and ready to take my mouth off her. Maybe it's to put off what I have to tell her for a few minutes more. Her begging turns into a delirious litany. When I do sit back, my face is a mess. I pull my fingers free and make sure she watches as I lick them clean.

"I want you inside me," she whispers, her gaze full of liquid heat. "Right now. I need your cock filling me up."

My heart clenches and my stomach dips.

"I—"

I break off, running my gaze over her body. It's not like I was waiting specifically for her, but I didn't go out of my way to do it either.

The truth of my love for her hits me right in the chest.

She's the only one I've ever cared for, the only one I've pictured doing this with. I swallow thickly. The times I've been with girls have been far and very few between, and even then it never felt right to do more than get them off with our clothes mostly on. Meeting her gaze, I lay my secret on the table.

"I haven't... There was only ever you. It was always you, Maisy."

TWENTY-FIVE
Maisy

My heart sits in my throat as the deep aching need intensifies between my legs. I never thought... He's always been so dominant the few times we've hooked up, I didn't even think he wasn't experienced.

Leaning up to cup Fox's jaw, I smile. "It's okay. I want you. You just made me come like four times. You can't do it wrong, just do what feels good."

Relief melts the lines of tension that I'm not judging him for never having sex before. That kind of stuff doesn't matter to me, it's all society pressure anyway. He crashes our mouths together in a wild kiss. We wind up in a tangle of limbs as we peel out of the rest of our clothes.

A huff leaves him when I push him back to study his inked chest. The tattoo of the ocean is amazing, the intricate waves rolling and rippling along his muscles, stretching across his heart and down his arm in a half sleeve. Hidden amongst the details is a second tattoo, this one a crow wearing a crown perched on a skull with its wings spread. My lips part as I trace it with my fingertips. A hoarse noise vibrates in his throat as I touch the ink I've been dying to see.

"It's beautiful."

"I told you I missed the ocean, too."

Grinning, I steal another kiss. His powerful thighs drive me crazy as I trap one between my legs. I have half a mind to rub my clit against his thigh until I come again, but I want to feel him inside me.

Fox breaks the kiss and curses under his breath, glancing at his discarded jeans with a dismayed look. "I don't have a condom. The guys...they used to tease me and slip one into my wallet, but I got rid of the last one when it expired."

A laugh rolls through me. "Good. Don't use expired condoms. That's as bad as being unprepared."

He grunts, pulling away. I lock my arms around his neck and keep him in place, with his cock gliding along my folds.

"I have a contraceptive hormonal implant and I'm clean."

My cheeks burn hot with the admission. I'm not ashamed or anything, because I own my body, but the implant wasn't my first pick for birth control. Mom didn't want to risk any kind of scandal, including teen pregnancy. Always controlling me in one way or another. As soon as

I was old enough, she made me ask the doctor about it and signed off her *permission*.

I force her and the awful sensation crawling up my throat from my mind and bring myself back into the present. "We're good to go."

Fox licks his lips, desire flaring in his gaze at the prospect of having me bare. "Are you sure? I've only touched you, but—"

I cover his mouth and smile. "I'm sure."

He studies me for a beat, then lowers himself over me, wrapping me in strong arms as he tortures the sensitive skin on the side of my neck. I moan as we rock together, his dick rubbing my clit instead of slipping inside. I open my legs wider in the hope he'll fuck me sometime this century, but I'm fine with doing this at his pace.

"Have you ever…?" The question is rumbled into my flushed skin.

I bite my lip, partly wishing I could tell him this was my first time, too. But I can't change the past and I don't regret that I've had sex before.

"Yeah. Last year during a yoga intensive retreat." I run my fingers through his hair when he shifts to peer at me through dark lashes. "It was fun, but that was all."

He tenses, shoulders flexing as he holds me tighter. "I kind of want to kill him for—"

"*She* isn't important right now," I stress, keeping my expression open. I've only come out to Thea and a tiny flutter moves through me.

Fox stills, blinking. "She? You're—"

"Bi, yes. But what matters is that I'm with who I want to be with right now." My fingers tighten in his messy hair at the back of his head. "Who I've always wanted to be with. You."

The relaxed, open smile he gives me pierces into my heart. It feels good that he accepts who I am just as much as I accept everything about him. "I'm going to fuck you now, Maisy Daisy."

A hot blush creeps up my neck, heating my cheeks at the nickname. I tuck my lips between my teeth and nod. He skims a hand up my leg and adjusts our position so I'm straddling him. When he lines up and presses inside, he watches my face as I sink down his length. The concentration in his expression makes my chest expand. He fills me inch by inch and I tip my head back, parting my lips.

"Good?"

"Yeah," I breathe, circling my hips. "So good."

"Thank fuck," he mutters, the concentration clearing as he thrusts up. "God, you feel incredible."

Fox holds onto my thighs as I move above him. I watch the emotions play out on his face, my breathing becoming strained as arousal pours over me from the way his blue eyes darken with pleasure. He groans and thrusts sharper while I ride him. He keeps the pace slow and careful. As good as it feels, I need more.

Bracing one hand on his tattooed chest, I grab hold of his hair and tug to get his full attention. The side of my mouth kicks up challengingly. "What are you doing? Sweet and gentle is fun, but it was never going to be us. Those times you were hate fucking me with your fingers?" I lean down to whisper hotly against his ear, pulling his hand to my neck. "I liked it. Don't treat me like I'll break, because I won't."

He releases a growl, grinning as he flips me over to take control. His hips snap and I gasp as his cock hits me deeper. His fingers wrap around my throat and hot and cold shivers run across my skin.

"Yes, like that," I hiss as the heat builds. "Don't stop."

"Look at me when I fuck you, daisy. Don't take your eyes off mine." I snap my eyes open at the command. He looks wild, dark hair hanging in his face, full lips parted, possessive gaze locked on mine. He punctuates his words with thrusts. "I want you to know it's me doing this to you. That you're *mine*. You always have been."

I nod, wrapping my legs around his hips.

Fox grunts, fingers tightening on my neck as he pins me to the bed. I'm getting wetter the harder he fucks me. Collapsing onto an elbow, he stops choking me in favor of holding my jaw in a firm grip. My nails rake down his back. He pants against my cheek, alternating between kissing and biting the side of my face as he drives into me.

"Fuck, Maisy," he chokes out. "I'm going to come hard enough to paint your goddamn insides so deep no one will ever claim your pussy after me."

"Never," I agree, arching against him as pleasure erupts in my core. "Oh god, I'm coming. Fuck, harder."

A rough sound tears from him, his thrusts speeding up with even more force as he chases me to orgasm. He pushes up far enough to watch my dazed expression with a hungry focus as I tremble from coming so hard. Moving his hand to grip my hair in his fist, he snaps his hips and stiffens with a low rumble. His cock throbs deep inside me and I gasp from the sensation.

We're both panting, coming down from the ecstasy racing through us. Fox pulls out and collapses beside me, reaching out and tugging me against his sweaty side. With his other hand, he reaches down and pulls my thigh across his torso. My pulse is throbbing between my legs and I shift just to feel the dirty gratification of our mingled come coating my inner thighs.

After a few minutes our breathing evens out.

"Damn," I murmur, lacking the brain power to say much more.

Fox chuckles, the low, raspy sound sending warm tingles over my skin and wrapping around my heart. He squeezes my thigh and turns to place a kiss in my hair. I tilt my head up and his lips find mine, the soft kiss at odds with how wild we were together. When we part, our gazes lock and we stare at each other.

It's comfortable. I don't feel the need to fill the silence, and neither does he. We simply exist in this moment. I'm bared to him down to my soul and feel like he's allowing me to look into his. There are no more walls between us.

He traces random patterns on my skin, holding me close. I feel like I'm right where I belong, the old warped piece that was gone from my heart for so long now firmly back in place.

* * *

When I wake up in Fox's bed, the apartment is empty and quiet. I stretch, enjoying the aches from yesterday and last night. The sight of Fox's belt still tied around a pipe above his bed where he restrained my wrists for round…who knows last night makes my mouth stretch in a delicious smile.

Music drifting from the lower level reaches me when I get up and drag one of his t-shirts over my head. It's big on me, hitting mid thigh and slipping off one shoulder. I skip everything else, pour a cup of coffee from the still-warm pot, and go off in search for him.

So far I've lucked out. My parents haven't done anything to find me. I wasn't kidding about smashing my phone if they tried to track it, but part of me is surprised they let me go after how controlling they've been. It leaves me waiting for the other shoe to drop. I need to check in with Holden and see what things are like at the house.

All other thoughts fly from my head when I creep down the stairs to the garage. Fox is in the middle of working, covered in a light sheen of sweat and grime. He's shirtless, tattoos on display, ripped black jeans hanging off his hips as he crosses to the workbench to grab a tool before heading back to the piece of metal he's bending to his will to form something. I park my ass on the step, watching in fascination with my coffee cup cradled in my hands.

It's as if the materials he uses have no choice but to obey his command to become what he wants. I don't know what it was originally, or what it will be, but it's beautiful. He hammers out a piece until it flattens, then uses another power tool to cut off a raw edge.

Fox looks up when he realizes I'm there, catching me out of his periphery. I grin when his gaze rakes over me from head to toe, the want obvious as he drags his teeth over his lower lip. Damn, a girl could get used to that.

"Hi." I keep eye contact as I take a sip of coffee.

Without a word he wipes his hands and crosses the garage, taking the steps two at a time until he reaches me halfway up. He slides his fingers into my hair and tilts my head back for a deep kiss.

Pulling back slowly, his eyes dip to what I'm wearing. "Nice shirt."

"I thought so," I say with a smirk. "You been up for a while?"

"I was under the impression people who did yoga got up with the sun. It's almost ten."

"That's when they aren't fucked within an inch of their life by an insatiable monster," I sass, indicating the finger-shaped bruises on my thighs to prove my point.

His gaze turns heated as I tease the hem of the shirt higher to follow the pattern of marks he left on me—bites, hickeys, and bruises covering my body. He takes my hand and sets my coffee aside on the step.

"Come here."

He tugs me down the steps, leading me to the Charger. Spinning me around, he captures my mouth again, nipping my lip before swiping his tongue over the sharp burst of pain. His large calloused hands fit to my waist, almost encircling it. I run my fingers over the scar on his knuckle as he guides me back until he has me splayed on the hood of his car.

"My dirty, rebellious little daisy," he murmurs, gaze pinning me in place as he slides a hand up my hip, pushing up his stolen shirt to reveal I have nothing on underneath. "You know what this means, right?"

I sink my teeth into my lip and shake my head.

With a crooked grin that's all mischief, he grabs the bottom of the shirt and rips it up so my lower body is completely bared to him.

"It means it's time for my breakfast. You don't wear panties around me and I'm going to fuck your pussy with my tongue, fingers, and cock. Got it?"

A bolt of electric heat races through my body as a moan escapes me. Fox pushes my legs wider and his sinful mouth descends on me. He sucks my clit into his mouth, chuckling at the noise that rips from my throat. My hands fly to the back of his head, holding on as he tortures me with his talented tongue.

The bay door is open, and though it seems like there isn't anyone else around in the row of warehouses where Fox has made his home, anyone could catch us if they drove up. It only makes the carnal exhilaration soar higher, calling to a deep hidden piece of myself I've suppressed for so long.

I'll never be able to look at his Charger again without blushing and thinking of this, him eating my pussy on the hood of his car.

"Yes," I sigh, threading my fingers through his hair as his tongue swipes with the perfect amount of pressure.

He doesn't shy away when my hips begin to rock, riding the sensual wave of building arousal. His face buries deeper between my legs and he lures me over the edge into an orgasm that ripples through my core. Damn, Sir Good Vibes has nothing on waking up to this first thing in the morning. My chest heaves with my panting breaths and I skate my fingers lazily over my nipples through Fox's shirt, enjoying the lingering aftershocks.

"That was amazing," I murmur.

"We're not done." Fox leans over me with a feral grin, planting his hands on either side of me on the matte black hood. "I love the way you look right now."

"How do I look?"

The question comes out breathless. A shiver wracks my body. Fisting the t-shirt I stole, he tugs me up.

"*Mine*," he rumbles against my lips before kissing me.

Tearing his mouth from mine, he turns me around and pushes in the middle of my back to encourage me to fold in half over the car. "Bend over."

Once I'm where he wants me, he lifts one of my knees up onto the hood. A breath shudders out of me from how turned on I am. The tip of his cock rubs up and down my folds as he teases me. He does it until I squirm.

"Come on," I plead, desperate for him to give it to me. For as much as I've awakened a beast in him, he's ignited a fiery need inside me. "More. Want you in me."

"Ask for it, baby," he demands, smacking my ass.

The words can't climb up my throat fast enough. "Please fuck me."

Fox slams into me, making my back arch and a cry catch in my throat. I manage to suck in a breath as he pulls out and thrusts again. My legs tremble, unable to move a lot in this position. I have to just take it and I love it, giving in to the feeling he stirs in me when he takes control. Tingles deep in my core have me close to coming again and we've barely started.

"You like it when I fuck you like that?"

A choked noise of assent escapes me. He grabs hold of my hair, just hard enough to feel it and his skin slaps against mine with his next thrust. I come hard, screaming as I ride it out.

"Mm, you squeeze my cock so good when you come all over it."

He leans over, kissing my spine as he slows down. The change hits me at a new angle and I squirm beneath him, trying to press back into each thrust. He chuckles, dragging his lips up my back. Long fingers reach around and press into my mouth. I curl my tongue around them and suck, loving this new sensation of being full with his muscular body stretched out over mine.

"Get these good and wet, wildflower, because I'm going to fucking own every part of you," he rasps against my hair.

Air gusts out of my lungs at the filthy promise. How does he know exactly what I want without me having to voice it? We've been apart for so long, but the ways our connection has matured into this intense compatibility almost scares me. No one else can give me this kind of fulfillment like he can. I know that deep in my bones.

I moan, slurping around his knuckles when he pulls free. With a quiet rumble, he changes the angle again, slamming his cock into me while he traces his wet fingers down the crack of my ass, circling around my hole. My breath hitches.

"I wish you could see how good you look right now, Maise." He massages my hole as his cock fills my pussy. When I relax enough one of his fingers enters my ass, he releases a low, satisfied groan. "Fuck, you're sucking me right in. Feel that?"

My head feels light and hazy, but I manage a nod as his finger sinks deeper. The sensation is strange, but my insides coil tight in excitement. He gives me time to adjust as he fucks my pussy and my ass, then adds a second finger after leaning down to spit in my crack. It's so vulgar, but it gets me obscenely hot. I can hear how wet I am as his cock pounds into me.

"Fox," I beg hoarsely, not even sure what I need.

"I've got you, baby. Just keep taking it." He squeezes my hip, pumping his fingers in time with his hips. He owns every inch of me, just like he promised. Body, heart, and fucking soul. "Good girl."

It becomes too much and I shake apart beneath him as I take it. The orgasm shatters me, unlike any I've had before, even better than all the things we did last night. My throat is scratchy as I scream through my release.

"Oh shit," Fox grits, his fingers digging into my hip as his dick pulses deep inside me, filling me with his come.

Carefully, he pulls his fingers free and braces his hands on the hood, caging me in. I can't move, still too delirious from such a mind-blowing orgasm, and he seems to be the same as his hot panting breaths coast over my damp skin. He stays inside me while he helps guide my leg off the car, then folds over my body, gathering me in his embrace. His lips press to the side of my face when I turn it to try to see him.

"You okay?"

"Yeah. That was… Wow. Good wow." I make a small noise and he understands, lips finding mine in a sweet kiss.

"Want me to carry you upstairs for a shower?"

"That sounds amazing, but not yet. Let me up?"

He peels away, our skin sticky. His hands hover over me as I stand, the large t-shirt falling down to cover me. Reaching overhead, I draw in a deep breath while stretching and focus on the energy moving through my body while he tugs his jeans back up his hips. I go through a couple other poses to get my blood flowing that leave me with only the delicious lingering aches of sex.

The first two times I saw the garage, we didn't stay long. Curiosity has me exploring, wanting to know more about Fox through the things he loves.

First I touch the motorcycle, finding the ding in the chrome. The memory filters through my head, making me smile as I think of his face when he sought me out to hide him before his dad killed him for the damage. We spent hours hidden away in my room watching cartoons. While I look around, he studies me, thumbs hooked in his jeans. I get distracted for a moment, admiring the hard planes of his sculpted body glistening with sweat.

"What?"

"Nothing, just admiring the excellent view," I sass.

He snorts, ruffling his dark tousled hair so it ends up even messier.

Biting my lip around a secret smile, I turn toward the workbench. Half-finished projects and his tools cover the surface, along with the piece he was working with when I came downstairs. I touch it, feeling the cool metal and trace the curve he's twisted it into.

"What are you making?"

"Not sure yet. I don't always have a plan when I'm making something. I usually just go with it until it feels done."

Thinking of the equally scrappy furniture pieces in his apartment, I glance over my shoulder. "Did you make the stuff upstairs too?" He nods. A soft smile tugs at my lips. "I like it. It's amazing that you can make something with your own hands. Your stuff has so much character. It's like I can feel you in them."

The compliment makes his handsome features morph into a perplexed expression. I don't think he thinks about sharing it with others. Warmth expands in my chest because he's sharing it with me.

"I remember how much you liked working on cars and learning about the mechanics, but this stuff is cool. How did you get into doing it?"

Coming around the Charger, he backs me against the workbench, bracing his hands on the edge. I take advantage of his proximity to trace his abs, grinning when his stomach twitches. Still ticklish. I file that away.

"It's mostly a hobby now. Something to keep my mind busy when it's too loud. I like working with my hands and tinkering with shit until it shapes into something. Sometimes it's useful, like the coffee table, and others it just is what it is." His gaze turns distant for a moment and he holds my hips, tugging me against his body like he needs me close enough to climb into his heart. "At first it was a habit I needed to survive. Once I went into the system, I wasn't used to having a lot."

I swallow at the melancholy in his tone, winding my arms around him to give him a hug. Resting my chin on his tattooed chest, I peer up at him while he tells me the story.

"Nothing belonged to you. That's the first thing you learn. It eats away at the hope most of those kids have that they'll find some damn stability in whatever home they're shoved into. But I already had everything ripped away from me, so it wasn't new." He sighs, rubbing my back like he needs to comfort me instead of the other way around. He laughs. "After I started living with my foster family in Thorne Point, Colt's mom caught me messing around with scrap metal from a junkyard on the outskirts of the city and tried to put my pieces in an avant garde art show. Eventually I stopped doing it because I had to, and kept at it more because I wanted to. I enjoy it."

"I'm glad," I murmur.

The smile he gives me makes my heart stop. I love the curve of it and I give him one of my own as I reach up to trace it.

When his lips connect with mine, I forget everything for a little while, existing where it's just the two of us without any of the pain of our past tarnishing this moment.

TWENTY-SIX
Fox

After making good on my offer to carry her upstairs, we cleaned up in the shower together. She protested that she could still walk, but a primal part of my brain needed to take care of her after she let me fuck her so roughly. I lose myself in running soapy hands over every inch of her body and massage her skin until she melts into me. My cock is ready for another round, but we have time.

"Stay in as long as you want. I have to call Colt to check in. I'll get him to mask your cell signal so your parents can't use it to find us."

She murmurs an agreement and I drop a quick kiss on her forehead before getting out.

"Let's go through the journals first, then we'll check the flash drive you brought," I tell her on my way out of the bathroom.

"Okay."

There's a part of me that wants to get back in under the hot spray of water with her. The part where she's entwined into my soul, tattooed on my heart. It takes effort, but I manage to force my feet to cross the room, discarding the towel around my waist to tug on a worn pair of jeans with rips in the knees.

Moving to the couch, I open the laptop and call Colton, setting my phone to speaker so I can work handsfree. I pull up the screenshots I took of the shady place we found Jacqueline at yesterday.

"*Foxy*," he greets cheerfully.

"Fuckface," I shoot back in the same tone.

Colt makes a cooing sound like I'm adorably amusing. I roll my eyes and push my fingers through the damp hair curling over my forehead.

"There was a warrant for impound out on your car and your bike. Two more popped up after I took care of the first one. I dropped a little present in their reporting system that'll crawl for any others and scramble them. You're welcome."

It figures Richard is trying to flex his power now that I'm getting closer.

"Thanks. I found something new. Jacqueline Landry skipped out on her normal schedule and when I traced her, she turned up at this remote address. It was another warehouse, looked shady as fuck. There was a logo on the place. SynCom."

"*Maybe a meeting?*"

"That's my thought. I sent it to you. See what you can pull on it? I'm thinking it's some kind of silent investor Nexus Lab doesn't want anyone to know about. Maisy confirmed it's connected when she told me Jacqueline's paychecks are paid through this company instead of the public front."

"*Oh?*" Colt's tone goes light and teasing. I can clearly see the kind of expression he has right now—grinning with his tongue stuck in his cheek while he spins around in his stupid fancy gamer chair. "*Your little flower is playing ball now?*"

I grunt and he chuckles. I haven't told him yet about how things have changed for me, but he's always teased me about her, especially when I found her on Instagram before I came back to Colorado. Staring at her photos for hours was so I could learn what I needed to, but he always thought it was more. Now I realize he was probably right. Asshole always sees through people, picking up on what they don't want found out.

"She's...yeah."

Luckily he lets it go instead of picking at it because he's a nosy bastard. The conversation jumps around for a few minutes while he gives Maisy's phone the same treatment he's given to mine and the Crows, making it untraceable. The water shuts off in the bathroom.

I trail off mid-sentence, gaze zeroed in on Maisy walking out of the bathroom in a cloud of steam. She's wearing one of my t-shirts again and I fucking know she's not wearing anything underneath because my wildflower likes her freedom. Her damp hair falls around her shoulders and she shoots me a crooked grin that makes my pants feel tighter with just one look. God, she's heaven and a curse wrapped into one perfect girl.

"*Fox?*" Colton prompts when the silence has stretched for a minute.

"Uh, yeah." Shit, what was I saying?

Maisy circles behind me on the couch and wraps her arms around my shoulders, giving me a kiss when I angle my head toward her like a moth to a flame, unable to focus on anything but her. She hums into it and I can feel the curve of her smile.

"Is that your brother?" she murmurs when we part.

"*You've got company,*" Colt says knowingly. Fucker probably has the biggest shit eating grin right now. "*Hey sweetheart. You sound hot. Tell me you're hot.*"

Maisy snorts, shooting me an amused glance as she comes around to sit next to me. I leave her be for a minute before giving in and dragging her onto my lap.

"Sure."

She says it without any shyness, owning herself. My arms tighten around her middle and my love for her expands in my chest. I inhale and the corners of my mouth twitch up. She still smells like flowers and coconut, but now there's something else.

Me.

After the shower and spending hours together, she smells like she's mine. It sends a pleased jolt through me.

"*Confident,*" Colt says with a hum. "*I like it.*"

Her light laughter makes something tug with want in my stomach. "It's not for you, sweetie," she says slyly. "I do it all for me. Everything else is bonus points."

"*Oh, damn. I think I just fell in love. Marry me?*"

A brief rush of jealousy flares, but I tamp down on it. My brother isn't a threat, but I can't help how possessive I feel about her—how possessive I've always felt around her. Maisy as a kid knew her worth and spoke out when she had an opinion, but as a woman her matured sense of self-assuredness is sexy as fuck.

"Sorry, Fox promised he'd marry me when he was nine. It was a proposal complete with a flower. You'll have to get in line."

All the air in the room feels like it's sucked out. She remembered my promise to her?

My throat bobs as I swallow and absently stroke her thigh, inching my fingers beneath the shirt and finding nothing but her warm skin. I squeeze a handful of her ass and nuzzle my face into her neck, trailing kisses and fighting the urge to leave another mark to claim her. I can't help how tactile I've become with her around, like I have this constant need to touch her in some way.

Colt makes a distressed sound like he's fatally wounded.

"So, he's told me you're his foster brother." Maisy leans toward the phone. "What was he like?"

I slide my lips together. If things were different, she wouldn't need to ask because she would've been with me. I never would've been separated from her. I picture it for a second, like I have many times, what it would be like if we remained close friends. How we'd have our first kiss by the tree we loved to climb as our friendship grew into something else.

"*He was a grumpy little shit,*" Colton says with a chuckle. "*Definition of doom and gloom. It was hilarious. Spill the tea, girl. What was he like before all the angst got to him?*"

Maisy launches into a story about the time me, her, and Holden swindled our entire block out of money on our lemonade stand racket so that we could buy a video game we wanted, a plan I masterminded. I huff out a laugh. It was my idea, but she's the one who organized us and brought all the customers in. Her whole body moves as she tells the story animatedly, her golden eyes lit up with fondness at the memory.

As they talk, I stay quiet, listening to the girl I never stopped loving and the first friend—family—I let in past the thorns stabbing into my heart meet each other. The way it makes my heart thud catches me off guard.

Colton shares another story of his own of the first time his parents dragged me to a Thorne Point high society party with their socialite friends and how he caught me sneaking canapés in my suit pocket.

It feels right that they're meeting and sharing these halves of my life that make up the whole, like my shattered life is colliding back into itself to mend the broken shards.

"*I'll update you when I find out,*" Colton says, breaking me out of my musings. "*Later.*"

The call ends and I stop playing, removing my hand from beneath the shirt she stole so we don't get sidetracked again.

"He seems great," she says, leaning against my chest as she curls up in my lap.

"Is this going to be a thing?" I tug on the material that looks way better on her than it does on me.

She grins. "Yup."

The corner of my mouth lifts. Good. When she wears my clothes it makes something hot and possessive slot into place inside me.

Maisy gets up, collecting the stack of magazines she had in her bag and hooking an arm through her hippie style purse before coming back to the couch. She splits the stack in half and nudges it toward me.

She settles in the corner of the couch with her own half, tucking her bare toes beneath my thighs while she leans against the arm. "What are we looking for?"

"Anything. I tried to look these up before online as PDFs to see if they talked about what they were researching, but I couldn't remember what they had samples of."

We work in a comfortable quiet as we begin scanning through the medical journals.

"Wait, I think this is it," Maisy says after getting partway through her share. She sits up, shifting to her knees to show me the magazine article. "Right here. I recognize it from the stashed patent files you showed me in your garage. Do you have the photos from that shipping facility?"

Tossing aside the magazine I was reading, I pull the laptop closer and bring up the images I took when I posed as an auditor assessing the company internally. I click through images of the shipping operation until she stops me with a hand on my wrist.

"The synthetic opioid! That's it."

"Looks like they didn't get to file the patent paperwork and the company pushed forward with producing it in large quantities."

Is this why my parents were killed? All over this drug?

"This is what they were shipping out," she murmurs. "A lot of it. When you were talking to the manager, I thought it seemed weird that they were only shipping out this. And only, what, five guys loading it onto the truck?"

I make a low noise of agreement, my heart thumping at this new development. For years I've tried to remember what those hidden papers in the old garage said, but my memories were too foggy from grief. It's been right in front of me this whole time.

Rubbing my jaw, I glance at her. "We should go back there to see if we can find out more."

TWENTY-SEVEN
Maisy

The shipping warehouse turns out to be a bust. We've circled the building twice, but after Fox lifted me onto his shoulders to peer in through a high window it became clear we were too late.

"It's empty." My shoulders droop. "Everything's gone, like they cleaned house as soon as they finished loading the outgoing shipment."

"I was afraid of that." His grip on my thighs flexes. "Damn it."

"We'll figure it out. You have those pictures. We can use them hopefully."

Fox sighs raggedly, lifting me down from his shoulders like I weigh nothing. His sharp jaw is clenched, a muscle quivering in his cheek. I reach up and smooth my thumbs over his face until his attention is back on me. He relaxes and lowers his forehead to rest against mine, hands finding my waist.

"Sorry," he rasps. "I thought maybe we'd be able to learn something more after such a big break."

"It's okay."

"Let's head back. It looks like it might rain."

Taking my hand, he leads me back to the low-hanging tree where he parked the Harley to hide it from anyone who might catch us here. He gets on and hands me the helmet before I swing my leg over the bike and take my place behind him. The leather of his jacket is cool to the touch as I slip my arms around him. Once the engine roars to life, we speed away from the mysteriously wiped shipping warehouse Nexus Lab used to distribute drugs they made.

We're only on the road for a few minutes before Fox tenses.

"What is it?" I shout to be heard over the wind.

He angles his head back to surreptitiously glance behind us, then faces front again. If he's uneasy, it can't be good. I want to look back, but his voice stops me.

"Hold on tight," he commands.

It's the only warning I get before he takes a sharp turn onto a gravel cut through that connects to another lane. As we hit it, heading in the opposite direction from Fox's warehouse studio apartment, I see it—the blacked out SUV tailing us.

My heart thuds loud enough in my ears to rival the growl of the motorcycle's engine. I hold on tight as Fox weaves us through the roads. This isn't like the last time he was followed, when we were in his car and had the cover of the more populated downtown area to get away. This time there's only long stretches of road surrounded by foothills and random warehouses in the shipping district.

Behind us, the SUV revs its engine as it speeds up, keeping hot on the bike's tail. Fox curses and takes another route. My fingers are sore from how tightly they're clenched in his leather jacket. We whip around corners and fly down roads, climbing up higher into the mountains where the motorcycle maneuvers faster than the SUV can.

When we finally lose the tail, Fox spends another twenty minutes taking us on a winding path, still not fully relaxing. We eventually make it back to his place. My limbs are stiff when we climb off the bike. His big rough hands help me by removing the helmet. He tugs me into his chest, locking his arms around me in a hug.

"Close call," I murmur, slipping my hands into his open jacket.

"Too close." He squeezes me tighter. "Come on. We have to see what your parents had on their computer."

As we take the stairs up from the garage, the clouds open up with a heavy rain that pounds the gravel lot outside, quickly creating puddles and rivers. Fox shrugs out of his leather jacket and pushes a hand beneath his muscle shirt, lifting it as he chases an itch. The downpour creates a white noise amplified by the metal roof and the large industrial windows that wrap around the second floor.

We return to our spots on the couch from earlier and I hand over the flash drive I used to copy the hard drive of the computer in my parents' home office. Fox plugs it in. My phone vibrates with a text and I pull it out of the back pocket of the cutoff shorts I changed into before we left for the shipping facility.

"It's Holden," I say when Fox shoots me a curious glance. "He's just checking in. Wants to make sure I'm okay." I run my fingers through my hair and give him a sidelong look. "You know, since it's my first time running away and all."

He snorts. "You're eighteen, not eight. I don't think they call that running away anymore."

"Semantics."

While Fox gets everything set up, I text my brother.

Maisy: I'm all good [peace sign emoji]
Holden: Where are you though? I hit up Thea because I assumed that's where you went and she said she hadn't seen you.
Maisy: I thought about it but she's been busy with her own stuff, I didn't want to dump more on her. She should just enjoy being married and focus on her bakery right now, not letting me couch surf.
Holden: So where are you then?
Maisy: Safe. That's all you need to know. Keep me posted on if Mom and Dad seem like

they're going to send out a search party because I'm being "over dramatic" [eye-roll emoji]
Holden: Actually I overheard them last night. They didn't know there wasn't music playing on my headphones when they were talking. They were acting kinda weird and Mom said she didn't think you knew anything and wasn't worried. She's sure you'll come around before things get out of hand.

I bite my lip and tell him thanks, tossing my phone onto the couch.

"Everything good?"

"Yeah." I scoot closer. "Holden's going to keep an eye on my parents and let me know if anything is up."

He nods while clicking into files from the copy of the hard drive. "Looks like there's a backlog of financial records and they kept track of meetings."

"That's good, right? Maybe there's a suspicious payout, like you said. Follow the money."

"Yeah." Fox's thick dark brows flatten over his stormy blue eyes. "Jesus, this says they met with the mayor at the time to bribe him to overlook Richard taking that other guy's place as chief. There's more, too. Mostly at that steakhouse, but sometimes random addresses."

I lean in to see what he points out on the computer screen. Seeing the proof of how deep the deception goes fills me with disgust. The steakhouse is known to be a hotspot for lucrative business deals and meetings amongst the power players in this town, but to find out they were doing stuff like this right out in the open doesn't sit right with me. I had no idea any of this was happening.

"This is like insurance. They keep track of it so that if they were ever caught, they could bring down the whole house with them."

Fox murmurs in agreement. "Whatever is going on, I think it funded a lot of the wealth in this town behind closed doors. Nexus Lab wasn't as big back then, but since it's grown to be one of the top producers in the last ten years, anyone connected got richer."

I slip my hand into his when his shoulders go rigid. He holds it like a lifeline and I want to take away all the pain he's carried.

Anyone who cooperated got richer, but people like his parents wound up dead. Could they have been trying to stop whoever was pulling the strings and blow the whistle on the whole thing?

"Do you think they did it to anyone who didn't play along? What happened to your parents, I mean?"

"Maybe. It's likely, but I...I've only been looking for anything connected to my parents."

"Hey," I say softly, encouraging him to turn his face to me. When he meets my gaze, my heart aches at the lost look in his eyes. "It's not your responsibility to solve everything. Whatever we find, we can send it somewhere. Like a tip line. But you're not a superhero, okay? Don't feel bad because bad things happen in the world."

His jaw works, but he nods, then tugs me closer. I climb into his lap and shield him from the computer by winding my arms around his neck for a hug. His strong arms band around my waist like a vice and slowly the tension in his body bleeds away while we sit there comforting each other. I comb my fingers through his thick hair and he leans into me with a rumble that vibrates in his chest.

We stay like that for a long time.

My heart feels heavy after going through what was hidden under the same roof I lived by my own parents. The deeper we dig, the more corruption and deception we find. It unsettles me that my parents had a hand in what we discovered.

Lies, bribery, death. All of Ridgeview is soaked in blood and it shakes me to my core that my parents are at the center of it all.

* * *

Colton calls Fox two days later with more answers. While he answers the call, I get a text. Grabbing my phone from the coffee table, I find a message from Thea and the girls in our group chat with a photo of Thea, Blair, and Gemma making silly faces.

Thea: We miss your face!!! Holden said you got in a fight with your parents. We're staging another jailbreak kidnapping and demand girl time. We've got your back!

A pang hits my chest. I want to go be with them. On any other normal day, I would be, but I've been sucked deep into this world Fox exists in, one that lurks beneath the bright surface. I can't drag my friends into this mess. Thea went through a scary situation last year and I won't be the one to put her in danger again. And while Blair and Gemma are total strong badasses, this isn't their problem either. It's mine and Fox's and it goes back ten years at the start of all of this mess.

Maisy: OMG excuse me, I just lost my heart to three beauties [heart eyes emoji]
Gemma: [Blowing a kiss emoji] We're a fine bunch.
Blair: [smirking emoji] [black heart emoji] Come hang, we're doing a beach day at the lake.
Maisy: I miss you too, babes. I'm laying low. You know how Dad gets track happy with my cell signal. Promise I'll swing by the bakery this week though.
Thea: [GIF of a puppy dog face] You sure you're okay?
Maisy: I'm good, I swear! I'll see you in a couple of days.
Thea: Okay, be safe and remember we love your bright face!
Maisy: You all better do a face mask for me [heart emoji] Put it on Dev, you know he secretly loves it [laughing emoji]

Gemma and Blair text back GIFs of laughing. The last time I roped him into doing face masks with us, I put his thick black hair in short little pig tails that looked like horns, making him live up to his old nickname as the school's dark devil.

I vow to tell them everything—including that I'm sort of with Fox now. As soon as we find the answers he's looking for to prove his parents murder, then I'll do the whole introduce him to my friends thing. The thought of Fox meshing with the rest of my friends almost makes me laugh. Despite being my oldest friend, he's totally different from everyone else's vibe in our social circle.

Putting my phone down, I tune into what Fox is talking to Colton about. He paces behind the couch, phone pressed to his ear while he rubs the back of his neck. It makes his t-shirt ride up, but I drag my attention off his body to focus. I don't know if it's good news or bad that's making him pace.

He catches me watching and sighs, switching to speaker phone and holding his phone out. "Repeat that."

"It's definitely a shell company. They bought out Nexus Lab eleven years ago," Colton's voice filters through the room. *"I dug up financials and it lines up with the growth Nexus Lab has had in the last decade. It wasn't until this shell bought them out that they became a national supplier."*

Fox and I exchange a look, his expression matching mine as my brows pull together.

"So who owns that?" I ask.

"That's the kicker." Colton uses a light and joking tone, but I sense he's as displeased by what he found as Fox. *"SynCom is traced back to a bigger company called Stalenko Corp. It's rumored to have Russian ties. I've heard some chatter about them in different hacker circles on the web in the last couple of years."*

Startled, I blink, turning to Fox. "Russian ties—like the mafia?"

"Yeah," he says gruffly. "Probably. It makes sense, how easy it's been to build a small pharmaceutical research and development company up into what it is today from the shadows. Direct supply chain if they're flooding the market with the drugs from the source, either dealing on the black market or maybe using their hold on such a large piece of the market pie to drive up the costs to legitimate buyers by astronomical amounts."

My eyes widen. "They'd also have access to control how much is made and where it's sent to."

"Cartels are probably pissed they didn't think of it first. Now the Russians have spent ten years building a nice little nest egg for themselves right alongside the opiate boom. Who needs to worry about product when it can be cooked up synthetically in a lab and be twice as potent."

Blood pounds in my ears. I'm vaguely aware of Fox ending the call with his brother as my head swims.

Criminals.

That's who my parents are working with. Working *for* probably.

All of Dad's smiles and his deep belly laughter and all the ways Mom used to be completely different flash through my head. They used to love their life and Holden and I back when they were a bright-eyed scientist and a cop with a moral code. Where did that go so wrong?

"Maise." Fox catches me by my shoulders with a worried expression. "Are you okay?"

"Yeah. I think…that was a lot to take in."

His mouth flattens to a grim line as he rubs my upper arms. A chill skates down my spine. "I know."

"How is this our lives? How are my parents working for a shell corporation with Russian ties?" My throat gets scratchy and hot when I consider that I still have my parents, even if they're secretly evil lapdogs for a foreign mob. He doesn't have any of his family left. "None of this is fucking normal."

"That's the point." Sighing, he pulls me closer and I lean my head against his chest as he rubs my back. "It makes it so much easier to manage an empire and carry out illegal business when they can pull strings through powerful business people with good public standing. No one suspects an ambitious woman with two high-achieving children and a husband who upholds the law in the middle of the country compared to a thug packing heat doing business in the middle of the night. It's how the most powerful crime families operate now. They'd probably make Forbes for their damn innovation and advancements wherever they've dipped their dirty hands to operate their puppets from the shadows."

I take comfort in his touch, melting against him. His heartbeat drums beneath where I rest my head and I listen to it, allowing it to center me with each deep breath I take to clear the dizziness.

Wanting to forget for just a second, I lift my head and seek him out. He meets me halfway, our mouths crashing together with a burning intensity beneath the kiss. His fingers tangle in my hair, cupping the back of my head as he holds me so tight I'm almost breathless. I press up on my toes, chasing the exhilarating feeling of his kiss with a desperate edge.

Fox rips his mouth from mine and cups my face, gaze bouncing back and forth as he meets my hooded eyes. I swallow back the wild woman I almost let take over.

"It'll be okay," he says in a strained tone.

I really hate that my parents could turn on their friends like this because of their own greed. Whatever the extent of their involvement is, they allowed it to poison everything in their life, all for the sake of the power it gave them, even if it meant people died for them to get ahead. It fills me with this urge to act and I follow the impulse.

"We have to go down there," I say.

"If they've got their people watching the shipping place, they probably have them on this, too."

It's not like him to want to be cautious. He's a take action type of person.

"We'll be careful."

The corner of his mouth kicks up and he tilts his head, giving me a once over that sends heat racing through me again. "Always in it for the thrill of trouble."

I grin. "So we're going?"

"Yes. But we need to blend in better than your scraps of fabric pretending to be yoga clothes and my ripped jeans in case people are there. We should make it look like we could be Nexus Lab employees again."

"It looked abandoned on Google street view."

"Still."

"I didn't bring much, but I'll see what I can throw together."

Luckily, I did put a pair of slim fitting black pants in my bag when I was throwing random things from my closet into it. They'll have to do. I pull them on as he dresses in a pair of dove gray slacks and a shirt. Once again I'm tempted by the sight of him dressed up from his usual rough appearance.

Fox's gaze trails the bare curve of my spine as I put my hair up in a sleek high ponytail, then put on a lace bralette and steal one of his few button down shirts from a rack he keeps in the corner. He lifts a brow, but says nothing. I get the message from his smirk, it amuses him that I keep stealing his clothes.

"This is more business chic than the vintage blouses and casual workout clothes I brought with me when I left my house," I point out once I'm ready. "I didn't account for how much undercover work I'd be doing when picking out my quick getaway wardrobe."

"Whatever you say," he says lightly, gaze traveling over me again. "You look good."

Kneeling by the black duffel bag that was in the back of his Charger when I stowed away, he takes out a handgun and checks the amount of bullets before slotting the clip back into place and tucking the weapon in the back of his pants. He puts his hand at the small of my back and guides me down to the garage.

"You think we need to be armed for this?"

"We have to be prepared for anything."

A chill skates down my neck at the ruthlessness in his tone. I change the subject.

"If you have suits, why didn't you ever wear the school uniform?"

"Because I don't play by the rules." He huffs out a laugh, putting his arm around my shoulders to draw me closer once we reach the bottom of the steps. "And because it helped people fear me if I looked like I could kill them with my bare hands. A preppy blazer wouldn't have done me any favors."

I sink my teeth into my lip. Is it wrong that what he said turns me on? Probably, but I don't care.

Chuckling, he plants a kiss on my cheek. "The rain let up. Let's go."

The ride there isn't long. It's closer than I expected to Fox's place. We take the Charger instead of the bike this time.

Instead of pulling in, we park on the no outlet lane and walk over. The place seems as deserted as the shipping facility was after it was wiped of any evidence of Nexus Lab using it. The building is run down, overgrown weeds doing their best to take over.

"Doesn't seem like anyone is around," I say after we test the front door and find it locked with a padlock.

"But Jacqueline definitely came here for something. It had to be important. She wouldn't break her strict routine and risk the way she likes to portray herself for something random."

"Something she didn't want to be seen doing," I add.

"Right. What about around here?" Fox's fingers circle my wrist and he takes us around the side of the building. "They might want it to put off this vibe like it's nothing important, or abandoned, but then have a back entrance or something on a sub level."

We barely make it ten steps before we're spotted.

"Hey!"

A sharp voice calls out, making us whip around. My stomach takes a nosedive. Fox moves quickly, putting me behind him protectively, one hand going to the back of his pants to grip the gun he tucked there.

"What are you doing here?"

TWENTY-EIGHT
Fox

The adrenaline racing through my veins doesn't slow when I spot the man who called us out. Once he's close, I see he's only maybe five years older than us in his mid-twenties with reddish brown hair and glasses with thick plastic frames. I'm still on the defensive, ready to protect Maisy from any threat. My grip on the gun doesn't ease.

"Who are you?" he demands.

"Who are *you*?" Maisy shoots back, inching out from behind me. She flicks her ponytail with confidence and gives the man a once over. "We're doing an internal audit and this is the property we're checking out today."

I want to smile, but I keep a stern expression. She's jumped to the cover I used when I snooped around the shipping facility.

The man raises a brow and adjusts his glasses, gaze flicking between us. "Really? Funny, because the internal records department is where I work and I've never seen either of you."

We both tense and I move close enough to grab her wrist, ready to fucking run if this guy calls backup.

"So let's try again. Who the hell are you kids and what are you doing here?"

"Kids?" I scoff. "You're not much older."

"I'm Maisy Landry. My mother is the CEO of Nexus Lab."

I swallow a curse. Damn it, Maisy.

She steps in front of me full of confidence like she's going to protect me with her family name, propping her hands on her hips.

This gets the guy's attention and he gives her a crooked grin that makes me growl under my breath. His gray eyes flick to me for a moment before his shoulders shake with a silent laugh. "I see. So, not internal auditors then."

It makes him relax that we don't work for the company.

"No. Now answer my question—who are you and why are you here?"

He holds out a hand. "Ethan Hannigan. Records department, as I said. Unlike you little sneaks, I'm seriously an employee."

I take in his casual shorts and button down. "Why would someone from the records department be out at an abandoned warehouse practically in the middle of nowhere on a

Saturday? Doesn't seem like it should be in the job description."

Ethan turns his lopsided grin on me. "Observant. And you are...?" He leaves the question hanging, then smirks. "Miss Landry's bodyguard? The suit's a nice touch, definitely makes you seem older. And you're armed. Smart."

"My boyfriend," Maisy says firmly, putting her hand in mine.

A stupid flutter fills my chest at the term and I have to work to keep my mouth from curving. For once, I pull on the pain of losing my parents and all the shit that happened to me after to help me keep from grinning like an idiot that the girl I love might feel the same about me.

Together we form a united front against Ethan. My gut tells me he's not what I first thought. If he was, we'd already be in the back of a blacked out SUV on our way to face whoever keeps trying to take me out just like my parents. It's enough for me to release the gun. But I'm still wary of trusting strangers and taking them at face value.

"How did you find this place?" Ethan asks, tucking his hands in his pockets.

"Followed my mom here when she was supposed to be at work," Maisy says, only partially lying.

Ethan hums like that makes total sense. "This is the first time I've been able to get out here. Every time I tried to follow, I'd lose the car taking her here. It's a little underwhelming from how suspicious it seems, huh?"

For whatever reason, he trusts that we aren't going to relay his admission of digging around to Jacqueline. He scans the tree branches waving over the damp concrete behind us and his expression shifts.

"We should probably get out of here before the security patrol comes around," he suggests. "They're a punctual bunch and they don't like uninvited guests."

"There's a diner nearby," I say.

Ethan nods. "I'll meet you there in twenty minutes. Grab a booth."

As I pull Maisy back toward the Charger, she keeps her voice down. "Are we just going to trust he's chill?"

I glance over my shoulder at the direction Ethan heads. "Didn't you see how much his demeanor changed once he found out we weren't official employees? I think he guessed we're snooping around like he is."

"What do you think his deal is?"

"That's what I want to find out. Come on."

We climb into the car. The drive to the diner is only a few minutes. It's mostly populated by truckers with its proximity to the interstate. The lunch rush is dwindling, the parking lot half full. We head inside and ask for a booth near the back. Maisy sits on my side and I keep an eye on the door while she chats to the waitress about our friend who will be joining us. It's not long before Ethan arrives with a leather satchel hanging off his shoulder, ambling over to our booth after a quick scan of the diner.

"So who are you really?" I prompt before his ass hits the fake red leather bench seat.

Ethan chuckles. "Damn, kid. Hasn't anyone taught you anything about the art of subtlety?"

"Don't really have time for subtlety." My fist clenches on the table, my other arm draped across the back of the seat around Maisy's shoulders.

Ethan holds up his hands as the waitress brings over a menu for him. He perks up and takes his time browsing over the specials. Maisy's elbow catches me in the side and I grunt. She lifts her brows and gestures toward Ethan with her head.

"I'm starved, aren't you?" She picks up her own menu, muttering out of the side of her mouth. "Let's order something so we don't stick out."

Ethan hums in approval, darting a look at us over the top of his laminated menu. Sighing, I flip mine open and order the first thing I see when the waitress comes around to collect our orders.

"Talk," I say once she drops off our drinks, unable to fully relax until I know what his deal is.

Pursing his lips, he stirs his Coke with the straw. "I work for Nexus Lab, but it's because I'm an undercover journalist. I've been investigating a network of elites tied to it. Politicians, other businesses—the works. The network stretches across the states."

Maisy's lips part and she leans across the table. I want to tug her back and keep her close. "What have you found out?"

Before he tells us, there's something else I want to know. "Why are you telling us? You met us less than an hour ago."

"Your name is Fox Wilder," Ethan says matter of factly. "You look just like your dad. I've got access to employee records and your parents' files were some of the first that tipped me off to some of the bigger things at work when I first began infiltrating the company."

My jaw clenches as I slump back against the seat. It's gratifying to know there are others who found what happened to my parents suspect. Maisy's hand lands on my leg beneath the table and she squeezes, leaning into me. I curl my arm further around her, catching a strand of her ponytail between my fingers.

"It's taken time to gain access, but I've been able to gather a good look at the history of the company," Ethan explains. "The money records are something else. Something changed a little over a decade ago that really put Nexus Lab on the map compared to its more humble beginnings."

We all pause when our food comes out. Ethan makes heart eyes at the burger set in front of him while Maisy digs into a breakfast special with a side of sausage links. I don't have the appetite for the sandwich I ordered, but I shove a chip into my mouth anyway. Maisy reaches over and steals one, making me smile reluctantly.

"So," Maisy prompts.

It takes Ethan a minute to continue, too busy taking a huge bite of his food and sighing in delight. "Gonna miss this."

Maisy and I glance at each other. She hitches a shoulder and presses her leg against mine, knee to hip.

"In the last couple of weeks I've been able to dig deeper without raising alarm now that I've built up my reputation and respect at the company. I came across a sealed file on employee termination. It seemed weird. I haven't had any luck cracking it—computers aren't really my thing." He meets my gaze directly and my stomach drops. "What caught my interest was the date. I checked the local papers and it lined up with your parents getting into an accident."

Everything he's telling us lines up with what Colton has found out for me, so I know what we're chasing is real.

"I have someone I trust who's good with computers. I want to prove my parents were murdered," I say. "That's it."

Ethan nods. "Of course. Take this." He rummages in his satchel and pulls out a flash drive. I palm it and tuck it into my pocket. He sticks another fry in his mouth. "The trail's leading me to the east coast. This is my last week at the company. I've already given notice because I've burned through my resources here."

"Why can't you stay and see it through?" Maisy asks.

"This is just one piece of the picture. I want the whole thing when I break this story. Everything I've got so far is on that drive."

"Thank you," Maisy says. "I'm glad we ran into you, or we might've missed out on knowing this."

"Probably would've gotten yourselves caught by the patrol, too," Ethan says with a pointed look as he drizzles ketchup over the rest of his fries. "Seriously, watch out for them. You'll find what I've pieced together on this in what I gave you, but when someone from their parent company has a meeting with the Nexus Lab board, it throws off this shady vibe. My co-worker goes white as a sheet whenever they come around."

I don't mention what we learned from Colton earlier about who owns the shell corporation that owns Nexus Lab. "Yeah. We'll be more careful."

"You'll have to be to prove what happened to your parents. Here's my number if you need me. Good luck."

With that, Ethan wipes his mouth with a napkin, slips me a business card, and tosses down enough cash to cover his meal before he nods to us and leaves.

Maisy sits back against the fake red leather. "Kismet."

"Bless you?" My brows dip. "The hell is that?"

She blows out an amused breath, lips curving. "It means fate, that something was meant to be. We seriously got lucky crossing paths with an undercover journalist who's been digging into the same thing you have."

"I don't believe in fate," I mutter, glancing out the window to watch the vehicles on the interstate fly by the exit for Ridgeview. "Shit's for fairytales."

"I believe you and I were meant to find each other again." Her hand finds mine and she leans her head on my shoulder. I almost laugh because I knew she'd call us fate. "You and me, that's how it's supposed to be. Just like we used to say."

That I can't argue with. It's the only way to explain the way my heart beats harder when she's around. How much less I'm ruled by the anger of my past because she keeps me grounded from spiraling out of control. How much better I fucking sleep without nightmares clawing at my mind because she's in my arms with her soothing floral and coconut scent wrapped around me.

"You're right." I turn back and drop a kiss on top of her head, inhaling her sweetness mingled with my shampoo. "It was a lucky break. We could've missed him and then we wouldn't have more information to comb through."

"See, the power of positive thinking." She sits up. "That's what Thea always says."

"The one with the bakery, right? Eloped in Paris?"

She nods with a fond smile. I'm hit by a pang of guilt. Maisy deserves to be enjoying her summer with her friends and living a normal life, but instead I've dragged her into my shadows and uncovered the seedy underbelly rotting this town from the ground up.

"Wait, how did you know about Paris?" She narrows her gaze. "I didn't tell you about that."

The corners of my mouth curl up in a smug smile. "I told you, daisy. Any move you made, I knew about it." Grasping her chin, I angle her face up and kiss her. She grins into it. "Ready to get out of here?"

"Yes. I want to know what Ethan's found in the time he's spent under the radar."

"Me too."

We leave the diner and I press Maisy back against the side of the Charger for another kiss before I hold her door open for her. She laughs as she slides in.

On our way back to my place, I grow quiet, contemplating everything we've learned in the last several hours. I can tell she's worried about me by the thousand and one looks she's shot at me in the last ten minutes alone.

She must finally reach a limit, because she reaches across the center console and takes my hand.

"What are you thinking?" Her soft voice is a balm to my aching soul.

I lick my lips, staring ahead at the road. My hand hangs over the wheel and I twitch my fingers, thinking how to put it.

"I have a bad feeling. All of this is bigger than I thought." I shake my head. "I only set out to prove the truth about my parents being murdered, that it was covered up. I never expected to discover this intricate web of lies and corruption. This shit runs so deep its roots burrow into Ridgeview."

"But now we can make it right."

Her optimism is a buoy to reach for in the churning sea I feel myself being pulled further into. I thread our fingers together, knuckles turning white from how tightly I grip her smaller hands. I just need to hold on and let her light guide me out of the darkness threatening to swallow me whole.

"I don't know what to do, Maise," I admit hoarsely.

Christ, I sound so goddamn broken and beat down by the hand I've been dealt. I wish more than anything nothing bad ever happened so she and I could've been two kids who grew up together and had a good life. But I know that's not how the world works. It's a cruel reality.

"No matter where this goes, I'm with you," she assures me with an admirable steel in her tone.

I manage to loosen my death grip on her hand and bring it up to my mouth for a kiss. That's when I see it in the rearview mirror. My body stiffens and time seems to slow in the seconds it takes me to suck in a sharp breath and focus on one thing: *drive*.

A loud bang goes off and Maisy screams. The back window blows out in a shower of broken glass. Fuck, this can't be happening!

"Get down!" I shout, trying to shield her while I drive.

There's no time to grab for the gun I stashed in the glove compartment. Instead of fighting back, I want to get us away to keep her safe. I slam my foot on the gas pedal, flooring it as I weave back and forth to make us a harder target to hit. The wind is loud, whipping into the car from the damage. I let my guard down and it might get us killed.

"Oh my god! What's happening?"

The blacked out SUV tries to close the distance and I see the shotgun again in the side mirror.

"Shit!"

Another bang rings out as I yank the wheel, but I'm not fast enough. The driver's side window shatters, sharp pieces catching me across the cheek and neck as I instinctively shy away with a grunt. Ignoring the pain, I grit my teeth and push the car harder to get us the hell out of there.

"You good?" I demand, praying no buckshot spread flew through the car.

Maisy tries to lift her head as my tires screech across the road when I take a turn too fast.

"Down, Maisy!" I press down on her shoulders and she curls up in a ball. "Someone's fucking shooting at us!"

"I figured that out," she yelps over the wind of the two destroyed windows. Reaching up, she latches on to my arm that's shielding her, grip desperate and scared. "They must have been watching and followed us."

"Hold on tight. I'll get us out of here."

My heart thumps hard as I white knuckle the wheel. I will get us out of this or we'll meet the same fate as my parents. I'll never let them take anything away from me again.

Especially not my daisy.

TWENTY-NINE
Maisy

Fox winces and I scrunch up my face in sympathy as I clean the cuts he got from the broken glass. He's sitting on a low stool shirtless, hair wet from the quick shower we took when we got back. His hands grip my hips as I dab at freshly dried blood on his cheek. He hasn't stopped touching me once, like he needs to physically know I'm safe by keeping me within reach.

"Sorry," I murmur when he grits his teeth from the sting of the alcohol wipe.

He grunts, jaw locked. I know he's not mad at me, but the force of his anger is a palpable thing. His body ripples with the need to tear something apart.

Someone fucking shot at us. If it wasn't serious before, it's clear how dangerous this is now.

I'm shaken by what happened on our way home from the diner, but staying strong. This is no time to lose my head. Neither of us got shot, thank god. I really hope Ethan wasn't followed. We made it away safely thanks to Fox's fast driving, managing to lose the blacked out SUV by luring them into the residential part of Ridgeview where they couldn't shoot at us without witnesses. That's what matters.

I peel open a small bandage and stick it over the long wound on Fox's neck, fingertips lingering on his warm damp skin. My body shakes with a shudder and air rushes past my lips. It hasn't stopped doing that, even after the shower. My pulse has calmed, but there is still something simmering beneath my skin. For now I ignore it, focusing on getting Fox patched up.

His dark blue eyes watch me with something like recognition reflecting back. I think he knows I'm more rattled than I'm letting on. He uses his thumbs to trace patterns on my hips and with a subtle press he guides me closer between his spread knees, near enough that I feel his breath coast down my chest and across my bare stomach.

My nipples tighten in response. A pulse of heat throbs between my legs and I swallow. I didn't bother to throw on more than a pair of tight workout shorts and a sports bra after the shower while he only tugged on the jeans he had on this morning.

When we stumbled up the steps to the second floor of Fox's warehouse, him half-dragging me, we stripped out of our clothes at the door. Pieces of glass clung to my hair, hitting the concrete floor with little pings as I shook it free. Fox pulled me right into the shower to wash off the danger and any lingering pieces too small to see. He took his time running his hands over my body first with a look of deep concentration and protectiveness until he was satisfied that I was glass-free. I did the same to him, carefully pushing my fingers into his thick hair while he silently watched.

Fox ended up with minor scrapes and one deeper cut on his neck. I was sore from how tensely I'd curled into a ball, crouched low and held in place by his arm as he drove us to safety, but the worst I'd end up with is some bruising from smacking into the center console from the tight turns. It's a miracle neither of us ended up with buckshot embedded in our skin.

Actually, it's lucky we made it away at all.

These are the people my mother and father work for. People willing to kill Fox, willing to kill *me* because I'm seen with him.

Do either of them know that I was shot at today?

Would they care?

They're willing to look the other way and go as far as covering up their friends' murder so their dirty bosses will keep paying them, so how far is too far? I don't know if I want to find out just how much they'd sacrifice for their greed.

"Hey." Fox grasps my wrist and cups my nape, bringing our foreheads together. The waves of anger subside a little as he focuses on me. "Stop thinking for a minute."

"How do you know that's what I was doing?" I whisper.

"Because you're shaking." He soothes his hand down my arm and rubs until the trembling passes. "It's okay. I'll keep you safe."

It's the most he's managed to say to me since the danger descended on us, like he had to work through everything clouding his own head too.

I close my eyes and slide my nose along his in a gentle nuzzle, taking comfort in his protective nature when it comes to me.

"Are you cold?" he asks in a low voice tinged in the shadows of his anger. "You could go into shock."

"No. I'm good."

Fox puts his big hands on my back and smooths them up and down every inch of my exposed skin. I can't help the way it makes me arch against him, a tiny sound catching in my throat. He keeps up the slow touches, stroking the curve of my spine with his calloused fingertips. My skin isn't cold, it's the opposite—I'm burning up inside and each tender touch nudges me closer to a cliff edge I feel like I need to dive off.

A strange hunger eats at me, one unlike any I've ever experienced. I've always had a healthy sexual appetite, but it's never been like this. My mind fills with images and I scrape my teeth over my lip, pushing aside the wish for Fox to pick me up by my thighs and toss me down on his bed.

"We should see what Ethan gave us on the flash drive," I say instead of entertaining the fantasies.

I move to go fish it out of Fox's pants, but his hold on me tightens, keeping me in place.

Leaning back, I peer at him curiously, but he doesn't let me get far. He adjusts on the stool and pulls me onto his lap. There's so much conflict swirling in his dark gaze when he cups my face and brushes his thumbs over my cheeks.

"I think we should stop," he finally says.

"Stop?"

Fox sighs heavily. "This is dangerous. I don't want you to get hurt." He pauses, throat bobbing. "That's the last thing I want now. If I have to choose between you and my revenge on this town, I choose you. My parents are dead, but you're alive and I'm not letting you go."

My heart cracks open and my breath hitches. I grasp his wrists as tears sting my eyes. Hearing him ready to give up on everything makes me ache, but at the same time hearing that I mean more to him than anything else makes me happy.

"Fox," I whisper. "I..."

His gaze pierces mine. It seems like he's holding his breath, waiting for me to confess how I feel about him. He has to know I'm in love with him, right? I think I always have been, since we were little kids.

"You said you've been searching for these answers for so long," I say.

"I know." He forces out a breath. "It's driven so much of my life, but it doesn't matter. I'd rather let it go if it means keeping you safe."

He's saying he's giving it up, but his body is wound tight, like it hasn't caught up with his head. He might be ready, but I'm not. He's pulled back the veil that shrouded my life and I'm done with the complacency. What's going on in this town is wrong and I want to see the consequences come down on them all.

"What if I say I'm not done?"

His brow wrinkles. "Maisy..."

"I'm serious. I think we should still keep going." I sit up straighter in his lap and set my jaw. "I'm not afraid and I want to see this to the end with you."

Fox studies me for a long stretch, cupping my shoulders like I'm something precious to be cradled and cherished.

"Are you sure?" His hands drop off my shoulders and skate down my back, stirring the heat in my center. The deep rumble of his voice is its own seductive and sensual temptation stroking my skin. "We could just leave. Follow the road wherever it takes us." Leaning in, he places an open-mouthed kiss on the column of my throat that makes my thighs clench. "Just you and me."

God, I want that. It's been my biggest dream for as long as I can remember. Damn him for dangling it in front of me.

We're so close to uncovering the truth, though. I can feel it. Fox needs that closure to be able to truly move on with his life.

I purse my lips. "I'm sure. We can't let them keep getting away with it all."

He stares at me for another moment, then nods. "The minute you're in danger again, we're stopping. Chasing ghosts isn't as important as you are to me."

A flutter moves through my chest and I smile. "Deal."

Pulled by the force of the thing still itching beneath my skin, I cover his mouth with mine. A sound sticks in his throat as he parts his lips for my tongue, holding my hips. The temperature in the room rises fast and I break off, panting and breathing him in. Zaps of the adrenaline that hasn't fully faded skitter across my body and I shudder. It's been building since we got away, since the shower with his hands on me under the water, since he kissed my neck and offered to give into the urge that always sits in the back of my mind to get in a car and drive.

It's all too much to ignore anymore and I need him.

Fox's eyes are heavy-lidded, tracking my tongue when I dart it out to wet my lower lip. My nipples harden, feeling sensitive with every tiny shift of my body in his lap.

"Is it..." I try to catch my breath. "Is it weird if I say I'm really horny right now?"

He chuckles, the sound dark and inviting, then captures my lips again, hands roaming freely. I moan into the searing kiss as pushes beneath my sports bra to squeeze my breast while teasing me with his tongue. The wild edge of his passion matches mine and seems on the verge of breaking free.

"Fuck me?" I breathe against his lips.

Fox leaves a lingering kiss at the corner of my mouth while grabbing the back of my thighs and lifting me into his arms as he stands. "You never have to ask twice, baby."

We leave the kitchenette area on one side of the converted warehouse space, but don't make it far. He drops me on the back of the couch and wastes no time peeling my tiny shorts off, tossing them aside before popping the button on his jeans. I watch in fascination as his powerful thighs are revealed and my breath grows short at the sight of his cock, hard and ready.

He slants his mouth over mine. Taking a fistful of my hair, he angles my head back so my neck is bared for him and breaks the kiss to lick a stripe up it. I shiver as he trails hot biting kisses back down.

"We could've died today." It's sinking in. The thrumming beneath my skin reaches a fever pitch. I meet his hooded eyes. "Make me feel alive?"

He keeps hold of my gaze as he releases my hair and drags his fingers down my body, over my folds, eliciting another shudder from me. He flicks his attention down briefly to watch his finger sink into me and I bite my lip, almost crying out in protest when he pulls it out. Holding up glistening fingers between us, his mouth curves into a seductive smirk.

"Thought so. Look at that, you're fucking soaked."

My cheeks prickle with heat, but I won't avert my gaze or hide from my arousal. Fox's smirk stretches wider and he kisses me hard, pushing my legs further apart.

Balanced on the back of the couch, I don't have much to hold onto, so I cling to his muscled shoulders and shudder as his cock enters me with one sharp thrust. My mouth falls open at the intense heat coiling in my core.

"Fox," I gasp, nails digging into his tattooed skin as I wrap my legs tighter around his waist.

There's a gleam in his eyes as he lifts one of my legs, stretching it high enough it drapes over his shoulder. He tests my flexibility and swipes his tongue in a slow arc over his lower lip when he finds the position is within my limit. Holding my hip with one hand, he grabs my nape with the other, trapping my leg. His thrusts are powerful and something dark and feral swirls in his eyes that stokes the fire burning in me. When he hits a spot that lights me up, my back arches and my nails rake across his skin, making him groan.

Our movements are passionate with an undercurrent of roughness that I crave.

His fingers clamp tighter on my nape as his skin slaps against mine. He pulls me closer and kisses me demandingly. I lean into it, a strangled cry sticking in my throat.

We almost died. Someone shot at us. But we're alive. *We're fucking alive.*

I break the kiss first, tilting my head back and closing my eyes. Fox curses, lips pressed to my neck.

"God, yes," I push out. "Don't stop."

"That what you need, baby?" His teeth scrape a sensitive spot on my neck, followed by his tongue. The vibration of his low laugh drags me closer to the edge. "Yeah, that's what I thought. Your pussy is begging for my cock."

I level him with a look, grabbing a fistful of his hair. He grins at me when I pull his face up from my neck. "Then keep going. Make me feel good."

"You want to come?" He snaps his hips to punctuate the question.

I nod, a moan escaping me as he hits that spot again.

"Hold on tight, or I'm going to fuck you so hard you fall off this couch."

Air punches out of me and my stomach dips with the spike of desire racing through me. The force of the next thrust makes my eyes roll back in my head. My entire body lights up, needing more, more, more. He takes me hard and fast, controlling and commanding my pleasure, and I have no choice but to obey.

A scream tears from my throat when I come. Fox's grip flexes on me. His thrusts turn more powerful as he chases his release. With a deep rumbling growl he stiffens and his cock pulses, filling my pussy.

This is what I needed—him making me feel how alive we are.

THIRTY
Maisy

Fox wasn't about to let me out of his sight for the foreseeable future, but I convinced him I needed to leave his converted warehouse or go stir crazy if I didn't get out for a bit.

The itch under my skin was killing me and I wouldn't tame myself or hold back from what I need anymore. My usual yoga routine wasn't helping. I needed fresh air and something normal to beat back the memories of being shot at yesterday. I promised to be careful while I hung out with Thea at her bakery. He tried to shove his gun in my purse, but since it wouldn't fit and I refused to carry it on me, he told me with finality that I had an hour before he picked me up.

"An hour and that's it," he reminds me when he drops me off on the main street lined with shopping boutiques, galleries, and a coffee shop. "I don't like leaving you here."

"I'm grabbing smoothies with my bestie, not walking into a life and death situation." He growls in displeasure and I bend to give him a quick kiss. "I'll be fine. Look, see? There are yoga moms. Totally safe."

As I gesture at the cheerful storefronts and the women I usually see in my classes pushing their kids in strollers amongst the other shoppers enjoying the summer day, his chiseled jaw works. Some people look our way, pausing to stare at him while they whisper to each other, probably spreading more lies about him.

"You should always be prepared," he says gruffly. "Be careful and keep an eye out. We still have no idea if they know you're with me. I'd rather no one found out if it keeps you safe."

I point to Thea's bakery in the middle of the block. "I'm going right there. Nothing's going to happen."

If I say it enough times, I'll believe it.

He brushes my waist. "If you need me, you call right away. I'll be back in an hour to get you."

I nod and watch him drive off, admiring the sight of him on his motorcycle. A pair of women in LuLulemons and trendy corduroy baseball caps wave to me as I head down the sidewalk.

"We missed you in class this week," one of them says.

"I know, sorry. I'm on a break for a while," I offer with a smile. When they exchange a glance and tilt their heads in silent yoga mom language—aka totally judging me—I add,

"Figuring out stuff for my freshman semester."

"Oh," they drawl in unison.

"Keep working on your crane pose, you'll get there." I infuse cheerfulness I don't feel into my tone. "It's all about practice, ladies."

I leave them behind and keep heading for the bakery.

A familiar voice nearby stops me in my tracks. *Mom*. Ducking under the shaded awning of a boutique, I hide behind a rack of clothes and pretend to browse until I spot her up ahead with Mayor Taylor and another man in tow. I've managed to avoid my parents around Ridgeview since I left, but I didn't think I'd run into her downtown in the middle of the day. Shouldn't she be at her office instead of having lunch with the mayor?

Then again, Fox and I traced her to that shady abandoned warehouse when she was supposed to be at work for an important meeting. Thinking of what happened after we went there yesterday sends a shudder rolling through me. I came out here to get away from the thoughts rattling around in my head.

It's weird to look at her now that I know she's working with criminals.

For a moment, I wonder if the mayor is in on their scheming. The old mayor was in some way, since they got him to overlook Dad's promotion with a bribe.

This is an opportunity I can't waste. I take out my phone and send a quick text to Thea letting her know I'm running late. She won't mind and this could be important to help us figure out more of what's going on.

Keeping my movements casual, I sneak my phone through the rack and snap photos of the three of them as they talk. They're too far to hear clearly. Mom seems tense and the guy with the mayor is frowning. I don't recognize him and it only tugs harder at my suspicion.

They turn and head my way. Crap. I shift around the boutique's sale racks and fake being absorbed in a vintage red suede number that, actually, I would love to have.

"Maisy." Not a question, barely a hint of surprise at running into me, and no trace of worry or remorse for the things she said to me the night I left.

I meet my mother's cool gaze. "Mom." My attention shifts over her shoulder to the mayor. "Mayor Taylor."

The third man stands close to the mayor. He has cropped hair and looks rough, even in a cheap suit stretched to its limit by his barrel chest. His steel gaze sweeps over me, making my skin crawl. Must be a new bodyguard.

"Nice to see you, Maisy," the mayor says. "I hope you're feeling better. Your mother mentioned you caught a bad stomach bug when I saw you last at the steakhouse."

"Right," I say, glancing accusingly at Mom. Any lie she can spin to keep her from looking bad is fair game. "I was sick to my stomach."

Partially true, since my parents tried to force sleazy Sam Blake on me as yet another way to control my life. Now I know all their dirty skeletons they hid from Holden and I.

It's subtle, but the corners of her mouth pinch in disapproval. She does a good job of acting like everything's normal while each slight gesture tells me I'll be sorry if I make a scene. Years of learned behavior rises in me, calling me to her will because it can't be unlearned overnight. I clench my teeth.

Do you know? I want to scream. *Do you know that the psychos paying you shot at me and Fox?*

"You should be at home," Mom says with a well-practiced casual air. She's a pro at doublespeaking to get her meaning across without raising alarms to anyone who doesn't know what she's really like. "It's too soon for you to be out and about after how seriously ill you were."

Translation: *stop fucking around and do as I say.*

Pressing my lips into a thin line, I stretch my arms overhead in a show of defiance. "I feel a lot better now."

"All the same, I'd rather see you go home, sweetheart."

The mayor's bodyguard is eerily transfixed on me. He gives me a yellow-toothed grin when I catch him staring at me for the third time instead of keeping an eye out for any potential threats, like a bodyguard is supposed to.

I roll my shoulders back. "I don't think I will."

Mom's eyes flash in annoyance. "Well. If you insist on being difficult."

Is it difficult or am I just thinking for myself? Not that she'd care. Her world only consists of what she wants to control.

"Jacqueline," the mayor says. "We should…"

"In a moment. We'll make it on time for the…" She pauses and her sleek bob swings when she turns back to me. The bodyguard shifts restlessly and she sighs. "Investors. I just want to make sure my daughter makes it home."

She grabs my wrist, nails digging in hard. I suck in a breath, shocked that she would do it in front of an audience. There isn't a shred of empathy or compassion in her gaze. If she doesn't know I was shot at, I doubt she'd be moved.

The truth of it is a punch to the gut. After seeing proof of her dirty business dealings, I can barely look at her. We haven't had a great relationship, or even an okay one for years, but it hurts to know she feels little for my well being.

A rumbling around the corner snags my attention. Fox's motorcycle turns down the road and relief washes over me. He must've stayed nearby. With his leather jacket, tousled dark hair, and the fresh cuts from our run in with the criminals my parents are working with, he looks every inch the dangerous bad boy whispered about throughout town. Mom and the others stiffen at the sight of him.

Oddly, she exchanges a look with the bodyguard, as if he's the one in control rather than her or the mayor.

"Bye, Mom."

Yanking my wrist from her talon-like nails, I keep my gaze locked with hers as I move toward the curb. The bike stops behind me and Fox's stony presence envelops me like a hug, warding off anyone else who dares get close while welcoming me into its embrace. Mom watches, enraged, as I get on the back of the bike and wrap my arms around Fox's waist.

"Maisy," she hisses.

Fox revs the engine, arrogantly cutting off whatever she tries to say next to save face and puts a hand over mine for a beat.

Mom cuts a sharp glance to the bodyguard, then the mayor, before looking back at me and silently commanding me to get off the motorcycle. I set my jaw. All I hear is the sound of glass shattering and the angry blast of gunshots.

Without another word, we peel away from my mother, the mayor, and his bodyguard. Later I'll apologize to Thea for ditching, but Fox couldn't have come at a better time.

It's like he knew I needed him. No matter what, he'll come for me.

THIRTY-ONE
Fox

Bright light filters through the industrial windows, making Maisy's hair shine in the summery morning rays. It's fanned out on the pillow as she sleeps. One of her hands is tucked beneath her cheek and the other reaches out to me, draped over my inked chest. Carefully, I roll toward her with a content, sleep-tinged sigh.

Having her in my arms, in my bed, to chase away the tortured images my mind fills with in sleep is wonderful. They haven't been bothering me as much. It's the best sleep I've gotten in years.

As I watch her, she cracks her eyes open groggily. My lips twitch and my heart turns over. For someone that loves to move and stretch her body with yoga, she doesn't love mornings. Maybe yoga is what helps her accept being awake.

"Morning," she whispers huskily.

With a cute little grunt, she snuggles closer and smiles at me. I caress her back and enjoy the feeling of her head resting on my chest. It's quiet and comfortable for a few minutes. This is nice, not having to worry about my problems or a plan or what happened two days ago, nothing but enjoying the beautiful girl in my arms.

"You feel okay?" she asks a while later.

"Yeah," I say, touching one of the scabbed over cuts on my cheek. "They'll heal in a few days. Not the worst I've dealt with."

She lifts her head, propping her chin on my pec to peer at me with her sleepy hazel eyes. "What do you want to do after all this is over?"

I go to answer, then pause. Do I have a life plan? My life has only been focused on revenge for so long. I never thought past it.

"I don't know," I say slowly.

Her calf slides against my leg beneath the sheets. I like it, all the little ways she touches me. She hums and shifts, folding her arms over my chest to rest her head on, her bare tits pressing into my skin. I lick my lips and skate my fingertips down her sides.

"What about the stuff you make? You could do something like the work you do with reclaimed materials. People would buy the things you build. Or do you like working on cars better?"

Her lips pucker in thought and I'm too busy breathing through a wave of fondness mingled with the tug of arousal low in my stomach when her body moves while she talks.

"You could open a workshop that gives you the space to do both." Her eyebrows waggle. "Y'know, because you're so multitalented."

As her voice dips with double meaning, she slides her soft body over mine, straddling me. Shit, I'm liking where this is going. My hands automatically find her hips and a pleased rumble vibrates in my throat.

"I...yes, I like that idea. Never thought about it much before."

I can barely string together a sentence, too distracted by the way she looks with the sheets pooled around her waist, hair mussed from sleep, hunger burning in her gaze. Proud of her body and happy to have me admire it. Her lashes flutter and she puts her hands on the ocean and crow on my chest as she continues in a hushed voice, painting a dream of the future.

Her skin is soft. I move one hand from her waist, pushing my palm up from her stomach, through the valley between her tits, not stopping until my fingers wrap around her throat. The corners of her mouth lift in approval. Using my hold on her neck, I pull her down to steal a kiss.

Mine, I think with a flare of possession.

"It'll be close enough to the beach to hear the seagulls," she mumbles against my lips between kisses. "Venice Beach, I think. Just a couple blocks away. And nearby, I'll have a beachfront yoga studio of my own. I've been thinking that's what I want to do, after my road trip. Just picture it."

I'm liking the idea more and more, but my thoughts haze over as she sits up and sinks onto my cock with this wicked half-lidded bliss on her face that has me ready to blow my load the minute I'm fully inside the wet heat of her pussy.

"Anything you want," I rasp, fitting my hands back to her waist and groaning when she starts to ride my cock. "As long as I'm with you."

All the things I thought I had to do seem less vital to living right now. This is all I need. When I'm with her, everything else fades away.

Victory gleams in her beautiful golden eyes and, god, I love her. I fucking love her.

* * *

It takes a few days, but I managed to get what I needed to fix the blown out glass on the Charger. After the repair is done, I climb the steps and find Maisy in a nest of sheets on the bed in a sports bra with the laptop, squinting at the screen. We hit a snag with the sealed employee file Ethan gave us that even Colt has had trouble decrypting, so she's combing through the copied hard drive from her parents' place searching for a way to get in.

I scrub a hand over my jaw as I watch her for a second, pushing away the thought of what happened the other day. Putting her life in danger is unacceptable. I'm still pissed those fuckers took a shot at her just to get at me. Even though she said we should keep going, I'm wondering if I should pull the plug on this.

Again I'm hit with the idea to put her on the back of the bike and just go. Leave Ridgeview in the dust while I take her wherever we want. Go find the life she talked about for us. I've spent so many years on this, but being with her makes me rethink what's important.

I cross the room and cup the back of her head, kissing her hair. "Any luck?"

"Not yet."

Maybe that's a good thing, I think grimly, partially hating myself for being so disrespectful to the memory of my dead parents.

It takes her another minute to give me her attention. I rub her shoulders and neck until her lashes flutter and she makes an appreciative noise. She's tense and I don't know if I'm good with her running herself into the ground like this. My mind whispers with the idea again, we could just leave and find the ocean. I slide my lips together and sigh. I miss the damn salt air and I want to breathe it in with her by my side.

"Don't forget to take a break. You've been at it for days." She nods, tilting her face up to accept the quick kiss I drop on her mouth before I pull away. "I'm going to workout."

I put on some music and lean my head side to side as I warm up, loosening my muscles until my limbs are ready. The first hit against the bag always feels the best. I let myself go, channeling all my rage at Nexus Lab and Stalenko Corp into my workout.

Feeling her gaze roaming over my form not long after, I smirk to myself. I'm not one to puff out my chest and preen, but it feels good to show my girl what I'm capable of as I unleash hit after hit to the punching bag. Sweat rolls down my body and I push myself harder for her benefit. The air in the room thickens. I have half a mind to abandon my workout and pin her to the bed instead, vent out the rest of my frustrations with my cock buried deep in her body.

It's a temptation that's always there, but I refocus on my breathing and go again.

Almost an hour later, Maisy sucks in a sharp breath and punches both her fists in the air. "I did it! Holy shit, I found it."

My gaze swings around, instinct always drawing me to her, and the heavy bag thumps into my side. I grunt, lifting my hands to steady it, then swipe an arm across my face to clear the sweat.

"You got in?"

"Yeah. There was a passcode with a number sequence tucked away within a subfolder." She rolls her lips between her teeth as she pushes the laptop away on the bed. "Um, the numbers line up with the date of the crash."

I scoff.

Of course they do.

Smug assholes, hiding everything in plain sight like they can't get caught for what they covered up. I blow out a breath and stalk across the room. Anxious ripples move through my stomach the closer I get to the bed, to Maisy, to the laptop with the answers I've been waiting for.

"So what's in the termination file?" I brace one hand behind her, leaning over to see the screen.

She pulls the laptop close again and scrolls through. "It's a notice of resignation. Your parents signatures are both on it."

I squint at where she points. "That's forged. Mom never made a loop for the L in Wilder. I remember because I used to try to copy her signature."

"It looks like other than that there's a PDF email thread, like it was printed out." She clicks on it, but the screen prompts her for another password. She tries the one she used to open the file and her shoulders relax in relief when we're granted access. "I think this IP address at the top means it was on a private company server. Look, it's from your dad's email at Nexus Lab, but it isn't with the company."

"That's your mom's email." I jab at the screen, unable to stop seething. Another email address catches my eye. "Wait, it was all of them and someone from Stalenko Corp. Why would they keep that if it connects them all? Password or not, if anyone found this it's solid proof. Scroll down."

My eyes fly back and forth, reading so fast the decade old email conversation blurs. The words jump out at me as I try to process what I'm seeing.

Previous payment is insufficient...risk of the supply chain tracing distribution of controlled substances back to the source...file a patent if our demands aren't met...

The responses from Stalenko Corp are clipped and unrelenting. They don't say it outright, but the threat between the lines is clear: cooperate or face the fatal consequences.

My fingers dig into the sheets and I lean over far enough that Maisy ends up almost folded in half beneath me while I try to get closer to the screen. As if being closer will change what's in front of me.

"Fox, are you okay?"

Maisy twists to put a hand on my chest. It caves as I stumble back from the bed, shoving my fingers into the sweaty roots of my hair.

"Fox." Her voice is gentle and tentative. She reaches out to brush my back. "Talk to me."

Thoughts collide in my head one after another. The undeniable truth is right there in black and white. Even Colton couldn't find it out.

My parents hid the samples and the patent paperwork they started in the garage because they were extorting Stalenko Corp for more money in the middle of helping them plan for Ridgeview to become the main manufacturer for the Russian syndicate's drug empire. They were in on it the entire time with Jacqueline Landry. Modern day criminals, working out their business deals over email instead of meeting in back alleys on foggy nights.

Memories from my childhood reshape and crystalize, moments where I saw them as innocent viscerally replaced with the harsher clarity of their whispers at night when they thought I was asleep.

Money.

They were always arguing about money and what they were going to do.

No.

In a swift move I grab the laptop, intent on throwing it through the goddamn window.

"Fox," Maisy says sharply, placing a hand on my inked arm.

My grip flexes as I drag in labored breaths. Red floods my vision and my heart pounds. I let her pry the laptop from my grip and she sets it aside. The ache in my jaw makes me rub at it and it takes effort to unclench my teeth. Spinning away from her, I begin to pace in time with my furious heartbeat.

A lie.

That's what I've chased for ten fucking years.

A lie.

That's what broke my heart and tore away my childhood strip by bloody strip until all that was left was what I am now—cold, savage, hellbent on going after what I want, what I thought was right.

A lie.

That's what plagued me with nightmares.

A goddamn lie.

Air burns my lungs as I struggle to catch my breath. Everything I thought I knew is a lie—lies on top of lies, that's all my life is made up of. An awful, broken sound echoes off the industrial windows and I realize it came from me.

"I thought," I choke out.

They were innocent. My family was murdered.

"I know," she murmurs with this sympathetic look that wrecks me.

"Fuck. It was just a dirty business deal gone wrong, so Stalenko took them out. I've fought to make this right for them for so fucking long."

I dedicated every ounce of energy to this. Fueled my thirst for vengeance with hatred for my best friend over a broken promise that didn't even matter. Because my parents were in on it all.

I knew corruption ran deep through the streets of Ridgeview, but I never thought it poisoned my parents.

"Fox, come on. You have to breathe."

She hovers close at the edge of the trail I'm burning into the concrete, unafraid of the violent fury coming off me in waves. I can't even look at her. I came back here ready to destroy everything in her life. All because I believed for so long that her family caused the destruction of mine—believed I was making things right when they've never been more wrong.

I should've pushed harder to let it all go when I was ready, because then we wouldn't be here. I wouldn't know the truth about my parents. Wouldn't know what really happened to them.

"Fuck!"

The yell bursts from me and the dam breaks. As I pace, the anger and hurt spill over, my heart beating faster and my vision tunneling. I kick hard at the couch and the heavy furniture scoots several inches. Maisy backs up a step and another rage-filled shout from me echoes off the walls.

Grabbing the next nearest thing blindly—the twisted scrap metal I worked on that she brought upstairs, calling it a conversation piece with a proud smirk—I hurl it across the room. It crashes somewhere in the kitchenette, the sound of breaking glass and carnage still not enough to make any of this better.

It's all I'm good for—destruction.

"All the goddamn shit I've done to get here! So many things, all of it bullshit. I dragged Colt into this. Dragged you in." The words slip free with each ragged gasp. The fragile control over myself is a whisper away from snapping entirely, leaving me dangling close to becoming unhinged. I feel myself dangerously near the edge as my thoughts take on a manic energy. "Destroy lives, that's what I came to do and I fucking did it. I fucked with yours like it was a game, plotted to take down your parents, made sure your brother's future crumbled. What was the goddamn point?!"

Maisy freezes. The patient concern for me disappears as her spine straightens.

"Wait, hold up, what?" Her voice rises. "What did you just say?"

Fresh betrayal shines in her hazel eyes.

It rips me from the precipice of losing control, reality crashing back over me as some of the overwhelming anger clears from my head. Panting and disoriented, I replay what I said and curse silently.

Holden was the first friend I ever made, before I became friends with Maisy, too. He taught me how to ride a bike when I was jealous Maisy learned before both of us. We'd race home from the bus stop, run into our houses, and meet back up to trade Pokémon, or play any of the latest games. He knew all my secret fears, and I knew his. We grew up side by side, partners in troublemaking.

We were best friends. Brothers before I had Colton and the Crows.

The rushing tide of memories of my childhood with the Landry siblings makes my chest constrict. Each one is more bittersweet than the last. I lost every good thing I had. Lost them. And what do I do? I come back and make enemies out of them. Because I wasn't satisfied with Jacqueline and Richard. I wanted to punish them all for the years I suffered.

Invisible shards of glass rake my throat and acidic self-loathing swirls in my stomach. "I took away his future by having his draft offer reversed. To make sure it stuck, I sent the college video clips of the fights he organized at the quarry in high school. He's...his face is clearly visible in them and sometimes he'd wear his letterman jacket."

"What the hell," she whispers. "You hung around him because you wanted to blackmail him? I thought… Damn it, Fox, I thought you were his friend."

The hurt lacing her tone is like being shoved onto hot coals with no protection from the blistering heat.

This was a long game. He used me as his enforcer and put me right in position to unravel the strings of his life. I took the video myself last fall in his senior year while making sure everyone else abided the rules.

Shaking her head, she begins to pace. "You know, when you messed with my grades, I didn't really get all that torn up about it. The grades, the life plan—that wasn't my dream in the first place. The rumors you stirred, even breaking into the yoga studio to freak me out, I moved past it. The car prank was disgusting, but it's just stuff. It didn't physically hurt me. I mean, whatever, right? You tried to break me with all that, but I'd have to care about those things for it to work. I was more hurt that you wouldn't talk to me for so long, but hung out with him. That's where your damage finally hit me hard."

Hearing her lay out my mistakes steals the rest of the air from the room.

"I believed they were innocent," I bite out, scrubbing my face. "Everything I did was for them and my sister. It didn't matter what I had to do."

I immediately want to take the explanation back. The words came out wrong. She doesn't take my defensive tone well, halting and narrowing her gaze. I open my mouth to apologize and explain better, but she beats me to it.

"You know, Holden really did love football and wanted to keep playing. He hasn't touched the game once all year. Hasn't watched it, either. You really fucked him over. He's told me he's happy, but that was when he thought he didn't earn that opportunity to play for a school he loved." Her mouth purses in frustration and she flings out an arm. "How could you do that to your best friend? I get that I broke my promise and understand why you hate my parents, but Holden? He didn't do shit to you and you destroyed his future as collateral damage. Don't you have limits? There's a difference between innocent people and the ones you think deserve to suffer."

Guilt rakes over my nerve endings. I was willing to do anything—whatever it took to get my revenge. Holden wasn't an innocent guy. He organized that fight ring and made money. Partied hard and lived his life wild. But he wasn't part of this. I could've spared him.

Maisy folds her arms over her chest. The distrust flashing in her gaze cuts deep. My jaw clenches, even as my heart splinters with a thousand fissures, the damn thing on the brink of implosion.

This is it. She should've run from me from the first moment and now it's happening. She finally sees the truth—what a monster I've become.

This time I can't chase her. I need to let her go if that's what she wants. I betrayed her and this is what I deserve for it.

I love her, but I went after everyone in her family. We don't get to ride off into the damn sunset together with the ruinous outcome of my actions laying between our feet.

"I'm sorry."

It's gruff, jagged around the edges, but what more can I say? The damage has been done for over a year.

She stares at me for a long moment. "I want to believe that, but I think this made me realize something really important. I've jumped from living my life under my parents' rules to living it for someone else. I got too caught up in all this. I don't want anyone to control me." She darts her gaze away, unwilling to look at me when she goes on. "I need to live my life for me."

My throat constricts. Fuck. Everything in me revolts. I don't want to lose her. Not like this. Not ever.

The confession of what I feel for her pushes to the surface, but I swallow it back. I have to respect her choice.

"I never want to take that away from you," I mutter. "I'm not holding you prisoner here."

She looks so lost for a moment that it eats me up inside. My stubborn, headstrong girl has spent too many years under someone else's control. I swallow, throat working as I close the distance between us. Regret tastes sour, sitting in the back of my mouth as a reminder of everything I've ruined for ghosts that didn't deserve my fierce loyalty.

Maisy touches my face and I close my eyes, breathing in deeply so I'll always remember her sweet, soothing scent.

"Take the Charger." A small gasp escapes her at my offer. "I don't want you to feel stranded. It's yours for as long as you need it. Go."

Across town, across the country, go wherever you want, little daisy.

"Okay." She sounds as wrecked as I am. "Thanks."

Her touch drops from my cheek and I already miss it. She rummages around the bed for clothes, her shoes. Keys jingle across the room, the sound ominous and final.

I keep my eyes closed the whole time because I can't stand to watch her go. Not when this is my fault.

As soon as I hear her drive off in my car, I sink to the floor, leaning against the back of the couch, and stare at nothing. The energy drains from my body like I'm slowly bleeding out. I expect to look down at the dusty concrete and find a pool of blood, but there's nothing there.

Just emptiness, like the hollow feeling carved out in my chest.

THIRTY-TWO
Maisy

It's weird driving Fox's matte black Charger. The windows have been fixed, but I can still hear the sound of the rear and driver's side windows shattering from over the weekend.

The muscles in my stomach tighten and I focus on taking measured breaths, rubbing my thumb over the quartz inlay in my brass bangle bracelet. Once my heart rate calms, I step out of the car and climb the steps to Thea and Connor's apartment with nothing but my phone because I left everything at his place like I'd be back.

Except his converted warehouse is the last place I want to be right now.

I need to get my head and my heart back in balance before I fall under someone else's control. I can't jump from my parents' rule to his.

First I drove around for a few hours, stopping at a peaceful grassy field to watch the sunset dip behind the Rockies while I meditated. Nature has this magic power and sitting there centered me. Once the warmth of the summer day bled away, I texted my best friend and she welcomed me with open arms because we always have each other's back.

Thea and Connor live in a chic, newer part of town in an apartment building built near the shopping district in the center of Ridgeview. The black metal railings leading up to their unit are modern with tension wire.

Letting myself in with a key Thea gave me, I shout, "Don't be naked!"

Thea's laughter rings out from the kitchen, her favorite spot in her home. She pokes her head around the doorway and beams at me. My heart swells at the sight of her, auburn curls piled on her head with flyaways framing her face.

"I thought you have no problem with nudity," she says as I kick off my shoes in the hallway, relishing the feeling of the cool tiled floors on my bare feet.

So much for letting her and Connor enjoy their private time as newlyweds. At least they welcomed me to couch surf with open arms. I definitely can't go home.

Not just because I don't know how I'll look my brother in the eye knowing I'm partly to blame for his college football draft being stolen from him. I'm still disgusted by what Fox and I discovered about my parents and I don't want to see either of them. There's no way I'm putting myself back in their clutches to try to control me again. Never.

Thinking of them only reminds me what I uncovered earlier in the afternoon that sent Fox flying off the handle. As mad as I am at him for keeping what he did to Holden from me, my heart is heavy for him. That was a shitty way to learn his parents were just as corrupt as mine.

"I don't. Bodies are totally natural." We go into the kitchen and I light up at my favorite batter in the mixing bowl, swiping a finger through it and sticking it in my mouth while Thea gives me a look. "But I don't want to walk into your home and watch while Connor dicks you down, babe. I'd rather be the main show than watch one."

Her cheeks turn a pretty shade of pink and she busies herself putting away ingredients. I fake a gasp and my mood lifts when a tiny squeak leaves her.

"You were totally doing it when I texted to say I was coming here, weren't you?" When she opens and closes her mouth, darting her blue eyes to the doorway I nod. "Knew it. Sorry for interrupting."

"It's fine. You know our door is always open for you. Want me to invite everyone else over? We can make a night of it."

"No, please." Some of my easygoing bravado fades and I rub my hands over my face. "Can it be just you and me for a bit?"

"Of course, Maise." Thea comes around the sleek white island to wrap her arms around me. "Connor's in the shower, but he can go to Devlin's if you need him to."

"Thanks."

A wave of gratefulness crests over me. I'm so glad I have such great friends and I feel more than a little bad I've kept them in the dark for so long. It's only been a little under two weeks since I went to live with Fox, but how much I've been missing after getting sucked into his dark world hits me like a punch.

"How's the bakery?" The opening is this week. God, I've been such a crappy best friend. "Everything ready?"

Thea lights up. "Yeah. I'm nervous as hell, but Connor's been keeping me distracted whenever I go off on a tangent."

I smirk at the loving curve of her mouth and the faraway look that fills her eyes for a moment. "I'll bet he has."

After she pours the batter into a baking tray and puts it in the oven, she washes her hands. I watch, leaning against the counter. She dries off, then nods toward the living room.

"What about that beach day you guys had?" We collapse on her couch, my head in her lap. "Tell me everything I missed while I've been laying low from my parents."

"About that," she says. "What's the deal? You normally come stay with me when they suck."

Biting my lip, I stare up at her. "I went to stay with Fox."

Her brows jump up, but she makes no judgements. "Blair and Devlin called it."

An amused breath gusts out of me. "Of course they did. Nothing gets by those two."

"So you worked things out from all his broody staring, I take it?" She leans over me and her voice lilts with excitement. "Did you ride his motorcycle?"

It's my turn to flush and I almost snort at the heat flooding my cheeks. I'm not embarrassed, but thinking about how we went from being at each other's throats to how it's been since he let me in makes me warm all over.

"Pretty much. And yes, it's… I can't even describe how amazing riding it is." I pause, waggling my eyebrows. "It's not the only thing I was riding."

Thea makes a scandalized noise that has both of us laughing and shoving at each other playfully.

I sigh, touching my leather bracelet as the amusement fades. "Until today."

"What happened?" Her voice is soft and soothing. She's always been nurturing and I close my eyes, letting her comfort me by running her fingers through my hair. "Tell me whatever you're comfortable with sharing."

I start at the beginning, explaining my childhood friendship with him in more detail than I gave her last year when he came back. Then I take her through his cold shoulder treatment, to everything changing after that fateful hookup at Jenna Taylor's party and how he tormented me but I sought him out anyway. I couldn't stay away from him if I tried. When I get to the story about sneaking into his car going from bribery to a car chase she yelps.

"Holy shit, Maisy," she says with wide eyes.

"I know. Things have been crazy and I'm sorry I didn't tell you. There's more."

Now that I've started unloading this, it feels good. I don't realize Connor is listening to me explain about all the corruption Fox and I have unearthed until he chimes in from the doorway where he's propped against the frame, fingers tucked in the waistband of his basketball shorts.

"You've been doing all this under our noses? Shit, I could've helped you. I know some guys."

Connor doesn't elaborate, but I guess from the mischief in his gray eyes the guys he knows are probably like Colton and the friends Fox has described. The type of people that skate outside of the law.

"So does Fox. We haven't been totally alone, but I didn't want to interrupt up your lives with this mess. You just got married and after all the crap you both had to deal with last year, I didn't want to add to any stress on top of opening the bakery."

Thea squeezes me. "You can always lean on your friends no matter what, okay?"

"Thanks babe," I murmur, soaking in the restorative energy of her magic hugs.

"Just let us know if we can do anything," she says. "We're here for you always."

"You know we've got your back. You're family and we protect our own."

I snort. "Has anyone told you and Dev you sound like mob bosses when you guys say that?"

His wide smile is full of wickedness. "Gotta keep our reps striking fear in the hearts of our enemies."

This time a laugh rolls through me, but it passes and I'm still left with the confused mix of feelings that haven't really left since Fox confessed about Holden.

How can he still own my heart but make me want to tackle him for hurting my brother? If

I did, would I fight him or kiss him?

"You still seem tense. Want me to roll a joint?" Connor offers.

"No thanks." I shake my head, wanting to be clear headed more than relaxed right now. "Can Thea and I chill on our own for a bit?"

He gives us a charming crooked grin and nods. "You got it." He comes over to the couch, bracing against the back of it to kiss Thea above me. "I'll go see if the guys are all good for the opening, sunshine."

"Thank you," Thea murmurs, face tilted up for one more kiss.

My chest cinches tight watching them. It makes me miss the rich scent of leather and earthy woods mixed with motor oil. Makes me miss *him*. How can someone become necessary for breathing in such a short time?

He gave me my own freedom by letting me take his car. I could go back there…or I could get on the highway and drive until the road runs out. My dreams have always been focused on traveling, but I keep shoving it aside.

But this is where I should be right now. I can't run from anything. My best friend is opening her bakery in two days and we've been planning the opening day for months.

"Peace out," Connor calls as he leaves the apartment.

"I'm in love with him." I don't wait, pushing the admission out and staring up at my best friend. Fox is the only person who makes me feel so alive. "But he did something bad. Well, a lot of bad things."

Thea puts a hand on my shoulder and helps me sit up. "We don't get to pick who we fall for. Did he hurt you? Because if he hurt you, then—"

"Yes, but not the way you're thinking." I curl up next to her and let her drape her arm over my shoulders. Playing with the hem of my loose shirt—god, another shirt I stole from Fox without even realizing—I exhale and tell her the rest of what happened today. "When we finally worked through the grudge he had about me, he kept this part about Holden a secret. I forgave him and we got each other back. I want to trust there's good in him, but when things get bad will he always take things so far?"

"Maybe. But that's him before he had you with him." She tilts her head. "It's a partnership. Connor's taken things too far, but together we find the balance."

Balance. That's what I want. If Fox didn't push me away, I could've pulled him back from the edge. I could've saved my brother from the heartache of his dream disintegrating right in front of him.

"What would make it better?"

I worry my lip for a moment. Holden still doesn't know. He's been better in the last few weeks now that he's settled at Ridgeview Community College. Not just better, he's been happy for the first time in a long time. I don't want to ruin that by telling him the truth. Maybe I'm overreacting to all of this. For once, I wish I wasn't so impulsive so I could've confronted

Fox instead of leaving.

"Talking it out, I guess. But I don't know, Holden's been pretty chill. I'd hate to rehash it if it's going to leave him reeling without the chance to reverse it. Fox said he sent incriminating video."

Thea frowns. "Does he still wish he could have gone there to play? Because if he doesn't, that might tell you the answer."

I shrug. "I don't know. He said he's glad it worked out, but it was taken from him. Given the chance? Maybe. But I think he met someone in one of his classes this semester."

"I think you should start by asking your brother since it has more to do with him."

Nodding, I slouch further on the couch. I'll text him later to broach the subject.

Thea's always been the logical one between the two of us. Now that I have the space away from the emotions racing through me when Fox angrily spit out what he did, it doesn't sting as badly when I prod at the memory. Betrayal still flares, but it's the same as when Fox explained the reason he hated me. An indignant sort of ache, but not such a deep cut I'll never move past it.

I try to picture if I had parents I idolized, would I end up like him? Every relationship poisoned by the demolition site of my heart? God, as angry as I was at him, my heart wobbles in sympathy.

I wonder what he's doing right now and hope he managed to calm down or find a better outlet for his anger than throwing shit around. Today was a shock for him, too, and I left him alone to handle it.

"If I love him, why does it hurt so much?"

How can I love someone that is capable of turning his back on my brother? How can I be ready to forgive him?

Thea wraps me up in another hug. "It's just how love is, messy and intense. Love is good and bad all at once."

She's right. More than that, I came here because I want to figure out what my priorities are. I jumped from standing up to my controlling, shady parents to throwing myself into Fox's crusade for the truth. Now that he has it, do we keep going or does it stop here?

Did I let myself bounce from one thing to the next because I'm afraid to take something I want for myself? I've pushed off my road trip indefinitely for so many reasons. It's scary to think I barely know my own self underneath all the layers I've put on over the years at my parents' command.

As I turn it over in my head, it rings true. That's been my problem, finally teased out from the murky shadows.

I'm scared. Too worried what happens if I make a mistake because I'm not used to making my own choices. And I used my shock about Holden to give the fear bigger wings.

My throat constricts and it takes a few tries to swallow past the lump that forms. I twist my fingers in Fox's stolen shirt, bringing the oversized neckline to my nose to take comfort in his faint scent lingering behind, like I've brought a piece of him with me.

It's still wrong, what he did. But Holden is happy and just like me, he's not physically hurt by Fox's manipulations.

"What do you need?" Thea prompts, breaking into my internal reflection. "Do you want to leave town for your trip? I know it's been hard to work it out, but you can take my car. We'll go together to your house and pack up all your stuff into the back."

A pang hits me hard. My first thought is Fox. I need him. I feel most like myself, my true self, when I'm with him. But I don't want to be the girl who can only be like that with him. That's why I asked him for space because everything was getting too crazy.

I need to live for me and make my own choices. But am I doing that if I stay for him, or should I stop letting excuses keep me from taking the road trip and moving to California?

As soon as I consider it, I know that's not what I need. The thought of leaving him behind hurts as much as it did when he was gone from my life. When I think of going to California now, I picture what we've both been talking about—both of us on the road together, him opening a workshop and me making my own path with a yoga studio of my own. I never wanted to do it alone, but I didn't realize I was waiting for the right person to do it with. Someone who knew from the beginning how much I dreamed of it.

I brush the old stones of my bracelet. When he gave them to me, he said they reminded him of me. I always thought the blue one looked like his eyes.

Fox is woven into my heart and soul, bound by our years-old connection and strengthened by everything we've been through together in the last couple of weeks.

That's what I needed to figure out. I couldn't see it until I stepped back. I was afraid I wasn't ready to discover myself, too scared to do something on my own.

While I search my head and heart for what I need, Thea waits patiently.

"I think living for myself doesn't have to mean that if I'm with Fox, I'm forgetting myself," I finally say.

Thea's eyes crinkle with her smile. "No one can outshine your light. Only enhance it."

"Yeah, you're right. It's about making my own choices."

Something I never had the luxury of with my parents breathing down my neck. Now that I know why they've been so meticulous my stomach turns in disappointment.

Screw them, though. They can't control me anymore. No one can, only me.

It's my choice to be with Fox and I'm not giving that up.

"Thanks for letting me talk it out, dude. You rock, forever and always."

Thea huffs in amusement and cups my cheeks. "I just asked the questions, you did all the heavy lifting."

I raise both arms and flex my biceps, enjoying the sound of her laugh. She pops up from the couch and disappears for a few minutes while I breathe through the lifted weight off my chest now that I found some clarity.

When she comes back, she has freshly baked cupcakes and holds up a bag of chips. "Want to gorge ourselves on snacks and marathon Bake Off until we pass out? I promise, you can eat all the cupcakes this time because I love you and you need it."

"Yes," I say, dragging it out in a lazy drawl. "You're the best."

"And don't you forget it."

"Never," I swear.

THIRTY-THREE
Fox

Darkness fell over the warehouse before I moved from the spot where I collapsed.

I could lose everything all over again. Revenge set me on this path, and if I hadn't followed it I would never have known the truth about my parents and what happened to them. It led me back to the girl who has always made my heart feel whole. But...it could be what poisons our relationship before it starts.

She never said we were done, even left most of her things behind, yet the dull ache in my chest has been a constant reminder of her absence as soon as I offered her the keys to the Charger.

There's a row of crystals she lined up on the windowsill near the bed. I pick up a pink one that looks the same as the other bracelet she wears, then put it back. Pushing my fingers through my hair until it's sticking on end, I sigh raggedly.

I should've told her everything at the start, as soon as I trusted her again and let her in. I'm an idiot for hiding what I've done. The last secret I kept from her never should've come out because I was in pain and losing control.

It's been two days since she left and every minute has been an agonizing blur of self-loathing, pushing my body past its limit so I pass out, then waking up drenched in a cold sweat in the middle of the night from a nightmare, bed fucking empty. No matter what I do, my demons come for me anyway. I keep at it. All so I don't chase after her and beg her to look at me, to see past the monstrous things I've done.

Keeping her was a pipe dream. I knew I was someone she should run from, but I swallowed her in my darkness anyway.

In the short time she'd been here, she filled this space with her light. Now it feels as empty as I do. I *miss* her. The rhythm of her breathing when she stops, drops, and does yoga at all hours of the day. The shape of her next to me in bed. The amused little curl of the corners of her mouth when I steal the coffee she can't ever finish. Damn it, the bright look that fills her eyes when she talks about how much California felt like a home she didn't know she'd miss even though she's only been once.

When she busted her way back into my heart, she put me back together. I've been broken for years, damaged beyond repair, but she made it better. She made me want more out of my life. As long as it meant having her by my side. I want to see her seek out every dream she has.

Taking in the state of the studio apartment, my stomach clenches. Destruction is all around me. For the first time in a long time, I don't want it. Any of it.

I go to the kitchenette in the corner and pick up the twisted scrap metal. My fingers follow the curved shape and if I squint, I can see the shape of a flower. I didn't know what this was before when I made it, one of those pieces I followed instinct instead of a plan.

I was making her. Making what I feel about her.

Swallowing past the roughness in my throat, I put it down and clean up the broken mugs and a bowl that shattered when I threw the thing I made across the room. Once I'm done, I move to the couch, bringing the abstract metal flower representing my girl with me. I put it on the coffee table and trace the shape with my gaze, seeing the curve of her smile, the arch of her back, the indescribable and intangible feeling of her excitement when she's on the back of my bike.

No wonder I followed the pull to create, willingly leaving her in my bed to get this out of my head. I was a man possessed until she crept down those stairs. I lean forward and curl my hand around it, imagining it's her under my palm.

Every single thing went into this piece and I feel naked staring at it.

Fuck, I can't live without her anymore. I don't want to. Learning to do it in the last ten years has been the worst kind of hell.

Maisy gave me back something I haven't had in a long time by reminding my heart it could still beat and feel—and it's always been for her. She's it for me. I can't let her go without a fight.

She's what's most important to me now.

Not my parents' ghosts.

Not taking down her parents for condemning me to a life of gruesome nightmares, emptiness, stripped of everything. The life my own parents had a hand in damning me with. But they couldn't take everything away from me. I fought and survived and found my way back to her.

You and me, that's how it's supposed to be. Her voice echoes in my head. We said it to each other as kids. We're not soulmates, not fate—nothing poetic like that. But we do fit together.

I was surviving before, but I wasn't living until Maisy Landry was mine again.

My hands flex at my side. Why am I sitting here pretending I'm a gentleman when I'm anything but? I'm not a good man. Maisy is *my* daisy and I'm going to go fight for her to prove it.

Determination settles in my bones and I grab my keys for the motorcycle while putting my phone to my ear. As soon as the call connects, I'm talking without waiting for a greeting.

"I need you to do something for me," I say, swinging a leg over the leather seat. "And I need it done yesterday."

My thumb swipes over the smooth material. Everything around me reminds me of her.

Colton's laugh filters through the phone. *"Really making a habit out of breaking the rules. If Wren finds out about these IOUs, he won't be a happy camper."*

That guy hasn't been happy since his light left this world. There's nothing left in him but brutality.

"I don't care." My voice doesn't shake as I give everything I have to make this right for her. "I'll pledge my entire life if I have to in payment."

Colton grunts, then goes quiet when he realizes I'm deadly serious. After a minute, he asks, *"What do you need?"*

I start the bike's ignition, mentally mapping every field of wildflowers I know of. I'll start with the one by our tree, where I found the purple daisies ten years ago.

"Holden Landry's admissions acceptance and football draft. Reverse it. Erase the blackmail evidence we sent."

"Uh, why?" Colt drawls. *"That's the opposite of what you've been working on."*

"It's important," I snap. Pausing to draw in a deep breath like Maisy was showing me this week before she left, I lower my voice. "Please, Colt. Just help me out with this. If I don't fix it…"

I don't finish, shutting down the thought. Life without Maisy isn't something I'm going to think about, which means failure is unacceptable.

"I'll see what I can do."

"Thanks. Text me."

Hanging up, I take off in search of the flowers that always remind me of Maisy with fire burning in my blood. I'll pick every wild daisy I find until there aren't any left. She deserves that and more, and I'll give her the whole fucking world before I'm done proving to her how much she matters to me.

* * *

By the time I make it to the bakery, I have to nudge my way through the opening day crowd spilling onto the sidewalk. A few people give me sharp looks and wide berth, the Wilder name still hard at work, but I ignore all that when I hear her laugh ring out inside. The light, airy sound ripples over me.

Maisy.

It's impossible to stop the way my heart stutters.

"Let me through," I say.

People move aside, glancing curiously at what I'm carrying and I reach the door. My hands shake slightly as I step over the threshold into the bustling bakery.

The fresh scent of cookies hits me first. Maisy's friend Thea stands behind a wood counter overflowing with treats beaming at the people waiting in line with Connor nearby, pride filling his gaze. A few conversations slow to a stop and I almost have to laugh. Everything is bright and cheerful in this place, and I'm darkening the door in ripped black jeans and a dark t-shirt, probably looking like a damn psycho.

All of that fades the moment I lay eyes on her across the room, perched on top of a table with Holden and one of her friends, heart-stopping smile wide and hazel eyes lit up with life. She's wearing a pair of cut off shorts with bleach splatters and a white stretched out muscle tank over the sports bra she had on the day she left. Her eyes meet mine and she stops. I want to cut open my chest and hand her my bleeding heart right then and there.

Because it's hers. It's always been hers. The damn thing beats only for her.

It sits in my throat as I take one staggering step toward her, then another. In three long strides I'm in front of her and for a second I hate this place because I can't pick out her floral and coconut scent. The irrational feeling passes after a beat.

Is this what love is? This crazy madness that latches onto the body?

"Fox," she says.

Holden shifts in his seat, away from the girl who seems to be with him to slide between me and his sister. I bite off the urge to snap at him to get out of my way.

"If you think I'm going to stand around while you hurt my sister some more—"

I cut him off. "The last thing I want to do is hurt her."

"Dude, move," Maisy says instead, nudging her brother aside. "I've got this."

Holden's brows flatten. "You're good?"

Maisy rolls her eyes. "Yes. Shoo. Go enjoy your date over there."

He swings his gaze back to me and I recognize the protectiveness in his expression. The girl with him takes his hand and tugs him toward the bakery counter.

"I'll be watching," Holden promises before turning around to hug the girl from behind, lifting her off her feet to make her laugh.

"So will we," mutters another of Maisy's friends with dark hair and a sharp gaze.

"Oh my god," Maisy says in exasperation, taking my wrist and tugging me closer to a mural of the sun and moon painted on the wall. She peers up at me with a worried pinch between her eyebrows. "Is everything okay? Did you find out something else?"

God, this girl. I hurt her and she still asks if I'm fine first.

Words fail me. They've never been my strong suit. The carefully thought out apology I planned while I picked flowers for an hour flies from my head.

Licking my lips, I try. "I brought you these."

Her gaze falls to the flowers in my hand. At least two of them are crushed from my choking grip, their stems bent. In my head it was a more romantic gesture than the reality, but her lips part.

"Purple daisies," she whispers.

"Yeah, I... They've always reminded me of you, Maise." I carefully touch the petals of one of the blooms sticking out. "Wild, stubborn, beautiful, and free."

Her eyes fly to my face, bouncing back and forth as she drinks me in greedily.

"You are. Doesn't matter what keeps you down, you'll overcome it. You bend to grow where nature will let you, but you also crop up wherever you want because nothing holds you back. You're a wildflower."

My wildflower.

A small sound escapes her and I want to reach out to bring her closer, but if I do I won't get this out. I rummage in my pocket for my phone and open the screenshot Colton sent me as I was pulling up in front of the bakery.

"I'm sorry. I know I fucked up, but I'll do whatever I have to so I can make it right."

"Fox, is this—?" She reads the text again, fingers curled around my phone.

"Yes. I reversed it. Well, Colt did, but if he still wants it, it's his. They'll take him next semester. I'm working on yours next."

"Don't bother," she mutters. "I'm not going to Northwestern."

Blood rushes in my ears and I focus on not crushing the daisies in my fist. "Are you going to leave?"

"Someday soon. Not by myself anymore, I hope."

"No."

It's out before I can hold it back. Because I don't want her to see the Pacific ocean again for the first time without me being there to watch her face as she takes it in.

"No?" She tilts her head and narrows her eyes. "What makes you think you can control what I want?"

"I know I can't. But I hate the thought of you with anyone else."

Just thinking about it makes me want to wrap my fingers around the neck of whoever would dare touch her and squeeze. A flash of possessive anger spears me as I take in the muscle tank hanging off her body and I hate that it's not one of my shirts. She laughs, breaking me out of the dark, murderous vision.

"Good thing I wasn't planning on that then."

The words that failed me before burst out of me in one breath. "I love you."

"You do?"

Maisy's throat works and I hold her gaze.

Nodding, I say it again. "I loved you back then and I love you now. It never went away, even when I believed you lied. Even when I thought I hated you, the whole time I was in love with you."

Taking another step, I close the distance between us, bending close enough to graze my lips over her temple. I touch the stones I gave her on the bracelet, a piece of me that she carries with her everywhere. She tilts her face up and all I want to do is wrap her in my arms and never let her go. I hold up the fistful of wildflowers between and offer my heart to her.

"You're my daisy," I rasp. "It's always been you."

THIRTY-FOUR
Maisy

Hearing him say those words starts a riot inside me. My heart skips a beat, tripping over itself like it wants to burst from my chest into his arms, where it belongs. Where *I* belong.

I draw in a shaking breath.

The second he walked in here I wanted to go to him, but I had to wait out the urge just to see what he would do. Since I left and talked it out with Thea, I knew what he meant to me.

Holding myself back from touching him, hugging him, kissing him was a sweet form of torture building the anticipation until I can't take it anymore. Now I can give in.

There are smudges beneath his eyes and stubble shadowing his jaw. He hasn't been sleeping.

Oh, Fox. I hope his nightmares haven't returned.

The daisies are choked in his desperate grip, some wilting and a little sad. But they're the same color as the one he gave me all those years ago when he promised I was his daisy and that he'd marry me someday.

I'm still his daisy.

Warmth blooms like the flowers he brought me, unfurling in my chest bringing a sense that feels a lot like happiness.

"I'll walk away from everything if it means you'll forgive me. I choose you, Maisy. I know how much you want to see the ocean. I know because the ocean is in my soul, too. We'll go together. I'll take you to California." He puts a hand over his heart where the ocean is inked into his skin. "I just needed you to know all this. I'll wait for as long as you need, forever if I have to. You and me, remember?"

My heart turns over and before he can say more, I press up on my toes, fisting his shirt before I kiss him. People around us cheer, but all I'm focused on is the slide of his lips against mine, the scrape of his stubble on my jaw, the soft relieved groan he pushes into my mouth when he wraps his arms around me.

The wobbling axis of my world rights itself in that moment.

Fox was never going to hold me back from what I want. Deep down, I knew that. I was scared to love him as much as I do because I worried it meant I'd lose myself in his black hole.

I was going to go back to his place after the opening to talk things out with him now that my head is clearer, but he was one step ahead of me. I didn't ask him to reverse Holden's ruined college draft, but he still made it better. He took action for his mistakes and it makes me fall for him even more than I already have.

Fox makes me feel alive. He's always known who I am and encouraged the wild streak I can't tame. He's who I'm meant to be with, who my heart sings for.

Pulling back from the kiss, I rest my forehead against his jaw, simmering with the joy bubbling through me. "I wasn't going to leave without you. You're who I meant I wanted to go with, like we said. Your workshop and my studio. Our own little adventure."

He squeezes me closer, probably crushing my handpicked bouquet of wildflowers even more. A laugh huffs out of me and I hug him back.

"I want you if it means the good and the bad. I'd relive the years of missing you, the pain of you coming back, all of it because it meant after all that my heart would be whole again." His lips touch the top of my head and I sink further into his strong embrace. "We found our way back to each other."

"We did," he murmurs.

Fox releases me and seals his lips over mine in a searing kiss I feel down to my toes. I smile into it. He pours so much into it that I sway slightly and he catches me. Cheers sound around us again and I recognize my friend's voices among them.

A throat clears and I lean back to find Holden hovering with the girl he met at school that he's been wrapped up in. I lift my brows in question.

"You're good?" he asks, glancing from me to Fox.

"I was until you interrupted."

The girl with him snorts and hooks her arm in his. "I told you to let them be, big guy."

Holden's cheeks fill with color and he rubs the back of his neck, muttering an apology under his breath. This girl is good for him and part of me is glad he ended up at the community college, or they'd never have met.

"Come on." I take the bouquet of flowers Fox picked for me and slip my hand into his. "I still haven't been able to introduce you to everyone."

I take him to the table where Devlin and Blair are. Gemma and Lucas joined them while Fox and I were working things out. When Connor sees us at the table, he pulls Thea away from the customers and they come over, too.

"You've grown a shadow," Devlin deadpans, making Connor snort.

"Dude," I say mildly. "Guys, this is Fox."

They introduce themselves and he keeps a hand tucked in my back pocket.

"That's your bike out front?" Lucas asks.

"Yeah. It was my dad's," Fox says. "I had to rebuild most of it until I got it back."

Lucas whistles low in understanding. "I have a 1990 Jeep I rebuilt. It's a labor of love." He throws a sardonic look at Gemma and plays with her hair. "Something some people don't appreciate."

A low laugh rolls through her. "That was one time, babe. One time. Besides, you were a dick then and you know you deserved it. Let it go."

"Never," he mutters, leaning in to kiss her cheek, making her smile affectionately.

Blair smirks. "Nothing wrong with stealing a man's pride and joy."

"I beg to differ," Devlin says, but there's fondness lacing his tone.

Thea comes around the table to size Fox up, hands on her hips. She's half his height, if that, but the fierce look on her face makes him stand at attention.

"Do I have to give you the shovel spiel?"

"The what?" Fox asks in bewilderment.

"The best friend, you-hurt-her-we-bury-you warning," Blair supplies with a gleam in her brown eyes.

"Oh." A short laugh leaves him and his hand flexes on my ass in my back pocket. "I'm pretty sure she'd bury me before you had the chance."

Thea's expression melts into a smile at the pride in his tone and Fox relaxes. "Good answer. Be right back."

She disappears into the back and returns shortly after with a fresh plate of cookies shaped like suns and moons baked in honor of her bakery opening. I'm so proud of her and as my friends all chat, I lean into Fox and feel a true sense of happiness. He doesn't exactly fit in with them easily, not when the rest of the guys have the bond of knowing each other from childhood, but he's not out of place either. He stays quiet, listening to us as we tease each other.

Holden joins in for a while, he and Fox talking in low murmurs while Gemma shows me photos of a hike she and Lucas drove north of their college for in the spring. I glance up and see them laughing together. It feels good, like the broken things between the three of us aren't beyond repair.

Our parents might have done irrevocable things, but we aren't them and we won't make their same mistakes.

Fox brushes his lips over my ear several minutes later. "Ready to get out of here?"

"Yes."

I say goodbye to my friends and congratulate Thea for the millionth time on doing what she always wanted. She hugs me tight in one of her magic embraces and tries to wink at me—tries and fails because she can't actually wink for shit—and I promise to check in with her later. Fox takes my hand.

Outside, the summer sun shines down on us, glinting off his motorcycle.

He hands over the helmet and closes his fingers over my wrists before I put it on. "Who's shirt is that?"

"This?" I look down. "Mine. Well, Holden's first, but I stole it from him three summers ago. He brought me clothes over at Thea and Connor's apartment yesterday since I didn't have anything."

He visibly relaxes, grabbing a handful of the material and tugging me in for a quick kiss. "Good," he rasps against my lips. "I don't have to kill anyone today."

Snorting, I push him off with a playful grin. "Were you going to deck Connor if I borrowed it from him?"

He mulls it over, jaw moving side to side. "Maybe. He'd hit back, but it would be worth it."

"No hitting my friends, even if they know how to fight."

"Fine." He smirks, raking his gaze over me. "No wearing anyone else's clothes. Only mine."

When he claims me like that, my stomach dips pleasantly. I've always liked when he wanted to be possessive of me, even when we were kids.

"Fine," I agree easily. "I like your shirts best anyway. Just a shirt and nothing else underneath, best feeling in the world."

The sound Fox releases is part-groan, part-growl and he grabs my hips. "Careful with that mouth, Maisy Daisy, or I'll fuck you right here in the middle of town."

My mouth curves and satisfaction rolls down my spine. "Promises, promises," I murmur in a seductive lilt that makes heat flare in his dark gaze. "Take me home?"

"Yeah. Get on."

Fitting my arms around him with the rumble of the motorcycle between our legs feels like home and freedom all at once.

"Hold on tight," he says over his shoulder.

Grinning into his back, I squeeze him. "Never letting go."

* * *

We're barely parked in the garage before I hop off the bike, needing to have his lips on mine after two days of being apart. He catches me in his arms, still straddling the bike as I grasp his face between my hands and capture his lips. Heat races over my skin as his palms drag over my body. At the needy sound that escapes me, he pops the buttons on my cut off shorts and stands from the bike in the same motion.

Yanking my body against his, he attacks my neck with his mouth, finding that sensitive spot that makes my thighs rub together against the pulse of heat in my core. His cock is a hard line against my stomach, but his focus is completely on me as he buries his big palms down the back of my shorts and pushes them off, rumbling in approval against my neck when he finds I don't have anything on beneath them.

"My wild girl," Fox rasps.

A grin tilts my lips at the reverence in his tone and my heart swells in my chest. *His wild girl*. That's who I am. Untamed and free and *myself*.

The shorts fall to my ankles and I kick them off without stopping my own exploration, hands roaming beneath his shirt and pushing it up. He reaches behind his head with one hand

and tugs the t-shirt off. Lifting me by my thighs, he guides my legs around his hips and carries me up the steps. My palms roam over his biceps, tracing the half sleeve tattoo on the left one.

We're barely through the door when his mouth captures mine again. His grip flexes on my ass and he seems like he doesn't want to let me go.

"Gonna make you mine," he says.

A light laugh shakes my shoulders. I feel like I'm floating on a cloud. "I never stopped being yours."

"Doesn't matter. You deserve to know I love you every second of the day."

He puts me down on the coffee table and flattens his palm in the center of my chest, pushing me down until I'm spread out for him across the reclaimed wood. He kneels at the edge between my thighs, placing hot kisses at random across my thighs.

The conversation piece I brought upstairs from the workshop stands next to my head. I'm glad to see its hypnotic curves haven't been damaged from him throwing it clear across the room when he was upset.

I reach up to touch it and Fox releases a rough sound.

"It's you."

I prop up on my elbows. "What?"

"I was...making you. I didn't realize it until you were gone." His thumbs trace tiny circles on my hips. "It's you, Maisy. How I see you. How I love you."

My breath hitches and I look at the mixed materials, the metal that shouldn't bend in that way but it does—both strong and fluid at once. Rooted in wood, but reaching for the sky. No one but him has ever taken the time to see me so clearly, to take that and create something beautiful. I lick my lips and lift my gaze to him knelt between my thighs like I'm something he cherishes. Worships.

"I love it," I whisper, setting it aside and combing my fingers through his dark fringe. "I love you."

The corner of his mouth kicks up in a crooked smile that makes my heart stutter. The fondness in his gaze melts into something more sensual.

"By the time I'm done, you'll never doubt that you're mine again. Because I've only ever been yours, Maisy Daisy. Since you were six years old, trailing after your brother and jealous he got to go to school before you. Let me show you."

Holding my gaze he lowers his mouth to my center and takes me to oblivion with my head thrown back.

The sexy smirk he shoots up the length of my body after I come should be illegal. He swipes the side of his mouth and licks the taste of me from his lips. Scooping me into his arms, we move to the bed.

"Not done with you yet," he says in a smoky whisper. "Sit on my face."

My stomach bottoms out. He doesn't wait, tugging me where he wants me and my fists scramble in the sheets at the swipe of his tongue on my pussy, my folds still sensitive from the first orgasm he teased out of me.

"Ride my tongue."

The command is muffled, his deep voice vibrating against my clit. It rips a gasp from me, but I rock my hips and tip my head back on a cry. He knows exactly how to bring me to the brink.

Not only because he's fucked me all over this warehouse, but because he *knows* me. My heart knows his and his knows mine. The truth of it wraps around me.

"Oh god," I breathe, dragging my nails over his tattooed chest and folding in half when my thighs start to shake. "God, I'm going to come again."

He chuckles against the swollen folds of my pussy and I tip over the edge, the waves of pleasure echoing from my core. He's not done. In fact, he shifts around like he's getting comfortable for the long haul, palms smoothing over my thighs and squeezing while he licks and sucks my clit with a deceptively sedate focus.

As much as I'm enjoying his pampering, my mouth waters at the sight of his erection straining against his jeans. I want to make him feel good, too. I lean over and plant a trail of kisses down his abs, licking a spot I know is ticklish. He grunts and I smile into his skin as I rub the front of his jeans. He slows down his tongue and brushes his fingers over my side.

"Let me make you feel good, too." I stroke him through his jeans. "If you think you're the only one allowed to lay claim, you're wrong, babe."

Fox hums against me and I unzip his jeans. He lifts up to help me shove them down far enough to free his cock. He's thick and hard, already past the point of ready to go. I waste no time swiping my tongue over the head and he groans in appreciation when I slip my lips around him. He returns to eating my pussy while I suck his cock and our moans become a symphony of pleasure filling the converted warehouse.

He kisses my folds slowly, then puts pressure on my clit that makes me draw in a sharp breath as I ride out the tingles racing over my skin. The vibrations of the noises I make have him thrusting his cock into my mouth and I relax, letting him fuck my face.

"Shit, your mouth is heaven," he chokes out as his thighs tense. "Fuck. *Fuck!*"

His come floods my mouth and I swallow it down while his arms wrap around me. He goes boneless after his orgasm and a primal sort of pride burns in my chest for making him come hard. After a minute, he strokes my back and guides me onto my side. He props up on an elbow to kick his jeans the rest of the way off and helps me out of my tank and sports bra so we're both naked.

I collapse against the sheets and stretch, rubbing my thighs together lazily to enjoy the lingering sensitivity.

"You think you're all done?"

I crack my eyes open and quirk my brows. Fox shoots me this sinful look that sends a shiver down my spine as he smooths a hand up my side.

"Just because I came doesn't mean I'm finished giving you orgasms, baby. Gonna keep fucking your pussy with my tongue while I finger your ass until my cock is ready to go again. I want you to be a filthy mess for me, little daisy." He bends over to kiss my hips, punctuating his next words with teeth and tongue. "Every. Single. Inch."

Air leaves me in a rush and I don't get the chance to respond before he does exactly what he promised. And after, when he enters me in one smooth thrust, he cradles me close until our bodies become one.

* * *

Sitting up in bed later, I suck on my swollen lower lip. It's tender from the hours Fox spent kissing me long and slow and unrelenting while I shook apart in his arms countless times until I didn't have another orgasm left in me. He's sprawled on his front beside me, one arm thrown possessively over my lap. We haven't stopped touching since we got back to the warehouse. He's worn out from how many rounds we just went.

"We have to get my dad out of office at least," I say.

He makes a barely audible sound, cracking an eye open to study me. "Are you sure?" He rubs my hip. "We could just let it all go. I have the answers, whether I wanted them or not. These people pulling the strings are dangerous. Fuck them."

"Yes, fuck them. That's my point."

He must see the determination in my expression because he drags himself up, curling around me so I'm resting against his chest. I hold onto the forearm banded across my chest and twist to see him.

"I don't want this town run by corruption. My friends will still live here when we leave. My brother still lives here." His chest moves with his sigh. "I can't stand that the person who is supposed to protect everyone and uphold the law is as dirty as the criminals he's arresting. I don't care if he's my dad. We can still make some of this right."

"So you still want to tangle with a criminal organization and a corporate drug operation?"

My lips press together. This is what we have to do. It might have started as Fox's crusade, but now his war is mine. I'll see it through until the end.

"Don't you? We can't run away yet."

His fingers thread through my hair. "It's not running if it's what we want."

"It is what I want, but we can't go to California without doing something about it first. Not when we know what they're doing."

His expression darkens, but he nods. "You're right. So, we do this, then we go?"

"Yes. No one else is going to stop them."

We might be young, but we're the only ones willing to do something to uproot the corruption in Ridgeview.

THIRTY-FIVE
Fox

THE warehouse is more crowded than I ever expected with Maisy's friends here to help. I was wary of letting more people into my circle, but she trusts them and I trust her. They showed up this morning and took over the space that didn't really feel like home until Maisy came to stay with me.

"Listen, you crow bastard," Connor Bishop snarks, stabbing a finger at his laptop where he's working with Colton over FaceTime with the video connection off. "You can't tell me you prefer clickjacking attacks over trojans. You just can't. Not after you were an asshole and infiltrated my shit."

They agreed to combine their tech skills to pin down the money trail we need to follow once and for all to connect Stalenko Corp to Richard's promotion. It turns out that Colton knew Connor and his wife better than we thought. They were tangled in the same mess that brought Wren and the Crows here last year as he hunted down the bastard that took his sister away from him.

"Just admit it's better!" Colton laughs over the call. "*Your firewall had a nice sized hole in it and I put my dick there. It was more than a year ago, get over it.*" Connor sputters, but Thea brings him a piece of the cake she brought with them and he forgets to be angry because he has eyes only for her. She kisses his head. "*Now quit trying to distract me with your opinions, peasant, and let the master work.*"

"Master?" Connor scoffs playfully with one arm around Thea. "Bro, you couldn't even crack this rotating cryptographic encryption sequence until you had my help just now."

"Play nice," Thea says.

"*Listen to your little cutie, Bishop.*"

Thea stops his growl with a kiss.

"Was it the smartest idea to let those two become friends?" Maisy murmurs to me as she takes a marker I was using to write on a white board. "They seem…"

"I know." Shaking my head, I give her a wry smirk. "I didn't know there were two of them."

She snickers and we turn back to the white board where we've laid out our strategy. Connor and Colt are stealing the secrets we need from the inside. Once we have those, we're bringing in the big guns. Ethan gave us his contacts, including federal investigators with a tip line. We have the incriminating email thread from ten years ago between my parents, Jacqueline Landry, and Stalenko Corp detailing their dirty plan. Plus the evidence I recorded during our stakeout of Richard accepting a bribe.

On top of that, Connor handed over his entire blackmail file on Richard Landry—which he made me pay for, the little fucker. When I told Colt, he cracked up about it and called it good business practice.

What's important is that Richard can't get out of this. They were idiots to keep track of their meetings and bribery over the years, and now we'll use it against him. Maisy and I are going to nail his ass to the wall and force him to resign, or every news outlet in Ridgeview will have a juicy new scandal to rock the town's idyllic mountainside foundation.

After I found out my parents weren't who I thought they were, I was ready to wash my hands of all this and walk away, but Maisy was right. If we don't do something about this, they get away with murder and continue to make money off the drugs they're funneling into the world.

"It's done." Devlin Murphy moves like a shadow, creeping up behind us.

It's unsettling he could sneak up on me. Blair pulled the same trick on me an hour ago when she showed up at my elbow and almost gave me a fucking heart attack. I think she knew it, too; she gave me this smug little smirk and I heard her husky laugh as she turned away.

He pushes fingers through his black hair and hands a legal pad to Maisy with notes from the phone call he's been on for most of the morning. "The DEA and FDA contacts your journalist friend gave you believed I was my dad on the phone and were pretty disturbed to hear about synthetic opiates being cooked up for sale to the black market. They insinuated there was an influx of the hard stuff flooding the streets and their west coast offices haven't been able to trace the source. They took down my number and said they'd be in touch if they needed to go over more questions."

"Thanks, Dev," Maisy says. "That gives this more credibility if it comes from someone as well known in the medical field as your dad is."

Devlin grimaces, like hearing it pains him. He shrugs. "Lucas and I are writing up testimonies, too." He motions with a nod of his head to the couch, where the guy who told me about his Jeep at the bakery sits with his girlfriend and Blair. "I paid your dad to keep Blair's arrest off the record when I bailed her out, and Lucas is recounting the poker nights at his house where your dad accepted bribes."

"Good," I say.

"Love a good takedown before lunch," Devlin says with a glint in his gaze that says everything I need to know about him. "Too bad there wasn't a need for any casual B and E this time around." His gaze cuts to Blair and fills with fondness. "I have missed a certain little thief's wily ways," he murmurs more to himself than us.

"Yes!" Connor cheers with his fists in the air while Colt makes a racket. He pulls Thea into his lap to celebrate. "Boo-fuckin'-*ya*, baby!"

I hope their celebration means good news. If they found the payout that has eluded the searching Maisy and I have done in the last few weeks, we'll finally be set.

It's strange to let this many people in, to have all this help when before it was hard enough to let Colton sniff out my secrets, to let Maisy see the full extent of the pain infecting my life. Yet somehow it feels right. I don't know her friends very well, but they dropped everything to help us.

"Think it'll be enough?" Maisy asks once Devlin goes back to the group on my couch.

"It'll have to be."

We're more than covered with incriminating proof to take Richard out. What remains to be seen is how it will affect Nexus Lab to operate without one of their obedient pieces on the board while we wait for the federal investigators to make their move.

* * *

It's sunny and bright the day Richard Landry faces the implosion of his career. The Ridgeview Police Department is quiet when I park the bike out front. The old Gold Rush era architecture makes it look like it belongs in a movie, matching many of the historic buildings in town.

Maisy gets off the back of the bike and holds her hand out for me to take. I grin as I lace our fingers together. Her and me, us against the goddamn world. She joked once about my warehouse being like the Batcave, but this is the first time I've felt a little like a hero.

Imagine it—me, the black shadow nightmare in this town, the hero of the story.

One thing's for sure, I've got the girl and I'm not letting her go.

"Let's do this," she says, spine straight and head held high. She looks like a firecracker, fierce and determined, set to go to war. I can't help pulling her into me for a kiss, sweeping my tongue into her mouth. The curve of her smile against my lips owns every beat of my heart. "Ready to fuck some shit up?"

It's taken us a few days to coordinate the proof we've gathered between what we already had and what her friends helped us dig up, but now we're ready.

"Yes. Let's go take a swing at an ugly empire."

Maisy pretends to fire off pistols with her fingers and winks at me, stirring a flutter in my chest. Hand in hand, we walk into the station. It's so obvious to me now, watching her slip into the good girl mask everyone around her saw her with. That was never the real her, just the way everyone expected her to act. She takes us right up to the front desk and tilts her head with this coy smile on her face.

"Hey, Officer Dean. How's your cat doing? I hope he adjusted to the diet."

"Maisy," the officer greets without suspecting anything. His gaze guts to me once with a hint of wariness, but returns to her. "Waffle is doing good, thanks for remembering."

"I'm so glad to hear it." She folds her arms over the high countertop. "We're supposed to meet my dad for lunch. Is he in his office?"

"Oh. I don't think he remembered." Officer Dean frowns. "He stepped out in a rush for a meeting."

"Can we wait for him in his office?"

She practically bats her lashes and has this guy eating right out of her hand. I have to fight back a smile.

"Well, you're not supposed to, but…"

"Oh, you're right." Maisy sighs. "I just wanted to surprise him."

The officer softens. Pushover. "You know what? Go ahead. He's been stressed lately and I think it'd cheer him up."

Maisy lights up. "You're a gem, Officer Dean. Thanks."

We leave the front desk behind and I lean close to murmur in her ear. "You're like a dangerous little honey trap."

"I'm saving the honey all for you," she says with a sly grin.

Richard's office sits in the corner of the building with big windows overlooking downtown Ridgeview. It's cushier than anyone would expect, even for a chief. I peer around while Maisy keeps an eye out for her dad.

A large polished mahogany desk sits in the center with an expensive leather chair. There's a family photo on the desk. I pick it up and the corners of my mouth tighten. It's from the trip both our families took to California. I'm in it, right between Maisy and Holden with our arms all linked around each other. We're grinning with sunburnt faces while Richard and Jacqueline stand off to the side. My mom is on our other side, but my dad isn't there. Instead of looking at the camera or his wife, Richard's gaze strays surreptitiously toward Mom. She's looking his way, too, peeking out of the corner of her eye while she tucks her hair behind her ear.

My heart thuds as I stare at the old photo. There's no way. I refuse to believe the hints of what I'm seeing, forcing my mind to shy away from the whispers of memories scratching at the edge of my awareness, that back up what my gut is telling me. Times the two of them would take us on outings. No. No fucking way Richard and my mom had a thing.

Swallowing hard, I put the photo down. It's the only one on the desk. For someone who wants to seem like a family man, he doesn't have anything else to remind him of them in here. The rest are photos with the mayor and with other prominent members of Ridgeview society. It's easy to guess money ties each of these men together. Favors. Bribery.

This is what Richard sold his soul for.

Muffled footsteps approach through the closed door. Richard comes in and his cheeks turn red when he realizes he's not alone. He rushes toward Maisy.

"You—I've been so worried!"

Before he reaches her, I step between them and shove him against the wall. "Don't touch her. You don't have the right."

Maisy calmly shuts the door. He fights against me. Despite his broad stature, I'm stronger, easily able to keep him in place.

"Why are *you* here? What do you think you're doing?"

Richard's face reddens more as he struggles to free himself. He goes for his holster, but I cut him off, twisting his arm.

"Were you just about to pull your weapon on your daughter and another civilian?"

"Civilian?" He barks out a harsh laugh. "With the whispers going around town about you, I'm sure you've probably done something to warrant an arrest."

"I thought you'd be happy to see me, Rich. No love lost for your old friends' son?" My lip curls and my fingers dig in harder to his designer three piece suit. I move to grab him by the throat. "I guess you did have me shipped off and figured I'd disappear so you didn't have to look at me to remind you of your sins."

His lips move, but he can't get any words out when I tighten the chokehold. His eyes bug out.

"Fox."

Pushing out a breath, I ease off from squeezing the life from Maisy's dad. He puts on a show of coughing and fighting me. It's futile. I'm bigger and stronger from the years I've spent keeping in shape while he sat behind a desk and enjoyed steak dinners with a side of cash under the table. Knowing he won't crack me, he appeals to her.

"Maisy, what is this? I told you to stay away from this boy. You're standing there while he assaults me? Sweetheart, look at me."

She won't. In my peripheral vision she keeps her gaze locked on me, remaining silent while he becomes increasingly agitated.

"Maisy!" Richard blusters. "Answer me, damn it. I've been lenient since you left the house, but this is too goddamn far. You need to come home. Your mother and I—"

"I just have one thing to say, Dad. *Arthur Jones*."

Richard jolts at the name of the man who was supposed to be chief of police before Richard was hastily installed into the position instead. Color drains from his face and he turns a sickly shade of gray. Maisy huffs and a humorless smile twists my lips.

"Yeah. The one who was supposed to have your position right now." I grab him by his silk tie and jerk him against the wall. "Funny, he had a heart attack about two months after you were sworn in. Shocked his family, since he was healthy before that. Weird, right? I have the obituary."

"You shouldn't be looking into this. You don't understand," Richard warns when I go for my phone.

Maisy turns away from us and I listen as she plugs the flash drive she brought into Richard's computer. I drag him away from the wall and sit him down at one of the seats in front of his desk while she turns the monitor around. All the evidence we've gathered is on the big screen. He releases a sound as if someone punched him in the stomach, shaking his head.

He's pathetic, unable to face what he's done. All the years I've spent imagining retribution, I never pictured him blubbering like this. The Richard Landry I remember from my childhood had a backbone, but it seems to have been whittled to nothing in the last decade. The single family photo is next to the screen, but I focus on him.

"Here's how this will go," I say, deceptively calm with an undercurrent of deadly fury lurking beneath the surface. "Resign, or this gets out. Everything you've done, the bribes you've taken, the blood on your hands—the people of this town are going to find out exactly who you are and your precious reputation will be ruined." We point out each piece of damning evidence we have against his years of being a crooked cop. Grabbing him by the collar, I lean down to snarl, "Your bosses don't like scandal, do they? And to be clear, I'm not talking about the taxpayers of Ridgeview. They might pretend to operate like a corporate investment firm, but we both know that's not what they really are."

"You're in over your head," he says hoarsely, picking up the photo I don't want to look at. Staring at it, his shoulders tremble and his throat bobs with a swallow. He turns to me with dead eyes. "You don't know what you're talking about."

"Don't I? You put me in the fucking foster system after my parents died, Rich!" I drag a hand through my hair as bitterness pricks my throat. "You signed off on the incident report, closed the case for the crash. You had to have seen the coroner's report. You knew my mom was pregnant. You helped cover up their murder."

Richard explodes from the chair, the photo clattering on the mahogany desk. He turns into a different person, shedding the flimsy remorse. Grabbing fistfuls of my leather jacket, he gets in my face.

"You're not walking out of this fucking station. I'm charging you with assault and then you're going to go away." His voice shakes with rage. "You'll never see my daughter again and poison her head with your lies. We've worked too hard to have it go up in smoke because you doctored proof."

I catch Maisy's disgusted expression from the corner of my eye as I stare down a man so different from the one I remember as a kid. His spittle hits my chin, eyes bloodshot and angry graying brows drawn into a deep wrinkle. This is not the same man who taught Holden and I how to hold and throw a football when we were seven at a block party in our old neighborhood.

"Dad!" Maisy shouts, coming around the desk. "Stop!"

He swipes an arm behind him and catches her off guard as she stumbles back, grabbing the corner of the desk to keep her balance. From the shock on her face, I guess he's never raised a hand to her before. I jerk, wanting to kill him for it.

"You think you solved the mystery?" Richard laughs, the sound dark and chilling. "You've got shit. This will go away. No one will believe biased testimonies."

Releasing me, he snatches the flash drive, drops it to the floor, and crushes it beneath his heel. Triumph has him standing tall against us.

"That's not the only copy, Dad. We've got backups of the proof. You can't run from this."

"Proof? Sweetheart, I know you're smarter than that. Don't be an idiot. Having your friends sign letters without witnesses to corroborate the story isn't proof of anything. There's no hardcopies of anything."

"What's your soul worth, you greedy bastard?" I ask coldly, stopping him in his tracks when he rounds the desk.

Confusion crosses his aged features until I throw down the final nail in the coffin, the payment buried in the Landry's financial records from an offshore account. Colton and Connor came through when they uncovered it after months of searching.

"Three quarters of a million." Richard's shoulders stiffen. I set my phone on the desk with a photo of the statement. He stares down in horror at the damning evidence. "Not a bad payout for murder, but you're still scum. Resign. Go away silently, or I'll make sure what the guys at Stalenko have threatened you with to keep you obedient will sound like a goddamn island vacation."

"How did you get that?" His voice is barely above a whisper. To himself, he stumbles over his words. "They swore no one would find it. Couldn't trace it back to us."

"It doesn't matter. If you don't resign, we're going to the press with this," Maisy says. "Step down, Dad. It's the right thing to do."

"Maisy," he says brokenly when he sees her clenched jaw. "Sweetie, I didn't... We had no choice. If we didn't follow orders, they'd kill our whole family."

"So you let them kill Fox's parents?" Her features twist in an appalled expression. "How did you justify that to sleep at night and look Holden and I in the eye for ten years?" There's only a faint tremor in her voice and I'm proud of her for standing up to him. "You're nothing more than a pawn and a coward. So you're going to do this, because if you don't I won't stop until you're behind bars where you belong."

Defeated, he sinks into the expensive desk chair and drags the discarded family photo, tracing his thumbs over the frame. The emotions flitting across his face sour the satisfaction I get seeing him knocked down to his knees. He touches my mom's side of the photo and my stomach revolts. *No.*

I snatch the photo from him and toss it aside. "What's it going to be, Richard? Do you have a shred of decency left in you?"

With a sigh, he begins to type. I move to stand over his chair from behind when he pauses to look at Maisy.

"Do the right thing," she says as she picks up the photo. "I remember this day," she whispers, gaze flickering. Richard flinches. "It seems like it was the last time we were all happy before..."

Before my parents died and everything changed.

Richard says nothing until he finishes drawing up his resignation letter. It's not until he signs it that I release a breath it seems I've been holding for ten years. Setting it aside, he turns to me with regret filling his gaze.

"I'm sorry, Fox. I never wanted it to be like this."

It's too little too fucking late.

"I loved your mother."

The room goes deadly silent and I stand rigid as another bomb drops on me. Maisy's eyes widen and she comes to my side to hold my hand as I grit my teeth.

"No," I bite out. "No you fucking didn't."

If it were true, how could he let her die. He's lying.

"We were...we wanted—"

"No!" I slam a fist down on the desk.

Richard swipes sweat from his brow and his shoulders slump. "It's the truth, son."

"Was the baby yours?"

"No. We were waiting for the right time."

It doesn't bring any relief.

"What are you saying?" Maisy demands, squeezing my hand.

Keeping his gaze pinned on me, he continues in a mournful voice. "It destroyed me when I found out about the crash. It wasn't supposed to happen. I wanted to protect her, too, but your dad just wanted more and more money. He wouldn't leave it until he got what he wanted. They weren't going to budge, so they eliminated them and made us cover it up."

"Stop it," I growl. "Just shut up."

I can't listen to this, or I'm going to explode. I don't know whether to wring his neck or deck him.

"How do you live with yourself? I don't even know you anymore," Maisy says. "I only wish I'd known sooner."

"Sweetheart," Richard begs. "I swear to you, everything I've ever done was to protect you and Holden. I just wanted to give you a good life. Please, please go home." He gets up, clearly intent on trying to patch things up with her. As he reaches out, Maisy takes a step back. "You're going to get hurt being around him. Just listen to me, honey."

"No! You think anything you say is going to make it better? I wanted my dad back!" Breathing heavily, her nails dig into my hand and it grounds me. I can't drown in my own misery when I have her at my side. "You lost me and Holden the minute you agreed to this insane deal. You and Mom destroyed our family. I don't want anything to do with you."

"Maisy, no, please—!"

She turns away from him. When he charges, my protective instinct takes over and I block him, hauling him by the lapels of his suit as I push him back.

"You'll never be able to hurt or control her again," I swear. "You'd have to go through me to get to her and I'll die before I let anyone touch her. Do you understand?"

"Maisy!" he tries again and I shake him hard enough his teeth clack.

"You're done, Richard." I let him go and he slumps against the wall.

"Bye Dad." Maisy won't look at him again.

Pausing at the door, I turn back. "Don't tell your wife or your bosses about this. When they ask why you resigned, you give them any reason you want but the truth. And if you warn them? We'll make sure this gets out."

Taking Maisy's hand, we leave behind a broken man as we walk out.

THIRTY-SIX
Maisy

The day after Dad steps down as Ridgeview's police chief, I invite Holden out for burgers at our favorite place in town.

Fox lets me take the Charger. Once we sorted things out between us, he told me I could consider it mine. The way he makes sure I feel free ignites a glowing ember of happiness in my chest.

After Dad admitted to loving Fox's mom, my stomach has been in knots. I don't know how to tell my brother what I know. God, all the things I know. It's enough to make my head spin. I meet Holden out front and relax when he ruffles my hair, then pulls me in for a hug.

"Did you hear about Dad?" he asks.

"Yeah."

"The house is so different without you," he says. "It's weird."

It hasn't been a full day, but since we left the station I've been worried Dad wouldn't take Fox's threat to heart. I'm afraid he'll warn Mom and Stalenko Corp anyway about the information we have on the whole operation.

"What's it been like at the house?" I ask as we head into the shop.

Inside it's decorated like a beach bar with bamboo counters and tropical plants. We place our orders and sit at one of the hightop tables with yellow stools. He shrugs and fiddles with a jar of drink umbrellas on the table.

"Well, at first it was fine. But I haven't been home much after they started fighting constantly in the days after you split. I think they want to get a divorce and they've been waiting for us to leave home before doing it. You believe that shit? Like they've made it easier for us by staying together."

I refuse to feel guilty for leaving after arguing with them. It's only the learned response I have that bucks up, so I shove it down. They had no right to treat me like they did.

"Have you been there since yesterday?" I watch him carefully.

"Yeah, I was there for dinner last night before I went out with some friends. Mom was pissed when Dad announced his resignation out of nowhere in the middle of eating. She threw her plate at him and called him a dickless coward."

My eyebrows fly up. Mom's always been the more cutthroat of our parents.

"What did he do?"

"Nothing." Holden swipes a hand over his mouth. "She stormed off and slammed the office door. I was sitting there with salmon halfway to my mouth and he just kept eating even though there were broken pieces of plate all over the floor and her dinner staining his shirt. Top ten most uncomfortable and awkward moments of my life, Maise."

When he doesn't mention how or why, I unclench my fists in my lap and pluck at the frayed threads of my shorts. The plan is going okay then. That makes me feel better. Now we're only waiting for the DEA agent Devlin was in touch with to review what we sent. The wait is killer.

Our food arrives and Holden changes the subject, stealing my milkshake for a sip before I've had any. "You'll never guess what happened. Like, fifteen minutes before I pulled up."

"What?"

"Ohio State reached out. A guy from the admissions office called and said there was some mix up, but if I still wanted to play for them I could transfer from the community college and start next semester there."

"Holden, that's great." I lean across the table and squeeze his wrist. "Will you go?"

One of his shoulders hitch. "I don't know yet. At first I was like what the fuck, you know? I'm hesitant because in the last year I think I'm actually glad I lost the draft."

Holden said that the night I left home. Whether he takes it or not, I feel better knowing it's there if he wants because Fox reversed what he did.

"Do you want to play football still?"

He mulls it over, taking a huge bite from his burger. "I think losing it is what made me realize I don't love the game as much as I thought I did. I've found other stuff I like. Community college really isn't that bad."

The corners of my mouth quirk up. I'm relieved to hear Holden found some peace after a year of moping over this. I wonder how much the girl he brought to Thea's opening day at the bakery had to do with this new leaf he's turned over.

"What about you?" he asks. "Will you go to Northwestern?"

"No." I don't even have to think about it. "I want to know—" *Myself* "—what the world's got to offer before I dive into college. If I do at all."

"That's good. There's no reason you have to decide now. Take a year, two. However long you need."

"I want to go to California."

"Yeah?" He grins. "Yeah, I can totally see that for you. When?"

"Soon." The longing in my voice is clear and I know he hears it when his expression turns soft.

We drift into lighter topics and I get to enjoy hanging out with my brother for the first time in so long. By the time we're finished with our burgers my stomach hurts from laughing so much. I feel lighter. We make plans to grab lunch again.

"Don't even think about starting your road trip without saying bye."

"I won't, promise. See you later." I wave after I steal Holden's last fry.

"Hey!"

Laughter fills my voice. "Should've been faster then, dude! Bye."

He waves me off as I head out. A smile lingers as I pull out my phone and find Fox checked in on my hang out with my brother.

Fox: Having a good time?
Maisy: Yeah. On my way home now.
Fox: Home. I like the sound of that. Come back fast so I can show you how much.
Maisy: Are you in the garage? Maybe I'll spread out on the hood of the Charger for you again.

I'm too busy grinning at the next flirtatious text I'm writing to pay much attention to a guy who leans out of an alleyway when I pass. Hands grab me from behind a beat later and my scream is cut off by his big hand covering my mouth. Panic surges and I try to break free without dropping my phone.

Some part of my brain knows my phone is important, I can't lose it if I'm taken to a second location.

Don't drop it. Don't let go.

My hand hurts from how tightly I grip it. All those times Dad worried about a kidnapping roll through my head. I thought he was paranoid, but I was so wrong.

Pain stings my arm and then my limbs stop obeying, feeling like lead weights. My eyelids weigh a million pounds. *Oh shit, I can't!* The harder I breathe, the more difficult it becomes to fight my attacker off.

Everything goes dark. I'm trapped in my mind screaming.

* * *

When I crack my eyes open they feel dry. I blink a few times, trying to get my sluggish brain to work through the fog. It's like I took too much of the cold medicine that always makes me groggy. I scrunch my face up and move, only to find my wrists are restrained by zip ties.

The fuck—?

"Jesus, about time." Disoriented, my head snaps up at the menacing, slightly accented voice coming from the shadows in the corner. "I only gave you half a dose of sedative."

"Where am I?" My tongue feels stuck to the roof of my mouth.

As soon as I ask, my stomach sinks. On the wall of the box-shaped room in large black stenciled letters is a familiar logo—SynCom. The shell company Russian thugs are using to pull the strings running Nexus Lab.

They brought me to the abandoned warehouse? Shit. I'm in serious trouble. Fox and I never had time to find a way into this place before Ethan interrupted us.

Blinking rapidly, I remember. I was on my way back to Fox after lunch with Holden. Someone grabbed me. My arm twinges with the phantom pain from where the needle stabbed into my skin. I don't feel my phone on me, unsure if I won the fight not to drop it or if this thug took it from me when he kidnapped me.

"You're nowhere special, little girl," my babysitter informs me.

He's a rough looking guy with yellow teeth and a barrel chest. Older than me by at least fifteen years, but not as old as my parents. What's worse, I recognize him. I thought he was Mayor Taylor's bodyguard when I ran into Mom in town. Sweat beads his brow and his hair is buzzed short. He stalks closer from across the room and nudges his heavy boot against the rung of the metal chair I'm tied to.

Against my instinct to keep him in my line of sight, I tear my gaze from him and take in the room we're in. It's dusty from disuse. There's a single door in the corner and a high window that's clouded over with grime letting in a minimal amount of light. The ceiling is low, like this is an office framed out of the larger warehouse.

"Why did you take me?" Some of the aftereffects of whatever he drugged me with lingers, clinging to my head like a stubborn cobweb. "And what the fuck did you give me?"

He barks out a laugh and my nose wrinkles at his sour cigarette-tinged breath wafting down on me. "A benzo. Midazolam. You must be a lightweight, princess, that shit's mild as fuck."

I grit my teeth and lean back when he bends to my level. He clamps a hand on the back of my neck and it feels nothing like it does when Fox holds me like that. A protest leaves me as he keeps me still while he lifts one of my eyelids, squinting at me.

"Probably still have some of it in your system. Be good and I'll give you some water in a bit. Can't have the pretty princess suffering."

I glance around the room. "And where will I pee? I don't see a bathroom."

He snorts and motions to the corner. "Right there." His eyes gleam and my stomach turns. "I like to watch."

The breath I draw in through my nose to calm myself is shaky. I squirm, feeling the bite of the plastic zip ties around my wrists and the scrape of rough rope rubbing my thighs raw. How the hell am I getting out of this?

"Why am I here?" I repeat, unsure if I want the answer.

The thug laughs again, like this is a game. "You're bait to catch your little boyfriend. One of our guys is waiting to catch him when he comes looking for you at that burger joint."

He turns away to grab another folding chair I didn't see before. There's a gun tucked in the back of his jeans. Raking my gaze over him while he's distracted, my heart sinks. I can't tell if he has my phone on him or not. Coming back, he pops the chair open in front of me and kicks back in it as if we're just chilling.

"Besides," he adds after stretching and folding his hands behind his head. "Two birds with one stone and all that." The amusement drops away, stripped back to the cruel nature beneath. "We'll use you to teach your mom a lesson about what happens when orders aren't followed."

My pulse races and my palms tingle with the horrible dread pouring over me. I thought my parents would let me go easily, and maybe they would have if I didn't get involved with plucking apart the threads of their empire, but I didn't stay away. I took charge with Fox, forcing Dad to resign, getting federal investigators to take a closer look.

Stalenko Corp has built up their operation over the last decade and all it took was Fox and I to make it wobble.

They wouldn't have touched me if they didn't think we were a threat.

Licking my lips, I push to see if he'll keep talking. "What sort of lesson?"

"Ransom. See?"

He digs out his phone and I tense when he pulls mine from his pocket, too. He shoves it away and I pray it's still turned on. *Find me, Fox.*

The photo I'm shown makes bile rise in my throat. I'm tied to the same chair as now, unconscious, my head pulled back by this guy while he takes a goddamn selfie angle photo.

It's sent to Mom's number. The read receipts are on. The message is marked as seen. No response.

Mom knows I'm here, in danger, but she hasn't done anything. The last remaining shred of hope she ever cared for me turns to dust. At whatever expression breaks past my mask of indifference, my kidnapper chuckles as if we're playing a game.

"Your mom was told to bring you to heel when you and your little boyfriend started poking around. Our security detail already knew about him, but we saw you on the surveillance feed sneaking around here. Once we realized who you were, we connected you back to your parents." He clicks his tongue in disapproval. "Naughty princess."

"What happens if my mom doesn't agree to pay the ransom?"

The ugly grin he gives me makes me wish I hadn't asked.

"Then," he says, taking a fistful of my hair and wrenching my head back.

I cry out, squeezing my eyes tight. Waiting until they open, his grin widens at the moisture clinging to my lashes. I press my lips together, refusing to let the thousands of protests past my lips like he wants when he forcefully fondles my breast through my tank top. I will not give him more power over me by crying and begging for this to stop, no matter how bad I want him off me. He watches the determination in my gaze and moves his rough touch lower, down my side, plucking teasingly at the waistband of my cutoffs. Disgust bubbles like acid in my stomach at the hunger in his gaze.

"Then you're all mine," he promises.

THIRTY-SEVEN
Fox

The last text response she sends cuts off in a string of unintelligible letters and autocorrected phrases that make no goddamn sense. One minute she's flirting and painting a sexy as fuck picture, the next it's like a switch is flipped. It immediately twists my stomach with a bad feeling that I confirm as soon as I hack into the CCTV feed for where she'd been.

The street in front of the beach-themed burger place where she met Holden is empty, no Maisy in sight. The Charger is still parked. There's no way she disappeared. She was just texting me five minutes ago.

I skim back through the recording a few minutes and my blood runs cold. Maisy has her head bent over her phone, unaware of the big burly guy trailing her. He's good, a professional that knows to keep back far enough that no one would suspect anything. Unless you've learned to see this shit like I have.

He goes for her and my heart jumps into my throat as my knuckles turn white from how tightly my fists ball. I gave her my gun to protect herself, but it's probably stashed in the glove compartment of the car. She gives him hell, kicking out, but his fist rams something in her arm and the fight seeps out of her as he uses his thick muscled arms to trap her against his chest until her body slumps. He pockets her phone and adjusts to distribute her weight.

"*Fuck!*"

Horror grips me by the throat as I watch the man drag Maisy to a blacked out SUV parked nearby. This can't be fucking happening. We've avoided them so many times and the minute I drop my guard, she's taken right off the street.

There's no time to waste. Jumping up, I rush around the apartment, grabbing anything I can that will help. I have to improvise and work with what I have on hand because nothing will keep me from getting her back and keeping her safe.

I send out a prayer to whatever might be listening as I throw my leg over the motorcycle. The gravel kicks up behind me as I tear out onto the road with my phone attached to the mount and a map tracing the location of her phone.

Hold on, Maisy. I'm coming.

* * *

Two blacked out SUVs are parked at Stalenko Corp's shell company warehouse where Maisy and I met Ethan Hannigan. I don't want to tip them off, so I cut the engine and walk the bike along the tree line. I keep low once I find a spot to leave it, calling on everything I've learned from Wren, Colton, and the rest of the Crows in the last few years. My gaze constantly sweeps for any threat. I freeze and crouch low behind a concrete loading slab at one side of the warehouse as a guy comes out of a nearby door, phone pressed to his ear as he slips sunglasses on.

"We'll make sure she understands what's at stake. Either she pays the ransom, or we kill the girl. Yeah. Yeah. Got it."

My heart drums a furious beat in my chest. It takes everything in me to stay hidden as the guy gets in one of the SUVs and pulls out. Hopefully that means they've left Maisy with a light detail inside. I will raze this fucking place to the ground before I let them harm her.

It takes more time than I'd like to case the perimeter to check for where the surveillance cameras are, taking their feeds out one by one with a methodical focus. When I make it to a door at the back, I use a knife from my kitchen to pick the lock.

A set of metal stairs leads up to a catwalk. I take them to get a better vantage to find where they're keeping Maisy. It's bigger inside than we first thought, but we barely had time before. From the catwalk that wraps around the perimeter and cuts across the middle, I can see they have several uses for this place to keep an eye on their operation under everyone's noses.

On the lower level, a man smoking a cigarette crosses to a door where the glow of a monitor spills out from the room. I start there, creeping down silently. Pausing outside the door, I listen.

"Is something up with the feed? What's all over the screen?"

"Dunno. They're all like that. Bird shit?"

Guess again. I sprayed WD-40 on the lenses. Their cameras will be toast and it keeps the feed blurry. Keeping low, I move into the room. A bank of computers shows the exterior security feed and a sports game on mute. Two guys are at the desk, the one with the cigarette leaning over the one seated.

This would be easier if I didn't have to take them out at the same time before they alert anyone else. While they're occupied, I peer around and find a brick propping the door open. Perfect, distraction and a weapon. I heft it and adjust my stance. Taking aim, I fling the brick at the guy with the cigarette and it catches him in the back of the neck.

"What the—"

Before either of them process the attack, I'm moving in. I smash the first guy's head to the desk to finish what the brick started and catch the seated guy around the neck in a stranglehold. The cigarette drops from the other guy's lips as his eyes roll back. He crumples to the floor while I clap my hand over the guy in the chair's mouth, tightening my arm until he goes slack.

Wasting no time, I drag their unconscious bodies to the floor and search them. I take their cell phones and smash them with the brick. On the cigarette guy, I find plastic ties in his pocket and use them to secure their wrists behind their backs, looping them both together. When I step back, I rake a hand through my hair and move to the bank of monitors. Nothing seems out of order. I tap a keyboard shortcut sequence Colt showed me and the monitors cut out, then reboot with blue screens of scrolling computer code.

My insides burn with the need to get to Maisy, but she wasn't on the screens before I cut them. I slip out of the room and head down a dimly lit hall. I freeze, pulse jumping when a grizzly looking guy with a beard exits a room ahead. He doesn't see me, turning away to head further into the hall. His head is bent like he's busy texting.

As quiet as I can be, I rush him from behind and use the momentum to shove him against a doorframe of an open door. At the same time, I sink a fist into his side. The man groans, doubling over where I hit him, instinctively swiping in defense. He lands a hit, catching me in the side with an elbow, throwing my footing off.

While he's still reeling, I grab the back of his shirt and drive my knee into his gut. He grunts, fingers scrabbling. One more blow to the head takes him down. Panting more from adrenaline than exertion, I catch him and lower him to the floor.

The hall has nothing useful, but inside the open door there's a room with pipes running up the exterior wall. I drag the guy over to them and pull his hands behind his back before I secure him to the pipes with the zip ties.

My thirst for destruction isn't over. It won't be until I find Maisy and get her out of here. At the end of the hall, I find I'm at the other end of the warehouse. There's another room built inside the space that looks like an office.

When I silently crack the door, I find Maisy inside and burning hot fury rockets through me. The guy who attacked her on the street is all over her. She's tied to a metal chair with rope around her legs. His hands lift her tank top while she juts her chin, face turned away.

My grip turns deadly on the door handle. It's only because he's within range to hurt Maisy that I don't charge him like my instincts scream at me to do. If I had my gun, I'd empty every single bullet into him. He's a dead man.

"Just want to look at what I get to play with later," he says gleefully, squeezing himself through his jeans. "Gonna bite those perky little tits until you scream, sweet thing."

She grits her teeth and takes measured breaths through her nose, ignoring his unwanted touches. Searing fire races through my veins. I want to rip this fucking asshole's head off with my bare hands for touching her.

Look at me. Look here, baby. I'll make it all better. Just hold on one more minute.

Staying silent, I creep inside. The thug is too busy molesting Maisy to notice me winding a length of electrical wire from my garage around my hands. She notices, though. Tears glisten in her eyes and spill down her cheeks.

It'll be okay, I mouth to her.

My brave girl gives me a fierce look and nods. The guy all over her chuckles and murmurs to her, assuming she's warming up to him exposing her.

"Get the fuck off her," I growl as I loop the wire around his neck and pull hard.

A strangled noise of shock catches in his throat as his spine snaps straight. His fingers scrabble at the wire pressed tight to his neck, but I'm taller and I got the jump on him. I keep my elbows tucked tight as I drag him away from Maisy. His legs kick out and flail.

When he goes slack, I wait a few seconds more, then drop him to the floor. Then I'm on him, using my hands to finish the job. His unconscious face turns purple.

"Fox, don't," Maisy calls. "Please don't kill him." She grunts, struggling against the bindings. "Just get me out of this fucking chair so we can leave."

My nostrils flare and I dig my thumbs harder into his jugular. I barely recognize my voice when words slip free. "He deserves it."

"Don't," she says again in a tight voice.

With a bitten off snarl, I let go and kick the fucker in the side before I hurry to crouch at her side.

"I'm sorry." I frame her face, sweeping my thumbs across her tear-stained cheeks.

"It's not your fault. It's our parents who brought this kind of danger here."

Her expression is grim and though she's doing her best to remain calm, I can tell by the tremor in her limbs as I untie the rope that she's seconds from her breaking point. I don't know how long that sick asshole was tormenting her like that, assaulting her body for his own pleasure. My teeth grind so hard my jaw aches.

Once the rope is loose enough, she curls into my chest with a small, anguished sound that cracks my heart in two. I fold her into my arms and stroke her tangled hair.

"Shh, it's okay. I'm here. I've got you."

Her wrists are pink and raw where the brittle plastic ties kept her restrained the more she fought against them. I carefully slide a pocket knife with a serrated slope in the blade between her wrists and the plastic, cutting the bindings away. She rubs them, cradling them close to her chest.

Cupping the back of her head, I pull her close and kiss her forehead.

"Look out!" Maisy yells, pushing me off balance from my crouch so I sprawl to the floor. "He has a gun!"

The thug lumbers toward us with an outraged bellow. His neck is red and angry from the wire and my hands, his eyes bloodshot where a vessel burst.

"You're dead!" he swears as he comes at me.

"You first," I spit.

Scrambling back, I swing around onto my knees and launch at his lower body with all my might, upsetting his center of balance and tackling him. He crashes to the floor and we both struggle for the gun he tries to aim at me. I slam his wrist down on the dusty concrete and he spits in my face, swinging at me and catching the side of my head with his fist. It knocks me to the side, but the punch isn't hard enough to do real damage.

"Fox!" Maisy's yell sounds to my left.

"Don't! Stay back!" I command.

"Like hell!"

The guy beneath me screams when she stomps on his hand while I grunt and rip the gun from him, using it to whip across his face to knock him out for a second time. I'm panting as I rise to my knees over his prone figure. Blood trickles from his temple from the force of the blow, but it's not enough to sate my need to end him.

"Did you kill him?" Maisy whispers.

"No. He's out cold." I climb to my feet and tuck the gun into the back of my jeans. "Better fucking stay that way this time. You okay?"

"Yeah."

"Come here." When she's close I kiss her, hands fisted in the back of her shirt. She makes a small sound and breaks away to bury her face in my chest. "You're okay now." I don't want to ask, but I force the question past my lips anyway. "Did he...did he touch you anywhere else?"

"No." Maisy pulls back far enough to wipe beneath her eyes and shakes her head. "He tried to scare me, but I don't think he was allowed to get away with too much on the off chance my mom was going to pay the ransom."

A relieved breath gusts out of me. "I subdued the others, but one got away before I snuck in. Eventually Stalenko Corp's higher ups are going to find out when he comes back. Let's tie him up like the rest and get the fuck out of here."

Maisy nods resolutely and picks up the discarded length of auto electrical wire. "I knew you'd find me."

"Always. I knew as soon as your text came through all autocorrected."

She curls her fingers around the wire, knuckles white. "Thank you."

Something in my chest shifts and expands. "You don't have to thank me, Maisy. I love you and I'll protect you."

She turns those beautiful hazel eyes on me, shining with a fresh bout of tears. "I love you, too."

Together we drag the thug across the room to a pipe running along the floor. She rifles through his pockets, retrieving her phone while I take out the zip ties I picked up and secure him to the pipe. I still want to kill him. More than that, I want to rip his skin off piece by piece and grind his bones to dust, but I need to get Maisy out of here.

THIRTY-EIGHT
Maisy

When we make it to Fox's hidden motorcycle outside, I turn to him with my heart sitting in my throat. "I had everything under control."

He chuckles and scrubs a hand over his face, then tugs me into his arms and speaks against the top of my head. "I love you."

I breathe him in for a moment, letting his strength soothe away the last couple hours of horror. He holds onto me tightly as if he never wants to let me go. A lump forms in my throat. I don't realize how much I'm shaking until he buffs his hands up and down my upper arms.

"Come on. I need to get you back before the adrenaline crash hits and you're not able to hold on." Framing my face, he tilts it up and gives me a smile tinged in darkness. "Before today I would've tied you up to make sure you'd have to hold on, but I think we can save that for another day."

A snort jerks my head. I have to laugh, because if I don't I'm on the brink of breaking down under the weight of it all. "You think?" My wrists still throb. The skin on my thighs is tender, putting off heat from rope burn. "Let's go."

The drive back is a challenge. Riding a motorcycle after being banged up highlights every ache in my body with each small bump in the road. I press my cheek into Fox's back and seek out the sensation of freedom that I love when we're on the bike to keep my mind off everything else. Thankfully it's not too far to his place.

Once we're at his converted warehouse, he sits me down on the same stool he used when I cleaned up his cuts after we were shot at. Those stormy blue eyes watch my expressions carefully as he checks me over. Physically, I'll be fine. Some minor bruises, skin abrasions, and the rest of the sedative dose will fade with time. The lasting damage is all psychological.

"I want to shower," I say.

No amount of strength of character or confidence in my body spares me from the mental horror I endured today. I can still feel his breath and disgusting hands on my skin, his rough grip lifting my shirt up to expose me, the sadistic way he laughed and got off on the power he held over me as I was tied up and unable to fight back.

My skin feels dirty and I want to scrub at it until I wash it all away. It won't take away the memory, but I won't feel better until I can do something to wipe away the lingering sensations of the violation of my body.

I never should have faced what I did today. Kidnapped. Held for ransom. *Assaulted*.

Dad swore yesterday that everything they did was to protect us. Bullshit. If they wanted to protect us, they wouldn't have welcomed that kind of danger into this town. Mom wouldn't have waited so long to save me from the criminals she works with. For all I know she saw the photo of me unconscious and bound then went about her day, not caring what happened to her daughter. The read receipt is burned into my brain and there's no coming back from that.

"Come on," Fox murmurs, taking my hand and leading me to the bathroom.

He starts the water, testing the temperature on his wrist before turning to me. I strip out of my tank top and fling it on the floor. A fierce rumble makes my gaze dart to him. His attention is on my breast, on the fingerprint shaped red marks. He holds a hand out, but curls his fingers into a tight fist, his skin stretched so the scar on his knuckles stands out.

Breathe, I coach myself, drawing on a meditative headspace to keep myself from shaking apart at the seams. In a hurry, I shuck off my shorts and step under the hot spray of water.

Fox turns to go. He promised he wouldn't leave me alone. A broken, panicked noise escapes me and he's back, jumping into the shower with me, still fully clothed.

"Shh." His arms hold me close while I cling to him, taking ragged breaths that make my chest heave. "I'm not going anywhere. I thought—I was going to give you privacy, but I'm here."

"Don't," I choke out.

"I know," he soothes in a jagged voice as he strokes my hair. "I promise that will never happen to you again."

We stay like that for a moment, his arms around me, keeping my trembling frame tucked against his chest. His clothes are soaked, the t-shirt sticking to his body while I stand there naked, half-wishing for the water to be scalding enough to burn the dirty layer of my skin off.

Straightening my spine, I reach for the bar of soap on the ledge. It smells spicy with a hint of the ocean we both confessed to missing, like a forest meeting the shoreline. It's *Fox*. I press it to my skin and start lathering. In a few movements I find myself scrubbing rough enough to chafe. I don't realize I'm panting until he gently pries the soap from my death grip.

"Let me."

Turning me around, he winds one arm around my middle and pulls me into his chest. I hold onto his arm to keep myself standing as he helps wash me. He doesn't let me go, supporting my weight when I sag against him, keeping his face pressed to the side of mine. I let my eyes close and focus on him.

The water shuts off and I crack my eyes open. He strips out of his wet clothes, the drenched material slapping to the floor. Stepping out, he offers a hand.

Fox dries me off and sits me down on the edge of the bed. The shower helped to make me feel more like myself. After he pulls on a pair of briefs, he rummages beneath the platform he built for the mattress out of found materials and kneels in front of me.

"Let me see your wrists." His voice is low, gentle, but infused with the power of his command. I offer my hands to him. "This will help."

Producing a tube of lotion, he squirts some onto his fingers and rubs it into my wrists with slow circles. My lashes flutter and a soft sigh leaves me. When he finishes with my wrists, he moves on, applying lotion to the irritated red patches of my thighs where the rope keeping me in the chair scraped me raw.

He glances up at the curious noise I make. "What?"

"I didn't think someone all rough and tough like you would bother with skincare," I tease.

Color tinges his cheeks and the corner of his mouth curls wryly. He scrapes his thumb nail over his lip and leers at me through his dark lashes. "It's not for my face." His brows lift and he traps the tip of his tongue between his teeth. "I didn't touch other girls, but a man has needs, Maise."

It takes a minute for his meaning to register to my sluggish mind. "Oh. Ohh, okay. I feel you." Smirking, I lean into him. "You and Righty? Same."

A husky laugh rumbles in his throat and he moves to my other thigh, taking his time to rub the lotion into my inflamed skin. As he cares for me, an intense wave of drowsiness has me swaying.

"Lay down, baby." He brushes damp tendrils of hair from my face and nudges me onto the bed. "I've got you."

I shift back, then freeze. "You won't leave?"

"No. I'm right here. Not going anywhere."

He follows me, opening his arms once he's settled. I burrow into them and breathe him in, nose tucked against the crook of his neck. He rubs my back in comforting circles.

"Are you cold?"

I shake my head. "Just hold me."

His arms cinch snugly around me. In his embrace, I'm safe, I'm loved, I'm protected.

"Thank you," I whisper, letting sleep claim me.

As I doze, I'm vaguely aware of him murmuring to me. I don't know what he says, but he never once leaves my side. He's there for me.

It's dark when I feel lucid again. I don't know if it was a lasting reaction to the sedative, the emotional overload, or a combination of it all, but when I wake up it's like I'm coming out of an intense nightmare. My limbs are heavy and the aches in my body are more prominent. I wish I could just fucking forget it all. Lock it in a damn vault in my mind and never face it again. I release a groan and roll over to find Fox's gaze on me in the dim shadows.

"You're awake," he says.

My cheek drags over his tattooed bicep beneath my head when I nod. He tucks my hair behind my ear, tracing the pads of his fingers down the side of my jaw.

"What happens now?" I ask.

He draws in a slow breath. "I know a guy not too far from here who has an endless supply of explosives. Well, Colt does. Part of his network. It's a day's drive away."

Phantom fingers squeeze my breasts too hard and air hitches in my throat. I picture fire and ash, imagine the man who took me screaming in agony while I watch his skin melt off his bones. For a second, I want it. It scares me I could feel so violently toward someone, but it doesn't make this go away.

"No. That makes us no better than them."

"I'm not a good man, Maisy." The way he grasps my jaw with his entire hand is firm, but not enough to hurt me. His gaze bores into mine. "They hurt you today and they deserve to burn for it."

A shiver runs down my spine. The sinister darkness in his tone calls to a part of myself I've never been aware of before. Maybe it's wrong to love this side of him, to know that he would destroy anything that dared hurt me. Maybe it's not what society deems normal, but it's me and it's him. That's all that matters to me.

"Not everyone working at Nexus Lab is guilty. We can't."

He sighs. "If the investigators don't make a move soon, we're doing this my way."

I concede. Days ago he was ready to walk away from this after he found the answers he was looking for about his parents. It's because of me that we're still seeing this through.

"After it's over, we're putting this town behind us." I shift closer when he buries his fingers in my hair and draws my forehead to his lips. "You and me."

"You and me," he responds.

THIRTY-NINE
Fox

STANDING out front of Nexus Lab to watch while law enforcement agency vehicles swarm the place is gratifying. The DEA and FDA special unit agents file in and out of the circus with boxes full of paperwork, computer towers, and panic-stricken employees who are having a hell of a Monday. My arm slides around Maisy's waist to pull her against my side and together we wait behind the barricades for the big finale.

I had Colt's guy with explosives on call, ready to pay him as much as he demanded to clean him out, but they finally came through. Ethan Hannigan tipped us off from wherever his trail took him and we arrived before the rest of the numerous news crews did.

It's been three days since Maisy was taken to the abandoned warehouse. I drove by it while she was with her brother, unwilling to leave her alone still. It was cleared out, as I suspected. Stalenko Corp probably pulled back so their lawyers could do the heavy lifting in connection to Nexus Lab taking the fall. I only hope this will all be enough for them to feel pressure from federal investigators breathing down their necks so they can't do this again.

Maisy tried to call her mom once, but it went to voicemail. She hasn't tried since. They're done, I think. Whatever chance there was that she could have some kind of relationship with her parents died the day her mom allowed her to be kidnapped and did nothing when she was hit up for ransom.

I can't decide whether it's worse to lose both parents in a suspicious accident, spend a decade believing they were innocent, only to find out they were far from it, or be forced to look them in the eye while they spend years controlling every move to maintain the wicked life they hide from their kids.

Both scenarios fucking suck. At least we have each other to lean on when we're bogged down by the misery of our shitty parents. Her friends are there for her. Thea bought her a journal after Maisy told her what happened and decided she didn't want to see a shrink yet. I've caught her scribbling in it after meditating.

"This is more people than I thought there'd be," Maisy says at my side.

"People love drama. They've come to see this madhouse so they can gossip about it when it's on the news."

She hums in agreement.

All around us, news anchors are describing the unfolding scene for the nightly lead in with the breaking story. It's not only local stations, but national coverage reporting the downfall of Nexus Lab. I overhear one of them detailing connections to several prominent businessmen here and satisfaction swirls in my gut.

We did this. We blew the lid off the deceitful underbelly of our corrupt town to expose the truth.

It isn't exactly what I hoped for when I came back to Colorado to seek retribution from the family that destroyed mine, but my hunt for revenge helped me find my way back to Maisy. I came here to ruin her life only to find out I still can't live without her. Everything I endured was worth it to find happiness with her.

For the longest time I thought we could never salvage the special connection we had as kids. I thought it died the same day my parents did. But I was wrong.

Maisy is my kismet, the one I'm supposed to love.

I thread my fingers through her hair, catching it in a loose grip. Using it for leverage, I angle her head back and hover my lips over hers. She gazes at me with passionate fire in her hazel eyes. It's a beautiful sight. She's more than the girl I fell in love with years ago and promised forever to. My wild daisy, the strongest fighter with a big heart and an adventurous spirit waiting to be let loose.

I never want to be apart from her again.

Tired of waiting, she closes the small gap between us to steal the kiss I didn't give her. I hum into it, cupping the back of her head as we kiss languidly. Victory tastes fucking sweet.

A commotion draws our attention to the front doors of the building. They fly open and two agents escort a furious Jacqueline Landry out in handcuffs. Maisy draws in a sharp breath as her mother's icy gaze passes over us. It's subtle, but Jacqueline stiffens. I almost wish she'd struggle and pitch a fit, but that's not who that bitch is. She'll save face until the end.

Dramatic fit or not, she knows we did this to her. It's enough.

Reporters rush to flank the group surrounding Jacqueline on her walk of shame, shouting questions and asking for a statement from the company's public face.

"What made you accept a deal like this?"

"Do you have anything to say about the raid on Nexus Lab? Were you aware the drugs your company produced were sold on the black market?"

"Is this related to your husband's sudden resignation from his position as police chief?"

"No comment," Jacqueline hisses.

I scoff and Maisy slides her arm around my waist. *Was it worth it?* That's what I want to ask her, Richard Landry, and my parents. If any of them could go back, would they let greed rule them again?

Jacqueline glares at the DEA agent that opens the back door of one of their vehicles near the barricade we're behind. It makes something old and decayed unlock in my chest as we watch her be folded into the back seat.

The Ridgeview, Colorado that anyone knew will never be the same after today. The secrets are spilled into the light.

Maisy turns to me. "I've seen enough. Have you?"

"Yeah."

Tossing one last glance at the car Jacqueline was stuffed into, I turn my back on a dark chapter in my life feeling lighter, walking hand in hand with the girl I love.

* * *

A week later, I'm breathing in the midsummer mountain air under the late afternoon sun with Maisy and her friends. The grassy sloping clearing we're lounging in is full of wildflowers and butterflies floating on the breeze. It's just off the road, our cars and my motorcycle parked in a gravel ditch at the edge of the field. Devlin and Connor kick a soccer ball back and forth shirtless while Lucas cracks open a beer and offers the first cool sip to Gemma sprawled between his legs.

Thea is braiding Maisy's hair in two french braids, Blair's already done in some intricate looking crown made of shiny dark hair.

She's been more herself this week, her smiles coming easier. I've been waiting for her to wake up from nightmares, but they don't plague her the same way they claimed my mind for years. What happened didn't break her.

The news has daily coverage on Jacqueline and the pharmaceutical company's illicit drug ring scandal. Jacqueline is the public fall guy, but details about the investigation have also come out with information on the mayor's involvement, and about my parents and their own sins that led to their fatal demise. It's strange, after finding out everything I thought I knew about them was a lie, I don't want to shy away from the whispers that continue when my name is mentioned.

It doesn't matter. Maisy knows who I am. That's all I need, a few good people who I consider my family to have my back.

Since the news broke, she's been spending a lot of time with her brother. We leave town today for the road trip she's dreamed of for half her life. She tells me Holden has plans to follow the girl he met at the local community college when she transfers for the fall semester to a different school. They're both done with Ridgeview. The only good thing this town has is her friends. Without them, we'd never come back here again.

"I brought you something." Maisy appears in front of me, shuffling on her knees in the grass. Her hair is braided, a wildflower tucked behind her ear.

I rake my teeth over my lip, grasping her hips. She holds up a daisy between us with thin purple petals, identical to the one I gave her when she was eight and the ones I picked for her to win her heart back. The corner of my mouth kicks up and I take the flower. She presses her lips to mine and I drag her into my lap, deepening our kiss.

Connor pauses his one-on-one soccer game with Devlin to howl like a coyote. Laughing, Maisy breaks away and tucks her face into my neck.

"The fuck is that supposed to mean?" I ask him.

He shoots me a mischievous grin. "Watch and learn, Foxy."

"No," I bark, nearly choking when Maisy's tongue darts out against my throat. "Don't pick that up from Colt."

His smirk is unrepentant as he scoops his wife into his arms and plants a kiss on her lips while she giggles. Lucas does the wild howl this time with his hands cupped around his mouth.

"What the fuck," I mutter. "Your friends are crazy."

Devlin chuckles as he drops to the grass nearby with the soccer ball tucked beneath his elbow. Blair wraps her arms around his shoulders from behind and kisses his cheek.

"It's the SLHS coyote call," Devlin explains. "I don't know how far back it goes, but when there's PDA, the mascot is the calling card. A right of passage in a way."

I shake my head. "This fucking town."

"Tell me about it," Blair says with an exasperated roll of her eyes. "High school here was weird as hell."

"You love it," Gemma says slyly, keeping her eyes closed and her face upturned to the sunshine while Lucas slips his hand beneath her shirt to caress her stomach.

"You learn to deal with it," Thea offers after she extricates herself from Connor. Her cheeks are pink and there's a brightness lighting her eyes up. "Who's hungry?"

A round of agreements go around. Maisy and Thea hand out sandwiches from a huge picnic basket. Laughter echoes off the treetops as we eat and enjoy the summer day. Gemma breaks out a camera and captures it all.

When the sun begins to dip lower, Maisy nudges me. "We should hit the road soon. I want to watch the sunset before we get to our first Airbnb."

The plan is to hop from rentals in the towns we pass through to camping in national parks as we meander our way to the west coast.

"Already?" Thea gives Maisy a sad smile. "I'm going to miss you."

"I'm going to California, I'm not dying, babe, jesus." Maisy wraps her in a bear hug until they tip over into the grass. The other two girls join the dog pile of affection. "I promise to keep up with the group chats. Instagram and text."

"Chase your dreams hard," Thea mumbles from somewhere in the mix of girls tangled together.

"You bet," Maisy says. "There's nothing holding me back from myself now."

"You're going to have the best damn time," Gemma says.

"FaceTime us if you get service in the parks at night?" Blair asks, glancing from Maisy to

Devlin. "I'd love to see what the stars look like out there."

He gives her this private smile that puts color in her cheeks.

"All the things," Maisy agrees, getting up and dusting off her cropped leggings.

My heart stutters at the sight of her, with grass sticking to her braids and one of my t-shirts knotted in the front so it shows off a strip of her taut stomach she's stunning. And *mine*.

After another round of goodbyes, we walk hand in hand to the line of cars by the edge of the clearing. The couples trail behind us, each with their arms around their partners. Maisy waves back at her friends and I follow suit, lifting a hand.

Maisy meets my eye and hooks her fingers in the belt loops of my jeans, luring me close for a kiss. I give her what she wants.

As a group, her friends give us a loud coyote howl that devolves into laughter.

"Ready?" I ask.

The curve of her smile is full of excitement. "So ready."

Framing her face between my hands, I kiss her again. "Good."

We climb on the bike and a flutter moves through my chest. This is it. Her arms slip around me and she squeezes my waist, resting her chin on my shoulder.

"Take me on an adventure," she whispers.

Grinning, I rev the rumbling engine and run my fingers over the braided leather bracelet carrying stones I gave her. She used to say the same exact thing when we played on our street as kids.

"Hold on tight, baby."

Her arms tighten and I gun it, taking us onto the road that will cross over the Rockies. The sun shines down in golden rays.

As we cross over the mountain range, Maisy lets out an elated cheer at the top of her lungs.

This is everything I want—the open road, my wild daisy girl wrapped around me, and the wind kissing our cheeks.

EPILOGUE
Maisy

2 Months Later

Summer is drawing to a close, but when we reach the west coast it feels like it will never end, keeping us in a perpetual bubble of sunshine and golden warmth. The beach I picked out on the map is deserted. I relish the sound of waves crashing and the taste of salt air on my tongue. I've missed this.

As soon as we got here an hour ago I snapped a photo and sent it to Holden and my friends. A giddiness swept over me as soon as my toes touched the sand. Tears pricked my eye while I stood at the water's edge brushing my fingers over the bracelet I made from Fox's stones when we came here as kids.

My brother and I are closer than ever since this road trip started, despite both of us no longer living in the same town. We have to hold onto each other because I don't think either of us will reach a place of trust with our parents again. Dad keeps trying to call, but I don't want to talk to him. As far as I'm concerned, Mom can rot behind bars for leaving me at the mercy of the people who attacked me. It's what they both deserve for all their misdeeds.

I have the love of those who actually care about me—my friends, my brother, my boyfriend. They're all important to me. They're more family than my parents have ever been.

Without them, I wouldn't have followed my dream to finally leave town. Now here I am in California at last.

I filled up the first journal Thea gave me and picked up another on our way out here. It's cathartic to reflect. I love pouring my thoughts into it, the good and bad, and documenting the memories we're making.

After we walked up and down the beach looking for new rocks to add to our collection we started on this trip, I sit on the bike in front of Fox, facing him with my legs straddling his powerful thighs. His hands are inside the oversized sides of my loose tank top, thumbs teasing the curves of my tits. I slide my arms around his neck and bite my lip.

"It's just us here. Like our own little world."

A rumble sounds in his chest and one of his hands slips further into my shirt, tracing my spine down to my ass. He hauls me closer so I can feel the hard ridge of him against my core.

My breath hitches and I rock against him.

"Do you feel free now, baby?" he murmurs against my parted lips.

The sinful rasp in his voice sends a bolt of heat right to my clit. With a soft moan, I nod. He kisses the corner of my mouth, grip flexing on my ass to grind against me.

Smirking, I peel off my top and let it flutter to the sand, feeling every ounce of freedom I've claimed. I no longer have to regulate myself or do anything I don't want to do. There are no reputations to uphold or expectations to meet. I can live on the wind, with Fox at my side where I'm happiest.

He bends to place a kiss on my throat, then lower to my sternum, then captures one of my nipples in his mouth. Waves crash against the shore and a pelican swoops overhead. A carefree laugh escapes me. His lips move back up to brush over mine.

I lean back, but his hand comes up to grasp my throat, pulling me back in.

"Not done with you yet," he whispers in a smoky, seductive tone before he kisses me again, deeper this time. "Never will be."

"I'm all yours and you're mine."

He takes me apart with his hands and mouth until we have a new memory of California, the first of many where he makes me feel wild on a beach.

I'm happy, fulfilled by chasing whims and traveling. I'm beginning to discover the parts of myself that have lived deep inside for too long, neglected before now.

The freedom is addictive after I've gone so long without it, hoping and wishing for it. There's a light in my heart every time the wind moves through my hair, with each choice I take for myself. What makes it sweeter is doing it all with the person who has my heart—him.

EPILOGUE
Fox

1 Year Later

Southern California suits us both in ways I never imagined. It's like our hearts knew we needed this to be our home the minute we first stepped foot in the state all those years ago on a combined family vacation, then spent every minute since missing it until we made our way here at the end of our road trip last summer.

Maisy turned her longing for the Pacific ocean into a bracelet with the small stones I found for her to hold onto the memory, while I inked it into my skin and sought out solace in a foggy cove in Maine until I returned to her.

Kismet, as my girl would say. She's got me believing in fate.

We did exactly what we dreamed up back in my converted warehouse in Ridgeview—she opened a yoga studio that opens right to the beach and I have a workshop-garage space where I spend my time making whatever my hands create on instinct. More often than not I think the shapes I twist out of the found materials remind me of Maisy, just like the piece we keep in the bedroom of our bungalow a few blocks from the coastline.

Wiping my greasy hands off on a rag, I step back from the classic '67 Camaro I've been tuning up for a customer while Maisy had her morning sessions at the studio. I want to finish up and beat her back to the house so I can get my surprise ready. My stomach dips at the thought of what I have planned and I toss the dirty rag onto the bench along the wall.

I wash up and close up the shop, strolling out into the alley that connects to the main strip of Venice Beach. As I walk the boulevard, I pull my hair into a small knot with one of the hair ties I stole from Maisy's nightstand tray I hammered out of a piece of copper I found in an antique shop. It's getting long, but Maisy likes it.

The walk back to our bungalow isn't long. The porch is covered in plants, wind chimes, and a couple of stray cats we fed once that have stuck around. I bend to rub the tubby orange one's clipped ear, smiling when he bumps his head against my knuckles.

"Big day today," I tell him as I unlock the door.

A quick glance at the clock lets me know I have just enough time to shower before she heads home from her yoga studio. I race through it, skipping a shirt and heading into the front room in just a low-slung pair of jeans with rips in the knees. After ducking outside to pick one of the wild daisies from our garden, I lay it on the coffee table next to her stack of journals and slip the finishing touch onto the stem.

I searched high and low for a ring, then it hit me. I needed to make it. Maisy has never been a girl that cares about diamonds, more happy to make a bracelet or necklace out of stones she finds meaning in. Jewelry wasn't something I'd tacked in my tinkering before, but Maisy is my muse and I'm damn proud of what I made.

The ring I crafted is her, me, *us*. Gold and silver metal twist together to shape it, twining around two stones, one her favorite crystal, amethyst, and the other a small piece of polished sea glass I picked up for her—both we found while walking on the beach. Around the stones I formed golden petals out of hammered metal.

Her muffled voice cooing to the porch cats has me sitting up straight on the couch. Despite the shower, my palms prickle with sweat. I rub them on my jeans and wait for her to come through the door.

"I'm home," she calls.

"I'm right here."

A warm smile turns on me and I swipe my tongue over my lower lip. I love this beautiful girl. Her light brown hair is up in a topknot and her loose workout crop top reveals her tan skin I'm itching to taste. I can never get enough.

Maisy drops her keys in a bowl I made and joins me on the couch with a content sigh. "How was your morning? Did you finish on the Camaro?"

"Just about." My arm drapes over her shoulder. "Got something for you."

"Yeah?"

I motion with a jerk of my chin to the table, where her daisy is waiting. She makes a happy noise and picks it up. Every day for the last year I've given her a flower I picked.

The ring slips off the stem and she catches it with quick reflexes before it drops to the floor.

"Hey, this is..." Maisy trails off as she gets a good look at the daisy-shaped ring in her palm.

Her gaze darts from the daisy, to the ring I made just for her, to me as I sink to the floor on one knee, pulling her down to sit on my thigh. Her arms automatically loop around my shoulders, absently tracing my tattoos. Those gorgeous hazel eyes widen.

"Oh." It comes out on a surprised sigh.

My gaze bounces between hers. "I promised a long time ago that I'd marry you one day because you're my daisy. What do you say?"

Maisy's breath hitches and she digs her fingers into my muscles. Her mouth curves into a wide grin. "I say yes."

A well of happiness overflows in my chest and I crush her to me, releasing a short laugh against her hair.

"You made this?" she asks when I lean back.

"Do you like it?"

"I love it." Her gaze is warm and fond as she tilts the ring side to side to study the details I put into it. "I recognize the stones. It's perfect."

I swoop in to kiss her, closing my fingers over the ring. With my forehead resting against hers, we both watch as I guide the engagement ring onto her finger.

"You're perfect, little daisy," I murmur. "You make me happy."

A soft, affectionate sound escapes her and I lift up, situating us back on the couch with her in my lap.

"So, locking it down, huh?" Maisy sasses.

I smack her thigh with a low growl. "You've known since you were eight that I wanted to marry you."

"Yeah, before you decided to hate me for ten years."

"Even then, I wanted you, baby. Especially then."

She cups my face with one hand and bumps her nose against mine.

My phone vibrates and I fish it out of my back pocket. "That's probably Lucas or Colt. They knew today was the day I was springing the question on you. They're not going to leave us alone to celebrate until I let them know how it went."

She laughs and tucks her face against my neck while she holds out the ring to admire it.

As soon as I unlock the phone, the screen glitches. An animation of a crow flies across the screen and lands on a skull. *Shit*. My stomach clenches. I promised Colton, and now Wren is calling to collect on the favors I owe to my brothers.

Cinching my arm tighter around Maisy, I tap on the animation and the encrypted message loads.

"Goddamn it," I mutter.

"What is it?" Maisy asks.

"We're going to have to delay our celebrating for a little bit." I tilt the screen toward her to show her the message. "I have to go to Thorne Point. It has to do with Ethan Hannigan."

Her brows draw together. "The journalist we met in Ridgeview?"

"Yeah. Something happened to him. He's missing."

"Oh shit," she murmurs, concern lacing her tone. "Do you think something bad happened?"

Shrugging, I shift her off my lap and get up. Damn, I'll have to get someone to cover the shop. I don't know how long this trip to the east coast will take. But this is what it means to be in with the Crows; when they call in favors, there's no hesitation. They helped me time and again, now I'll do the same for them.

"I'll be back as soon as I can," I promise.

"Fox Michael Wilder." Maisy crosses her arms and plants herself in front of me to stop me in my tracks. "If you think I'm letting you go all the way to Maine to help Colton without me, you're wrong. We're going together."

My heart fucking melts. "Okay. We go together. Me and you."

"Me and you," she repeats with a resolute nod. "No matter what."

Wherever we go, it's always together.

BONUS SERIES EPILOGUE
Devlin

8 Years Later

Family means something in Ridgeview. To our group, our family is the one we chose. It's grown over the years and the small ember that began in my damaged heart is now a full blaze.

We support each other. We have each other's backs. Same as when we were just kids with the weight of the world on our shoulders.

As life has gotten busy with marriage and kids, we started a new tradition to remind ourselves to slow down. It doesn't matter if some of us leave Ridgeview, like Maisy and Fox making their home in California, or if we stick to what we know, like Lucas and Gemma living in Silver Lake Forest Estates. Lucas designed the house they had built on the lake we both grew up on, the one we're chilling at now.

What counts is that twice a year we get everyone together for a week at the lake. It began back when Blair was pregnant with Phoenix and it's continued.

"Here."

Condensation from a cold beer bottle drips on my shoulder and I hiss when Blair pushes it into my neck. She's still the wicked little demon I caught, then married all those years ago. Her husky laugh makes the corner of my mouth tug up.

"Don't think I won't seek retribution for that later, angel." I take the beer and tug her into my lap.

The beach lounger wobbles, digging deeper into the sand until she finds her balance, always graceful. Her mouth pulls into a Cheshire cat grin as she settles against my chest.

"Counting on it," Blair says.

As I take a pull from the beer, my hand tucks around her waist, toying with the bikini ties on the red little number she has on. I always love her in my color.

"Momma," Aurora says at one side of the beach chair we're sharing.

Her twin brother Jasper is playing in the sand on my other side.

"What baby?" Blair asks, brushing her shiny brown hair away from her face.

"Up for cuddle."

A raspy laugh vibrates in my chest and I hold my arm out to our three year old to help her up. "Come here, my little star."

Aurora lights up with a big smile that I love and she launches at me. I gather both my girls in my arms. Jasper's attention leaves his plastic shovel. Not one to be left out, he gets in on the action, climbing to his feet and gripping my leg to hoist himself up on his own. He's always resourceful and likes to do things his way.

The four of us settle on the lounger under the shade of an umbrella and watch Phoenix laughing his head off while Fox plays with him and Caleb, Lucas and Gemma's son, in the shallows of the lake. The three of them splash around and the boys shriek while Fox catches them in his arms and spins them to make bigger waves. Caleb is a couple years younger than Phoenix—around the same age as the twins—but he has always looked at his cousin like he hung the moon. It's about the same way I probably used to look at Lucas, like an older brother to idolize.

A sense of contentment buzzes in me as I brush Blair's long hair aside and skim the tip of my nose over her jaw. Aurora sticks her thumb in her mouth and rests against Blair while she wraps our little girl in her arms. Jasper sits on the lounger cushion between my legs, releasing deep belly laughs when I tease him like I'm going to trap him with my knees.

"Tonight," I murmur against the shell of Blair's ear. "Under the stars."

She shoots me a secret smile, the one she reserves for me. The one that makes my pulse race, that makes me love her more fiercely every day we have together.

The stars really came through for me, giving me everything I ever wished for and more.

Laughter further down the beach echoes into the spindly treetops framing the beach. Thea and Maisy have Luna and Maisy's one year old son Morgan in their laps. From here I can make out the abstract shapes of rainbows they're building in the warm sand with rocks and shells they've picked from their walk earlier. Luna is beaming and Thea drops a kiss on her head. Maisy bumps her shoulder into Thea's and the three girls laugh at something I can't hear while the baby is fascinated by sticking his toes in the sand.

Nearby, Lucas and Bishop man the grill. Bishop flips burgers while Lucas heckles him, hiding his grin behind his youngest's wispy blonde curls. Little Charlie finds this hilarious and whips around to catch her dad before he hides.

"It says grill master, right here." Bishop gestures with the spatula to the ridiculous design on the apron he has on, then makes a shooing motion. "Outta my kitchen."

"I see no master before me, only the pupil who will never surpass the true master." Lucas plays up the comical dramatics with his daughter as his sidekick.

"Charlie girl, you're supposed to be on Uncle B's side," Bishop says, giving her big puppy eyes.

She giggles harder and squirms in Lucas' arms.

"Nah, man, my girl's a daddy's girl. Isn't that right?" Lucas bounces her playfully, sparking a fresh round of high-pitched squeals of delight. "Up top, baby girl."

Charlie puts her palm against his when he holds it up. She hasn't quite figured out high-fiving yet, but she's getting there. She's as clever as her mom.

Gemma snorts from her spot, stretched out on a beach towel close to my lounger. She tips her sunglasses down her nose to watch her husband and our friend elbow each other. Bishop rolls his eyes at Lucas' comment about his grilling skills, but shoots him a good-natured cocky grin.

"Can't decide which of them is the baby over there," Gemma jokes.

Blair's shoulders shake with amusement. "The answer is all of them."

"Only one of them shits in a diaper though," I say.

A smirk tugs at my mouth and the three of us chuckle. It sends me back to when we were younger with a wave of nostalgia and I'm struck by how the fact we all connected is the once in a lifetime kind of friendship.

Fox emerges from the lake, dripping water, dark hair slicked back with the boys hanging at his hips from his grip around their waists.

Phoenix lifts his head and catches my eye as Fox carries him up the beach. The corner of my mouth kicks up at how happy he looks. His childhood is so different from mine. It's full of joy and happiness. None of our kids worry that they're not wanted or not enough. We all shower them in love, support—anything they need, we make sure they get it.

When they pass where Luna is making rainbows with her mom and Maisy, Phoenix wriggles free. Caleb follows, chasing after Phoenix on shorter legs as Luna lifts a bucket and leads them. They're probably planning to look for frogs, just like me and Lucas used to do. Gemma gets up from her towel and strolls after them to keep an eye on things as they explore the reeds poking out of the shallows past the cleared out swimming area.

Fox bends over to kiss Maisy and scoops Morgan into his arms. Maisy and Thea join him as he ambles over to the picnic table and grill with Lucas and Bishop. Thea breaks away to wrap her arms around Bishop's waist from behind.

"Kiss the cook, sunshine."

Bishop angles his cheek and points. His grin stretches when she leans up to trail kisses across his skin, lingering at his mouth when she captures his lips. Her wide brimmed straw hat topples off her head. Bishop hums in contentment and gives her one last peck.

"That's the kind of sugar I like," he crows, retrieving her hat for her.

"You like it all," Thea teases. "Those look about done. I'll get the other snacks ready."

"I'll help," Maisy offers.

"Nah, I'll get it. Here—"

Bishop hands the spatula off to Lucas and follows his wife. I catch his low, flirtatious murmurs as he cups her shoulders and buries his face in her neck from behind. She giggles.

Maisy gives Fox a playful swat on the ass, winks, then goes to join Gemma and the kids on their quest at the edge of the lake. Gemma leans down to see what Caleb is showing her and dutifully takes a picture when he poses with his find. Smirking, she ruffles his hair and he hugs her leg. Close by, Luna and Phoenix have their heads bent close together, absorbed in their task. Those two have been attached at the hip since birth.

"You could do it in wood." Lucas' voice drifts over from the grill. "It'll be easier to work with for the scope of the structure."

He waves the spatula, pausing what he's explaining to Fox to flip a burger. The pair of them match with their babies in their arms and relaxed grins while they talk shop. Ever since Lucas built Cinder a luxury cat tree, he and Fox have been dabbling in projects together here and there over the years.

"Yeah, I might," Fox agrees. "That'll give it more character. Is that live edge supplier still open? I'll have it shipped back to the workshop."

"It is. Drive out together tomorrow to check it out?"

"Sounds good."

Lucas gives Bishop a nod and he cups his hands around his mouth to call from the picnic table. "Lunch is ready."

Gemma and Maisy herd the kids up to our spot while Thea and Bishop bring over the stuff she packed up this morning. Lucas and Fox come over with the babies, and Blair and I get up to help serve everything. The eight of us work as a team to wrangle our seven toddlers until they're all situated. We laugh as we eat, teasing each other in the way that families do.

After we finish lunch, the twins wind up napping together on my lounger, wrapped in the towel Blair tucked around them. Maisy and Fox put Morgan in his travel playpen under Thea and Bishop's care while they go out for a swim. Gemma stretches out on her towel again, smiling crookedly and taking photos on her phone of Lucas and baby Charlie. He holds her hands for balance while she stands between his legs and digs her feet in the sand. The pride he glows with is the same I feel watching my kids accomplish something new.

With the twins asleep and Phoenix occupied with Luna, I take Blair's hand and walk with her to the edge of the water. The memory of the time we played chicken together against Gemma and Lucas pops into my head, drawing a smirk. I pull her closer and kiss her temple.

"What was that for?" she asks, skimming her feet through the cool shallow water lapping at the shore.

"Because I love you. Do I need any other reason than that?"

Her eyes light up with a gleam and she cups either side of my neck, tugging me down for another kiss. When we part, she gives me a beautiful smile. "Love you, too."

We walk hand in hand along the edge of the lake that is home to many of our memories.

This vacation is just as perfect as it is every year. It's always a good time when I have my family around me.

If I had to do it all over again, I would. Fighting through the pain was worth it to find Blair, to solidify my relationship with my best friends—my brothers. To find this group of people that work together.

Phoenix and Luna run across our path with mischief lighting up their gazes. Our son captures my best friend's daughter's tiny hand in his and he doesn't let go as Luna urges him to hurry. Blair and I exchange a look and she smirks.

Most of all, it was worth it for them. Our kids. The next generation of troublemakers in Ridgeview.

BONUS EXTRAS
THE NEXT GENERATION OF TROUBLEMAKERS

Gemma & Lucas Saint
    Caleb Saint, 3
    Charlotte "Charlie" Saint, 1

Blair & Devlin Murphy
    Phoenix Nash Murphy, 5
    Aurora Macy & Jasper Orion Murphy, 3

Thea & Connor Bishop
    Luna Ivy Bishop, 5

Maisy & Fox Wilder
    Morgan Avery Wilder, 2

ABOUT THE AUTHOR
ROMANCE WITH DARING EDGE

Veronica Eden is an international bestselling author of dark new adult romances + reverse harem romances with spitfire heroines and irresistible heroes.

She loves exploring complicated feelings, magical worlds, epic adventures, and the bond of characters that embrace us against the world. She has always been drawn to gruff antiheroes, clever villains, and the twisty-turns of morally gray decisions. She believes sometimes the villain should get the girl and is a sucker for a deliciously devilish antihero. Veronica Eden is the pen name of romance author Mara Townsend. When not writing, she can be found soaking up sunshine at the beach, snuggling in a pile with her untamed pack of animals (her husband, dog and cat), and surrounding herself with as many plants as she can get her hands on.

* * *

CONTACT + FOLLOW
Email: veronicaedenauthor@gmail.com
Website: veronicaedenauthor.com
FB Reader Group: bit.ly/veronicafbgroup
Amazon: amazon.com/author/veronicaeden

ALSO BY VERONICA EDEN

Sign up for the mailing list to get first access and ARC opportunities! Follow Veronica on BookBub for new release alerts!

DARK ROMANCE
Sinners and Saints Series
Wicked Saint
Tempting Devil
Ruthless Bishop
Savage Wilder

Crowned Crows Series
Crowned Crows of Thorne Point

Standalone
Unmasked Heart

REVERSE HAREM ROMANCE
Bound by Bounty Series
(COMING SOON)

Standalone
More Than Bargained

CONTEMPORARY ROMANCE
Standalone
Jingle Wars

Printed in Poland
by Amazon Fulfillment
Poland Sp. z o.o., Wrocław
28 April 2021

fa2e16ae-f053-4375-aea0-5192688f1f33R01